KT-151-279

PENGUIN BOOKS

RUDYARD KIPLING: SELECTED STORIES

Rudyard Kipling, son of John Lockwood Kipling, the author of *Beast and Man in India*, was born in Bombay in 1865. He was educated at the United Services College, Westward Ho!, and was engaged in journalistic work in India from 1882 to 1889. His fame rests principally on his short stories, dealing with India, the sea, the jungle and its beasts, the army, the navy and a multitude of other subjects. His verse, as varied in subject as his prose, also enjoyed great popularity. Among his more famous publications are *Plain Tales from The Hills* (1888), *Life's Handicap* (1891), *Barrack-Room Ballads* (1892), *The Jungle Book* (1894), *The Day's Work* (1898), *Kim* (1901), *Just So Stories* (1902), *Puck of Pook's Hill* (1906), and *Rewards and Fairies* (1910). Kipling, who was awarded a Nobel Prize for Literature in 1907, died in 1936.

Andrew Rutherford is Warden of Goldsmiths' College, University of London. Formerly Regius Professor of English in the University of Aberdeen, he is a well-known authority on Kipling and has edited *Plain Tales from the Hills*, *Early Verse by Rudyard Kipling 1879–1889*, *Kipling's Mind and Art* and two volumes of Kipling's later stories (in Penguin Modern Classics).

Rudyard Kipling

SELECTED
STORIES

EDITED
BY ANDREW RUTHERFORD

PENGUIN BOOKS

Penguin Books Ltd, Harmondsworth, Middlesex, England
Viking Penguin Inc., 40 West 23rd Street, New York, New York 10010, U.S.A.
Penguin Books Australia Ltd, Ringwood, Victoria, Australia
Penguin Books Canada Ltd, 2801 John Street, Markham, Ontario, Canada L3R 1B4
Penguin Books (N.Z.) Ltd, 182–190 Wairau Road, Auckland 10, New Zealand

This selection published in Penguin Books 1987

Made and printed in Great Britain by
Richard Clay Ltd, Bungay, Suffolk
Typeset in Monophoto Ehrhardt

Contents

Introduction

Rudyard Kipling (1865–1936) is beyond question the greatest short-story writer in the English language, and this collection illustrates the richness and variety of his achievement.

It opens with the first story he published as a young journalist in India – a dramatic monologue spoken by a Portuguese half-caste in an opium den in Lahore. Already we see here, in 'The Gate of the Hundred Sorrows', Kipling's eager interest in mankind in all its varieties and his willingness, as he himself once put it, 'to think in another man's skin'. Gabral Misquitta is the first of a long series of Kipling narrators – Pathans, Sikhs, Hindus, Anglo-Indian officials, loafers, private soldiers, Scots engineers, English peasants, characters from past ages as well as from the present – who offer their unique perspectives on life to us in their own authentic idiom.

The collection ends with an acknowledged masterpiece, 'The Gardener', written half a century later in the aftermath of the Great War, in which Kipling's only son had been killed on his first day in action. Helen Turrell's similar bereavement is treated in an impersonal, complex, elliptical mode of narration typical of the later Kipling: it controls intensities of grief and compassion, and shows him as a sophisticated artist combining, in Coleridge's phrase, 'a more than usual state of emotion with more than usual order'.

The stories of the years between show a remarkable range of subject-matter and technique. India, where Kipling had been born, where he had spent his early years and where he worked for seven years as a journalist between the ages of sixteen and twenty-three, was a rich source of material and inspiration, even after he had left it for America and England. In the vulgar mind indeed he has been typecast as the spokesman for Anglo-India (in the sense of the British community in India) and the propagandist of Empire. The political views which he shared with many millions both before and after him should not, however, be made a stick with which to beat his literary reputation. Historically considered, British imperialism of the later nineteenth century was a complex phenomenon defying simplistic condemnation, and there are many Credit as well as Debit entries in the moral balance-sheet of British rule in India. Furthermore, Kipling's attitude to his material is

Selected Stories

more varied than the stereotype would suggest. Anglo-Indian life, that strange mutation from Victorian norms, is described both sympathetically and satirically: its vices, vanities and follies are exposed, yet its achievements and its ethic of self-sacrifice and service are finely celebrated in stories which now stand as records of a vanished world. There were powerful pressures to conformism and to prejudice in that world, and to these Kipling sometimes yielded; but he also had impulses to rebellion – to the repudiation of its orthodoxies and taboos. 'A stone's throw out from either hand/From that well-ordered road we tread /And all the world is wild and strange,' he wrote in the verse-heading to one of his earliest stories; and we find him passing from the narrower confines of Anglo-India to explore the tragic loves of Englishmen and Indian women in 'Lispeth', 'Beyond the Pale', 'Without Benefit of Clergy'; and to enter into the minds of characters whose lives are lived on assumptions radically different from his own: the Afghan horse-dealer of 'Dray Wara Yow Dee', racked by his obsessive thirst for vengeance; Little Tobrah, who kills his blind sister by pushing her down a well since 'it is better to die than to starve'; and saintly mendicants, renouncers of the world, like Purun Baghat and Kim's Lama. This ability to project himself imaginatively into other minds, into representatives of what might seem alien humanity, is one of Kipling's great strengths as an artist.

He shows the same capacity for imaginative empathy in his treatment of animals and of machinery – in his rendering the game of polo in 'The Maltese Cat' from the viewpoint of the polo ponies, or in his virtuosic presentation of the running-in of the *Dimbula* in 'The Ship that Found Herself'. He found indeed new worlds to conquer when he turned, in that highly technological age, to machines and the men who work them, like the ships' engineers of 'Bread upon the Waters' and 'The Devil and the Deep Sea'. Early in his career he had deliberately crossed the boundaries of class in a revolutionary attempt to render the working-class speech, the attitudes and background, the loves and sorrows, of ordinary British soldiers, and some of his greatest successes in both verse and prose had been couched in a modified version of the language of the barrack-room. His interest extends, however, to many other types and examples of 'people who *do* things': the Sons of Martha who carry out the work of the world, whether as soldiers, administrators, peasants, engine-drivers, deep-sea fishermen, engineers, farmers or builders, were always closer to his heart than the intellectuals he stigmatized as the Sons of Mary (see Luke 10:38–42); and he strove mightily in his fiction to commemorate their qualities and their achievements.

When he settled at Bateman's at Burwash in 1902 he found still

2

further challenges in the sheer unfamiliarity, the foreignness of England: the social and psychological discoveries of the protagonist in 'My Son's Wife' make this an anthropological study as well as a moral fable. And Kipling brought to the Sussex countryside, its people and traditions, the same fascinated attention he had given earlier to life in the Punjab. He explores its past as well as its present in stories like 'Marklake Witches' and 'The Knife and the Naked Chalk', summoning up characters from history or pre-history and demonstrating not so much the differences as the continuity of their experience and values with our own.

There are also forays into autobiography, like 'Baa Baa, Black Sheep', which is based on the events of his own childhood. There are political fables, like the study of decadence in 'The Mother Hive'. There are psychological case-histories like 'Mary Postgate'. And there is an inexhaustible interest in the world around him, an insatiable curiosity about the diversity of creatures it contains. To read a wide selection of Kipling's fiction is to be astonished by the range and the vitality of his invention, the sureness and the subtlety of his technique. 'But enough of this,' as Dryden wrote of Chaucer; 'there is such a variety of game springing up before me, that I am distracted in my choice, and know not which to follow. It is sufficient to say, according to the proverb, that here is God's plenty.'

⧉ The Gate of the Hundred Sorrows[1] ⧉

If I can attain Heaven for a pice,[2] why should you be envious?
Opium Smoker's Proverb.

This is no work of mine. My friend, Gabral Misquitta, the half-caste, spoke it all, between moonset and morning, six weeks before he died; and I took it down from his mouth as he answered my questions. So:

It lies between the Coppersmith's Gully and the pipe-stem sellers' quarter, within a hundred yards, too, as the crow flies, of the Mosque of Wazir Khan. I don't mind telling anyone this much, but I defy him to find the Gate, however well he may think he knows the City.[3] You might even go through the very gully it stands in a hundred times, and be none the wiser. We used to call the gully, 'The Gully of the Black Smoke', but its native name is altogether different of course. A loaded donkey couldn't pass between the walls; and, at one point, just before you reach the Gate, a bulged house-front makes people go along all sideways.

It isn't really a gate though. It's a house. Old Fung-Tching had it first five years ago. He was a boot-maker in Calcutta. They say that he murdered his wife there when he was drunk. That was why he dropped bazar-rum and took to the Black Smoke instead. Later on, he came up north and opened the Gate as a house where you could get your smoke in peace and quiet. Mind you, it was a *pukka*,[4] respectable opium-house, and not one of those stifling, sweltering *chandoo-khanas*,[5] that you can find all over the City. No; the old man knew his business thoroughly, and he was most clean for a Chinaman. He was a one-eyed little chap, not much more than five feet high, and both his middle fingers were gone. All the same, he was the handiest man at rolling black pills I have ever seen. Never seemed to be touched by the Smoke, either; and what he took day and night, night and day, was a caution. I've been at it five years, and I can do my fair share of the Smoke with anyone; but I was a child to Fung-Tching that way. All the same, the old man was keen on his money: very keen; and that's what I can't understand. I heard he saved a good deal before he died, but his nephew has got all that now; and the old man's gone back to China to be buried.

He kept the big upper room, where his best customers gathered, as

neat as a new pin. In one corner used to stand Fung-Tching's Joss —
almost as ugly as Fung-Tching — and there were always sticks burning
under his nose; but you never smelt 'em when the pipes were going
thick. Opposite the Joss was Fung-Tching's coffin. He had spent a good
deal of his savings on that, and whenever a new man came to the Gate he
was always introduced to it. It was lacquered black, with red and gold
writings on it, and I've heard that Fung-Tching brought it out all the
way from China. I don't know whether that's true or not, but I know
that, if I came first in the evening, I used to spread my mat just at the
foot of it. It was a quiet corner, you see, and a sort of breeze from the
gully came in at the window now and then. Besides the mats, there was
no other furniture in the room — only the coffin and the old Joss all
green and blue and purple with age and polish.

Fung-Tching never told us why he called the place 'The Gate of the
Hundred Sorrows'. (He was the only Chinaman I know who used bad-
sounding fancy names. Most of them are flowery. As you'll see in
Calcutta.) We used to find that out for ourselves. Nothing grows on you
so much, if you're white, as the Black Smoke. A yellow man is made
different. Opium doesn't tell on him scarcely at all; but white and black
suffer a good deal. Of course, there are some people that the Smoke
doesn't touch any more than tobacco would at first. They just doze a bit,
as one would fall asleep naturally, and next morning they are almost fit
for work. Now, I was one of that sort when I began, but I've been at it
for five years pretty steadily, and it's different now. There was an old
aunt of mine, down Agra way, and she left me a little at her death.
About sixty rupees a month secured. Sixty isn't much. I can recollect a
time, seems hundreds and hundreds of years ago, that I was getting my
three hundred a month, and pickings, when I was working on a big
timber-contract in Calcutta.

I didn't stick to that work for long. The Black Smoke does not allow
of much other business; and even though I am very little affected by it
as men go, I couldn't do a day's work now to save my life. After all, sixty
rupees is what I want. When old Fung-Tching was alive he used to draw
the money for me, give me about half of it to live on (I eat very little),
and the rest he kept himself. I was free of the Gate at any time of the
day and night, and could smoke and sleep there when I liked, so I didn't
care. I know the old man made a good thing out of it; but that's no
matter. Nothing matters much to me; and besides, the money always
came fresh and fresh each month.

There was ten of us met at the Gate when the place was first opened.
Me, and two Baboos [6] from a Government Office somewhere in

Anarkulli,[7] but they got the sack and couldn't pay (no man who has to work in the daylight can do the Black Smoke for any length of time straight on); a Chinaman that was Fung-Tching's nephew; a bazar-woman that had got a lot of money somehow; an English loafer – Mac-Somebody I think, but I have forgotten – that smoked heaps, but never seemed to pay anything (they said he had saved Fung-Tching's life at some trial in Calcutta when he was a barrister); another Eurasian, like myself, from Madras; a half-caste woman, and a couple of men who said they had come from the North. I think they must have been Persians or Afghans or something. There are not more than five of us living now, but we come regular. I don't know what happened to the Baboos; but the bazar-woman she died after six months of the Gate, and I think Fung-Tching took her bangles and nose-ring for himself. But I'm not certain. The Englishman, he drank as well as smoked, and he dropped off. One of the Persians got killed in a row at night by the big well near the mosque a long time ago, and the Police shut up the well, because they said it was full of foul air. They found him dead at the bottom of it. So you see, there is only me, the Chinaman, the half-caste woman that we call the *Memsahib* (she used to live with Fung-Tching), the other Eurasian, and one of the Persians. The *Memsahib* looks very old now. I think she was a young woman when the gate was opened; but we are all old for the matter of that. Hundreds and hundreds of years old. It is very hard to keep count of time in the Gate, and, besides, time doesn't matter to me. I draw my sixty rupees fresh and fresh every month. A very, very long while ago, when I used to be getting three hundred and fifty rupees a month, and pickings, on a big timber-contract at Calcutta, I had a wife of sorts. But she's dead now. People said that I killed her by taking to the Black Smoke. Perhaps I did, but it's so long since that it doesn't matter. Sometimes when I first came to the Gate, I used to feel sorry for it; but that's all over and done with long ago, and I draw my sixty rupees fresh and fresh every month, and am quite happy. Not *drunk* happy, you know, but always quiet and soothed and contented.

How did I take to it? It began at Calcutta. I used to try it in my own house, just to see what it was like. I never went very far, but I think my wife must have died then. Anyhow, I found myself here, and got to know Fung-Tching. I don't remember rightly how that came about; but he told me of the Gate and I used to go there, and, somehow, I have never got away from it since. Mind you, though, the Gate was a respectable place in Fung-Tching's time where you could be comfortable, and not at all like the *chandoo-khanas* where the niggers go. No; it was clean and quiet, and not crowded. Of course, there were others beside us ten and the man; but we always had a mat apiece, with a wadded woollen headpiece, all covered with black and red dragons and things; just like the coffin in the corner.

At the end of one's third pipe the dragons used to move about and fight. I've watched 'em many and many a night through. I used to regulate my Smoke that way, and now it takes a dozen pipes to make 'em stir. Besides, they are all torn and dirty, like the mats, and old Fung-Tching is dead. He died a couple of years ago, and gave me the pipe I always use now – a silver one, with queer beasts crawling up and down the receiver-bottle below the cup. Before that, I think, I used a big bamboo stem with a copper cup, a very small one, and a green jade mouthpiece. It was a little thicker than a walking-stick stem, and smoked sweet, very sweet. The bamboo seemed to suck up the smoke. Silver doesn't, and I've got to clean it out now and then, that's a great deal of trouble, but I smoke it for the old man's sake. He must have made a good thing out of me, but he always gave me clean mats and pillows, and the best stuff you could get anywhere.

When he died, his nephew Tsin-ling took up the Gate, and he called it the 'Temple of the Three Possessions'; but we old ones speak of it as the 'Hundred Sorrows', all the same. The nephew does things very shabbily, and I think the *Memsahib* must help him. She lives with him; same as she used to do with the old man. The two let in all sorts of low people, niggers and all, and the Black Smoke isn't as good as it used to be. I've found burnt bran in my pipe over and over again. The old man would have died if that had happened in his time. Besides, the room is never cleaned, and all the mats are torn and cut at the edges. The coffin is gone – gone to China again – with the old man and two ounces of Smoke inside it, in case he should want 'em on the way.

The Joss doesn't get so many sticks burnt under his nose as he used to; that's a sign of ill-luck, as sure as Death. He's all brown, too, and no one ever attends to him. That's the *Memsahib's* work, I know; because, when Tsin-ling tried to burn gilt paper before him, she said it was a waste of money, and, if he kept a stick burning very slowly, the Joss wouldn't know the difference. So now we've got the sticks mixed with a lot of glue, and they take half an hour longer to burn, and smell stinky. Let alone the smell of the room by itself. No business can get on if they try that sort of thing. The Joss doesn't like it. I can see that. Late at night, sometimes, he turns all sorts of queer colours – blue and green and red – just as he used to do when old Fung-Tching was alive; and he rolls his eyes and stamps his feet like a devil.

I don't know why I don't leave the place and smoke quietly in a little room of my own in the bazar. Most like, Tsin-ling would kill me if I went away – he draws my sixty rupees now – and besides, it's so much trouble, and I've grown to be very fond of the Gate. It's not much to look at. Not what it was in the old man's time, but I couldn't leave it. I've seen so many come in and out. And I've seen so many die here on the mats that I should be afraid of dying in the open now. I've seen some things that people would call strange enough; but nothing is strange when you're on the Black Smoke, except the Black Smoke. And if it was, it wouldn't matter. Fung-Tching used to be very particular about his people, and never got in anyone who'd give trouble by dying messy and such. But the nephew isn't half so careful. He tells everywhere that he keeps a 'first chop' [8] house. Never tries to get men in quietly, and make them comfortable like Fung-Tching did. That's why the Gate is getting a little bit more known than it used to be. Among the niggers of course. The nephew daren't get a white, or, for matter of that, a mixed skin into the place. He has to keep us three of course – me and the *Memsahib* and the other Eurasian. We're fixtures. But he wouldn't give us credit for a pipeful – not for anything.

One of these days, I hope, I shall die in the Gate. The Persian and the Madras man are terribly shaky now. They've got a boy to light their pipes for them. I always do that myself. Most like, I shall see them carried out before me. I don't think I shall ever outlive the *Memsahib* or Tsin-ling. Women last longer than men at the Black Smoke, and Tsin-ling has a deal of the old man's blood in him, though he does smoke cheap stuff. The bazar-woman knew when she was going two days before her time; and she died on a clean mat with a nicely wadded pillow, and the old man hung up her pipe just above the Joss. He was always fond of her, I fancy. But he took her bangles just the same.

I should like to die like the bazar-woman – on a clean, cool mat with a pipe of good stuff between my lips. When I feel I'm going, I shall ask Tsin-ling for them, and he can draw my sixty rupees a month, fresh and fresh, as long as he pleases. Then I shall lie back, quiet and comfortable, and watch the black and red dragons have their last big fight together; and then . . .

Well, it doesn't matter. Nothing matters much to me – only I wish Tsin-ling wouldn't put bran into the Black Smoke.

⨎ The Story of Muhammad Din [1] ⨎

Who is the happy man? He that sees in his own house at home, little
children crowned with dust, leaping and falling and crying.

Munichandra, translated by Professor Peterson. [2]

The polo-ball was an old one, scarred, chipped, and dinted. It stood on
the mantelpiece among the pipe-stems which Imam Din, *khitmatgar*, [3]
was cleaning for me.

'Does the Heaven-born want this ball?' said Imam Din deferentially.

The Heaven-born set no particular store by it; but of what use was a
polo-ball to a *khitmatgar*?

'By Your Honour's favour, I have a little son. He has seen this ball,
and desires it to play with. I do not want it for myself.'

No one would for an instant accuse portly old Imam Din of wanting
to play with polo-balls. He carried out the battered thing into the verandah; and there followed a hurricane of joyful squeaks, a patter of
small feet, and the *thud-thud-thud* of the ball rolling along the ground.
Evidently the little son had been waiting outside the door to secure his
treasure. But how had he managed to see that polo-ball?

Next day, coming back from office half an hour earlier than usual, I
was aware of a small figure in the dining-room – a tiny, plump figure in
a ridiculously inadequate shirt which came, perhaps, half-way down the
tubby stomach. It wandered round the room, thumb in mouth, crooning
to itself as it took stock of the pictures. Undoubtedly this was the 'little
son'.

He had no business in my room, of course; but was so deeply absorbed
in his discoveries that he never noticed me in the doorway. I stepped into
the room and startled him nearly into a fit. He sat down on the ground
with a gasp. His eyes opened, and his mouth followed suit. I knew what
was coming, and fled, followed by a long, dry howl which reached the
servants' quarters far more quickly than any command of mine had ever
done. In ten seconds Imam Din was in the dining-room. Then despairing
sobs arose, and I returned to find Imam Din admonishing the small
sinner who was using most of his shirt as a handkerchief.

'This boy,' said Imam Din judicially, 'is a *budmash* [4] – a big *budmash*.

He will, without doubt, go to the *jail-khana*⁵ for his behaviour.' Renewed yells from the penitent, and an elaborate apology to myself from Imam Din.

'Tell the baby,' said I, 'that the *Sahib* is not angry, and take him away.' Imam Din conveyed my forgiveness to the offender, who had now gathered all his shirt round his neck, stringwise, and the yell subsided into a sob. The two set off for the door. 'His name,' said Imam Din, as though the name was part of the crime, 'is Muhammad Din, and he is a *budmash*.' Freed from present danger, Muhammad Din turned round in his father's arms, and said gravely, 'It is true that my name is Muhammad Din, *Tahib*, but I am not a *budmash*. I am a *man*!'

From that day dated my acquaintance with Muhammad Din. Never again did he come into my dining-room, but on the neutral ground of the garden, we greeted each other with much state, though our conversation was confined to '*Talaam, Tahib*' from his side, and '*Salaam, Muhammad Din*' from mine. Daily on my return from office, the little white shirt, and the fat little body used to rise from the shade of the creeper-covered trellis where they had been hid; and daily I checked my horse here, that my salutation might not be slurred over or given unseemly.

Muhammad Din never had any companions. He used to trot about the compound, in and out of the castor-oil bushes, on mysterious errands of his own. One day I stumbled upon some of his handiwork far down the grounds. He had half buried the polo-ball in dust, and stuck six shrivelled old marigold flowers in a circle round it. Outside that circle again was a rude square, traced out in bits of red brick alternating with fragments of broken china; the whole bounded by a little bank of dust. The waterman from the well-curb put in a plea for the small architect, saying that it was only the play of a baby and did not much disfigure my garden.

Heaven knows that I had no intention of touching the child's work then or later; but, that evening, a stroll through the garden brought me unawares full on it; so that I trampled, before I knew, marigold-heads, dust-bank, and fragments of broken soap-dish into confusion past all hope of mending. Next morning, I came upon Muhammad Din crying softly to himself over the ruin I had wrought. Someone had cruelly told him that the *Sahib* was very angry with him for spoiling the garden, and had scattered his rubbish, using bad language the while. Muhammad Din laboured for an hour at effacing every trace of the dust-bank and pottery fragments, and it was with a tearful and apologetic face that he said, '*Talaam, Tahib*,' when I came home from office. A hasty inquiry resulted in Imam Din informing Muhammad Din that, by my singular favour, he was permitted to disport himself as he pleased. Whereat the child took heart and fell to tracing the ground-plan of an edifice which was to eclipse the marigold-polo-ball creation.

For some months the chubby little eccentricity revolved in his humble orbit among the castor-oil bushes and in the dust; always fashioning magnificent palaces from stale flowers thrown away by the bearer, smooth water-worn pebbles, bits of broken glass, and feathers pulled, I fancy, from my fowls – always alone, and always crooning to himself.

A gaily-spotted sea-shell was dropped one day close to the last of his little buildings; and I looked that Muhammad Din should build something more than ordinarily splendid on the strength of it. Nor was I disappointed. He meditated for the better part of an hour, and his crooning rose to a jubilant song. Then he began tracing in the dust. It would certainly be a wondrous palace, this one, for it was two yards long and a yard broad in ground-plan. But the palace was never completed.

Next day there was no Muhammad Din at the head of the carriage-drive, and no '*Talaam, Tahib*' to welcome my return. I had grown accustomed to the greeting, and its omission troubled me. Next day Imam Din told me that the child was suffering slightly from fever and needed quinine. He got the medicine, and an English Doctor.

'They have no stamina, these brats,' said the Doctor, as he left Imam Din's quarters.

A week later, though I would have given much to have avoided it, I met on the road to the Mussulman burying-ground Imam Din, accompanied by one other friend, carrying in his arms, wrapped in a white cloth, all that was left of little Muhammad Din.

The Other Man [1]

When the Earth was sick and the Skies were grey
And the woods were rotted with rain,
The Dead Man rode through the autumn day
To visit his love again.

Old Ballad.

Far back in the 'seventies', before they had built any Public-Offices at Simla,[2] and the broad road round Jakko[3] lived in a pigeon-hole in the P.W.D.[4] hovels, her parents made Miss Gaurey marry Colonel Schreiderling. He could not have been much more than thirty-five years her senior; and, as he lived on two hundred rupees a month and had money of his own, he was well off. He belonged to good people, and suffered in the cold weather from lung-complaints. In the hot weather he dangled on the brink of heat-apoplexy; but it never quite killed him.

Understand, I do not blame Schreiderling. He was a good husband according to his lights, and his temper only failed him when he was being nursed. Which was some seventeen days in each month. He was almost generous to his wife about money-matters, and that, for him, was a concession. Still Mrs Schreiderling was not happy. They married her when she was this side of twenty and had given all her poor little heart to another man. I have forgotten his name, but we will call him the Other Man. He had no money and no prospects. He was not even good-looking; and I think he was in the Commissariat or Transport. But, in spite of all these things, she loved him very badly; and there was some sort of an engagement between the two when Schreiderling appeared and told Mrs Gaurey that he wished to marry her daughter. Then the other engagement was broken off – washed away by Mrs Gaurey's tears, for that lady governed her house by weeping over disobedience to her authority and the lack of reverence she received in her old age. The daughter did not take after her mother. She never cried. Not even at the wedding.

The Other Man bore his loss quietly, and was transferred to as bad a station as he could find. Perhaps the climate consoled him. He suffered from intermittent fever, and that may have distracted him from his other trouble. He was weak about the heart also. Both ways. One of the valves was affected, and the fever made it worse. This showed itself later on.

Then many months passed, and Mrs Schreiderling took to being ill. She did not pine away like people in story-books, but she seemed to pick up every form of illness that went about a Station, from simple fever upwards. She was never more than ordinarily pretty at the best of times; and the illnesses made her ugly. Schreiderling said so. He prided himself on speaking his mind.

When she ceased being pretty, he left her to her own devices, and went back to the lairs of his bachelordom. She used to trot up and down Simla Mall in a forlorn sort of way, with a grey Terai hat[5] well on the back of her head, and a shocking bad saddle under her. Schreiderling's generosity stopped at the horse. He said that any saddle would do for a woman as nervous as Mrs Schreiderling. She never was asked to dance, because she did not dance well; and she was so dull and uninteresting, that her box very seldom had any cards in it. Schreiderling said that if he had known she was going to be such a scarecrow after her marriage, he would never have married her. He always prided himself on speaking his mind, did Schreiderling.

He left her at Simla one August, and went down to his regiment. Then she revived a little, but she never recovered her looks. I found out at the Club that the Other Man was coming up sick – very sick – on an off chance of recovery. The fever and the heart-valves had nearly killed him. She knew that too, and she knew – what I had no interest in knowing – when he was coming up. I suppose he wrote to tell her. They had not seen each other since a month before the wedding. And here comes the unpleasant part of the story.

A late call kept me down at the Dovedell Hotel till dusk one evening. Mrs Schreiderling had been flitting up and down the Mall all the afternoon in the rain. Coming up along the Cart-road, a tonga[6] passed me, and my pony, tired with standing so long, set off at a canter. Just by the road down to the Tonga Office Mrs Schreiderling, dripping from head to foot, was waiting for the tonga. I turned uphill as the tonga was no affair of mine; and just then she began to shriek. I went back at once and saw, under the Tonga Office lamps, Mrs Schreiderling kneeling in the wet road by the back seat of the newly-arrived tonga, screaming hideously. Then she fell face down in the dirt as I came up.

Sitting in the back seat, very square and firm, with one hand on the awning-stanchion and the wet pouring off his hat and moustache, was the Other Man – dead. The sixty-mile uphill jolt had been too much for his valve, I suppose. The tonga-driver said, 'This Sahib died two stages out of Solon. Therefore, I tied him with a rope, lest he should fall out by the way, and so came to Simla. Will the Sahib give me *bukshish*?[7] *It*,' pointing to the Other Man, 'should have given one rupee.'

The Other Man sat with a grin on his face, as if he enjoyed the joke of his arrival; and Mrs Schreiderling, in the mud, began to groan. There was no one except us four in the office and it was raining heavily. The first thing was to take Mrs Schreiderling home, and the second was to prevent her name from being mixed up with the affair. The tonga-driver received five rupees to find a bazar rickshaw for Mrs Schreiderling. He was to tell the Tonga Babu afterwards of the Other Man, and the Babu was to make such arrangements as seemed best.

Mrs Schreiderling was carried into the shed out of the rain, and for three-quarters of an hour we two waited for the rickshaw. The Other Man was left exactly as he had arrived. Mrs Schreiderling would do everything but cry, which might have helped her. She tried to scream as soon as her senses came back, and then she began praying for the Other Man's soul. Had she not been as honest as the day, she would have prayed for her own soul too. I waited to hear her do this, but she did not. Then I tried to get some of the mud off her habit. Lastly, the rickshaw came, and I got her away – partly by force. It was a terrible business from beginning to end; but most of all when the rickshaw had to squeeze between the wall and the tonga, and she saw by the lamplight that thin, yellow hand grasping the awning-stanchion.

She was taken home just as everyone was going to a dance at Vice-regal Lodge – 'Peterhoff'[8] it was then – and the doctor found out that she had fallen from her horse, that I had picked her up at the back of Jakko, and really deserved great credit for the prompt manner in which I had secured medical aid. She did not die – men of Schreiderling's stamp marry women who don't die easily. They live and grow ugly.

She never told of her one meeting, since her marriage, with the Other Man; and, when the chill and cough following the exposure of that evening allowed her abroad, she never by word or sign alluded to having met me by the Tonga Office. Perhaps she never knew.

She used to trot up and down the Mall, on that shocking bad saddle, looking as if she expected to meet someone round the corner every minute. Two years afterwards she went Home, and died – at Bourne-mouth, I think.

Schreiderling, when he grew maudlin at Mess, used to talk about 'my poor dear wife'. He always set great store on speaking his mind, did Schreiderling.

⟦ Lispeth [1] ⟧

Look, you have cast out Love! What Gods are these
    You bid me please?
The Three in One, the One in Three? Not so!
    To my own Gods I go.
It may be they shall give me greater ease
Than your cold Christ and tangled Trinities.
                                    The Convert.

She was the daughter of Sonoo, a Hill-man of the Himalayas, and Jadéh his wife. One year their maize failed, and two bears spent the night in their only opium poppy-field just above the Sutlej Valley on the Kotgarh [2] side; so, next season, they turned Christian, and brought their baby to the Mission to be baptized. The Kotgarh Chaplain christened her Elizabeth, and 'Lispeth' is the Hill or *pahari* pronunciation.

Later, cholera came into the Kotgarh Valley and carried off Sonoo and Jadéh, and Lispeth became half servant, half companion, to the wife of the then Chaplain of Kotgarh. This was after the reign of the Moravian missionaries [3] in that place, but before Kotgarh had quite forgotten her title of 'Mistress of the Northern Hills'.

Whether Christianity improved Lispeth, or whether the gods of her own people would have done as much for her under any circumstances, I do not know; but she grew very lovely. When a Hill-girl grows lovely she is worth travelling fifty miles over bad ground to look upon. Lispeth had a Greek face – one of these faces people paint so often, and see so seldom. She was of a pale, ivory colour, and, for her race, extremely tall. Also, she possessed eyes that were wonderful; and, had she not been dressed in the abominable print-cloths affected by Missions, you would, meeting her on the hillside unexpectedly, have thought her the original Diana [4] of the Romans going out to slay.

Lispeth took to Christianity readily, and did not abandon it when she reached womanhood, as do some Hill-girls. Her own people hated her because she had, they said, become a white woman and washed herself daily; and the Chaplain's wife did not know what to do with her. One cannot ask a stately goddess, five foot ten in her shoes, to clean plates and dishes. She played with the Chaplain's children and took classes in the Sunday School, and read all the books in the house, and grew more and more beautiful, like the Princesses in fairy tales. The Chaplain's wife said that the girl ought to take service in Simla as a nurse or something 'genteel'. But Lispeth did not want to take service. She was very happy where she was.

When travellers – there were not many in those years – came in to Kotgarh, Lispeth used to lock herself into her own room for fear they might take her away to Simla, or out into the unknown world.

One day, a few months after she was seventeen years old, Lispeth went out for a walk. She did not walk in the manner of English ladies – a mile and a half out, with a carriage-ride back again. She covered between twenty and thirty miles in her little constitutionals, all about and about, between Kotgarh and Narkunda.[5] This time she came back at full dusk, stepping down the breakneck descent into Kotgarh with something heavy in her arms. The Chaplain's wife was dozing in the drawing-room when Lispeth came in breathing heavily and very exhausted with her burden. Lispeth put it down on the sofa, and said simply, 'This is my husband. I found him on the Bagi Road. He has hurt himself. We will nurse him, and when he is well, your husband shall marry him to me.'

This was the first mention Lispeth had ever made of her matrimonial views, and the Chaplain's wife shrieked with horror. However, the man on the sofa needed attention first. He was a young Englishman, and his head had been cut to the bone by something jagged. Lispeth said she had found him down the hillside, and had brought him in. He was breathing queerly and was unconscious.

He was put to bed and tended by the Chaplain, who knew something of medicine; and Lispeth waited outside the door in case she could be useful. She explained to the Chaplain that this was the man she meant to marry; and the Chaplain and his wife lectured her severely on the impropriety of her conduct. Lispeth listened quietly, and repeated her first proposition. It takes a great deal of Christianity to wipe out uncivilized Eastern instincts, such as falling in love at first sight. Lispeth, having found the man she worshipped, did not see why she should keep silent as to her choice. She had no intention of being sent away, either. She was going to nurse that Englishman until he was well enough to marry her. This was her programme.

After a fortnight of slight fever and inflammation, the Englishman recovered coherence and thanked the Chaplain and his wife, and Lispeth

– especially Lispeth – for their kindness. He was a traveller in the East, he said – they never talked about 'globe-trotters' in those days, when the P. & O.[6] fleet was young and small – and had come from Dehra Dun to hunt for plants and butterflies among the Simla hills. No one at Simla, therefore, knew anything about him. He fancied that he must have fallen over the cliff while reaching out for a fern on a rotten tree-trunk, and that his coolies must have stolen his baggage and fled. He thought he would go back to Simla when he was a little stronger. He desired no more mountaineering.

He made small haste to go away, and recovered his strength slowly. Lispeth objected to being advised either by the Chaplain or his wife; therefore the latter spoke to the Englishman, and told him how matters stood in Lispeth's heart. He laughed a good deal, and said it was very pretty and romantic, but, as he was engaged to a girl at Home, he fancied that nothing would happen. Certainly he would behave with discretion. He did that. Still he found it very pleasant to talk to Lispeth, and walk with Lispeth, and say nice things to her, and call her pet names while he was getting strong enough to go away. It meant nothing at all to him, and everything in the world to Lispeth. She was very happy while the fortnight lasted, because she had found a man to love.

Being a savage by birth, she took no trouble to hide her feelings, and the Englishman was amused. When he went away, Lispeth walked with him up the Hill as far as Narkunda, very troubled and very miserable. The Chaplain's wife, being a good Christian and disliking anything in the shape of fuss or scandal – Lispeth was beyond her management entirely – had told the Englishman to tell Lispeth that he was coming back to marry her. 'She is but a child you know, and, I fear, at heart a heathen,' said the Chaplain's wife. So all the twelve miles up the Hill the Englishman, with his arm round Lispeth's waist, was assuring the girl that he would come back and marry her; and Lispeth made him promise over and over again. She wept on the Narkunda Ridge till he had passed out of sight along the Muttiani path.

Then she dried her tears and went in to Kotgarh again, and said to the Chaplain's wife, 'He will come back and marry me. He has gone to his own people to tell them so.' And the Chaplain's wife soothed Lispeth and said, 'He will come back.' At the end of two months, Lispeth grew impatient, and was told that the Englishman had gone over the seas to England. She knew where England was, because she had read little geography primers; but, of course, she had no conception of the nature of the sea, being a Hill-girl. There was an old puzzle-map of the World in the house. Lispeth had played with it when she was a child. She unearthed it again, and put it together of evenings, and cried to herself, and tried to imagine where her Englishman was. As she had no ideas of distance or steamboats, her notions were somewhat wild. It would not have made the least difference had she been perfectly correct; for the Englishman had no intention of coming back to marry a Hill-girl. He forgot all about her by the time he was butterfly-hunting in Assam. He wrote a book on the East afterwards. Lispeth's name did not appear there.

At the end of three months, Lispeth made daily pilgrimage to Narkunda to see if her Englishman was coming along the road. It gave her comfort, and the Chaplain's wife finding her happier thought that she was getting over her 'barbarous and most indelicate folly'. A little later, the walks ceased to help Lispeth and her temper grew very bad. The Chaplain's wife thought this a profitable time to let her know the real state of affairs – that the Englishman had only promised his love to keep her quiet – that he had never meant anything, and that it was wrong and improper of Lispeth to think of marriage with an Englishman, who was of a superior clay, besides being promised in marriage to a girl of his own people. Lispeth said that all this was clearly impossible because he had said he loved her, and the Chaplain's wife had, with her own lips, asserted that the Englishman was coming back.

'How can what he and you said be untrue?' a. ed Lispeth.

'We said it as an excuse to keep you quiet, child,' said the Chaplain's wife.

'Then you have lied to me,' said Lispeth, 'you and he?'

The Chaplain's wife bowed her head, and said nothing. Lispeth was silent, too, for a little time; then she went out down the valley, and returned in the dress of a Hill-girl – infamously dirty, but without the nose-stud and ear-rings. She had her hair braided into the long pigtail, helped out with black thread, that Hill-women wear.

'I am going back to my own people,' said she. 'You have killed Lispeth. There is only left old Jadéh's daughter – the daughter of a *pahari*[7] and the servant of *Tarka Devi*.[8] You are all liars, you English.'

By the time that the Chaplain's wife had recovered from the shock of the announcement that Lispeth had 'verted to her mother's gods, the girl had gone; and she never came back.

She took to her own unclean people savagely, as if to make up the arrears of the life she had stepped out of; and, in a little time, she married a woodcutter who beat her after the manner of *paharis*, and her beauty faded soon.

'There is no law whereby you can account for the vagaries of the heathen,' said the Chaplain's wife, 'and I believe that Lispeth was always at heart an infidel.' Seeing she had been taken into the Church of England at the mature age of five weeks, this statement does not do credit to the Chaplain's wife.

Lispeth was a very old woman when she died. She had always a perfect command of English, and when she was sufficiently drunk, could sometimes be induced to tell the story of her first love-affair.

It was hard then to realize that the bleared, wrinkled creature, exactly like a wisp of charred rag, could ever have been 'Lispeth of the Kotgarh Mission'.

Venus Annodomini [1]

And the years went on, as the years must do;
But our great Diana was always new –
Fresh, and blooming, and blonde, and fair,
With azure eyes and with aureate hair;
And all the folk, as they came or went,
Offered her praise to her heart's content.
Diana of Ephesus.

She had nothing to do with Number Eighteen in the Braccio Nuovo [2] of the Vatican, between Visconti's Ceres and the God of the Nile. She was purely an Indian deity – an Anglo-Indian deity, that is to say – and we called her *the* Venus Annodomini, to distinguish her from other Annodominis of the same everlasting order. There was a legend among the Hills that she had once been young; but no living man was prepared to come forward and say boldly that the legend was true. Men rode up to Simla, and stayed, and went away and made their name and did their life's work, and returned again to find the Venus Annodomini exactly as they had left her. She was as immutable as the Hills. But not quite so green. All that a girl of eighteen could do in the way of riding, walking, dancing, picnicking and over-exertion generally, the Venus Annodomini did, and showed no sign of fatigue or trace of weariness. Besides perpetual youth, she had discovered, men said, the secret of perpetual health; and her fame spread about the land. From a mere woman, she grew to be an Institution, insomuch that no young man could be said to be properly formed, who had not, at some time or another, worshipped at the shrine of the Venus Annodomini. There was no one like her, though there were many imitations. Six years in her eyes were no more than six months to ordinary women; and ten made less visible impression on her than does a week's fever on an ordinary woman. Everyone adored her, and in return she was pleasant and courteous to nearly everyone. Youth had been a habit of hers for so long, that she could not part with it – never realized, in fact, the necessity of parting with it – and took for her more chosen associates young people.

Among the worshippers of the Venus Annodomini was young Gayerson. 'Very Young Gayerson' he was called to distinguish him from his

father 'Young' Gayerson, a Bengal Civilian,[3] who affected the customs
– as he had the heart – of youth. 'Very Young' Gayerson was not
content to worship placidly and for form's sake, as the other young
men did, or to accept a ride or a dance, or a talk from the Venus
Annodomini in a properly humble and thankful spirit. He was exacting, and, therefore, the Venus Annodomini repressed him. He worried
himself nearly sick in a futile sort of way over her; and his devotion
and earnestness made him appear either shy or boisterous or rude, as
his mood might vary, by the side of the older men who, with him,
bowed before the Venus Annodomini. She was sorry for him. He
reminded her of a lad who, three-and-twenty years ago, had professed
a boundless devotion for her, and for whom in return she had felt
something more than a week's weakness. But that lad had fallen away
and married another woman less than a year after he had worshipped
her; and the Venus Annodomini had almost – not quite – forgotten
his name. 'Very Young' Gayerson had the same big blue eyes and the
same way of pouting his underlip when he was excited or troubled.
But the Venus Annodomini checked him sternly none the less. Too
much zeal was a thing that she did not approve of; preferring instead,
a tempered and sober tenderness.

'Very Young' Gayerson was miserable, and took no trouble to con-
ceal his wretchedness. He was in the Army – a Line regiment I think,
but am not certain – and, since his face was a looking-glass and his
forehead an open book, by reason of his innocence, his brothers-
in-arms made his life a burden to him and embittered his naturally
sweet disposition. No one except 'Very Young' Gayerson, and he never
told his views, knew how old 'Very Young' Gayerson believed the
Venus Annodomini to be. Perhaps he thought her five-and-twenty, or
perhaps she told him that she was this age. 'Very Young' Gayerson
would have forded the Indus in flood to carry her lightest word, and
had implicit faith in her. Everyone liked him, and everyone was sorry
when they saw him so bound a slave of the Venus Annodomini. Everyone, too, admitted that it was not her fault; for the Venus Annodomini
differed from Mrs Hauksbee and Mrs Reiver[4] in this particular – she
never moved a finger to attract anyone; but, like Ninon de L'Enclos,[5]
all men were attracted to her. One could admire and respect Mrs
Hauksbee, despise and avoid Mrs Reiver, but one was forced to adore
the Venus Annodomini.

'Very Young' Gayerson's papa held a Division or a Collectorate or
something administrative in a particularly unpleasant part of Bengal –
full of Babus who edited newspapers proving that 'Young' Gayerson

was a 'Nero' and a 'Scylla' and a 'Charybdis'; and, in addition to the Babus, there was a good deal of dysentery and cholera abroad for nine months of the year. 'Young' Gayerson – he was about five-and-forty – rather liked Babus, they amused him, but he objected to dysentery, and when he could get away, went to Darjiling [6] for the most part. This particular season he fancied that he would come up to Simla and see his boy. The boy was not altogether pleased. He told the Venus Annodomini that his father was coming up, and she flushed a little and said that she should be delighted to make his acquaintance. Then she looked long and thoughtfully at 'Very Young' Gayerson, because she was very, very sorry for him, and he was a very, very big idiot.

'My daughter is coming out in a fortnight, Mr Gayerson,' she said.

'Your *what?*' said he.

'Daughter,' said the Venus Annodomini. 'She's been out for a year at Home already, and I want her to see a little of India. She is nineteen and a very sensible nice girl I believe.'

'Very Young' Gayerson, who was a short twenty-two years old, nearly fell out of his chair with astonishment; for he had persisted in believing, against all belief, in the youth of the Venus Annodomini. She, with her back to the curtained window, watched the effect of her sentences and smiled.

'Very Young' Gayerson's papa came up twelve days later, and had not been in Simla four-and-twenty hours, before two men, old acquaintains of his, had told him how 'Very Young' Gayerson had been conducting himself.

'Young' Gayerson laughed a good deal, and inquired who the Venus Annodomini might be. Which proves that he had been living in Bengal where nobody knows anything except the rate of Exchange. Then he said boys will be boys, and spoke to his son about the matter. 'Very Young' Gayerson said that he felt wretched and unhappy; and 'Young' Gayerson said that he repented of having helped to bring a fool into the world. He suggested that his son had better cut his leave short and go down to his duties. This led to an unfilial answer, and relations were strained, until 'Young' Gayerson demanded that they should call on the Venus Annodomini. 'Very Young' Gayerson went with his papa, feeling, somehow, uncomfortable and small.

The Venus Annodomini received them graciously and 'Young' Gayerson said, 'By Jove! It's Kitty!' 'Very Young' Gayerson would have listened for an explanation, if his time had not been taken up with trying to talk to a large, handsome, quiet, well-dressed girl – introduced to him by the Venus Annodomini as her daughter. She was far older in manner, style, and repose than 'Very Young' Gayerson; and, as he realized this thing, he felt sick.

Presently, he heard the Venus Annodomini saying, 'Do you know that your son is one of my most devoted admirers?'

'I don't wonder,' said 'Young' Gayerson. Here he raised his voice, 'He follows his father's footsteps. Didn't I worship the ground you trod on, ever so long ago, Kitty – and you haven't changed since then. How strange it all seems!'

'Very Young' Gayerson said nothing. His conversation with the daughter of the Venus Annodomini was, through the rest of the call, fragmentary and disjointed.

'At five tomorrow then,' said the Venus Annodomini. 'And mind you are punctual.'

'At five punctually,' said 'Young' Gayerson. 'You can lend your old father a horse I daresay, youngster, can't you? I'm going for a ride tomorrow afternoon.'

'Certainly,' said 'Very Young' Gayerson. 'I am going down tomorrow morning. My ponies are at your service, Sir.'

The Venus Annodomini looked at him across the half-light of the room, and her big grey eyes filled with moisture. She rose and shook hands with him.

'Goodbye, Tom,' whispered the Venus Annodomini.

His Wedded Wife[1]

Cry 'Murder!' in the market-place, and each
Will turn upon his neighbour anxious eyes
That ask – 'Art thou the man?' We hunted Cain,
Some centuries ago, across the world.
That bred the fear our own misdeeds maintain
Today.

Vibart's Moralities.

Shakespeare says something about worms, or it may be giants or beetles,[2] turning if you tread on them too severely. The safest plan is never to tread on a worm – not even on the last new subaltern from Home, with his buttons hardly out of their tissue-paper, and the red of sappy English beef in his cheeks. This is a story of the worm that turned. For the sake of brevity, we will call Henry Augustus Ramsay Faizanne, 'The Worm', though he really was an exceedingly pretty boy, without a hair on his face, and with a waist like a girl's, when he came out to the Second 'Shikarris'[3] and was made unhappy in several ways. The 'Shikarris' are a high-caste regiment, and you must be able to do things well – play a banjo, or ride more than little, or sing, or act – to get on with them.

The Worm did nothing except fall off his pony, and knock chips out of gate-posts with his trap. Even that became monotonous after a time. He objected to whist, cut the cloth at billiards, sang out of tune, kept very much to himself, and wrote to his Mamma and sisters at Home. Four of these five things were vices which the 'Shikarris' objected to and set themselves to eradicate. Everyone knows how subalterns are, by brother subalterns, softened and not permitted to be ferocious. It is good and wholesome, and does no one any harm, unless tempers are lost; and then there is trouble. There was a man once –

The 'Shikarris' *shikarred* The Worm very much, and he bore everything without winking. He was so good and so anxious to learn, and flushed so pink, that his education was cut short, and he was left to his own devices by everyone except the Senior Subaltern, who continued to make life a burden to The Worm. The Senior Subaltern meant no harm; but his chaff was coarse and he didn't quite understand where to stop.

25

He had been waiting too long for his Company; and that always sours a man. Also he was in love, which made him worse.

One day, after he had borrowed The Worm's trap for a lady who never existed, had used it himself all the afternoon, had sent a note, to The Worm, purporting to come from the lady, and was telling the Mess all about it, The Worm rose in his place and said, in his quiet, lady-like voice – 'That was a very pretty sell; but I'll lay you a month's pay to a month's pay when you get your step, that I work a sell on you that you'll remember for the rest of your days, and the Regiment after you when you're dead or broke.' [4] The Worm wasn't angry in the least, and the rest of the Mess shouted. Then the Senior Subaltern looked at The Worm from the boots upwards, and down again, and said – 'Done, Baby.' The Worm held the rest of the Mess to witness that the bet had been taken, and retired into a book with a sweet smile.

Two months passed, and the Senior Subaltern still educated The Worm, who began to move about a little more as the hot weather came on. I have said that the Senior Subaltern was in love. The curious thing is that a girl was in love with the Senior Subaltern. Though the Colonel said awful things, and the Majors snorted, and the married Captains looked unutterable wisdom, and the juniors scoffed, those two were engaged.

The Senior Subaltern was so pleased with getting his Company and his acceptance at the same time that he forgot to bother The Worm. The girl was a pretty girl, and had money of her own. She does not come into this story at all.

One night, at the beginning of the hot weather, all the Mess, except The Worm who had gone to his own room to write Home letters, were sitting on the platform outside the Mess House. The Band had finished playing, but no one wanted to go in. And the Captains' wives were there also. The folly of a man in love is unlimited. The Senior Subaltern had been holding forth on the merits of the girl he was engaged to, and the ladies were purring approval while the men yawned, when there was a rustle of skirts in the dark, and a tired, faint voice lifted itself.

'Where's my husband?'

I do not wish in the least to reflect on the morality of the 'Shikarris'; but it is on record that four men jumped up as if they had been shot. Three of them were married men. Perhaps they were afraid that their wives had come from Home unbeknownst. The fourth said that he had acted on the impulse of the moment. He explained this afterwards.

Then the voice cried, 'O Lionel!' Lionel was the Senior Subaltern's name. A woman came into the little circle of light by the candles on the peg-tables, stretching out her hands to the dark where the Senior Subaltern was, and sobbing. We rose to our feet, feeling that things were going to happen and ready to believe the worst. In this bad, small world of ours, one knows so little of the life of the next man – which, after all, is entirely his own concern – that one is not surprised when a crash comes. Anything might turn up any day for anyone. Perhaps the Senior Subaltern had been trapped in his youth. Men are crippled that way occasionally. We didn't know; we wanted to hear; and the Captains' wives were as anxious as we. If he had been trapped, he was to be excused; for the woman from nowhere, in the dusty shoes and grey travelling-dress, was very lovely, with black hair and great eyes full of tears. She was tall, with a fine figure, and her voice had a running sob in it pitiful to hear. As soon as the Senior Subaltern stood up, she threw her arms round his neck, and called him 'my darling', and said she could not bear waiting alone in England, and his letters were so short and cold, and she was his to the end of the world, and would he forgive her? This did not sound quite like a lady's way of speaking. It was too demonstrative.

Things seemed black indeed, and the Captains' wives peered under their eyebrows at the Senior Subaltern, and the Colonel's face set like the Day of Judgment framed in grey bristles, and no one spoke for a while.

Next the Colonel said, very shortly, 'Well, Sir?' and the woman sobbed afresh. The Senior Subaltern was half choked with the arms round his neck, but he gasped out – 'It's a damned lie! I never had a wife in my life!' – 'Don't swear,' said the Colonel. 'Come into the Mess. We must sift this clear somehow,' and he sighed to himself, for he believed in his 'Shikarris', did the Colonel.

We trooped into the ante-room, under the full lights, and there we saw how beautiful the woman was. She stood up in the middle of us all, sometimes choking with crying, then hard and proud, and then holding out her arms to the Senior Subaltern. It was like the fourth act of a tragedy. She told us how the Senior Subaltern had married her when he was Home on leave eighteen months before; and she seemed to know all that we knew, and more too, of his people and his past life. He was white and ashy-grey, trying now and again to break into the torrent of her words; and we, noting how lovely she was and what a criminal he looked, esteemed him a beast of the worst kind. We felt sorry for him, though.

I shall never forget the indictment of the Senior Subaltern by his wife. Nor will he. It was so sudden, rushing out of the dark, unannounced, into our dull lives. The Captains' wives stood back; but their eyes were alight, and you could see that they had already convicted and sentenced the Senior Subaltern. The Colonel seemed five years older. One Major was shading his eyes with his hand and watching the woman from underneath it. Another was chewing his moustache and smiling quietly as if he were witnessing a play. Full in the open space in the centre, by the whist-tables, the Senior Subaltern's terrier was hunting for fleas. I remember all this as clearly as though a photograph were in my hand. I remember the look of horror on the Senior Subaltern's face. It was rather like seeing a man hanged; but much more interesting. Finally, the woman wound up by saying that the Senior Subaltern carried a double F. M. in tattoo on his left shoulder. We all knew that, and to our innocent minds it seemed to clinch the matter. But one of the bachelor Majors said very politely, 'I presume that your marriage-certificate would be more to the purpose?'

That roused the woman. She stood up and sneered at the Senior Subaltern for a cur, and abused the Major and the Colonel and all the rest. Then she wept, and then she pulled a paper from her breast, saying imperially, 'Take that! And let my husband – my lawfully wedded husband – read it aloud – if he dare!'

There was a hush, and the men looked into each other's eyes as the Senior Subaltern came forward in a dazed and dizzy way, and took the paper. We were wondering, as we stared, whether there was anything against anyone of us that might turn up later on. The Senior Subaltern's throat was dry; but, as he ran his eye over the paper, he broke out into a hoarse cackle of relief, and said to the woman, 'You young blackguard!' But the woman had fled through a door, and on the paper was written, 'This is to certify that I, The Worm, have paid in full my debts to the Senior Subaltern, and, further, that the Senior Subaltern is my debtor, by agreement on the 23d of February, as by the Mess attested, to the extent of one month's Captain's pay, in the lawful currency of the Indian Empire.'

Then a deputation set off for The Worm's quarters and found him, betwixt and between, unlacing his stays, with the hat, wig, and serge dress, on the bed. He came over as he was, and the 'Shikarris' shouted till the Gunners' Mess sent over to know if they might have a share of the fun. I think we were all, except the Colonel and the Senior Subaltern, a little disappointed that the scandal had come to nothing. But that is human nature. There could be no two words about The Worm's acting. It leaned as near to a nasty tragedy as anything this side of a joke can. When most of the Subalterns sat upon him with sofa-cushions to find out why he had not said that acting was his strong point, he answered very quietly, 'I don't think you ever asked me. I used to act at Home with my sisters.' But no acting with girls could account for The Worm's display that night. Personally, I think it was in bad taste. Besides being dangerous. There is no sort of use in playing with fire, even for fun.

The 'Shikarris' made him President of the Regimental Dramatic Club; and, when the Senior Subaltern paid up his debt, which he did at once, The Worm sank the money in scenery and dresses. He was a good Worm; and the 'Shikarris' are proud of him. The only drawback is that he has been christened 'Mrs Senior Subaltern'; and, as there are now two Mrs Senior Subalterns in the Station, this is sometimes confusing to strangers.

Later on, I will tell you of a case something like this, but with all the jest left out and nothing in it but real trouble.

In the Pride of his Youth [1]

'Stopped in the straight when the race was his own!
Look at him cutting it – cur to the bone!'
'Ask, ere the youngster be rated and chidden,
What did he carry and how was he ridden?
Maybe they used him too much at the start;
Maybe Fate's weight-cloths [2] are breaking his heart.'
                                        Life's Handicap.

When I was telling you of the joke that The Worm played off on the Senior Subaltern, I promised a somewhat similar tale, but with all the jest left out. This is that tale.

Dicky Hatt was kidnapped in his early, early youth – neither by landlady's daughter, housemaid, barmaid, nor cook, but by a girl so nearly of his own caste that only a woman could have said she was just the least little bit in the world below it. This happened a month before he came out to India, and five days after his one-and-twentieth birthday. The girl was nineteen – six years older than Dicky in the things of this world, that is to say – and, for the time, twice as foolish as he.

Excepting, always, falling off a horse there is nothing more fatally easy than marriage before the Registrar. The ceremony costs less than fifty shillings, and is remarkably like walking into a pawn-shop. After the declarations of residence have been put in, four minutes will cover the rest of the proceedings – fees, attestation, and all. Then the Registrar slides the blotting-pad over the names, and says grimly with his pen between his teeth, 'Now you're man and wife'; and the couple walk out into the street feeling as if something were horribly illegal somewhere.

But that ceremony holds and can drag a man to his undoing just as thoroughly as the 'long as ye both shall live' curse from the altar-rails, with the bridesmaids giggling behind, and 'The Voice that breathed o'er Eden' lifting the roof off. In this manner was Dicky Hatt kidnapped, and he considered it vastly fine, for he had received an appointment in India which carried a magnificent salary from the Home point of view. The marriage was to be kept secret for a year. Then Mrs Dicky Hatt was to come out, and the rest of life was to be a glorious golden mist. That was how they sketched it under the Addison Road Station lamps; and, after one short month, came Gravesend [3] and Dicky steaming out to his new life, and the girl crying in a thirty-shillings a week bed-and-living-room, in a back street off Montpelier Square near the Knightsbridge Barracks.

But the country that Dicky came to was a hard land where men of twenty-one were reckoned very small boys indeed, and life was expensive. The salary that loomed so large six thousand miles away did not go far. Particularly when Dicky divided it by two, and remitted more than the fair half, at $1-6\frac{7}{8}$,[4] to Montpelier Square. One hundred and thirty-five rupees out of three hundred and thirty is not much to live on; but it was absurd to suppose that Mrs Hatt could exist forever on the £20 held back by Dicky from his outfit allowance. Dicky saw this and remitted at once; always remembering that Rs. 700 were to be paid, twelve months later, for a first-class passage out for a lady. When you add to these trifling details the natural instincts of a boy beginning a new life in a new country and longing to go about and enjoy himself, and the necessity for grappling with strange work – which, properly speaking, should take up a boy's undivided attention – you will see that Dicky started handicapped. He saw it himself for a breath or two; but he did not guess the full beauty of his future.

As the hot weather began, the shackles settled on him and ate into his flesh. First would come letters – big, crossed, seven-sheet letters – from his wife, telling him how she longed to see him, and what a Heaven upon earth would be their property when they met. Then some boy of the chummery wherein Dicky lodged would pound on the door of his bare little room, and tell him to come out to look at a pony – the very thing to suit him. Dicky could not afford ponies. He had to explain this. Dicky could not afford living in the chummery, modest as it was. He had to explain this before he moved to a single room next the office where he worked all day. He kept house on a green oilcloth table-cover, one chair, one bedstead, one photograph, one tooth-glass very strong and thick, a seven-rupee eight-anna filter, and messing by contract at thirty-seven rupees a month. Which last item was extortion. He had no punkah, for a punkah costs fifteen rupees a month; but he slept on the roof of the office with all his wife's letters under his pillow. Now and again he was asked out to dinner, where he got both a punkah and an iced drink. But this was seldom, for people objected to recognizing a boy who had evidently the instincts of a Scotch tallow-chandler, and who lived in such a nasty fashion. Dicky could not subscribe to any amusement, so he found no amusement except the pleasure of turning over his Bank-book and reading what it said about 'loans on approved security'. That cost nothing. He remitted through a Bombay Bank, by the way, and the Station knew nothing of his private affairs.

Every month he sent Home all he could possibly spare for his wife and for another reason which was expected to explain itself shortly, and would require more money.

About this time Dicky was overtaken with the nervous, haunting fear that besets married men when they are out of sorts. He had no pension to look to. What if he should die suddenly, and leave his wife unprovided for? The thought used to lay hold of him in the still, hot nights on the roof, till the shaking of his heart made him think that he was going to die then and there of heart-disease. Now this is a frame of mind which no boy has a right to know. It is a strong man's trouble; but, coming when it did, it nearly drove poor punkah-less, perspiring Dicky Hatt mad. He could tell no one about it.

A certain amount of 'screw'[5] is as necessary for a man as for a billiard-ball. It makes them both do wonderful things. Dicky needed money badly, and he worked for it like a horse. But, naturally, the men who owned him knew that a boy can live very comfortably on a certain income – pay in India is a matter of age not merit, you see, and, if their particular boy wished to work like two boys, Business forbid that they should stop him. But Business forbid that they should give him an increase of pay at his present ridiculously immature age. So Dicky won certain rises of salary – ample for a boy – not enough for a wife and a child – certainly too little for the seven-hundred-rupee passage that he and Mrs Hatt had discussed so lightly once upon a time. And with this he was forced to be content.

Somehow, all his money seemed to fade away in Home drafts and the crushing Exchange, and the tone of the Home letters changed and grew querulous. 'Why wouldn't Dicky have his wife and the baby out? Surely he had a salary – a fine salary – and it was too bad of him to enjoy himself in India. But would he – could he – make the next draft a little more elastic?' Here followed a list of baby's kit, as long as a Parsee's bill. Then Dicky, whose heart yearned to his wife and the little son he had never seen – which, again, is a feeling no boy is entitled to – enlarged the draft and wrote queer half-boy, half-man letters, saying that life was not so enjoyable after all and would the little wife wait yet a little longer? But the little wife, however much she approved of money, objected to waiting, and there was a strange, hard sort of ring in her letters that Dicky didn't understand. How could he, poor boy?

Later on still – just as Dicky had been told – *àpropos* of another youngster who had 'made a fool of himself' as the saying is – that matrimony would not only ruin his further chances of advancement, but would lose him his present appointment – came the news that the baby, his own little, little son, had died and, behind this, forty lines of an angry woman's scrawl, saying the death might have been averted if certain things, all costing money, had been done, or if the mother and the baby had been with Dicky. The letter struck at Dicky's naked heart; but, not being officially entitled to a baby, he could show no sign of trouble.

How Dicky won through the next four months, and what hope he kept alight to force him into his work, no one dare say. He pounded on, the seven-hundred-rupee passage as far away as ever, and his style of living unchanged, except when he launched into a new filter. There was the strain of his office-work, and the strain of his remittances, and the knowledge of his boy's death, which touched the boy more, perhaps, than it would have touched a man; and, beyond all, the enduring strain of his daily life. Grey-headed seniors who approved of his thrift and his fashion of denying himself everything pleasant, reminded him of the old saw that says –

> 'If a youth would be distinguished in his art, art, art,
> He must keep the girls away from his heart, heart, heart.'

And Dicky, who fancied he had been through every trouble that a man is permitted to know, had to laugh and agree; with the last line of his balanced Bank-book jingling in his head day and night.

But he had one more sorrow to digest before the end. There arrived a letter from the little wife – the natural sequence of the others if Dicky had only known it – and the burden of that letter was 'gone with a handsomer man than you'. It was a rather curious production, without stops, something like this – 'She was not going to wait for ever and the baby was dead and Dicky was only a boy and he would never set eyes on her again and why hadn't he waved his handkerchief to her when he left Gravesend and God was her judge she was a wicked woman but Dicky was worse enjoying himself in India and this other man loved the ground she trod on and would Dicky ever forgive her for she would never forgive Dicky; and there was no address to write to.'

Instead of thanking his stars that he was free, Dicky discovered exactly how an injured husband feels – again, not at all the knowledge to which a boy is entitled – for his mind went back to his wife as he remembered her in the thirty-shilling 'suite' in Montpelier Square, when the dawn of his last morning in England was breaking, and she was crying in the bed.

Whereat he rolled about on his bed and bit his fingers. He never stopped to think whether, if he had met Mrs Hatt after those two years, he would have discovered that he and she had grown quite different and new persons. This, theoretically, he ought to have done. He spent the night after the English Mail came in rather severe pain.

Next morning, Dicky Hatt felt disinclined to work. He argued that he had missed the pleasure of youth. He was tired, and he had tasted all the sorrow in life before three-and-twenty. His Honour was gone – that was the man; and now he, too, would go to the Devil – that was the boy in him. So he put his head down on the green oil-cloth tablecover, and wept before resigning his post, and all it offered.

But the reward of his services came. He was given three days to reconsider himself, and the Head of the establishment, after some telegraphings, said that it was a most unusual step, but, in view of the ability that Mr Hatt had displayed at such and such a time, at such and such junctures, he was in a position to offer him an infinitely superior post – first on probation and later, in the natural course of things, on confirmation. 'And how much does the post carry?' said Dicky. 'Six hundred and fifty rupees,' said the Head slowly, expecting to see the young man sink with gratitude and joy.

And it came then! The seven-hundred-rupee-passage, and enough to have saved the wife, and the little son, and to have allowed of assured and open marriage, came then. Dicky burst into a roar of laughter – laughter he could not check – nasty, jangling merriment that seemed as if it would go on for ever. When he had recovered himself he said, quite seriously, 'I'm tired of work. I'm an old man now. It's about time I retired. And I will.'

'The boy's mad!' said the Head.

I think he was right; but Dicky Hatt never reappeared to settle the question.

The Daughter of the Regiment [1]

Jain 'Ardin' was a Sarjint's wife,
  A Sarjint's wife wus she.
She married of 'im in Orldershort
  An' comed acrost the sea.
(*Chorus*) 'Ave you never 'eard tell o' Jain 'Ardin'?
                    Jain 'Ardin'?
                    Jain 'Ardin'?
    'Ave you never 'eard tell o' Jain 'Ardin'?
The pride o' the Compan*ee*?
                Old Barrack-Room Ballad.

'A gentleman who doesn't know the Circassian Circle ought not to stand up for it – puttin' everybody out.' That was what Miss McKenna said, and the Sergeant who was my *vis-à-vis* looked the same thing. I was afraid of Miss McKenna. She was six feet high, all yellow freckles and red hair, and was simply clad in white satin shoes, a pink muslin dress, an apple-green stuff sash, and black silk gloves, with yellow roses in her hair. Wherefore I fled from Miss McKenna and sought my friend Private Mulvaney, who was at the cant– refreshment-table.

'So you've been dancin' with little Jhansi [2] McKenna, Sorr – she that's goin' to marry Corp'ril Slane? Whin you next conversh wid your lorruds an' your ladies, tell thim you've danced wid little Jhansi. 'Tis a thing to be proud av.'

But I wasn't proud. I was humble. I saw a story in Private Mulvaney's eye; and besides, if he stayed too long at the bar, he would, I knew, qualify for more pack-drill. Now to meet an esteemed friend doing pack-drill outside the guard-room is embarrassing, especially if you happen to be walking with his Commanding Officer.

'Come on to the parade-ground, Mulvaney, it's cooler there, and tell me about Miss McKenna. What is she, and who is she, and why is she called "Jhansi"?'

'D'ye mane to say you've never heard av Ould Pummeloe's [3] daughter? An' you thinkin' you know things! I'm wid ye in a minut' whin me poipe's lit.'

We came out under the stars. Mulvaney sat down on one of the

35

artillery bridges, and began in the usual way: his pipe between his teeth, his big hands clasped and dropped between his knees, and his cap well on the back of his head –

'Whin Mrs Mulvaney, that is, was Miss Shadd that was, you were a dale younger than you are now, an' the Army was dif'rint in sev'ril e-senshuls. Bhoys have no call for to marry nowadays, an' that's why the Army has so few rale, good, honust, swearin', strapagin', tinder-hearted, heavy-futted wives as ut used to have whin I was a Corp'ril. I was rejuced afthwards – but no matther – I was a Corp'ril wanst. In thim times, a man lived *an'* died wid his regiment; an' by natur', he married whin he was a *man*. Whin I was Corp'ril – Mother av Hivin, how the rigimint has died an' been borrun since that day! – my Colour-Sar'jint was Ould McKenna, an' a married man tu. An' his woife – his first woife, for he married three times did McKenna – was Bridget McKenna, from Portarlington, like mesilf. I've misremembered fwhat her first name was; but in B Comp'ny we called her "Ould Pummeloe", by reason av her figure, which was entirely cir-cum-fe-renshill. Like the big dhrum! Now that woman – God rock her sowl to rest in glory! – was for everlastin' havin' childher; an' McKenna, whin the fifth or sixth come squallin' on to the musther-roll, swore he wud number thim off in future. But Ould Pummeloe she prayed av him to christen them after the names av the stations they was borrun in. So there was Colaba McKenna, an' Muttra McKenna, an' a whole Presidincy⁴ av other McKennas, an' little Jhansi, dancin' over yonder. Whin the childher wasn't bornin', they was dying; for, av our childher die like sheep in these days, they died like flies thin. I lost me own little Shadd – but no matther. 'Tis long ago, and Mrs Mulvaney niver had another.

'I'm digresshin. Wan divil's hot summer, there come an order from some mad ijjit, whose name I misremember, for the rigimint to go up-country. Maybe they wanted to know how the new rail carried throops. They knew! On me sowl, they knew before they was done! Old Pummeloe had just buried Muttra McKenna; an', the season bein' onwholesim, only little Jhansi McKenna, who was four year ould thin, was left on hand.

'Foive childer gone in fourteen months. 'Twas harrd, wasn't ut?

'So we wint up to our new station in that blazin' heat – may the curse av Saint Lawrence⁵ conshume the man who gave the ordher! Will I iver forget that move? They gave us two wake thrains to the rigimint; an' we was eight hundher' and sivinty strong. There was A, B, C, an' D Companies in the secon' thrain, wid twelve women, no orficers' ladies, an' thirteen childher. We was to go six hundher' miles, an' railways was

new in thim days. Whin we had been a night in the belly av the thrain –
the men ragin' in their shirts an' dhrinkin' anything they cud find, an'
eatin' bad fruit-stuff whin they cud, for we cudn't stop 'em – I was a
Corp'ril thin – the cholera bruk out wid the dawnin' av the day.

'Pray to the Saints, you may niver see cholera in a throop-thrain! 'Tis
like the judgmint av God hittin' down from the nakid sky! We run into a
rest-camp – as ut might have been Ludianny, but not by any means so
comfortable. The Orficer Commandin' sent a telegrapt up the line,
three hundher' mile up, askin' for help. Faith, we wanted ut, for ivry
sowl av the followers ran for the dear life as soon as the thrain stopped;
an' by the time that telegrapt was writ, there wasn't a naygur in the
station exceptin' the telegrapt-clerk – an' he only bekaze he was held
down to his chair by the scruff av his sneakin' black neck. Thin the day
began wid the noise in the carr'ges, an' the rattle av the men on the
platform fallin' over, arms an' all, as they stud for to answer the Comp'ny
muster-roll before goin' over to the camp. 'Tisn't for me to say what like
the cholera was like. May be the Doctor cud ha' tould, av he hadn't
dropped on to the platform from the door av a carriage where we was
takin' out the dead. He died wid the rest. Some bhoys had died in the
night. We tuk out siven, and twenty more was sickenin' as we tuk thim.
The women was huddled up anyways, screamin' wid fear.

'Sez the Commandin' Orficer whose name I misremember, "Take the
women over to that tope [6] av trees yonder. Get thim out av the camp.
'Tis no place for thim."

'Ould Pummeloe was sittin' on her beddin'-rowl, thryin' to kape little
Jhansi quiet. "Go off to that tope!" sez the Orficer. "Go out av the
men's way!"

'"Be dammed av I do!" sez Ould Pummeloe, an' little Jhansi, squattin'
by her mother's side, squeaks out, "Be damned av I do," tu. Thin Ould
Pummeloe turns to the women an' she sez, "Are ye goin' to let the bhoys
die while you're picnickin', ye sluts?" sez she. "'Tis wather they want.
Come on an' help."

'Wid that, she turns up her sleeves an' steps out for a well behind the
rest-camp – little Jhansi trottin' behind wid a *lotah* [7] an' string, an' the
other women followin' like lambs, wid horse-buckets and cookin' pots.
Whin all the things was full, Ould Pummeloe marches back into camp –
'twas like a battlefield wid all the glory missin' – at the hid av the
rigimint av women.

'"McKenna, me man!" she sez, wid a voice on her like grand-roun's
challenge, "tell the bhoys to be quiet. Ould Pummeloe's comin' to look
afther thim – wid free dhrinks."

'Thin we cheered, an' the cheerin' in the lines was louder than the noise av the poor divils wid the sickness on thim. But not much.

'You see, we was a new an' raw rigimint in those days, an' we cud make neither head nor tail av the sickness; an' so we was useless. The men was goin' roun' an' about like dumb sheep, waitin' for the nex' man to fall over, an' sayin' undher their spache, "Fwhat is ut? In the name av God, *fwhat* is ut?" 'Twas horrible. But through ut all, up an' down, an' down an' up, wint Ould Pummeloe an' little Jhansi – all we cud see av the baby, undher a dead man's helmut wid the chin-strap swingin' about her little stummick – up an' down wid the wather an' fwhat brandy there was.

'Now an' thin Ould Pummeloe, the tears runnin' down her fat, red face, sez, "Me bhoys, me poor, dead, darlin' bhoys!" But, for the most, she was thryin' to put heart into the men an' kape thim stiddy; and little Jhansi was tellin' thim all they wud be "betther in the mornin'". 'Twas a thrick she'd picked up from hearin' Ould Pummeloe whin Muttra was burnin' out wid fever. In the mornin'! 'Twas the iverlastin' mornin' at St Pether's Gate was the mornin' for seven-an'-twenty good men; and twenty more was sick to the death in that bitter, burnin' sun. But the women worked like angils as I've said, an' the men like divils, till two doctors come down from above, and we was rescued.

'But, just before that, Ould Pummeloe, on her knees over a bhoy in my squad – right-cot man to me he was in the barrick – tellin' him the worrud av the Church that niver failed a man yet, sez, "Hould me up, bhoys! I'm feelin' bloody sick!" 'Twas the sun, not the cholera, did ut. She misremembered she was only wearin' her ould black bonnet, an' she died wid "McKenna, me man," houldin' her up, an' the bhoys howled whin they buried her.

'That night, a big wind blew, an' blew, an' blew, an' blew the tents flat. But it blew the cholera away an' niver another case there was all the while we was waitin' – ten days in quarintin'. Av you will belave me, the thrack av the sickness in the camp was for all the wurruld the thrack av a man walkin' four times in a figur-av-eight through the tents. They say 'tis the Wandherin' Jew takes the cholera wid him. I believe ut.

'An' *that*,' said Mulvaney illogically, 'is the cause why little Jhansi McKenna is fwhat she is. She was brought up by the Quartermaster Sergeant's wife whin McKenna died, but she b'longs to B Comp'ny; and this tale I'm tellin' you – *wid* a proper appreciashin av Jhansi McKenna – I've belted into ivry recruity av the Comp'ny as he was drafted. 'Faith, 'twas me belted Corp'ril Slane into askin' the girl!'

'Not really?'

'Man, I did! She's no beauty to look at, but she's Ould Pummeloe's daughter, an' 'tis my juty to provide for her. Just before Slane got his promotion I sez to him, "Slane," sez I, "tomorrow 'twill be insubordinashin av me to chastise you; but, by the sowl av Ould Pummeloe, who is now in glory, av you don't give me your wurrud to ask Jhansi McKenna at wanst, I'll peel the flesh off yer bones wid a brass huk tonight. 'Tis a dishgrace to B Comp'ny she's been single so long!" sez I. Was I goin' to let a three-year-ould [8] preshume to discoorse wid me – my will bein' set? No! Slane wint an' asked her. He's a good bhoy is Slane. Wan av these days he'll get into the Com'ssariat an' dhrive a buggy wid his – savin's. So I provided for Ould Pummeloe's daughter; an' now you go along an' dance agin wid her.'

And I did.

I felt a respect for Miss Jhansi McKenna; and I went to her wedding later on.

Perhaps I will tell you about that one of these days. [9]

❴ Thrown Away ¹ ❵

And some are sulky, while some will plunge.
  [*So ho! Steady! Stand still, you!*]
Some you must gentle, and some you must lunge.²
  [*There! There! Who wants to kill you?*]
Some – there are losses in every trade –
Will break their hearts ere bitted and made,
Will fight like fiends as the rope cuts hard,
And die dumb-mad in the breaking-yard.
                    Toolungala Stockyard Chorus.

To rear a boy under what parents call the 'sheltered life system' is, if the boy must go into the world and fend for himself, not wise. Unless he be one in a thousand he has certainly to pass through many unnecessary troubles; and may, possibly, come to extreme grief simply from ignorance of the proper proportions of things.

Let a puppy eat the soap in the bath-room or chew a newly-blacked boot. He chews and chuckles until, by and by, he finds out that blacking and Old Brown Windsor make him very sick; so he argues that soap and boots are not wholesome. Any old dog about the house will soon show him the unwisdom of biting big dogs' ears. Being young, he remembers and goes abroad, at six months, a well-mannered little beast with a chastened appetite. If he had been kept away from boots, and soap, and big dogs till he came to the trinity full-grown and with developed teeth, consider how fearfully sick and thrashed he would be! Apply that notion to the 'sheltered life', and see how it works. It does not sound pretty, but it is the better of two evils.

There was a Boy once who had been brought up under the 'sheltered life' theory; and the theory killed him dead. He stayed with his people all his days, from the hour he was born till the hour he went into Sandhurst nearly at the top of the list. He was beautifully taught in all that wins marks by a private tutor, and carried the extra weight of 'never having given his parents an hour's anxiety in his life'. What he learnt at Sandhurst beyond the regular routine is of no great consequence. He looked about him, and he found soap and blacking, so to speak, very good. He ate a little, and came out of Sandhurst not so high as he went in. Then there was an interval and a scene with his people, who expected much from him. Next a year of living unspotted from the world in a third-rate depôt battalion where all the juniors were children and all the seniors old women; and lastly he came out to India where he was cut off from the support of his parents, and had no one to fall back on in time of trouble except himself.

Now India is a place beyond all others where one must not take things too seriously – the mid-day sun always excepted. Too much work and too much energy kill a man just as effectively as too much assorted vice or too much drink. Flirtation does not matter, because everyone is being transferred and either you or she leave the Station, and never return. Good work does not matter, because a man is judged by his worst output and another man takes all the credit of his best as a rule. Bad work does not matter, because other men do worse and incompetents hang on longer in India than anywhere else. Amusements do not matter, because you must repeat them as soon as you have accomplished them once, and most amusements only mean trying to win another person's money. Sickness does not matter, because it's all in the day's work, and if you die, another man takes over your place and your office in the eight hours between death and burial. Nothing matters except Home-furlough and acting allowances, and these only because they are scarce. It is a slack country where all men work with imperfect instruments; and the wisest thing is to escape as soon as ever you can to some place where amusement is amusement and a reputation worth the having.

But this Boy – the tale is as old as the Hills – came out, and took all things seriously. He was pretty and was petted. He took the pettings seriously and fretted over women not worth saddling a pony to call upon. He found his new free life in India very good. It does look attractive in the beginning, from a subaltern's point of view – all ponies, partners, dancing, and so on. He tasted it as the puppy tastes the soap. Only he came late to the eating, with a grown set of teeth. He had no sense of balance – just like the puppy – and could not understand why he was not treated with the consideration he received under his father's roof. This hurt his feelings.

He quarrelled with other boys and, being sensitive to the marrow, remembered these quarrels, and they excited him. He found whist, and gymkhanas, and things of that kind (meant to amuse one after office) good; but he took them seriously too, just as seriously as he took the 'head' that followed after drink. He lost his money over whist and gymkhanas because they were new to him.

He took his losses seriously, and wasted as much energy and interest over a two-goldmohur³ race for maiden⁴ *ekka*-ponies⁵ with their manes hogged, as if it had been the Derby. One half of this came from inexperience – much as the puppy squabbles with the corner of the hearthrug – and the other half from the dizziness bred by stumbling out of his quiet life into the glare and excitement of a livelier one. No one told him about the soap and the blacking, because an average man takes it for granted that an average man is ordinarily careful in regard to them. It was pitiful to watch The Boy knocking himself to pieces, as an overhandled colt falls down and cuts himself when he gets away from the groom.

This unbridled license in amusements not worth the trouble of breaking line for, much less rioting over, endured for six months – all through one cold weather – and then we thought that the heat and the knowledge of having lost his money and health and lamed his horses would sober The Boy down, and he would stand steady. In ninety-nine cases out of a hundred this would have happened. You can see the principle working in any Indian Station. But this particular case fell through because The Boy was sensitive and took things seriously – as I may have said some seven times before. Of course, we could not tell how his excesses struck him personally. They were nothing very heartbreaking or above the average. He might be crippled for life financially, and want a little nursing. Still the memory of his performances would wither away in one hot weather, and the bankers would help him to tide over the money-troubles. But he must have taken another view altogether and have believed himself ruined beyond redemption. His Colonel talked to him severely when the cold weather ended. That made him more wretched than ever; and it was only an ordinary 'Colonel's wigging'!

What follows is a curious instance of the fashion in which we are all linked together and made responsible for one another. *The* thing that kicked the beam in The Boy's mind was a remark that a woman made when he was talking to her. There is no use in repeating it, for it was only a cruel little sentence, rapped out before thinking, that made him flush to the roots of his hair. He kept himself to himself for three days, and then put in for two days' leave to go shooting near a Canal Engineer's Rest House⁶ about thirty miles out. He got his leave, and that night at Mess was noisier and more offensive than ever. He said that he was 'going to shoot big game', and left at half-past ten o'clock in an *ekka*. Partridge – which was the only thing a man could get near the Rest House – is not big game; so everyone laughed.

Next morning one of the Majors came in from short leave, and heard that The Boy had gone out to shoot 'big game'. The Major had taken an interest in The Boy, and had, more than once, tried to check him. The Major put up his eyebrows when he heard of the expedition and went to The Boy's rooms where he rummaged.

Presently he came out and found me leaving cards on the Mess. There was no one else in the ante-room.

He said, 'The Boy has gone out shooting. *Does* a man shoot *tetur*[7] with a revolver and writing-case?'

I said, 'Nonsense, Major!' for I saw what was in his mind.

He said, 'Nonsense or no nonsense, I'm going to the Canal now – at once. I don't feel easy.'

Then he thought for a minute, and said, 'Can you lie?'

'You know best,' I answered. 'It's my profession.'

'Very well,' said the Major, 'you must come out with me now – at once – in an *ekka* to the Canal to shoot black-buck. Go and put on *shikar*-kit[8] – *quick* – and drive here with a gun.'

The Major was a masterful man; and I knew that he would not give orders for nothing. So I obeyed, and on return found the Major packed up in an *ekka* – gun-cases and food slung below – all ready for a shooting-trip.

He dismissed the driver and drove himself. We jogged along quietly while in the station; but, as soon as we got to the dusty road across the plains, he made that pony fly. A country-bred[9] can do nearly anything at a pinch. We covered the thirty miles in under three hours, but the poor brute was nearly dead.

Once I said, 'What's the blazing hurry, Major?'

He said quietly, 'The Boy has been alone, by himself for – one, two, five – fourteen hours now! I tell you, I don't feel easy.'

This uneasiness spread itself to me, and I helped to beat the pony.

When we came to the Canal Engineer's Rest House the Major called for The Boy's servant; but there was no answer. Then we went up to the house, calling for The Boy by name; but there was no answer.

'Oh, he's out shooting,' said I.

Just then, I saw through one of the windows a little hurricane-lamp burning. This was at four in the afternoon. We both stopped dead in the verandah, holding our breath to catch every sound; and we heard, inside the room, the '*brr – brr – brr*' of a multitude of flies. The Major said nothing, but he took off his helmet and we entered very softly.

The Boy was dead on the bed in the centre of the bare, lime-washed room. He had shot his head nearly to pieces with his revolver. The gun-cases were still strapped, so was the bedding, and on the table lay The

Boy's writing-case with photographs. He had gone away to die like a poisoned rat!

The Major said to himself softly, 'Poor Boy! Poor, *poor* devil!' Then he turned away from the bed and said, 'I want your help in this business.'

Knowing The Boy was dead by his own hand, I saw exactly what that help would be, so I passed over to the table, took a chair, lit a cheroot, and began to go through the writing-case; the Major looking over my shoulder and repeating to himself, 'We came too late! – Like a rat in a hole! – Poor, *poor* devil!'

The Boy must have spent half the night in writing to his people, to his Colonel, and to a girl at Home; and as soon as he had finished, must have shot himself, for he had been dead a long time when we came in.

I read all that he had written, and passed over each sheet to the Major as I finished it.

We saw from his accounts how very seriously he had taken everything. He wrote about 'disgrace which he was unable to bear' – 'indelible shame' – 'criminal folly' – 'wasted life', and so on; besides a lot of private things to his father and mother much too sacred to put into print. The letter to the girl at Home was the most pitiful of all; and I choked as I read it. The Major made no attempt to keep dry-eyed. I respected him for that. He read and rocked himself to and fro, and simply cried like a woman without caring to hide it. The letters were so dreary and hopeless and touching. We forgot all about The Boy's follies, and only thought of the poor Thing on the bed and the scrawled sheets in our hands. It was utterly impossible to let the letters go Home. They would have broken his father's heart and killed his mother after killing her belief in her son.

At last the Major dried his eyes openly, and said, 'Nice sort of thing to spring on an English family! What shall we do?'

I said, knowing what the Major had brought me out for – 'The Boy died of cholera. We were with him at the time. We can't commit ourselves to half-measures. Come along.'

Then began one of the most grimly comic scenes I have ever taken part in – the concoction of a big, written lie, bolstered with evidence, to soothe The Boy's people at Home. I began the rough draft of the letter, the Major throwing in hints here and there while he gathered up all the stuff that The Boy had written and burnt it in the fireplace. It was a hot, still evening when we began, and the lamp burned very badly. In due course I made the draft to my satisfaction, setting forth how The Boy was the pattern of all virtues, beloved by his regiment, with every promise of a great career before him, and so on; how we had helped him through the sickness – it was no time for little lies you will understand – and how he had died without pain. I choked while I was putting down these things and thinking of the poor people who would read them. Then I laughed at the grotesqueness of the affair, and the laughter mixed itself up with the choke – and the Major said that we both wanted drinks.

I am afraid to say how much whisky we drank before the letter was finished. It had not the least effect on us. Then we took off The Boy's watch, locket, and ring.

Lastly, the Major said, 'We must send a lock of hair too. A woman values that.'

But there were reasons why we could not find a lock fit to send. The Boy was black-haired, and so was the Major, luckily. I cut off a piece of the Major's hair above the temple with a knife, and put it into the packet we were making. The laughing-fit and the chokes got hold of me again, and I had to stop. The Major was nearly as bad; and we both knew that the worst part of the work was to come.

We sealed up the packet, photographs, locket, seals, ring, letter, and lock of hair with The Boy's sealing-wax and The Boy's seal.

Then the Major said, 'For God's sake let's get outside – away from the room – and think!'

We went outside, and walked on the banks of the Canal for an hour, eating and drinking what we had with us, until the moon rose. I know now exactly how a murderer feels. Finally, we forced ourselves back to the room with the lamp and the Other Thing in it, and began to take up the next piece of work. I am not going to write about this. It was too horrible. We burned the bedstead and dropped the ashes into the Canal; we took up the matting of the room and treated that in the same way. I went off to a village and borrowed two big hoes – I did not want the villagers to help – while the Major arranged – the other matters. It took us four hours' hard work to make the grave. As we worked, we argued out whether it was right to say as much as we remembered of the Burial of the Dead. We compromised things by saying the Lord's Prayer with a private unofficial prayer for the peace of the soul of The Boy. Then we filled in the grave and went into the verandah – not the house – to lie down to sleep. We were dead-tired.

When we woke the Major said wearily, 'We can't go back till tomorrow. We must give him a decent time to die in. He died early *this* morning, remember. That seems more natural.' So the Major must have been lying awake all the time, thinking.

45

I said, 'Then why didn't we bring the body back to cantonments?'

The Major thought for a minute. 'Because the people bolted when they heard of the cholera. And the *ekka* has gone!'

That was strictly true. We had forgotten all about the *ekka*-pony, and he had gone home.

So we were left there alone, all that stifling day, in the Canal Rest House, testing and re-testing our story of The Boy's death to see if it was weak in any point. A native appeared in the afternoon, but we said that a *Sahib* was dead of cholera, and he ran away. As the dusk gathered, the Major told me all his fears about The Boy, and awful stories of suicide or nearly-carried-out suicide – tales that made one's hair crisp. He said that he himself had once gone into the same Valley of the Shadow [10] as The Boy, when he was young and new to the country; so he understood how things fought together in The Boy's poor jumbled head. He also said that youngsters, in their repentant moments, consider their sins much more serious and ineffaceable than they really are. We talked together all through the evening and rehearsed the story of the death of The Boy. As soon as the moon was up, and The Boy, theoretically, just buried, we struck across country for the Station. We walked from eight till six o'clock in the morning; but though we were dead-tired, we did not forget to go to The Boy's rooms and put away his revolver with the proper amount of cartridges in the pouch. Also to set his writing-case on the table. We found the Colonel and reported the death, feeling more like murderers than ever. Then we went to bed and slept the clock round; for there was no more in us.

The tale had credence as long as was necessary; for everyone forgot about The Boy before a fortnight was over. Many people, however, found time to say that the Major had behaved scandalously in not bringing in the body for a regimental funeral. The saddest thing of all was the letter from The Boy's mother to the Major and me – with big inky blisters all over the sheet. She wrote the sweetest possible things about our great kindness, and the obligation she would be under to us as long as she lived.

All things considered, she was under an obligation; but not exactly as she meant.

⁅ Beyond the Pale ¹ ⁆

Love heeds not caste nor sleep a broken bed. I went in search of love and
lost myself.   *Hindu Proverb.*

A man should, whatever happens, keep to his own caste, race and breed.
Let the White go to the White and the Black to the Black. Then,
whatever trouble falls is in the ordinary course of things – neither
sudden, alien nor unexpected.

This is the story of a man who wilfully stepped beyond the safe limits
of decent everyday society, and paid for it heavily.

He knew too much in the first instance; and he saw too much in the
second. He took too deep an interest in native life; but he will never do
so again.

Deep away in the heart of the City, behind Jitha Megji's *bustee*,² lies
Amir Nath's Gully, which ends in a dead-wall pierced by one grated
window. At the head of the Gully is a big cowbyre, and the walls on either
side of the Gully are without windows. Neither Suchet Singh nor Gaur
Chand approve of their women-folk looking into the world. If Durga
Charan had been of their opinion, he would have been a happier man
today, and little Bisesa would have been able to knead her own bread. Her
room looked out through the grated window into the narrow dark Gully
where the sun never came and where the buffaloes wallowed in the blue
slime. She was a widow, about fifteen years old, and she prayed the Gods,
day and night, to send her a lover; for she did not approve of living alone.

One day, the man – Trejago his name was – came into Amir Nath's
Gully on an aimless wandering; and, after he had passed the buffaloes,
stumbled over a big heap of cattle-food.

Then he saw that the Gully ended in a trap, and heard a little laugh
from behind the grated window. It was a pretty little laugh, and Trejago,
knowing that, for all practical purposes, the old *Arabian Nights* are good
guides, went forward to the window, and whispered that verse of 'The
Love Song of Har Dyal' which begins:

Can a man stand upright in the face of the naked Sun; or a Lover in the
Presence of his Beloved?

If my feet fail me, O Heart of my Heart, am I to blame, being blinded by the
glimpse of your beauty?

There came the faint *tchink* of a woman's bracelets from behind the grating, and a little voice went on with the song at the fifth verse:

Alas! alas! Can the Moon tell the Lotus of her love when the Gate of Heaven is shut and the clouds gather for the rains?

They have taken my Beloved, and driven her with the pack-horses to the North.

There are iron chains on the feet that were set on my heart.

Call to the bowmen to make ready –

The voice stopped suddenly, and Trejago walked out of Amir Nath's Gully, wondering who in the world could have capped 'The Love Song of Har Dyal' so neatly.

Next morning, as he was driving to office, an old woman threw a packet into his dogcart. In the packet was the half of a broken glass-bangle, one flower of the blood-red *dhak*,[3] a pinch of *bhusa* or cattle-food, and eleven cardamoms. That packet was a letter – not a clumsy compromising letter, but an innocent unintelligible lover's epistle.

Trejago knew far too much about these things, as I have said. No Englishman should be able to translate object-letters. But Trejago spread all the trifles on the lid of his office-box and began to puzzle them out.

A broken glass-bangle stands for a Hindu widow all India over; because, when her husband dies, a woman's bracelets are broken on her wrists. Trejago saw the meaning of the little bit of glass. The flower of the *dhak* means diversely 'desire', 'come', 'write' or 'danger', according to the other things with it. One cardamom means 'jealousy'; but when any article is duplicated in an object-letter, it loses its symbolic meaning and stands merely for one of a number indicating time, or, if incense, curds, or saffron be sent also, place. The message ran then – 'A widow – *dhak* flower and *bhusa* – at eleven o'clock.' The pinch of *bhusa* enlightened Trejago. He saw – this kind of letter leaves much to instinctive knowledge – that the *bhusa* referred to the big heap of cattle-food over which he had fallen in Amir Nath's Gully, and that the message must come from the person behind the grating; she being a widow. So the message ran then – 'A widow, in the Gully in which is the heap of *bhusa*, desires you to come at eleven o'clock.'

Trejago threw all the rubbish into the fireplace and laughed. He knew that men in the East do not make love under windows at eleven in the forenoon, nor do women fix appointments a week in advance. So he went, that very night at eleven, into Amir Nath's Gully, clad in a *boorka*,[4] which cloaks a man as well as a woman. Directly the gongs of the City

made the hour, the little voice behind the grating took up 'The Love
Song of Har Dyal' at the verse where the Pathan girl calls upon Har
Dyal to return. The song is really pretty in the Vernacular. In English
you miss the wail of it. It runs something like this –

> Alone upon the housetops, to the North
>   I turn and watch the lightning in the sky, –
> The glamour of thy footsteps in the North,
>   *Come back to me, Beloved, or I die!*
>
> Below my feet the still bazar is laid
>   Far, far, below the weary camels lie, –
> The camels and the captives of thy raid.
>   *Come back to me, Beloved, or I die!*
>
> My father's wife is old and harsh with years,
>   And drudge of all my father's house am I. –
> My bread is sorrow and my drink is tears,
>   *Come back to me, Beloved, or I die!*

As the song stopped, Trejago stepped up under the grating and whispered – 'I am here.'

Bisesa was good to look upon.

That night was the beginning of many strange things, and of a double
life so wild that Trejago today sometimes wonders if it were not all a
dream. Bisesa, or her old handmaiden who had thrown the object-letter,
had detached the heavy grating from the brick-work of the wall; so that
the window slid inside, leaving only a square of raw masonry into which
an active man might climb.

In the day-time, Trejago drove through his routine of office-work, or
put on his calling-clothes and called on the ladies of the Station; wondering how long they would know him if they knew of poor little Bisesa.
At night, when all the City was still, came the walk under the evil-
smelling *boorka*, the patrol through Jitha Megji's *bustee*, the quick turn
into Amir Nath's Gully between the sleeping cattle and the dead walls,
and then, last of all, Bisesa, and the deep, even breathing of the old
woman who slept outside the door of the bare little room that Durga
Charan allotted to his sister's daughter. Who or what Durga Charan was,
Trejago never inquired; and why in the world he was not discovered and
knifed never occurred to him till his madness was over, and Bisesa . . .
But this comes later.

Bisesa was an endless delight to Trejago. She was as ignorant as a
bird; and her distorted versions of the rumours from the outside world
that had reached her in her room, amused Trejago almost as much as her

lisping attempts to pronounce his name – 'Christopher'. The first syllable was always more than she could manage, and she made funny little gestures with her roseleaf hands, as one throwing the name away, and then, kneeling before Trejago asked him, exactly as an English-woman would do, if he were sure he loved her. Trejago swore that he loved her more than anyone else in the world. Which was true.

After a month of this folly, the exigencies of his other life compelled Trejago to be especially attentive to a lady of his acquaintance. You may take it for a fact that anything of this kind is not only noticed and discussed by a man's own race but by some hundred and fifty natives as well. Trejago had to walk with this lady and talk to her at the Band-stand, and once or twice to drive with her; never for an instant dreaming that this would affect his dearer, out-of-the-way life. But the news flew, in the usual mysterious fashion, from mouth to mouth till Bisesa's duenna heard of it and told Bisesa. The child was so troubled that she did the household work evilly, and was beaten by Durga Charan's wife in consequence.

A week later, Bisesa taxed Trejago with the flirtation. She understood no gradations and spoke openly. Trejago laughed and Bisesa stamped her little feet – little feet, light as marigold flowers, that could lie in the palm of a man's one hand.

Much that is written about Oriental passion and impulsiveness is exaggerated and compiled at secondhand, but a little of it is true; and when an Englishman finds that little, it is quite as startling as any passion in his own proper life. Bisesa raged and stormed, and finally threatened to kill herself if Trejago did not at once drop the alien *Memsahib* who had come between them. Trejago tried to explain, and to show her that she did not understand these things from a Western standpoint. Bisesa drew herself up, and said simply –

'I do not. I know only this – it is not good that I should have made you dearer than my own heart to me, *Sahib*. You are an Englishman. I am only a black girl' – she was fairer than bar-gold in the Mint, – 'and the widow of a black man.'

Then she sobbed and said – 'But on my soul and my Mother's soul, I love you. There shall no harm come to you, whatever happens to me.'

Trejago argued with the child, and tried to soothe her, but she seemed quite unreasonably disturbed. Nothing would satisfy her save that all relations between them should end. He was to go away at once. And he went. As he dropped out of the window, she kissed his forehead twice, and he walked home wondering.

A week, and then three weeks, passed without a sign from Bisesa.

Trejago, thinking that the rupture had lasted quite long enough, went down to Amir Nath's Gully for the fifth time in the three weeks, hoping that his rap at the sill of the shifting grating would be answered. He was not disappointed.

There was a young moon, and one stream of light fell down into Amir Nath's Gully, and struck the grating which was drawn away as he knocked. From the black dark, Bisesa held out her arms into the moonlight. Both hands had been cut off at the wrists, and the stumps were nearly healed.

Then, as Bisesa bowed her head between her arms and sobbed, someone in the room grunted like a wild beast, and something sharp – knife, sword, or spear – thrust at Trejago in his *boorka*. The stroke missed his body, but cut into one of the muscles of the groin, and he limped slightly from the wound for the rest of his days.

The grating went into its place. There was no sign whatever from inside the house – nothing but the moonlight strip on the high wall, and the blackness of Amir Nath's Gully behind.

The next thing Trejago remembers, after raging and shouting like a madman between those pitiless walls, is that he found himself near the river as the dawn was breaking, threw away his *boorka* and went home bareheaded.

What was the tragedy – whether Bisesa had, in a fit of causeless despair, told everything, or the intrigue had been discovered and she tortured to tell; whether Durga Charan knew his name and what became of Bisesa – Trejago does not know to this day. Something horrible had happened, and the thought of what it must have been comes upon Trejago in the night now and again, and keeps him company till the morning. One special feature of the case is that he does not know where lies the front of Durga Charan's house. It may open on to a courtyard common to two or more houses, or it may lie behind any one of the gates of Jitha Megji's *bustee*. Trejago cannot tell. He cannot get Bisesa – poor little Bisesa – back again. He has lost her in the City where each man's house is as guarded and as unknowable as the grave; and the grating that opens into Amir Nath's Gully has been walled up.

But Trejago pays his calls regularly, and is reckoned a very decent sort of man.

There is nothing peculiar about him, except a slight stiffness, caused by a riding-strain, in the right leg.

⟨ A Wayside Comedy ¹ ⟩

Because to every purpose there is time and judgment, therefore the
misery of man is great upon him.   *Ecclesiastes* viii. 6.

Fate and the Government of India have turned the Station of Kashima
into a prison; and, because there is no help for the poor souls who are
now lying there in torment, I write this story, praying that the
Government of India may be moved to scatter the European population
to the four winds.

Kashima is bounded on all sides by the rock-tipped circle of the
Dosehri hills. In spring, it is ablaze with roses. In summer, the roses die
and the hot winds blow from the hills. In autumn, the white mists from
the *jhils* ² cover the place as with water, and in winter, the frosts nip
everything young and tender to earth-level. There is but one view in
Kashima – a stretch of perfectly flat pasture and plough-land, running
up to the grey-blue scrub of the Dosehri hills.

There are no amusements, except snipe and tiger shooting; but the
tigers have been long since hunted from their lairs in the rock-caves, and
the snipe only come once a year. Narkarra – one hundred and forty-
three miles by road – is the nearest Station to Kashima. But Kashima
never goes to Narkarra, where there are at least twelve English people. It
stays within the circle of the Dosehri hills.

All Kashima acquits Mrs Vansuythen of any intention to do harm;
but all Kashima knows that she, and she alone, brought about their pain.

Boulte, the Engineer, Mrs Boulte, and Captain Kurrell know this.
They are the English population of Kashima, if we except Major Vansuythen, who is of no importance whatever, and Mrs Vansuythen, who
is the most important of all.

You must remember, though you will not understand, that all laws
weaken in a small and hidden community where there is no public
opinion. When a man is absolutely alone in a Station he runs a certain risk
of falling into evil ways. This risk is multiplied by every addition to the
population up to twelve – the Jury-number. After that, fear and conse-
quent restraint begin, and human action becomes less grotesquely jerky.

There was deep peace in Kashima till Mrs Vansuythen arrived. She was a charming woman, everyone said so everywhere; and she charmed everyone. In spite of this, or, perhaps, because of this, since Fate is so perverse, she cared only for one man, and he was Major Vansuythen. Had she been plain or stupid, this matter would have been intelligible to Kashima. But she was a fair woman, with very still grey eyes, the colour of a lake just before the light of the sun touches it. No man who had seen those eyes could, later on, explain what fashion of woman she was to look upon. The eyes dazzled him. Her own sex said that she was 'not bad-looking, but spoilt by pretending to be so grave'. And yet her gravity was natural. It was not her habit to smile. She merely went through life, looking at those who passed; and the women objected while the men fell down and worshipped.

She knows and is deeply sorry for the evil she has done to Kashima; but Major Vansuythen cannot understand why Mrs Boulte does not drop in to afternoon tea at least three times a week. 'When there are only two women in one Station, they ought to see a great deal of each other,' says Major Vansuythen.

Long and long before ever Mrs Vansuythen came out of those far-away places where there is society and amusement, Kurrell had discovered that Mrs Boulte was the one woman in the world for him and – you dare not blame them. Kashima was as out of the world as Heaven or the Other Place, and the Dosehri hills kept their secret well. Boulte had no concern in the matter. He was in camp for a fortnight at a time. He was a hard, heavy man, and neither Mrs Boulte nor Kurrell pitied him. They had all Kashima and each other for their very very own; and Kashima was the Garden of Eden in those days. When Boulte returned from his wanderings he would call him 'old fellow', and the three would dine together. Kashima was happy then when the Judgment of God seemed almost as distant as Narkarra or the railway that ran down to the sea. But the Government sent Major Vansuythen to Kashima, and with him came his wife.

The etiquette of Kashima is much the same as that of a desert island. When a stranger is cast away there, all hands go down to the shore to make him welcome. Kashima assembled at the masonry platform close to the Narkarra Road, and spread tea for the Vansuythens. That ceremony was reckoned a formal call, and made them free of the Station, its rights and privileges. When the Vansuythens settled down they gave a tiny house-warming to all Kashima; and that made Kashima free of their house, according to the immemorial usage of the Station.

Then the Rains came, when no one could go into camp, and the

Narkarra Road was washed away by the Kasun River, and in the cup-like pastures of Kashima the cattle waded knee-deep. The clouds dropped down from the Dosehri hills and covered everything.

At the end of the Rains Boulte's manner towards his wife changed and became demonstratively affectionate. They had been married twelve years, and the change startled Mrs Boulte, who hated her husband with the hate of a woman who has met with nothing but kindness from her mate, and, in the teeth of this kindness, has done him a great wrong. Moreover, she had her own trouble to fight with – her watch to keep over her own property, Kurrell. For two months the Rains had hidden the Dosehri hills and many other things besides; but, when they lifted, they showed Mrs Boulte that her man among men, her Ted – for she called him Ted in the old days when Boulte was out of earshot – was slipping the links of the allegiance.

'The Vansuythen Woman has taken him,' Mrs Boulte said to herself; and when Boulte was away, wept over her belief, in the face of the over-vehement blandishments of Ted. Sorrow in Kashima is as fortunate as Love because there is nothing to weaken it save the flight of Time. Mrs Boulte had never breathed her suspicion to Kurrell because she was not certain; and her nature led her to be very certain before she took steps in any direction. That is why she behaved as she did.

Boulte came into the house one evening, and leaned against the door-post of the drawing-room, chewing his moustache. Mrs Boulte was putting some flowers into a vase. There is a pretence of civilization even in Kashima.

'Little woman,' said Boulte quietly, 'do you care for me?'

'Immensely,' said she, with a laugh. 'Can you ask it?'

'But I'm serious,' said Boulte. '*Do* you care for me?'

Mrs Boulte dropped the flowers, and turned round quickly. 'Do you want an honest answer?'

'Ye-es, I've asked for it.'

Mrs Boulte spoke in a low, even voice for five minutes, very distinctly, that there might be no misunderstanding her meaning. When Samson broke the pillars of Gaza,[3] he did a little thing, and one not to be compared with the deliberate pulling down of a woman's homestead about her own ears. There was no wise female friend to advise Mrs Boulte, the singularly cautious wife, to hold her hand. She struck at Boulte's heart, because her own was sick with suspicion of Kurrell, and worn out with the long strain of watching alone through the Rains. There was no plan or purpose in her speaking. The sentences made themselves; and Boulte listened, leaning against the door-post with his hands in his pockets. When all was over, and Mrs Boulte began to breathe through her nose before breaking out into tears, he laughed and stared straight in front of him at the Dosehri hills.

'Is that all?' he said. 'Thanks, I only wanted to know, you know.'

'What are you going to do?' said the woman, between her sobs.

'Do! Nothing. What should I do? Kill Kurrell, or send you Home, or apply for leave to get a divorce? It's two days' *dâk*⁴ into Narkarra.' He laughed again and went on: 'I'll tell you what *you* can do. You can ask Kurrell to dinner tomorrow – no, on Thursday, that will allow you time to pack – and you can bolt with him. I give you my word I won't follow.'

He took up his helmet and went out of the room, and Mrs Boulte sat till the moonlight streaked the floor, thinking and thinking and thinking. She had done her best upon the spur of the moment to pull the house down; but it would not fall. Moreover, she could not understand her husband, and she was afraid. Then the folly of her useless truthfulness struck her, and she was ashamed to write to Kurrell, saying, 'I have gone mad and told everything. My husband says that I am free to elope with you. Get a *dâk* for Thursday, and we will fly after dinner.' There was a cold-bloodedness about that procedure which did not appeal to her. So she sat still in her own house and thought.

At dinner-time Boulte came back from his walk, white and worn and haggard, and the woman was touched at his distress. As the evening wore on she muttered some expression of sorrow, something approaching to contrition. Boulte came out of a brown study and said, 'Oh, *that*! I wasn't thinking about that. By the way, what does Kurrell say to the elopement?'

'I haven't seen him,' said Mrs Boulte. 'Good God, is that all?'

But Boulte was not listening, and her sentence ended in a gulp.

The next day brought no comfort to Mrs Boulte, for Kurrell did not appear, and the new life that she, in the five minutes' madness of the previous evening, had hoped to build out of the ruins of the old, seemed to be no nearer.

Boulte ate his breakfast, advised her to see her Arab pony fed in the verandah, and went out. The morning wore through, and at mid-day the tension became unendurable. Mrs Boulte could not cry. She had finished her crying in the night, and now she did not want to be left alone. Perhaps the Vansuythen Woman would talk to her; and, since talking opens the heart, perhaps there might be some comfort to be found in her company. She was the only other woman in the Station.

In Kashima there are no regular calling-hours. Everyone can drop in upon everyone else at pleasure. Mrs Boulte put on a big *terai* hat,⁵ and walked across to the Vansuythens' house to borrow last week's *Queen*. The two compounds touched, and instead of going up the drive, she crossed through the gap in the cactus-hedge, entering the house from the back. As she passed through the dining-room, she heard, behind the *purdah*[6] that cloaked the drawing-room door, her husband's voice, saying:

'But on my Honour! On my Soul and Honour, I tell you she doesn't care for me. She told me so last night. I would have told you then if Vansuythen hadn't been with you. If it is for *her* sake that you'll have nothing to say to me, you can make your mind easy. It's Kurrell –'

'What?' said Mrs Vansuythen, with a hysterical little laugh. 'Kurrell! Oh, it can't be! You two must have made some horrible mistake. Perhaps you – you lost your temper, or misunderstood, or something. Things *can't* be as wrong as you say.'

Mrs Vansuythen had shifted her defence to avoid the man's pleading and was desperately trying to keep him to a side-issue.

'There must be some mistake,' she insisted, 'and it can be all put right again.'

Boulte laughed grimly.

'It can't be Captain Kurrell! He told me that he had never taken the least – the least interest in your wife, Mr Boulte. Oh, *do* listen! He said he had not. He swore he had not,' said Mrs Vansuythen.

The *purdah* rustled, and the speech was cut short by the entry of a little thin woman, with big rings round her eyes. Mrs Vansuythen stood up with a gasp.

'What was that you said?' asked Mrs Boulte. 'Never mind that man. What did Ted say to you? What did he say to you? What did he say to you?'

Mrs Vansuythen sat down helplessly on the sofa, overborne by the trouble of her questioner.

'He said – I can't remember exactly what he said – but I understood him to say – that is – But, really, Mrs Boulte, isn't it rather a strange question?'

'*Will* you tell me what he said?' repeated Mrs Boulte. Even a tiger will fly before a bear robbed of her whelps, and Mrs Vansuythen was only an ordinarily good woman. She began in a sort of desperation: 'Well, he said that he never cared for you at all, and, of course, there was not the least reason why he should have, and – and – that was all.'

'You said he *swore* he had not cared for me. Was that true?'

'Yes,' said Mrs Vansuythen very softly.

Mrs Boulte wavered for an instant where she stood, and then fell forward fainting.

'What did I tell you?' said Boulte, as though the conversation had been unbroken. 'You can see for yourself. She cares for *him*.' The light began to break into his dull mind, and he went on: 'And he – what was *he* saying to you?'

But Mrs Vansuythen, with no heart for explanations or impassioned protestations, was kneeling over Mrs Boulte.

'Oh, you brute!' she cried. 'Are *all* men like this? Help me to get her into my room – and her face is cut against the table. Oh, *will* you be quiet, and help me to carry her? I hate you, and I hate Captain Kurrell. Lift her up carefully, and now – go! Go away!'

Boulte carried his wife into Mrs Vansuythen's bedroom, and departed before the storm of that lady's wrath and disgust, impenitent and burning with jealousy. Kurrell had been making love to Mrs Vansuythen – would do Vansuythen as great a wrong as he had done Boulte, who caught himself considering whether Mrs Vansuythen would faint if she discovered that the man she loved had forsworn her.

In the middle of these meditations, Kurrell came cantering along the road and pulled up with a cheery 'Good mornin'. Been mashing Mrs Vansuythen as usual, eh? Bad thing for a sober, married man, that. What will Mrs Boulte say?'

Boulte raised his head and said slowly: 'Oh, you liar!' Kurrell's face changed. 'What's that?' he asked quickly.

'Nothing much,' said Boulte. 'Has my wife told you that you two are free to go off whenever you please? She has been good enough to explain the situation to me. You've been a true friend to me, Kurrell – old man – haven't you?'

Kurrell groaned, and tried to frame some sort of idiotic sentence about being willing to give 'satisfaction'. But his interest in the woman was dead, had died out in the Rains, and, mentally, he was abusing her for her amazing indiscretion. It would have been so easy to have broken off the thing gently and by degrees, and now he was saddled with – Boulte's voice recalled him.

'I don't think I should get any satisfaction from killing you, and I'm pretty sure you'd get none from killing me.'

Then in a querulous tone, ludicrously disproportioned to his wrongs, Boulte added:

'Seems rather a pity that you haven't the decency to keep to the woman, now you've got her. You've been a true friend to *her* too, haven't you?'

Kurrell stared long and gravely. The situation was getting beyond him.

'What do you mean?' he said.

Boulte answered more to himself than the questioner: 'My wife came over to Mrs Vansuythen's just now; and it seems you'd been telling Mrs Vansuythen that you'd never cared for Emma. I suppose you lied, as usual. What had Mrs Vansuythen to do with you, or you with her? Try to speak the truth for once in a way.'

Kurrell took the double insult without wincing, and replied by another question: 'Go on. What happened?'

'Emma fainted,' said Boulte simply. 'But, look here, what had you been saying to Mrs Vansuythen?'

Kurrell laughed. Mrs Boulte had, with unbridled tongue, made havoc of his plans; and he could at least retaliate by hurting the man in whose eyes he was humiliated and shown dishonourable.

'Saying to her? What *does* a man tell a lie like that for? I suppose I said pretty much what you've said, unless I'm a good deal mistaken.'

'I spoke the truth,' said Boulte, again more to himself than Kurrell. 'Emma told me she hated me. She has no right in me.'

'No! I suppose not. You're only her husband, y'know. And what did Mrs Vansuythen say after you had laid your disengaged heart at her feet?'

Kurrell felt almost virtuous as he put the question.

'I don't think that matters,' Boulte replied; 'and it doesn't concern you.'

'But it does! I tell you it does' – began Kurrell shamelessly.

The sentence was cut by a roar of laughter from Boulte's lips. Kurrell was silent for an instant, and then he, too, laughed – laughed long and loudly, rocking in his saddle. It was an unpleasant sound – the mirthless mirth of these men on the long white line of the Narkarra Road. There were no strangers in Kashima, or they might have thought that captivity within the Dosehri hills had driven half the European population mad. The laughter ended abruptly, and Kurrell was the first to speak.

'Well, what are you going to do?'

Boulte looked up the road, and at the hills. 'Nothing,' said he quietly. 'What's the use? It's too ghastly for anything. We must let the old life go on. I can only call you a hound and a liar, and I can't go on calling you names for ever. Besides which, I don't feel that I'm much better. We can't get out of this place. What *is* there to do?'

Kurrell looked round the rat-pit of Kashima and made no reply. The injured husband took up the wondrous tale.

'Ride on, and speak to Emma if you want to. God knows *I* don't care what you do.'

He walked forward, and left Kurrell gazing blankly after him. Kurrell did not ride on either to sce Mrs Boulte or Mrs Vansuythen. He sat in his saddle and thought, while his pony grazed by the roadside.

The whir of approaching wheels roused him. Mrs Vansuythen was driving home Mrs Boulte, white and wan, with a cut on her forehead.

'Stop, please,' said Mrs Boulte. 'I want to speak to Ted.'

Mrs Vansuythen obeyed, but as Mrs Boulte leaned forward, putting her hand upon the splash-board of the dog-cart, Kurrell spoke.

'I've seen your husband, Mrs Boulte.'

There was no necessity for any further explanation. The man's eyes were fixed, not upon Mrs Boulte, but her companion. Mrs Boulte saw the look.

'Speak to him!' she pleaded, turning to the woman at her side. 'Oh, speak to him! Tell him what you told me just now. Tell him you hate him! Tell him you hate him!'

She bent forward and wept bitterly, while the *sais*,[7] impassive, went forward to hold the horse. Mrs Vansuythen turned scarlet and dropped the reins. She wished to be no party to such unholy explanations.

'I've nothing to do with it,' she began coldly; but Mrs Boulte's sobs overcame her, and she addressed herself to the man. 'I don't know what I am to say, Captain Kurrell. I don't know what I can call you. I think you've − you've behaved abominably, and she has cut her forehead terribly against the table.'

'It doesn't hurt. It isn't anything,' said Mrs Boulte feebly. '*That* doesn't matter. Tell him what you told me. Say you don't care for him. Oh, Ted, *won't* you believe her?'

'Mrs Boulte has made me understand that you were − that you were fond of her once upon a time,' went on Mrs Vansuythen.

'Well!' said Kurrell brutally. 'It seems to me that Mrs Boulte had better be fond of her own husband first.'

'Stop!' said Mrs Vansuythen. 'Hear me first. I don't care − I don't want to know anything about you and Mrs Boulte; but I want *you* to know that I hate you, that I think you are a cur, and that I'll never, *never* speak to you again. Oh, I don't dare to say what I think of you, you − man!'

'I want to speak to Ted,' moaned Mrs Boulte, but the dog-cart rattled on, and Kurrell was left on the road, shamed, and boiling with wrath against Mrs Boulte.

He waited till Mrs Vansuythen was driving back to her own house, and, she being freed from the embarrassment of Mrs Boulte's presence, learned for the second time her opinion of himself and his actions.

In the evenings it was the wont of all Kashima to meet at the platform on the Narkarra Road, to drink tea and discuss the trivialities of the day. Major Vansuythen and his wife found themselves alone at the gathering-place for almost the first time in their remembrance; and the cheery Major, in the teeth of his wife's remarkably reasonable suggestion that the rest of the Station might be sick, insisted upon driving round to the two bungalows and unearthing the population.

'Sitting in the twilight!' said he, with great indignation, to the Boultes. 'That'll never do! Hang it all, we're one family here! You *must* come out, and so must Kurrell. I'll make him bring his banjo.'

So great is the power of honest simplicity and a good digestion over guilty consciences that all Kashima did turn out, even down to the banjo; and the Major embraced the company in one expansive grin. As he grinned, Mrs Vansuythen raised her eyes for an instant and looked at all Kashima. Her meaning was clear. Major Vansuythen would never know anything. He was to be the outsider in that happy family whose cage was the Dosehri hills.

'You're singing villainously out of tune, Kurrell,' said the Major truthfully. 'Pass me that banjo.'

And he sang in excruciating wise till the stars came out and all Kashima went to dinner.

That was the beginning of the New Life of Kashima – the life that Mrs Boulte made when her tongue was loosened in the twilight.

Mrs Vansuythen has never told the Major; and since he insists upon keeping up a burdensome geniality, she has been compelled to break her vow of not speaking to Kurrell. This speech, which must of necessity preserve the semblance of politeness and interest, serves admirably to keep alight the flames of jealousy and dull hatred in Boulte's bosom, as it awakens the same passions in his wife's heart. Mrs Boulte hates Mrs Vansuythen because she has taken Ted from her, and, in some curious fashion, hates her because Mrs Vansuythen – and here the wife's eyes see far more clearly than the husband's – detests Ted. And Ted – that gallant captain and honourable man – knows now that it is possible to hate a woman once loved, to the verge of wishing to silence her for ever with blows. Above all is he shocked that Mrs Boulte cannot see the error of her ways.

Boulte and he go out tiger-shooting together in all friendship. Boulte has put their relationship on a most satisfactory footing.

'You're a blackguard,' he says to Kurrell, 'and I've lost any self-respect I may ever have had; but when you're with me, I can feel certain that you are not with Mrs Vansuythen, or making Emma miserable.'

Kurrell endures anything that Boulte may say to him. Sometimes they are away for three days together, and then the Major insists upon his wife going over to sit with Mrs Boulte; although Mrs Vansuythen has repeatedly declared that she prefers her husband's company to any in the world. From the way in which she clings to him, she would certainly seem to be speaking the truth.

But of course, as the Major says, 'in a little Station we must all be friendly'.

⟨ Dray Wara Yow Dee [1] ⟩

For jealousy is the rage of a man: therefore he will not spare in the day of
vengeance.   *Proverbs* vi: 34.

Almonds and raisins, Sahib? Grapes from Kabul? Or a pony of the
rarest if the Sahib will only come with me. He is thirteen-three,[2] Sahib,
plays polo, goes in a cart, carries a lady and – Holy Kurshed[3] and the
Blessed Imams,[4] it is the Sahib himself! My heart is made fat and my
eye glad. May you never be tired! As is cold water in the Tirah,[5] so is the
sight of a friend in a far place. And what do *you* in this accursed land?[6]
South of Delhi, Sahib, you know the saying – 'Rats are the men and
trulls the women.' It was an order? Ahoo! An order is an order till one is
strong enough to disobey. O my brother, O my friend, we have met in an
auspicious hour! Is all well in the heart and the body and the house? In a
lucky day have we two come together again.

I am to go with you? Your favour is great. Will there be picket-room
in the compound? I have three horses and the bundles and the horse-
boy. Moreover, remember that the police here hold me a horse-thief.
What do these Lowland bastards know of horse-thieves? Do you remember that time in Peshawur when Kamal[7] hammered on the gates of
Jumrud[8] – mountebank that he was – and lifted the Colonel's horses all
in one night? Kamal is dead now, but his nephew has taken up the
matter, and there will be more horses a-missing if the Khyber Levies do
not look to it.

The Peace of God and the favour of His Prophet be upon this house
and all that is in it! Shafiz Ullah, rope the mottled mare under the tree
and draw water. The horses can stand in the sun, but double the felts
over the loins. Nay, my friend, do not trouble to look them over. They
are to sell to the Officer-fools who know so many things of the horse.
The mare is heavy in foal; the grey is a devil unlicked; and the dun – but
you know the trick of the peg. When they are sold I go back to Pubbi, or,
it may be, the Valley of Peshawur.

O friend of my heart, it is good to see you again. I have been bowing
and lying all day to the Officer-Sahibs in respect to those horses; and my
mouth is dry for straight talk. *Auggrh!* Before a meal tobacco is good.

Do not join me, for we are not in our own country. Sit in the verandah and I will spread my cloth here. But first I will drink. *In the name of God returning thanks, thrice!* This is sweet water, indeed – sweet as the water of Sheoran when it comes from the snows.

They are all well and pleased in the North – Khoda Baksh and the others. Yar Khan has come down with the horses from Kurdistan – six-and-thirty head only, and a full half pack-ponies – and has said openly in the Kashmir Serai that you English should send guns and blow the Amir[9] into Hell. There are *fifteen* tolls now on the Kabul road; and at Dakka, when he thought he was clear, Yar Khan was stripped of all his Balkh stallions by the Governor! This is a great injustice, and Yar Khan is hot with rage. And of the others: Mahbub Ali is still at Pubbi, writing God knows what. Tugluq Khan is in jail for the business of the Kohat Police Post. Faiz Beg came down from Ismail-ki-Dhera with a Bokhariot belt for thee, my brother, at the closing of the year, but none knew whither thou hadst gone: there was no news left behind. The Cousins have taken a new run near Pakpattan to breed mules for the Government carts, and there is a story in the Bazar of a priest. Oho! Such a salt tale! Listen –

Sahib, why do you ask that? My clothes are foulcd because of the dust on the road. My eyes are sad because of the glare of the sun. My feet are swollen because I have washed them in bitter water, and my cheeks are hollow because the food here is bad. Fire burn your money! What do I want with it? I am rich. I thought you were my friend. But you are like the others – a Sahib. Is a man sad? Give him money, say the Sahibs. Is he dishonoured? Give him money, say the Sahibs. Hath he a wrong upon his head? Give him money, say the Sahibs. Such are the Sahibs, and such art thou – even thou.

Nay, do not look at the feet of the dun. Pity it is that I ever taught you to know the legs of a horse. Footsore? Be it so. What of that? The roads are hard. And the mare footsore? She bears a double burden, Sahib.

And now, I pray you, give me permission to depart. Great favour and honour has the Sahib done me, and graciously has he shown his belief that the horses are stolen. Will it please him to send me to the Thana?[10] To call a sweeper and have me led away by one of these lizard-men? I am the Sahib's friend. I have drunk water in the shadow of his house, and he has blackened my face. Remains there anything more to do? Will the Sahib give me eight annas to make smooth the injury and – complete the insult – ?

Forgive me, my brother. I knew not – I know not now – what I say.

Yes, I lied to you! I will put dust on my head – and I am an Afridi! The horses have been marched footsore from the Valley to this place, and my eyes are dim, and my body aches for the want of sleep, and my heart is dried up with sorrow and shame. But as it was my shame, so by God the Dispenser of Justice – by Allah-al-Mumīt![11] – it shall be my own revenge!

We have spoken together with naked hearts before this, and our hands have dipped into the same dish, and thou hast been to me as a brother. Therefore I pay thee back with lies and ingratitude – as a Pathan. Listen now! When the grief of the soul is too heavy for endurance it may be a little eased by speech; and, moreover, the mind of a true man is as a well, and the pebble of confession dropped therein sinks and is no more seen. From the Valley have I come on foot, league by league, with a fire in my chest like the fire of the Pit. And why? Hast thou, then, so quickly forgotten our customs, among this folk who sell their wives and their daughters for silver? Come back with me to the North and be among men once more. Come back when this matter is accomplished and I call for thee! The bloom of the peach-orchards is upon all the Valley, and *here* is only dust and a great stink. There is a pleasant wind among the mulberry trees, and the streams are bright with snow-water, and the caravans go up and the caravans go down, and a hundred fires sparkle in the gut of the Pass, and tent-peg answers hammer-nose, and pack-horse squeals to pack-horse across the drift-smoke of the evening. It is good in the North now. Come back with me. Let us return to our own people! Come!

Whence is my sorrow? Does a man tear out his heart and make fritters thereof over a slow fire for aught other than a woman? Do not laugh, friend of mine, for your time will also be. A woman of the Abazai was she, and I took her to wife to staunch the feud between our village and the men of Ghor. I am no longer young? The lime has touched my beard? True. I had no need of the wedding? Nay, but I loved her. What saith Rahman? [12] 'Into whose heart Love enters, there is Folly *and naught else*. By a glance of the eye she hath blinded thee; and by the eyelids and the fringe of the eyelids taken thee into the captivity without ransom, *and naught else.*' Dost thou remember that song at the sheep-roasting in the Pindi camp [13] among the Uzbegs of the Amir?

The Abazai are dogs and their women the servants of sin. There was a lover of her own people, but of that her father told me naught. My friend, curse for me in your prayers, as I curse at each praying from the Fakr to the Isha,[14] the name of Daoud Shah, Abazai, whose head is still upon his neck, whose hands are still upon his wrists, who has done me dishonour, who has made my name a laughing-stock among the women of Little Malikand.

I went into Hindustan at the end of two months – to Cherat. I was gone twelve days only; but I had said that I would be fifteen days absent. This I did to try her, for it is written: 'Trust not the incapable.' Coming up the gorge alone in the falling of the light, I heard the voice of a man singing at the door of my house; and it was the voice of Daoud Shah, and the song that he sang was *'Dray wara yow dee'* – 'All three are one'. It was as though a heel-rope had been slipped round my heart and all the Devils were drawing it tight past endurance. I crept silently up the hill-road, but the fuse of my matchlock was wetted with the rain, and I could not slay Daoud Shah from afar. Moreover, it was in my mind to kill the woman also. Thus he sang, sitting outside my house, and, anon, the woman opened the door, and I came nearer, crawling on my belly among the rocks. I had only my knife to my hand. But a stone slipped under my foot, and the two looked down the hillside, and he, leaving his matchlock, fled from my anger, because he was afraid for the life that was in him. But the woman moved not till I stood in front of her, crying: 'O woman, what is this that thou hast done?' And she, void of fear, though she knew my thought, laughed, saying: 'It is a little thing. I loved him, and *thou* art a dog and cattle-thief coming by night. Strike!' And I, being still blinded by her beauty, for, O my friend, the women of the Abazai are very fair, said: 'Hast thou no fear?' And she answered: 'None – but only the fear that I do not die.' Then said I: 'Have no fear.' And she bowed her head, and I smote it off at the neck-bone so that it leaped between my feet. Thereafter the rage of our people came upon me, and I hacked off the breasts, that the men of Little Malikand might know the crime, and cast the body into the watercourse that flows to the Kabul River. *Dray wara yow dee! Dray wara yow dee!* The body without the head, the soul without light, and my own darkling heart – all three are one – all three are one!

That night, making no halt, I went to Ghor and demanded news of Daoud Shah. Men said: 'He is gone to Pubbi for horses. What wouldst thou of him? There is peace between the villages.' I made answer: 'Ay! The peace of treachery and the love that the Devil Atala [15] bore to Gurel.' So I fired thrice into the tower-gate and laughed and went my way.

In those hours, brother and friend of my heart's heart, the moon and the stars were as blood above me, and in my mouth was the taste of dry earth. Also, I broke no bread, and my drink was the rain of the valley of Ghor upon my face.

At Pubbi I found Mahbub Ali, the writer, sitting upon his charpoy,[16] and gave up my arms according to your Law.[17] But I was not grieved, for it was in my heart that I should kill Daoud Shah with my bare hands thus – as a man strips a bunch of raisins. Mahbub Ali said: 'Daoud Shah has even now gone hot-foot to Peshawur, and he will pick up his horses upon the road to Delhi, for it is said that the Bombay Tramway Company are buying horses there by the truckload; eight horses to the truck.' And that was a true saying.

Then I saw that the hunting would be no little thing, for the man was gone into your borders to save himself against my wrath. And shall he save himself so? Am I not alive? Though he run northward to the Dora and the snow, or southerly to the Black Water, I will follow him, as a lover follows the footsteps of his mistress, and coming upon him I will take him tenderly – Aho! so tenderly! – in my arms, saying: 'Well hast thou done and well shalt thou be repaid.' And out of that embrace Daoud Shah shall not go forth with the breath in his nostrils. *Auggrh!* Where is the pitcher? I am as thirsty as a mother mare in the first month.

Your Law! What is your Law to me? When the horses fight on the runs do they regard the boundary pillars; or do the kites of Ali Musjid [18] forbear because the carrion lies under the shadow of the Ghor Kuttri? [19] The matter began across the Border. It shall finish where God pleases. Here; in my own country; or in Hell. All three are one.

Listen now, sharer of the sorrow of my heart, and I will tell of the hunting. I followed to Peshawur from Pubbi, and I went to and fro about the streets of Peshawur like a houseless dog, seeking for my enemy. Once I thought that I saw him washing his mouth in the conduit in the big square, but when I came up he was gone. It may be that it was he, and, seeing my face, he had fled.

A girl of the bazar said that he would go to Nowshera. I said: 'O heart's heart, does Daoud Shah visit thee?' And she said: 'Even so.' I said: 'I would fain see him, for we be friends parted for two years. Hide me, I pray, here in the shadow of the window-shutter, and I will wait for his coming.' And the girl said: 'O Pathan, look into my eyes!' And I turned, leaning upon her breast, and looked into her eyes, swearing that I spoke the very Truth of God. But she answered: 'Never friend waited friend with such eyes. Lie to God and the Prophet, but to a woman ye cannot lie. Get hence! There shall no harm befall Daoud Shah by cause of me.'

I would have strangled that girl but for the fear of your Police; and thus the hunting would have come to naught. Therefore I only laughed and departed, and she leaned over the window-bar in the night and mocked me down the street. Her name is Jamun. When I have made my account with the man I will return to Peshawur and – her lovers shall desire her no more for her beauty's sake. She shall not be *Jamun*, but *Ak*,[20] the cripple among trees. Ho! ho! *Ak* shall she be!

At Peshawur I bought the horses and grapes, and the almonds and dried fruits, that the reason of my wanderings might be open to the Government, and that there might be no hindrance upon the road. But when I came to Nowshera he was gone; and I knew not where to go. I stayed one day at Nowshera, and in the night a Voice spoke in my ears as I slept among the horses. All night it flew round my head and would not cease from whispering. I was upon my belly, sleeping as the Devils sleep, and it may have been that the Voice was the voice of a Devil. It said: 'Go south, and thou shalt come upon Daoud Shah.' Listen, my brother and chiefest among friends – listen! Is the tale a long one? Think how it was long to me. I have trodden every league of the road from Pubbi to this place; and from Nowshera my guide was only the Voice and the lust of vengeance.

To the Uttock I went, but that was no hindrance to me. Ho! ho! A man may turn the word twice, even in his trouble. The Uttock was no *uttock* [obstacle] to me; and I heard the Voice above the noise of the waters beating on the big rock, saying: 'Go to the right.' So I went to Pindigheb, and in those days my sleep was taken from me utterly, and the head of the woman of the Abazai was before me night and day, even as it had fallen between my feet. *Dray wara yow dee! Dray wara yow dee!* Fire, ashes, and my couch, all three are one – all three are one!

Now I was far from the winter path of the dealers who had gone to Sialkot, and so south by the rail and the Big Road to the line of cantonments; but there was a Sahib in camp at Pindigheb who bought from me a white mare at a good price, and told me that one Daoud Shah had passed to Shahpur with horses. Then I saw that the warning of the Voice was true, and made swift to come to the Salt Hills. The Jhelum was in flood, but I could not wait, and, in the crossing, a bay stallion was washed down and drowned. Herein was God hard to me – not in respect of the beast, of that I had no care – but in this snatching. While I was upon the right bank urging the horses into the water, Daoud Shah was upon the left; for – *Alghias! Alghias!*[21] – the hoofs of my mare scattered the hot ashes of his fires when we came up the hither bank in the light of morning. But he had fled. His feet were made swift by the terror of Death. And I went south from Shahpur as the kite flies. I dared not turn aside lest I should miss my vengeance – which is my right. From Shahpur

I skirted by the Jhelum, for I thought that he would avoid the Desert of the Rechna. But, presently, at Sahiwal, I turned away upon the road to Jhang, Samundri, and Gugera, till, upon a night, the mottled mare breasted the fence of the rail that runs to Montgomery. And that place was Okara, and the head of the woman of the Abazai lay upon the sand between my feet.

Thence I went to Fazilka, and they said that I was mad to bring starved horses there. The Voice was with me, and I was *not* mad, but only wearied, because I could not find Daoud Shah. It was written that I should not find him at Rania nor Bahadurgarh, and I came into Delhi from the west, and there also I found him not. My friend, I have seen many strange things in my wanderings. I have seen the Devils rioting across the Rechna as the stallions riot in spring. I have heard the *Djinns* [22] calling to each other from holes in the sand, and I have seen them pass before my face. There are no Devils, say the Sahibs? They are very wise, but they do not know all things about Devils or – horses. Ho! ho! I say to you who are laughing at my misery, that I have seen the Devils at high noon whooping and leaping on the shoals of the Chenab. [23] And was I afraid? My brother, when the desire of a man is set upon one thing alone, he fears neither God nor Man nor Devil. If my vengeance failed, I would splinter the Gates of Paradise with the butt of my gun, or I would cut my way into Hell with my knife, and I would call upon Those who Govern there for the body of Daoud Shah. What love so deep as hate?

Do not speak. I know the thought in your heart. Is the white of this eye clouded? How does the blood beat at the wrist? There is no madness in my flesh, but only the vehemence of the desire that has eaten me up. Listen!

South of Delhi I knew not the country at all. Therefore I cannot say where I went, but I passed through many cities. I knew only that it was laid upon me to go south. When the horses could march no more, I threw myself upon the earth and waited till the day. There was no sleep with me in that journeying; and that was a heavy burden. Dost thou know, brother of mine, the evil of wakefulness that cannot break – when the bones are sore for lack of sleep – and the skin of the temples twitches with weariness, and yet – there is no sleep – there is no sleep? *Dray wara yow dee! Dray wara yow dee!* The eye of the Sun, the eye of the Moon, and my own unrestful eyes – all three are one – all three are one!

There was a city the name whereof I have forgotten, and there the Voice called all night. That was ten days ago. It has cheated me afresh. I have come hither from a place called Hamirpur, and, behold, it is my Fate that I should meet with thee to my comfort, and the increase of friendship. This is a good omen. By the joy of looking upon thy face the weariness has gone from my feet, and the sorrow of my so long travel is forgotten. Also my heart is peaceful; for I know that the end is near.

It may be that I shall find Daoud Shah in this city going northward, since a Hill-man will ever head back to his Hills when the spring warns. And shall he see those hills of our country? Surely I shall overtake him! Surely my vengeance is safe! Surely God hath him in the hollow of His hand against my claiming! There shall no harm befall Daoud Shah till I come; for I would fain kill him quick and whole with the life sticking firm in his body. A pomegranate is sweetest when the cloves break away unwilling from the rind. Let it be in the daytime, that I may see his face, and my delight may be crowned.

And when I have accomplished the matter and my Honour is made clean, I shall return thanks unto God, the Holder of the Scales of the Law, and I shall sleep. From the night, through the day, and into the night again I shall sleep; and no dream shall trouble me.

And now, O my brother, the tale is all told. *Ahi! Ahi! Alghias! Ahi!*

⚡ Little Tobrah [1] ⚡

'Prisoner's head did not reach to the top of the dock,' as the English newspapers say. This case, however, was not reported because nobody cared by so much as a hempen rope for the life or death of Little Tobrah. The assessors in the red court-house sat upon him all through the long hot afternoon, and whenever they asked him a question he salaamed and whined. Their verdict was that the evidence was inconclusive, and the Judge concurred. It was true that the dead body of Little Tobrah's sister had been found at the bottom of the well, and Little Tobrah was the only human being within a half mile radius at the time; but the child might have fallen in by accident. Therefore Little Tobrah was acquitted, and told to go where he pleased. This permission was not so generous as it sounds, for he had nowhere to go to, nothing in particular to eat, and nothing whatever to wear.

He trotted into the court-compound, and sat upon the well-kerb, wondering whether an unsuccessful dive into the black water below would end in a forced voyage [2] across the other Black Water. [3] A groom put down an emptied nose-bag on the bricks, and Little Tobrah, being hungry, set himself to scrape out what wet grain the horse had overlooked.

'O Thief – and but newly set free from the terror of the Law! Come along!' said the groom, and Little Tobrah was led by the ear to a large and fat Englishman, who heard the tale of the theft.

'Hah!' said the Englishman three times (only he said a stronger word). 'Put him into the net and take him home.' So Little Tobrah was thrown into the net of the cart, and, nothing doubting that he should be stuck like a pig, was driven to the Englishman's house. 'Hah!' said the Englishman as before. 'Wet grain, by Jove! Feed the little beggar, some of you, and we'll make a riding-boy of him! See? Wet grain, good Lord!'

'Give an account of yourself,' said the Head of the Grooms to Little Tobrah after the meal had been eaten, and the servants lay at ease in their quarters behind the house. 'You are not of the groom caste, unless it be for the stomach's sake. How came you into the court, and why? Answer, little devil's spawn!'

'There was not enough to eat,' said Little Tobrah calmly. 'This is a good place.'

70

'Talk straight talk,' said the Head Groom, 'or I will make you clean out the stable of that large red stallion who bites like a camel.'

'We be *Telis*, oil-pressers,' said Little Tobrah, scratching his toes in the dust. 'We were *Telis* – my father, my mother, my brother, the elder by four years, myself, and the sister.'

'She who was found dead in the well?' said one who had heard something of the trial.

'Even so,' said Little Tobrah gravely. 'She who was found dead in the well. It befell upon a time, which is not in my memory, that the sickness came to the village where our oil-press stood, and first my sister was smitten as to her eyes, and went without sight, for it was *mata* – the small-pox. Thereafter, my father and my mother died of that same sickness, so we were alone – my brother who had twelve years, I who had eight, and the sister who could not see. Yet were there the bullock and the oil-press remaining, and we made shift to press the oil as before. But Surjun Dass, the grain-seller, cheated us in his dealings; and it was always a stubborn bullock to drive. We put marigold flowers for the Gods upon the neck of the bullock, and upon the great grinding-beam that rose through the roof; but we gained nothing thereby, and Surjun Dass was a hard man.'

'*Bapri-bap*,'[4] muttered the grooms' wives, 'to cheat a child so! But *we* know what the *bunnia*-folk[5] are, sisters.'

'The press was an old press, and we were not strong men – my brother and I; nor could we fix the neck of the beam firmly in the shackle.'

'Nay, indeed,' said the gorgeously-clad wife of the Head Groom, joining the circle. 'That is a strong man's work. When I was a maid in my father's house –'

'Peace, woman,' said the Head Groom. 'Go on, boy.'

'It is nothing,' said Little Tobrah. 'The big beam tore down the roof upon a day which is not in my memory, and with the roof fell much of the hinder wall, and both together upon our bullock, whose back was broken. Thus we had neither home, nor press, nor bullock – my brother, myself, and the sister who was blind. We went crying away from that place, hand-in-hand, across the fields; and our money was seven annas and six pie. There was a famine in the land. I do not know the name of the land. So, on a night when we were sleeping, my brother took the five annas that remained to us and ran away. I do not know whither he went. The curse of my father be upon him. But I and the sister begged food in the villages, and there was none to give. Only all men said – "Go to the Englishmen and they will give." I did not know what the Englishmen were; but they said that they were white, living in tents. I went forward;

but I cannot say whither I went, and there was no more food for myself or the sister. And upon a hot night, she weeping and calling for food, we came to a well, and I bade her sit upon the kerb, and thrust her in, for, in truth, she could not see; and it is better to die than to starve.'

'Ai! Ahi!' wailed the grooms' wives in chorus; 'he thrust her in, for it is better to die than to starve!'

'I would have thrown myself in also, but that she was not dead and called to me from the bottom of the well, and I was afraid and ran. And one came out of the crops saying that I had killed her and defiled the well, and they took me before an Englishman, white and terrible, living in a tent, and me he sent here. But there were no witnesses, and it is better to die than to starve. She, furthermore, could not see with her eyes, and was but a little child.'

'Was but a little child,' echoed the Head Groom's wife. 'But who art thou, weak as a fowl and small as a day-old colt, what art *thou*?'

'I who was empty am now full,' said Little Tobrah, stretching himself upon the dust. 'And I would sleep.'

The groom's wife spread a cloth over him while Little Tobrah slept the sleep of the just.

⟦ Black Jack [1] ⟧

To the wake av Tim O'Hara
Came company,
All St Patrick's Alley
Was there to see.
        Robert Buchanan.[2]

As the Three Musketeers share their silver, tobacco, and liquor together, as they protect each other in barracks or camp, and as they rejoice together over the joy of one, so do they divide their sorrows. When Ortheris's irrepressible tongue has brought him into cells for a season, or Learoyd has run amok through his kit and accoutrements, or Mulvaney has indulged in strong waters, and under their influence reproved his Commanding Officer, you can see the trouble in the faces of the untouched two. And the rest of the Regiment know that comment or jest is unsafe. Generally the three avoid Orderly-Room and the Corner Shop [3] that follows, leaving both to the young bloods who have not sown their wild oats; but there are occasions –

For instance, Ortheris was sitting on the drawbridge of the main gate of Fort Amara, with his hands in his pockets and his pipe, bowl down, in his mouth. Learoyd was lying at full length on the turf of the glacis, kicking his heels in the air, and I came round the corner and asked for Mulvaney.

Ortheris spat into the Ditch and shook his head. 'No good seein' 'im now,' said Ortheris; ''e's a bloomin' camel. Listen.'

I heard on the flags of the verandah opposite to the cells, which are close to the Guard-Room, a measured step that I could have identified out of the tramp of an army. There were twenty paces *crescendo*, a pause, and then twenty *diminuendo*.

'That's 'im,' said Ortheris; 'my Gawd, that's 'im! All for a bloomin' button you could see your face in an' a bit o' lip that a bloomin' Hark-angel would 'a' guv back.'

Mulvaney was doing pack-drill – was compelled, that is to say, to walk up and down for certain hours in full marching order, with rifle, bayonet, ammunition, knapsack, and overcoat. And his offence was being dirty on parade! I nearly fell into the Fort Ditch with astonishment and wrath, for Mulvaney is the smartest man that ever mounted guard, and would as soon think of turning out uncleanly as of dispensing with his trousers.

'Who was the Sergeant that checked him?' I asked.

'Mullins, o' course,' said Ortheris. 'There ain't no other man would whip 'im on the peg⁴ so. But Mullins ain't a man. 'E's a dirty little pig-scraper, that's wot 'e is.'

'What did Mulvaney say? He's not the make of man to take that quietly.'

'Say! Bin better for 'im if 'e'd shut 'is mouth. Lord, 'ow we laughed! "Sargint," 'e sez, "ye say I'm dirty. Well," sez 'e, "when your wife lets you blow your own nose for yourself, perhaps you'll know wot dirt is. You're himperfec'ly eddicated, Sargint," sez 'e, an' then we fell in. But after p'rade, 'e was up an' Mullins was swearin' 'imself black in the face at Ord'ly-Room that Mulvaney 'ad called 'im a swine an' Lord knows wot all. You know Mullins. 'E'll 'ave 'is 'ead broke in one o' these days. 'E's too big a bloomin' liar for ord'nary consumption. "Three hours' can an' kit," sez the Colonel; "not for bein' dirty on p'rade, but for 'avin' said somethin' to Mullins, tho' I do not believe," sez 'e, "you said wot 'e said you said." An' Mulvaney fell away sayin' nothin'. You know 'e never speaks to the Colonel for fear o' gettin' 'imself fresh copped.'

Mullins, a very young and very much married Sergeant, whose manners were partly the result of innate depravity and partly of imperfectly digested Board School, came over the bridge, and most rudely asked Ortheris what he was doing.

'Me?' said Ortheris. 'Ow! I'm waiting for my C'mission. Seed it comin' along yit?'

Mullins turned purple and passed on. There was the sound of a gentle chuckle from the glacis where Learoyd lay.

''E expects to get his C'mission some day,' explained Ortheris. 'Gawd 'elp the Mess that 'ave to put their 'ands into the same kiddy⁵ as 'im! Wot time d'you make it, sir? Fower! Mulvaney'll be out in 'arf an hour. You don't want to buy a dorg, sir, do you? A pup you can trust – 'arf Rampur by the Colonel's grey'ound.'

'Ortheris,' I answered sternly, for I knew what was in his mind, 'do you mean to say that –'

'I didn't mean to arx money o' you, any'ow,' said Ortheris. 'I'd 'a' sold you the dorg good an' cheap, but – but – I know Mulvaney'll want somethin' after we've walked 'im orf, an' I ain't got nothin', nor 'e 'asn't neither. I'd sooner sell you the dorg, sir. 'Strewth I would!'

A shadow fell on the drawbridge, and Ortheris began to rise into the air, lifted by a huge hand upon his collar.

'Onnything but t' braass,' said Learoyd quietly, as he held the Londoner over the Ditch. 'Onnything but t' braass, Orth'ris, ma son! Ah've got one rupee eight annas ma own.' He showed two coins, and replaced Ortheris on the drawbridge rail.

'Very good,' I said; 'where are you going to?'

'Goin' to walk 'im orf w'en 'e comes out – two miles or three or fower,' said Ortheris.

The footsteps within ceased. I heard the dull thud of a knapsack falling on a bedstead, followed by the rattle of arms. Ten minutes later, Mulvaney, faultlessly dressed, his lips tight and his face as black as a thunderstorm, stalked into the sunshine on the drawbridge. Learoyd and Ortheris sprang from my side and closed in upon him, both leaning towards him as horses lean upon the pole. In an instant they had disappeared down the sunken road to the cantonments, and I was left alone. Mulvaney had not seen fit to recognize me; so I knew that his trouble must be heavy upon him.

I climbed one of the bastions and watched the figures of the Three Musketeers grow smaller and smaller across the plain. They were walking as fast as they could put foot to the ground, and their heads were bowed. They fetched a great compass round the parade-ground, skirted the Cavalry lines, and vanished in the belt of trees that fringes the low land by the river.

I followed slowly, and sighted them – dusty, sweating, but still keeping up their long, swinging tramp – on the river bank. They crashed through the Forest Reserve, headed towards the Bridge of Boats, and presently established themselves on the bow of one of the pontoons. I rode cautiously till I saw three puffs of white smoke rise and die out in the clear evening air, and knew that peace had come again. At the bridge-head they waved me forward with gestures of welcome.

'Tie up your 'orse,' shouted Ortheris, 'an' come on, sir. We're all goin' 'ome in this 'ere bloomin' boat.'

From the bridge-head to the Forest Officer's bungalow is but a step. The mess-man was there, and would see that a man held my horse. Did the Sahib require aught else – a peg,[6] or beer? Ritchie Sahib had left half-a-dozen bottles of the latter, but since the Sahib was a friend of Ritchie Sahib, and he, the mess-man, was a poor man –

I gave my order quietly, and returned to the bridge. Mulvaney had taken off his boots, and was dabbling his toes in the water; Learoyd was lying on his back on the pontoon; and Ortheris was pretending to row with a big bamboo.

'I'm an ould fool,' said Mulvaney reflectively, 'dhraggin' you two out here bekaze I was undher the Black Dog – sulkin' like a child. Me that was sodgerin' when Mullins, an' be damned to him, was shquealin' on a counterpin for five shillin' a week – an' that not paid! Bhoys, I've tuck you five miles out av natural pivarsity. Phew!'

'Wot's the odds as long as you're 'appy?' said Ortheris, applying himself afresh to the bamboo. 'As well 'ere as anywhere else.'

Learoyd held up a rupee and an eight-anna bit, and shook his head sorrowfully. 'Five miles from t' Canteen, all along o' Mulvaaney's blaasted pride.'

'I know ut,' said Mulvaney penitently. 'Why will ye come wid me? An' yet I wud be mortial sorry av ye did not – any time – though I am ould enough to know betther. But I will do penance. I will take a dhrink av wather.'

Ortheris squeaked shrilly. The butler of the Forest bungalow was standing near the railings with a basket, uncertain how to clamber down to the pontoon.

'Might 'a' know'd you'd 'a' got liquor out o' bloomin' desert, sir,' said Ortheris gracefully to me. Then to the mess-man: 'Easy with them there bottles. They're worth their weight in gold. Jock, ye long-armed beggar, get out o' that an' hike 'em down.'

Learoyd had the basket on the pontoon in an instant, and the Three Musketeers gathered round it with dry lips. They drank my health in due and ancient form, and thereafter tobacco tasted sweeter than ever. They absorbed all the beer, and disposed themselves in picturesque attitudes to admire the setting sun – no man speaking for a while.

Mulvaney's head dropped upon his chest, and we thought that he was asleep.

'What on earth did you come so far for?' I whispered to Ortheris.

'To walk 'im orf, o' course. When 'e's been checked we allus walks 'im orf. 'E ain't fit to be spoke to those times – nor 'e ain't fit to leave alone neither. So we takes 'im till 'e is.'

Mulvaney raised his head, and stared straight into the sunset. 'I had my rifle,' said he dreamily, 'an' I had my bay'nit, an' Mullins came round the corner, an' he looked in my face an' grinned dishpiteful. "*You* can't blow your own nose," sez he. Now, I cannot tell fwhat Mullins's expayrience may ha' been, but, Mother av God, he was nearer to his death that minut' than I have iver been to mine – and that's less than the thicknuss av a hair!'

'Yes,' said Ortheris calmly, 'you'd look fine with all your buttons took orf, an' the Band in front o' you, walkin' roun' slow time. We're both front-rank men, me an' Jock, when the Rig'ment's in 'ollow square. Bloomin' fine you'd look. "The Lord giveth an' the Lord taketh awai, – Heasy with that there drop! – Blessed be the naime o' the Lord."' He gulped in a quaint and suggestive fashion.

'Mullins! What's Mullins?' said Learoyd slowly. 'Ah'd taake a coomp'ny o' Mullinses – ma hand behind me. Sitha, Mulvaaney, don't be a fool.'

'*You* were not checked for fwhat you did not do, an' made a mock av afther. 'Twas for less than that the Tyrone [7] wud ha' sent O'Hara to Hell, instid av lettin' him go by his own choosin', whin Rafferty shot him,' retorted Mulvaney.

'And who stopped the Tyrone from doing it?' I asked.

'This ould fool who's sorry he did not shtick that pig Mullins.' His head dropped again. When he raised it he shivered and put his hands on the shoulders of his two companions.

'Ye've walked the Divil out av me, bhoys,' said he.

Ortheris shot out the red-hot dottle of his pipe on the back of the hairy fist. 'They say 'Ell's 'otter than that,' said he, as Mulvaney swore aloud. 'You be warned so. Look yonder!' – he pointed across the river to a ruined temple – 'Me an' you an' '*im*' – he indicated me by a jerk of his head – 'was there one day when Hi made a bloomin' show o' myself. You an' 'im stopped me doin' such – an' Hi was on'y wishful for to desert. [8] You are makin' a bigger bloomin' show o' yourself now.'

'Don't mind him, Mulvaney,' I said; 'Dinah Shadd won't let you hang yourself yet awhile, and you don't intend to try it either. Let's hear about the Tyrone and O'Hara. Rafferty shot him for fooling with his wife. What happened before that?'

'There's no fool like an ould fool. Ye know ye can do anythin' wid me whin I'm talkin'. Did I say I wud like to cut Mullins's liver out? I deny the imputashin, for fear that Orth'ris here wud report me – Ah! You wud tip me into the river, wud you? Set quiet, little man. Anyways, Mullins is not worth the throuble av an extry p'rade, an' I will trate him wid outrajis contimpt. The Tyrone an' O'Hara! O'Hara an' the Tyrone, begad! Ould days are hard to bring back into the mouth, but they're always inside the head.'

Followed a long pause.

'O'Hara was a Divil. Though I saved him, for the honour av the Rig'mint, from his death that time, I say it now. He was a Divil – a long, bould, black-haired Divil.'

'Which way?' asked Ortheris.

'Wimmen.'

'Then I know another.'

'Not more than in reason, if you mane me, ye warped walkin'-shtick. I have been young, an' for why shud I not have tuk what I cud? Did I iver, whin I was Corp'ril, use the rise av my rank – wan step an' that taken away, more's the sorrow an' the fault av me! – to prosecute nefarious inthrigues, as O'Hara did? Did I, whin I was Corp'ril, lay my spite upon a man an' make his life a dog's life from day to day? Did I lie, as O'Hara lied, till the young wans in the Tyrone turned white wid the fear av the Judgment av God killin' thim all in a lump, as ut killed the woman at Devizes?[9] I did not! I have sinned my sins an' I have made my confesshin, an' Father Victor knows the worst av me. O'Hara was tuk, before he cud spake, on Rafferty's door-stip, an' no man knows the worst av him. But this much I know!

'The Tyrone was recruited any fashion in the ould days. A draf' from Connemara – a draf' from Portsmouth – a draf' from Kerry, an' that was a blazin' bad draf' – here, there, and ivrywhere – but the large av thim was Irish – Black Irish. Now there are Irish an' Irish. The good are good as the best, but the bad are wurrse than the wurrst. 'Tis this way. They clog together in pieces as fast as thieves, an' no wan knows fwhat they will do till wan turns informer an' the gang is bruk. But ut begins agin, a day later, meetin' in holes an' corners an' swearin' bloody oaths an' shtickin' a man in the back an' runnin' away, an' thin waiting for the blood-money on the reward papers – to see if ut's worth enough. Those are the Black Irish, an' 'tis they that bring dishgrace upon the name av Ireland, an' thim I wud kill – as I nearly killed wan wanst.

'But to reshume. My room – 'twas before I was married – was wid twelve av the scum av the earth – the pickin's av the gutther – mane men that wud neither laugh nor talk nor yet get dhrunk as a man shud. They thried some av their dog's thricks on me, but I dhrew a line around my cot, an' the man that thransgressed ut wint into hospital for three days good.

'O'Hara had put his spite on the room – he was my Colour-Sargint – an' nothing cud we do to plaze him. I was younger than I am now, an' I tuk fwhat I got in the way av dhressing-down and punishmint-dhrill wid me tongue in me cheek. But it was diff'rint wid the others, an' why I cannot say, excipt that some men are borrun mane an' go to dhirty murther where a fist is more than enough. Afther a whoile, they changed their chune to me an' was desp'rit frien'ly – all twelve av thim cursin' O'Hara in chorus.

' "Eyah!" sez I, "O'Hara's a divil and I'm not for denyin' ut, but is

he the only man in the wurruld? Let him go. He'll get tired av findin'
our kit foul an' our 'coutrements onproperly kep'."

'"We will *not* let him go," sez they.

'"Thin take him," sez I, "an' a dashed poor yield you will get for
your throuble."

'"Is he not misconductin' himself wid Slimmy's wife?" sez another.

'"She's common to the Rig'mint," sez I. "Fwhat has made ye this
partic'lar on a suddint?"

'"Has he not put his spite on the roomful av us? Can we do anythin'
that he will not check us for?" sez another.

'"That's thrue," sez I.

'"Will ye not help us to do aught," sez another – "a big bould man
like you?"

'"I will break his head upon his shoulthers av he puts hand on me,"
sez I. "I will give him the lie av he says that I'm dhirty an' I wud not
mind duckin' him in the Artillery troughs if ut was not that I'm thryin'
for me shtripes."

'"Is that all ye will do?" sez another. "Have ye no more spunk than
that, ye blood-dhrawn calf?'

'"Blood-dhrawn I may be," says I, gettin' back to my cot an' makin'
my line round ut; "but ye know that the man who comes acrost this mark
will be more blood-dhrawn than me. No man gives me the name in my
mouth," I sez. "Ondhersthand, I will have no part wid you in anythin'
ye do, nor will I raise my fist to my shuperior. Is any wan comin' on?"
sez I.

'They made no move, tho' I gave thim full time, but stud growlin' an'
snarlin' together at wan ind av the room. I tuk up my cap and wint out to
Canteen, thinkin' no little av mesilf, an' there I grew most ondacintly
dhrunk in my legs. My head was all reasonable.

'"Houligan," I sez to a man in E Comp'ny that was by way av bein' a
frind av mine; "I'm overtuk from the belt down. Do you give me the
touch av your shoulther to presarve me formashin an' march me acrost
the ground into the high grass. I'll sleep ut off there," sez I; an' Houligan
– he's dead now, but good he was whoile he lasted – walked wid me,
givin' me the touch whin I wint wide, ontil we came to the high grass,
an', my faith, sky an' earth was fair rowlin' undher me. I made for
where the grass was thickust, an' there I slep' off my liquor wid an aisy
conscience. I did not desire to come on the books too frequint; my
characther havin' been shpotless for the good half av a year.

'Whin I roused, the dhrink was dyin' out in me, an' I felt as though a
she-cat had littered in me mouth. I had not learned to hould my liquor

wid comfort in thim days. 'Tis little betther I am now. "I will get
Houligan to pour a bucket over my head," thinks I, an' I wud ha' risen,
but I heard some wan say: "Mulvaney can take the blame av ut for the
backslidin' hound he is."

'" Oho!" sez I, an' me head ringing like a guard-room gong: "fwhat is
the blame that this young man must take to oblige Tim Vulmea?" For
'twas Tim Vulmea that shpoke.

'I turned on me belly an' crawled through the grass, a bit at a time, to
where the spache came from. There was the twelve av my room sittin'
down in a little patch, the dhry grass wavin' above their heads an' the sin
av black murther in their hearts. I put the stuff aside to get clear view.

'"Fwhat's that?" sez wan man, jumpin' up.

'"A dog," says Vulmea. "You're a nice hand to this job! As I said,
Mulvaney will take the blame – av ut comes to a pinch."

'"'Tis harrd to swear a man's life away," sez a young wan.

'"Thank ye for that," thinks I. "Now, fwhat the divil are you paragins
conthrivin' agin' me?"

'"'Tis as aisy as dhrinkin' your quart," sez Vulmea. "At sivin or
thereon, O'Hara will come acrost to the Married Quarters, goin' to call
on Slimmy's wife, the swine! Wan av us 'll pass the wurrud to the room
an' we shtart the divil an' all av a shine – laughin' an' crackin' on [10] an'
t'rowin' our boots about. Thin O'Hara will come to give us the ordher to
be quiet, the more by token bekaze the room lamp will be knocked over in
the larkin'. He will take the straight road to the ind door where there's
the lamp in the verandah, an' that'll bring him clear agin' the light as he
shtands. He will not be able to look into the dhark. Wan av us will loose
off, an' a close shot ut will be, an' shame to the man that misses. 'Twill
be Mulvaney's rifle, she that is at the head av the rack – there's no
mishtakin' that long-shtocked, cross-eyed bitch even in the dhark."

'The thief misnamed my ould firin'-piece out av jealousy – I was
pershuaded av that – an' ut made me more angry than all.

'But Vulmea goes on: "O'Hara will dhrop, an' by the time the light's
lit agin, there'll be some six av us on the chest av Mulvaney, cryin'
murther an' rape. Mulvaney's cot is near the ind door, an' the shmokin'
rifle will be lyin' undher him whin we've knocked him over. We know,
an' all the Rig'mint knows, that Mulvaney has given O'Hara more lip
than any man av us. Will there be any doubt at the Coort-Martial? Wud
twelve honust sodger-bhoys swear away the life av a dear, quiet, swate-
timpered man such as is Mulvaney – wid his line av pipe-clay roun' his
cot, threatenin' us wid murther av we overshtepped ut, as we can truthful
testify?"

'"Mary, Mother av Mercy!" thinks I to mesilf; "ut is this to have an unruly mimber an' fistes fit to use! The hounds!"

'The big dhrops ran down my face, for I was wake wid the liquor an' had not the full av my wits about me. I laid sthill an' heard thim workin' thimsilves up to swear me life away by tellin' tales av ivry time I had put my mark on wan or another; an', my faith, they was few that was not so dishtinguished. 'Twas all in the way av fair fight, though, for niver did I raise my hand excipt whin they had provoked me to ut.

'"'Tis all well," sez wan av thim, "but who's to do this shootin'?"

'"Fwhat matther?" sez Vulmea. "'Tis Mulvaney will do that – at the Coort-Martial."

'"He will so," sez the man, "but whose hand is put to the thrigger – *in the room?*"

'"Who'll do ut?" sez Vulmea, lookin' round, but divil a man answered. They began to dishpute till Kiss, that was always playin' Shpoil Five, sez: "Thry the kyards!" Wid that he opind his tunic an' tuk out the greasy palammers,[11] an' they all fell in wid the notion.

'"Deal on!" sez Vulmea, wid a big rattlin' oath, "an' the Black Curse av Shielygh come to the man that will not do his jooty as the kyards say. Amin!"

'"Black Jack is the masther," sez Kiss, dealin'. Black Jack, sorr, I shud expaytiate to you, is the Ace av Shpades which from time immimorial has been intimately connect wid battle, murther, an' suddin death.

'*Wanst* Kiss dealt, an' there was no sign, but the men was whoite wid the workin's av their sowls. *Twice* Kiss dealt, an' there was a grey shine on their cheeks like the mess av an egg. *Three* times Kiss dealt, an' they was blue. "Have ye not lost him?" sez Vulmea, wipin' the sweat on him; "let's ha' done quick!" "Quick ut is," sez Kiss, throwin' him the kyard; an' ut fell face up on his knee – Black Jack!

'Thin they all cackled wid laughin'. "Jooty thrippence," sez wan av thim, "an' damned cheap at that price!" But I cud see they all dhrew a little away from Vulmea an' lef' him sittin' playin' wid the kyard. Vulmea sez no wurrud for a whoile but licked his lips – cat-ways. Thin he threw up his head an' made the men swear by ivry oath known to stand by him not alone in the room but at the Coort-Martial that was to set on *me*! He tould off five av the biggest to stretch me on my cot whin the shot was fired, an' another man he tould off to put out the light, an' yet another to load my rifle. He wud not do that himsilf; an' that was quare, for 'twas but a little thing considherin'.

'Thin they swore over again that they wud not bethray wan another, an' crep' out av the grass in diff'rint ways, two by two. A mercy ut was that they did not come on me. I was sick wid fear in the pit av me stummick – sick, sick, sick! Afther they was all gone, I wint back to Canteen an' called for a quart to put a thought in me. Vulmea was there, dhrinkin' heavy, an' politeful to me beyond reason. "Fwhat will I do? – fwhat will I do?" thinks I to mesilf whin Vulmea wint away.

'Prisintly the Arm'rer-Sargint comes in stiffin'[12] an' crackin' on, not plazed wid any wan, bekaze the Martini-Henry[13] bein' new to the Rig'mint in those days we used to play the mischief wid her arrangemints. 'Twas a long time before I cud get out av the way av thryin' to pull back the backsight an' turnin' her over afther firin' – as if she was a Snider.

'"Fwhat tailor-men do they give me to work wid?" sez the Arm'rer-Sargint. "Here's Hogan, his nose flat as a table, laid by for a week, an' ivry Comp'ny sendin' their arrums in knocked to small shivreens."

'"Fwhat's wrong wid Hogan, Sargint?" sez I.

'"Wrong!" sez the Arm'rer-Sargint; "I showed him, as though I had been his mother, the way av shtrippin' a 'Tini, an' he shtrup her clane an' aisy. I tould him to put her to agin' an' fire a blank into the blow-pit to show how the dhirt hung on the groovin'. He did that, but he did not put in the pin av the fallin'-block, an' av coorse whin he fired he was strook by the block jumpin' clear. Well for him 'twas but a blank – a full charge wud ha' cut his eye out."

'I looked a thrifle wiser than a boiled sheep's head. "How's that, Sargint?" sez I.

'"This way, ye blundherin' man, an' don't you be doin' ut," sez he. Wid that he shows me a Waster action – the breech av her all cut away to show the inside – an' so plazed he was to grumble that he dimonsthrated fwhat Hogan had done twice over. "An' that comes av not knowin' the wepping you're provided wid," sez he.

'"Thank ye, Sargint," sez I; "I will come to you agin for further informashin."

'"Ye will not," sez he. "Kape your clanin'-rod away from the breech-pin or you will get into throuble."

'I wint outside an' I cud ha' danced wid delight for the grandeur av ut. "They will load my rifle, good luck to thim, whoile I'm away," thinks I, and back I wint to the Canteen to give thim their clear chanst.

'The Canteen was fillin' wid men at the ind av the day. I made feign to be far gone in dhrink, an', wan by wan, all my roomful came in wid Vulmea. I wint away, walkin' thick an' heavy, but not so thick an' heavy that any man cud ha' tuk me. Sure an' thrue, there was a kyartridge gone from my pouch an' lyin' snug in my rifle. I was hot wid rage agin' thim all, and I worried the bullet out wid me teeth as fast as I cud, the room bein' empty. Then I tuk my boot an' the clanin'-rod and knocked out the pin av the fallin'-block. Oh, 'twas music whin that pin rowled on the flure! I put ut into my pouch an' shtuck a dab av dhirt on the holes in the plate, puttin' the fallin'-block back. "That'll do your business, Vulmea," sez I, lyin' aisy on me cot. "Come an' sit on me chest, the whole room av you, an' I will take you to me bosom for the biggest divils that iver cheated halter." I wud have no mercy on Vulmea. His eye or his life — little I cared!

'At dusk they came back, the twelve av thim, an' they had all been dhrinkin'. I was shammin' sleep on the cot. Wan man wint outside in the verandah. Whin he whishtled they began to rage roun' the room an' carry on tremenjus. But I niver want to hear men laugh as they did — sky-larkin' too! 'Twas like mad jackals.

'"Shtop that blasted noise!" sez O'Hara in the dark, an' pop goes the room lamp. I cud hear O'Hara runnin' up an' the rattlin' av my rifle in the rack an' the men breathin' heavy as they stud roun' my cot. I cud see O'Hara in the light av the verandah lamp, an' thin I heard the crack av my rifle. She cried loud, poor darlint, bein' mishandled. Next minut' five men were houldin' me down. "Go aisy," I sez; "fwhat's ut all about?"'

'Thin Vulmea, on the flure, raised a howl you cud hear from wan ind av cantonmints to the other. "I'm dead, I'm butchered, I'm blind!" sez he. "Saints have mercy on my sinful sowl! Sind for Father Constant! Oh, sind for Father Constant an' let me go clane!" By that I knew he was not so dead as I cud ha' wished.

'O'Hara picks up the lamp in the verandah wid a hand as stiddy as a rest. "Fwhat damned dog's thrick is this av yours?" sez he, and turns the light on Tim Vulmea that was shwimmin' in blood from top to toe. The fallin'-block had sprung free behin' a full charge av powther — good care I tuk to bite down the brass afther takin' out the bullet, that there might be somethin' to give ut full worth — an' had cut Tim from the lip to the corner av the right eye, lavin' the eyelid in tatthers, an' so up an' along by the forehead to the hair. 'Twas more av a rakin' plough, if you will ondhersthand, than a clane cut; an' niver did I see a man bleed as Vulmea did. The dhrink an' the stew that he was in pumped the blood strong. The minut' the men sittin' on my chest heard O'Hara spakin' they scatthered each wan to his cot, an' cried out very politeful: "Fwhat is ut, Sargint?"

'"Fwhat is ut!" sez O'Hara, shakin' Tim. "Well an' good do you know fwhat ut is, ye skulkin' ditch-lurkin' dogs! Get a *dooli*,[14] an' take this whimperin' scutt away. There will be more heard av ut than any av you will care for."

'Vulmea sat up rockin' his head in his hand an' moanin' for Father Constant.

'"Be done!" sez O'Hara, dhraggin' him up by the hair. "You're none so dead that you cannot go fifteen years for thryin' to shoot me."

'"I did not," sez Vulmea; "I was shootin' mesilf."

'"That's quare," sez O'Hara, "for the front av my jackut is black wid your powther." He tuk up the rifle that was still warm an' began to laugh. "I'll make your life Hell to you," sez he, "for attempted murther an' kapin' your rifle onproperly. You'll be hanged first an' thin put undher stoppages¹⁵ for four fifteen. The rifle's done for," sez he.

'"Why, 'tis *my* rifle!" sez I, comin' up to look. "Vulmea, ye divil, fwhat were you doin' wid her — answer me that?"

'"Lave me alone," sez Vulmea; "I'm dyin'!"

'"I'll wait till you're betther," sez I, "an' thin we two will talk ut out umbrageous."

'O'Hara pitched Tim into the *dooli*, none too tinder, but all the bhoys kep' by their cots, which was not the sign av innocint men. I was huntin' ivrywhere for my fallin'-block, but not findin' ut at all. I niver found ut.

'"*Now* fwhat will I do?" sez O'Hara, swinging the verandah light in his hand an' lookin' down the room. I had hate and contimpt av O'Hara an' I have now, dead tho' he is, but for all that will I say he was a brave man. He is baskin' in Purgathory this tide, but I wish he cud hear that, whin he stud lookin' down the room an' the bhoys shivered before the eye av him, I knew him for a brave man an' I liked him *so*.

'"Fwhat will I do?" sez O'Hara agin, an' we heard the voice av a woman low an' sof' in the verandah. 'Twas Slimmy's wife, come over at the shot, sittin on wan av the benches an' scarce able to walk.

'"O Denny! — Denny, dear," sez she, "have they kilt you?"

'O'Hara looked down the room again an' showed his teeth to the gum. Thin he spat on the flure.

'"You're not worth ut," sez he. "Light that lamp, ye dogs," an' wid that he turned away, an' I saw him walkin' off wid Slimmy's wife; she thryin' to wipe off the powther-black on the front av his jackut wid her handkerchief. "A brave man you are," thinks I — "a brave man an' a bad woman."

'No wan said a wurrud for a time. They was all ashamed, past spache.

'"Fwhat d'you think he will do?" sez wan av thim at last. "He knows we're all in ut."

'"Are we so?" sez I from my cot. "The man that sez that to me will be hurt. I do not know," sez I, "fwhat ondherhand divilmint you have conthrived, but by fwhat I've seen I know that you cannot commit murther wid another man's rifle – such shakin' cowards you are. I'm goin' to slape," I sez, "an' you can blow my head off whoile I lay." I did not slape, though, for a long time. Can ye wonder?

'Next morn the news was through all the Rig'mint, an' there was nothin' that the men did not tell. O'Hara reports, fair an' aisy, that Vulmea was come to grief through tamperin' wid his rifle in barricks, all for to show the mechanism. An', by my sowl, he had the impart'nince to say that he was on the shpot at the time an' cud certify that ut was an accidint! You might ha' knocked my roomful down wid a straw whin they heard that. 'Twas lucky for thim that the bhoys were always thryin' to find out how the new rifle was made, an' a lot av thim had come up for aisin' the pull by shtickin' bits av grass an' such in the part av the lock that showed near the thrigger. The first issues of the 'Tinis was not covered in, an' I mesilf have aised the pull av mine time an' agin. A light pull is ten points on the range to me.

'"I will not have this foolishness!" sez the Colonel. "I will twist the tail off Vulmea!" sez he; but whin he saw him, all tied up an' groanin' in hospital, he changed his will. "Make him an early convalescint," sez he to the Doctor, an' Vulmea was made so for a warnin'. His big bloody bandages an' face puckered up to wan side did more to kape the bhoys from messin' wid the insides av their rifles than any punishmint.

'O'Hara gave no reason for fhwat he'd said, an' all my roomful were too glad to ask, tho' he put his spite upon thim more wearin' than before. Wan day, howiver, he tuk me apart very polite, for he cud be that at his choosin'.

'"You're a good sodger, tho' you're a damned insolint man," sez he.

'"Fair wurruds, Sargint," sez I, "or I may be insolint agin."

'"'Tis not like you," sez he, "to lave your rifle in the rack widout the breech-pin, for widout the breech-pin she was whin Vulmea fired. I shud ha' found the break av ut in the eyes av the holes, else," he sez.

'"Sargint," sez I, "fwhat wud your life ha' been worth av the breech-pin had been in place, for, on my sowl, my life wud be worth just as much to me av I tould you whether ut was or was not? Be thankful the bullet was not there," I sez.

'"That's thrue," sez he, pulling his moustache; "but I do not believe that you, for all your lip, were in that business."

'"Sargint," sez I, "I cud hammer the life out av a man in ten minut's wid my fistes if that man dishplazed me; for I am a good sodger, an' I will be threated as such, an' whoile my fistes are my own they're strong enough for all the work I have to do. *They* do not fly back towards me!" sez I, lookin' him betune the eyes.

'"You're a good man," sez he, lookin' me betune the eyes – an' oh, he was a gran'-built man to see! – "you're a good man," he sez, "an' I cud wish, for the pure frolic av ut, that I was not a Sargint, or that you were not a Privit; an' you will think me no coward whin I say this thing."

'"I do not," sez I. "I saw you whin Vulmea mishandled the rifle. But, Sargint," I sez, "take the wurrud from me now, spakin' as man to man wid the shtripes off, tho' 'tis little right I have to talk, me bein' fwhat I am by natur'. This time ye tuk no harm, an' next time ye may not, but, in the ind, so sure as Slimmy's wife came into the verandah, so sure will ye take harm – an' bad harm. Have thought, Sargint," sez I. "Is ut worth ut?"

'"Ye're a bould man," sez he, breathin' harrd. "A very bould man. But I am a bould man tu. Do you go your ways, Privit Mulvaney, an' I will go mine."

'We had no further spache thin or afther, but, wan by another, he drafted the twelve av my room out into other rooms an' got thim spread among the Comp'nies, for they was not a good breed to live together, an' the Comp'ny Orf'cers saw ut. They wud ha' shot me in the night av they had known fwhat I knew; but that they did not.

'An', in the ind, as I said, O'Hara met his death from Rafferty for foolin' wid his wife. He wint his own way too well – Eyah, too well! Shtraight to that affair, widout turnin' to the right or to the lef', he wint, an' may the Lord have mercy on his sowl. Amin!'

''Ear! 'ear!' said Ortheris, pointing the moral with a wave of his pipe. 'An' this is 'im 'oo would be a bloomin' Vulmea all for the sake of Mullins an' a bloomin' button! Mullins never went after a woman in his life. Mrs Mullins, she saw 'im one day –'

'Ortheris,' I said hastily, for the romances of Private Ortheris are all too daring for publication, 'look at the sun. It's a quarter past six!'

'Oh, Lord! Three-quarters of an hour for five an' a 'arf miles! We'll 'ave to run like Jimmy O.'

The Three Musketeers clambered on to the bridge, and departed hastily in the direction of the cantonment road. When I overtook them I offered them two stirrups and a tail, which they accepted enthusiastically. Ortheris held the tail, and in this manner we trotted steadily through the shadows by an unfrequented road.

At the turn into the cantonments we heard carriage wheels. It was the Colonel's barouche, and in it sat the Colonel's wife and daughter. I caught a suppressed chuckle, and my beast sprang forward with a lighter step.

The Three Musketeers had vanished into the night.

⟨ On the City Wall ¹ ⟩

Then she let them down by a cord through the window; for her house was
upon the town wall, and she dwelt upon the wall.   *Joshua* ii: 15.

Lalun is a member of the most ancient profession in the world. Lilith ²
was her very-great-grand-mamma, and that was before the days of Eve,
as everyone knows. In the West, people say rude things about Lalun's
profession, and write lectures about it, and distribute the lectures to
young persons in order that Morality may be preserved. In the East,
where the profession is hereditary, descending from mother to daughter,
nobody writes lectures or takes any notice; and that is a distinct proof of
the inability of the East to manage its own affairs.

Lalun's real husband, for even ladies of Lalun's profession in the East
must have husbands, was a big jujube-tree.³ Her Mamma, who had
married a fig-tree, spent ten thousand rupees on Lalun's wedding,
which was blessed by forty-seven clergymen of Mamma's Church, and
distributed five thousand rupees in charity to the poor. And that was
the custom of the land. The advantages of having a jujube-tree for a
husband are obvious. You cannot hurt his feelings, and he looks im-
posing.

Lalun's husband stood on the plain outside the City walls, and Lalun's
house was upon the east wall facing the river. If you fell from the broad
window-seat you dropped thirty feet sheer into the City Ditch. But if
you stayed where you should and looked forth, you saw all the cattle of
the City being driven down to water, the students of the Government
College playing cricket, the high grass and trees that fringed the river-
bank, the great sand-bars that ribbed the river, the red tombs of dead
Emperors beyond the river, and very far away through the blue heat-
haze a glint of the snows of the Himalayas.

Wali Dad used to lie in the window-seat for hours at a time watching
this view. He was a young Mohammedan who was suffering acutely
from education of the English variety and knew it. His father had sent
him to a Mission-school to get wisdom, and Wali Dad had absorbed
more than ever his father or the Missionaries intended he should. When
his father died, Wali Dad was independent and spent two years ex-

perimenting with the creeds of the Earth and reading books that are of no use to anybody.

After he had made an unsuccessful attempt to enter the Roman Catholic Church and the Presbyterian fold at the same time (the Missionaries found him out and called him names; but they did not understand his trouble), he discovered Lalun on the City wall and became the most constant of her few admirers. He possessed a head that English artists at home would rave over and paint amid impossible surroundings – a face that female novelists would use with delight through nine hundred pages. In reality he was only a clean-bred young Mohammedan, with pencilled eyebrows, small-cut nostrils, little feet and hands, and a very tired look in his eyes. By virtue of his twenty-two years he had grown a neat black beard which he stroked with pride and kept delicately scented. His life seemed to be divided between borrowing books from me and making love to Lalun in the window-seat. He composed songs about her, and some of the songs are sung to this day in the City from the Street of the Mutton-Butchers to the Copper-Smiths' ward.

One song, the prettiest of all, says that the beauty of Lalun was so great that it troubled the hearts of the British Government and caused them to lose their peace of mind. That is the way the song is sung in the streets; but, if you examine it carefully and know the key to the explanation, you will find that there are three puns in it – on 'beauty', 'heart', and 'peace of mind' – so that it runs: 'By the subtlety of Lalun the administration of the Government was troubled and it lost such-and-such a man.' When Wali Dad sings that song his eyes glow like hot coals, and Lalun leans back among the cushions and throws bunches of jasmine-buds at Wali Dad.

But first it is necessary to explain something about the Supreme Government which is above all and below all and behind all. Gentlemen come from England, spend a few weeks in India, walk round this great Sphinx of the Plains, and write books upon its ways and its works, denouncing or praising it as their own ignorance prompts. Consequently all the world knows how the Supreme Government conducts itself. But no one, not even the Supreme Government, knows everything about the administration of the Empire. Year by year England sends out fresh drafts for the first fighting-line, which is officially called the Indian Civil Service. These die, or kill themselves by overwork, or are worried to death, or broken in health and hope in order that the land may be protected from death and sickness, famine and war, and may eventually become capable of standing alone. It will never stand alone, but the idea is a pretty one, and men are willing to die for it, and yearly the work of pushing and coaxing and scolding and petting the country into good living goes forward. If an advance be made all credit is given to the native, while the Englishmen stand back and wipe their foreheads. If a failure occurs the Englishmen step forward and take the blame. Overmuch tenderness of this kind has bred a strong belief among many natives that the native is capable of administering the country, and many devout Englishmen believe this also, because the theory is stated in beautiful English with all the latest political colours.

There are other men who, though uneducated, see visions and dream dreams, and they, too, hope to administer the country in their own way – that is to say, with a garnish of Red Sauce. Such men must exist among two hundred million people, and, if they are not attended to, may cause trouble and even break the great idol called *Pax Britannica*, which, as the newspapers say, lives between Peshawur and Cape Comorin. Were the Day of Doom to dawn tomorrow, you would find the Supreme Government 'taking measures to allay popular excitement', and putting guards upon the graveyards that the Dead might troop forth orderly. The youngest Civilian would arrest Gabriel on his own responsibility if the Archangel could not produce a Deputy-Commissioner's permission to 'make music or other noises' as the licence says.

Whence it is easy to see that mere men of the flesh who would create a tumult must fare badly at the hands of the Supreme Government. And they do. There is no outward sign of excitement; there is no confusion; there is no knowledge. When due and sufficient reasons have been given, weighed and approved, the machinery moves forward, and the dreamer of dreams and the seer of visions is gone from his friends and following. He enjoys the hospitality of Government; there is no restriction upon his movements within certain limits; but he must not confer any more with his brother dreamers. Once in every six months the Supreme Government assures itself that he is well and takes formal acknowledgment of his existence. No one protests against his detention, because the few people who know about it are in deadly fear of seeming to know him; and never a single newspaper 'takes up his case' or organizes demonstrations on his behalf, because the newspapers of India have got behind that lying proverb which says the Pen is mightier than the Sword, and can walk delicately.

So now you know as much as you ought about Wali Dad, the educational mixture, and the Supreme Government.

Lalun has not yet been described. She would need, so Wali Dad says, a thousand pens of gold, and ink scented with musk. She has been variously compared to the Moon, the Dil Sagar Lake, a spotted quail, a gazelle, the Sun on the Desert of Kutch, the Dawn, the Stars, and the young bamboo. These comparisons imply that she is beautiful exceedingly according to the native standards, which are practically the same as those of the West. Her eyes are black and her hair is black, and her eyebrows are black as leeches; her mouth is tiny and says witty things; her hands are tiny and have saved much money; her feet are tiny and have trodden on the naked hearts of many men. But, as Wali Dad sings: 'Lalun *is* Lalun, and when you have said that, you have only come to the Beginnings of Knowledge.'

The little house on the City wall was just big enough to hold Lalun, and her maid, and a pussycat with a silver collar. A big pink-and-blue cut-glass chandelier hung from the ceiling of the reception room. A petty Nawab had given Lalun the horror, and she kept it for politeness' sake. The floor of the room was of polished chunam,[4] white as curds. A latticed window of carved wood was set in one wall; there was a profusion of squabby pluffy cushions and fat carpets everywhere, and Lalun's silver hookah, studded with turquoises, had a special little carpet all to its shining self. Wali Dad was nearly as permanent a fixture as the chandelier. As I have said, he lay in the window-seat and meditated on Life and Death and Lalun – 'specially Lalun. The feet of the young men of the City tended to her doorways and then – retired, for Lalun was a particular maiden, slow of speech, reserved of mind, and not in the least inclined to orgies which were nearly certain to end in strife. 'If I am of no value, I am unworthy of this honour,' said Lalun. 'If I am of value, they are unworthy of Me.' And that was a crooked sentence.

In the long hot nights of latter April and May all the City seemed to assemble in Lalun's little white room to smoke and to talk. Shiahs[5] of the grimmest and most uncompromising persuasion; Sufis[6] who had lost all belief in the Prophet and retained but little in God; wandering Hindu priests passing southward on their way to the Central India fairs and other affairs; Pundits in black gowns, with spectacles on their noses and undigested wisdom in their insides; bearded headmen of the wards; Sikhs with all the details of the latest ecclesiastical scandal in the Golden Temple; red-eyed priests from beyond the Border, looking like trapped wolves and talking like ravens; M.A.'s of the University, very superior and very voluble – all these people and more also you might find in the white room. Wali Dad lay in the window-seat and listened to the talk.

'It is Lalun's *salon*,' said Wali Dad to me, 'and it is electic – is not that the word? Outside of a Freemasons' Lodge I have never seen such gatherings. *There* I dined once with a Jew – a Yahoudi!' He spat into the City Ditch with apologies for allowing national feelings to overcome him. 'Though I have lost every belief in the world,' said he, 'and try to be proud of my losing, I cannot help hating a Jew. Lalun admits no Jews here.'

'But what in the world do all these men do?' I asked.

'The curse of our country,' said Wali Dad. 'They talk. It is like the Athenians [7] – always hearing and telling some new thing. Ask the Pearl and she will show you how much she knows of the news of the City and the Province. Lalun knows everything.'

'Lalun,' I said at random – she was talking to a gentleman of the Kurd persuasion who had come in from God-knows-where – 'when does the 175th Regiment go to Agra?'

'It does not go at all,' said Lalun, without turning her head. 'They have ordered the 118th to go in its stead. That Regiment goes to Lucknow in three months, unless they give a fresh order.'

'That is so,' said Wali Dad, without a shade of doubt. 'Can you, with your telegrams and your newspapers, do better? Always hearing and telling some new thing,' he went on. 'My friend, has your God ever smitten a European nation for gossiping in the bazars? India has gossiped for centuries – always standing in the bazars until the soldiers go by. Therefore – you are here today instead of starving in your own country, and I am not a Mohammedan – I am a Product – a Demnition Product. [8] *That* also I owe to you and yours: that I cannot make an end to my sentence without quoting from your authors.' He pulled at the hookah and mourned, half feelingly, half in earnest, for the shattered hopes of his youth. Wali Dad was always mourning over something or other – the country of which he despaired, or the creed in which he had lost faith, or the life of the English which he could by no means understand.

Lalun never mourned. She played little songs on the *sitar*, [9] and to hear her sing, 'O Peacock, cry again', was always a fresh pleasure. She knew all the songs that have ever been sung, from the war-songs of the South, that make the old men angry with the young men and the young men angry with the State, to the love-songs of the North, where the swords whinny-whicker like angry kites in the pauses between the kisses, and the Passes fill with armed men, and the Lover is torn from his Beloved and cries *Ai! Ai! Ai!* evermore. She knew how to make up tobacco for the pipe so that it smelt like the Gates of Paradise and wafted you gently through them. She could embroider strange things in gold and silver, and dance softly with the moonlight when it came in at the window. Also she knew the hearts of men, and the heart of the City, and whose wives were faithful and whose untrue, and more of the secrets of the Government Offices than are good to be set down in this place. Nasiban, her maid, said that her jewellery was worth ten thousand pounds, and that, some night, a thief would enter and murder her for its possession; but Lalun said that all the City would tear that thief limb from limb, and that he, whoever he was, knew it.

So she took her *sitar* and sat in the window-seat, and sang a song of old days that had been sung by a girl of her profession in an armed camp on the eve of a great battle[10] – the day before the Fords of the Jumna ran red and Sivaji fled fifty miles to Delhi with a Toorkh stallion at his horse's tail and another Lalun on his saddle-bow. It was what men call a Mahratta *laonee*,[11] and it said:

> Their warrior forces Chimnajee
> > Before the Peishwa led,
> The Children of the Sun and Fire
> > Behind him turned and fled.

And the chorus said:

> With them there fought who rides so free
> > With sword and turban red,
> The warrior-youth who earns his fee
> > At peril of his head.

'At peril of his head,' said Wali Dad in English to me. 'Thanks to your Government, all our heads are protected, and with the educational facilities at my command' – his eyes twinkled wickedly – 'I might be a distinguished member of the local administration. Perhaps, in time, I might even be a member of a Legislative Council.'

'Don't speak English,' said Lalun, bending over her *sitar* afresh. The chorus went out from the City wall to the blackened wall of Fort Amara which dominates the City. No man knows the precise extent of Fort Amara. Three kings built it hundreds of years ago, and they say that there are miles of underground rooms beneath its walls. It is peopled with many ghosts, a detachment of Garrison Artillery, and a Company of Infantry. In its prime it held ten thousand men and filled its ditches with corpses.

'At peril of his head,' sang Lalun again and again.

A head moved on one of the ramparts – the grey head of an old man – and a voice, rough as shark-skin on a sword-hilt, sent back the last line of the chorus and broke into a song that I could not understand, though Lalun and Wali Dad listened intently.

'What is it?' I asked. 'Who is it?'

'A consistent man,' said Wali Dad. 'He fought you in '46, when he

was a warrior-youth; refought you in '57, and he tried to fight you in
'71, but you had learned the trick of blowing men from guns too well.
Now he is old; but he would still fight if he could.'

'Is he a Wahabi,[12] then? Why should he answer to a Mahratta *laonee* if
he be Wahabi – or Sikh?' said I.

'I do not know,' said Wali Dad. 'He has lost, perhaps, his religion.
Perhaps he wishes to be a King. Perhaps he *is* a King. I do not know his
name.'

'That is a lie, Wali Dad. If you know his career you must know his
name.'

'That is quite true. I belong to a nation of liars. I would rather not tell
you his name. Think for yourself.'

Lalun finished her song, pointed to the Fort, and said simply: 'Khem
Singh.'

'Hm,' said Wali Dad. 'If the Pearl chooses to tell you, the Pearl is a
fool.'

I translated to Lalun, who laughed. 'I choose to tell what I choose to
tell. They kept Khem Singh in Burma,' said she. 'They kept him there
for many years until his mind was changed in him. So great was the
kindness of the Government. Finding this, they sent him back to his
own country that he might look upon it before he died. He is an old
man, but when he looks upon this his country his memory will come.
Moreover, there be many who remember him.'

'He is an Interesting Survival,' said Wali Dad, pulling at the pipe. 'He
returns to a country now full of educational and political reform, but, as
the Pearl says, there are many who remember him. He was once a great
man. There will never be any more great men in India. They will all,
when they are boys, go whoring after strange gods, and they will become
citizens – "fellow-citizens" – "illustrious fellow-citizens". What is it
that the native papers call them?'

Wali Dad seemed to be in a very bad temper. Lalun looked out of the
window and smiled into the dust-haze. I went away thinking about
Khem Singh, who had once made history with a thousand followers, and
would have been a princeling but for the power of the Supreme
Government aforesaid.

The Senior Captain Commanding Fort Amara was away on leave,
but the Subaltern, his Deputy, had drifted down to the Club, where I
found him and inquired of him whether it was really true that a political
prisoner had been added to the attractions of the Fort. The Subaltern
explained at great length, for this was the first time that he had held
command of the Fort, and his glory lay heavy upon him.

'Yes,' said he, 'a man was sent in to me about a week ago from down the line – a thorough gentleman, whoever he is. Of course I did all I could for him. He had his two servants and some silver cooking-pots, and he looked for all the world like a native officer. I called him Subadar[13] Sahib. Just as well to be on the safe side, y'know. "Look here, Subadar Sahib," I said, "you're handed over to my authority, and I'm supposed to guard you. Now I don't want to make your life hard, but you must make things easy for me. All the Fort is at your disposal, from the flagstaff to the dry Ditch, and I shall be happy to entertain you in any way I can, but you mustn't take advantage of it. Give me your word that you won't try to escape, Subadar Sahib, and I'll give you my word that you shall have no heavy guard put over you." I thought the best way of getting at him was by going at him straight, y'know; and it was, by Jove! The old man gave me his word, and moved about the Fort as contented as a sick crow. He's a rummy chap – always asking to be told where he is and what the buildings about him are. I had to sign a slip of blue paper when he turned up, acknowledging receipt of his body and all that, and I'm responsible, y'know, that he doesn't get away. Queer thing, though, looking after a Johnnie old enough to be your grandfather, isn't it? Come to the Fort one of these days and see him.'

For reasons which will appear, I never went to the Fort while Khem Singh was then within its walls. I knew him only as a grey head seen from Lalun's window – a grey head and a harsh voice. But natives told me that, day by day, as he looked upon the fair lands round Amara, his memory came back to him and, with it, the old hatred against the Government that had been nearly effaced in far-off Burma. So he raged up and down the West face of the Fort from morning till noon and from evening till the night, devising vain things in his heart, and croaking war-songs when Lalun sang on the City wall. As he grew more acquainted with the Subaltern he unburdened his old heart of some of the passions that had withered it. 'Sahib,' he used to say, tapping his stick against the parapet, 'when I was a young man I was one of twenty thousand horsemen who came out of the City and rode round the plain here. Sahib, I was the leader of a hundred, then of a thousand, then of five thousand, and now!' – he pointed to his two servants. 'But from the beginning to today I would cut the throats of all the Sahibs in the land if I could. Hold me fast, Sahib, lest I get away and return to those who would follow me. I forgot them when I was in Burma, but now that I am in my own country again, I remember everything.'

'Do you remember that you have given me your Honour not to make your tendance a hard matter?' said the Subaltern.

'Yes, to you, only to you, Sahib,' said Khem Singh. 'To you because you are of a pleasant countenance. If my turn comes again, Sahib, I will not hang you nor cut your throat.'

'Thank you,' said the Subaltern gravely, as he looked along the line of guns that could pound the City to powder in half an hour. 'Let us go into our own quarters, Khem Singh. Come and talk with me after dinner.'

Khem Singh would sit on his own cushion at the Subaltern's feet, drinking heavy, scented aniseed brandy in great gulps, and telling strange stories of Fort Amara, which had been a palace in the old days, of Begums and Ranees [14] tortured to death – in the very vaulted chamber that now served as a mess-room; would tell stories of Sobraon [15] that made the Subaltern's cheeks flush and tingle with pride of race, and of the Kuka rising [16] from which so much was expected and the fore-knowledge of which was shared by a hundred thousand souls. But he never told tales of '57 [17] because, as he said, he was the Subaltern's guest, and '57 is a year that no man, Black or White, cares to speak of. Once only, when the aniseed brandy had slightly affected his head, he said: 'Sahib, speaking now of a matter which lay between Sobraon and the affair of the Kukas, it was ever a wonder to us that you stayed your hand at all, and that, having stayed it, you did not make the land one prison. Now I hear from without that you do great honour to all men of our country and by your own hands are destroying the Terror of your Name which is your strong rock and defence. This is a foolish thing. Will oil and water mix? Now in '57 –'

'I was not born then, Subadar Sahib,' said the Subaltern, and Khem Singh reeled to his quarters.

The Subaltern would tell me of these conversations at the Club, and my desire to see Khem Singh increased. But Wali Dad, sitting in the window-seat of the house on the City wall, said that it would be a cruel thing to do, and Lalun pretended that I preferred the society of a grizzled old Sikh to hers.

'Here is tobacco, here is talk, here are many friends and all the news of the City, and, above all, here is myself. I will tell you stories and sing you songs, and Wali Dad will talk his English nonsense in your ears. Is that worse than watching the caged animal yonder? Go tomorrow then, if you must, but today such-and-such an one will be here, and he will speak of wonderful things.'

It happened that Tomorrow never came, and the warm heat of the latter Rains gave place to the chill of early October almost before I was aware of the flight of the year. The Captain Commanding the Fort returned from leave and took over charge of Khem Singh according to the laws of seniority. The Captain was not a nice man. He called all natives 'niggers', which, besides being extreme bad form, shows gross ignorance.

'What's the use of telling off two Tommies to watch that old nigger?' said he.

'I fancy it soothes his vanity,' said the Subaltern. 'The men are ordered to keep well out of his way, but he takes them as a tribute to his importance, poor old chap.'

'I won't have Line men taken off regular guards in this way. Put on a couple of Native Infantry.'

'Sikhs?' said the Subaltern, lifting his eyebrows.

'Sikhs, Pathans, Dogras – they're all alike, these black vermin,' and the Captain talked to Khem Singh in a manner which hurt that old gentleman's feelings. Fifteen years before, when he had been caught for the second time, everyone looked upon him as a sort of tiger. He liked being regarded in this light. But he forgot that the world goes forward in fifteen years, and many Subalterns are promoted to Captaincies.

'The Captain-pig is in charge of the Fort?' said Khem Singh to his native guard every morning. And the native guard said: 'Yes, Subadar Sahib,' in deference to his age and his air of distinction; but they did not know who he was.

In those days the gathering in Lalun's little white room was always large and talked more than before.

'The Greeks,' said Wali Dad, who had been borrowing my books, 'the inhabitants of the city of Athens, where they were always hearing and telling some new thing, rigorously secluded their women – who were fools. Hence the glorious institution of the heterodox women [18] – is it not? – who were amusing and *not* fools. All the Greek philosophers delighted in their company. Tell me, my friend, how it goes now in Greece and the other places upon the Continent of Europe. Are your women-folk also fools?'

'Wali Dad,' I said, 'you never speak to us about your women-folk and we never speak about ours to you. That is the bar between us.'

'Yes,' said Wali Dad, 'it is curious to think that our common meeting-place should be here, in the house of a common – how do you call *her*?' He pointed with the pipe-mouth to Lalun.

'Lalun is nothing but Lalun,' I said, and that was perfectly true. 'But if you took your place in the world, Wali Dad, and gave up dreaming dreams –'

'I might wear an English coat and trousers. I might be a leading

Mohammedan pleader. I might be received even at the Commissioner's tennis-parties where the English stand on one side and the natives on the other, in order to promote social intercourse throughout the Empire. Heart's Heart,' said he to Lalun quickly, 'the Sahib says that I ought to quit you.'

'The Sahib is always talking stupid talk,' returned Lalun with a laugh. 'In this house I am a Queen and thou art a King. The Sahib' – she put her arms above her head and thought for a moment – 'the Sahib shall be our Vizier [19] – thine and mine, Wali Dad – because he has said that thou shouldst leave me.'

Wali Dad laughed immoderately, and I laughed too. 'Be it so,' said he. 'My friend, are you willing to take this lucrative Government appointment? Lalun, what shall his pay be?'

But Lalun began to sing, and for the rest of the time there was no hope of getting a sensible answer from her or Wali Dad. When the one stopped, the other began to quote Persian poetry with a triple pun in every other line. Some of it was not strictly proper, but it was all very funny, and it only came to an end when a fat person in black, with gold pince-nez, sent up his name to Lalun, and Wali Dad dragged me into the twinkling night to walk in a big rose-garden and talk heresies about Religion and Governments and a man's career in life.

The Mohurrum, the great mourning-festival of the Mohammedans, was close at hand, and the things that Wali Dad said about religious fanaticism would have secured his expulsion from the loosest-thinking Muslim sect. There were the rose-bushes round us, the stars above us, and from every quarter of the City came the boom of the big Mohurrum drums. You must know that the City is divided in fairly equal proportions between the Hindus and the Mussulmans, and where both creeds belong to the fighting races, a big religious festival gives ample chance for trouble. When they can – that is to say, when the authorities are weak enough to allow it – the Hindus do their best to arrange some minor feast-day of their own in time to clash with the period of general mourning for the martyrs Hasan and Hussain, the heroes of the Mohurrum. Gilt and painted paper representations of their tombs are borne with shouting and wailing, music, torches, and yells, through the principal thoroughfares of the City; which fakements are called *tazias*. Their passage is rigorously laid down beforehand by the Police, and detachments of Police accompany each *tazia*, lest the Hindus should throw bricks at it and the peace of the Queen and the heads of Her loyal subjects should thereby be broken. Mohurrum time in a 'fighting' town means anxiety to all the officials, because, if a riot breaks out, the officials and not the rioters are held responsible. The former must foresee everything, and while not making their precautions ridiculously elaborate, must see that they are at least adequate.

'Listen to the drums!' said Wali Dad. 'That is the heart of the people – empty and making much noise. How, think you, will the Mohurrum go this year? *I* think that there will be trouble.'

He turned down a side-street and left me alone with the stars and a sleepy Police patrol. Then I went to bed and dreamed that Wali Dad had sacked the City and I was made Vizier, with Lalun's silver pipe for mark of office.

All day the Mohurrum drums beat in the City, and all day deputations of tearful Hindu gentlemen besieged the Deputy-Commissioner with assurances that they would be murdered ere next dawning by the Mohammedans. 'Which,' said the Deputy-Commissioner, in confidence to the Head of Police, 'is a pretty fair indication that the Hindus are going to make 'emselves unpleasant. I think we can arrange a little surprise for them. I have given the heads of both Creeds fair warning. If they choose to disregard it, so much the worse for them.'

There was a large gathering in Lalun's house that night, but of men that I had never seen before, if I except the fat gentleman in black with the gold pince-nez. Wali Dad lay in the window-seat, more bitterly scornful of his Faith and its manifestations than I had ever known him. Lalun's maid was very busy cutting up and mixing tobacco for the guests. We could hear the thunder of the drums as the processions accompanying each *tazia* marched to the central gathering-place in the plain outside the City, preparatory to their triumphant re-entry and circuit within the walls. All the streets seemed ablaze with torches, and only Fort Amara was black and silent.

When the noise of the drums ceased, no one in the white room spoke for a time. 'The first *tazia* has moved off,' said Wali Dad, looking to the plain.

'That is very early,' said the man with the pince-nez. 'It is only half-past eight.' The company rose and departed.

'Some of them were men from Ladakh,'[20] said Lalun, when the last had gone. 'They brought me brick-tea such as the Russians sell, and a tea-urn from Peshawur. Show me, now, how the English Memsahibs make tea.'

The brick-tea was abominable. When it was finished Wali Dad suggested going into the streets. 'I am nearly sure that there will be trouble tonight,' he said. 'All the City thinks so, and *Vox Populi* is *Vox Dei*,[21] as the Babus say. Now I tell you that at the corner of the Padshahi Gate you will find my horse all this night if you want to go about and to see things. It is a most disgraceful exhibition. Where is the pleasure of saying "*Ya Hasan! Ya Hussain!*" twenty thousand times in a night?'

All the processions – there were two-and-twenty of them – were now well within the City walls. The drums were beating afresh, the crowd were howling '*Ya Hasan! Ya Hussain!*' and beating their breasts, the brass bands were playing their loudest, and at every corner where space allowed, Mohammedan preachers were telling the lamentable story of the death of the Martyrs. It was impossible to move except with the crowd, for the streets were not more than twenty feet wide. In the Hindu quarters the shutters of all the shops were up and cross-barred. As the first *tazia*, a gorgeous erection, ten feet high, was borne aloft on the shoulders of a score of stout men into the semi-darkness of the Gully of the Horsemen, a brickbat crashed through its talc and tinsel sides.

'Into thy hands, O Lord!' murmured Wali Dad profanely, as a yell went up from behind, and a native officer of Police jammed his horse through the crowd. Another brickbat followed, and the *tazia* staggered and swayed where it had stopped.

'Go on! In the name of the Sirkar,[22] go forward!' shouted the Police-man, but there was an ugly cracking and splintering of shutters, and the crowd halted, with oaths and growlings, before the house whence the brickbat had been thrown.

Then, without any warning, broke the storm – not only in the Gully of the Horsemen, but in half-a-dozen other places. The *tazias* rocked like ships at sea, the long pole-torches dipped and rose round them while the men shouted: 'The Hindus are dishonouring the *tazias*! Strike! strike! Into their temples for the Faith!' The six or eight Policemen with each *tazia* drew their batons, and struck as long as they could in the hope of forcing the mob forward, but they were overpowered, and as contingents of Hindus poured into the streets, the fight became general. Half a mile away where the *tazias* were yet untouched the drums and the shrieks of '*Ya Hasan! Ya Hussain!*' continued, but not for long. The priests at the corners of the streets knocked the legs from the bedsteads that supported their pulpits and smote for the Faith, while stones fell from the silent houses upon friend and foe, and the packed streets bellowed: '*Din! Din! Din!*'[23] A *tazia* caught fire, and was dropped for a flaming barrier between Hindu and Mussulman at the corner of the Gully. Then the crowd surged forward, and Wali Dad drew me close to the stone pillar of a well.

'It was intended from the beginning!' he shouted in my ear, with more heat than blank unbelief should be guilty of. 'The bricks were carried up to the houses beforehand. These swine of Hindus! We shall be killing kine in their temples tonight!'

Tazia after *tazia*, some burning, others torn to pieces, hurried past us and the mob with them, howling, shrieking, and striking at the house doors in their flight. At last we saw the reason of the rush. Hugonin, the Assistant District Superintendent of Police, a boy of twenty, had got together thirty constables and was forcing the crowd through the streets. His old grey Police-horse showed no sign of uneasiness as it was spurred breast-on into the crowd, and the long dog-whip with which he had armed himself was never still.

'They know we haven't enough Police to hold 'em,' he cried as he passed me, mopping a cut on his face. 'They *know* we haven't! Aren't any of the men from the Club coming down to help? Get on, you sons of burnt fathers!' The dog-whip cracked across the writhing backs, and the constables smote afresh with baton and gun-butt. With these passed the lights and the shouting, and Wali Dad began to swear under his breath. From Fort Amara shot up a single rocket; then two side by side. It was the signal for troops.

Petitt, the Deputy-Commissioner, covered with dust and sweat, but calm and gently smiling, cantered up the clean-swept street in rear of the main body of the rioters. 'No one killed yet,' he shouted. 'I'll keep 'em on the run till dawn! Don't let 'em halt, Hugonin! Trot 'em about till the troops come.'

The science of the defence lay solely in keeping the mob on the move. If they had breathing-space they would halt and fire a house, and then the work of restoring order would be more difficult, to say the least of it. Flames have the same effect on a crowd as blood has on a wild beast.

Word had reached the Club, and men in evening-dress were beginning to show themselves and lend a hand in heading off and breaking up the shouting masses with stirrup-leathers, whips, or chance-found staves. They were not very often attacked, for the rioters had sense enough to know that the death of a European would not mean not one hanging but many, and possibly the appearance of the thrice-dreaded Artillery. The clamour in the City redoubled. The Hindus had descended into the streets in real earnest and ere long the mob returned. It was a strange sight. There were no *tazias* – only their riven platforms – and there were no Police. Here and there a City dignitary, Hindu or Mohammedan, was vainly imploring his co-religionists to keep quiet and behave themselves – advice for which his white beard was pulled. Then a native officer of Police, unhorsed but still using his spurs with effect, would be borne along, warning all the crowd of the danger of insulting the Government. Everywhere men struck aimlessly with sticks, grasping each other by the throat, howling and foaming with rage, or beat with their bare hands on the doors of the houses.

'It is a lucky thing that they are fighting with natural weapons,' I said to Wali Dad, 'else we should have half the City killed.'

I turned as I spoke and looked at his face. His nostrils were distended, his eyes were fixed, and he was smiting himself softly on the breast. The crowd poured by with renewed riot – a gang of Mussulmans hard pressed by some hundred Hindu fanatics. Wali Dad left my side with an oath, and shouting: '*Ya Hasan! Ya Hussain!*' plunged into the thick of the fight, where I lost sight of him.

I fled by a side alley to the Padshahi Gate, where I found Wali Dad's horse, and thence rode to the Fort. Once outside the City wall, the tumult sank to a dull roar, very impressive under the stars and reflecting great credit on the fifty thousand angry able-bodied men who were making it. The troops who, at the Deputy-Commissioner's instance, had been ordered to rendezvous quietly near the Fort, showed no signs of being impressed. Two companies of Native Infantry, a squadron of Native Cavalry, and a company of British Infantry were kicking their heels in the shadow of the East face, waiting for orders to march in. I am sorry to say that they were all pleased, unholily pleased, at the chance of what they called 'a little fun'. The senior officers, to be sure, grumbled at having been kept out of bed, and the English troops pretended to be sulky, but there was joy in the hearts of all the subalterns, and whispers ran up and down the line: 'No ball-cartridge – what a beastly shame!' 'D'you think the beggars will really stand up to us?' 'Hope I shall meet my money-lender there. I owe him more than I can afford.' 'Oh, they won't let us even unsheath swords.' 'Hurrah! Up goes the fourth rocket. Fall in, there!'

The Garrison Artillery, who to the last cherished a wild hope that they might be allowed to bombard the City at a hundred yards' range, lined the parapet above the East gateway and cheered themselves hoarse as the British Infantry doubled along the road to the Main Gate of the City. The Cavalry cantered on to the Padshahi Gate, and the Native Infantry marched slowly to the Gate of the Butchers. The surprise was intended to be of a distinctly unpleasant nature, and to come on top of the defeat of the Police, who had been just able to keep the Moham-medans from firing the houses of a few leading Hindus. The bulk of the riot lay in the north and north-west wards. The east and south-east were by this time dark and silent, and I rode hastily to Lalun's house, for I wished to tell her to send someone in search of Wali Dad. The house was unlighted, but the door was open, and I climbed upstairs in the darkness. One small lamp in the white room showed Lalun and her maid leaning half out of the window, breathing heavily and evidently pulling at something that refused to come.

'Thou art late – very late,' gasped Lalun without turning her head. 'Help us now, O Fool, if thou hast not spent thy strength howling among the *tazias*. Pull! Nasiban and I can do no more! O Sahib, is it you? The Hindus have been hunting an old Mohammedan round the Ditch with clubs. If they find him again they will kill him. Help us to pull him up.'

I put my hands to the long red silk waist-cloth that was hanging out of the window, and we three pulled and pulled with all the strength at our command. There was something very heavy at the end, and it swore in an unknown tongue as it kicked against the City wall.

'Pull, oh, pull!' said Lalun at the last. A pair of brown hands grasped the window-sill and a venerable Mohammedan tumbled upon the floor, very much out of breath. His jaws were tied up, his turban had fallen over one eye, and he was dusty and angry.

Lalun hid her face in her hands for an instant and said something about Wali Dad that I could not catch.

Then, to my extreme gratification, she threw her arms round my neck and murmured pretty things. I was in no haste to stop her; and Nasiban, being a handmaiden of tact, turned to the big jewel-chest that stands in the corner of the white room and rummaged among the contents. The Mohammedan sat on the floor and glared.

'One service more, Sahib, since thou hast come so opportunely,' said Lalun. 'Wilt thou' – it is very nice to be thou-ed by Lalun – 'take this old man across the City – the troops are everywhere, and they might hurt him, for he is old – to the Kumharsen Gate? There I think he may find a carriage to take him to his house. He is a friend of mine, and thou art – more than a friend – therefore I ask this.'

Nasiban bent over the old man, tucked something into his belt, and I raised him up and led him into the streets. In crossing from the east to the west of the City there was no chance of avoiding the troops and the crowd. Long before I reached the Gully of the Horsemen I heard the shouts of the British Infantry crying cheerily: '*Hutt*,[24] ye beggars! *Hutt*, ye devils! Get along! Go forward, there!' Then followed the ringing of rifle-butts and shrieks of pain. The troops were banging the bare toes of the mob with their gun-butts – for not a bayonet had been fixed. My companion mumbled and jabbered as we walked on until we were carried back by the crowd and had to force our way to the troops. I caught him by the wrist and felt a bangle there – the iron bangle of the Sikhs – but I had no suspicions, for Lalun had only ten minutes before put her arms round me. Thrice we were carried back by the crowd, and when we made our way past the British Infantry it was to meet the Sikh Cavalry driving another mob before them with the butts of their lances.

'What are these dogs?' said the old man.

'Sikhs of the Cavalry, Father,' I said, and we edged our way up the line of horses two abreast and found the Deputy-Commissioner, his helmet smashed on his head, surrounded by a knot of men who had come down from the Club as amateur constables and had helped the Police mightily.

'We'll keep 'em on the run till dawn,' said Petitt. 'Who's your villainous friend?'

I had only time to say: 'The Protection of the Sirkar!' when a fresh crowd flying before the Native Infantry carried us a hundred yards nearer to the Kumharsen Gate, and Petitt was swept away like a shadow.

'I do not know – I cannot see – this is all new to me!' moaned my companion. 'How many troops are there in the City?'

'Perhaps five hundred,' I said.

'A lakh²⁵ of men beaten by five hundred – and Sikhs among them! Surely, surely, I am an old man, but – the Kumharsen Gate is new. Who pulled down the stone lions? Where is the conduit? Sahib, I am a very old man, and, alas, I – I cannot stand.' He dropped in the shadow of the Kumharsen Gate where there was no disturbance. A fat gentleman wearing gold pince-nez came out of the darkness.

'You are most kind to bring my old friend,' he said suavely. 'He is a landholder of Akala. He should not be in a big City when there is religious excitement. But I have a carriage here. You are quite truly kind. Will you help me to put him into the carriage? It is very late.'

We bundled the old man into a hired victoria that stood close to the gate, and I turned back to the house on the City wall. The troops were driving the people to and fro, while the Police shouted, 'To your houses! Get to your houses!' and the dog-whip of the Assistant District Superintendent cracked remorselessly. Terror-stricken *bunnias*²⁶ clung to the stirrups of the Cavalry, crying that their houses had been robbed (which was a lie), and the burly Sikh horsemen patted them on the shoulder and bade them return to those houses lest a worse thing should happen. Parties of five or six British soldiers, joining arms, swept down the side-gullies, their rifles on their backs, stamping, with shouting and song, upon the toes of Hindu and Mussulman. Never was religious enthusiasm more systematically squashed; and never were poor breakers of the peace more utterly weary and footsore. They were routed out of holes and corners, from behind well-pillars and byres, and bidden to go to their houses. If they had no houses to go to, so much the worse for their toes.

On returning to Lalun's door I stumbled over a man at the threshold. He was sobbing hysterically and his arms flapped like the wings of a goose. It was Wali Dad, Agnostic and Unbeliever, shoeless, turbanless, and frothing at the mouth, the flesh on his chest bruised and bleeding from the vehemence with which he had smitten himself. A broken torch-handle lay by his side, and his quivering lips murmured, '*Ya Hasan! Ya Hussain!*' as I stooped over him. I pushed him a few steps up the staircase, threw a pebble at Lalun's City window and hurried home.

Most of the streets were very still, and the cold wind that comes before the dawn whistled down them. In the centre of the Square of the Mosque a man was bending over a corpse. The skull had been smashed in by gun-butt or bamboo-stave.

'It is expedient that one man should die for the people,'[27] said Petitt grimly, raising the shapeless head. 'These brutes were beginning to show their teeth too much.'

And from afar we could hear the soldiers singing 'Two Lovely Black Eyes' as they drove the remnant of the rioters within doors.

Of course you can guess what happened? I was not so clever. When the news went abroad that Khem Singh had escaped from the Fort, I did not, since I was then living this story, not writing it, connect myself, or Lalun, or the fat gentleman of the gold pince-nez, with his disappearance. Nor did it strike me that Wali Dad was the man who should have convoyed him across the City, or that Lalun's arms round my neck were put there to hide the money that Nasiban gave to Khem Singh, and that Lalun had used me and my white face as even a better safeguard than Wali Dad who proved himself so untrustworthy. All that I knew at the time was that, when Fort Amara was taken up with the riots, Khem Singh profited by the confusion to get away, and that his two Sikh guards also escaped.

But later on I received full enlightenment; and so did Khem Singh. He fled to those who knew him in the old days, but many of them were dead and more were changed, and all knew something of the Wrath of the Government. He went to the young men, but the glamour of his name had passed away, and they were entering native regiments or Government offices, and Khem Singh could give them neither pension, decorations, nor influence – nothing but a glorious death with their back to the mouth of a gun. He wrote letters and made promises, and the letters fell into bad hands, and a wholly insignificant subordinate officer of Police tracked them down and gained promotion thereby. Moreover, Khem Singh was old, and aniseed brandy was scarce, and he had left his silver cooking-pots in Fort Amara with his nice warm bedding, and the gentleman with the gold pince-nez was told by Those who had employed him that Khem Singh as a popular leader was not worth the money paid.

'Great is the mercy of these fools of English!' said Khem Singh when the situation was put before him. 'I will go back to Fort Amara of my own free will and gain honour. Give me good clothes to return in.'

So, at his own time, Khem Singh knocked at the wicket-gate of the Fort and walked to the Captain and the Subaltern, who were nearly grey-headed on account of correspondence that daily arrived from Simla marked 'Private'.

'I have come back, Captain Sahib,' said Khem Singh. 'Put no more guards over me. It is no good out yonder.'

A week later I saw him for the first time to my knowledge, and he made as though there were an understanding between us.

'It was well done, Sahib,' said he, 'and greatly I admired your astuteness in thus boldly facing the troops when I, whom they would have doubtless torn to pieces, was with you. Now there is a man in Fort Ooltagarh whom a bold man could with ease help to escape. This is the position of the Fort as I draw it on the sand –'

But I was thinking how I had become Lalun's Vizier after all.

At the Pit's Mouth [1]

Men say it was a stolen tide –
    The Lord that sent it He knows all,
But in mine ear will aye abide
    The message that the bells let fall,
And awesome bells they were to me,
That in the dark rang 'Enderby'.
                    Jean Ingelow.[2]

Once upon a time there was a Man and his Wife and a Tertium Quid.[3]

All three were unwise, but the Wife was the unwisest. The Man should have looked after his Wife, who should have avoided the Tertium Quid, who, again, should have married a wife of his own, after clean and open flirtations, to which nobody can possibly object, round Jakko [4] or Observatory Hill.[5] When you see a young man with his pony in a white lather and his hat on the back of his head, flying downhill at fifteen miles an hour to meet a girl who will be properly surprised to meet him, you naturally approve of that young man, and wish him Staff appointments, and take an interest in his welfare, and, as the proper time comes, give them sugar-tongs or side-saddles according to your means and generosity.

The Tertium Quid flew downhill on horseback, but it was to meet the Man's Wife; and when he flew uphill it was for the same end. The Man was in the Plains, earning money for his Wife to spend on dresses and four-hundred-rupee bracelets, and inexpensive luxuries of that kind. He worked very hard, and sent her a letter or a postcard daily. She also wrote to him daily, and said that she was longing for him to come up to Simla. The Tertium Quid used to lean over her shoulder and laugh as she wrote the notes. Then the two would ride to the Post Office together.

Now, Simla is a strange place and its customs are peculiar; nor is any man who has not spent at least ten seasons there qualified to pass judgment on circumstantial evidence, which is the most untrustworthy in the Courts. For these reasons, and for others which need not appear, I decline to state positively whether there was anything irretrievably wrong in the relations between the Man's Wife and the Tertium Quid. If there was, and hereon you must form your own opinion, it was the Man's Wife's fault. She was kittenish in her manners, wearing generally an air of soft and fluffy innocence. But she was deadlily learned and evil-instructed; and, now and again, when the mask dropped, men saw this, shuddered and – almost drew back. Men are occasionally particular, and the least particular men are always the most exacting.

Simla is eccentric in its fashion of treating friendships. Certain attachments which have set and crystallized through half-a-dozen seasons acquire almost the sanctity of the marriage bond, and are revered as such. Again, certain attachments equally old, and, to all appearance, equally venerable, never seem to win any recognized official status; while a chance-sprung acquaintance, not two months born, steps into the place which by right belongs to the senior. There is no law reducible to print which regulates these affairs.

Some people have a gift which secures them infinite toleration, and others have not. The Man's Wife had not. If she looked over the garden wall, for instance, women taxed her with stealing their husbands. She complained pathetically that she was not allowed to choose her own friends. When she put up her big white muff to her lips, and gazed over it and under her eyebrows at you as she said this thing, you felt that she had been infamously misjudged, and that all the other women's instincts were all wrong. Which was absurd. She was not allowed to own the Tertium Quid in peace; and was so strangely constructed that she would not have enjoyed peace had she been so permitted. She preferred some semblance of intrigue to cloak even her most commonplace actions.

After two months of riding, first round Jakko, then Elysium, then Summer Hill, then Observatory Hill, then under Jutogh, and lastly up and down the Cart Road, as far as the Tara Devi gap in the dusk, she said to the Tertium Quid, 'Frank, people say we are too much together, and people are so horrid.'

The Tertium Quid pulled his moustache, and replied that horrid people were unworthy of the consideration of nice people.

'But they have done more than talk – they have written – written to my hubby – I'm sure of it,' said the Man's Wife, and she pulled a letter from her husband out of her saddle-pocket and gave it to the Tertium Quid.

It was an honest letter, written by an honest man, then stewing in the Plains on two hundred rupees a month (for he allowed his wife eight hundred and fifty), and in a silk banian[6] and cotton trousers. It said that, perhaps, she had not thought of the unwisdom of allowing her name to be so generally coupled with the Tertium Quid's; that she was too much of a child to understand the dangers of that sort of thing; that he, her husband, was the last man in the world to interfere jealously with her little amusements and interests, but that it would be better were she to drop the Tertium Quid quietly and for her husband's sake. The letter was sweetened with many pretty little pet names, and it amused the Tertium Quid considerably. He and She laughed over it, so that you, fifty yards away, could see their shoulders shaking while the horses slouched along side by side.

Their conversation was not worth repeating. The upshot of it was that, next day, no one saw the Man's Wife and the Tertium Quid together. They had both gone down to the Cemetery, which, as a rule, is only visited officially by the inhabitants of Simla.

A Simla funeral with the clergyman riding, the mourners riding, and the coffin creaking as it swings between the bearers, is one of the most depressing things on this earth, particularly when the procession passes under the wet, dank dip beneath the Rockcliffe Hotel, where the sun is shut out, and all the hill streams are wailing and weeping together as they go down the valleys.

Occasionally folk tend the graves, but we in India shift and are transferred so often that, at the end of the second year, the Dead have no friends – only acquaintances who are far too busy amusing themselves up the hill to attend to old partners. The idea of using a Cemetery as a rendezvous is distinctly a feminine one. A man would have said simply, 'Let people talk. We'll go down the Mall.' A woman is made differently, especially if she be such a woman as the Man's Wife. She and the Tertium Quid enjoyed each other's society among the graves of men and women whom they had known and danced with aforetime.

They used to take a big horse-blanket and sit on the grass a little to the left of the lower end, where there is a dip in the ground, and where the occupied graves stop short and the ready-made ones are not ready. Each well-regulated Indian Cemetery keeps half-a-dozen graves permanently open for contingencies and incidental wear and tear. In the Hills these are more usually baby's size, because children who come up weakened and sick from the Plains often succumb to the effects of the Rains in the Hills or get pneumonia from their *ayahs*[7] taking them through damp pinewoods after the sun has set. In cantonments, of course, the man's size is more in request; these arrangements varying with the climate and population.

One day when the Man's Wife and the Tertium Quid had just arrived in the Cemetery, they saw some coolies breaking ground. They had marked out a full-size grave, and the Tertium Quid asked them whether any Sahib was sick. They said that they did not know; but it was an order that they should dig a Sahib's grave.

'Work away,' said the Tertium Quid, 'and let's see how it's done.'

The coolies worked away, and the Man's Wife and the Tertium Quid watched and talked for a couple of hours while the grave was being deepened. Then a coolie, taking the earth in baskets as it was thrown up, jumped over the grave.

'That's queer,' said the Tertium Quid. 'Where's my ulster?'

'What's queer?' said the Man's Wife.

'I have got a chill down my back – just as if a goose had walked over my grave.'

'Why do you look at the thing, then?' said the Man's Wife. 'Let us go.'

The Tertium Quid stood at the head of the grave, and stared without answering for a space. Then he said, dropping a pebble down, 'It is nasty – and cold: horribly cold. I don't think I shall come to the Cemetery any more. I don't think grave-digging is cheerful.'

The two talked and agreed that the Cemetery was depressing. They also arranged for a ride next day out from the Cemetery through the Mashobra Tunnel up to Fagoo and back, because all the world was going to a garden-party at Viceregal Lodge, and all the people of Mashobra would go too.

Coming up the Cemetery road, the Tertium Quid's horse tried to bolt uphill, being tired with standing so long, and managed to strain a back sinew.

'I shall have to take the mare tomorrow,' said the Tertium Quid, 'and she will stand nothing heavier than a snaffle.'

They made their arrangements to meet in the Cemetery, after allowing all the Mashobra people time to pass into Simla. That night it rained heavily, and, next day, when the Tertium Quid came to the trysting-place, he saw that the new grave had a foot of water in it, the ground being a tough and sour clay.

'Jove! That looks beastly,' said the Tertium Quid. 'Fancy being boarded up and dropped into that well!'

They then started off to Fagoo, the mare playing with the snaffle and picking her way as though she were shod with satin, and the sun shining divinely. The road below Mashobra to Fagoo is officially styled the Himalayan–Thibet Road; but in spite of its name it is not much more than six feet wide in most places, and the drop into the valley below may be anything between one and two thousand feet.

'Now we're going to Thibet,' said the Man's Wife merrily, as the horses drew near to Fagoo. She was riding on the cliff side.

'Into Thibet,' said the Tertium Quid, 'ever so far from people who say horrid things, and hubbies who write stupid letters. With you – to the end of the world!'

A coolie carrying a log of wood came round a corner, and the mare went wide to avoid him – forefeet in and haunches out, as a sensible mare should go.

'To the world's end,' said the Man's Wife, and looked unspeakable things over her near shoulder at the Tertium Quid.

He was smiling, but, while she looked, the smile froze stiff, as it were, on his face, and changed to a nervous grin – the sort of grin men wear when they are not quite easy in their saddles. The mare seemed to be sinking by the stern, and her nostrils cracked while she was trying to realize what was happening. The rain of the night before had rotted the drop-side of the Himalayan–Thibet Road, and it was giving way under her. 'What are you doing?' said the Man's Wife. The Tertium Quid gave no answer. He grinned nervously and set his spurs into the mare, who rapped with her forefeet on the road, and the struggle began. The Man's Wife screamed, 'Oh, Frank, get off!'

But the Tertium Quid was glued to the saddle – his face blue and white – and he looked into the Man's Wife's eyes. Then the Man's Wife clutched at the mare's head and caught her by the nose instead of the bridle. The brute threw up her head and went down with a scream, the Tertium Quid upon her, and the nervous grin still set on his face.

The Man's Wife heard the tinkle-tinkle of little stones and loose earth falling off the roadway, and the sliding roar of the man and horse going down. Then everything was quiet, and she called on Frank to leave his mare and walk up. But Frank did not answer. He was underneath the mare, nine hundred feet below, spoiling a patch of Indian corn.

As the revellers came back from Viceregal Lodge in the mists of the evening, they met a temporarily insane woman, on a temporarily mad horse, swinging round the corners, with her eyes and her mouth open, and her head like the head of a Medusa.[8] She was stopped by a man at the risk of his life, and taken out of the saddle, a limp heap, and put on the bank to explain herself. This wasted twenty minutes, and then she was sent home in a lady's rickshaw, still with her mouth open and her hands picking at her riding-gloves.

She was in bed through the following three days, which were rainy; so she missed attending the funeral of the Tertium Quid, who was lowered into eighteen inches of water, instead of the twelve to which he had first objected.

⟨ The Man who would be King [1] ⟩

Brother to a Prince and fellow to a beggar if he be found worthy.

The Law, as quoted,[2] lays down a fair conduct of life, and one not easy to follow. I have been fellow to a beggar again and again under circumstances which prevented either of us finding out whether the other was worthy. I have still to be brother to a Prince, though I once came near to kinship with what might have been a veritable King, and was promised the reversion of a Kingdom – army, law-courts, revenue, and policy all complete. But, today, I greatly fear that my King is dead, and if I want a crown I must go hunt it for myself.

The beginning of everything was in a railway train upon the road to Mhow from Ajmir. There had been a Deficit in the Budget, which necessitated travelling, not Second-class, which is only half as dear as First-class, but by Intermediate, which is very awful indeed. There are no cushions in the Intermediate class, and the population are either Intermediate, which is Eurasian, or Native, which for a long night journey is nasty, or Loafer, which is amusing though intoxicated. Intermediates do not buy from refreshment-rooms. They carry their food in bundles and pots, and buy sweets from the native sweetmeat-sellers, and drink the roadside water. That is why in the hot weather Intermediates are taken out of the carriages dead, and in all weathers are most properly looked down upon.

My particular Intermediate happened to be empty till I reached Nasirabad, when a big black-browed gentleman in shirt-sleeves entered, and, following the custom of Intermediates, passed the time of day. He was a wanderer and a vagabond like myself, but with an educated taste for whisky. He told tales of things he had seen and done, of out-of-the-way corners of the Empire into which he had penetrated, and of adventures in which he risked his life for a few days' food.

'If India was filled with men like you and me, not knowing more than the crows where they'd get their next day's rations, it isn't seventy millions of revenue the land would be paying – it's seven hundred millions,' said he; and as I looked at his mouth and chin I was disposed to agree with him.

We talked politics – the politics of Loaferdom, that sees things from the underside where the lath and plaster is not smoothed off – and we talked postal arrangements because my friend wanted to send a telegram back from the next station to Ajmir, the turning-off place from the Bombay to the Mhow line as you travel westward. My friend had no money beyond eight annas, which he wanted for dinner, and I had no money at all, owing to the hitch in the Budget before mentioned. Further, I was going into a wilderness where, though I should resume touch with the Treasury, there were no telegraph offices. I was, therefore, unable to help him in any way.

'We might threaten a Station-master, and make him send a wire on tick,' said my friend, 'but that'd mean inquiries for you and for me, and *I*'ve got my hands full these days. Did you say you are travelling back along this line within any days?'

'Within ten,' I said.

'Can't you make it eight?' said he. 'Mine is rather urgent business.'

'I can send your telegram within ten days if that will serve you,' I said.

'I couldn't trust the wire to fetch him, now I think of it. It's this way. He leaves Delhi on the 23rd for Bombay. That means he'll be running through Ajmir about the night of the 23rd.'

'But I'm going into the Indian Desert,' I explained.

'Well *and* good,' said he. 'You'll be changing at Marwar Junction to get into Jodhpore territory – you must do that – and he'll be coming through Marwar Junction in the early morning of the 24th by the Bombay Mail. Can you be at Marwar Junction on that time? 'Twon't be inconveniencing you because I know that there's precious few pickings to be got out of these Central India States – even though you pretend to be correspondent of the *Backwoodsman*.' [3]

'Have you ever tried that trick?' I asked.

'Again and again, but the Residents [4] find you out, and then you get escorted to the border before you've time to get your knife into them. But about my friend here. I *must* give him a word o' mouth to tell him what's come to me or else he won't know where to go. I would take it more than kind of you if you was to come out of Central India in time to catch him at Marwar Junction, and say to him: "He has gone South for the week." He'll know what that means. He's a big man with a red beard, and a great swell he is. You'll find him sleeping like a gentleman with all his luggage round him in a second-class compartment. But don't you be afraid. Slip down the window, and say: "He has gone South for the week," and he'll tumble. It's only cutting your time of stay in those parts by two days. I ask you as a stranger – going to the West,' he said with emphasis.

'Where have *you* come from?' said I.

'From the East,' said he, 'and I am hoping that you will give him the message on the Square – for the sake of my Mother as well as your own.'

Englishmen are not usually softened by appeals to the memory of their mothers, but for certain reasons,[5] which will be fully apparent, I saw fit to agree.

'It's more than a little matter,' said he, 'and that's why I asked you to do it – and now I know that I can depend on you doing it. A second-class carriage at Marwar Junction, and a red-haired man asleep in it. You'll be sure to remember. I get out at the next station, and I must hold on there till he comes or sends me what I want.'

'I'll give the message if I catch him,' I said, 'and for the sake of your Mother as well as mine I'll give you a word of advice. Don't try to run the Central India States just now as the correspondent of the *Back-woodsman*. There's a real one knocking about there, and it might lead to trouble.'

'Thank you,' said he simply, 'and when will the swine be gone? I can't starve because he's ruining my work. I wanted to get hold of the De-gumber Rajah down here about his father's widow, and give him a jump.'

'What did he do to his father's widow, then?'

'Filled her up with red pepper and slippered her to death as she hung from a beam. I found that out myself, and I'm the only man that would dare going into the State to get hush-money for it. They'll try to poison me, same as they did in Chortumna when I went on the loot there. But you'll give the man at Marwar Junction my message?'

He got out at a little roadside station, and I reflected. I had heard, more than once, of men personating correspondents of newspapers and bleeding small Native States with threats of exposure, but I had never met any of the caste before. They lead a hard life, and generally die with great suddenness. The Native States have a wholesome horror of English newspapers which may throw light on their peculiar methods of government, and do their best to choke correspondents with champagne, or drive them out of their mind with four-in-hand barouches. They do not understand that nobody cares a straw for the internal administration of Native States so long as oppression and crime are kept within decent limits, and the ruler is not drugged, drunk, or diseased from one end of the year to the other. They are the dark places of the earth, full of unimaginable cruelty, touching the Railway and the Telegraph on one side, and, on the other, the days of Harun-al-Raschid.[6] When I left the train I did business with divers Kings, and in eight days passed through many changes of life. Sometimes I wore dress-clothes and consorted with Princes and Politicals,[7] drinking from crystal and eating from silver. Sometimes I lay out upon the ground and devoured what I could get, from a plate made of leaves, and drank the running water, and slept under the same rug as my servant. It was all in the day's work.

Then I headed for the Great Indian Desert upon the proper date, as I had promised, and the night mail set me down at Marwar Junction, where a funny, little, happy-go-lucky, native-managed railway runs to Jodhpore. The Bombay Mail from Delhi makes a short halt at Marwar. She arrived as I got in, and I had just time to hurry to her platform and go down the carriages. There was only one second-class on the train. I slipped the window and looked down upon a flaming red beard, half covered by a railway rug. That was my man, fast asleep, and I dug him gently in the ribs. He woke with a grunt, and I saw his face in the light of the lamps. It was a great and shining face.

'Tickets again?' said he.

'No,' said I. 'I am to tell you that he has gone South for the week. He has gone South for the week!'

The train had begun to move out. The red man rubbed his eyes. 'He has gone South for the week,' he repeated. 'Now that's just like his impidence. Did he say that I was to give you anything? Cause I won't.'

'He didn't,' I said, and dropped away, and watched the red lights die out in the dark. It was horribly cold because the wind was blowing off the sands. I climbed into my own train – not an Intermediate carriage this time – and went to sleep.

If the man with the beard had given me a rupee I should have kept it as a memento of a rather curious affair. But the consciousness of having done my duty was my only reward.

Later on I reflected that two gentlemen like my friends could not do any good if they forgathered and personated correspondents of newspapers, and might, if they blackmailed one of the little rat-trap states of Central India or Southern Rajputana, get themselves into serious difficulties. I therefore took some trouble to describe them as accurately as I could remember to people who would be interested in deporting them; and succeeded, so I was later informed, in having them headed back from the Degumber borders.

Then I became respectable, and returned to an office where there were no Kings and no incidents outside the daily manufacture of a newspaper. A newspaper office seems to attract every conceivable sort of person, to the prejudice of discipline. Zenana[8]-mission ladies arrive, and beg that the Editor will instantly abandon all his duties to describe a Christian prize-giving in a back-slum of a perfectly inaccessible village; Colonels who have been overpassed for command sit down and sketch the outline of a series of ten, twelve, or twenty-four leading articles on Seniority *versus* Selection; Missionaries wish to know why they have not been permitted to escape from their regular vehicles of abuse and swear at a brother-missionary under special patronage of the editorial We; stranded theatrical companies troop up to explain that they cannot pay for their advertisements, but on their return from New Zealand or Tahiti will do so with interest; inventors of patent punkah-pulling machines, carriage couplings, and unbreakable swords and axle-trees, call with specifications in their pockets and hours at their disposal; tea-companies enter and elaborate their prospectuses with the office pens; secretaries of ball-committees clamour to have the glories of their last dance more fully described; strange ladies rustle in and say, 'I want a hundred lady's cards printed *at once*, please,' which is manifestly part of an Editor's duty; and every dissolute ruffian that ever tramped the Grand Trunk Road makes it his business to ask for employment as a proof-reader. And, all the time, the telephone-bell is ringing madly, and Kings are being killed on the Continent, and Empires are saying, 'You're another,' and Mister Gladstone[9] is calling down brimstone upon the British Dominions and the little black copy-boys are whining, '*kaa-pi chay-ha-yeh*' [copy wanted] like tired bees, and most of the paper is as blank as Modred's shield.[10]

But that is the amusing part of the year. There are six other months when none ever comes to call, and the thermometer walks inch by inch up to the top of the glass, and the office is darkened to just above reading-light, and the press-machines are red-hot of touch, and nobody writes anything but accounts of amusements in the Hill-stations, or obituary notices. Then the telephone becomes a tinkling terror, because it tells you of the sudden deaths of men and women that you knew intimately, and the prickly-heat covers you with a garment, and you sit down and write: 'A slight increase of sickness is reported from the Khuda Janta Khan District. The outbreak is purely sporadic in its nature, and, thanks to the energetic efforts of the District authorities, is now almost at an end. It is, however, with deep regret we record the death, etc.'

Then the sickness really breaks out, and the less recording and reporting the better for the peace of the subscribers. But the Empires and the Kings continue to divert themselves as selfishly as before, and the

Foreman thinks that a daily paper really ought to come out once in twenty-four hours, and all the people at the Hill-stations in the middle of their amusements say: 'Good gracious! Why can't the paper be sparkling? I'm sure there's plenty going on up here.'

That is the dark half of the moon, and, as the advertisements say, 'must be experienced to be appreciated'.

It was in that season, and a remarkably evil season, that the paper began running the last issue of the week on Saturday night, which is to say Sunday morning, after the custom of a London paper. This was a great convenience, for immediately after the paper was put to bed, the dawn would lower the thermometer from 96° to almost 84° for half an hour, and in that chill – you have no idea how cold is 84° on the grass until you begin to pray for it – a very tired man could get off to sleep ere the heat roused him.

One Saturday night it was my pleasant duty to put the paper to bed alone. A King or a courtier or courtesan or a Community was going to die or get a new Constitution, or do something that was important on the other side of the world, and the paper was to be held open till the latest possible minute in order to catch the telegram.

It was a pitchy black night, as stifling as a June night can be, and the *loo*, the red-hot wind from the westward, was booming among the tinder-dry trees and pretending that the rain was on its heels. Now and again a spot of almost boiling water would fall on the dust with the flop of a frog, but all our weary world knew that was only pretence. It was a shade cooler in the press-room than the office, so I sat there, while the type ticked and clicked, and the night-jars hooted at the windows, and the all but naked compositors wiped the sweat from their foreheads, and called for water. The thing that was keeping us back, whatever it was, would not come off, though the *loo* dropped and the last type was set, and the whole round earth stood still in the choking heat, with its finger on its lip, to wait the event. I drowsed, and wondered whether the telegraph was a blessing, and whether this dying man, or struggling people, might be aware of the inconvenience the delay was causing. There was no special reason beyond the heat and worry to make tension, but, as the clock-hands crept up to three o'clock, and the machines spun their fly-wheels two or three times to see that all was in order before I said the word that would set them off, I could have shrieked aloud.

Then the roar and rattle of the wheels shivered the quiet into little bits. I rose to go away, but two men in white clothes stood in front of me. The first one said: 'It's him!' The second said: 'So it is!' And they both laughed almost as loudly as the machinery roared, and mopped their foreheads. 'We seed there was a light burning across the road, and we were sleeping in that ditch there for coolness, and I said to my friend here, "The office is open. Let's come along and speak to him as turned us back from the Degumber State,"' said the smaller of the two. He was the man I had met in the Mhow train, and his fellow was the red-haired man of Marwar Junction. There was no mistaking the eyebrows of the one or the beard of the other.

I was not pleased, because I wished to go to sleep, not to squabble with loafers. 'What do you want?' I asked.

'Half an hour's talk with you, cool and comfortable, in the office,' said the red-bearded man. 'We'd *like* some drink – the Contrack doesn't begin yet, Peachey, so you needn't look – but what we really want is advice. We don't want money. We ask you as a favour, because we found out you did us a bad turn about Degumber State.'

I led from the press-room to the stifling office with the maps on the walls, and the red-haired man rubbed his hands. 'That's something like,' said he. 'This was the proper shop to come to. Now, sir, let me introduce to you Brother Peachey Carnehan, that's him, and Brother Daniel Dravot, that is *me*, and the less said about our professions the better, for we have been most things in our time. Soldier, sailor, compositor, photographer, proof-reader, street-preacher, *and* correspondent of the *Backwoodsman* when we thought the paper wanted one. Carnehan is sober, and so am I. Look at us first, and see that's sure. It will save you cutting into my talk. We'll take one of your cigars apiece, and you shall see us light up.'

I watched the test. The men were absolutely sober, so I gave them each a tepid whisky and soda.

'Well *and* good,' said Carnehan of the eyebrows, wiping the froth from his moustache. 'Let *me* talk now, Dan. We have been all over India, mostly on foot. We have been boiler-fitters, engine-drivers, petty contractors, and all that, and we have decided that India isn't big enough for such as us.'

They certainly were too big for the office. Dravot's beard seemed to fill half the room and Carnehan's shoulders the other half, as they sat on the big table. Carnehan continued: 'The country isn't half worked out because they that governs it won't let you touch it. They spend all their blessed time in governing it, and you can't lift a spade, nor chip a rock, nor look for oil, nor anything like that, without all the Government saying, "Leave it alone, and let us govern." Therefore, such *as* it is, we will let it alone, and go away to some other place where a man isn't crowded and can come to his own. We are not little men, and there is nothing that we are afraid of except Drink, and we have signed a Con-track on that. *Therefore*, we are going away to be Kings.'

'Kings in our own right,' muttered Dravot.

'Yes, of course,' I said. 'You've been tramping in the sun, and it's a very warm night, and hadn't you better sleep over the notion? Come tomorrow.'

'Neither drunk nor sunstruck,' said Dravot. 'We have slept over the notion half a year, and require to see Books and Atlases, and we have decided that there is only one place now in the world that two strong men can Sar-a-*whack*.[11] They call it Kafiristan.[12] By my reckoning it's the top right-hand corner of Afghanistan, not more than three hundred miles from Peshawur. They have two-and-thirty heathen idols there, and we'll be the thirty-third and fourth. It's a mountainous country, and the women of those parts are very beautiful.'

'But that is provided against in the Contrack,' said Carnehan. 'Neither Woman nor Liqu-or, Daniel.'

'And that's all we know, except that no one has gone there, and they fight; and in any place where they fight, a man who knows how to drill men can always be a King. We shall go to those parts and say to any King we find – "D'you want to vanquish your foes?" and we will show him how to drill men; for that we know better than anything else. Then we will subvert that King and seize his Throne and establish a Dy-nasty.'

'You'll be cut to pieces before you're fifty miles across the Border,' I said. 'You have to travel through Afghanistan to get to that country. It's one mass of mountains and peaks and glaciers, and no Englishman has been through it. The people are utter brutes, and even if you reached them you couldn't do anything.'

'That's more like,' said Carnehan. 'If you could think us a little more mad we would be more pleased. We have come to you to know about this country, to read a book about it, and to be shown maps. We want you to tell us that we are fools and to show us your books.' He turned to the bookcases.

'Are you at all in earnest?' I said.

'A little,' said Dravot sweetly. 'As big a map as you have got, even if it's all blank where Kafiristan is, and any books you've got. We can read, though we aren't very educated.'

I uncased the big thirty-two-miles-to-the-inch map of India, and two smaller Frontier maps, hauled down volume INF-KAN of the *Encyclopaedia Britannica*, and the men consulted them.

'See here!' said Dravot, his thumb on the map. 'Up to Jagdallak, Peachey and me know the road. We was there with Roberts' Army.[13]

We'll have to turn off to the right at Jagdallak through Laghman territory. Then we get among the hills – fourteen thousand feet – fifteen thousand – it will be cold work there, but it don't look very far on the map.'

I handed him Wood on the *Sources of the Oxus*. Carnehan was deep in the *Encyclopaedia*.

'They're a mixed lot,' said Dravot reflectively; 'and it won't help us to know the names of their tribes. The more tribes the more they'll fight, and the better for us. From Jagdallak to Ashang – H'mm!'

'But all the information about the country is as sketchy and inaccurate as can be,' I protested. 'No one knows anything about it really. Here's the file of the *United Services' Institute*. Read what Bellew says.'

'Blow Bellew!' said Carnehan. 'Dan, they're a stinkin' lot of heathens, but this book here says they think they're related to us English.'

I smoked while the men pored over Raverty, Wood, the maps, and the *Encyclopaedia*.

'There is no use your waiting,' said Dravot politely. 'It's about four o'clock now. We'll go before six o'clock if you want to sleep, and we won't steal any of the papers. Don't you sit up. We're two harmless lunatics, and if you come tomorrow evening down to the Serai we'll say good-bye to you.'

'You *are* two fools,' I answered. 'You'll be turned back at the Frontier or cut up the minute you set foot in Afghanistan. Do you want any money or a recommendation down-country? I can help you to the chance of work next week.'

'Next week we shall be hard at work ourselves, thank you,' said Dravot. 'It isn't so easy being a King as it looks. When we've got our Kingdom in going order we'll let you know, and you can come up and help us to govern it.'

'Would two lunatics make a Contrack like that?' said Carnehan, with subdued pride, showing me a greasy half-sheet of notepaper on which was written the following. I copied it, then and there, as a curiosity:

This Contract between me and you persuing witnesseth in the name of God – Amen and so forth.

(*One*) *That me and you will settle this matter together; i.e. to be Kings of Kafiristan.*

(*Two*) *That you and me will not, while this matter is being settled, look at any Liquor, nor any Woman black, white, or brown, so as to get mixed up with one or the other harmful.*

(*Three*) *That we conduct ourselves with Dignity and Discretion, and if one of us gets into trouble the other will stay by him.*

Signed by you and me this day.
Peachey Taliaferro Carnehan.
Daniel Dravot.
Both Gentlemen at Large.

'There was no need for the last article,' said Carnehan, blushing modestly; 'but it looks regular. Now you know the sort of men that loafers are — we *are* loafers, Dan, until we get out of India — and *do* you think that we would sign a Contrack like that unless we was in earnest? We have kept away from the two things that make life worth having.'

'You won't enjoy your lives much longer if you are going to try this idiotic adventure. Don't set the office on fire,' I said, 'and go away before nine o'clock.'

I left them still poring over the maps and making notes on the back of the 'Contrack'. 'Be sure to come down to the Serai tomorrow,' were their parting words.

The Kumharsen Serai is the great four-square sink of humanity where the strings of camels and horses from the North load and unload. All the nationalities of Central Asia may be found there, and most of the folk of India proper. Balkh and Bokhara there meet Bengal and Bombay, and try to draw eye-teeth. You can buy ponies, turquoises, Persian pussy-cats, saddle-bags, fat-tailed sheep and musk in the Kumharsen Serai, and get many strange things for nothing. In the afternoon I went down to see whether my friends intended to keep their word or were lying there drunk.

A priest attired in fragments of ribbons and rags stalked up to me, gravely twisting a child's paper whirligig. Behind him was his servant bending under the load of a crate of mud toys. The two were loading up two camels, and the inhabitants of the Serai watched them with shrieks of laughter.

'The priest is mad,' said a horse-dealer to me. 'He is going up to Kabul to sell toys to the Amir. He will either be raised to honour or have his head cut off. He came in here this morning and has been behaving madly ever since.'

'The witless are under the protection of God,' stammered a flat-cheeked Uzbeg in broken Hindi. 'They foretell future events.'

'Would they could have foretold that my caravan would have been cut up by the Shinwaris almost within shadow of the Pass!' grunted the Yusufzai agent of a Rajputana trading-house whose goods had been diverted into the hands of other robbers just across the Border, and whose misfortunes were the laughing-stock of the bazar. 'Ohé, priest, whence come you and whither do you go?'

'From Roum [14] have I come,' shouted the priest, waving his whirligig; 'from Roum, blown by the breath of a hundred devils across the sea! O thieves, robbers, liars, the blessing of Pir Khan [15] on pigs, dogs, and perjurers! Who will take the Protected of God to the North to sell charms that are never still to the Amir? The camels shall not gall, the sons shall not fall sick, and the wives shall remain faithful while they are away, of the men who give me place in their caravan. Who will assist me to slipper the King of the Roos [16] with a golden slipper with a silver heel? The protection of Pir Khan be upon his labours!' He spread out the skirts of his gaberdine and pirouetted between the lines of tethered horses.

'There starts a caravan from Peshawur to Kabul in twenty days, *Huzrut*,'[17] said the Yusufzai trader. 'My camels go therewith. Do thou also go and bring us good luck.'

'I will go even now!' shouted the priest. 'I will depart upon my winged camels, and be at Peshawur in a day! Ho! Hazar [18] Mir Khan,' he yelled to his servant, 'drive out the camels, but let me first mount my own.'

He leaped on the back of his beast as it knelt, and, turning round to me, cried: 'Come thou also, Sahib, a little along the road, and I will sell thee a charm – an amulet that shall make thee King of Kafiristan.'

Then the light broke upon me, and I followed the two camels out of the Serai till we reached open road and the priest halted.

'What d'you think o' that?' said he in English. 'Carnehan can't talk their patter, so I've made him my servant. He makes a handsome servant. 'Tisn't for nothing that I've been knocking about the country for fourteen years. Didn't I do that talk neat? We'll hitch on to a caravan at Peshawur till we get to Jagdallak, and then we'll see if we can get donkeys for our camels, and strike into Kafiristan. Whirligigs for the Amir, oh, Lor! Put your hand under the camel-bags and tell me what you feel.'

I felt the butt of a Martini,[19] and another and another.

'Twenty of 'em,' said Dravot placidly. 'Twenty of 'em and ammunition to correspond, under the whirligigs and the mud dolls.'

'Heaven help you if you are caught with those things!' I said. 'A Martini is worth her weight in silver among the Pathans.'

'Fifteen hundred rupees of capital – every rupee we could beg, borrow, or steal – are invested on these two camels,' said Dravot. 'We won't get caught. We're going through the Khyber with a regular caravan. Who'd touch a poor mad priest?'

'Have you got everything you want?' I asked, overcome with astonishment.

'Not yet, but we shall soon. Give us a memento of your kindness, *Brother*. You did me a service, yesterday, and that time in Marwar. Half my Kingdom shall you have, as the saying is.' I slipped a small charm compass from my watch-chain and handed it up to the priest.

'Good-bye,' said Dravot, giving me a hand cautiously. 'It's the last time we'll shake hands with an Englishman these many days. Shake hands with him, Carnehan,' he cried, as the second camel passed me.

Carnehan leaned down and shook hands. Then the camels passed away along the dusty road, and I was left alone to wonder. My eye could detect no failure in the disguises. The scene in the Serai proved that they were complete to the native mind. There was just the chance, therefore, that Carnehan and Dravot would be able to wander through Afghanistan without detection. But, beyond, they would find death – certain and awful death.

Ten days later a native correspondent, giving me the news of the day from Peshawur, wound up his letter with: 'There has been much laughter here on account of a certain mad priest who is going in his estimation to sell petty gauds and insignificant trinkets which he ascribes as great charms to H.H. the Amir of Bokhara. He passed through Peshawur and associated himself to the Second Summer caravan that goes to Kabul. The merchants are pleased because through superstition they imagine that such mad fellows bring good fortune.'

The two, then, were beyond the Border. I would have prayed for them, but, that night, a real King died in Europe, and demanded an obituary notice.

The wheel of the world swings through the same phases again and again. Summer passed and winter thereafter, and came and passed again. The daily paper continued and I with it, and upon the third summer there fell a hot night, a night-issue, and a strained waiting for something to be telegraphed from the other side of the world, exactly as had happened before. A few great men had died in the past two years, the machines worked with more clatter, and some of the trees in the office garden were a few feet taller. But that was all the difference.

I passed over to the press-room, and went through just such a scene as I have already described. The nervous tension was stronger than it had been two years before, and I felt the heat more acutely. At three o'clock I cried, 'Print off,' and turned to go, when there crept to my chair what was left of a man. He was bent into a circle, his head was sunk between his shoulders, and he moved his feet one over the other like a bear. I could hardly see whether he walked or crawled – this rag-wrapped, whining cripple who addressed me by name, crying that he was come back. 'Can you give me a drink?' he whimpered. 'For the Lord's sake, give me a drink!'

I went back to the office, the man following with groans of pain, and I turned up the lamp.

'Don't you know me?' he gasped, dropping into a chair, and he turned his drawn face, surmounted by a shock of grey hair, to the light.

I looked at him intently. Once before had I seen eyebrows that met over the nose in an inch-broad black band, but for the life of me I could not recall where.

'I don't know you,' I said, handing him the whisky. 'What can I do for you?'

He took a gulp of the spirit raw, and shivered in spite of the suffocating heat.

'I've come back,' he repeated; 'and I was the King of Kafiristan – me and Dravot – crowned Kings we was! In this office we settled it – you setting there and giving us the books. I am Peachey – Peachey Taliaferro Carnehan, and you've been setting here ever since – oh, Lord!'

I was more than a little astonished, and expressed my feelings accordingly.

'It's true,' said Carnehan, with a dry cackle, nursing his feet, which were wrapped in rags. 'True as gospel. Kings we were, with crowns upon our heads – me and Dravot – poor Dan – oh, poor, poor Dan, that would never take advice, not though I begged of him!'

'Take the whisky,' I said, 'and take your own time. Tell me all you can recollect of everything from beginning to end. You got across the Border on your camels, Dravot dressed as a mad priest and you his servant. Do you remember that?'

'I ain't mad – yet, but I shall be that way soon. Of course I remember. Keep looking at me, or maybe my words will go all to pieces. Keep looking at me in my eyes and don't say anything.'

I leaned forward and looked into his face as steadily as I could. He dropped one hand upon the table and I grasped it by the wrist. It was twisted like a bird's claw, and upon the back was a ragged red diamond-shaped scar.

'No, don't look there. Look at *me*,' said Carnehan. 'That comes afterwards, but for the Lord's sake don't distrack me. We left with that caravan, me and Dravot playing all sorts of antics to amuse the people we were with. Dravot used to make us laugh in the evenings when all the people was cooking their dinners – cooking their dinners, and . . . what did they do then? They lit little fires with sparks that went into Dravot's beard, and we all laughed – fit to die. Little red fires they was, going into Dravot's big red beard – so funny.' His eyes left mine and he smiled foolishly.

'You went as far as Jagdallak with that caravan,' I said at a venture, 'after you had lit those fires. To Jagdallak where you turned off to try to get into Kafiristan.'

'No, we didn't neither. What are you talking about? We turned off before Jagdallak, because we heard the roads was good. But they wasn't good enough for our two camels – mine and Dravot's. When we left the caravan, Dravot took off all his clothes and mine too, and said we would be heathen, because the Kafirs didn't allow Mohammedans to talk to them. So we dressed betwixt and between, and such a sight as Daniel Dravot I never saw yet nor expect to see again. He burned half his beard, and slung a sheep-skin over his shoulder, and shaved his head into patterns. He shaved mine, too, and made me wear outrageous things to look like a heathen. That was in a most mountaineous country, and our camels couldn't go along any more because of the mountains. They were tall and black, and coming home I saw them fight like wild goats – there are lots of goats in Kafiristan. And these mountains, they never keep still, no more than the goats. Always fighting they are, and don't let you sleep at night.'

'Take some more whisky,' I said very slowly. 'What did you and Daniel Dravot do when the camels could go no farther because of the rough roads that led into Kafiristan?'

'What did which do? There was a party called Peachey Taliaferro Carnehan that was with Dravot. Shall I tell you about him? He died out there in the cold. Slap from the bridge fell old Peachey, turning and twisting in the air like a penny whirligig that you can sell to the Amir – No; they was two for three-ha'pence, those whirligigs, or I am much mistaken and woeful sore . . . And then these camels were no use, and Peachey said to Dravot – "For the Lord's sake let's get out of this before our heads are chopped off," and with that they killed the camels all among the mountains, not having anything in particular to eat, but first they took off the boxes with the guns and the ammunition, till two men came along driving four mules. Dravot up and dances in front of them, singing: "Sell me four mules." Says the first man: "If you are rich enough to buy, you are rich enough to rob"; but before ever he could put his hand to his knife, Dravot breaks his neck over his knee, and the other party runs away. So Carnehan loaded the mules with the rifles that was taken off the camels, and together we starts forward into those bitter cold mountaineous parts, and never a road broader than the back of your hand.'

He paused for a moment, while I asked him if he could remember the nature of the country through which he had journeyed.

'I am telling you as straight as I can, but my head isn't as good as it might be. They drove nails through it to make me hear better how Dravot died. The country was mountaineous, and the mules were most contrary, and the inhabitants was dispersed and solitary. They went up and up, and down and down, and that other party, Carnehan, was imploring of Dravot not to sing and whistle so loud, for fear of bringing down the tremenjus avalanches. But Dravot says that if a King couldn't sing it wasn't worth being King, and whacked the mules over the rump, and never took no heed for ten cold days. We came to a big level valley all among the mountains, and the mules were near dead, so we killed them, not having anything in special for them or us to eat. We sat upon the boxes, and played odd and even with the cartridges that was jolted out.

'Then ten men with bows and arrows ran down that valley, chasing twenty men with bows and arrows, and the row was tremenjus. They was fair men – fairer than you or me – with yellow hair and remarkable well built. Says Dravot, unpacking the guns: "This is the beginning of the business. We'll fight for the ten men," and with that he fires two rifles at the twenty men, and drops one of them at two hundred yards from the rock where he was sitting. The other men began to run, but Carnehan and Dravot sits on the boxes picking them off at all ranges, up and down the valley. Then we goes up to the ten men that had run across the snow too, and they fires a footy little arrow at us. Dravot he shoots above their heads and they all falls down flat. Then he walks over them and kicks them, and then he lifts them up and shakes hands all round to make them friendly like. He calls them and gives them the boxes to carry, and waves his hand for all the world as though he was King already. They takes the boxes and him across the valley and up the hill into a pine wood on the top, where there was half-a-dozen big stone idols. Dravot he goes to the biggest – a fellow they call Imbra – and lays a rifle and a cartridge at his feet, rubbing his nose respectful with his own nose, patting him on the head, and saluting in front of it. He turns round to the men and nods his head and says: "That's all right. I'm in the know too, and all these old jim-jams are my friends." Then he opens his mouth and points down it, and when the first man brings him food, he says: "No"; and when the second man brings him food, he says:

"No"; but when one of the old priests and the boss of the village brings him food, he says: "Yes", very haughty, and eats it slow. That was how we came to our first village, without any trouble, just as though we had tumbled from the skies. But we tumbled from one of those damned rope-bridges, you see, and – you couldn't expect a man to laugh much after that?'

'Take some more whisky and go on,' I said. 'That was the first village you came into. How did you get to be King?'

'I wasn't King,' said Carnehan. 'Dravot he was the King, and a handsome man he looked with the gold crown on his head and all. Him and the other party stayed in that village, and every morning Dravot sat by the side of old Imbra, and the people came and worshipped. That was Dravot's order. Then a lot of men came into the valley, and Carnehan and Dravot picks them off with the rifles before they knew where they was, and runs down into the valley and up again the other side and finds another village, same as the first one, and the people all falls down flat on their faces, and Dravot says: "Now what is the trouble between you two villages?" and the people points to a woman, as fair as you or me, that was carried off, and Dravot takes her back to the first village and counts up the dead – eight there was. For each dead man Dravot pours a little milk on the ground and waves his arms like a whirligig, and "That's all right," says he. Then he and Carnehan takes the big boss of each valley by the arm and walks them down into the valley, and shows them how to scratch a line with a spear right down the valley, and gives each a sod of turf from both sides of the line. Then all the people comes down and shouts like the devil and all, and Dravot says: "Go and dig the land, and be fruitful and multiply," which they did, though they didn't understand. Then we asks the names of things in their lingo – bread and water and fire and idols and such, and Dravot leads the priest of each village up to the idol, and says he must sit there and judge the people, and if anything goes wrong he is to be shot.

'Next week they was all turning up the land in the valley as quiet as bees and much prettier, and the priests heard all the complaints and told Dravot in dumb show what it was about. "That's just the beginning," says Dravot. "They think we're Gods." He and Carnehan picks out twenty good men and shows them how to click off a rifle, and form fours, and advance in line, and they was very pleased to do so, and clever to see the hang of it. Then he takes out his pipe and his baccy-pouch and leaves one at one village, and one at the other, and off we two goes to see what was to be done in the next valley. That was all rock, and there was a little village there, and Carnehan says: "Send 'em to the old valley to plant," and takes 'em there, and gives 'em some land that wasn't took before. They were a poor lot, and we blooded 'em with a kid before letting 'em into the new Kingdom. That was to impress the people, and then they settled down quiet, and Carnehan went back to Dravot, who had got into another valley, all snow and ice and most mountaineous. There was no people there and the Army got afraid, so Dravot shoots one of them, and goes on till he finds some people in a village, and the Army explains that unless the people wants to be killed they had better not shoot their little matchlocks; for they had matchlocks. We makes friends with the priest, and I stays there alone with two of the Army, teaching the men how to drill, and a thundering big Chief comes across the snow with kettle-drums and horns twanging, because he heard there was a new God kicking about. Carnehan sights for the brown of the men half a mile across the snow and wings one of them. Then he sends a message to the Chief that, unless he wished to be killed, he must come and shake hands with me and leave his arms behind. The Chief comes alone first, and Carnehan shakes hands with him and whirls his arms about, same as Dravot used, and very much surprised that Chief was, and strokes my eyebrows. Then Carnehan goes alone to the Chief, and asks him in dumb show if he had an enemy he hated. "I have," says the Chief. So Carnehan weeds out the pick of his men, and sets the two of the Army to show them drill, and at the end of two weeks the men can manoeuvre about as well as Volunteers. So he marches with the Chief to a great big plain on the top of a mountain, and the Chief's men rushes into a village and takes it; we three Martinis firing into the brown of the enemy. So we took that village too, and I gives the Chief a rag from my coat and says, "Occupy till I come"; which was scriptural. By way of a reminder, when me and the Army was eighteen hundred yards away, I drops a bullet near him standing on the snow, and all the people falls flat on their faces. Then I sends a letter to Dravot wherever he be by land or by sea.'

At the risk of throwing the creature out of train I interrupted: 'How could you write a letter up yonder?'

'The letter? – Oh! – The letter ! Keep looking at me between the eyes, please. It was a string-talk letter, that we'd learned the way of it from a blind beggar in the Punjab.'

I remembered that there had once come to the office a blind man with a knotted twig and a piece of string which he wound round the twig according to some cipher of his own. He could, after the lapse of days or weeks, repeat the sentence which he had reeled up. He had reduced the alphabet to eleven primitive sounds, and tried to teach me his method, but I could not understand.

'I sent that letter to Dravot,' said Carnehan; 'and told him to come back because this Kingdom was growing too big for me to handle, and then I struck for the first valley, to see how the priests were working. They called the village we took along with the Chief, Bashkai, and the first village we took, Er-Heb. The priests at Er-Heb was doing all right, but they had a lot of pending cases about land to show me, and some men from another village had been firing arrows at night. I went out and looked for that village, and fired four rounds at it from a thousand yards. That used all the cartridges I cared to spend, and I waited for Dravot, who had been away two or three months, and I kept my people quiet.

'One morning I heard the devil's own noise of drums and horns, and Dan Dravot marches down the hill with his Army and a tail of hundreds of men, and, which was the most amazing, a great gold crown on his head. 'My Gord, Carnehan,' says Daniel, "this is a tremenjus business, and we've got the whole country as far as it's worth having. I am the son of Alexander by Queen Semiramis,[20] and you're my younger brother and a God too! It's the biggest thing we've ever seen. I've been marching and fighting for six weeks with the Army, and every footy little village for fifty miles has come in rejoiceful; and more than that, I've got the key of the whole show, as you'll see, and I've got a crown for you! I told 'em to make two of 'em at a place called Shu, where the gold lies in the rock like suet in mutton. Gold I've seen, and turquoise I've kicked out of the cliffs, and there's garnets in the sands of the river, and here's a chunk of amber that a man brought me. Call up all the priests and, here, take your crown."

'One of the men opens a black hair bag, and I slips the crown on. It was too small and too heavy, but I wore it for the glory. Hammered gold it was – five pound weight, like a hoop of a barrel.

'"Peachey," says Dravot, "we don't want to fight no more. The Craft's[21] the trick, so help me!" and he brings forward that same Chief that I left at Baskhai – Billy Fish we called him afterwards, because he was so like Billy Fish that drove the big tank-engine at Mach on the Bolan in the old days. "Shake hands with him," says Dravot, and I shook hands and nearly dropped, for Billy Fish gave me the Grip. I said nothing, but tried him with the Fellow Craft Grip. He answers all right, and I tried the Master's Grip, but that was a slip. "A Fellow Craft he is!" I says to Dan. "Does he know the Word?" – "He does," says Dan, "and all the priests know. It's a miracle! The Chiefs and the priests can work a Fellow Craft Lodge in a way that's very like ours, and they've cut the marks on the rocks, but they don't know the Third Degree, and they've come to find out. It's Gord's Truth! I've known these long years that the Afghans knew up to the Fellow Craft Degree, but this is a miracle. A God and a Grand-Master of the Craft am I, and a Lodge in the Third Degree I will open, and we'll raise the head priests and the Chiefs of the villages."

'"It's against all the law," I says, "holding a Lodge without warrant from anyone; and you know we never held office in any Lodge."

'"It's a master-stroke o' policy," says Dravot. "It means running the country as easy as a four-wheeled bogie on a down grade. We can't stop to inquire now, or they'll turn against us. I've forty Chiefs at my heel, and passed and raised according to their merit they shall be. Billet these men on the villages, and see that we run up a Lodge of some kind. The temple of Imbra will do for the Lodge-room. The women must make aprons as you show them. I'll hold a levee of Chiefs tonight and Lodge tomorrow."

'I was fair run off my legs, but I wasn't such a fool as not to see what a pull this Craft business gave us. I showed the priests' families how to make aprons of the degrees, but for Dravot's apron the blue border and marks was made of turquoise lumps on white hide, not cloth. We took a great square stone in the temple for the Master's chair, and little stones for the officers' chairs, and painted the black pavement with white squares, and did what we could to make things regular.

'At the levee which was held that night on the hillside with big bonfires, Dravot gives out that him and me were Gods and sons of Alexander, and Past Grand-Masters in the Craft, and was come to make Kafiristan a country where every man should eat in peace and drink in quiet, and 'specially obey us. Then the Chiefs come round to shake hands, and they were so hairy and white and fair it was just shaking hands with old friends. We gave them names according as they was like men we had known in India – Billy Fish, Holly Dilworth, Pikky Kergan, that was Bazar-master when I was at Mhow, and so on, and so on.

'*The* most amazing miracles was at Lodge next night. One of the old priests was watching us continuous, and I felt uneasy, for I knew we'd have to fudge the Ritual, and I didn't know what the men knew. The old priest was a stranger come in from beyond the village of Bashkai. The minute Dravot puts on the Master's apron that the girls had made for him, the priest fetches a whoop and a howl, and tries to overturn the stone that Dravot was sitting on. "It's all up now," I says. "That comes of meddling with the Craft without warrant!" Dravot never winked an eye, not when ten priests took and tilted over the Grand-Master's chair – which was to say the stone of Imbra. The priest begins rubbing the bottom end of it to clear away the black dirt, and presently he shows all the other priests the Master's Mark, same as was on Dravot's apron, cut into the stone. Not even the priests of the temple of Imbra knew it was there. The old chap falls flat on his face at Dravot's feet and kisses 'em. "Luck again," says Dravot, across the Lodge to me; "they say it's the missing Mark that no one could understand the why of. We're more than safe now." Then he bangs the butt of his gun for a gavel and says: "By virtue of the authority vested in me by my own right hand and the help of Peachey, I declare myself Grand-Master of all Freemasonry in Kafiristan in this the Mother Lodge o' the country, and King of Kafiristan equally with Peachey!" At that he puts on his crown and I puts on mine – I was doing Senior Warden – and we opens the Lodge in most ample form. It was a amazing miracle! The priests moved in Lodge through the first two degrees almost without telling, as if the memory was coming back to them. After that, Peachey and Dravot raised such as was worthy – high priests and Chiefs of far-off villages. Billy Fish was the first, and I can tell you we scared the soul out of him. It was not in any way according to Ritual, but it served our turn. We didn't raise more than ten of the biggest men, because we didn't want to make the Degree common. And they was clamouring to be raised.

'"In another six months," says Dravot, "we'll hold another Communication, and see how you are working." Then he asks them about their villages, and learns that they was fighting one against the other, and was sick and tired of it. And when they wasn't doing that they was fighting with the Mohammedans. "You can fight those when they come into our country," says Dravot. "Tell off every tenth man of your tribes for a Frontier guard, and send two hundred at a time to this valley to be drilled. Nobody is going to be shot or speared any more so long as he does well, and I know that you won't cheat me, because you're white people – sons of Alexander – and not like common, black Mohammedans. You are *my* people, and by God," says he, running off into English at the end, "I'll make a damned fine Nation of you, or I'll die in the making!"

'I can't tell all we did for the next six months, because Dravot did a lot I couldn't see the hang of, and he learned their lingo in a way I never could. My work was to help the people plough, and now and again go out with some of the Army and see what the other villages were doing, and make 'em throw rope-bridges across the ravines which cut up the country horrid. Dravot was very kind to me, but when he walked up and down in the pine-wood pulling that bloody red beard of his with both fists I knew he was thinking plans I could not advise about, and I just waited for orders.

'But Dravot never showed me disrespect before the people. They were afraid of me and the Army, but they loved Dan. He was the best of friends with the priests and the Chiefs; but anyone could come across the hills with a complaint, and Dravot would hear him out fair, and call four priests together and say what was to be done. He used to call in Billy Fish from Bashkai, and Pikky Kergan from Shu, and an old Chief we called Kafoozelum — it was like enough to his real name — and hold councils with 'em when there was any fighting to be done in small villages. That was his Council of War, and the four priests of Bashkai, Shu, Khawak, and Madora was his Privy Council. Between the lot of 'em they sent me, with forty men and twenty rifles and sixty men carrying turquoises, into the Ghorband country to buy those hand-made Martini rifles, that come out of the Amir's workshops at Kabul, from one of the Amir's Herati regiments that would have sold the very teeth out of their mouths for turquoises.

'I stayed in Ghorband a month, and gave the Governor there the pick of my baskets for hush-money, and bribed the Colonel of the regiment some more, and, between the two and the tribespeople, we got more than a hundred hand-made Martinis, a hundred good Kohat *jezails*²² that'll throw to six hundred yards, and forty man-loads of very bad ammunition for the rifles. I came back with what I had, and distributed 'em among the men that the Chiefs sent in to me to drill. Dravot was too busy to attend to those things, but the old Army that we first made helped me, and we turned out five hundred men that could drill, and two hundred that knew how to hold arms pretty straight. Even those corkscrewed, handmade guns was a miracle to them. Dravot talked big about powder-shops and factories, walking up and down in the pine-wood when the winter was coming on.

'"I won't make a Nation," says he. "I'll make an Empire! These men aren't niggers; they're English! Look at their eyes — look at their mouths. Look at the way they stand up. They sit on chairs in their own houses. They're the Lost Tribes, or something like it, and they've grown to be English. I'll take a census in the spring if the priests don't get frightened. There must be a fair two million of 'em in these hills. The villages are full o' little children. Two million people — two hundred and fifty thousand fighting men — and all English! They only want the rifles and a little drilling. Two hundred and fifty thousand men, ready to cut in on Russia's right flank when she tries for India! Peachey, man," he says, chewing his beard in great hunks, "we shall be Emperors — Emperors of the Earth! Rajah Brooke²³ will be a suckling to us. I'll treat with the Viceroy on equal terms. I'll ask him to send me twelve picked English – twelve that I know of – to help us govern a bit. There's Mackray, Sergeant-pensioner at Segowli – many's the good dinner he's given me, and his wife a pair of trousers. There's Donkin, the Warder of Tounghoo Jail. There's hundreds that I could lay my hand on if I was in India. The Viceroy shall do it for me. I'll send a man through in the spring for those men, and I'll write for a Dispensation from the Grand Lodge for what I've done as Grand-Master. That – and all the Sniders that'll be thrown out when the native troops in India take up the Martini. They'll be worn smooth, but they'll do for fighting in these hills. Twelve English, a hundred thousand Sniders run through the Amir's country in driblets – I'd be content with twenty thousand in one year – and we'd be an Empire. When everything was shipshape, I'd hand over the crown – this crown I'm wearing now – to Queen Victoria on my knees, and she'd say: 'Rise up, Sir Daniel Dravot.' Oh, it's big! It's big, I tell you! But there's so much to be done in every place – Bashkai, Khawak, Shu, and everywhere else."

' "What is it?" I says. "There are no more men coming in to be drilled this autumn. Look at those fat, black clouds. They're bringing the snow."

' "It isn't that," says Daniel, putting his hand very hard on my shoulder; "and I don't wish to say anything that's against you, for no other living man would have followed me and made me what I am as you have done. You're a first-class Commander-in-Chief, and the people know you; but – it's a big country, and somehow you can't help me, Peachey, in the way I want to be helped."

' "Go to your blasted priests, then!" I said, and I was sorry when I made that remark, but it did hurt me sore to find Daniel talking so superior, when I'd drilled all the men, and done all he told me.

' "Don't let's quarrel, Peachey," says Daniel without cursing. "You're a King too, and the half of this Kingdom is yours; but can't you see, Peachey, we want cleverer men than us now – three or four of 'em, that we can scatter about for our Deputies. It's a hugeous great State, and I can't always tell the right thing to do, and I haven't time for all I want to do, and here's winter coming on and all." He stuffed half his beard into his mouth, all red like the gold of his crown.

' "I'm sorry, Daniel," says I. "I've done all I could. I've drilled the men and shown the people how to stack their oats better; and I've brought in those tinware rifles from Ghorband – but I know what you're driving at. I take it Kings always feel oppressed that way."

' "There's another thing too," says Dravot, walking up and down.

"The winter's coming and these people won't be giving much trouble, and if they do we can't move about. I want a wife."

'"For Gord's sake, leave the women alone!" I says. "We've both got all the work we can, though I *am* a fool. Remember the Contrack, and keep clear o' women."

'"The Contrack only lasted till such time as we were Kings; and Kings we have been these months past," says Dravot, weighing his crown in his hand. "You go get a wife, too, Peachey – a nice, strappin', plump girl that'll keep you warm in the winter. They're prettier than English girls, and we can take the pick of 'em. Boil 'em once or twice in hot water and they'll come out like chicken and ham."

'"Don't tempt me!" I says. "I will not have any dealings with a woman not till we are a dam' sight more settled than we are now. I've been doing the work o' two men, and you've been doing the work o' three. Let's lie off a bit, and see if we can get some better tobacco from Afghan country and run in some good liquor; but no women."

'"Who's talking o' *women*?" says Dravot. "I said *wife* – a Queen to breed a King's son for the King. A Queen out of the strongest tribe, that'll make them your blood-brothers, and that'll lie by your side and tell you all the people thinks about you and their own affairs. That's what I want."

'"Do you remember that Bengali woman I kept at Mogul Serai when I was a platelayer?" says I. "A fat lot o' good she was to me. She taught me the lingo and one or two other things; but what happened? She ran away with the Station-master's servant and half my month's pay. Then she turned up at Dadur Junction in tow of a half-caste, and had the impidence to say I was her husband – all among the drivers in the running-shed too!"

'"We've done with that," says Dravot; "these women are whiter than you or me, and a Queen I will have for the winter months."

'"For the last time o' asking, Dan, do *not*," I says. "It'll only bring us harm. The Bible says that Kings ain't to waste their strength on women, 'specially when they've got a raw new Kingdom to work over."

'"For the last time of answering, I will," said Dravot, and he went away through the pine-trees looking like a big red devil, the sun being on his crown and beard and all.

'But getting a wife was not as easy as Dan thought. He put it before the Council, and there was no answer till Billy Fish said that he'd better ask the girls. Dravot damned them all round. "What's wrong with me?" he shouts, standing by the idol Imbra. "Am I a dog or am I not enough of a man for your wenches? Haven't I put the shadow of my hand over this country? Who stopped the last Afghan raid?" It was me really, but Dravot was too angry to remember. "Who bought your guns? Who repaired the bridges? Who's the Grand-Master of the Sign cut in the stone?" says he, and he thumped his hand on the block that he used to sit on in Lodge, and at Council, which opened like Lodge always. Billy Fish said nothing and no more did the others. "Keep your hair on, Dan," said I; "and ask the girls. That's how it's done at Home, and these people are quite English."

'"The marriage of the King is a matter of State," says Dan, in a red-hot rage, for he could feel, I hope, that he was going against his better mind. He walked out of the Council-room, and the others sat still, looking at the ground.

'"Billy Fish," says I to the Chief of Bashkai, "what's the difficulty here? A straight answer to a true friend."

'"You know," says Billy Fish. "How should a man tell you who knows everything? How can daughters of men marry Gods or Devils? It's not proper."

'I remembered something like that in the Bible; but if, after seeing us as long as they had, they still believed we were Gods, 'twasn't for me to undeceive them.

'"A God can do anything," says I. "If the King is fond of a girl he'll not let her die." – "She'll have to," says Billy Fish. "There are all sorts of Gods and Devils in these mountains, and now and again a girl marries one of them and isn't seen any more. Besides, you two know the Mark cut in the stone. Only the Gods know that. We thought you were men till you showed the Sign of the Master."

'I wished then that we had explained about the loss of the genuine secrets of a Master-Mason at the first go-off; but I said nothing. All that night there was a blowing of horns in a little dark temple half-way down the hill, and I heard a girl crying fit to die. One of the priests told us that she was being prepared to marry the King.

'"I'll have no nonsense of that kind," says Dan. "I don't want to interfere with your customs, but I'll take my own wife." – "The girl's a little bit afraid," says the priest. "She thinks she's going to die, and they are a-heartening of her up down in the temple."

'"Hearten her very tender, then," says Dravot, "or I'll hearten you with the butt of a gun so you'll never want to be heartened again." He licked his lips, did Dan, and stayed up walking about more than half the night, thinking of the wife that he was going to get in the morning. I wasn't any means comfortable, for I knew that dealings with a woman in foreign parts, though you was a crowned King twenty times over, could not but be risky. I got up very early in the morning while Dravot was asleep, and I saw the priests talking together in whispers, and the Chiefs talking together too, and they looked at me out of the corners of their eyes.

'"What is up, Fish?" I says to the Baskhai man, who was wrapped up in his furs and looking splendid to behold.

'"I can't rightly say," says he; "but if you can make the King drop all this nonsense about marriage, you'll be doing him and me and yourself a great service."

'"That I do believe," says I. "But sure, you know, Billy, as well as me, having fought against and for us, that the King and me are nothing more than two of the finest men that God Almighty ever made. Nothing more, I do assure you."

'"That may be," says Billy Fish, "and yet I should be sorry if it was." He sinks his head upon his great fur cloak for a minute and thinks. "King," says he, "be you man or God or Devil, I'll stick by you today. I have twenty of my men with me, and they will follow me. We'll go to Bashkai until the storm blows over."

'A little snow had fallen in the night, and everything was white except them greasy fat clouds that blew down and down from the north. Dravot came out with his crown on his head, swinging his arms and stamping his feet, and looking more pleased than Punch.

'"For the last time, drop it, Dan," says I in a whisper. "Billy Fish here says that there will be a row."

'"A row among my people!" says Dravot. "Not much. Peachey, you're a fool not to get a wife too. Where's the girl?" says he with a voice as loud as the braying of a jackass. "Call up all the Chiefs and priests, and let the Emperor see if his wife suits him."

'There was no need to call anyone. They were all there leaning on their guns and spears round the clearing in the centre of the pine-wood. A lot of priests went down to the little temple to bring up the girl, and the horns blew fit to wake the dead. Billy Fish saunters round and gets as close to Daniel as he could, and behind him stood his twenty men with matchlocks. Not a man of them under six feet. I was next to Dravot, and behind me was twenty men of the regular Army. Up comes the girl, and a strapping wench she was, covered with silver and turquoises, but white as death, and looking back every minute at the priests.

'"She'll do," said Dan, looking her over. "What's to be afraid of, lass? Come and kiss me." He puts his arm round her. She shuts her eyes, gives a bit of a squeak, and down goes her face in the side of Dan's flaming red beard.

'"The slut's bitten me!" says he, clapping his hand to his neck, and, sure enough, his hand was red with blood. Billy Fish and two of his matchlock-men catches hold of Dan by the shoulders and drags him into the Bashkai lot, while the priests howls in their lingo: "Neither God nor Devil but a man!" I was all taken aback, for a priest cut at me in front, and the Army behind began firing into the Bashkai men.

'"God A'mighty!" says Dan. "What is the meaning o' this?"

'"Come back! Come away!" says Billy Fish. "Ruin and Mutiny's the matter. We'll break for Bashkai if we can."

'I tried to give some sort of orders to my men – the men o' the regular Army – but it was no use, so I fired into the brown of 'em with an English Martini and drilled three beggars in a line. The valley was full of shouting, howling people, and every soul was shrieking, "Not a God nor a Devil but only a man!" The Bashkai troops stuck to Billy Fish all they were worth, but their matchlocks wasn't half as good as the Kabul breech-loaders, and four of them dropped. Dan was bellowing like a bull, for he was very wrathy; and Billy Fish had a hard job to prevent him running out at the crowd.

'"We can't stand," says Billy Fish. "Make a run for it down the valley! The whole place is against us." The matchlock-men ran, and we went down the valley in spite of Dravot. He was swearing horrible and crying out he was a King. The priests rolled great stones on us, and the regular Army fired hard, and there wasn't more than six men, not counting Dan, Billy Fish, and me, that came down to the bottom of the valley alive.

'Then they stopped firing and the horns in the temple blew again. "Come away – for God's sake come away!" says Billy Fish. "They'll send runners out to all the villages before ever we get to Bashkai. I can protect you there, but I can't do anything now."

'My own notion is that Dan began to go mad in his head from that hour. He stared up and down like a stuck pig. Then he was all for walking back alone and killing the priests with his bare hands; which he could have done. "An Emperor am I," says Daniel, "and next year I shall be a Knight of the Queen."

'"All right, Dan," says I; "but come along now while there's time."

'"It's your fault," says he, "for not looking after your Army better. There was mutiny in the midst, and you didn't know – you damned engine-driving, plate-laying, missionary's-pass-hunting hound!" He sat upon a rock and called me every name he could lay tongue to. I was too heart-sick to care, though it was all his foolishness that brought the smash.

'"I'm sorry, Dan," says I, "but there's no accounting for natives. This business is our 'Fifty-Seven.²⁴ Maybe we'll make something out of it yet, when we've got to Bashkai."

'"Let's get to Bashkai, then," says Dan, "and, by God, when I come back here again I'll sweep the valley so there isn't a bug in a blanket left!"

'We walked all that day, and all that night Dan was stumping up and down on the snow, chewing his beard and muttering to himself.

'"There's no hope o' getting clear," said Billy Fish. "The priests will have sent runners to the villages to say that you are only men. Why didn't you stick on as Gods till things was more settled? I'm a dead man," says Billy Fish, and he throws himself down on the snow and begins to pray to his Gods.

'Next morning we was in a cruel bad country – all up and down, no level ground at all, and no food either. The six Bashkai men looked at Billy Fish hungry-ways as if they wanted to ask something, but they said never a word. At noon we came to the top of a flat mountain all covered with snow, and when we climbed up into it, behold, there was an Army in position waiting in the middle!

'"The runners have been very quick," says Billy Fish, with a little bit of a laugh. "They are waiting for us."

'Three or four men began to fire from the enemy's side, and a chance shot took Daniel in the calf of the leg. That brought him to his senses. He looks across the snow at the Army, and sees the rifles that we had brought into the country.

'"We're done for," says he. "They are Englishmen, these people – and it's my blasted nonsense that has brought you to this. Get back, Billy Fish, and take your men away. You've done what you could, and now cut for it. Carnehan," says he, "shake hands with me and go along with Billy. Maybe they won't kill you. I'll go and meet 'em alone. It's me that did it. Me, the King!"

'"Go!" says I. "Go to Hell, Dan! I'm with you here. Billy Fish, you clear out, and we two will meet those folk."

'"I'm a Chief," says Billy Fish, quite quiet. "I stay with you. My men can go."

'The Bashkai fellows didn't wait for a second word, but ran off, and Dan and me and Billy Fish walked across to where the drums were drumming and the horns were horning. It was cold – awful cold. I've got that cold in the back of my head now. There's a lump of it there.'

The punkah-coolies had gone to sleep. Two kerosene lamps were blazing in the office, and the perspiration poured down my face and splashed on the blotter as I leaned forward. Carnehan was shivering, and I feared that his mind might go. I wiped my face, took a fresh grip of the piteously mangled hands, and said: 'What happened after that?'

The momentary shift of my eyes had broken the clear current.

'What was you pleased to say?' whined Carnehan. 'They took them without any sound. Not a little whisper all along the snow, not though the King knocked down the first man that set hand on him – not though old Peachey fired his last cartridge into the brown of 'em. Not a single solitary sound did those swines make. They just closed up tight, and I tell you their furs stunk. There was a man called Billy Fish, a good friend of us all, and they cut his throat, sir, then and there, like a pig; and the King kicks up the bloody snow and says: "We've had a dashed fine run for our money. What's coming next?" But Peachey, Peachey Taliaferro, I tell you, sir, in confidence as betwixt two friends, he lost his head, sir. No, he didn't neither. The King lost his head, so he did, all along o' one of those cunning rope-bridges. Kindly let me have the paper-cutter, sir. It tilted this way. They marched him a mile across that snow to a rope-bridge over a ravine with a river at the bottom. You may have seen such. They prodded him behind like an ox. "Damn your eyes!" says the King. "D'you suppose I can't die like a gentleman?" He turns to Peachey – Peachey that was crying like a child. "I've brought you to this, Peachey," says he. "Brought you out of your happy life to be killed in Kafiristan, where you was late Commander-in-Chief of the Emperor's forces. Say you forgive me, Peachey." – "I do," says Peachey. "Fully and freely do I forgive you, Dan." – "Shake hands, Peachey," says he. "I'm going now." Out he goes, looking neither right nor left, and when he was plumb in the middle of those dizzy dancing ropes – "Cut, you beggars," he shouts; and they cut, and old Dan fell, turning round and round and round, twenty thousand miles, for he took half an hour to fall till he struck the water, and I could see his body caught on a rock with the gold crown close beside.

'But do you know what they did to Peachey between two pine-trees? They crucified him, sir, as Peachey's hands will show. They used wooden pegs for his hands and his feet; and he didn't die. He hung there and screamed, and they took him down next day, and said it was a miracle that he wasn't dead. They took him down – poor old Peachey that hadn't done them any harm – that hadn't done them any –'

He rocked to and fro and wept bitterly, wiping his eyes with the back of his scarred hands and moaning like a child for some ten minutes.

'They was cruel enough to feed him up in the temple, because they said he was more of a God than old Daniel that was a man. Then they turned him out on the snow, and told him to go home, and Peachey came home in about a year, begging along the roads quite safe; for Daniel Dravot he walked before and said: "Come along, Peachey. It's a big thing we're doing." The mountains they danced at night, and the mountains they tried to fall on Peachey's head, but Dan he held up his hand, and Peachey came along bent double. He never let go of Dan's hand, and he never let go of Dan's head. They gave it to him as a present in the temple, to remind him not to come again, and though the crown was pure gold, and Peachey was starving, never would Peachey sell the same. You knew Dravot, sir! You knew Right Worshipful Brother Dravot! Look at him now!'

He fumbled in the mass of rags round his bent waist; brought out a black horsehair bag embroidered with silver thread, and shook therefrom on to my table – the dried, withered head of Daniel Dravot! The morning sun that had long been paling the lamps struck the red beard and blind sunken eyes; struck, too, a heavy circlet of gold studded with raw turquoises, that Carnehan placed tenderly on the battered temples.

'You behold now,' said Carnehan, 'the Emperor in his habit as he lived [25] – the King of Kafiristan with his crown upon his head. Poor old Daniel that was a monarch once!'

I shuddered, for, in spite of defacements manifold, I recognized the head of the man of Marwar Junction. Carnehan rose to go. I attempted to stop him. He was not fit to walk abroad. 'Let me take away the whisky, and give me a little money,' he gasped. 'I was a King once. I'll go to the Deputy-Commissioner and ask to set in the Poorhouse till I get my health. No, thank you, I can't wait till you get a carriage for me. I've urgent private affairs – in the South – at Marwar.'

He shambled out of the office and departed in the direction of the Deputy-Commissioner's house. That day at noon I had occasion to go down the blinding hot Mall, and I saw a crooked man crawling along the white dust of the roadside, his hat in his hand, quavering dolorously after the fashion of street-singers at Home. There was not a soul in sight, and he was out of all possible earshot of the houses. And he sang through his nose, turning his head from right to left:

> 'The Son of God goes forth to war,
>   A kingly crown to gain;
> His blood-red banner streams afar!
>   Who follows in his train?' [26]

I waited to hear no more, but put the poor wretch into my carriage and drove him to the nearest missionary for eventual transfer to the

Asylum. He repeated the hymn twice while he was with me, whom he did not in the least recognize, and I left him singing it to the missionary.

Two days later I inquired after his welfare of the Superintendent of the Asylum.

'He was admitted suffering from sunstroke. He died early yesterday morning,' said the Superintendent. 'Is it true that he was half an hour bare-headed in the sun at mid-day?'

'Yes,' said I, 'but do you happen to know if he had anything upon him by any chance when he died?'

'Not to my knowledge,' said the Superintendent.

And there the matter rests.

⁅ Baa Baa, Black Sheep [1] ⁆

Baa Baa, Black Sheep,
Have you any wool?
Yes, Sir, yes, Sir, three bags full.
One for the Master, one for the Dame —
None for the Little Boy that cries down the lane.
Nursery Rhyme.

The First Bag

When I was in my father's house, I was in a better place. [2]

They were putting Punch to bed – the *ayah* [3] and the *hamal* [4] and Meeta, the big *Surti* [5] boy, with the red-and-gold turban. Judy, already tucked inside her mosquito-curtains, was nearly asleep. Punch had been allowed to stay up for dinner. Many privileges had been accorded to Punch within the last ten days, and a greater kindness from the people of his world had encompassed his ways and works, which were mostly obstreperous. He sat on the edge of his bed and swung his bare legs defiantly.

'Punch-*baba* going to bye-lo?' said the *ayah* suggestively.

'No,' said Punch. 'Punch-*baba* wants the story about the Ranee [6] that was turned into a tiger. Meeta must tell it, and the *hamal* shall hide behind the door and make tiger-noises at the proper time.'

'But Judy-*baba* will wake up,' said the *ayah*.

'Judy-*baba* is waked,' piped a small voice from the mosquito-curtains. 'There was a Ranee that lived at Delhi. Go on, Meeta,' and she fell fast asleep again while Meeta began the story.

Never had Punch secured the telling of that tale with so little opposition. He reflected for a long time. The *hamal* made the tiger-noises in twenty different keys.

''Top!' said Punch authoritatively. 'Why doesn't Papa come in and say he is going to give me *put-put*?'

'Punch-*baba* is going away,' said the *ayah*. 'In another week there will be no Punch-*baba* to pull my hair any more.' She sighed softly, for the boy of the household was very dear to her heart.

'Up the Ghauts [7] in a train?' said Punch, standing on his bed. 'All the way to Nassick [8] where the Ranee-Tiger lives?'

'Not to Nassick this year, little Sahib,' said Meeta, lifting him on his shoulder. 'Down to the sea where the coconuts are thrown, and across the sea in a big ship. Will you take Meeta with you to *Belait*?'[9]

'You shall all come,' said Punch, from the height of Meeta's strong arms. 'Meeta and the *ayah* and the *hamal* and Bhini-in-the-Garden, and the salaam-Captain-Sahib-snake-man.'

There was no mockery in Meeta's voice when he replied: 'Great is the Sahib's favour,' and laid the little man down in the bed, while the *ayah*, sitting in the moonlight at the doorway, lulled him to sleep with an interminable canticle such as they sing in the Roman Catholic Church at Parel.[10] Punch curled himself into a ball and slept.

Next morning Judy shouted that there was a rat in the nursery, and thus he forgot to tell her the wonderful news. It did not much matter, for Judy was only three and she would not have understood. But Punch was five; and he knew that going to England would be much nicer than a trip to Nassick.

Papa and Mamma sold the brougham and the piano, and stripped the house, and curtailed the allowance of crockery for the daily meals, and took long counsel together over a bundle of letters bearing the Rocklington postmark.

'The worst of it is that one can't be certain of anything,' said Papa, pulling his moustache. 'The letters in themselves are excellent, and the terms are moderate enough.'

'The worst of it is that the children will grow up away from me,' thought Mamma; but she did not say it aloud.

'We are only one case among hundreds,' said Papa bitterly. 'You shall go Home again in five years, dear.'

'Punch will be ten then – and Judy eight. Oh, how long and long and long the time will be! And we have to leave them among strangers.'

'Punch is a cheery little chap. He's sure to make friends wherever he goes.'

'And who could help loving my Ju?'

They were standing over the cots in the nursery late at night, and I think that Mamma was crying softly. After Papa had gone away, she knelt down by the side of Judy's cot. The *ayah* saw her and put up a prayer that the Memsahib might never find the love of her children taken away from her and given to a stranger.

Mamma's own prayer was a slightly illogical one. Summarized it ran: 'Let strangers love my children and be as good to them as I should be, but let *me* preserve their love and their confidence for ever and ever. Amen.' Punch scratched himself in his sleep, and Judy moaned a little.

Next day they all went down to the sea, and there was a scene at the Apollo Bunder [11] when Punch discovered that Meeta could not come too, and Judy learned that the *ayah* must be left behind. But Punch found a thousand fascinating things in the rope, block, and steam-pipe line on the big P. & O. steamer long before Meeta and the *ayah* had dried their tears.

'Come back, Punch-*baba*,' said the *ayah*.

'Come back,' said Meeta, 'and be a *Burra Sahib* [a big man].'

'Yes,' said Punch, lifted up in his father's arms to wave good-bye. 'Yes, I will come back, and I will be a *Burra Sahib Bahadur* [a very big man indeed]!'

At the end of the first day Punch demanded to be set down in England, which he was certain must be close at hand. Next day there was a merry breeze, and Punch was very sick. 'When I come back to Bombay,' said Punch on his recovery, 'I will come by the road – in a broom-*gharri*.[12] This is a very naughty ship.'

The Swedish boatswain consoled him, and he modified his opinions as the voyage went on. There was so much to see and to handle and ask questions about that Punch nearly forgot the *ayah* and Meeta and the *hamal*, and with difficulty remembered a few words of the Hindustani once his second speech.

But Judy was much worse. The day before the steamer reached Southampton, Mamma asked her if she would not like to see the *ayah* again. Judy's blue eyes turned to the stretch of sea that had swallowed all her tiny past, and she said: '*Ayah!* What *ayah*?'

Mamma cried over her and Punch marvelled. It was then that he heard for the first time Mamma's passionate appeal to him never to let Judy forget Mamma. Seeing that Judy was young, ridiculously young, and that Mamma, every evening for four weeks past, had come into the cabin to sing her and Punch to sleep with a mysterious rune that he called 'Sonny, my soul',[13] Punch could not understand what Mamma meant. But he strove to do his duty; for, the moment Mamma left the cabin, he said to Judy: 'Ju, you bemember Mamma?'

''Torse I do,' said Judy.

'Then *always* bemember Mamma, 'r else I won't give you the paper ducks that the red-haired Captain Sahib cut out for me.'

So Judy promised always to 'bemember Mamma'.

Many and many a time was Mamma's command laid upon Punch, and Papa would say the same thing with an insistence that awed the child.

'You must make haste and learn to write, Punch,' said Papa, 'and then you'll be able to write letters to us in Bombay.'

'I'll come into your room,' said Punch, and Papa choked.

Papa and Mamma were always choking in those days. If Punch took Judy to task for not 'bemembering', they choked. If Punch sprawled on the sofa in the Southampton lodging-house and sketched his future in purple and gold, they choked; and so they did if Judy put up her mouth for a kiss.

Through many days all four were vagabonds on the face of the earth – Punch with no one to give orders to, Judy too young for anything, and Papa and Mamma grave, distracted, and choking.

'Where,' demanded Punch, wearied of a loathsome contrivance on four wheels with a mound of luggage atop – '*where* is our broom-*gharri*? This thing talks so much that *I* can't talk. Where is our *own* broom-*gharri*? When I was at Bandstand before we comed away, I asked Inverarity Sahib why he was sitting in it, and he said it was his own. And I said, "I will *give* it you" – I like Inverarity Sahib – and I said, "Can you put your legs through the pully-wag loops by the windows?" And Inverarity Sahib said No, and laughed. I can put my legs through the pully-wag loops. I can put my legs through *these* pully-wag loops. Look! Oh, Mamma's crying again! I didn't know I wasn't not to do *so*.'

Punch drew his legs out of the loops of the four-wheeler: the door opened and he slid to the earth, in a cascade of parcels, at the door of an austere little villa whose gates bore the legend 'Downe Lodge'. Punch gathered himself together and eyed the house with disfavour. It stood on a sandy road, and a cold wind tickled his knickerbockered legs.

'Let us go away,' said Punch. 'This is not a pretty place.'

But Mamma and Papa and Judy had left the cab, and all the luggage was being taken into the house. At the doorstep stood a woman in black, and she smiled largely, with dry chapped lips. Behind her was a man, big, bony, grey, and lame as to one leg – behind him a boy of twelve, black-haired and oily in appearance. Punch surveyed the trio, and advanced without fear, as he had been accustomed to do in Bombay when callers came and he happened to be playing in the verandah.

'How do you do?' said he. 'I am Punch.' But they were all looking at the luggage – all except the grey man, who shook hands with Punch, and said he was 'a smart little fellow'. There was much running about and banging of boxes, and Punch curled himself up on the sofa in the dining-room and considered things.

'I don't like these people,' said Punch. 'But never mind. We'll go away soon. We have always went away soon from everywhere. I wish we was gone back to Bombay *soon*.'

The wish bore no fruit. For six days Mamma wept at intervals, and showed the woman in black all Punch's clothes – a liberty which Punch resented. 'But p'raps she's a new white *ayah*,' he thought. 'I'm to call her Antirosa, but she doesn't call *me* Sahib. She says just Punch,' he confided to Judy. 'What is Antirosa?'

Judy didn't know. Neither she nor Punch had heard anything of an animal called an aunt. Their world had been Papa and Mamma, who knew everything, permitted everything, and loved everybody – even Punch when he used to go into the garden at Bombay and fill his nails with mould after the weekly nail-cutting, because, as he explained between two strokes of the slipper to his sorely-tried father, his fingers 'felt so new at the ends'.

In an undefined way Punch judged it advisable to keep both parents between himself and the woman in black and the boy with black hair. He did not approve of them. He liked the grey man, who had expressed a wish to be called 'Uncleharri'. They nodded at each other when they met, and the grey man showed him a little ship with rigging that took up and down.

'She is a model of the *Brisk* – the little *Brisk* that was sore exposed that day at Navarino.'[14] The grey man hummed the last words and fell into a reverie. 'I'll tell you about Navarino, Punch, when we go for walks together; and you mustn't touch the ship, because she's the *Brisk*.'

Long before that walk, the first of many, was taken, they roused Punch and Judy in the chill dawn of a February morning to say Goodbye; and of all people in the wide earth to Papa and Mamma – both crying this time. Punch was very sleepy and Judy was cross.

'Don't forget us,' pleaded Mamma. 'Oh, my little son, don't forget us, and see that Judy remembers too.'

'I've told Judy to bemember,' said Punch, wriggling, for his father's beard tickled his neck. 'I've told Judy – ten – forty – 'leven thousand times. But Ju's so young – quite a baby – isn't she?'

'Yes,' said Papa, 'quite a baby, and you must be good to Judy, and make haste to learn to write and – and – and –'

Punch was back in his bed again. Judy was fast asleep, and there was the rattle of a cab below. Papa and Mamma had gone away. Not to Nassick; that was across the sea. To some place much nearer, of course, and equally of course they would return. They came back after dinner-parties, and Papa had come back after he had been to a place called 'The Snows', and Mamma with him, to Punch and Judy at Mrs Inverarity's house in Marine Lines. Assuredly they would come back again. So Punch fell asleep till the true morning, when the black-haired boy met him with the information that Papa and Mamma had gone to Bombay, and that he and Judy were to stay at Downe Lodge 'for ever'. Antirosa, tearfully appealed to for a contradiction, said that Harry had spoken the truth, and that it behoved Punch to fold up his clothes neatly on going to bed. Punch went out and wept bitterly with Judy, into whose fair head he had driven some ideas of the meaning of separation.

When a matured man discovers that he has been deserted by Providence, deprived of his God, and cast without help, comfort, or sympathy, upon a world which is new and strange to him, his despair, which may find expression in evil living, the writing of his experiences, or the more satisfactory diversion of suicide, is generally supposed to be impressive. A child, under exactly similar circumstances as far as its knowledge goes, cannot very well curse God and die. It howls till its nose is red, its eyes are sore, and its head aches. Punch and Judy, through no fault of their own, had lost all their world. They sat in the hall and cried; the black-haired boy looking on from afar.

The model of the ship availed nothing, though the grey man assured Punch that he might pull the rigging up and down as much as he pleased; and Judy was promised free entry into the kitchen. They wanted Papa and Mamma, gone to Bombay beyond the seas, and their grief while it lasted was without remedy.

When the tears ceased the house was very still. Antirosa had decided that it was better to let the children 'have their cry out', and the boy had gone to school. Punch raised his head from the floor and sniffed mournfully. Judy was nearly asleep. Three short years had not taught her how to bear sorrow with full knowledge. There was a distant, dull boom in the air – a repeated heavy thud. Punch knew that sound in Bombay in the monsoon. It was the sea – the sea that must be traversed before anyone could get to Bombay.

'Quick, Ju!' he cried. 'We're close to the sea. I can hear it! Listen! That's where they've went. P'raps we can catch them if we was in time. They didn't mean to go without us. They've only forgot.'

'Iss,' said Judy. 'They've only forgotted. Less go to the sea.'

The hall-door was open and so was the garden-gate.

'It's very, very big, this place,' he said, looking cautiously down the road, 'and we will get lost. But *I* will find a man and order him to take me back to my house – like I did in Bombay.'

He took Judy by the hand, and the two ran hatless in the direction of the sound of the sea. Downe Lodge was almost the last of a range of newly-built houses running out, through a field of brick-mounds, to a heath where gipsies occasionally camped and where the Garrison Artillery of Rocklington practised. There were few people to be seen, and the children might have been taken for those of the soldiery who ranged far. Half an hour the wearied little legs tramped across heath, potato-patch, and sand-dune.

'I'se so tired,' said Judy, 'and Mamma will be angry.'

'Mamma's *never* angry. I suppose she is waiting at the sea now while Papa gets tickets. We'll find them and go along with them. Ju, you mustn't sit down. Only a little more and we'll come to the sea. Ju, if you sit down I'll *thmack* you!' said Punch.

They climbed another dune, and came upon the great grey sea at low tide. Hundreds of crabs were scuttling about the beach, but there was no trace of Papa and Mamma, not even of a ship upon the waters – nothing but sand and mud for miles and miles.

And 'Uncleharri' found them by chance – very muddy and very forlorn – Punch dissolved in tears, but trying to divert Judy with an 'ickle trab', and Judy wailing to the pitiless horizon for 'Mamma, Mamma!' – and again 'Mamma!'

The Second Bag

> Ah, well-a-day, for we are souls bereaved!
> Of all the creatures under Heaven's wide cope
> We are most hopeless, who had once most hope,
> And most beliefless, who had most believed.
>   *A. H. Clough.*[15]

All this time not a word about Black Sheep. He came later, and Harry, the black-haired boy, was mainly responsible for his coming.

Judy – who could help loving little Judy? – passed, by special permit, into the kitchen and thence straight to Aunty Rosa's heart. Harry was Aunty Rosa's one child, and Punch was the extra boy about the house. There was no special place for him or his little affairs, and he was forbidden to sprawl on sofas and explain his ideas about the manufacture of this world and his hopes for his future. Sprawling was lazy and wore out sofas, and little boys were not expected to talk. They were talked to, and the talking-to was intended for the benefit of their morals. As the unquestioned despot of the house at Bombay, Punch could not quite understand how he came to be of no account in this his new life.

Harry might reach across the table and take what he wanted; Judy might point and get what she wanted. Punch was forbidden to do either. The grey man was his great hope and stand-by for many months after Mamma and Papa left, and he had forgotten to tell Judy to 'bemember Mamma'.

This lapse was excusable, because in the interval he had been introduced by Aunty Rosa to two very impressive things – an abstraction called God, the intimate friend and ally of Aunty Rosa, generally believed to live behind the kitchen-range because it was hot there – and a dirty brown book filled with unintelligible dots and marks. Punch was always anxious to oblige everybody. He therefore welded the story of the Creation on to what he could recollect of his Indian fairy tales, and scandalized Aunty Rosa by repeating the result to Judy. It was a sin, a grievous sin, and Punch was talked to for a quarter of an hour. He could not understand where the iniquity came in, but was careful not to repeat the offence, because Aunty Rosa told him that God had heard every word he had said and was very angry. If this were true why didn't God come and say so, thought Punch, and dismissed the matter from his mind. Afterwards he learned to know the Lord as the only thing in the world more awful than Aunty Rosa – as a Creature that stood in the background and counted the strokes of the cane.

But the reading was, just then, a much more serious matter than any creed. Aunty Rosa sat him upon a table and told him that A B meant ab. 'Why?' said Punch. 'A is a and B is bee. *Why* does A B mean ab?'

'Because I tell you it does,' said Aunty Rosa, 'and you've got to say it.'

Punch said it accordingly, and for a month, hugely against his will, stumbled through the brown book, not in the least comprehending what it meant. But Uncle Harry, who walked much and generally alone, was wont to come into the nursery and suggest to Aunty Rosa that Punch should walk with him. He seldom spoke, but he showed Punch all Rocklington, from the mud-banks and the sand of the back-bay to the great harbours where ships lay at anchor, and the dock-yards where the hammers were never still, and the marine-store shops, and the shiny brass counters in the Offices where Uncle Harry went once every three months with a slip of blue paper and received sovereigns in exchange; for he held a wound-pension. Punch heard, too, from his lips the story of the battle of Navarino, where the sailors of the Fleet, for three days afterwards, were deaf as posts and could only sign to each other. 'That was because of the noise of the guns,' said Uncle Harry, 'and I have got the wadding of a bullet somewhere inside me now.'

Punch regarded him with curiosity. He had not the least idea what wadding was, and his notion of a bullet was a dockyard cannon-ball bigger than his own head. How could Uncle Harry keep a cannon-ball inside him? He was afraid to ask, for fear Uncle Harry might be angry.

Punch had never known what anger – real anger – meant until one terrible day when Harry had taken his paint-box to paint a boat with, and Punch had protested. Then Uncle Harry had appeared on the scene and, muttering something about 'strangers' children', had with a stick smitten the black-haired boy across the shoulders till he wept and yelled, and Aunty Rosa came in and abused Uncle Harry for cruelty to his own flesh and blood, and Punch shuddered to the tips of his shoes. 'It wasn't my fault,' he explained to the boy, but both Harry and Aunty Rosa said that it was, and that Punch had told tales, and for a week there were no more walks with Uncle Harry.

But that week brought a great joy to Punch.

He had repeated till he was thrice weary the statement that 'The Cat lay on the Mat and the Rat came in.'

'Now I can truly read,' said Punch, 'and now I will never read anything in the world.'

He put the brown book in the cupboard where his school-books lived and accidentally tumbled out a venerable volume, without covers, labelled *Sharpe's Magazine*. There was the most portentous picture of a Griffin on the first page, with verses below. The Griffin carried off one sheep a day from a German village, till a man came with a 'falchion' and split the Griffin open. Goodness only knew what a falchion was, but there was the Griffin and his history was an improvement upon the eternal Cat.

'This,' said Punch, 'means things, and now I will know all about everything in all the world.' He read till the light failed, not understanding a tithe of the meaning, but tantalized by glimpses of new worlds hereafter to be revealed.

'What is a "falchion"? What is a "e-wee lamb"? What is a "base *uss*urper"? What is a "verdant mead"?' he demanded, with flushed cheeks, at bedtime, of the astonished Aunty Rosa.

'Say your prayers and go to sleep,' she replied, and that was all the help Punch then or afterwards found at her hands in the new and delightful exercise of reading.

'Aunty Rosa only knows about God and things like that,' argued Punch. 'Uncle Harry will tell me.'

The next walk proved that Uncle Harry could not help either; but he allowed Punch to talk, and even sat down on a bench to hear about the Griffin. Other walks brought other stories as Punch ranged farther afield, for the house held large store of old books that no one ever opened – from *Frank Fairlegh*[16] in serial numbers, and the earlier poems of Tennyson, contributed anonymously to *Sharpe's Magazine*, to '62 Exhibition Catalogues, gay with colours and delightfully incomprehensible, and odd leaves of *Gulliver's Travels*.

As soon as Punch could string a few pot-hooks together he wrote to Bombay, demanding by return of post 'all the books in all the world'. Papa could not comply with this modest indent, but sent *Grimm's Fairy Tales* and a *Hans Andersen*. That was enough. If he were only left alone Punch could pass, at any hour he chose, into a land of his own, beyond reach of Aunty Rosa and her God, Harry and his teasements, and Judy's claims to be played with.

'Don't disturve me, I'm reading. Go and play in the kitchen,' grunted Punch. 'Aunty Rosa lets *you* go there.' Judy was cutting her second teeth and was fretful. She appealed to Aunty Rosa, who descended on Punch.

'I was reading,' he explained, 'reading a book. I *want* to read.'

'You're only doing that to show off,' said Aunty Rosa. 'But we'll see. Play with Judy now, and don't open a book for a week.'

Judy did not pass a very enjoyable playtime with Punch, who was consumed with indignation. There was a pettiness at the bottom of the prohibition which puzzled him.

'It's what I like to do,' he said, 'and she's found out that and stopped me. Don't cry, Ju – it wasn't your fault – *please* don't cry, or she'll say I made you.'

Ju loyally mopped up her tears, and the two played in their nursery, a room in the basement and half underground, to which they were regularly sent after the mid-day dinner while Aunty Rosa slept. She drank wine – that is to say, something from a bottle in the cellaret – for her stomach's sake, but if she did not fall asleep she would sometimes come into the nursery to see that the children were really playing. Now bricks, wooden hoops, ninepins, and chinaware cannot amuse for ever, especially when all Fairyland is to be won by the mere opening of a book, and, as often as not, Punch would be discovered reading to Judy or telling her interminable tales. That was an offence in the eyes of the law, and Judy would be whisked off by Aunty Rosa, while Punch was left to play alone, 'and be sure that I hear you doing it'.

It was not a cheering employ, for he had to make a playful noise. At last, with infinite craft, he devised an arrangement whereby the table could be supported as to three legs on toy bricks, leaving the fourth clear to bring down on the floor. He could work the table with one hand and hold the book with the other. This he did till an evil day when Aunty Rosa pounced upon him unawares and told him that he was 'acting a lie'.

'If you're old enough to do that,' she said – her temper was always worst after dinner – 'you're old enough to be beaten.'

'But – I'm – I'm not a animal!' said Punch aghast. He remembered Uncle Harry and the stick, and turned white. Aunty Rosa had hidden a light cane behind her, and Punch was beaten then and there over the shoulders. It was a revelation to him. The room-door was shut, and he was left to weep himself into repentance and work out his own gospel of life.

Aunty Rosa, he argued, had the power to beat him with many stripes. It was unjust and cruel, and Mamma and Papa would never have allowed it. Unless perhaps, as Aunty Rosa seemed to imply, they had sent secret orders. In which case he was abandoned indeed. It would be discreet in the future to propitiate Aunty Rosa, but then again, even in matters in which he was innocent, he had been accused of wishing to 'show off'. He had 'shown off' before visitors when he had attacked a strange gentleman – Harry's uncle, not his own – with requests for information about the Griffin and the falchion, and the precise nature of the Tilbury[16] in which Frank Fairlegh rode – all points of paramount interest which he was bursting to understand. Clearly it would not do to pretend to care for Aunty Rosa.

At this point Harry entered and stood afar off, eyeing Punch, a dishevelled heap in the corner of the room, with disgust.

'You're a liar – a young liar,' said Harry, with great unction, 'and you're to have tea down here because you're not fit to speak to us. And you're not to speak to Judy again till Mother gives you leave. You'll corrupt her. You're only fit to associate with the servant. Mother says so.'

Having reduced Punch to a second agony of tears, Harry departed upstairs with the news that Punch was still rebellious.

Uncle Harry sat uneasily in the dining-room. 'Damn it all, Rosa,' said he at last, 'can't you leave the child alone? He's a good enough little chap when I meet him.'

'He puts on his best manners with you, Henry,' said Aunty Rosa, 'but I'm afraid, I'm very much afraid, that he is the Black Sheep of the family.'

Harry heard and stored up the name for future use. Judy cried till she was bidden to stop, her brother not being worth tears; and the evening concluded with the return of Punch to the upper regions and a private sitting at which all the blinding horrors of Hell were revealed to Punch with such store of imagery as Aunty Rosa's narrow mind possessed.

Most grievous of all was Judy's round-eyed reproach, and Punch went to bed in the depths of the Valley of Humiliation. He shared his room with Harry and knew the torture in store. For an hour and a half he had to answer that young gentleman's questions as to his motives for telling a lie, and a grievous lie, the precise quantity of punishment inflicted by Aunty Rosa, and had also to profess his deep gratitude for such religious instruction as Harry thought fit to impart.

From that day began the downfall of Punch, now Black Sheep.

'Untrustworthy in one thing, untrustworthy in all,' said Aunty Rosa, and Harry felt that Black Sheep was delivered into his hands. He would wake him up in the night to ask him why he was such a liar.

'I don't know,' Punch would reply.

'Then don't you think you ought to get up and pray to God for a new heart?'

'Y-yess.'

'Get out and pray, then!' And Punch would get out of bed with raging hate in his heart against all the world, seen and unseen. He was always tumbling into trouble. Harry had a knack of cross-examining him as to his day's doings, which seldom failed to lead him, sleepy and savage, into half-a-dozen contradictions – all duly reported to Aunty Rosa next morning.

'But it *wasn't* a lie,' Punch would begin, charging into a laboured explanation that landed him more hopelessly in the mire. 'I said that I didn't say my prayers *twice* over in the day, and *that* was on Tuesday. *Once* I did. I *know* I did, but Harry said I didn't,' and so forth, till the tension brought tears, and he was dismissed from the table in disgrace.

'You usen't to be as bad as this,' said Judy, awestricken at the catalogue of Black Sheep's crimes. 'Why are you so bad now?'

'I don't know,' Black Sheep would reply. 'I'm not, if I only wasn't bothered upside-down. I knew what I *did*, and I want to say so; but Harry always makes it out different somehow, and Aunty Rosa doesn't believe a word I say. Oh, Ju! Don't *you* say I'm bad too.'

'Aunty Rosa says you are,' said Judy. 'She told the Vicar so when he came yesterday.'

'Why does she tell all the people outside the house about me? It isn't fair,' said Black Sheep. 'When I was in Bombay, and was bad – *doing* bad, not made-up bad like this – Mamma told Papa, and Papa told me he knew, and that was all. *Outside* people didn't know too – even Meeta didn't know.'

'I don't remember,' said Judy wistfully. 'I was all little then. Mamma was just as fond of you as she was of me, wasn't she?'

''Course she was. So was Papa. So was everybody.'

'Aunty Rosa likes me more than she does you. She says that you are a Trial and a Black Sheep, and I'm not to speak to you more than I can help.'

'Always? Not outside of the times when you mustn't speak to me at all?'

Judy nodded her head mournfully. Black Sheep turned away in despair, but Judy's arms were round his neck.

'Never mind, Punch,' she whispered. 'I *will* speak to you just the same as ever and ever. You're my own own brother though you are – though Aunty Rosa says you're bad, and Harry says you are a little coward. He says that if I pulled your hair hard, you'd cry.'

'Pull, then,' said Punch.

Judy pulled gingerly.

'Pull harder – as hard as you can! There! I don't mind how much you pull it *now*. If you'll speak to me same as ever I'll let you pull it as much as you like – pull it out if you like. But I know if Harry came and stood by and made you do it I'd cry.'

So the two children sealed the compact with a kiss, and Black Sheep's heart was cheered within him, and by extreme caution and careful avoidance of Harry he acquired virtue, and was allowed to read undisturbed for a week. Uncle Harry took him for walks, and consoled him with rough tenderness, never calling him Black Sheep. 'It's good for you, I suppose, Punch,' he used to say. 'Let us sit down. I'm getting tired.' His steps led him now not to the beach, but to the Cemetery of Rocklington, amid the potato-fields. For hours the grey man would sit on a tombstone, while Black Sheep would read epitaphs, and then with a sigh would stump home again.

'I shall lie there soon,' said he to Black Sheep, one winter evening, when his face showed white as a worn silver coin under the light of the lych gate. 'You needn't tell Aunty Rosa.'

A month later he turned sharp round, ere half a morning walk was completed, and stumped back to the house. 'Put me to bed, Rosa,' he muttered. 'I've walked my last. The wadding has found me out.'

They put him to bed, and for a fortnight the shadow of his sickness lay upon the house, and Black Sheep went to and fro unobserved. Papa had sent him some new books, and he was told to keep quiet. He retired into his own world, and was perfectly happy. Even at night his felicity was unbroken. He could lie in bed and string himself tales of travel and adventure while Harry was downstairs.

'Uncle Harry's going to die,' said Judy, who now lived almost entirely with Aunty Rosa.

'I'm very sorry,' said Black Sheep soberly. 'He told me that a long time ago.'

Aunty Rosa heard the conversation. 'Will nothing check your wicked tongue?' she said angrily. There were blue circles round her eyes.

Black Sheep retreated to the nursery and read *Cometh up as a Flower* [18] with deep and uncomprehending interest. He had been forbidden to open it on account of its 'sinfulness', but the bonds of the Universe were crumbling, and Aunty Rosa was in great grief.

'I'm glad,' said Black Sheep. 'She's unhappy now. It wasn't a lie, though. *I* knew. He told me not to tell.'

That night Black Sheep woke with a start. Harry was not in the room, and there was a sound of sobbing on the next floor. Then the voice of Uncle Harry, singing the song of the Battle of Navarino, came through the darkness:

> 'Our vanship was the *Asia* –
> The *Albion* and *Genoa*!'

'He's getting well,' thought Black Sheep, who knew the song through all its seventeen verses. But the blood froze at his little heart as he thought. The voice leapt an octave, and ran shrill as a boatswain's pipe:

> 'And next came on the lovely *Rose*,
> The *Philomel*, her fire-ship, closed,
> And the little *Brisk* was sore exposed
> That day at Navarino.'

'That day at Navarino, Uncle Harry!' shouted Black Sheep, half wild with excitement and fear of he knew not what.

A door opened, and Aunty Rosa screamed up the staircase: 'Hush! For God's sake hush, you little devil! Uncle Harry is *dead*!'

The Third Bag

> Journeys end in lovers' meeting,
> Every wise man's son doth know. [19]

'I wonder what will happen to me now,' thought Black Sheep, when semi-pagan rites peculiar to the burial of the Dead in middle-class houses had been accomplished, and Aunty Rosa, awful in black crape, had returned to this life. 'I don't think I've done anything bad that she knows of. I suppose I will soon. She will be very cross after Uncle Harry's dying, and Harry will be cross too. I'll keep in the nursery.'

Unfortunately for Punch's plans, it was decided that he should be sent to a day-school which Harry attended. This meant a morning walk with Harry, and perhaps an evening one; but the prospect of freedom in the interval was refreshing. 'Harry'll tell everything I do, but I won't do anything,' said Black Sheep. Fortified with this virtuous resolution, he went to school only to find that Harry's version of his character had preceded him, and that life was a burden in consequence. He took stock of his associates. Some of them were unclean, some of them talked in dialect, many dropped their h's, and there were two Jews and a negro, or someone quite as dark, in the assembly. 'That's a *hubshi*,'[20] said Black Sheep to himself. 'Even Meeta used to laugh at a *hubshi*. I don't think this is a proper place.' He was indignant for at least an hour, till he reflected that any expostulation on his part would be by Aunty Rosa construed into 'showing off', and that Harry would tell the boys.

'How do you like school?' said Aunty Rosa at the end of the day.

'I think it is a very nice place,' said Punch quietly.

'I suppose you warned the boys of Black Sheep's character?' said Aunty Rosa to Harry.

'Oh yes,' said the censor of Black Sheep's morals. 'They know all about him.'

'If I was with my father,' said Black Sheep, stung to the quick, 'I shouldn't *speak* to those boys. He wouldn't let me. They live in shops. I saw them go into shops – where their fathers live and sell things.'

'You're too good for that school, are you?' said Aunty Rosa, with a bitter smile. 'You ought to be grateful, Black Sheep, that those boys speak to you at all. It isn't every school that takes little liars.'

Harry did not fail to make much capital out of Black Sheep's ill-considered remark; with the result that several boys, including the *hubshi*, demonstrated to Black Sheep the eternal equality of the human race by smacking his head, and his consolation from Aunty Rosa was that it 'served him right for being vain'. He learned, however, to keep his opinions to himself, and by propitiating Harry in carrying books and the like to get a little peace. His existence was not too joyful. From nine till twelve he was at school, and from two to four, except on Saturdays. In the evenings he was sent down into the nursery to prepare his lessons for the next day, and every night came the dreaded cross-questionings at Harry's hand. Of Judy he saw but little. She was deeply religious – at six years of age Religion is easy to come by – and sorely divided between her natural love for Black Sheep and her love for Aunty Rosa, who could do no wrong.

The lean woman returned that love with interest, and Judy, when she dared, took advantage of this for the remission of Black Sheep's penalties. Failures in lessons at school were punished at home by a week without reading other than school-books, and Harry brought the news of such a failure with glee. Further, Black Sheep was then bound to repeat his lessons at bedtime to Harry, who generally succeeded in making him break down, and consoled him by gloomiest forebodings for the morrow. Harry was at once spy, practical joker, inquisitor, and Aunty Rosa's deputy executioner. He filled his many posts to admiration. From his actions, now that Uncle Harry was dead, there was no appeal. Black Sheep had not been permitted to keep any self-respect at school: at home he was, of course, utterly discredited, and grateful for any pity that the servant-girls – they changed frequently at Downe Lodge because they, too, were liars – might show. 'You're just fit to row in the same boat with Black Sheep,' was a sentiment that each new Jane or Eliza might expect to hear, before a month was over, from Aunty Rosa's lips; and Black Sheep was used to ask new girls whether they had yet been compared to him. Harry was 'Master Harry' in their mouths; Judy was officially 'Miss Judy'; but Black Sheep was never anything more than Black Sheep *tout court*.[21]

As time went on and the memory of Papa and Mamma became wholly overlaid by the unpleasant task of writing them letters, under Aunty Rosa's eye, each Sunday, Black Sheep forgot what manner of life he had led in the beginning of things. Even Judy's appeals to 'try and remember about Bombay' failed to quicken him.

'I can't remember,' he said. 'I know I used to give orders and Mamma kissed me.'

'Aunty Rosa will kiss you if you are good,' pleaded Judy.

'Ugh! I don't want to be kissed by Aunty Rosa. She'd say I was doing it to get something more to eat.'

The weeks lengthened into months, and the holidays came; but just before the holidays Black Sheep fell into deadly sin.

Among the many boys whom Harry had incited to 'punch Black Sheep's head because he daren't hit back', was one more aggravating than the rest, who, in an unlucky moment, fell upon Black Sheep when Harry was not near. The blows stung, and Black Sheep struck back at random with all the power at his command. The boy dropped and whimpered. Black Sheep was astounded at his own act, but, feeling the unresisting body under him, shook it with both his hands in blind fury and then began to throttle his enemy; meaning honestly to slay him. There was a scuffle, and Black Sheep was torn off the body by Harry and some colleagues, and cuffed home tingling but exultant. Aunty Rosa was out. Pending her arrival, Harry set himself to lecture Black Sheep on the sin of murder – which he described as the offence of Cain.

'Why didn't you fight him fair? What did you hit him when he was down for, you little cur?'

Black Sheep looked up at Harry's throat and then at a knife on the dinner-table.

'I don't understand,' he said wearily. 'You always set him on me and told me I was a coward when I blubbed. Will you leave me alone until Aunty Rosa comes in? She'll beat me if you tell her I ought to be beaten; so it's all right.'

'It's all wrong,' said Harry magisterially. 'You nearly killed him, and I shouldn't wonder if he dies.'

'Will he die?' said Black Sheep.

'I daresay,' said Harry, 'and then you'll be hanged, and go to Hell.'

'All right,' said Black Sheep, picking up the table-knife. 'Then I'll kill *you* now. You say things and do things and – and *I* don't know how things happen, and you never leave me alone – and I don't care *what* happens!'

He ran at the boy with the knife, and Harry fled upstairs to his room, promising Black Sheep the finest thrashing in the world when Aunty Rosa returned. Black Sheep sat at the bottom of the stairs, the table-knife in his hand, and wept for that he had not killed Harry. The servant-girl came up from the kitchen, took the knife away, and consoled him. But Black Sheep was beyond consolation. He would be badly beaten by Aunty Rosa; then there would be another beating at Harry's hands; then Judy would not be allowed to speak to him; then the tale would be told at school, and then –

There was no one to help and no one to care, and the best way out of the business was by death. A knife would hurt, but Aunty Rosa had told him, a year ago, that if he sucked paint he would die. He went into the nursery, unearthed the now disused Noah's Ark, and sucked the paint off as many animals as remained. It tasted abominably, but he had licked Noah's Dove clean by the time Aunty Rosa and Judy returned. He went upstairs and greeted them with: 'Please, Aunty Rosa, I believe I've nearly killed a boy at school, and I've tried to kill Harry, and when you've done all about God and Hell, will you beat me and get it over?'

The tale of the assault as told by Harry could only be explained on the ground of possession by the Devil. Wherefore Black Sheep was not only most excellently beaten, once by Aunty Rosa, and once, when thoroughly cowed down, by Harry but he was further prayed for at family prayers, together with Jane, who had stolen a cold rissole from the pantry, and snuffled audibly as her sin was brought before the Throne of Grace. Black Sheep was sore and stiff but triumphant. He would die that very night and be rid of them all. No, he would ask for no forgiveness from Harry, and at bed-time would stand no questioning at Harry's hands, even though addressed as 'Young Cain'.

'I've been beaten,' said he, 'and I've done other things. I don't care what I do. If you speak to me tonight, Harry, I'll get out and try to kill you. Now you can kill me if you like.'

Harry took his bed into the spare room, and Black Sheep lay down to die.

It may be that the makers of Noah's Arks know that their animals are likely to find their way into young mouths, and paint them accordingly. Certain it is that the common, weary next morning broke through the windows and found Black Sheep quite well and a good deal ashamed of himself, but richer by the knowledge that he could, in extremity, secure himself against Harry for the future.

When he descended to breakfast on the first day of the holidays, he was greeted with the news that Harry, Aunty Rosa, and Judy were going away to Brighton, while Black Sheep was to stay in the house with the servant. His latest outbreak suited Aunty Rosa's plans admirably. It gave her good excuse for leaving the extra boy behind. Papa in Bombay, who really seemed to know a young sinner's wants to the hour, sent, that week, a package of new books. And with these, and the society of Jane on board-wages, Black Sheep was left alone for a month.

The books lasted for ten days. They were eaten too quickly in long gulps of twelve hours at a time. Then came days of doing absolutely nothing, of dreaming dreams and marching imaginary armies up and down stairs, of counting the number of banisters, and of measuring the length and breadth of every room in handspans – fifty down the side, thirty across, and fifty back again. Jane made many friends, and, after receiving Black Sheep's assurance that he would not tell of her absences, went out daily for long hours. Black Sheep would follow the rays of the sinking sun from the kitchen to the dining-room and thence upward to his own bedroom until all was grey dark, and he ran down to the kitchen fire and read by its light. He was happy in that he was left alone and could read as much as he pleased. But, later, he grew afraid of the shadows of window curtains and the flapping of doors and the creaking of shutters. He went out into the garden, and the rustling of the laurel-bushes frightened him.

He was glad when they all returned – Aunty Rosa, Harry, and Judy – full of news, and Judy laden with gifts. Who could help loving loyal little Judy? In return for all her merry babblement, Black Sheep confided to her that the distance from the hall-door to the top of the first landing was exactly one-hundred and eighty-four handspans. He had found it out himself!

Then the old life recommenced; but with a difference, and a new sin. To his other iniquities Black Sheep had now added a phenomenal clumsiness – was as unfit to trust in action as he was in word. He himself could not account for spilling everything he touched, upsetting glasses as he put his hand out, and bumping his head against doors that were manifestly shut. There was a grey haze upon all his world, and it narrowed month by month, until at last it left Black Sheep almost alone with the flapping curtains that were so like ghosts, and the nameless terrors of broad daylight that were only coats on pegs after all.

Holidays came and holidays went, and Black Sheep was taken to see many people whose faces were all exactly alike; was beaten when occasion demanded, and tortured by Harry on all possible occasions; but defended by Judy through good and evil report, though she hereby drew upon herself the wrath of Aunty Rosa.

The weeks were interminable and Papa and Mamma were clean forgotten. Harry had left school and was a clerk in a Banking-Office.

Freed from his presence, Black Sheep resolved that he should no longer be deprived of his allowance of pleasure-reading. Consequently when he failed at school he reported that all was well, and conceived a large contempt for Aunty Rosa as he saw how easy it was to deceive her. 'She says I'm a little liar when I don't tell lies, and now I do, she doesn't know,' thought Black Sheep. Aunty Rosa had credited him in the past with petty cunning and stratagem that had never entered into his head. By the light of the sordid knowledge that she had revealed to him he paid her back full tale. In a household where the most innocent of his motives, his natural yearning for a little affection, had been interpreted into a desire for more bread and jam, or to ingratiate himself with strangers and so put Harry into the background, his work was easy. Aunty Rosa could penetrate certain kinds of hypocrisy, but not all. He set his child's wits against hers and was no more beaten. It grew monthly more and more of a trouble to read the school-books, and even the pages of the open-print story-books danced and were dim. So Black Sheep brooded in the shadows that fell about him and cut him off from the world, inventing horrible punishments for 'dear Harry', or plotting another line of the tangled web of deception that he wrapped round Aunty Rosa.

Then the crash came and the cobwebs were broken. It was impossible to foresee everything. Aunty Rosa made personal inquiries as to Black Sheep's progress and received information that startled her. Step by step, with a delight as keen as when she convicted an underfed housemaid of the theft of cold meats, she followed the trail of Black Sheep's delinquencies. For weeks and weeks, in order to escape banishment from the book-shelves, he had made a fool of Aunty Rosa, of Harry, of God, of all the world! Horrible, most horrible, and evidence of an utterly depraved mind.

Black Sheep counted the cost. 'It will only be one big beating and then she'll put a card with "Liar" on my back, same as she did before. Harry will whack me and pray for me, and she will pray for me at prayers and tell me I'm a Child of the Devil and give me hymns to learn. But I've done all my reading and she never knew. She'll say she knew all along. She's an old liar too,' said he.

For three days Black Sheep was shut in his own bedroom – to prepare his heart. 'That means two beatings. One at school and one here. *That* one will hurt most.' And it fell even as he thought. He was thrashed at school before the Jews and the *hubshi* for the heinous crime of carrying home false reports of progress. He was thrashed at home by Aunty Rosa on the same count, and then the placard was produced. Aunty Rosa stitched it between his shoulders and bade him go for a walk with it upon him.

'If you make me do that,' said Black Sheep very quietly, 'I shall burn this house down, and perhaps I'll kill you. I don't know whether I *can* kill you – you're so bony – but I'll try.'

No punishment followed this blasphemy, though Black Sheep held himself ready to work his way to Aunty Rosa's withered throat, and grip there till he was beaten off. Perhaps Aunty Rosa was afraid, for Black Sheep, having reached the Nadir of Sin, bore himself with a new recklessness.

In the midst of all the trouble there came a visitor from over the seas to Downe Lodge, who knew Papa and Mamma, and was commissioned to see Punch and Judy. Black Sheep was sent to the drawing-room and charged into a solid tea-table laden with china.

'Gently, gently, little man,' said the visitor, turning Black Sheep's face to the light slowly. 'What's that big bird on the palings?'

'What bird?' asked Black Sheep.

The visitor looked deep down into Black Sheep's eyes for half a minute, and then said suddenly: 'Good God, the little chap's nearly blind!'

It was a most businesslike visitor. He gave orders, on his own responsibility, that Black Sheep was not to go to school or open a book until Mamma came home. 'She'll be here in three weeks, as you know, of course,' said he, 'and I'm Inverarity Sahib. I ushered you into this wicked world, young man, and a nice use you seem to have made of your time. You must do nothing whatever. Can you do that?'

'Yes,' said Punch in a dazed way. He had not known that Mamma was coming. There was a chance, then, of another beating. Thank Heaven, Papa wasn't coming too. Aunty Rosa had said of late that he ought to be beaten by a man.

For the next three weeks Black Sheep was strictly allowed to do nothing. He spent his time in the old nursery looking at the broken toys, for all of which account must be rendered to Mamma. Aunty Rosa hit him over the hands if even a wooden boat were broken. But that sin was of small importance compared to the other revelations, so darkly hinted at by Aunty Rosa. 'When your Mother comes, and hears what I have to tell her, she may appreciate you properly,' she said grimly, and mounted guard over Judy lest that small maiden should attempt to comfort her brother, to the peril of her soul.

And Mamma came — in a four-wheeler — fluttered with tender excitement. Such a Mamma! She was young, frivolously young, and beautiful, with delicately flushed cheeks, eyes that shone like stars, and a voice that needed no appeal of outstretched arms to draw little ones to her heart. Judy ran straight to her, but Black Sheep hesitated. Could this wonder be 'showing off'? She would not put out her arms when she knew of his crimes. Meantime was it possible that by fondling she wanted to get anything out of Black Sheep? Only all his love and all his confidence; but that Black Sheep did not know. Aunty Rosa withdrew and left Mamma, kneeling between her children, half laughing, half crying, in the very hall where Punch and Judy had wept five years before.

'Well, chicks, do you remember me?'

'No,' said Judy frankly, 'but I said, "God bless Papa and Mamma" ev'vy night.'

'A little,' said Black Sheep. 'Remember I wrote to you every week, anyhow. That isn't to show off, but 'cause of what comes afterwards.'

'What comes after? What should come after, my darling boy?' And she drew him to her again. He came awkwardly, with many angles. 'Not used to petting,' said the quick Mother-soul. 'The girl is.'

'She's too little to hurt anyone,' thought Black Sheep, 'and if I said I'd kill her, she'd be afraid. I wonder what Aunty Rosa will tell.'

There was a constrained late dinner, at the end of which Mamma picked up Judy and put her to bed with endearments manifold. Faithless little Judy had shown her defection from Aunty Rosa already. And that lady resented it bitterly. Black Sheep rose to leave the room.

'Come and say good-night,' said Aunty Rosa offering a withered cheek.

'Huh!' said Black Sheep. 'I never kiss you, and I'm not going to show off. Tell that woman what I've done, and see what she says.'

Black Sheep climbed into bed feeling that he had lost Heaven after a glimpse through the gates. In half an hour 'that woman' was bending over him. Black Sheep flung up his right arm. It wasn't fair to come and hit him in the dark. Even Aunty Rosa never tried that. But no blow followed.

'Are you showing off? I won't tell you anything more than Aunty Rosa has, and *she* doesn't know everything,' said Black Sheep as clearly as he could for the arms round his neck.

'Oh, my son – my little, little son! It was my fault – *my* fault, darling – and yet how could we help it? Forgive me, Punch.' The voice died out in a broken whisper, and two hot tears fell on Black Sheep's forehead.

'Has she been making you cry too?' he asked. 'You should see Jane cry. But you're nice, and Jane is a Born Liar – Aunty Rosa says so.'

'Hush, Punch, hush! My boy, don't talk like that. Try to love me a little bit – a little bit. You don't know how I want it. Punch-*baba*, come back to me! I am your Mother – your own Mother – and never mind the rest. I know – yes, I know, dear. It doesn't matter now. Punch, won't you care for me a little?'

It is astonishing how much petting a big boy of ten can endure when he is quite sure that there is no one to laugh at him. Black Sheep had never been made much of before, and here was this beautiful woman treating him – Black Sheep, the Child of the Devil and the inheritor of undying flame – as though he were a small God.

'I care for you a great deal, Mother dear,' he whispered at last, 'and I'm glad you've come back; but are you sure Aunty Rosa told you everything?'

'Everything. What *does* it matter? But –' the voice broke with a sob that was also laughing – 'Punch, my poor, dear, half-blind darling, don't you think it was a little foolish of you?'

'*No.* It saved a lickin'.'

Mamma shuddered and slipped away in the darkness to write a long letter to Papa. Here is an extract:

. . . Judy is a dear, plump little prig who adores the woman, and wears with as much gravity as her religious opinions – only eight, Jack! – a venerable horsehair atrocity which she calls her Bustle! I have just burnt it, and the child is asleep in my bed as I write. She will come to me at once. Punch I cannot quite understand. He is well nourished, but seems to have been worried into a system of small deceptions which the woman magnifies into deadly sins. Don't you recollect our own upbringing, dear, when the Fear of the Lord was so often the beginning of falsehood? I shall win Punch to me before long. I am taking the children away into the country to get them to know me, and, on the whole, I am content, or shall be when you come home, dear boy, and then, thank God, we shall be all under one roof again at last!

Three months later, Punch, no longer Black Sheep, has discovered that he is the veritable owner of a real, live, lovely Mamma, who is also a sister, comforter, and friend, and that he must protect her till the Father comes home. Deception does not suit the part of a protector, and, when one can do anything without question, where is the use of deception?

'Mother would be awfully cross if you walked through that ditch,' says Judy, continuing a conversation.

'Mother's never angry,' says Punch. 'She'd just say, "You're a little *pagal* [idiot]"; and that's not nice, but I'll show.'

Punch walks through the ditch and mires himself to the knees. 'Mother dear,' he shouts, 'I'm just as dirty as I can pos-*sib*-ly be!'

'Then change your clothes as quickly as you pos-*sib*-ly can!' Mother's clear voice rings out from the house. 'And don't be a little *pagal*!'

'There! Told you so,' says Punch. 'It's all different now, and we are just as much Mother's as if she had never gone.'

Not altogether, O Punch, for when young lips have drunk deep of the bitter waters of Hate, Suspicion, and Despair, all the Love in the world will not wholly take away that knowledge; though it may turn darkened eyes for a while to the light, and teach Faith where no Faith was.

The Head of the District [1]

There's a convict more in the Central Jail,
　　Behind the old mud wall;
There's a lifter less on the Border trail,
　　And the Queen's Peace over all,
　　　　Dear boys,
　　The Queen's Peace over all.

For we must bear our leader's blame,
　　On us the shame will fall,
If we lift our hand from a fettered land
　　And the Queen's Peace over all,
　　　　Dear boys,
　　The Queen's Peace over all!
　　　　　The Running of Shindand.

I

The Indus had risen in flood without warning. Last night it was a fordable shallow; tonight five miles of raving muddy water parted bank and caving bank, and the river was still rising under the moon. A litter borne by six bearded men, all unused to the work, stopped in the white sand that bordered the whiter plain.

'It's God's will,' they said. 'We dare not cross tonight, even in a boat. Let us light a fire and cook food. We be tired men.'

They looked at the litter inquiringly. Within, the Deputy Commissioner of the Kot-Kumharsen district lay dying of fever. They had brought him across country, six fighting-men of a frontier clan that he had won over to the paths of a moderate righteousness, when he had broken down at the foot of their inhospitable hills. And Tallantire, his assistant, rode with them, heavy-hearted as heavy-eyed with sorrow and lack of sleep. He had served under the sick man for three years, and had learned to love him as men associated in toil of the hardest learn to love – or hate. Dropping from his horse he parted the curtains of the litter and peered inside.

'Orde – Orde, old man, can you hear? We have to wait till the river goes down, worse luck.'

'I hear,' returned a dry whisper. 'Wait till the river goes down. I

164

thought we should reach camp before the dawn. Polly knows. She'll meet me.'

One of the litter-men stared across the river and caught a faint twinkle of light on the far side. He whispered to Tallantire, 'There are his campfires, and his wife. They will cross in the morning, for they have better boats. Can he live so long?'

Tallantire shook his head. Yardley-Orde was very near to death. What need to vex his soul with hopes of a meeting that could not be? The river gulped at the banks, brought down a cliff of sand, and snarled the more hungrily. The litter-men sought for fuel in the waste – dried camelthorn and refuse of the camps that had waited at the ford. Their swordbelts clinked as they moved softly in the haze of the moonlight, and Tallantire's horse coughed to explain that he would like a blanket.

'I'm cold too,' said the voice from the litter. 'I fancy this is the end. Poor Polly!'

Tallantire rearranged the blankets; Khoda Dad Khan, seeing this, stripped off his own heavy-wadded sheepskin coat and added it to the pile. 'I shall be warm by the fire presently,' said he. Tallantire took the wasted body of his chief into his arms and held it against his breast. Perhaps if they kept him very warm Orde might live to see his wife once more. If only blind Providence would send a three-foot fall in the river!

'That's better,' said Orde faintly. 'Sorry to be a nuisance, but is – is there anything to drink?'

They gave him milk and whisky, and Tallantire felt a little warmth against his own breast. Orde began to mutter.

'It isn't that I mind dying,' he said. 'It's leaving Polly and the district. Thank God! we have no children. Dick, you know, I'm dipped – awfully dipped – debts in my first five years' service. It isn't much of a pension, but enough for her. She has her mother at home. Getting there is the difficulty. And – and – you see, not being a soldier's wife –'

'We'll arrange the passage home, of course,' said Tallantire quietly.

'It's not nice to think of sending round the hat; but, good Lord! how many men I lie here and remember that had to do it! Morten's dead – he was of my year. Shaughnessy is dead, and he had children; I remember he used to read us their school-letters; what a bore we thought him! Evans is dead – Kot-Kumharsen killed him! Ricketts of Myndonie is dead – and I'm going too. "Man that is born of a woman is small potatoes and few in the hill."[2] That reminds me, Dick; the four Khusru Kheyl villages in our border want a one-third remittance this spring. That's fair; their crops are bad. See that they get it, and speak to Ferris about the canal. I should like to have lived till that was finished; it means so much for the North-Indus villages – but Ferris is an idle beggar – wake him up. You'll have charge of the district till my successor comes. I wish they would appoint you permanently; you know the folk. I suppose it will be Bullows, though. Good man, but too weak for frontier work; and he doesn't understand the priests. The blind priest at Jagai will bear watching. You'll find it in my papers – in the uniform case, I think. Call the Khusru Kheyl men up; I'll hold my last public audience. Khoda Dad Khan!'

The leader of the men sprang to the side of the litter, his companions following.

'Men, I'm dying,' said Orde quickly, in the vernacular; 'and soon there will be no more Orde Sahib to twist your tails and prevent you from raiding cattle.'

'God forbid this thing!' broke out the deep bass chorus. 'The Sahib is not going to die.'

'Yes, he is; and then he will know whether Mahomed speaks truth, or Moses. But you must be good men when I am not here. Such of you as live in our borders must pay your taxes quietly as before. I have spoken of the villages to be gently treated this year. Such of you as live in the hills must refrain from cattle-lifting, and burn no more thatch, and turn a deaf ear to the voice of the priests, who, not knowing the strength of the Government, would lead you into foolish wars, wherein you will surely die and your crops be eaten by strangers. And you must not sack any caravans, and must leave your arms at the police-post when you come in; as has been your custom, and my order. And Tallantire Sahib will be with you, but I do not know who takes my place. I speak now true talk, for I am as it were already dead, my children – for though ye be strong men, ye are children.'

'And thou art our father and our mother,' broke in Khoda Dad Khan with an oath. 'What shall we do, now there is no one to speak for us, or to teach us to go wisely!'

'There remains Tallantire Sahib. Go to him; he knows your talk and your heart. Keep the young men quiet, listen to the old men, and obey. Khoda Dad Khan, take my ring. The watch and chain go to thy brother. Keep those things for my sake, and I will speak to whatever God I may encounter and tell him that the Khusru Kheyl are good men. Ye have my leave to go.'

Khoda Dad Khan, the ring upon his finger, choked audibly as he caught the well-known formula that closed an interview. His brother turned to look across the river. The dawn was breaking, and a speck of white showed on the dull silver of the stream. 'She comes,' said the man under his breath. 'Can he live for another two hours?' And he pulled the newly-acquired watch out of his belt and looked uncomprehendingly at the dial, as he had seen Englishmen do.

For two hours the bellying sail tacked and blundered up and down the river, Tallantire still clasping Orde in his arms, and Khoda Dad Khan chafing his feet. He spoke now and again of the district and his wife, but, as the end neared, more frequently of the latter. They hoped he did not know that she was even then risking her life in a crazy native boat to regain him. But the awful foreknowledge of the dying deceived them. Wrenching himself forward, Orde looked through the curtains and saw how near was the sail. 'That's Polly,' he said simply, though his mouth was wried with agony. 'Polly and – the grimmest practical joke ever played on a man. Dick – you'll – have – to – explain.'

And an hour later Tallantire met on the bank a woman in a gingham riding-habit and a sun-hat who cried out to him for her husband – her boy and her darling – while Khoda Dad Khan threw himself face-down on the sand and covered his eyes.

II

The very simplicity of the notion was its charm. What more easy to win a reputation for far-seeing statesmanship, originality, and, above all, deference to the desires of the people, than by appointing a child of the country to the rule of that country? Two hundred millions of the most loving and grateful folk under Her Majesty's dominion would laud the fact, and their praise would endure for ever. Yet he was indifferent to praise or blame, as befitted the Very Greatest of All the Viceroys.[3] His administration was based upon principle, and the principle must be enforced in season and out of season. His pen and tongue had created the New India, teeming with possibilities – loud-voiced, insistent, a nation among nations – all his very own. Wherefore the Very Greatest of All the Viceroys took another step in advance, and with it counsel of those who should have advised him on the appointment of a successor to Yardley-Orde. There was a gentleman and a member of the Bengal Civil Service who had won his place and a university degree to boot in fair and open competition with the sons of the English. He was cultured, of the world, and, if report spoke truly, had wisely and, above all, sympathetically ruled a crowded district in South-Eastern Bengal. He had been to England and charmed many drawing-rooms there. His name, if the Viceroy recollected aright, was Mr Grish Chunder Dé, MA. In short, did anybody see any objection to the appointment, always on principle, of a man of the people to rule the people? The district in South-Eastern Bengal might with advantage, he apprehended, pass over to a younger civilian of Mr G. C. Dé's nationality (who had written a remarkably clever pamphlet on the political value of sympathy in administration); and Mr G. C. Dé could be transferred northward to Kot-Kumharsen. The Viceroy was averse, on principle, to interfering with appointments under control of the Provincial Governments. He wished it to be understood that he merely recommended and advised in this instance. As regarded the mere question of race, Mr Grish Chunder Dé was more English than the English, and yet possessed of that peculiar sympathy and insight which the best among the best Service in the world could only win to at the end of their service.

The stern, black-bearded kings who sit about the Council-board of India divided on the step, with the inevitable result of driving the Very Greatest of All the Viceroys into the borders of hysteria, and a bewildered obstinacy pathetic as that of a child.

'The principle is sound enough,' said the weary-eyed Head of the Red Provinces in which Kot-Kumharsen lay, for he too held theories. 'The only difficulty is –'

'Put the screw on the district officials; brigade Dé with a very strong Deputy Commissioner on each side of him; give him the best assistant in the Province; rub the fear of God into the people beforehand; and if anything goes wrong, say that his colleagues didn't back him up. All these lovely little experiments recoil on the District-Officer in the end,' said the Knight of the Drawn Sword[4] with a truthful brutality that made the Head of the Red Provinces shudder. And on a tacit understanding of this kind the transfer was accomplished, as quietly as might be for many reasons.

It is sad to think that what goes for public opinion in India did not generally see the wisdom of the Viceroy's appointment. There were not lacking indeed hireling organs, notoriously in the pay of a tyrannous bureaucracy, who more than hinted that His Excellency was a fool, a dreamer of dreams, a doctrinaire, and, worst of all, a trifler with the lives of men. 'The Viceroy's Excellence Gazette', published in Calcutta, was at pains to thank 'Our beloved Viceroy for once more and again thus gloriously vindicating the potentialities of the Bengali nations for extended executive and administrative duties in foreign parts beyond our ken. We do not at all doubt that our excellent fellow-townsman, Mr Grish Chunder Dé, Esq., MA, will uphold the prestige of the Bengali, notwithstanding what underhand intrigue and *peshbundi*[5] may be set on foot to insidiously nip his fame and blast his prospects among the proud

civilians,[6] some of which will now have to serve under a despised
native and take orders too. How will you like that, Misters? We entreat
our beloved Viceroy still to substantiate himself superiorly to race-
prejudice and colour-blindness, and to allow the flower of this now
our Civil Service all the full pays and allowances granted to his more
fortunate brethren.'

III

'When does this man take over charge? I'm alone just now, and I gather
that I'm to stand fast under him.'

'Would you have cared for a transfer?' said Bullows keenly. Then,
laying his hand on Tallantire's shoulder: 'We're all in the same boat;
don't desert us. And yet, why the devil should you stay, if you can get
another charge?'

'It was Orde's,' said Tallantire simply.

'Well, it's Dé's now. He's a Bengali of the Bengalis, crammed with
code and case law; a beautiful man so far as routine and deskwork go,
and pleasant to talk to. They naturally have always kept him in his own
home district, where all his sisters and his cousins and his aunts[7] lived,
somewhere south of Dacca. He did no more than turn the place into a
pleasant little family preserve, allowed his subordinates to do what they
liked, and let everybody have a chance at the shekels. Consequently he's
immensely popular down there.'

'I've nothing to do with that. How on earth am I to explain to the
district that they are going to be governed by a Bengali? Do you – does
the Government, I mean – suppose that the Khusru Kheyl will sit quiet
when they once know? What will the Mahomedan heads of villages say?
How will the police – Muzbi Sikhs and Pathans – how will *they* work
under him? We couldn't say anything if the Government appointed a
sweeper; but my people will say a good deal, you know that. It's a piece
of cruel folly!'

'My dear boy, I know all that, and more. I've represented it, and have
been told that I am exhibiting "culpable and puerile prejudice". By
Jove, if the Khusru Kheyl don't exhibit something worse than that I
don't know the Border! The chances are that you will have the district
alight on your hands, and I shall have to leave my work and help you
pull through. I needn't ask you to stand by the Bengali man in every
possible way. You'll do that for your own sake.'

'For Orde's. I can't say that I care twopence personally.'

'Don't be an ass. It's grievous enough, God knows, and the Government will know later on; but that's no reason for your sulking. *You* must try to run the district; *you* must stand between him and as much insult as possible; *you* must show him the ropes; *you* must pacify the Khusru Kheyl, and just warn Curbar of the Police to look out for trouble by the way. I'm always at the end of a telegraph-wire, and willing to peril my reputation to hold the district together. You'll lose yours, of course. If you keep things straight, and he isn't actually beaten with a stick when he's on tour, he'll get all the credit. If anything goes wrong, you'll be told that you didn't support him loyally.'

'I know what I've got to do,' said Tallantire wearily, 'and I'm going to it. But it's hard.'

'The work is with us, the event is with Allah – as Orde used to say when he was more than usually in hot water.' And Bullows rode away.

That two gentlemen in Her Majesty's Bengal Civil Service should thus discuss a third, also in that service, and a cultured and affable man withal, seems strange and saddening. Yet listen to the artless babble of the Blind Mullah of Jagai, the priest of the Khusru Kheyl, sitting upon a rock overlooking the Border. Five years before, a chance-hurled shell from a screw-gun [8] battery had dashed earth in the face of the Mullah, then urging a rush of Ghazis [9] against half a dozen British bayonets. So he became blind, and hated the English none the less for the little accident. Yardley-Orde knew his failing, and had many times laughed at him therefor.

'Dogs you are,' said the Blind Mullah to the listening tribesmen round the fire. 'Whipped dogs! Because you listened to Orde Sahib and called him father and behaved as his children, the British Government have proven how they regard you. Orde Sahib ye know is dead.'

'Ai! ai! ai!' said half a dozen voices.

'He was a man. Comes now in his stead, whom think ye? A Bengali of Bengal – an eater of fish from the South.'

'A lie!' said Khoda Dad Khan. 'And but for the small matter of thy priesthood, I'd drive my gun butt-first down thy throat.'

'Oho, art thou there, lickspittle of the English? Go in tomorrow across the Border to pay service to Orde Sahib's successor, and thou shalt slip thy shoes at the tent-door of a Bengali, as thou shalt hand thy offering to a Bengali's black fist. This I know; and in my youth, when a young man spoke evil to a Mullah holding the doors of Heaven and Hell, the gun-butt was not rammed down the Mullah's gullet. No!'

The Blind Mullah hated Khoda Dad Khan with Afghan hatred, both being rivals for the headship of the tribe; but the latter was feared for bodily as the other for spiritual gifts. Khoda Dad Khan looked at Orde's ring and grunted, 'I go in tomorrow because I am not an old fool, preaching war against the English. If the Government, smitten with madness, have done this, then . . .'

'Then,' croaked the Mullah, 'thou wilt take out the young men and strike at the four villages within the Border?'

'Or wring thy neck, black raven of Jehannum,[10] for a bearer of ill-tidings.'

Khoda Dad Khan oiled his long locks with great care, put on his best Bokhara belt, a new turban-cap, and fine green shoes, and accompanied by a few friends came down from the hills to pay a visit to the new Deputy Commissioner of Kot-Kumharsen. Also he bore tribute – four or five priceless gold mohurs of Akbar's[11] time in a white handkerchief. These the Deputy Commissioner would touch and remit. The little ceremony used to be a sign that, so far as Khoda Dad Khan's personal influence went, the Khusru Kheyl would be good boys – till the next time; especially if Khoda Dad Khan happened to like the new Deputy Commissioner. In Yardley-Orde's consulship his visit concluded with a sumptuous dinner and perhaps forbidden liquors; certainly with some wonderful tales and great good-fellowship. Then Khoda Dad Khan would swagger back to his hold, vowing that Orde Sahib was one prince and Tallantire Sahib another, and that whosoever went a-raiding into British territory would be flayed alive. On this occasion he found the Deputy Commissioner's tents looking much as usual. Regarding himself as privileged he strode through the open door to confront a suave, portly Bengali in English costume writing at a table. Unversed in the elevating influence of education, and not in the least caring for university degrees, Khoda Dad Khan promptly set the man down for a Babu – the native clerk of the Deputy Commissioner – a hated and despised animal.

'Ugh!' said he cheerfully. 'Where's your master, Babujee?'

'I am the Deputy Commissioner,' said the gentleman in English.

Now he overvalued the effects of university degrees, and stared Khoda Dad Khan in the face. But if from your earliest infancy you have been accustomed to look on battle, murder, and sudden death, if spilt blood affects your nerves as much as red paint, and, above all, if you have faithfully believed that the Bengali was the servant of all Hindustan, and that all Hindustan was vastly inferior to your own large, lustful self, you can endure, even though uneducated, a very large amount of looking over. You can even stare down a graduate of an Oxford college if the latter has been born in a hothouse, of stock bred in a hothouse, and fearing physical pain as some men fear sin; especially if your opponent's mother has frightened him to sleep in his youth with horrible stories of devils inhabiting Afghanistan, and dismal legends of the black North. The eyes behind the gold spectacles sought the floor. Khoda Dad Khan chuckled, and swung out to find Tallantire hard by. 'Here,' said he roughly, thrusting the coins before him, 'touch and remit. That answers for *my* good behaviour. But, O Sahib, has the Government gone mad to send a black Bengali dog to us? And am I to pay service to such an one? And are you to work under him? What does it mean?'

'It is an order,' said Tallantire. He had expected something of this kind. 'He is a very clever S-sahib.'

'He a Sahib! He's a *kala admi* – a black man – unfit to run at the tail of a potter's donkey. All the peoples of the earth have harried Bengal. It is written. Thou knowest when we of the North wanted women or plunder whither went we? To Bengal – where else? What child's talk is this of Sahibdom – after Orde Sahib too! Of a truth the Blind Mullah was right.'

'What of him?' asked Tallantire uneasily. He mistrusted that old man with his dead eyes and his deadly tongue.

'Nay, now, because of the oath that I sware to Orde Sahib when we watched him die by the river yonder, I will tell. In the first place, is it true that the English have set the heel of the Bengali on their own neck, and that there is no more English rule in the land?'

'I am here,' said Tallantire, 'and I serve the Maharanee of England.'

'The Mullah said otherwise, and further that because we loved Orde Sahib the Government sent us a pig to show that we were dogs, who till now have been held by the strong hand. Also that they were taking away the white soldiers, that more Hindustanis might come, and that all was changing.'

This is the worst of ill-considered handling of a very large country. What looks so feasible in Calcutta, so right in Bombay, so unassailable in Madras, is misunderstood by the North, and entirely changes its complexion on the banks of the Indus. Khoda Dad Khan explained as clearly as he could that, though he himself intended to be good, he really could not answer for the more reckless members of his tribe under the leadership of the Blind Mullah. They might or they might not give trouble, but they certainly had no intention whatever of obeying the new Deputy Commissioner. Was Tallantire perfectly sure that in the event of any systematic border-raiding the force in the district could put it down promptly?

'Tell the Mullah if he talks any more fool's talk,' said Tallantire curtly, 'that he takes his men on to certain death, and his tribe to blockade, trespass-fine, and blood-money. But why do I talk to one who no longer carries weight in the counsels of the tribe?'

Khoda Dad Khan pocketed that insult. He had learned something that he much wanted to know, and returned to his hills to be sarcastically complimented by the Mullah, whose tongue raging round the camp-fires was deadlier flame than ever dung-cake fed.

IV

Be pleased to consider here for a moment the unknown district of Kot-Kumharsen. It lay cut lengthways by the Indus under the line of the Khusru hills – ramparts of useless earth and tumbled stone. It was seventy miles long by fifty broad, maintained a population of something less than two hundred thousand, and paid taxes to the extent of forty thousand pounds a year on an area that was by rather more than half sheer, hopeless waste. The cultivators were not gentle people, the miners for salt were less gentle still, and the cattle-breeders least gentle of all. A police-post in the top right-hand corner and a tiny mud fort in the top left-hand corner prevented as much salt-smuggling and cattle-lifting as the influence of the civilians could not put down; and in the bottom right-hand corner lay Jumala, the district headquarters – a pitiful knot of lime-washed barns facetiously rented as houses, reeking with frontier fever, leaking in the rain, and ovens in the summer.

It was to this place that Grish Chunder Dé was travelling, there formally to take over charge of the district. But the news of his coming had gone before. Bengalis were as scarce as poodles among the simple Borderers, who cut each other's heads open with their long spades and worshipped impartially at Hindu and Mahomedan shrines. They crowded to see him, pointing at him, and diversely comparing him to a gravid milch-buffalo, or a broken-down horse, as their limited range of metaphor prompted. They laughed at his police-guard, and wished to know how long the burly Sikhs were going to lead Bengali apes. They inquired whether he had brought his women with him, and advised him explicitly not to tamper with theirs. It remained for a wrinkled hag by the roadside to slap her lean breasts as he passed, crying, 'I have suckled six that could have eaten six thousand of *him*. The Government shot them, and made this That a king!' Whereat a blue-turbaned huge-boned plough-mender shouted, 'Have hope, mother o' mine! He may yet go the way of thy wastrels.' And the children, the little brown puff-balls, regarded curiously. It was generally a good thing for infancy to stray into Orde Sahib's tent, where copper coins were to be won for the mere wishing, and tales of the most authentic, such as even their mothers knew but the first half of. No! This fat black man could never tell them how Pir Prith hauled the eye-teeth out of ten devils; how the big stones came to lie all in a row on top of the Khusru hills, and what happened if you shouted through the village-gate to the grey wolf at even 'Badl Khas is dead.' Meantime Grish Chunder Dé talked hastily and much to Tallantire, after the manner of those who are 'more English than the English' – of Oxford and 'home', with much curious book-knowledge of bump-suppers, cricket-matches, hunting-runs, and other unholy sports of the alien. 'We must get these fellows in hand,' he said once or twice uneasily; 'get them well in hand, and drive them on a tight rein. No use, you know, being slack with your district.'

And a moment later Tallantire heard Debendra Nath Dé, who brotherliwise had followed his kinsman's fortune and hoped for the shadow of his protector as a pleader, whisper in Bengali, 'Better are dried fish at Dacca than drawn swords at Delhi. Brother of mine, these men are devils, as our mother said. And you will always have to ride upon a horse!'

That night there was a public audience in a broken-down little town thirty miles from Jumala, when the new Deputy Commissioner, in reply to the greetings of the subordinate native officials, delivered a speech. It was a carefully thought-out speech, which would have been very valuable had not his third sentence begun with three innocent words, '*Hamara hookum hai* – It is my order.' Then there was a laugh, clear and bell-like, from the back of the big tent, where a few border landholders sat, and the laugh grew and scorn mingled with it, and the lean, keen face of Debendra Nath Dé paled, and Grish Chunder turning to Tallantire spake: '*You* – you put up this arrangement.' Upon that instant the noise of hoofs rang without, and there entered Curbar, the District Super-intendent of Police, sweating and dusty. The State had tossed him into a corner of the province for seventeen weary years, there to check smuggling of salt, and to hope for promotion that never came. He had forgotten how to keep his white uniform clean, had screwed rusty spurs into patent-leather shoes, and clothed his head indifferently with a helmet or a turban. Soured, old, worn with heat and cold, he waited till he should be entitled to sufficient pension to keep him from starving.

'Tallantire,' said he, disregarding Grish Chunder Dé, 'come outside. I want to speak to you.' They withdrew. 'It's this,' continued Curbar. 'The Khusru Kheyl have rushed and cut up half a dozen of the coolies on Ferris's new canal-embankment; killed a couple of men and carried off a woman. I wouldn't trouble you about that – Ferris is after them and Hugonin, my assistant, with ten mounted police. But that's only the beginning, I fancy. Their fires are out on the Hassan Ardeb heights, and unless we're pretty quick there'll be a flare-up all along our Border. They are sure to raid the four Khusru villages on our side of the line: there's been bad blood between them for years; and you know the Blind Mullah has been preaching a holy war since Orde went out. What's your notion?'

'Damn!' said Tallantire thoughtfully. 'They've begun quick. Well, it seems to me I'd better ride off to Fort Ziar and get what men I can there to picket among the lowland villages, if it's not too late. Tommy Dodd commands at Fort Ziar, I think. Ferris and Hugonin ought to teach the canal-thieves a lesson, and – No, we can't have the Head of the Police ostentatiously guarding the Treasury. You go back to the canal. I'll wire Bullows to come in to Jumala with a strong police-guard, and sit on the Treasury. They won't touch the place, but it looks well.'

'I – I – I insist upon knowing what this means,' said the voice of the Deputy Commissioner, who had followed the speakers.

'Oh!' said Curbar, who being in the Police could not understand that fifteen years of education must, on principle, change the Bengali into a Briton. 'There has been a fight on the Border, and heaps of men are killed. There's going to be another fight, and heaps more will be killed.'

'What for?'

'Because the teeming millions of this district don't exactly approve of you, and think that under your benign rule they are going to have a good time. It strikes me that you had better make arrangements. I act, as you know, by your orders. What do you advise?'

'I – I take you all to witness that I have not yet assumed charge of the district,' stammered the Deputy Commissioner, not in the tones of the 'more English'.

'Ah, I thought so. Well, as I was saying, Tallantire, your plan is sound. Carry it out. Do you want an escort?'

'No; only a decent horse. But how about wiring to headquarters?'

'I fancy, from the colour of his cheeks, that your superior officer will send some wonderful telegrams before the night's over. Let him do that, and we shall have half the troops of the province coming up to see what's the trouble. Well, run along, and take care of yourself – the Khusru Kheyl jab upwards from below, remember. Ho! Mir Khan, give Tallantire Sahib the best of the horses, and tell five men to ride to Jumala with the Deputy Commissioner Sahib Bahadur. There is a hurry toward.'

There was; and it was not in the least bettered by Debendra Nath Dé clinging to a policeman's bridle and demanding the shortest, the very shortest way to Jumala. Now originality is fatal to the Bengali. Debendra Nath should have stayed with his brother, who rode steadfastly for Jumala on the railway-line, thanking gods entirely unknown to the most catholic of universities that he had not taken charge of the district, and could still – happy resource of a fertile race! – fall sick.

And I grieve to say that when he reached his goal two policemen, not devoid of rude wit, who had been conferring together as they bumped in their saddles, arranged an entertainment for his behoof. It consisted of first one and then the other entering his room with prodigious details of war, the massing of bloodthirsty and devilish tribes, and the burning of towns. It was almost as good, said these scamps, as riding with Curbar after evasive Afghans. Each invention kept the hearer at work for half an hour on telegrams which the sack of Delhi would hardly have justified. To every power that could move a bayonet or transfer a terrified man, Grish Chunder Dé appealed telegraphically. He was alone, his assistants had fled, and in truth he had not taken over charge of the district. Had the telegrams been despatched many things would have occurred; but since the only signaller in Jumala had gone to bed, and the station-master, after one look at the tremendous pile of paper, discovered that railway regulations forbade the forwarding of imperial messages, police-men Ram Singh and Nihal Singh were fain to turn the stuff into a pillow and slept on it very comfortably.

Tallantire drove his spurs into a rampant skewbald stallion with china-blue eyes, and settled himself for the forty-mile ride to Fort Ziar. Knowing his district blindfold, he wasted no time hunting for short cuts, but headed across the richer grazing-ground to the ford where Orde had died and been buried. The dusty ground deadened the noise of his horse's hoofs, the moon threw his shadow, a restless goblin, before him, and the heavy dew drenched him to the skin. Hillock, scrub that brushed against the horse's belly, unmetalled road where the whip-like foliage of the tamarisks lashed his forehead, illimitable levels of lowland furred with bent and speckled with drowsing cattle, waste, and hillock anew, dragged themselves past, and the skewbald was labouring in the deep sand of the Indus-ford. Tallantire was conscious of no distinct thought till the nose of the dawdling ferry-boat grounded on the farther side, and his horse shied snorting at the white headstone of Orde's grave. Then he uncovered, and shouted that the dead might hear, 'They're out, old man! Wish me luck.' In the chill of the dawn he was hammering with a stirrup-iron at the gate of Fort Ziar, where fifty sabres of that tattered regiment, the Belooch Beshaklis,[12] were supposed to guard Her Majesty's interests along a few hundred miles of Border. This particular fort was commanded by a subaltern, who, born of the ancient family of the Derouletts, naturally answered to the name of Tommy Dodd.[13] Him Tallantire found robed in a sheepskin coat, shaking with fever like an aspen, and trying to read the native apothecary's list of invalids.

'So you've come, too,' said he. 'Well, we're all sick here, and I don't think I can horse thirty men; but we're bub – bub – bub blessed willing. Stop, does this impress you as a trap or a lie?' He tossed a scrap of paper to Tallantire, on which was written painfully in crabbed Gurmukhi, 'We cannot hold young horses. They will feed after the moon goes down in the four border villages issuing from the Jagai pass on the next night.' Then in English round hand – 'Your sincere friend.'

'Good man!' said Tallantire. 'That's Khoda Dad Khan's work, I know. It's the only piece of English he could ever keep in his head, and he is immensely proud of it. He is playing against the Blind Mullah for his own hand – the treacherous young ruffian!'

'Don't know the politics of the Khusru Kheyl, but if you're satisfied, I am. That was pitched in over the gatehead last night, and I thought we might pull ourselves together and see what was on. Oh, but we're sick with fever here and no mistake! Is this going to be a big business, think you?' said Tommy Dodd.

Tallantire gave him briefly the outlines of the case, and Tommy Dodd whistled and shook with fever alternately. That day he devoted to strategy, the art of war, and the enlivenment of the invalids, till at dusk there stood ready forty-two troopers, lean, worn, and dishevelled, whom Tommy Dodd surveyed with pride, and addressed thus, 'O men! If you die you will go to Hell. Therefore endeavour to keep alive. But if you go to Hell that place cannot be hotter than this place, and we are not told that we shall there suffer from fever. Consequently be not afraid of dying. File out there!' They grinned, and went.

V

It will be long ere the Khusru Kheyl forget their night attack on the lowland villages. The Mullah had promised an easy victory and unlimited plunder; but behold, armed troopers of the Queen had risen out of the very earth, cutting, slashing, and riding down under the stars, so that no man knew where to turn, and all feared that they had brought an army about their ears, and ran back to the hills. In the panic of that flight more men were seen to drop from wounds inflicted by an Afghan knife jabbed upwards, and yet more from long-range carbine-fire. Then there rose a cry of treachery, and when they reached their own guarded heights, they had left, with some forty dead and sixty wounded, all their confidence in the Blind Mullah on the plains below. They clamoured, swore, and argued round the fires; the women wailing for the lost, and the Mullah shrieking curses on the returned.

Then Khoda Dad Khan, eloquent and unbreathed, for he had taken no part in the fight, rose to improve the occasion. He pointed out that the tribe owed every item of its present misfortune to the Blind Mullah, who had lied in every possible particular and talked them into a trap. It was undoubtedly an insult that a Bengali, the son of a Bengali, should presume to administer the Border, but that fact did not, as the Mullah pretended, herald a general time of license and lifting; and the inexplicable madness of the English had not in the least impaired their power of guarding their marches. On the contrary, the baffled and out-generalled tribe would now, just when their food-stock was lowest, be blockaded from any trade with Hindustan until they had sent hostages for good behaviour, paid compensation for disturbance, and blood-money at the rate of thirty-six English pounds per head for every villager that they might have slain. 'And ye know that those lowland dogs will make oath that we have slain scores. Will the Mullah pay the fines or must we sell our guns?' A low growl ran round the fires. 'Now, seeing that all this is the Mullah's work, and that we have gained nothing but promises of Paradise thereby, it is in my heart that we of the Khusru Kheyl lack a shrine whereat to pray. We are weakened, and henceforth how shall we dare to cross into the Madar Kheyl border, as has been our custom, to kneel to Pir Sajji's tomb? The Madar men will fall upon us, and rightly. But our Mullah is a holy man. He has helped two score of us into Paradise this night. Let him therefore accompany his flock, and we will build over his body a dome of the blue tiles of Mooltan, and burn lamps at his feet every Friday night. He shall be a saint: we shall have a shrine; and there our women shall pray for fresh seed to fill the gaps in our fighting-tale. How think you?'

A grim chuckle followed the suggestion, and the soft *wheep, wheep* of unscabbarded knives followed the chuckle. It was an excellent notion, and met a long felt want of the tribe. The Mullah sprang to his feet, glaring with withered eyeballs at the drawn death he could not see, and calling down the curses of God and Mahomed on the tribe. Then began a game of blind man's buff round and between the fires, whereof Khuruk Shah, the tribal poet, has sung in verse that will not die.

They tickled him gently under the armpit with the knife-point. He leaped aside screaming, only to feel a cold blade drawn lightly over the back of his neck, or a rifle-muzzle rubbing his beard. He called on his adherents to aid him, but most of these lay dead on the plains, for Khoda Dad Khan had been at some pains to arrange their decease. Men described to him the glories of the shrine they would build, and the little children clapping their hands cried, 'Run, Mullah, run! There's a man behind you!' In the end, when the sport wearied, Khoda Dad Khan's brother sent a knife home between his ribs. 'Wherefore,' said Khoda Dad Khan with charming simplicity, 'I am now Chief of the Khusru Kheyl!' No man gainsaid him; and they all went to sleep very stiff and sore.

On the plain below Tommy Dodd was lecturing on the beauties of a cavalry charge by night, and Tallantire, bowed on his saddle, was gasping hysterically because there was a sword dangling from his wrist flecked with the blood of the Khusru Kheyl, the tribe that Orde had kept in leash so well. When a Rajpoot trooper pointed out that the skewbald's right ear had been taken off at the root by some blind slash of its unskilled rider, Tallantire broke down altogether, and laughed and sobbed till Tommy Dodd made him lie down and rest.

'We must wait about till the morning,' said he. 'I wired to the Colonel just before we left, to send a wing of the Beshaklis after us. He'll be furious with me for monopolizing the fun, though. Those beggars in the hills won't give us any more trouble.'

'Then tell the Beshaklis to go on and see what has happened to Curbar on the canal. We must patrol the whole line of the Border. You're quite sure, Tommy, that – that stuff was – was only the skewbald's ear?'

'Oh, quite,' said Tommy. 'You just missed cutting off his head. *I* saw you when we went into the mess. Sleep, old man.'

Noon brought two squadrons of Beshaklis and a knot of furious brother officers demanding the court-martial of Tommy Dodd for 'spoiling the picnic', and a gallop across country to the canal-works where Ferris, Curbar, and Hugonin were haranguing the terror-stricken coolies on the enormity of abandoning good work and high pay, merely because half a dozen of their fellows had been cut down. The sight of a troop of the Beshaklis restored wavering confidence, and the police-hunted section of the Khusru Kheyl had the joy of watching the canal-bank humming with life as usual, while such of their men as had taken refuge in the water-courses and ravines were being driven out by the troopers. By sundown began the remorseless patrol of the Border by police and trooper, most like the cow-boys' eternal ride round restless cattle.

'Now,' said Khoda Dad Khan to his fellows, pointing out a line of twinkling fires below, 'ye may see how far the old order changes. After their horse will come the little devil-guns that they can drag up to the tops of the hills, and, for aught I know, to the clouds when we crown the hills. If the tribe-council thinks good, I will go to Tallantire Sahib – who loves me – and see if I can stave off at least the blockade. Do I speak for the tribe?'

'Ay, speak for the tribe in God's name. How those accursed fires wink! Do the English send their troops on the wire – or is this the work of the Bengali?'

As Khoda Dad Khan went down the hill he was delayed by an interview with a hard-pressed tribesman, which caused him to return hastily for something he had forgotten. Then, handing himself over to the two troopers who had been chasing his friend, he claimed escort to Tallantire Sahib, then with Bullows at Jumala. The Border was safe, and the time for reasons in writing had begun.

'Thank Heaven!' said Bullows, 'that the trouble came at once. Of course we can never put down the reason in black and white, but all India will understand. And it is better to have a sharp short outbreak than five years of impotent administration inside the Border. It costs less. Grish Chunder Dé has reported himself sick, and has been transferred to his own province without any sort of reprimand. He was strong on not having taken over the district.'

'Of course,' said Tallantire bitterly. 'Well, what am I supposed to have done that was wrong?'

'Oh, you will be told that you exceeded all your powers, and should have reported, and written, and advised for three weeks until the Khusru Kheyl could really come down in force. But I don't think the authorities will dare to make a fuss about it. They've had their lesson. Have you seen Curbar's version of the affair? He can't write a report, but he can speak the truth.'

'What's the use of the truth? He'd much better tear up the report. I'm sick and heartbroken over it all. It was so utterly unnecessary – except in that it rid us of that Babu.'

Entered unabashed Khoda Dad Khan, a stuffed forage-net in his hand, and the troopers behind him.

'May you never be tired!' said he cheerily. 'Well, Sahibs, that was a good fight, and Naim Shah's mother is in debt to you, Tallantire Sahib. A clean cut, they tell me, through jaw, wadded coat, and deep into the collarbone. Well done! But I speak for the tribe. There has been a fault – a great fault. Thou knowest that I and mine, Tallantire

Sahib, kept the oath we sware to Orde Sahib on the banks of the Indus.'

'As an Afghan keeps his knife – sharp on one side, blunt on the other,' said Tallantire.

'The better swing in the blow, then. But I speak God's truth. Only the Blind Mullah carried the young men on the tip of his tongue, and said that there was no more Border-law because a Bengali had been sent, and we need not fear the English at all. So they came down to avenge that insult and get plunder. Ye know what befell, and how far I helped. Now five score of us are dead or wounded, and we are all shamed and sorry, and desire no further war. Moreover, that ye may better listen to us, we have taken off the head of the Blind Mullah, whose evil counsels have led us to folly. I bring it for proof,' – and he heaved on the floor the head. 'He will give no more trouble, for *I* am chief now, and so I sit in a higher place at all audiences. Yet there is an offset to this head. That was another fault. One of the men found that black Bengali beast, through whom this trouble arose, wandering on horseback and weeping. Reflecting that he had caused loss of much good life, Alla Dad Khan, whom, if you choose, I will tomorrow shoot, whipped off this head, and I bring it to you to cover your shame, that ye may bury it. See, no man kept the spectacles, though they were of gold.'

Slowly rolled to Tallantire's feet the crop-haired head of a spectacled Bengali gentleman, open-eyed, open-mouthed – the head of Terror incarnate. Bullows bent down. 'Yet another blood-fine and a heavy one, Khoda Dad Khan, for this is the head of Debendra Nath, the man's brother. The Babu is safe long since. All but the fools of the Khusru Kheyl know that.'

'Well, I care not for carrion. Quick meat for me. The thing was under our hills asking the road to Jumala, and Alla Dad Khan showed him the road to Jehannum, being, as thou sayest, but a fool. Remains now what the Government will do to us. As to the blockade –'

'Who art thou, seller of dog's flesh,' thundered Tallantire, 'to speak of terms and treaties? Get hence to the hills – go, and wait there starving, till it shall please the Government to call thy people out for punishment – children and fools that ye be! Count your dead, and be still. Rest assured that the Government will send you a *man!*'

'Ay,' returned Khoda Dad Khan, 'for we also be men.'

As he looked Tallantire between the eyes, he added, 'And by God, Sahib, may thou be that man!'

The Courting of Dinah Shadd [1]

What did the colonel's lady think?
  Nobody never knew.
Somebody asked the sergeant's wife
  An' she told 'em true.
When you git to a man in the case
  They're like a row o' pins,
For the colonel's lady an' Judy O'Grady
  Are sisters under their skins.
Barrack-Room Ballad.

All day I had followed at the heels of a pursuing army engaged on one of the finest battles that ever camp of exercise beheld. Thirty thousand troops had, by the wisdom of the Government of India, been turned loose over a few thousand square miles of country to practise in peace what they would never attempt in war. Consequently cavalry charged unshaken infantry at the trot. Infantry captured artillery by frontal attacks delivered in line of quarter columns, and mounted infantry skirmished up to the wheels of an armoured train which carried nothing more deadly than a twenty-five-pounder Armstrong, two Nordenfeldts,[2] and a few score volunteers all cased in three-eighths-inch boiler-plate. Yet it was a very lifelike camp. Operations did not cease at sundown; nobody knew the country and nobody spared man or horse. There was unending cavalry scouting and almost unending forced work over broken ground. The Army of the South had finally pierced the centre of the Army of the North, and was pouring through the gap hot-foot to capture a city of strategic importance. Its front extended fanwise, the sticks being represented by regiments strung out along the line of route backwards to the divisional transport columns and all the lumber that trails behind an army on the move. On its right the broken left of the Army of the North was flying in mass, chased by the Southern horse and hammered by the Southern guns till these had been pushed far beyond the limits of their last support. Then the flying sat down to rest, while the elated commandant of the pursuing force telegraphed that he held all in check and observation.

Unluckily he did not observe that three miles to his right flank a flying column of Northern horse with a detachment of Ghoorkhas and British troops had been pushed round as fast as the failing light allowed, to cut across the entire rear of the Southern Army – to break, as it were, all the ribs of the fan where they converged by striking at the transport, reserve ammunition, and artillery supplies. Their instructions were to go in, avoiding the few scouts who might not have been drawn off by the pursuit, and create sufficient excitement to impress the Southern Army with the wisdom of guarding their own flank and rear before they captured cities. It was a pretty manoeuvre, neatly carried out.

Speaking for the second division of the Southern Army, our first intimation of the attack was at twilight, when the artillery were labouring in deep sand, most of the escort were trying to help them out, and the main body of the infantry had gone on. A Noah's Ark of elephants, camels, and the mixed menagerie of an Indian transport-train bubbled and squealed behind the guns, when there appeared from nowhere in particular British infantry to the extent of three companies, who sprang to the heads of the gun-horses and brought all to a standstill amid oaths and cheers.

'How's that, umpire?' said the major commanding the attack, and with one voice the drivers and limber gunners answered 'Hout!' while the colonel of artillery sputtered.

'All your scouts are charging our main body,' said the major. 'Your flanks are unprotected for two miles. I think we've broken the back of this division. And listen – there go the Ghoorkhas!'

A weak fire broke from the rear-guard more than a mile away, and was answered by cheerful howlings. The Ghoorkhas, who should have swung clear of the second division, had stepped on its tail in the dark, but drawing off hastened to reach the next line of attack, which lay almost parallel to us five or six miles away.

Our column swayed and surged irresolutely – three batteries, the divisional ammunition reserve, the baggage, and a section of the hospital and bearer corps. The commandant ruefully promised to report himself 'cut up' to the nearest umpire, and commending his cavalry and all other cavalry to the special care of Eblis,[3] toiled on to resume touch with the rest of the division.

'We'll bivouac here tonight,' said the major, 'I have a notion that the Ghoorkhas will get caught. They may want us to re-form on. Stand easy till the transport gets away.'

A hand caught my beast's bridle and led him out of the choking dust; a larger hand deftly canted me out of the saddle; and two of the hugest hands in the world received me sliding. Pleasant is the lot of the special correspondent who falls into such hands as those of Privates Mulvaney, Ortheris, and Learoyd.

'An' that's all right,' said the Irishman calmly. 'We thought we'd find you somewheres here by. Is there anything av yours in the transport? Orth'ris'll fetch ut out.'

Ortheris did 'fetch ut out', from under the trunk of an elephant, in the shape of a servant and an animal both laden with medical comforts. The little man's eyes sparkled.

'If the brutil an' licentious soldiery av these parts gets sight av the thruck,' said Mulvaney, making practised investigation, 'they'll loot ev'rything. They're bein' fed on iron-filin's an' dog-biscuit these days, but glory's no compensation for a belly-ache. Praise be, we're here to protect you, sorr. Beer, sausage, bread (soft an' that's a cur'osity), soup in a tin, whisky by the smell av ut, an' fowls! Mother av Moses, but ye take the field like a confectioner! 'Tis scand'lus.'

''Ere's a orficer,' said Ortheris significantly. 'When the sergent's done lushin'⁴ the privit may clean the pot.'

I bundled several things into Mulvaney's haversack before the major's hand fell on my shoulder and he said tenderly, 'Requisitioned for the Queen's service. Wolseley was quite wrong⁵ about special correspondents: they are the soldier's best friends. Come and take pot-luck with us tonight.'

And so it happened amid laughter and shoutings that my well-considered commissariat melted away to reappear later at the mess-table, which was a waterproof sheet spread on the ground. The flying column had taken three days' rations with it, and there be few things nastier than Government rations – especially when Government is experimenting with German toys. Erbswurst, tinned beef of surpassing tinniness, compressed vegetables, and meat-biscuits may be nourishing, but what Thomas Atkins needs is bulk in his inside. The major, assisted by his brother officers, purchased goats for the camp, and so made the experiment of no effect. Long before the fatigue-party sent to collect brushwood had returned, the men were settled down by their valises, kettles and pots had appeared from the surrounding country, and were dangling over fires as the kid and the compressed vegetable bubbled together; there rose a cheerful clinking of mess-tins; outrageous demands for 'a little more stuffin' with that there liver-wing'; and gust on gust of chaff as pointed as a bayonet and as delicate as a gun-butt.

'The boys are in a good temper,' said the major. 'They'll be singing presently. Well, a night like this is enough to keep them happy.'

Over our heads burned the wonderful Indian stars, which are not all pricked in on one plane, but, preserving an orderly perspective, draw the eye through the velvet darkness of the void up to the barred doors of heaven itself. The earth was a grey shadow more unreal than the sky. We could hear her breathing lightly in the pauses between the howling of the jackals, the movement of the wind in the tamarisks, and the fitful mutter of musketry-fire leagues away to the left. A native woman from some unseen hut began to sing, the mail-train thundered past on its way to Delhi, and a roosting crow cawed drowsily. Then there was a belt-loosening silence about the fires, and the even breathing of the crowded earth took up the story.

The men, full fed, turned to tobacco and song – their officers with them. The subaltern is happy who can win the approval of the musical critics in his regiment, and is honoured among the more intricate step-dancers. By him, as by him who plays cricket cleverly, Thomas Atkins will stand in time of need, when he will let a better officer go on alone. The ruined tombs of forgotten Mussulman saints heard the ballad of *Agra Town*, *The Buffalo Battery*, *Marching to Kabul*, *The long, long Indian Day*, *The Place where the Punkah-coolie died*, and that crashing chorus which announces,

> Youth's daring spirit, manhood's fire,
> Firm hand and eagle eye,
> Must he acquire, who would aspire
> To see the grey boar die.

Today, of all those jovial thieves who appropriated my commissariat and lay and laughed round that waterproof sheet, not one remains. They went to camps that were not of exercise and battles without umpires. Burmah, the Soudan, and the frontier – fever and fight – took them in their time.

I drifted across to the men's fires in search of Mulvaney, whom I found strategically greasing his feet by the blaze. There is nothing particularly lovely in the sight of a private thus engaged after a long day's march, but when you reflect on the exact proportion of the 'might, majesty, dominion, and power' of the British Empire which stands on those feet you take an interest in the proceedings.

'There's a blister, bad luck to ut, on the heel,' said Mulvaney. 'I can't touch ut. Prick ut out, little man.'

Ortheris took out his house-wife, eased the trouble with a needle, stabbed Mulvaney in the calf with the same weapon, and was swiftly kicked into the fire.

'I've bruk the best av my toes over you, ye grinnin' child av disruption,' said Mulvaney, sitting cross-legged and nursing his feet; then seeing me, 'Oh, ut's you, sorr! Be welkim, an' take that maraudin' scutt's place. Jock, hold him down on the cindhers for a bit.'

But Ortheris escaped and went elsewhere, as I took possession of the hollow he had scraped for himself and lined with his greatcoat. Learoyd on the other side of the fire grinned affably and in a minute fell fast asleep.

'There's the height av politeness for you,' said Mulvaney, lighting his pipe with a flaming branch. 'But Jock's eaten half a box av your sardines at wan gulp, an' I think the tin too. What's the best wid you, sorr, an' how did you happen to be on the losin' side this day whin we captured you?'

'The Army of the South is winning all along the line,' I said.

'Then that line's the hangman's rope, savin' your presence. You'll learn tomorrow how we rethreated to dhraw thim on before we made thim trouble, an' that's what a woman does. By the same tokin, we'll be attacked before the dawnin' an' ut would be betther not to slip your boots. How do I know that? By the light av pure reason. Here are three companies av us ever so far inside av the enemy's flank an' a crowd av roarin', tarin', squealin' cavalry gone on just to turn out the whole hornet's nest av them. Av course the enemy will pursue, by brigades like as not, an' thin we'll have to run for ut. Mark my words. I am av the opinion av Polonius [6] whin he said, "Don't fight wid ivry scutt for the pure joy av fightin', but if you do, knock the nose av him first an' frequint." We ought to ha' gone on an' helped the Ghoorkhas.'

'But what do you know about Polonius?' I demanded. This was a new side of Mulvaney's character.

'All that Shakespeare iver wrote an' a dale more that the gallery shouted,' said the man of war, carefully lacing his boots. 'Did I not tell you av Silver's theatre in Dublin whin I was younger than I am now an' a patron av the drama? Ould Silver wud never pay actor-man or woman their just dues, an' by consequince his comp'nies was collapsible at the last minut. Thin the bhoys wud clamour to take a part, an' oft as not ould Silver made them pay for the fun. Faith, I've seen Hamlut played wid a new black eye an' the queen as full as a cornucopia. I remimber wanst Hogin that 'listed in the Black Tyrone [7] an' was shot in South Africa, he sejuced ould Silver into givin' him Hamlut's part instid av me that had a fine fancy for rhetoric in those days. Av course I wint into the gallery an' began to fill the pit wid other people's hats, an' I passed the time av day to Hogin walkin' through Denmark like a hamstrung mule wid a pall on his back. "Hamlut," sez I, "there's a hole in your heel. Pull up your shtockin's, Hamlut," sez I. "Hamlut, Hamlut, for the love av decincy dhrop that skull an' pull up your shtockin's." The whole house begun to tell him that. He stopped his soliloquishms mid-between. "My shtockin's may be comin' down or they may not," sez he, screwin' his eye into the gallery, for well he knew who I was. "But afther this performince is over me an' the Ghost'll trample the tripes out av you, Terence, wid your ass's bray!" An' that's how I come to know about Hamlut. Eyah! Those days, those days! Did you iver have onendin' devilmint an' nothin' to pay for it in your life, sorr?'

'Never, without having to pay,' I said.

'That's thrue! 'Tis mane whin you considher on ut; but ut's the same wid horse or fut. A headache if you dhrink, an' a belly-ache if you eat too much, an' a heart-ache to kape all down. Faith, the beast only gets the colic, an' he's the lucky man.'

He dropped his head and stared into the fire, fingering his moustache the while. From the far side of the bivouac the voice of Corbet-Nolan, senior subaltern of B company, uplifted itself in an ancient and much appreciated song of sentiment, the men moaning melodiously behind him.

> The north wind blew coldly, she drooped from that hour,
> My own little Kathleen, my sweet little Kathleen,
> Kathleen, my Kathleen, Kathleen O'Moore!

With forty-five O's in the last word: even at that distance you might have cut the soft South Irish accent with a shovel.

'For all we take we must pay, but the price is cruel high,' murmured Mulvaney when the chorus had ceased.

'What's the trouble?' I said gently, for I knew that he was a man of an inextinguishable sorrow.

'Hear now,' said he. 'Ye know what I am now. *I* know what I mint to be at the beginnin' av my service. I've tould you time an' again, an' what I have not Dinah Shadd has. An' what am I? Oh, Mary Mother av Hiven, an ould dhrunken, untrustable baste av a privit that has seen the reg'ment change out from colonel to drummer-boy, not wanst or twice, but scores av times! Ay, scores! An' me not so near gettin' promotion as in the first! An' me livin' on an' kapin' clear av clink, not by my own good conduck, but the kindness av some orf'cer-bhoy young enough to be son to me? Do I not know ut? Can I not tell whin I'm passed over at p'rade, tho' I'm rockin' full av liquor an' ready to fall all in wan piece, such as even a suckin' child might see, bekaze, "Oh, 'tis only ould Mulvaney!" An' whin I'm let off in ord'ly-room through some thrick of the tongue an' a ready answer an' the ould man's mercy, is ut smilin' I feel whin I fall away an' go back to Dinah Shadd, thryin' to carry ut all off as a joke? Not I! 'Tis hell to me, dumb hell through ut all; an' next time whin the fit comes I will be as bad again. Good cause the reg'ment has to know me for the best soldier in ut. Better cause have I to know mesilf for the worst man. I'm only fit to tache the new drafts what I'll niver learn myself; an' I am sure, as tho' I heard ut, that the minut wan av these pink-eyed recruities gets away from my "Mind ye now," an' "Listen to this, Jim, bhoy," – sure I am that the sergint houlds me up to him for a warnin'. So I tache, as they say at musketry-instruction, by direct and ricochet fire. Lord be good to me, for I have stud some throuble!'

'Lie down and go to sleep,' said I, not being able to comfort or advise. 'You're the best man in the regiment, and, next to Ortheris, the biggest fool. Lie down and wait till we're attacked. What force will they turn out? Guns, think you?'

'Try that wid your lorrds an' ladies, twistin' an turnin' the talk, tho' you mint ut well. Ye cud say nothin' to help me, an' yet ye niver knew what cause I had to be what I am.'

'Begin at the beginning and go on to the end,' I said royally. 'But rake up the fire a bit first.'

I passed Ortheris's bayonet for a poker.

'That shows how little we know what we do,' said Mulvaney, putting it aside. 'Fire takes all the heart out av the steel, an' the next time, may be, that our little man is fighting for his life his bradawl'll break, an' so you'll ha' killed him, manin' no more than to kape yourself warm. 'Tis a recruity's thrick that. Pass the clanin'-rod, sorr.'

I snuggled down abashed; and after an interval the voice of Mulvaney began.

'Did I iver tell you how Dinah Shadd came to be wife av mine?'

I dissembled a burning anxiety that I had felt for some months – ever since Dinah Shadd, the strong, the patient, and the infinitely tender, had of her own good love and free will washed a shirt for me, moving in a barren land where washing was not.

'I can't remember,' I said casually. 'Was it before or after you made love to Annie Bragin, and got no satisfaction?'

The story of Annie Bragin is written in another place.[8] It is one of the many less respectable episodes in Mulvaney's chequered career.

'Before – before – long before, was that business av Annie Bragin an' the corp'ril's ghost. Niver woman was the worse for me whin I had married Dinah. There's a time for all things, an' I know how to kape all things in place – barrin' the dhrink, that kapes me in my place wid no hope av comin' to be aught else.'

'Begin at the beginning,' I insisted. 'Mrs Mulvaney told me that you married her when you were quartered in Krab Bokhar barracks.'

'An' the same is a cess-pit,' said Mulvaney piously. 'She spoke thrue, did Dinah. 'Twas this way. Talkin' av that, have ye iver fallen in love, sorr?'

I preserved the silence of the damned. Mulvaney continued –

'Thin I will assume that ye have not. *I* did. In the days av my youth, as I have more than wanst tould you, I was a man that filled the eye an' delighted the sowl av women. Niver man was hated as I have bin. Niver man was loved as I – no, not within half a day's march av ut! For the first five years av my service, whin I was what I wud give my sowl to be now, I tuk whatever was within my reach an' digested ut – an' that's more than most men can say. Dhrink I tuk, an' ut did me no harm. By the Hollow av Hiven, I cud play wid four women at wanst, an' kape them from findin' out anythin' about the other three, an' smile like a full-blown marigold through ut all. Dick Coulhan, av the battery we'll have down on us tonight, could drive his team no better than I mine, an' I hild the worser cattle! An' so I lived, an' so I was happy till afther that business wid Annie Bragin – she that turned me off as cool as a meat-safe, an' taught me where I stud in the mind av an honest woman. 'Twas no sweet dose to swallow.

'Afther that I sickened awhile an' tuk thought to my reg'mental work; conceiting mesilf I wud study an' be a sargint, an' a major-gineral twinty minutes afther that. But on top av my ambitiousness there was an empty place in my sowl, an' me own opinion av mesilf cud not fill ut. Sez I to mesilf, "Terence, you're a great man an' the best set-up in the reg'mint. Go on an' get promotion." Sez mesilf to me, "What for?" Sez I to mesilf, "For the glory av ut!" Sez mesilf to me, "Will that fill these two strong arrums av yours, Terence?" – "Go to the devil," sez I to mesilf. "Go to the married lines," sez mesilf to me. "'Tis the same thing," sez I to mesilf. "Av you're the same man, ut is," said mesilf to me; an' wid that I considhered on ut a long while. Did you iver feel that way, sorr?'

I snored gently, knowing that if Mulvaney were uninterrupted he would go on. The clamour from the bivouac fires beat up to the stars, as the rival singers of the companies were pitted against each other.

'So I felt that way an' a bad time ut was. Wanst, bein' a fool, I wint into the married lines more for the sake av spakin' to our ould colour-sergint Shadd than for any thruck wid women-folk. I was a corp'ril then – rejuced afterwards, but a corp'ril then. I've got a photograft av mesilf to prove ut. "You'll take a cup av tay wid us?" sez Shadd. "I will that," I sez, "tho' tay is not my divarsion."

"'Twud be better for you if ut were," sez ould Mother Shadd, an' she had ought to know, for Shadd, in the ind av his service, dhrank bung-full each night.

'Wid that I tuk off my gloves — there was pipeclay in thim, so that they stud alone — an' pulled up my chair, lookin' round at the china ornaments an' bits av things in the Shadds' quarters. They were things that belonged to a man, an' no camp-kit, here today an' dishipated next. "You're comfortable in this place, sergint," sez I. "'Tis the wife that did ut, boy," sez he, pointin' the stem av his pipe to ould Mother Shadd, an' she smacked the top av his bald head apon the compliment. "That manes you want money," sez she.

'An' thin — an' thin whin the kettle was to be filled, Dinah came in — my Dinah — her sleeves rowled up to the elbow an' her hair in a winkin' glory over her forehead, the big blue eyes beneath twinklin' like stars on a frosty night, an' the tread av her two feet lighter than waste-paper from the colonel's basket in ord'ly-room whin ut's emptied. Bein' but a shlip av a girl she went pink at seein' me, an' I twisted me moustache an' looked at a picture forninst the wall. Niver show a woman that ye care the snap av a finger for her, an' begad she'll come bleatin' to your boot-heels!'

'I suppose that's why you followed Annie Bragin till everybody in the married quarters laughed at you,' said I, remembering that unhallowed wooing and casting off the disguise of drowsiness.

'I'm layin' down the gin'ral theory av the attack,' said Mulvaney, driving his boot into the dying fire. 'If you read the *Soldier's Pocket Book*, which niver any soldier reads, you'll see that there are exceptions. Whin Dinah was out av the door (an' twas as tho' the sunlight had shut too) — "Mother av Hiven, sergint," sez I, "but is that your daughter?" — "I've believed that way these eighteen years," sez ould Shadd, his eyes twinklin'; "but Mrs Shadd has her own opinion, like iv'ry woman." — "'Tis wid yours this time, for a mericle," sez Mother Shadd. "Thin why in the name av fortune did I niver see her before?" sez I. "Bekaze you've been thrapesin' round wid the married women these three years past. She was a bit av a child till last year, an' she shot up wid the spring," sez ould Mother Shadd. "I'll thrapese no more," sez I. "D'you mane that?" sez ould Mother Shadd, lookin' at me side-ways like a hen looks at a hawk whin the chickens are runnin' free. "Try me, an' tell," sez I. Wid that I pulled on my gloves, dhrank off the tay, an' went out av the house as stiff as at gin'ral p'rade, for well I knew that Dinah Shadd's eyes were in the small av my back out av the scullery window. Faith! that was the only time I mourned I was not a cav'l'ry man for the pride av the spurs to jingle.

'I wint out to think, an' I did a powerful lot av thinkin', but ut all came round to that shlip av a girl in the dotted blue dhress, wid the blue eyes an' the sparkil in them. Thin I kept off canteen, an' I kept to the married quarthers, or near by, on the chanst av meetin' Dinah. Did I meet her? Oh, my time past, did I not; wid a lump in my throat as big as my valise an' my heart goin' like a farrier's forge on a Saturday morning? 'Twas "Good day to ye, Miss Dinah," an "Good day t'you, corp'ril," for a week or two, and divil a bit further could I get bekaze av the respect I had to that girl that I cud ha' broken betune finger an' thumb.'

Here I giggled as I recalled the gigantic figure of Dinah Shadd when she handed me my shirt.

'Ye may laugh,' grunted Mulvaney. 'But I'm speakin' the trut', an' 'tis you that are in fault. Dinah was a girl that wud ha' taken the imperiousness out av the Duchess av Clonmel in those days. Flower hand, foot av shod air, an' the eyes av the livin' mornin' she had that is my wife today – ould Dinah, and niver aught else than Dinah Shadd to me.

''Twas after three weeks standin' off an' on, an' niver makin' headway excipt through the eyes, that a little drummer-boy grinned in me face whin I had admonished him wid the buckle av my belt for riotin' all over the place. "An' I'm not the only wan that doesn't kape to barricks," sez he. I tuk him by the scruff av his neck – my heart was hung on a hair-thrigger those days, you will onderstand – an' "Out wid ut," sez I, "or I'll lave no bone av you unbreakable." – "Speak to Dempsey," sez he howlin'. "Dempsey which?" sez I, "ye unwashed limb av Satan." – "Av the Bob-tailed Dhragoons," sez he. "He's seen her home from her aunt's house in the civil lines four times this fortnight." – "Child!" sez I, dhroppin' him, "your tongue's stronger than your body. Go to your quarters. I'm sorry I dhressed you down."

'At that I went four ways to wanst huntin' Dempsey. I was mad to think that wid all my airs among women I shud ha' been chated by a basin-faced fool av a cav'lryman not fit to trust on a trunk. Presintly I found him in our lines – the Bobtails was quartered next us – an' a tallowy, topheavy son av a she-mule he was wid his big brass spurs an' his plastrons on his epigastrons [9] an' all. But he niver flinched a hair.

'"A word wid you, Dempsey," sez I. "You've walked wid Dinah Shadd four times this fortnight gone."

'"What's that to you?" sez he. "I'll walk forty times more, an' forty on top av that, ye shovel-futted clod-breakin' infantry lance-corp'ril."

'Before I cud gyard he had his gloved fist home on my cheek an' down I went full-sprawl. "Will that content you?" sez he, blowin' on his knuckles for all the world like a Scots Greys orf'cer. "Content!" sez I. "For your own sake, man, take off your spurs, peel your jackut, an' onglove. 'Tis the beginnin' av the overture; stand up!"

'He stud all he know, but he niver peeled his jacket, an' his shoulders had no fair play. I was fightin' for Dinah Shadd an' that cut on my cheek. What hope had he forninst me? "Stand up," sez I, time an' agin whin he was beginnin' to quarter the ground an' gyard high an' go large. "This isn't ridin'-school," I sez. "O man, stand up an' let me get in at ye." But whin I saw he wud be runnin' about, I grup his shtock in my left an' his waist-belt in my right an' swung him clear to my right front, head undher, he hammerin' my nose till the wind was knocked out av him on the bare ground. "Stand up," sez I, "or I'll kick your head into your chest!" and I wud ha' done ut too, so ragin' mad I was.

'"My collar bone's bruk," sez he. "Help me back to lines. I'll walk wid her no more." So I helped him back.'

'And was his collar-bone broken?' I asked, for I fancied that only Learoyd could neatly accomplish that terrible throw.

'He pitched on his left shoulder-point. Ut was. Next day the news was in both barricks, an' whin I met Dinah Shadd wid a cheek on me like all the reg'mintal tailor's samples there was no "Good mornin', corp'ril," or aught else. "An' what have I done, Miss Shadd," sez I, very bould, plantin' mesilf forninst her, "that ye should not pass the time of day?"

'"Ye've half-killed rough-rider Dempsey," sez she, her dear blue eyes fillin' up.

'"May be," sez I. "Was he a friend av yours that saw ye home four times in the fortnight?"

'"Yes," sez she, but her mouth was down at the corners. "An' – an' what's that to you?" she sez.

'"Ask Dempsey," sez I, purtendin' to go away.

'"Did you fight for me then, ye silly man?" she sez, tho' she knew ut all along.

'"Who else?" sez I, an' I tuk wan pace to the front.

'"I wasn't worth ut," sez she, fingerin' in her apron.

'"That's for me to say," sez I. "Shall I say ut?"

'"Yes," sez she in a saint's whisper, an' at that I explained mesilf; and she tould me what ivry man that is a man, an' many that is a woman, hears wanst in his life.

'"But what made ye cry at startin', Dinah, darlin'?" sez I.

'"Your – your bloody cheek," sez she, duckin' her little head down on

my sash (I was on duty for the day) an' whimperin' like a sorrowful
angil.

'Now a man cud take that two ways. I tuk ut as pleased me best an' my
first kiss wid ut. Mother av Innocence! but I kissed her on the tip av the
nose an' undher the eye; an' a girl that lets a kiss come tumbleways like
that has never been kissed before. Take note av that, sorr. Thin we wint
hand in hand to ould Mother Shadd like two little childher, an' she said
'twas no bad thing, an' ould Shadd nodded behind his pipe, an' Dinah
ran away to her own room. That day I throd on rollin' clouds. All earth
was too small to hould me. Begad, I cud ha' hiked the sun out av the sky
for a live coal to my pipe, so magnificent I was. But I tuk recruities at
squad-drill instid, an' began wid general battalion advance whin I shud
ha' been balance-steppin' them. Eyah! that day! that day!'

A very long pause. 'Well?' said I.

' 'Twas all wrong,' said Mulvaney, with an enormous sigh. 'An' I
know that ev'ry bit av ut was my own foolishness. That night I tuk
maybe the half av three pints – not enough to turn the hair of a man in
his natural senses. But I was more than half drunk wid pure joy, an' that
canteen beer was so much whisky to me. I can't tell how it came about,
but *bekaze* I had no thought for anywan except Dinah, *bekaze* I
hadn't slipped her little white arms from my neck five minuts, *bekase* the
breath of her kiss was not gone from my mouth, I must go through the
married lines on my way to quarters, an' I must stay talkin' to a red-
headed Mullingar heifer av a girl, Judy Sheehy, that was daughter to
Mother Sheehy, the wife of Nick Sheehy, the canteen-sergint – the
Black Curse av Shielygh be on the whole brood that are above groun'
this day!

' "An' what are ye houldin' your head that high for, corp'ril?" sez
Judy. "Come in an' thry a cup av tay," she sez, standin' in the doorway.
Bein' an ontrustable fool, an' thinkin' av anything but tay, I wint.

' "Mother's at canteen," sez Judy, smoothin' the hair av hers that was
like red snakes, an' lookin' at me corner-ways out av her green cats' eyes.
"Ye will not mind, corp'ril?"

' "I can endure," sez I; ould Mother Sheehy bein' no divarsion av
mine, nor her daughter too. Judy fetched the tea things an' put thim on
the table, leanin' over me very close to get thim square. I dhrew back,
thinkin' av Dinah.

' "Is ut afraid you are av a girl alone?" sez Judy.

' "No," sez I. "Why should I be?"

' "That rests wid the girl," sez Judy, dhrawin' her chair next to mine.

' "Thin there let ut rest," sez I; an' thinkin' I'd been a trifle onpolite,

I sez, "The tay's not quite sweet enough for my taste. Put your little finger in the cup, Judy. 'Twill make ut necthar."

'"What's necthar?" sez she.

'"Somethin' very sweet," sez I; an' for the sinful life av me I cud not help lookin' at her out av the corner av my eye, as I was used to look at a woman.

'"Go on wid ye, corp'ril," sez she. "You're a flirrt."

'"On me sowl I'm not," sez I.

'"Then you're a cruel handsome man, an' that's worse," sez she, heaving big sighs an' lookin' crossways.

'"You know your own mind," sez I.

'"'Twud be better for me if I did not," she sez.

'"There's a dale to be said on both sides av that," sez I, unthinkin'.

'"Say your own part av ut, then, Terence, darlin'," sez she; "for begad I'm thinkin' I've said too much or too little for an honest girl," an' wid that she put her arms round my neck an' kissed me.

'"There's no more to be said afther that," sez I, kissin' her back again – Oh the mane scutt that I was, my head ringin' wid Dinah Shadd! How does ut come about, sorr, that when a man has put the comether on wan woman, he's sure bound to put it on another? 'Tis the same thing at musketry. Wan day ivry shot goes wide or into the bank, an' the next, lay high lay low, sight or snap, ye can't get off the bull's-eye for ten shots runnin'.'

'That only happens to a man who has had a good deal of experience. He does it without thinking,' I replied.

'Thankin' you for the complimint, sorr, ut may be so. But I'm doubtful whether you mint ut for a complimint. Hear now; I sat there wid Judy on my knee tellin' me all manner av nonsinse an' only sayin' "yes" an' "no", when I'd much better ha' kept tongue betune teeth. An' that was not an hour afther I had left Dinah! What I was thinkin' av I cannot say. Presintly, quiet as a cat, ould Mother Sheehy came in velvet-dhrunk. She had her daughter's red hair, but 'twas bald in patches, an' I cud see in her wicked ould face, clear as lightnin', what Judy wud be twenty years to come. I was for jumpin' up, but Judy niver moved.

'"Terence has promust, mother," sez she, an' the could sweat bruk out all over me. Ould Mother Sheehy sat down of a heap an' began playin' wid the cups. "Thin you're a well-matched pair," she sez very thick. "For he's the biggest rogue that iver spoiled the Queen's shoe-leather, an' –"

'"I'm off, Judy," sez I. "Ye should not talk nonsinse to your mother. Get her to bed, girl."

'"Nonsinse!" sez the ould woman, prickin' up her ears like a cat an' grippin' the table-edge. "'Twill be the most nonsinsical nonsinse for you, ye grinnin' badger, if nonsinse 'tis. Git clear, you. I'm goin' to bed."

'I ran out into the dhark, my head in a stew an' my heart sick, but I had sinse enough to see that I'd brought ut all on mysilf. "It's this to pass the time av day to a panjandhrum av hell-cats," sez I. "What I've said, an' what I've not said do not matther. Judy an' her dam will hould me for a promust man, an' Dinah will give me the go, an' I desarve ut. I will go an' get dhrunk," sez I, "an' forget about ut, for 'tis plain I'm not a marrin' man."

'On my way to canteen I ran against Lascelles, colour-sergeant that was av E Comp'ny, a hard, hard man, wid a torment av a wife. "You've the head av a drowned man on your shoulders," sez he; "an' you're goin' where you'll get a worse wan. Come back," sez he. "Let me go," sez I. "I've thrown my luck over the wall wid my own hand!" – "Then that's not the way to get ut back again," sez he. "Have out wid your throuble, ye fool-bhoy." An' I tould him how the matther was.

'He sucked in his lower lip. "You've been thrapped," sez he. "Ju Sheehy wud be the betther for a man's name to hers as soon as can. An' ye thought ye'd put the comether on her – that's the natural vanity of the baste. Terence, you're a big born fool, but you're not bad enough to marry into that comp'ny. If you said anythin', an' for all your prot-estations I'm sure ye did – or did not, which is worse – eat ut all – lie like the father of all lies, but come out av ut free av Judy. Do I not know what ut is to marry a woman that was the very spit an' image av Judy whin she was young? I'm gettin' old an' I've larnt patience, but you, Terence, you'd raise hand on Judy an' kill her in a year. Never mind if Dinah gives you the go, you've desarved ut; never mind if the whole reg'mint laughs you all day. Get shut av Judy an' her mother. They can't dhrag you to church, but if they do, they'll dhrag you to hell. Go back to your quarters and lie down," sez he. Thin over his shoulder, "You *must* ha' done with thim."

'Next day I wint to see Dinah, but there was no tucker in me as I walked. I knew the throuble wud come soon enough widout any handlin' av mine, an' I dreaded ut sore.

'I heard Judy callin' me, but I hild straight on to the Shadds' quarthers, an' Dinah wud ha' kissed me but I put her back.

'"Whin all's said, darlin'," sez I, "you can give ut me if ye will, tho' I misdoubt 'twill be so easy to come by then."

'I had scarce begun to put the explanation into shape before Judy an' her mother came to the door. I think there was a verandah, but I'm forgettin'.

'"Will ye not step in?" sez Dinah, pretty and polite, though the Shadds had no dealin's with the Sheehys. Old Mother Shadd looked up quick, an' she was the fust to see the throuble; for Dinah was her daughter.

'"I'm pressed for time today," sez Judy as bould as brass; "an' I've only come for Terence – my promust man. 'Tis strange to find him here the day afther the day."

'Dinah looked at me as though I had hit her, an' I answered straight.

'"There was some nonsinse last night at the Sheehys' quarthers, an' Judy's carryin' on the joke, darlin'," sez I.

'"At the Sheehys' quarthers?" sez Dinah very slow, an' Judy cut in wid: "He was there from nine till ten, Dinah Shadd, an' the betther half av that time I was sittin' on his knee, Dinah Shadd. Ye may look and ye may look an' ye may look me up an' down, but ye won't look away that Terence is my promust man. Terence, darlin', 'tis time for us to be comin' home."

'Dinah Shadd niver said word to Judy. "Ye left me at half-past eight," she sez to me, "an' I niver thought that ye'd leave me for Judy – promises or no promises. Go back wid her, you that have to be fetched by a girl! I'm done with you," sez she, and she ran into her own room, her mother followin'. So I was alone wid those two women and at liberty to spake my sentiments."

'"Judy Sheehy," sez I, "if you made a fool av me betune the lights you shall not do ut in the day. I niver promised you words or lines."

'"You lie," sez ould Mother Sheehy, "an' may ut choke you where you stand!" She was far gone in dhrink.

'"An' tho' ut choked me where I stud I'd not change," sez I. "Go home, Judy. I take shame for a decent girl like you dhraggin' your mother out bare-headed on this errand. Hear now, and have ut for an answer. I gave my word to Dinah Shadd yesterday, an', more blame to me, I was wid you last night talkin' nonsinse but nothin' more. You've chosen to thry to hould me on ut. I will not be held thereby for anythin' in the world. Is that enough?"

'Judy wint pink all over. "An' I wish you joy av the perjury," sez she, duckin' a curtsey. "You've lost a woman that would ha' wore her hand to the bone for your pleasure; an' 'deed, Terence, ye were not thrapped ..." Lascelles must ha' spoken plain to her. "I am such as Dinah is – 'deed I am! Ye've lost a fool av a girl that'll niver look at you again, an' ye've lost what ye niver had – your common honesty. If you manage your men as you manage your love-makin', small wondher they call you the worst corp'ril in the comp'ny. Come away, mother," sez she.

'But divil a fut would the ould woman budge! "D'you hould by that?" sez she, peerin' up under her thick grey eyebrows.

'"Ay, an' wud," sez I, "tho' Dinah gave me the go twinty times. I'll have no thruck with you or yours," sez I. "Take your child away, ye shameless woman."

'"An' am I shameless?" sez she, bringin' her hands up above her head. "Thin what are you, ye lyin', schamin', weak-kneed, dhirty-souled son av a sutler? Am *I* shameless? Who put the open shame on me an' my child that we shud go beggin' through the lines in the broad daylight for the broken word of a man? Double portion of my shame be on you, Terence Mulvaney, that think yourself so strong! By Mary and the saints, by blood and water an' by ivry sorrow that came into the world since the beginnin', the black blight fall on you and yours, so that you may niver be free from pain for another when ut's not your own! May your heart bleed in your breast drop by drop wid all your friends laughin' at the bleedin'! Strong you think yourself? May your strength be a curse to you to dhrive you into the divil's hands against your own will! Clear-eyed you are? May your eyes see clear evry step av the dark path you take till the hot cindhers av hell put thim out! May the ragin' dry thirst in my own ould bones go to you that you shall niver pass bottle full nor glass empty. God preserve the light av your onderstandin' to you, my jewel av a bhoy, that ye may niver forget what you mint to be an' do, whin you're wallowin' in the muck! May ye see the betther and follow the worse as long as there's breath in your body; an' may ye die quick in a strange land, watchin' your death before ut takes you, an' onable to stir hand or foot!"

'I heard a scufflin' in the room behind, and thin Dinah Shadd's hand dhropped into mine like a rose-leaf into a muddy road.

'"The half av that I'll take," sez she, "an' more too if I can. Go home, ye silly talkin' woman – go home an' confess."

'"Come away! Come away!" sez Judy pullin' her mother by the shawl. '"'Twas none av Terence's fault. For the love av Mary stop the talkin'!"

'"An' you!" said ould Mother Sheehy, spinnin' round forninst Dinah. "Will ye take the half av that man's load? Stand off from him, Dinah Shadd, before he takes you down too – you that look to be a quarther-master-sergeant's wife in five years. You look too high, child. You shall *wash* for the quarther-master-sergeant, whin he plases to give you the job out av charity; but a privit's wife you shall be to the end, an' evry sorrow of a privit's wife you shall know and niver a joy but wan, that shall go from you like the running tide from a rock. The pain av bearin' you shall know but niver the pleasure av giving the breast; an' you shall put away a man-child into the common ground wid niver a priest to say a prayer over him, an' on that man-child ye shall think ivry day av your life. Think long, Dinah Shadd, for you'll niver have another tho' you pray till your knees are bleedin'. The mothers av childer shall mock you behind your back when you're wringing over the wash-tub. You shall know what ut is to help a dhrunken husband home an' see him go to the gyard-room. Will that plase you, Dinah Shadd, that won't be seen talkin' to my daughter? You shall talk to worse than Judy before all's over. The sergints' wives shall look down on you contemptuous, daughter av a sergint, an' you shall cover ut all up wid a smiling face whin your heart's burstin'. Stand off av him, Dinah Shadd, for I've put the Black Curse of Shielygh upon him an' his own mouth shall make ut good."

'She pitched forward on her head an' began foamin' at the mouth. Dinah Shadd ran out wid water, an' Judy dhragged the ould woman into the verandah till she sat up.

'"I'm old an' forlore," she sez, thremblin' an' cryin', "and 'tis like I say a dale more than I mane."

'"When you're able to walk – go," says ould Mother Shadd. "This house has no place for the likes av you that have cursed my daughter."

'"Eyah!" said the ould woman. "Hard words break no bones, an' Dinah Shadd'll kape the love av her husband till my bones are green corn. Judy darlin', I misremember what I came here for. Can you lend us the bottom av a taycup av tay, Mrs Shadd?"

'But Judy dhragged her off cryin' as tho' her heart wud break. An' Dinah Shadd an' I, in ten minutes we had forgot ut all.'

'Then why do you remember it now?' said I.

'Is ut like I'd forget? Ivry word that wicked ould woman spoke fell thrue in my life afterwards, an' I cud ha' stud ut all – stud ut all – excipt when my little Shadd was born. That was on the line av march three months afther the regiment was taken with cholera. We were betune Umballa an' Kalka thin, an' I was on picket. Whin I came off duty the women showed me the child, an' ut turned on uts side an' died as I looked. We buried him by the road, an' Father Victor was a day's march behind wid the heavy baggage, so the comp'ny captain read a prayer. An' since then I've been a childless man, an' all else that ould Mother Sheehy put upon me an' Dinah Shadd. What do you think, sorr?'

I thought a good deal, but it seemed better then to reach out for Mulvaney's hand. The demonstration nearly cost me the use of three

The Courting of Dinah Shadd

fingers. Whatever he knows of his weaknesses, Mulvaney is entirely ignorant of his strength.

'But what do you think?' he repeated, as I was straightening out the crushed fingers.

My reply was drowned in yells and outcries from the next fire, where ten men were shouting for 'Orth'ris', 'Privit Orth'ris', 'Mistah Or–ther–ris!' 'Deah boy', 'Cap'n Orth'ris', 'Field-Marshal Orth'ris', 'Stanley, you pen'north o' pop, come 'ere to your own comp'ny!' And the cockney, who had been delighting another audience with recondite and Rabelaisian yarns, was shot down among his admirers by the major force.

'You've crumpled my dress-shirt 'orrid,' said he, 'an' I shan't sing no more to this 'ere bloomin' drawin'-room.'

Learoyd, roused by the confusion, uncoiled himself, crept behind Ortheris, and slung him aloft on his shoulders. 'Sing, ye bloomin' hummin' bird!' said he, and Ortheris, beating time on Learoyd's skull, delivered himself, in the raucous voice of the Ratcliffe Highway, of this song:

> My girl she give me the go onst,
>   When I was a London lad,
> An' I went on the drink for a fortnight,
>   An' then I went to the bad.
> The Queen she give me a shillin'
>   To fight for 'er over the seas;
> But Guv'ment built me a fever-trap,
>   An' Injia give me disease.
>
> #### Chorus
> Ho! don't you 'eed what a girl says,
>   An' don't you go for the beer;
> But I was an ass when I was at grass,
>   An' that is why I'm here.
>
> I fired a shot at a Afghan,
>   The beggar 'e fired again,
> An' I lay on my bed with a 'ole in my 'ed,
>   An' missed the next campaign!
> I up with my gun at a Burman
>   Who carried a bloomin' *dah*,[10]
> But the cartridge stuck and the bay'nit bruk,
>   An' all I got was the scar.
>
> #### Chorus
> Ho! don't you aim at a Afghan,
>   When you stand on the sky-line clear;

An' don't you go for a Burman
    If none o' your friends is near.

I served my time for a corp'ral,
    An' wetted my stripes with pop,
For I went on the bend with a intimate friend,
    An' finished the night in the 'shop'.
I served my time for a sergeant;
    The colonel 'e sez 'No!
The most you'll see is a full C.B.'[11]
    An' . . . very next night 'twas so.

Chorus

Ho! don't you go for a corp'ral
    Unless your 'ed is clear;
But I was an ass when I was at grass,
    An' that is why I'm 'ere.

I've tasted the luck o' the army
    In barrack an' camp an' clink,
An' I lost my tip[12] through the bloomin' trip
    Along o' the women an' drink.
I'm down at the heel o' my service,
    An' when I am laid on the shelf,
My very wust friend from beginning to end
    By the blood of a mouse was myself!

Chorus

Ho! don't you 'eed what a girl says,
    An' don't you go for the beer;
But I was an ass when I was at grass
    An' that is why I'm 'ere.

'Ay, listen to our little man now, singin' an' shoutin' as tho' trouble had niver touched him. D' you remember when he went mad with the home-sickness?'[13] said Mulvaney, recalling a never-to-be-forgotten season when Ortheris waded through the deep waters of affliction and behaved abominably. 'But he's talkin' bitter truth, though. Eyah!

'My very worst frind from beginnin' to ind
    By the blood av a mouse was mesilf!'

When I woke I saw Mulvaney, the night-dew gemming his moustache, leaning on his rifle at picket, lonely as Prometheus[14] on his rock, with I know not what vultures tearing his liver.

The Man Who Was [1]

The Earth gave up her dead that tide,
  Into our camp he came,
And said his say, and went his way,
  And left our hearts aflame.

Keep tally — on the gun-butt score
  The vengeance we must take,
When God shall bring full reckoning,
  For our dead comrade's sake.

Ballad.

Let it be clearly understood that the Russian is a delightful person till he tucks in his shirt. As an Oriental he is charming. It is only when he insists upon being treated as the most easterly of western peoples instead of the most westerly of easterns that he becomes a racial anomaly extremely difficult to handle. The host never knows which side of his nature is going to turn up next.

Dirkovitch was a Russian — a Russian of the Russians — who appeared to get his bread by serving the Czar as an officer in a Cossack regiment, and corresponding for a Russian newspaper with a name that was never twice alike. He was a handsome young Oriental, fond of wandering through unexplored portions of the earth, and he arrived in India from nowhere in particular. At least no living man could ascertain whether it was by way of Balkh, Badakshan, Chitral, Beluchistan, or Nepaul, or anywhere else. The Indian Government, being in an unusually affable mood, gave orders that he was to be civilly treated and shown everything that was to be seen. So he drifted, talking bad English and worse French, from one city to another, till he foregathered with Her Majesty's White Hussars [2] in the city of Peshawur, which stands at the mouth of that narrow swordcut in the hills that men call the Khyber Pass. He was undoubtedly an officer, and he was decorated after the manner of the Russians with little enamelled crosses, and he could talk, and (though this has nothing to do with his merits) he had been given up as a hopeless task, or cask, by the Black Tyrone, [3] who individually and collectively, with hot whisky and honey, mulled brandy, and mixed spirits of every kind, had striven in all hospitality to make him drunk. And when the

Black Tyrone, who are exclusively Irish, fail to disturb the peace of head of a foreigner – that foreigner is certain to be a superior man.

The White Hussars were as conscientious in choosing their wine as in charging the enemy. All that they possessed, including some wondrous brandy, was placed at the absolute disposition of Dirkovitch, and he enjoyed himself hugely – even more than among the Black Tyrones.

But he remained distressingly European through it all. The White Hussars were 'My dear true friends', 'Fellow-soldiers glorious', and 'Brothers inseparable'. He would unburden himself by the hour on the glorious future that awaited the combined arms of England and Russia when their hearts and their territories should run side by side, and the great mission of civilizing Asia should begin. That was unsatisfactory, because Asia is not going to be civilized after the methods of the West. There is too much Asia and she is too old. You cannot reform a lady of many lovers, and Asia has been insatiable in her flirtations aforetime. She will never attend Sunday school or learn to vote save with swords for tickets.

Dirkovitch knew this as well as anyone else, but it suited him to talk special-correspondently and to make himself as genial as he could. Now and then he volunteered a little, a very little information about his own sotnia[4] of Cossacks, left apparently to look after themselves somewhere at the back of beyond. He had done rough work in Central Asia, and had seen rather more help-yourself fighting than most men of his years. But he was careful never to betray his superiority, and more than careful to praise on all occasions the appearance, drill, uniform, and organization of Her Majesty's White Hussars. And indeed they were a regiment to be admired. When Lady Durgan, widow of the late Sir John Durgan, arrived in their station, and after a short time had been proposed to by every single man at mess, she put the public sentiment very neatly when she explained that they were all so nice that unless she could marry them all, including the colonel and some majors already married, she was not going to content herself with one hussar. Wherefore she wedded a little man in a rifle regiment, being by nature contradictious; and the White Hussars were going to wear crape on their arms, but compromised by attending the wedding in full force, and lining the aisle with un-utterable reproach. She had jilted them all – from Basset-Holmer the senior captain to little Mildred the junior subaltern, who could have given her four thousand a year and a title.

The only persons who did not share the general regard for the White Hussars were a few thousand gentlemen of Jewish extraction who lived across the border, and answered to the name of Pathan. They had once met the regiment officially and for something less than twenty minutes, but the interview, which was complicated with many casualties, had filled them with prejudice. They even called the White Hussars children of the devil and sons of persons whom it would be perfectly impossible to meet in decent society. Yet they were not above making their aversion fill their money-belts. The regiment possessed carbines – beautiful Martini-Henry carbines that would lob a bullet into an enemy's camp at one thousand yards, and were even handier than the long rifle. Therefore they were coveted all along the border, and since demand inevitably breeds supply, they were supplied at the risk of life and limb for exactly their weight in coined silver – seven and one half pounds weight of rupees, or sixteen pounds sterling reckoning the rupee at par. They were stolen at night by snaky-haired thieves who crawled on their stomachs under the nose of the sentries; they disappeared mysteriously from locked arm-racks, and in the hot weather, when all the barrack doors and windows were open, they vanished like puffs of their own smoke. The border people desired them for family vendettas and contingencies. But in the long cold nights of the northern Indian winter they were stolen most extensively. The traffic of murder was liveliest among the hills at that season, and prices ruled high. The regimental guards were first doubled and then trebled. A trooper does not much care if he loses a weapon – Government must make it good – but he deeply resents the loss of his sleep. The regiment grew very angry, and one rifle-thief bears the visible marks of their anger upon him to this hour. That incident stopped the burglaries for a time, and the guards were reduced accordingly, and the regiment devoted itself to polo with unexpected results; for it beat by two goals to one that very terrible polo corps the Lushkar Light Horse,[5] though the latter had four ponies apiece for a short hour's fight, as well as a native officer who played like a lambent flame across the ground.

They gave a dinner to celebrate the event. The Lushkar team came, and Dirkovitch came, in the fullest full uniform of a Cossack officer, which is as full as a dressing-gown, and was introduced to the Lushkars, and opened his eyes as he regarded. They were lighter men than the Hussars, and they carried themselves with the swing that is the peculiar right of the Punjab Frontier Force[6] and all Irregular Horse. Like everything else in the Service it has to be learnt, but, unlike many things, it is never forgotten, and remains on the body till death.

The great beam-roofed mess-room of the White Hussars was a sight to be remembered. All the mess plate was out on the long table – the same table that had served up the bodies of five officers after a forgotten fight long and long ago – the dingy, battered standards faced the door of entrance, clumps of winter-roses lay between the silver candlesticks, and the portraits of eminent officers deceased looked down on their successors from between the heads of sambhur, nilghai, markhor,[7] and, pride of all the mess, two grinning snow-leopards that had cost Basset-Holmer four months' leave that he might have spent in England, instead of on the road to Thibet and the daily risk of his life by ledge, snow-slide, and grassy slope.

The servants in spotless white muslin and the crest of their regiments on the brow of their turbans waited behind their masters, who were clad in the scarlet and gold of the White Hussars, and the cream and silver of the Lushkar Light Horse. Dirkovitch's dull green uniform was the only dark spot at the board, but his big onyx eyes made up for it. He was fraternizing effusively with the captain of the Lushkar team, who was wondering how many of Dirkovitch's Cossacks his own dark wiry down-countrymen could account for in a fair charge. But one does not speak of these things openly.

The talk rose higher and higher, and the regimental band played between the courses, as is the immemorial custom, till all tongues ceased for a moment with the removal of the dinner-slips [8] and the first toast of obligation, when an officer rising said, 'Mr Vice, the Queen,' and little Mildred from the bottom of the table answered, 'The Queen, God bless her,' and the big spurs clanked as the big men heaved themselves up and drank the Queen upon whose pay they were falsely supposed to settle their mess-bills. That Sacrament of the Mess never grows old, and never ceases to bring a lump into the throat of the listener wherever he be by sea or by land. Dirkovitch rose with his 'brothers glorious', but he could not understand. No one but an officer can tell what the toast means; and the bulk have more sentiment than comprehension. Immediately after the little silence that follows on the ceremony there entered the native officer who had played for the Lushkar team. He could not, of course, eat with the mess, but he came in at dessert, all six feet of him, with the blue and silver turban atop, and the big black boots below. The mess rose joyously as he thrust forward the hilt of his sabre in token of fealty for the colonel of the White Hussars to touch, and dropped into a vacant chair amid shouts of: '*Rung ho*, Hira Singh!' (which being translated means 'Go in and win'). 'Did I whack you over the knee, old man?' 'Ressaidar Sahib, what the devil made you play that kicking pig of a pony in the last ten minutes?' '*Shabash*,[9] Ressaidar [10] Sahib!' Then the voice of the colonel, 'The health of Ressaidar Hira Singh!'

After the shouting had died away Hira Singh rose to reply, for he was the cadet of a royal house, the son of a king's son, and knew what was due on these occasions. Thus he spoke in the vernacular: 'Colonel Sahib and officers of this regiment. Much honour have you done me. This will I remember. We came down from afar to play you. But we were beaten.' ('No fault of yours, Ressaidar Sahib. Played on our own ground y' know. Your ponies were cramped from the railway. Don't apologize!') 'Therefore perhaps we will come again if it be so ordained.' ('Hear! Hear! Hear, indeed! Bravo! Hsh!') 'Then we will play you afresh' ('Happy to meet you.') 'till there are left no feet upon our ponies. Thus far for sport.' He dropped one hand on his sword-hilt and his eye wandered to Dirkovitch lolling back in his chair. 'But if by the will of God there arises any other game which is not the polo game, then be assured, Colonel Sahib and officers, that we will play it out side by side, though *they*,' again his eye sought Dirkovitch, 'though *they* I say have fifty ponies to our one horse.' And with a deep-mouthed *Rung ho!* that sounded like a musket-butt on flagstones, he sat down amid leaping glasses.

Dirkovitch, who had devoted himself steadily to the brandy – the terrible brandy aforementioned – did not understand, nor did the expurgated translations offered to him at all convey the point. Decidedly Hira Singh's was the speech of the evening, and the clamour might have continued to the dawn had it not been broken by the noise of a shot without that sent every man feeling at his defenceless left side. Then there was a scuffle and a yell of pain.

'Carbine-stealing again!' said the adjutant, calmly sinking back in his chair. 'This comes of reducing the guards. I hope the sentries have killed him.'

The feet of armed men pounded on the verandah flags, and it was as though something was being dragged.

'Why don't they put him in the cells till the morning?' said the colonel testily. 'See if they've damaged him, sergeant.'

The mess sergeant fled out into the darkness and returned with two troopers and a corporal, all very much perplexed.

'Caught a man stealin' carbines, sir,' said the corporal. 'Leastways 'e was crawlin' towards the barracks, sir, past the main road sentries, an' the sentry 'e sez, sir –'

The limp heap of rags upheld by the three men groaned. Never was seen so destitute and demoralized an Afghan. He was turbanless, shoeless, caked with dirt, and all but dead with rough handling. Hira Singh started slightly at the sound of the man's pain. Dirkovitch took another glass of brandy.

'*What* does the sentry say?' said the colonel.

'Sez 'e speaks English, sir,' said the corporal.

'So you brought him into mess instead of handing him over to the sergeant! If he spoke all the Tongues of the Pentecost you've no business –'

Again the bundle groaned and muttered. Little Mildred had risen from his place to inspect. He jumped back as though he had been shot.

'Perhaps it would be better, sir, to send the men away,' said he to the colonel, for he was a much privileged subaltern. He put his arms round the rag-bound horror as he spoke, and dropped him into a chair. It may not have been explained that the littleness of Mildred lay in his being six feet four and big in proportion. The corporal seeing that an officer was disposed to look after the capture, and that the colonel's eye was beginning to blaze, promptly removed himself and his men. The mess was left alone with the carbine-thief, who laid his head on the table and wept bitterly, hopelessly, and inconsolably, as little children weep.

Hira Singh leapt to his feet. 'Colonel Sahib,' said he, 'that man is no Afghan, for they weep *Ai! Ai!* Nor is he of Hindustan, for they weep *Oh! Ho!* He weeps after the fashion of the white men, who say *Ow! Ow!*'

'Now where the dickens did you get that knowledge, Hira Singh?' said the captain of the Lushkar team.

'Hear him!' said Hira Singh simply, pointing at the crumpled figure that wept as though it would never cease.

'He said, "My God!"' said little Mildred. 'I heard him say it.'

The colonel and the mess-room looked at the man in silence. It is a horrible thing to hear a man cry. A woman can sob from the top of her palate, or her lips, or anywhere else, but a man must cry from his diaphragm, and it rends him to pieces.

'Poor devil!' said the colonel, coughing tremendously. 'We ought to send him to hospital. He's been man-handled.'

Now the adjutant loved his carbines. They were to him as his grandchildren, the men standing in the first place. He grunted rebelliously: 'I can understand an Afghan stealing, because he's built that way. But I can't understand his crying. That makes it worse.'

The brandy must have affected Dirkovitch, for he lay back in his chair and stared at the ceiling. There was nothing special in the ceiling beyond a shadow as of a huge black coffin. Owing to some peculiarity in the construction of the mess-room this shadow was always thrown when the candles were lighted. It never disturbed the digestion of the White Hussars. They were in fact rather proud of it.

'Is he going to cry all night?' said the colonel, 'or are we supposed to sit up with little Mildred's guest until he feels better?'

The man in the chair threw up his head and stared at the mess. 'Oh, my God!' he said, and every soul in the mess rose to his feet. Then the Lushkar captain did a deed for which he ought to have been given the Victoria Cross – distinguished gallantry in a fight against overwhelming curiosity. He picked up his team with his eyes as the hostess picks up the ladies at the opportune moment, and pausing only by the colonel's chair to say, 'This isn't *our* affair, you know, sir,' led them into the verandah and the gardens. Hira Singh was the last to go, and he looked at Dirkovitch. But Dirkovitch had departed into a brandy-paradise of his own. His lips moved without sound, and he was studying the coffin on the ceiling.

'White – white all over,' said Basset-Holmer, the adjutant. 'What a pernicious renegade he must be! I wonder where he came from?'

The colonel shook the man gently by the arm, and 'Who are you?' said he.

There was no answer. The man stared round the mess-room and smiled in the colonel's face. Little Mildred, who was always more of a woman than a man till 'Boot and saddle' [11] was sounded, repeated the question in a voice that would have drawn confidences from a geyser. The man only smiled. Dirkovitch at the far end of the table slid gently from his chair to the floor. No son of Adam in this present imperfect world can mix the Hussars' champagne with the Hussars' brandy by five and eight glasses of each without remembering the pit whence he was digged [12] and descending thither. The band began to play the tune with which the White Hussars from the date of their formation have concluded all their functions. They would sooner be disbanded than abandon that tune; it is a part of their system. The man straightened himself in his chair and drummed on the table with his fingers.

'I don't see why we should entertain lunatics,' said the colonel. 'Call a guard and send him off to the cells. We'll look into the business in the morning. Give him a glass of wine first though.'

Little Mildred filled a sherry-glass with the brandy and thrust it over to the man. He drank, and the tune rose louder, and he straightened himself yet more. Then he put out his long-taloned hands to a piece of plate opposite and fingered it lovingly. There was a mystery connected with that piece of plate, in the shape of a spring which converted what was a seven-branched candlestick, three springs on each side and one in the middle, into a sort of wheel-spoke candelabrum. He found the spring, pressed it, and laughed weakly. He rose from his chair and inspected a picture on the wall, then moved on to another picture, the mess watching him without a word. When he came to the mantelpiece he

shook his head and seemed distressed. A piece of plate representing a
mounted hussar in full uniform caught his eye. He pointed to it, and
then to the mantelpiece with inquiry in his eyes.

'What is it – Oh what is it?' said little Mildred. Then as a mother
might speak to a child, 'That is a horse. Yes, a horse.'

Very slowly came the answer in a thick, passionless guttural – 'Yes, I –
have seen. But – where is *the* horse?'

You could have heard the hearts of the mess beating as the men drew
back to give the stranger full room in his wanderings. There was no
question of calling the guard.

Again he spoke – very slowly, 'Where is *our* horse?'

There is but one horse in the White Hussars, and his portrait hangs
outside the door of the mess-room. He is the piebald drum-horse, the
king of the regimental band, that served the regiment for seven-and-
thirty years, and in the end was shot for old age. Half the mess tore
the thing down from its place and thrust it into the man's hands. He
placed it above the mantelpiece, it clattered on the ledge as his poor
hands dropped it, and he staggered towards the bottom of the table,
falling into Mildred's chair. Then all the men spoke to one another
something after this fashion, 'The drum-horse hasn't hung over the
mantelpiece since '67.' 'How does he know?' 'Mildred, go and speak
to him again.' 'Colonel, what are you going to do?' 'Oh, dry up, and
give the poor devil a chance to pull himself together.' 'It isn't possible
anyhow. The man's a lunatic.'

Little Mildred stood at the colonel's side talking in his ear. 'Will you
be good enough to take your seats please, gentlemen!' he said, and the
mess dropped into the chairs. Only Dirkovitch's seat, next to little
Mildred's, was blank, and little Mildred himself had found Hira Singh's
place. The wide-eyed mess-sergeant filled the glasses in dead silence.
Once more the colonel rose, but his hand shook, and the port spilled on
the table as he looked straight at the man in little Mildred's chair and
said hoarsely, 'Mr Vice, the Queen.' There was a little pause, but the
man sprang to his feet and answered without hesitation, 'The Queen,
God bless her!' and as he emptied the thin glass he snapped the shank
between his fingers.

Long and long ago, when the Empress of India was a young woman
and there were no unclean ideals in the land, it was the custom of a few
messes to drink the Queen's toast in broken glass, to the vast delight of
the mess-contractors. The custom is now dead, because there is nothing
to break anything for, except now and again the word of a Government,
and that has been broken already.

'That settles it,' said the colonel, with a gasp. 'He's not a sergeant. What in the world is he?'

The entire mess echoed the word, and the volley of questions would have scared any man. It was no wonder that the ragged, filthy invader could only smile and shake his head.

From under the table, calm and smiling, rose Dirkovitch, who had been roused from healthful slumber by feet upon his body. By the side of the man he rose, and the man shrieked and grovelled. It was a horrible sight coming so swiftly upon the pride and glory of the toast that had brought the strayed wits together.

Dirkovitch made no offer to raise him, but little Mildred heaved him up in an instant. It is not good that a gentleman who can answer to the Queen's toast should lie at the feet of a subaltern of Cossacks.

The hasty action tore the wretch's upper clothing nearly to the waist, and his body was seamed with dry black scars. There is only one weapon in the world that cuts in parallel lines, and it is neither the cane nor the cat. Dirkovitch saw the marks, and the pupils of his eyes dilated. Also his face changed. He said something that sounded like *Shto ve takete*, and the man fawning answered, *Chetyre*.

'What's that?' said everybody together.

'His number. That is number four, you know,' Dirkovitch spoke very thickly.

'What has a Queen's officer to do with a qualified number?' said the colonel, and an unpleasant growl ran round the table.

'How can I tell?' said the affable Oriental with a sweet smile. 'He is a – how you have it? – escape – run-a-way, from over there.' He nodded towards the darkness of the night.

'Speak to him if he'll answer you, and speak to him gently,' said little Mildred, settling the man in a chair. It seemed most improper to all present that Dirkovitch should sip brandy as he talked in purring, spitting Russian to the creature who answered so feebly and with such evident dread. But since Dirkovitch appeared to understand no one said a word. All breathed heavily, leaning forward, in the long gaps of the conversation. The next time that they have no engagements on hand the White Hussars intend to go to St Petersburg in a body to learn Russian.

'He does not know how many years ago,' said Dirkovitch facing the mess, 'but he says it was very long ago in a war. I think there was an accident. He says he was of this glorious and distinguished regiment in the war.'

'The rolls! The rolls! Holmer, get the rolls!' said little Mildred, and the adjutant dashed off bare-headed to the orderly-room, where the muster-rolls of the regiment were kept. He returned just in time to hear Dirkovitch conclude, 'Therefore, my dear friends, I am most sorry to say there was an accident which would have been reparable if he had apologized to that our colonel, which he had insulted.'

Then followed another growl which the colonel tried to beat down. The mess was in no mood just then to weigh insults to Russian colonels.

'He does not remember, but I think that there was an accident, and so he was not exchanged among the prisoners, but he was sent to another place – how do you say? – the country. *So*, he says, he came here. He does not know how he came. Eh? He was at Chepany' – the man caught the word, nodded, and shivered – 'at Zhigansk and Irkutsk. I cannot understand how he escaped. He says, too, that he was in the forests for many years, but how many years he has forgotten – that with many things. It was an accident; done because he did not apologize to that our colonel. Ah!'

Instead of echoing Dirkovitch's sigh of regret, it is sad to record that the White Hussars livelily exhibited un-Christian delight and other emotions, hardly restrained by their sense of hospitality. Holmer flung the frayed and yellow regimental rolls on the table, and the men flung themselves at these.

'Steady! Fifty-six – fifty-five – fifty-four,' said Holmer. 'Here we are. "Lieutenant Austin Limmason. *Missing*." That was before Sebastopol.[13] What an infernal shame! Insulted one of their colonels, and was quietly shipped off. Thirty years of his life wiped out.'

'But he never apologized. Said he'd see him damned first,' chorused the mess.

'Poor chap! I suppose he never had the chance afterwards. How did he come here?' said the colonel.

The dingy heap in the chair could give no answer.

'Do you know who you are?'

It laughed weakly.

'Do you know that you are Limmason – Lieutenant Limmason of the White Hussars?'

Swiftly as a shot came the answer, in a slightly surprised tone, 'Yes, I'm Limmason, of course.' The light died out in his eyes, and the man collapsed, watching every motion of Dirkovitch with terror. A flight from Siberia may fix a few elementary facts in the mind, but it does not seem to lead to continuity of thought. The man could not explain how, like a homing pigeon, he had found his way to his own old mess again. Of what he had suffered or seen he knew nothing. He cringed before Dirkovitch as instinctively as he had pressed the spring of the candlestick, sought the picture of the drum-horse, and answered to the toast of the Queen. The rest was a blank that the dreaded Russian tongue could only in part remove. His head bowed on his breast, and he giggled and cowered alternately.

The devil that lived in the brandy prompted Dirkovitch at this extremely inopportune moment to make a speech. He rose, swaying slightly, gripped the table-edge, while his eyes glowed like opals, and began:

'Fellow-soldiers glorious – true friends and hospitables. It was an accident, and deplorable – most deplorable.' Here he smiled sweetly all round the mess. 'But you will think of this little, little thing. So little, is it not? The Czar! Posh! I slap my fingers – I snap my fingers at him. Do I believe in him? No! But in us Slav who has done nothing, *him* I believe. Seventy – how much – millions peoples that have done nothing – not one thing. Posh! Napoleon was an episode.' He banged a hand on the table. 'Hear you, old peoples, we have done nothing in the world – out here. All our work is to do; and it shall be done, old peoples. Get a-way!' He waved his hand imperiously, and pointed to the man. 'You see him. He is not good to see. He was just one little – oh, so little – accident, that no one remembered. Now he is *That!* So will you be, brother soldiers so brave – so will you be. But you will never come back. You will all go where he is gone, or' – he pointed to the great coffin-shadow on the ceiling, and muttering, 'Seventy millions – get a-way, you old peoples,' fell asleep.

'Sweet, and to the point,' said little Mildred. 'What's the use of getting wroth? Let's make this poor devil comfortable.'

But that was a matter suddenly and swiftly taken from the loving hands of the White Hussars. The lieutenant had returned only to go away again three days later, when the wail of the Dead March, and the tramp of the squadrons, told the wondering Station, who saw no gap in the mess-table, that an officer of the regiment had resigned his newfound commission.

And Dirkovitch, bland, supple, and always genial, went away too by a night train. Little Mildred and another man saw him off, for he was the guest of the mess, and even had he smitten the colonel with the open hand, the law of that mess allowed no relaxation of hospitality.

'Good-bye, Dirkovitch, and a pleasant journey,' said little Mildred.

'*Au revoir*,' said the Russian.

'Indeed! But we thought you were going home?'

'Yes, but I will come again. My dear friends, is that road shut?' He pointed to where the North Star burned over the Khyber Pass.

'By Jove! I forgot. Of course. Happy to meet you, old man, any time you like. Got everything you want? Cheroots, ice, bedding? That's all right. Well, *au revoir*, Dirkovitch.'

'Um,' said the other man, as the tail-lights of the train grew small. 'Of – all – the – unmitigated –!'

Little Mildred answered nothing, but watched the North Star and hummed a selection from a recent Simla burlesque that had much delighted the White Hussars. It ran –

> I'm sorry for Mister Bluebeard,
> I'm sorry to cause him pain;
> But a terrible spree there's sure to be
> When he comes back again.

Without Benefit of Clergy [1]

Before my Spring I garnered Autumn's gain,
Out of her time my field was white with grain,
  The year gave up her secrets to my woe.
Forced and deflowered each sick season lay,
In mystery of increase and decay;
I saw the sunset ere men saw the day,
  Who am too wise in that I should not know.

Bitter Waters.

I

'But if it be a girl?'

'Lord of my life, it cannot be. I have prayed for so many nights, and sent gifts to Sheikh Badl's [2] shrine so often, that I know God will give us a son – a man-child that shall grow into a man. Think of this and be glad. My mother shall be his mother till I can take him again, and the mullah of the Pattan mosque shall cast his nativity – God send he be born in an auspicious hour! – and then, and then thou wilt never weary of me, thy slave.'

'Since when hast thou been a slave, my queen?'

'Since the beginning – till this mercy came to me. How could I be sure of thy love when I knew that I had been bought with silver?'

'Nay, that was the dowry. I paid it to thy mother.'

'And she has buried it, and sits upon it all day long like a hen. What talk is yours of dower! I was bought as though I had been a Lucknow dancing-girl instead of a child.'

'Art thou sorry for the sale?'

'I have sorrowed; but today I am glad. Thou wilt never cease to love me now? – answer, my king.'

'Never – never. No.'

'Not even though the *mem-log* [3] – the white women of thy own blood – love thee? And remember, I have watched them driving in the evening; they are very fair.'

'I have seen fire-balloons by the hundred. I have seen the moon, and – then I saw no more fire-balloons.'

213

Ameera clapped her hands and laughed. 'Very good talk,' she said. Then with an assumption of great stateliness, 'It is enough. Thou hast my permission to depart – if thou wilt.'

The man did not move. He was sitting on a low red-lacquered couch in a room furnished only with a blue and white floor-cloth, some rugs, and a very complete collection of native cushions. At his feet sat a woman of sixteen, and she was all but all the world in his eyes. By every rule and law she should have been otherwise, for he was an Englishman, and she a Mussulman's daughter bought two years before from her mother, who, being left without money, would have sold Ameera shrieking to the Prince of Darkness if the price had been sufficient.

It was a contract entered into with a light heart; but even before the girl had reached her bloom she came to fill the greater portion of John Holden's life. For her, and the withered hag her mother, he had taken a little house overlooking the great red-walled city, and found – when the marigolds had sprung up by the well in the courtyard, and Ameera had established herself according to her own ideas of comfort, and her mother had ceased grumbling at the inadequacy of the cooking-places, the distance from the daily market, and at matters of house-keeping in general – that the house was to him his home. Anyone could enter his bachelor's bungalow by day or night, and the life that he led there was an unlovely one. In the house in the city his feet only could pass beyond the outer courtyard to the women's rooms; and when the big wooden gate was bolted behind him he was king in his own territory, with Ameera for queen. And there was going to be added to this kingdom a third person whose arrival Holden felt inclined to resent. It interfered with his perfect happiness. It disarranged the orderly peace of the house that was his own. But Ameera was wild with delight at the thought of it, and her mother not less so. The love of a man, and particularly a white man, was at the best an inconstant affair, but it might, both women argued, be held fast by a baby's hands. 'And then,' Ameera would always say, 'then he will never care for the white *mem-log*. I hate them all – I hate them all.'

'He will go back to his own people in time,' said the mother; 'but by the blessing of God that time is yet afar off.'

Holden sat silent on the couch thinking of the future, and his thoughts were not pleasant. The drawbacks of a double life are manifold. The Government, with singular care, had ordered him out of the station for a fortnight on special duty in the place of a man who was watching by the bedside of a sick wife. The verbal notification of the transfer had been edged by a cheerful remark that Holden ought to think himself lucky in being a bachelor and a free man. He came to break the news to Ameera.

'It is not good,' she said slowly, 'but it is not all bad. There is my mother here, and no harm will come to me – unless indeed I die of pure joy. Go thou to thy work and think no troublesome thoughts. When the days are done I believe . . . nay, I am sure. And – and then I shall lay *him* in thy arms, and thou wilt love me for ever. The train goes tonight, at midnight is it not? Go now, and do not let thy heart be heavy by cause of me. But thou wilt not delay in returning? Thou wilt not stay on the road to talk to the bold white *mem-log*. Come back to me swiftly, my life.'

As he left the courtyard to reach his horse that was tethered to the gate-post, Holden spoke to the white-haired old watchman who guarded the house, and bade him under certain contingencies despatch the filled-up telegraph-form that Holden gave him. It was all that could be done, and with the sensations of a man who has attended his own funeral Holden went away by the night mail to his exile. Every hour of the day he dreaded the arrival of the telegram, and every hour of the night he pictured to himself the death of Ameera. In consequence his work for the State was not of first-rate quality, nor was his temper towards his colleagues of the most amiable. The fortnight ended without a sign from his home, and, torn to pieces by his anxieties, Holden returned to be swallowed up for two precious hours by a dinner at the club, wherein he heard, as a man hears in a swoon, voices telling him how execrably he had performed the other man's duties, and how he had endeared himself to all his associates. Then he fled on horseback through the night with his heart in his mouth. There was no answer at first to his blows on the gate, and he had just wheeled his horse round to kick it in when Pir Khan appeared with a lantern and held his stirrup.

'Has aught occurred?' said Holden.

'The news does not come from my mouth, Protector of the Poor, but –' He held out his shaking hand as befitted the bearer of good news who is entitled to a reward.

Holden hurried through the courtyard. A light burned in the upper room. His horse neighed in the gateway, and he heard a shrill little wail that sent all the blood into the apple of his throat. It was a new voice, but it did not prove that Ameera was alive.

'Who is there?' he called up the narrow brick staircase.

There was a cry of delight from Ameera, and then the voice of the mother, tremulous with old age and pride – 'We be two women and and – the – man – thy – son.'

On the threshold of the room Holden stepped on a naked dagger, that was laid there to avert ill-luck, and it broke at the hilt under his impatient heel.

'God is great!' cooed Ameera in the half-light. 'Thou hast taken his misfortunes on thy head.'

'Ay, but how is it with thee, life of my life? Old woman, how is it with her?'

'She has forgotten her sufferings for joy that the child is born. There is no harm; but speak softly,' said the mother.

'It only needed thy presence to make me all well,' said Ameera. 'My king, thou hast been very long away. What gifts hast thou for me? Ah, ah! It is I that bring gifts this time. Look, my life, look. Was there ever such a babe? Nay, I am too weak even to clear my arm from him.'

'Rest then, and do not talk. I am here, *bachari* [little woman].'

'Well said, for there is a bond and a heel-rope [*peecharee*] between us now that nothing can break. Look – canst thou see in this light? He is without spot or blemish. Never was such a man-child. *Ya illah!*⁴ he shall be a pundit – no, a trooper of the Queen. And, my life, dost thou love me as well as ever, though I am faint and sick and worn? Answer truly.'

'Yea. I love as I have loved, with all my soul. Lie still, pearl, and rest.'

'Then do not go. Sit by my side here – so. Mother, the lord of this house needs a cushion. Bring it.' There was an almost imperceptible movement on the part of the new life that lay in the hollow of Ameera's arm. 'Aho!' she said, her voice breaking with love. 'The babe is a champion from his birth. He is kicking me in the side with mighty kicks. Was there ever such a babe! And he is ours to us – thine and mine. Put thy hand on his head, but carefully, for he is very young, and men are unskilled in such matters.'

Very cautiously Holden touched with the tips of his fingers the downy head.

'He is of the Faith,' said Ameera; 'for lying here in the night-watches I whispered the call to prayer and the profession of faith into his ears. And it is most marvellous that he was born upon a Friday, as I was born. Be careful of him, my life; but he can almost grip with his hands.'

Holden found one helpless little hand that closed feebly on his finger. And the clutch ran through his body till it settled about his heart. Till then his sole thought had been for Ameera. He began to realize that there was someone else in the world, but he could not feel that it was a veritable son with a soul. He sat down to think and Ameera dozed lightly.

'Get hence, *sahib*,' said her mother under her breath. 'It is not good that she should find you here on waking. She must be still.'

'I go,' said Holden submissively. 'Here be rupees. See that my *baba* gets fat and finds all that he needs.'

The chink of silver roused Ameera. 'I am his mother, and no hireling,' she said weakly. 'Shall I look to him more or less for the sake of money? Mother, give it back. I have borne my lord a son.'

The deep sleep of weakness came upon her almost before the sentence was completed. Holden went down to the courtyard very softly with his heart at ease. Pir Khan, the old watchman, was chuckling with delight. 'This house is now complete,' he said, and without further comment thrust into Holden's hands the hilt of a sabre worn many years ago when he, Pir Khan, served the Queen in the police. The bleat of a tethered goat came from the well-kerb.

'There be two,' said Pir Khan, 'two goats of the best. I bought them, and they cost much money; and since there is no birth-party assembled their flesh will be all mine. Strike craftily, *sahib*! 'Tis an ill-balanced sabre at the best. Wait till they raise their heads from cropping the marigolds.'

'And why?' said Holden, bewildered.

'For the birth-sacrifice. What else? Otherwise the child being un-guarded from fate may die. The Protector of the Poor knows the fitting words to be said.'

Holden had learned them once with little thought that he would ever speak them in earnest. The touch of the cold sabre-hilt in his palm turned suddenly to the clinging grip of the child up-stairs – the child that was his own son – and a dread of loss filled him.

'Strike!' said Pir Khan. 'Never life came into the world but life was paid for it. See, the goats have raised their heads. Now! With a drawing cut!'

Hardly knowing what he did, Holden cut twice as he muttered the Mahomedan prayer that runs: 'Almighty! In place of this my son I offer life for life, blood for blood, head for head, bone for bone, hair for hair, skin for skin.' The waiting horse snorted and bounded in his pickets at the smell of the raw blood that spirted over Holden's riding-boots.

'Well smitten!' said Pir Khan wiping the sabre. 'A swordsman was lost in thee. Go with a light heart, Heaven-born. I am thy servant, and the servant of thy son. May the Presence live a thousand years and . . . the flesh of the goats is all mine?' Pir Khan drew back richer by a month's pay. Holden swung himself into the saddle and rode off through the low-hanging wood-smoke of the evening. He was full of riotous ex-ultation, alternating with a vast vague tenderness directed towards no particular object, that made him choke as he bent over the neck of his uneasy horse. 'I never felt like this in my life,' he thought. 'I'll go to the club and pull myself together.'

A game of pool was beginning, and the room was full of men. Holden entered, eager to get to the light and the company of his fellows, singing at the top of his voice –

'In Baltimore a-walking, a lady I did meet!'

'Did you?' said the club-secretary from his corner. 'Did she happen to tell you that your boots were wringing wet? Great goodness, man, it's blood!'

'Bosh!' said Holden, picking his cue from the rack. 'May I cut in? It's dew. I've been riding through high crops. My faith! my boots are in a mess though!

> 'And if it be a girl she shall wear a wedding-ring,
> And if it be a boy he shall fight for his king,
> With his dirk, and his cap, and his little jacket blue,
> He shall walk the quarter-deck –'

'Yellow on blue – green next player,' said the marker monotonously. '*He shall walk the quarter-deck* – Am I green, marker? *He shall walk the quarter-deck* – eh! that's a bad shot – *As his daddy used to do*!'

'I don't see that you have anything to crow about,' said a zealous junior civilian acidly. 'The Government is not exactly pleased with your work when you relieved Sanders.'

'Does that mean a wigging from headquarters?' said Holden with an abstracted smile. 'I think I can stand it.'

The talk beat up round the ever-fresh subject of each man's work, and steadied Holden till it was time to go to his dark empty bungalow, where his butler received him as one who knew all his affairs. Holden remained awake for the greater part of the night, and his dreams were pleasant ones.

II

'How old is he now?'

'*Ya illah!* What a man's question! He is all but six weeks old; and on this night I go up to the house-top with thee, my life, to count the stars. For that is auspicious. And he was born on a Friday under the sign of the Sun, and it has been told to me that he will outlive us both and get wealth. Can we wish for aught better, beloved?'

'There is nothing better. Let us go up to the roof, and thou shalt count the stars – but a few only, for the sky is heavy with cloud.'

'The winter rains are late, and maybe they come out of season. Come, before all the stars are hid. I have put on my richest jewels.'

'Thou hast forgotten the best of all.'

'*Ai!* Ours. He comes also. He has never yet seen the skies.'

Ameera climbed the narrow staircase that led to the flat roof. The child, placid and unwinking, lay in the hollow of her right arm, gorgeous in silver-fringed muslin with a small skull-cap on his head. Ameera wore all that she valued most. The diamond nose-stud that takes the place of the Western patch in drawing attention to the curve of the nostril, the gold ornament in the centre of the forehead studded with tallow-drop emeralds and flawed rubies, the heavy circlet of beaten gold that was fastened round her neck by the softness of the pure metal, and the chinking curb-patterned silver anklets hanging low over the rosy ankle-bone. She was dressed in jade-green muslin as befitted a daughter of the Faith, and from shoulder to elbow and elbow to wrist ran bracelets of silver tied with floss silk, frail glass bangles slipped over the wrist in proof of the slenderness of the hand, and certain heavy gold bracelets that had no part in her country's ornaments, but, since they were Holden's gift and fastened with a cunning European snap, delighted her immensely.

They sat down by the low white parapet of the roof, overlooking the city and its lights.

'They are happy down there,' said Ameera. 'But I do not think that they are as happy as we. Nor do I think the white *mem-log* are as happy. And thou?'

'I know they are not.'

'How dost thou know?'

'They give their children over to the nurses.'

'I have never seen that,' said Ameera with a sigh, 'nor do I wish to see. *Ahi!*' – she dropped her head on Holden's shoulder – 'I have counted forty stars, and I am tired. Look at the child, love of my life, he is counting too.'

The baby was staring with round eyes at the dark of the heavens. Ameera placed him in Holden's arms, and he lay there without a cry.

'What shall we call him among ourselves?' she said. 'Look! Art thou ever tired of looking? He carries thy very eyes. But the mouth –'

'Is thine, most dear. Who should know better than I?'

''Tis such a feeble mouth. Oh, so small! And yet it holds my heart between its lips. Give him to me now. He has been too long away.'

'Nay, let him lie; he has not yet begun to cry.'

'When he cries thou wilt give him back – eh? What a man of mankind thou art! If he cried he were only the dearer to me. But, my life, what little name shall we give him?'

The small body lay close to Holden's heart. It was utterly helpless and very soft. He scarcely dared to breathe for fear of crushing it. The caged green parrot that is regarded as a sort of guardian-spirit in most native households moved on its perch and fluttered a drowsy wing.

'There is the answer,' said Holden. 'Mian Mittu has spoken. He shall be the parrot. When he is ready he will talk mightily and run about. Mian Mittu is the parrot in thy — in the Mussulman tongue, is it not?'

'Why put me so far off?' said Ameera fretfully. 'Let it be like unto some English name — but not wholly. For he is mine.'

'Then call him Tota, for that is likest English.'

'Ay, Tota, and that is still the parrot. Forgive me, my lord, for a minute ago, but in truth he is too little to wear all the weight of Mian Mittu for name. He shall be Tota — our Tota to us. Hearest thou, oh, small one? Littlest, thou art Tota.' She touched the child's cheek, and he waking wailed, and it was necessary to return him to his mother, who soothed him with the wonderful rhyme of *Aré koko, Jaré koko!* which says —

> 'Oh crow! Go crow! Baby's sleeping sound,
> And the wild plums grow in the jungle, only a penny a pound.
> Only a penny a pound, *baba*, only a penny a pound.'

Reassured many times as to the price of those plums, Tota cuddled himself down to sleep. The two sleek, white well-bullocks in the court-yard were steadily chewing the cud of their evening meal; old Pir Khan squatted at the head of Holden's horse, his police sabre across his knees, pulling drowsily at a big water-pipe that croaked like a bull-frog in a pond. Ameera's mother sat spinning in the lower verandah, and the wooden gate was shut and barred. The music of a marriage-procession came to the roof above the gentle hum of the city, and a string of flying-foxes crossed the face of the low moon.

'I have prayed,' said Ameera after a long pause, 'I have prayed for two things. First, that I may die in thy stead if thy death is demanded, and in the second, that I may die in the place of the child. I have prayed to the Prophet and to Beebee Miriam [the Virgin Mary]. Thinkest thou either will hear?'

'From thy lips who would not hear the lightest word?'

'I asked for straight talk, and thou hast given me sweet talk. Will my prayers be heard?'

'How can I say? God is very good.'

'Of that I am not sure. Listen now. When I die, or the child dies, what is thy fate? Living, thou wilt return to the bold white *mem-log*, for kind calls to kind.'

'Not always.'

'With a woman, no; with a man it is otherwise. Thou wilt in this life, later on, go back to thine own folk. That I could almost endure, for I should be dead. But in thy very death thou wilt be taken away to a strange place and a paradise that I do not know.'

'Will it be paradise?'

'Surely, for who would harm thee? But we two – I and the child – shall be elsewhere, and we cannot come to thee, nor canst thou come to us. In the old days, before the child was born, I did not think of these things; but now I think of them always. It is very hard talk.'

'It will fall as it will fall. Tomorrow we do not know, but today and love we know well. Surely we are happy now.'

'So happy that it were well to make our happiness assured. And thy Beebee Miriam should listen to me; for she is also a woman. But then she would envy me! It is not seemly for men to worship a woman.'

Holden laughed aloud at Ameera's little spasm of jealousy.

'Is it not seemly? Why didst thou not turn me from worship of thee, then?'

'Thou a worshipper! And of me? My king, for all thy sweet words, well I know that I am thy servant and thy slave, and the dust under thy feet. And I would not have it otherwise. See!'

Before Holden could prevent her she stooped forward and touched his feet; recovering herself with a little laugh she hugged Tota closer to her bosom. Then, almost savagely –

'Is it true that the bold white *mem-log* live for three times the length of my life? Is it true that they make their marriages not before they are old women?'

'They marry as do others – when they are women.'

'That I know, but they wed when they are twenty-five. Is that true?'

'That is true.'

'*Ya illah!* At twenty-five! Who would of his own will take a wife even of eighteen? She is a woman – aging every hour. Twenty-five! I shall be an old woman at that age, and – Those *mem-log* remain young for ever. How I hate them!'

'What have they to do with us?'

'I cannot tell. I know only that there may now be alive on this earth a woman ten years older than I who may come to thee and take thy love ten years after I am an old woman, grey-headed, and the nurse of Tota's son. That is unjust and evil. They should die too.'

'Now, for all thy years thou art a child, and shalt be picked up and carried down the staircase.'

'Tota! Have a care for Tota, my lord! Thou at least art as foolish as any babe!' Ameera tucked Tota out of harm's way in the hollow of her neck, and was carried downstairs laughing in Holden's arms, while Tota opened his eyes and smiled after the manner of the lesser angels.

He was a silent infant, and, almost before Holden could realize that he was in the world, developed into a small gold-coloured little god and unquestioned despot of the house overlooking the city. Those were months of absolute happiness to Holden and Ameera – happiness withdrawn from the world, shut in behind the wooden gate that Pir Khan guarded. By day Holden did his work with an immense pity for such as were not so fortunate as himself, and a sympathy for small children that amazed and amused many mothers at the little station-gatherings. At nightfall he returned to Ameera – Ameera, full of the wondrous doings of Tota; how he had been seen to clap his hands together and move his fingers with intention and purpose – which was manifestly a miracle – how later, he had of his own initiative crawled out of his low bedstead on to the floor and swayed on both feet for the space of three breaths.

'And they were long breaths, for my heart stood still with delight,' said Ameera.

Then Tota took the beasts into his councils – the well-bullocks, the little grey squirrels, the mongoose that lived in a hole near the well, and especially Mian Mittu, the parrot, whose tail he grievously pulled, and Mian Mittu screamed till Ameera and Holden arrived.

'Oh villain! Child of strength! This to thy brother on the house-top! *Tobah, tobah!* [5] Fie! Fie! But I know a charm to make him wise as Suleiman and Aflatoun [Solomon and Plato]. Now look,' said Ameera. She drew from an embroidered bag a handful of almonds. 'See! we count seven. In the name of God!'

She placed Mian Mittu, very angry and rumpled, on the top of his cage, and seating herself between the babe and the bird she cracked and peeled an almond less white than her teeth. 'This is a true charm, my life, and do not laugh. See! I give the parrot one-half and Tota the other.' Mian Mittu with careful beak took his share from between Ameera's lips, and she kissed the other half into the mouth of the child, who ate it slowly with wondering eyes. 'This I will do each day of seven, and without doubt he who is ours will be a bold speaker and wise. Eh, Tota, what wilt thou be when thou art a man and I am grey-headed?' Tota tucked his fat legs into adorable creases. He could crawl, but he was not going to waste the spring of his youth in idle speech. He wanted Mian Mittu's tail to tweak.

When he was advanced to the dignity of a silver belt – which, with a magic square engraved on silver and hung round his neck, made up the greater part of his clothing – he staggered on a perilous journey down the garden to Pir Khan, and proffered him all his jewels in exchange for one little ride on Holden's horse, having seen his mother's mother chaffering with pedlars in the verandah. Pir Khan wept and set the untried feet on his own grey head in sign of fealty, and brought the bold adventurer to his mother's arms, vowing that Tota would be a leader of men ere his beard was grown.

One hot evening, while he sat on the roof between his father and mother watching the never-ending warfare of the kites that the city boys flew, he demanded a kite of his own with Pir Khan to fly it, because he had a fear of dealing with anything larger than himself, and when Holden called him a 'spark', he rose to his feet and answered slowly in defence of his new-found individuality, '*Hum' park nahin hai. Hum admi hai* [I am no spark, but a man].'

The protest made Holden choke and devote himself very seriously to a consideration of Tota's future. He need hardly have taken the trouble. The delight of that life was too perfect to endure. Therefore it was taken away as many things are taken away in India – suddenly and without warning. The little lord of the house, as Pir Khan called him, grew sorrowful and complained of pains who had never known the meaning of pain. Ameera, wild with terror, watched him through the night, and in the dawning of the second day the life was shaken out of him by fever – the seasonal autumn fever. It seemed altogether impossible that he could die, and neither Ameera nor Holden at first believed the evidence of the little body on the bedstead. Then Ameera beat her head against the wall and would have flung herself down the well in the garden had Holden not restrained her by main force.

One mercy only was granted to Holden. He rode to his office in broad daylight and found waiting him an unusually heavy mail that demanded concentrated attention and hard work. He was not, however, alive to this kindness of the gods.

III

The first shock of a bullet is no more than a brisk pinch. The wrecked body does not send in its protest to the soul till ten or fifteen seconds later. Holden realized his pain slowly, exactly as he had realized his happiness, and with the same imperious necessity for hiding all trace of it. In the beginning he only felt that there had been a loss, and that Ameera needed comforting, where she sat with her head on her knees shivering as Mian Mittu from the house-top called, *Tota! Tota! Tota!* Later all his world and the daily life of it rose up to hurt him. It was an outrage that any one of the children at the band-stand in the evening should be alive and clamorous, when his own child lay dead. It was more than mere pain when one of them touched him, and stories told by over-fond fathers of their children's latest performances cut him to the quick. He could not declare his pain. He had neither help, comfort, nor sympathy; and Ameera at the end of each weary day would lead him through the hell of self-questioning reproach which is reserved for those who have lost a child, and believe that with a little – just a little more care – it might have been saved.

'Perhaps,' Ameera would say, 'I did not take sufficient heed. Did I, or did I not? The sun on the roof that day when he played so long alone and I was – *ahi!* braiding my hair – it may be that the sun then bred the fever. If I had warned him from the sun he might have lived. But, oh my life, say that I am guiltless! Thou knowest that I loved him as I love thee. Say that there is no blame on me, or I shall die – I shall die!'

'There is no blame – before God, none. It was written, and how could we do aught to save? What has been, has been. Let it go, beloved.'

'He was all my heart to me. How can I let the thought go when my arm tells me every night that he is not here? *Ahi! Ahi!* Oh, Tota, come back to me – come back again, and let us be all together as it was before!'

'Peace, peace! For thine own sake, and for mine also, if thou lovest me – rest.'

'By this I know thou dost not care; and how shouldst thou? The white men have hearts of stone and souls of iron. Oh, that I had married a man of mine own people – though he beat me – and had never eaten the bread of an alien!'

'Am I an alien – mother of my son?'

'What else – *Sahib*? . . . Oh, forgive me – forgive! The death has driven me mad. Thou art the life of my heart, and the light of my eyes, and the breath of my life, and – and I have put thee from me, though it was but for a moment. If thou goest away, to whom shall I look for help? Do not be angry. Indeed, it was the pain that spoke and not thy slave.'

'I know, I know. We be two who were three. The greater need therefore that we should be one.'

They were sitting on the roof as of custom. The night was a warm one in early spring, and sheet-lightning was dancing on the horizon to a broken tune played by far-off thunder. Ameera settled herself in Holden's arms.

'The dry earth is lowing like a cow for the rain, and I – I am afraid. It was not like this when we counted the stars. But thou lovest me as much as before, though a bond is taken away? Answer!'

'I love more because a new bond has come out of the sorrow that we have eaten together, and that thou knowest.'

'Yea, I knew,' said Ameera in a very small whisper. 'But it is good to hear thee say so, my life, who art so strong to help. I will be a child no more, but a woman and an aid to thee. Listen! Give me my *sitar* [6] and I will sing bravely.'

She took the light silver-studded *sitar* and began a song of the great hero Rajah Rasalu. [7] The hand failed on the strings, the tune halted, checked, and at a low note turned off to the poor little nursery-rhyme about the wicked crow –

'And the wild plums grow in the jungle, only a penny a pound.
Only a penny a pound, *baba* – only . . .'

Then came the tears, and the piteous rebellion against fate till she slept, moaning a little in her sleep, with the right arm thrown clear of the body as though it protected something that was not there. It was after this night that life became a little easier for Holden. The ever-present pain of loss drove him into his work, and the work repaid him by filling up his mind for nine or ten hours a day. Ameera sat alone in the house and brooded, but grew happier when she understood that Holden was more at ease, according to the custom of women. They touched happiness again, but this time with caution.

'It was because we loved Tota that he died. The jealousy of God was upon us,' said Ameera. 'I have hung up a large black jar before our window to turn the evil eye from us, and we must make no protestations of delight, but go softly underneath the stars, lest God find us out. Is that not good talk, worthless one?'

She had shifted the accent on the word that means 'beloved', in proof of the sincerity of her purpose. But the kiss that followed the new christening was a thing that any deity might have envied. They went about henceforward saying, 'It is naught, it is naught'; and hoping that all the Powers heard.

The Powers were busy on other things. They had allowed thirty million people four years of plenty, wherein men fed well and the crops were certain, and the birth-rate rose year by year; the districts reported a purely agricultural population varying from nine hundred to two thousand to the square mile of the overburdened earth; and the Member for Lower Tooting, wandering about India in top-hat and frock-coat, talked largely of the benefits of British rule, and suggested as the one thing needful the establishment of a duly qualified electoral system and a general bestowal of the franchise. His long-suffering hosts smiled and made him welcome, and when he paused to admire, with pretty picked words, the blossom of the blood-red *dhak*-tree that had flowered untimely for a sign of what was coming, they smiled more than ever.

It was the Deputy Commissioner of Kot-Kumharsen, staying at the club for a day, who lightly told a tale that made Holden's blood run cold as he overheard the end.

'He won't bother anyone any more. Never saw a man so astonished in my life. By Jove, I thought he meant to ask a question in the House about it. Fellow-passenger in his ship – dined next him – bowled over by cholera and died in eighteen hours. You needn't laugh, you fellows. The Member for Lower Tooting is awfully angry about it; but he's more scared. I think he's going to take his enlightened self out of India.'

'I'd give a good deal if he were knocked over. It might keep a few vestrymen of his kidney to their own parish. But what's this about cholera? It's full early for anything of that kind,' said the warden of an unprofitable salt-lick.

'Don't know,' said the Deputy Commissioner reflectively. 'We've got locusts with us. There's sporadic cholera all along the north – at least we're calling it sporadic for decency's sake. The spring crops are short in five districts, and nobody seems to know where the rains are. It's nearly March now. I don't want to scare anybody, but it seems to me that Nature's going to audit her accounts with a big red pencil this summer.'

'Just when I wanted to take leave, too!' said a voice across the room.

'There won't be much leave this year, but there ought to be a great deal of promotion. I've come in to persuade the Government to put my pet canal on the list of famine-relief works. It's an ill-wind that blows no good. I shall get that canal finished at last.'

'Is it the old programme then,' said Holden; 'famine, fever, and cholera?'

'Oh no. Only local scarcity and an unusual prevalence of seasonal sickness. You'll find it all in the reports if you live till next year. You're a lucky chap. *You* haven't got a wife to send out of harm's way. The hill-stations ought to be full of women this year.'

'I think you're inclined to exaggerate the talk in the *bazars*,' said a young civilian in the Secretariat. 'Now I have observed –'

'I daresay you have,' said the Deputy Commissioner, 'but you've a great deal more to observe, my son. In the meantime, I wish to observe to you –' and he drew him aside to discuss the construction of the canal that was so dear to his heart. Holden went to his bungalow and began to understand that he was not alone in the world, and also that he was afraid for the sake of another – which is the most soul-satisfying fear known to man.

Two months later, as the Deputy had foretold, Nature began to audit her accounts with a red pencil. On the heels of the spring-reapings came a cry for bread, and the Government, which had decreed that no man should die of want, sent wheat. Then came the cholera from all four quarters of the compass. It struck a pilgrim-gathering of half a million at a sacred shrine. Many died at the feet of their god; the others broke and ran over the face of the land carrying the pestilence with them. It smote a walled city and killed two hundred a day. The people crowded the trains, hanging on to the footboards and squatting on the roofs of the carriages, and the cholera followed them, for at each station they dragged out the dead and the dying. They died by the roadside, and the horses of the Englishmen shied at the corpses in the grass. The rains did not come, and the earth turned to iron lest man should escape death by hiding in her. The English sent their wives away to the hills and went about their work, coming forward as they were bidden to fill the gaps in the fighting-line. Holden, sick with fear of losing his chiefest treasure on earth, had done his best to persuade Ameera to go away with her mother to the Himalayas.

'Why should I go?' said she one evening on the roof.

'There is sickness, and people are dying, and all the white *mem-log* have gone.'

'All of them?'

'All – unless perhaps there remain some old scald-head [8] who vexes her husband's heart by running risk of death.'

'Nay; who stays is my sister, and thou must not abuse her, for I will be a scald-head too. I am glad all the bold *mem-log* are gone.'

'Do I speak to a woman or a babe? Go to the hills, and I will see to it that thou goest like a queen's daughter. Think, child. In a red-lacquered bullock cart, veiled and curtained, with brass peacocks upon the pole and red cloth hangings. I will send two orderlies for guard and –'

'Peace! Thou art the babe in speaking thus. What use are those toys to me? *He* would have patted the bullocks and played with the housings. For his sake, perhaps – thou hast made me very English – I might have gone. Now, I will not. Let the *mem-log* run.'

'Their husbands are sending them, beloved.'

'Very good talk. Since when hast thou been my husband to tell me what to do? I have but borne thee a son. Thou art only all the desire of my soul to me. How shall I depart when I know that if evil befall thee by the breadth of so much as my littlest finger-nail – is that not small? – I should be aware of it though I were in paradise. And here, this summer thou mayest die – *ai, janee,*[9] die! and in dying they might call to tend thee a white woman, and she would rob me in the last of thy love!'

'But love is not born in a moment or on a death-bed!'

'What dost thou know of love, stoneheart? She would take thy thanks at least and, by God and the Prophet and Beebee Miriam the mother of thy Prophet, that I will never endure. My lord and my love, let there be no more foolish talk of going away. Where thou art, I am. It is enough.' She put an arm round his neck and a hand on his mouth.

There are not many happinesses so complete as those that are snatched under the shadow of the sword. They sat together and laughed, calling each other openly by every pet name that could move the wrath of the gods. The city below them was locked up in its own torments. Sulphur fires blazed in the streets; the conches in the Hindu temples screamed and bellowed, for the gods were inattentive in those days. There was a service in the great Mahomedan shrine, and the call to prayer from the minarets was almost unceasing. They heard the wailing in the houses of the dead, and once the shriek of a mother who had lost a child and was calling for its return. In the grey dawn they saw the dead borne out through the city gates, each litter with its own little knot of mourners. Wherefore they kissed each other and shivered.

It was a red and heavy audit, for the land was very sick and needed a little breathing-space ere the torrent of cheap life should flood it anew. The children of immature fathers and undeveloped mothers made no resistance. They were cowed and sat still, waiting till the sword should be sheathed in November if it were so willed. There were gaps among the English, but the gaps were filled. The work of superintending famine-relief, cholera-sheds, medicine-distribution, and what little sanitation was possible, went forward because it was so ordered.

Holden had been told to keep himself in readiness to move to replace the next man who should fall. There were twelve hours in each day when he could not see Ameera, and she might die in three. He was considering what his pain would be if he could not see her for three months, or if she died out of his sight. He was absolutely certain that her death would be demanded – so certain, that when he looked up from the telegram and saw Pir Khan breathless in the doorway, he laughed aloud. 'And?' said he –

'When there is a cry in the night and the spirit flutters into the throat, who has a charm that will restore? Come swiftly, Heaven-born! It is the black cholera.'

Holden galloped to his home. The sky was heavy with clouds, for the long-deferred rains were near and the heat was stifling. Ameera's mother met him in the courtyard, whimpering, 'She is dying. She is nursing herself into death. She is all but dead. What shall I do, *sahib*?'

Ameera was lying in the room in which Tota had been born. She made no sign when Holden entered, because the human soul is a very lonely thing and, when it is getting ready to go away, hides itself in a misty borderland where the living may not follow. The black cholera does its work quietly and without explanation. Ameera was being thrust out of life as though the Angel of Death had himself put his hand upon her. The quick breathing seemed to show that she was either afraid or in pain, but neither eyes nor mouth gave any answer to Holden's kisses. There was nothing to be said or done. Holden could only wait and suffer. The first drops of the rain began to fall on the roof and he could hear shouts of joy in the parched city.

The soul came back a little and the lips moved. Holden bent down to listen. 'Keep nothing of mine,' said Ameera. 'Take no hair from my head. *She* would make thee burn it later on. That flame I should feel. Lower! Stoop lower! Remember only that I was thine and bore thee a son. Though thou wed a white woman tomorrow, the pleasure of receiving in thy arms thy first son is taken from thee for ever. Remember me when thy son is born – the one that shall carry thy name before all men. His misfortunes be on my head. I bear witness – I bear witness' – the lips were forming the words on his ear – 'that there is no God but – thee, beloved!'

Then she died. Holden sat still, and all thought was taken from him – till he heard Ameera's mother lift the curtain.

'Is she dead, *sahib*?'

'She is dead.'

'Then I will mourn, and afterwards take an inventory of the furniture in this house. For that will be mine. The *sahib* does not mean to resume it? It is so little, so very little, *sahib*, and I am an old woman. I would like to lie softly.'

'For the mercy of God be silent a while. Go out and mourn where I cannot hear.'

'*Sahib*, she will be buried in four hours.'

'I know the custom. I shall go ere she is taken away. That matter is in thy hands. Look to it, that the bed on which – on which she lies –'

'Aha! That beautiful red-lacquered bed. I have long desired –'

'That the bed is left here untouched for my disposal. All else in the house is thine. Hire a cart, take everything, go hence, and before sunrise let there be nothing in this house but that which I have ordered thee to respect.'

'I am an old woman. I would stay at least for the days of mourning, and the rains have just broken. Whither shall I go?'

'What is that to me? My order is that there is a going. The house-gear is worth a thousand rupees and my orderly shall bring thee a hundred rupees tonight.'

'That is very little. Think of the cart-hire.'

'It shall be nothing unless thou goest, and with speed. O woman, get hence and leave me with my dead!'

The mother shuffled down the staircase, and in her anxiety to take stock of the house-fittings forgot to mourn. Holden stayed by Ameera's side and the rain roared on the roof. He could not think connectedly by reason of the noise, though he made many attempts to do so. Then four sheeted ghosts glided dripping into the room and stared at him through their veils. They were the washers of the dead. Holden left the room and went out to his horse. He had come in a dead, stifling calm through ankle-deep dust. He found the courtyard a rain-lashed pond alive with frogs; a torrent of yellow water ran under the gate, and a roaring wind drove the bolts of the rain like buckshot against the mud-walls. Pir Khan was shivering in his little hut by the gate, and the horse was stamping uneasily in the water.

'I have been told the *sahib's* order,' said Pir Khan. 'It is well. This house is now desolate. I go also, for my monkey-face would be a reminder of that which has been. Concerning the bed, I will bring that to thy house yonder in the morning; but remember, *sahib*, it will be to thee a knife turning in a green wound. I go upon a pilgrimage, and I will take no money. I have grown fat in the protection of the Presence whose sorrow is my sorrow. For the last time I hold his stirrup.'

He touched Holden's foot with both hands and the horse sprang out into the road, where the creaking bamboos were whipping the sky and all the frogs were chuckling. Holden could not see for the rain in his face. He put his hands before his eyes and muttered –

'Oh you brute! You utter brute!'

The news of his trouble was already in his bungalow. He read the knowledge in his butler's eyes when Ahmed Khan brought in food, and for the first and last time in his life laid a hand upon his master's shoulder, saying, 'Eat, *sahib*, eat. Meat is good against sorrow. I also have known. Moreover the shadows come and go, *sahib*; the shadows come and go. These be curried eggs.'

Holden could neither eat nor sleep. The heavens sent down eight inches of rain in that night and washed the earth clean. The waters tore down walls, broke roads, and scoured open the shallow graves on the Mahomedan burying-ground. All next day it rained, and Holden sat still in his house considering his sorrow. On the morning of the third day he received a telegram which said only, 'Ricketts, Myndonie. Dying. Holden relieve. Immediate.' Then he thought that before he departed he would look at the house wherein he had been master and lord. There was a break in the weather, and the rank earth steamed with vapour.

He found that the rains had torn down the mud pillars of the gateway, and the heavy wooden gate that had guarded his life hung lazily from one hinge. There was grass three inches high in the courtyard; Pir Khan's lodge was empty, and the sodden thatch sagged between the beams. A grey squirrel was in possession of the verandah, as if the house had been untenanted for thirty years instead of three days. Ameera's mother had removed everything except some mildewed matting. The *tick-tick* of the little scorpions as they hurried across the floor was the only sound in the house. Ameera's room and the other one where Tota had lived were heavy with mildew; and the narrow staircase leading to the roof was streaked and stained with rain-borne mud. Holden saw all these things, and came out again to meet in the road Durga Dass, his landlord – portly, affable, clothed in white muslin, and driving a Cee-spring buggy. He was over-looking his property to see how the roofs stood the stress of the first rains.

'I have heard,' said he, 'you will not take this place any more, *sahib*?'

'What are you going to do with it?'

'Perhaps I shall let it again.'

'Then I will keep it on while I am away.'

Durga Dass was silent for some time. 'You shall not take it on, *sahib*,' he said. 'When I was a young man I also – but today I am a member of the Municipality. Ho! Ho! No. When the birds have gone what need to keep the nest? I will have it pulled down – the timber will sell for something always. It shall be pulled down, and the Municipality shall make a road across, as they desire, from the burning-ghaut [10] to the city wall, so that no man may say where this house stood.'

On Greenhow Hill [1]

To Love's low voice she lent a careless ear;
Her hand within his rosy fingers lay,
A chilling weight. She would not turn or hear;
But with averted face went on her way.
But when pale Death, all featureless and grim,
Lifted his bony hand, and beckoning
Held out his cypress-wreath, she followed him,
And Love was left forlorn and wondering,
That she who for his bidding would not stay,
At Death's first whisper rose and went away.

Rivals. [2]

'*Ohé, Ahmed Din! Shafiz Ullah ahoo!* Bahadur Khan, where are you? Come out of the tents, as I have done, and fight against the English. Don't kill your own kin! Come out to me!'

The deserter from a native corps was crawling round the outskirts of the camp, firing at intervals, and shouting invitations to his old comrades. Misled by the rain and the darkness, he came to the English wing of the camp, and with his yelping and rifle-practice disturbed the men. They had been making roads all day, and were tired.

Ortheris was sleeping at Learoyd's feet. 'Wot's all that?' he said thickly. Learoyd snored, and a Snider bullet ripped its way through the tent wall. The men swore. 'It's that bloomin' deserter from the Aurangabadis,' [3] said Ortheris. 'Git up, someone, an' tell 'im 'e's come to the wrong shop.'

'Go to sleep, little man,' said Mulvaney, who was steaming nearest the door. 'I can't arise an' expaytiate with him. 'Tis rainin' entrenchin' tools outside.'

''Tain't because you bloomin' can't. It's 'cause you bloomin' won't, ye long, limp, lousy, lazy beggar, you. 'Ark to 'im 'owlin'!'

'Wot's the good of argifying? Put a bullet into the swine! 'E's keepin' us awake!' said another voice.

A subaltern shouted angrily, and a dripping sentry whined from the darkness –

''Tain't no good, sir. I can't see 'im. 'E's 'idin' somewhere down 'ill.'

Ortheris tumbled out of his blanket. 'Shall I try to get 'im, sir?' said he.

'No,' was the answer. 'Lie down. I won't have the whole camp shooting all round the clock. Tell him to go and pot his friends.'

Ortheris considered for a moment. Then, putting his head under the tent wall, he called, as a bus conductor calls in a block, ''Igher up, there! 'Igher up!'

The men laughed, and the laughter was carried down wind to the deserter, who, hearing that he had made a mistake, went off to worry his own regiment half a mile away. He was received with shots; the Aurangabadis were very angry with him for disgracing their colours.

'An' that's all right,' said Ortheris, withdrawing his head as he heard the hiccough of the Sniders in the distance. 'S'elp me Gawd, tho', that man's not fit to live – messin' with my beauty-sleep this way.'

'Go out and shoot him in the morning, then,' said the subaltern incautiously. 'Silence in the tents now. Get your rest, men.'

Ortheris lay down with a happy little sigh, and in two minutes there was no sound except the rain on the canvas and the all-embracing and elemental snoring of Learoyd.

The camp lay on a bare ridge of the Himalayas, and for a week had been waiting for a flying column to make connection. The nightly rounds of the deserter and his friends had become a nuisance.

In the morning the men dried themselves in hot sunshine and cleaned their grimy accoutrements. The native regiment was to take its turn of road-making that day while the Old Regiment loafed.

'I'm goin' to lay for a shot at that man,' said Ortheris, when he had finished washing out his rifle. ''E comes up the watercourse every evenin' about five o'clock. If we go and lie out on the north 'ill a bit this afternoon we'll get 'im.'

'You're a bloodthirsty little mosquito,' said Mulvaney, blowing blue clouds into the air. 'But I suppose I will have to come wid you. Fwhere's Jock?'

'Gone out with the Mixed Pickles, 'cause 'e thinks 'isself a bloomin' marksman,' said Ortheris with scorn.

The 'Mixed Pickles' were a detachment of picked shots, generally employed in clearing spurs of hills when the enemy were too impertinent. This taught the young officers how to handle men, and did not do the enemy much harm. Mulvaney and Ortheris strolled out of camp, and passed the Aurangabadis going to their road-making.

'You've got to sweat today,' said Ortheris genially. 'We're going to get your man. You didn't knock 'im out last night by any chance, any of you?'

'No. The pig went away mocking us. I had one shot at him,' said a private. 'He's my cousin and *I* ought to have cleared our dishonour. But good luck to you.'

They went cautiously to the north hill, Ortheris leading, because, as he explained, 'this is a long-range show, an' I've got to do it.' His was an almost passionate devotion to his rifle, whom, by barrack-room report, he was supposed to kiss every night before turning in. Charges and scuffles he held in contempt, and, when they were inevitable, slipped between Mulvaney and Learoyd, bidding them to fight for his skin as well as their own. They never failed him. He trotted along, questing like a hound on a broken trail, through the wood of the north hill. At last he was satisfied, and threw himself down on the soft pine-needled slope that commanded a clear view of the watercourse and a brown, bare hillside beyond it. The trees made a scented darkness in which an army corps could have hidden from the sun-glare without.

''Ere's the tail o' the wood,' said Ortheris. ''E's got to come up the watercourse, 'cause it gives 'im cover. We'll lay 'ere. 'Tain't not arf so bloomin' dusty neither.'

He buried his nose in a clump of scentless white violets. No one had come to tell the flowers that the season of their strength was long past, and they had bloomed merrily in the twilight of the pines.

'This is something like,' he said luxuriously. 'Wot a 'evinly clear drop for a bullet acrost. How much d'you make it, Mulvaney?'

'Seven hunder. Maybe a trifle less, bekaze the air's so thin.'

Wop! wop! wop! went a volley of musketry on the rear face of the north hill.

'Curse them Mixed Pickles firin' at nothin'! They'll scare arf the country.'

'Thry a sightin' shot in the middle of the row,' said Mulvaney, the man of many wiles. 'There's a red rock yonder he'll be sure to pass. Quick!'

Ortheris ran his sight up to six hundred yards and fired. The bullet threw up a feather of dust by a clump of gentians at the base of the rock.

'Good enough!' said Ortheris, snapping the scale down. 'You snick your sights to mine or a little lower. You're always firin' high. But remember, first shot to me. O Lordy! but it's a lovely afternoon.'

The noise of the firing grew louder, and there was a tramping of men in the wood. The two lay very quiet, for they knew that the British soldier is desperately prone to fire at anything that moves or calls. Then Learoyd appeared, his tunic ripped across the breast by a bullet, looking ashamed of himself. He flung down on the pine-needles, breathing in snorts.

'One o' them damned gardeners o' th' Pickles,' said he, fingering the rent. 'Firin' to th' right flank, when he knowed I was there. If I knew who he was I'd 'a' rippen the hide offan him. Look at ma tunic!'

'That's the spishil trustability av a marksman. Train him to hit a fly wid a stiddy rest at seven hunder, an' he loose on anythin' he sees or hears up to th' mile. You're well out av that fancy-firin' gang, Jock. Stay here.'

'Bin firin' at the bloomin' wind in the bloomin' treetops,' said Ortheris with a chuckle. 'I'll show you some firin' later on.'

They wallowed in the pine-needles, and the sun warmed them where they lay. The Mixed Pickles ceased firing, and returned to camp, and left the wood to a few scared apes. The watercourse lifted up its voice in the silence, and talked foolishly to the rocks. Now and again the dull thump of a blasting charge three miles away told that the Aurangabadis were in difficulties with their road-making. The men smiled as they listened and lay still, soaking in the warm leisure. Presently Learoyd, between the whiffs of his pipe –

'Seems queer – about 'im yonder – desertin' at all.'

''E'll be a bloomin' side queerer when I've done with 'im,' said Ortheris. They were talking in whispers, for the stillness of the wood and the desire of slaughter lay heavy upon them.

'I make no doubt he had his reasons for desertin'; but, my faith! I make less doubt ivry man has good reason for killin' him,' said Mulvaney.

'Happen there was a lass tewed up[4] wi' it. Men do more than more for th' sake of a lass.'

'They make most av us 'list. They've no manner av right to make us desert.'

'Ah; they make us 'list, or their fathers do,' said Learoyd softly, his helmet over his eyes.

Ortheris's brows contracted savagely. He was watching the valley. 'If it's a girl I'll shoot the beggar twice over, an' second time for bein' a fool. You're blasted sentimental all of a sudden. Thinkin' o' your last near shave?'

'Nay, lad; ah was but thinkin' o' what has happened.'

'An' fwhat has happened, ye lumberin' child av calamity, that you're lowing like a cow-calf at the back av the pasture, an' suggestin' invidious excuses for the man Stanley's goin' to kill. Ye'll have to wait another hour yet, little man. Spit it out, Jock, an' bellow melojus to the moon. It

235

Selected Stories

takes an earthquake or a bullet graze to fetch aught out av you. Discourse, Don Juan! The a-moors av Lotharius[5] Learoyd! Stanley, kape a rowlin' rig'mental eye on the valley.'

'It's along o' yon hill there,' said Learoyd, watching the bare sub-Himalayan spur that reminded him of his Yorkshire moors. He was speaking more to himself than his fellows. 'Ay,' said he, 'Rumbolds Moor stands up ower Skipton town, an' Greenhow Hill stands up ower Pately Brig. I reckon you've never heeard tell o' Greenhow Hill, but yon bit o' bare stuff if there was nobbut a white road windin' is like ut; strangely like. Moors an' moors an' moors, wi' never a tree for shelter, an' grey houses wi' flagstone rooves, and pewits cryin', an' a windhover goin' to and fro just like these kites. And cold! A wind that cuts you like a knife. You could tell Greenhow Hill folk by the red-apple colour o' their cheeks an' nose tips, and their blue eyes, driven into pin-points by the wind. Miners mostly, burrowin' for lead i' th' hillsides, followin' the trail of th' ore vein same as a field-rat. It was the roughest minin' I ever seen. Yo'd come on a bit o' creakin' wood windlass like a well-head, an' you was let down i' th' bight of a rope, fendin' yoursen off the side wi' one hand, carryin' a candle stuck in a lump o' clay with t'other, an' clickin' hold of a rope with t'other hand.'

'An' that's three of them,' said Mulvaney. 'Must be a good climate in those parts.'

Learoyd took no heed.

'An' then yo' came to a level, where you crept on your hands and knees through a mile o' windin' drift, an' you come out into a cave-place as big as Leeds Townhall, with a engine pumpin' water from workin's 'at went deeper still. It's a queer country, let alone minin', for the hill is full of those natural caves, an' the rivers an' the becks drops into what they call pot-holes, an' come out again miles away.'

'Wot was you doin' there?' said Ortheris.

'I was a young chap then, an' mostly went wi' 'osses, leadin' coal and lead ore; but at th' time I'm tellin' on I was drivin' the waggon-team i' th' big sumph.[6] I didn't belong to that country-side by rights. I went there because of a little difference at home, an' at fust I took up wi' a rough lot. One night we'd been drinkin', an' I must ha' hed more than I could stand, or happen th' ale was none so good. Though i' them days, By for God, I never seed bad ale.' He flung his arms over his head, and gripped a vast handful of white violets. 'Nah,' said he, 'I never seed the ale I could not drink, the bacca I could not smoke, nor the lass I could not kiss. Well, we mun have a race home, the lot on us. I lost all th' others, an' when I was climbin' ower one of them walls built o' loose

236

stones, I comes down into the ditch, stones and all, an' broke my arm. Not as I knawed much about it, for I fell on th' back of my head, an' was knocked stupid like. An' when I come to mysen it were mornin', an' I were lyin' on the settle i' Jesse Roantree's house-place, an' 'Liza Roantree was settin' sewin'. I ached all ovver, and my mouth were like a lime-kiln. She gave me a drink out of a china mug wi' gold letters – "A Present from Leeds" – as I looked many and many a time at after. "Yo're to lie still while Dr Warbottom comes, because your arm's broken, and father has sent a lad to fetch him. He found yo' when he was goin' to work, an' carried you here on his back," sez she. "Oa!" sez I; an' I shet my eyes, for I felt ashamed o' mysen. "Father's gone to his work these three hours, an' he said he'd tell 'em to get somebody to drive the tram." The clock ticked, an' a bee comed in the house, an' they rung i' my head like mill-wheels. An' she give me another drink an' settled the pillow. "Eh, but yo're young to be getten drunk an' such like, but yo' won't do it again, will yo'?" – "Noa," sez I, "I wouldn't if she'd not but stop they mill-wheels clatterin'.'"

'Faith, it's a good thing to be nursed by a woman when you're sick!' said Mulvaney. 'Dir' cheap at the price av twenty broken heads.'

Ortheris turned to frown across the valley. He had not been nursed by many women in his life.

'An' then Dr Warbottom comes ridin' up, an' Jesse Roantree along with 'im. He was a high-larned doctor, but he talked wi' poor folk same as theirsens. "What's ta bin agaate on naa?" he sings out. "Brekkin' tha thick head?" An' he felt me all ovver. "That's none broken. Tha' nobbut knocked a bit sillier than ordinary, an' that's daaft eneaf." An' soa he went on, callin' me all the names he could think on, but settin' my arm, wi' Jesse's help, as careful as could be. "Yo' mun let the oaf bide here a bit, Jesse," he says, when he hed strapped me up an' given me a dose o' physic; "an' you an' 'Liza will tend him, though he's scarcelins worth the trouble. An' tha'll lose tha work," sez he, "an' tha'll be upon th' Sick Club for a couple o' months an' more. Doesn't tha think tha's a fool?"'

'But whin was a young man, high or low, the other av a fool, I'd like to know?' said Mulvaney. 'Sure, folly's the only safe way to wisdom, for I've thried it.'

'Wisdom!' grinned Ortheris, scanning his comrades with uplifted chin. 'You're bloomin' Solomons, you two, ain't you?'

Learoyd went calmly on, with a steady eye like an ox chewing the cud.

'And that was how I comed to know 'Liza Roantree. There's some tunes as she used to sing – aw, she were always singin' – that fetches

Greenhow Hill before my eyes as fair as yon brow across there. And she would learn me to sing bass, an' I was to go to th' chapel wi' 'em, where Jesse and she led the singin', th' old man playin' the fiddle. He was a strange chap, old Jesse, fair mad wi' music, an' he made me promise to learn the big fiddle when my arm was better. It belonged to him, and it stood up in a big case alongside o' th' eight-day clock, but Willie Satterthwaite, as played it in the chapel, had getten deaf as a door-post, and it vexed Jesse, as he had to rap him ower his head wi' th' fiddle-stick to make him give ower sawin' at th' right time.

'But there was a black drop in it all, an' it was a man in a black coat that brought it. When th' Primitive Methodist preacher came to Greenhow, he would always stop wi' Jesse Roantree, an' he laid hold of me from th' beginning. It seemed I wor a soul to be saved, and he meaned to do it. At th' same time I jealoused[7] at he were keen o' savin' 'Liza Roantree's soul as well, and I could ha' killed him many a time. An' this went on till one day I broke out, an' borrowed th' brass for a drink from 'Liza. After fower days I come back, wi' my tail between my legs, just to see 'Liza again. But Jesse were at home an' th' preacher – th' Reverend Amos Barraclough. 'Liza said naught, but a bit o' red come into her face as were white of a regular thing. Says Jesse, tryin' his best to be civil, "Nay, lad, it's like this. You've getten to choose which way it's goin' to be. I'll ha' nobody across ma doorstep as goes a-drinkin', an' borrows my lass's money to spend i' their drink. Ho'd tha tongue, 'Liza," sez he, when she wanted to put in a word 'at I were welcome to th' brass, and she were none afraid that I wouldn't pay it back. Then the Reverend cuts in, seein' as Jesse were losin' his temper, an' they fair beat me among them. But it were 'Liza, as looked an' said naught, as did more than either o' their tongues, an' soa I concluded to get converted.'

'Fwhat!' shouted Mulvaney. Then, checking himself, he said softly, 'Let be! Let be! Sure the Blessed Virgin is the mother of all religion an' most women; an' there's a dale av piety in a girl if the men would only let ut stay there. I'd ha' been converted myself under the circumstances.'

'Nay, but,' pursued Learoyd with a blush, 'I meaned it.'

Ortheris laughed as loudly as he dared, having regard to his business at the time.

'Ay, Ortheris, you may laugh, but you didn't know yon preacher Barraclough – a little white-faced chap, wi' a voice as 'ud wile a bird off an a bush, and a way o' layin' hold of folks as made them think they'd never had a live man for a friend before. You never saw him, an' – an' – you never seed 'Liza Roantree – never seed 'Liza Roantree . . . Happen it was as much 'Liza as th' preacher and her father, but anyways they all meaned it, an' I was fair shamed o' mysen, an' so I become what they called a changed charácter. And when I think on, it's hard to believe as yon chap going to prayer-meetin's, chapel, and class-meetin's were me. But I never had naught to say for mysen, though there was a deal o' shoutin', and old Sammy Strother, as were almost clemmed [8] to death and doubled up with the rheumatics, would sing out, "Joyful! Joyful!" and 'at it were better to go up to heaven in a coal-basket than down to hell i' a coach an' six. And he would put his old claw on my shoulder, sayin', "Doesn't tha feel it, tha great lump? Doesn't tha feel it?" An' sometimes I thought I did, and then again I thought I didn't, an' how was that?'

'The iverlastin' nature av mankind,' said Mulvaney. 'An', furthermore, I misdoubt you were built for the Primitive Methodians. They're a new corps anyways. I hold by the Ould Church, for she's the mother of them all – ay, an' the father, too. I like her bekaze she's most remarkable regimental in her fittings. I may die in Honolulu, Nova Zambra, or Cape Cayenne, but wherever I die, me bein' fwhat I am, an' a priest handy, I go under the same orders an' the same words an' the same unction as tho' the Pope himself come down from the roof av St Peter's to see me off. There's neither high nor low, nor broad nor deep, nor betwixt nor between wid her, an' that's what I like. But mark you, she's no manner av Church for a wake man, bekaze she takes the body and the soul av him, onless he has his proper work to do. I remember when my father died that was three months comin' to his grave; begad he'd ha' sold the shebeen above our heads for ten minutes' quittance of purgathory. An' he did all he could. That's why I say ut takes a strong man to deal with the Ould Church, an' for that reason you'll find so many women go there. An' that sames a conundrum.'

'Wot's the use o' worrittin' 'bout these things?' said Ortheris. 'You're bound to find all out quicker nor you want to, any'ow.' He jerked the cartridge out of the breech-block into the palm of his hand. ''Ere's my chaplain,' he said, and made the venomous black-headed bullet bow like a marionette. ''E's goin' to teach a man all about which is which, an' wot's true, after all, before sundown. But wot 'appened after that, Jock?'

'There was one thing they boggled at, and almost shut th' gate i' my face for, and that were my dog Blast, th' only one saved out o' a litter o' pups as was blowed up when a keg o' minin' powder loosed off in th' store-keeper's hut. They liked his name no better than his business, which were fightin' every dog he comed across; a rare good dog, wi' spots o' black and pink on his face, one ear gone, and lame o' one side wi' being driven in a basket through an iron roof, a matter of half a mile.

'They said I mun give him up 'cause he were worldly and low; and would I let mysen be shut out of heaven for the sake on a dog? "Nay," says I, "if th' door isn't wide enough for th' pair on us, we'll stop outside, for we'll none be parted." And th' preacher spoke up for Blast, as had a likin' for him from th' first – I reckon that was why I come to like th' preacher – and wouldn't hear o' changin' his name to Bless, as some o' them wanted. So th' pair on us became reg'lar chapel-members. But it's hard for a young chap o' my build to cut traces from the world, th' flesh, an' the devil all uv a heap. Yet I stuck to it for a long time, while th' lads as used to stand about th' town-end an' lean ower th' bridge, spittin' into th' beck o' a Sunday, would call after me, "Sitha, Learoyd, when's ta bean to preach, 'cause we're comin' to hear tha." – "Ho'd tha jaw. He hasn't getten th' white choaker on ta morn," another lad would say, and I had to double my fists hard i' th' bottom of my Sunday coat, and say to mysen, "If 'twere Monday and I warn't a member o' the Primitive Methodists, I'd leather all th' lot of yond'." That was th' hardest of all – to know that I could fight and I mustn't fight.'

Sympathetic grunts from Mulvaney.

'So what wi' singin', practisin', and class-meetin's, and th' big fiddle, as he made me take between my knees, I spent a deal o' time i' Jesse Roantree's house-place. But often as I was there, th' preacher fared to me to go oftener, and both th' old man an' th' young woman were pleased to have him. He lived i' Pately Brig, as were a goodish step off, but he come. He come all the same. I liked him as well or better as any man I'd ever seen i' one way, and yet I hated him wi' all my heart i' t'other, and we watched each other like cat and mouse, but civil as you please, for I was on my best behaviour, and he was that fair and open that I was bound to be fair with him. Rare good company he was, if I hadn't wanted to wring his cliver little neck half of the time. Often and often when he was goin' from Jesse's I'd set him a bit on the road.'

'See 'im 'ome, you mean?' said Ortheris.

'Ay. It's a way we have i' Yorkshire o' seein' friends off. Yon was a friend as I didn't want to come back, and he didn't want me to come back neither, and so we'd walk together towards Pately, and then he'd set me back again, and there we'd be wal two o'clock i' the mornin' settin' each other to an' fro like a blasted pair o' pendulums twixt hill and valley, long after th' light had gone out i' 'Liza's window, as both on us had been looking at, pretending to watch the moon.'

'Ah!' broke in Mulvaney, 'ye'd no chanst against the maraudin' psalm-singer. They'll take the airs an' the graces instid av the man nine times out av ten, an' they only find the blunder later – the wimmen.'

'That's just where yo're wrong,' said Learoyd, reddening under the freckled tan of his cheeks. 'I was th' first wi 'Liza, an' yo'd think that were enough. But th' parson were a steady-gaited sort o' chap, and Jesse were strong o' his side, and all th' women i' the congregation dinned it to 'Liza 'at she were fair fond to take up wi' a wastrel ne'er-do-weel like me, as was scarcelins respectable an' a fighting dog at his heels. It was all very well for her to be doing me good and saving my soul, but she must mind as she didn't do herself harm. They talk o' rich folk bein' stuck up an' genteel, but for cast-iron pride o' respectability there's naught like poor chapel folk. It's as cold as th' wind o' Greenhow Hill – ay, and colder, for 'twill never change. And now I come to think on it, one at strangest things I know is 'at they couldn't abide th' thought o' soldiering. There's a vast o' fightin' i' th' Bible, and there's a deal of Methodists i' th' army; but to hear chapel folk talk you'd think that soldierin' were next door, an' t'other side, to hangin'. I' their meetin's all their talk is o' fightin'. When Sammy Strother were stuck for summat to say in his prayers, he'd sing out, "Th' sword o' th' Lord and o' Gideon." They were allus at it about puttin' on th' whole armour o' righteousness, an' fightin' the good fight o' faith. And then, atop o' 't all, they held a prayer-meetin' ower a young chap as wanted to 'list, and nearly deafened him, till he picked up his hat and fair ran away. And they'd tell tales in th' Sunday-school o' bad lads as had been thumped and brayed [9] for bird-nesting o' Sundays and playin' truant o' week-days, and how they took to wrestlin', dog-fightin', rabbit-runnin', and drinkin', till at last, as if 'twere a hepitaph on a gravestone, they damned him across th' moors wi', "an' then he went and 'listed for a soldier", an' they'd all fetch a deep breath, and throw up their eyes like a hen drinkin'.'

'Fwhy is ut?' said Mulvaney, bringing down his hand on his thigh with a crack. 'In the name av God, fwhy is ut? I've seen ut, tu. They cheat an' they swindle an' they lie an' they slander, an' fifty times fifty worse; but the last an' the worst by their reckonin' is to serve the Widdy [10] honest. It's like the talk av childer – seein' things all round.'

'Plucky lot of fightin' good fights of whatsername they'd do if we didn't see they had a quiet place to fight in. And such fightin' as theirs is! Cats on the tiles. T'other callin' to which to come on. I'd give a month's pay to get some o' them broad-backed beggars in London sweatin' through a day's road-makin' an' a night's rain. They'd carry on a deal afterwards – same as we're supposed to carry on. I've bin turned out of a measly arf-license pub down Lambeth way, full o' greasy kebmen, 'fore now,' said Ortheris with an oath.

'Maybe you were dhrunk,' said Mulvaney soothingly.

'Worse nor that. The Forders [11] were drunk. *I* was wearin' the Queen's uniform.'

'I'd no particular thought to be a soldier i' them days,' said Learoyd, still keeping his eye on the bare hill opposite, 'but this sort o' talk put it i' my head. They was so good, th' chapel folk, that they tumbled ower t'other side. But I stuck to it for 'Liza's sake, specially as she was learning me to sing the bass part in a horotorio as Jesse were gettin' up. She sung like a throstle hersen, and we had practisin's night after night for a matter of three months.'

'I know what a horotorio is,' said Ortheris pertly. 'It's a sort of chaplain's sing-song – words all out of the Bible, and hullabaloojah choruses.'

'Most Greenhow Hill folks played some instrument or t'other, an' they all sung so you might have heard them miles away, and they were so pleased wi' the noise they made they didn't fair to want anybody to listen. The preacher sung high seconds when he wasn't playin' the flute, an' they set me, as hadn't got far with big fiddle, again Willie Satterthwaite, to jog his elbow when he had to get a' gate playin'. Old Jesse was happy if ever a man was, for he were th' conductor an' th' first fiddle an' th' leadin' singer, beatin' time wi' his fiddle-stick, till at times he'd rap with it on the table, and cry out, "Now, you mun all stop; it's my turn." And he'd face round to his front, fair sweating wi' pride, to sing th' tenor solos. But he were grandest i' th' choruses, waggin' his head, flinging his arms round like a windmill, and singin' hisself black in the face. A rare singer were Jesse.

'Yo see, I was not o' much account wi' 'em all exceptin' to 'Liza Roantree, and I had a deal o' time settin' quiet at meetings and horotorio practices to hearken their talk, and if it were strange to me at beginnin', it got stranger still at after, when I was shut on it, and could study what it meaned.

'Just after th' horotorios came off, 'Liza, as had allus been weakly like, was took very bad. I walked Dr Warbottom's horse up and down a deal of times while he were inside, where they wouldn't let me go, though I fair ached to see her. "She'll be better i' noo, lad – better i' noo," he used to say. "Tha mun ha' patience." Then they said if I was quiet I might go in, and th' Reverend Amos Barraclough used to read to her lyin' propped up among th' pillows. Then she began to mend a bit, and they let me carry her on to th' settle, and when it got warm again she went about same as afore. Th' preacher and me and Blast was a deal together i' them days, and i' one way we was rare good comrades. But I could ha' stretched him time and again with a good will. I mind one day he said he would like to go down into th' bowels o' th' earth, and see how th' Lord had builded th' framework o' th' everlastin' hills. He were one of them chaps as had a gift o' sayin' things. They rolled off the tip of his clever tongue, same as Mulvaney here, as would ha' made a rare good preacher if he had nobbut given his mind to it. I lent him a suit o' miner's kit as almost buried th' little man, and his white face down i' th' coat-collar and hat-flap looked like the face of a boggart,[12] and he cowered down i' the' bottom o' the waggon. I was drivin' a tram[13] as led up a bit of an incline up to th' cave where the engine was pumpin', and where th' ore was brought up and put into th' waggons as went down o' themselves, me puttin' th' brake on and th' horses a-trottin' after. Long as it was daylight we were good friends, but when we got fair into th' dark, and could nobbut see th' day shinin' at the hole like a lamp at a street-end, I feeled downright wicked. Ma religion dropped all away from me when I looked back at him as were always comin' between me and 'Liza. The talk was 'at they were to be wed when she got better, an' I couldn't get her to say yes or nay to it. He began to sing a hymn in his thin voice, and I came out wi' a chorus that was all cussin' an' swearin' at my horses, an' I began to know how I hated him. He were such a little chap, too. I could drop him wi' one hand down Garstang's Copper-hole – a place where th' beck slithered ower th' edge on a rock, and fell wi' a bit of a whisper into a pit as no rope i' Greenhow could plumb.'

Again Learoyd rooted up the innocent violets. 'Ay, he should see th' bowels o' th' earth an' never naught else. I could take him a mile or two along th' drift, and leave him wi' his candle doused to cry hallelujah, wi' none to hear him and say amen. I was to lead him down th' ladder-way to th' drift where Jesse Roantree was workin', and why shouldn't he slip on th' ladder, wi' my feet on his fingers till they loosed grip, and I put him down wi' my heel? If I went fust down th' ladder I could click hold on him and chuck him over my head, so as he should go squshin' down the shaft, breakin' his bones at ev'ry timberin' as Bill Appleton did when he was fresh,[14] and hadn't a bone left when he wrought to th' bottom. Niver a blasted leg to walk from Pately. Niver an arm to put round 'Liza Roantree's waist. Niver no more – niver no more.'

The thick lips curled back over the yellow teeth, and that flushed face was not pretty to look upon. Mulvaney nodded sympathy, and Ortheris, moved by his comrade's passion, brought up the rifle to his shoulder, and searched the hillside for his quarry, muttering ribaldry about a sparrow, a spout, and a thunder-storm. The voice of the watercourse supplied the necessary small talk till Learoyd picked up his story.

'But it's none so easy to kill a man like yon. When I'd given up my horses to th' lad as took my place and I was showin' th' preacher th' workin's, shoutin' into his ear across th' clang o' th' pumpin' engines, I saw he were afraid o' naught; and when the lamplight showed his black eyes, I could feel as he was masterin' me again. I were no better nor Blast chained up short and growlin' i' the depths of him while a strange dog went safe past.

' "Th'art a coward and a fool," I said to mysen; an' I wrestled i' my mind again' him till, when we come to Garstang's Copper-hole, I laid hold o' the preacher and lifted him up over my head, and held him into the darkest on it. "Now, lad," I says, "it's to be one or t'other on us – thee or me – for 'Liza Roantree. Why, isn't thee afraid for thysen?" I says, for he were still i' my arms as a sack. "Nay; I'm but afraid for thee, my poor lad, as knows naught," says he. I set him down on th' edge, an' th' beck run stiller, an' there was no more buzzin' in my head like when th' bee come through th' window o' Jesse's house. "What dost tha mean?" says I.

' "I've often thought as thou ought to know," says he, "but 'twas hard to tell thee. 'Liza Roantree's for neither on us, nor for nobody o' this earth. Dr Warbottom says – and he knows her, and her mother before her – that she is in a decline, and she cannot live six months longer. He's known it for many a day. Steady, John! Steady!" says he. And that weak little man pulled me further back and set me again' him, and talked it all over quiet and still, me turnin' a bunch o' candles in my hand, and counting them ower and ower again as I listened. A deal on it were th' regular preachin' talk, but there were a vast lot as made me begin to think as he were more of a man than I'd ever given him credit for, till I were cut as deep for him as I were for mysen.

'Six candles we had, and we crawled and climbed all that day while they lasted, and I said to mysen, " 'Liza Roantree hasn't six months to live." And when we came into th' daylight again we were like dead men to look at, an' Blast come behind us without so much as waggin' his tail. When I saw 'Liza again she looked at me a minute and says, "Who's telled tha? For I see tha knows." And she tried to smile as she kissed me, and I fair broke down.

'Yo'see, I was a young chap i' them days, and had seen naught o' life, let alone death, as is allus a-waitin'. She told me as Dr Warbottom said as Greenhow air was too keen, and they were goin' to Bradford, to Jesse's brother David, as worked i' a mill, and I mun hold up like a man and a Christian, and she'd pray for me. Well, and they went away, and the preacher that same back end o' th' year were appointed to another circuit, as they call it, and I were left alone on Greenhow Hill.

'I tried, and I tried hard, to stick to th' chapel, but 'tweren't th' same thing at after. I hadn't 'Liza's voice to follow i' th' singin', nor her eyes a'shinin' acrost their heads. And i' th' class-meetings they said as I mun have some experiences to tell, and I hadn't a word to say for mysen.

'Blast and me moped a good deal, and happen we didn't behave ourselves over well, for they dropped us and wondered however they'd come to take us up. I can't tell how we got through th' time, while i' th' winter I gave up my job and went to Bradford. Old Jesse were at th' door o' th' house, in the long street o' little houses. He'd been sendin' th' children 'way as were clatterin' their clogs in th' causeway, for she were asleep.

'"Is it thee?" he says; "but you're not to see her. I'll none have her wakened for a nowt like thee. She's goin' fast, and she mun go in peace. Thou'lt never be good for naught i' th' world, and as long as thou lives thou'll never play the big fiddle. Get away, lad, get away!" So he shut the door softly i' my face.

'Nobody never made Jesse my master, but it seemed to me he was about right, and I went away into the town and knocked up against a recruiting sergeant. The old tales o' th' chapel folk came buzzin' into my head. I was to get away, and this were th' regular road for the likes o' me. I 'listed there and then, took th' Widow's shillin', and had a bunch o' ribbons pinned i' my hat.

'But next day I found my way to David Roantree's door, and Jesse came to open it. Says he, "Thou's come back again wi' th' devil's colours flyin' – thy true colours, as I always telled thee."

'But I begged and prayed of him to let me see her nobbut to say good-bye, till a woman calls down th' stair-way, "She says John Learoyd's to come up." Th' old man shifts aside in a flash, and lays his hand on my arm, quite gentle like. "But thou'lt be quiet, John," says he, "for she's rare and weak. Thou was allus a good lad."

'Her eyes were all alive wi' light, and her hair was thick on the pillow round her, but her cheeks were thin – thin to frighten a man that's strong. "Nay, father, yo' mayn't say th' devil's colours. Them ribbons is pretty." An' she held out her hands for th' hat, an' she put all straight as a woman will wi' ribbons. "Nay, but what they're pretty," she says. "Eh, but I'd ha' liked to see thee i' thy red coat, John, for thou was allus my own lad – my very own lad, and none else."

'She lifted up her arms, and they come round my neck i' a gentle grip, and they slacked away, and she seemed fainting. "Now yo' mun get away, lad," says Jesse, and I picked up my hat and I came downstairs.

'Th' recruiting sergeant were waitin' for me at th' corner public-house. "Yo've seen your sweetheart?" says he. "Yes, I've seen her," says I. "Well, we'll have a quart now, and you'll do your best to forget her," says he, bein' one o' them smart, bustlin' chaps. "Ay, sergeant," says I. "Forget her." And I've been forgettin' her ever since.'

He threw away the wilted clump of white violets as he spoke. Ortheris suddenly rose to his knees, his rifle at his shoulder, and peered across the valley in the clear afternoon light. His chin cuddled the stock, and there was a twitching of the muscles of the right cheek as he sighted; Private Stanley Ortheris was engaged on his business. A speck of white crawled up the watercourse.

'See that beggar? . . . Got 'im.'

Seven hundred yards away, and a full two hundred down the hillside, the deserter of the Aurangabadis pitched forward, rolled down a red rock, and lay very still, with his face in a clump of blue gentians, while a big raven flapped out of the pine wood to make investigation.

'That's a clean shot, little man,' said Mulvaney.

Learoyd thoughtfully watched the smoke clear away. 'Happen there was a lass tewed up wi' him, too,' said he.

Ortheris did not reply. He was staring across the valley, with the smile of the artist who looks on the completed work.

'Rikki-Tikki-Tavi' [1]

At the hole where he went in
Red-Eye called to Wrinkle-Skin.
Hear what little Red-Eye saith:
'Nag,[2] come up and dance with death!'

Eye to eye and head to head,
    (*Keep the measure, Nag.*)
This shall end when one is dead;
    (*At thy pleasure, Nag.*)
Turn for turn and twist for twist –
    (*Run and hide thee, Nag.*)
Hah! The hooded Death has missed!
    (*Woe betide thee, Nag!*)

This is the story of the great war that Rikki-tikki-tavi fought single-handed, through the bath-rooms of the big bungalow in Segowlee cantonment. Darzee, the tailor-bird, helped him, and Chuchundra, the musk-rat, who never comes out into the middle of the floor, but always creeps round by the wall, gave him advice; but Rikki-tikki did the real fighting.

He was a mongoose, rather like a little cat in his fur and his tail, but quite like a weasel in his head and his habits. His eyes and the end of his restless nose were pink; he could scratch himself anywhere he pleased, with any leg, front or back, that he chose to use; he could fluff up his tail till it looked like a bottle-brush, and his war-cry, as he scuttled through the long grass, was: '*Rikki-tikk-tikki-tikki-tchk!*'

One day, a high summer flood washed him out of the burrow where he lived with his father and mother, and carried him, kicking and clucking, down a roadside ditch. He found a little wisp of grass floating there, and clung to it till he lost his senses. When he revived, he was lying in the hot sun on the middle of a garden path, very draggled indeed, and a small boy was saying: 'Here's a dead mongoose. Let's have a funeral.'

'No,' said his mother; 'let's take him in and dry him. Perhaps he isn't really dead.'

They took him into the house, and a big man picked him up between his finger and thumb, and said he was not dead but half choked; so they wrapped him in cotton-wool, and warmed him, and he opened his eyes and sneezed.

'Now,' said the big man (he was an Englishman who had just moved into the bungalow); 'don't frighten him, and we'll see what he'll do.'

It is the hardest thing in the world to frighten a mongoose, because he is eaten up from nose to tail with curiosity. The motto of all the mongoose family is, 'Run and find out'; and Rikki-tikki was a true mongoose. He looked at the cotton-wool, decided that it was not good to eat, ran all round the table, sat up and put his fur in order, scratched himself, and jumped on the small boy's shoulder.

'Don't be frightened, Teddy,' said his father. 'That's his way of making friends.'

'Ouch! He's tickling under my chin,' said Teddy.

Rikki-tikki looked down between the boy's collar and neck, snuffed at his ear, and climbed down to the floor, where he sat rubbing his nose.

'Good gracious,' said Teddy's mother, 'and that's a wild creature! I suppose he's so tame because we've been kind to him.'

'All mongooses are like that,' said her husband. 'If Teddy doesn't pick him up by the tail, or try to put him in a cage, he'll run in and out of the house all day long. Let's give him something to eat.'

They gave him a little piece of raw meat. Rikki-tikki liked it immensely, and when it was finished he went out into the verandah and sat in the sunshine and fluffed up his fur to make it dry to the roots. Then he felt better.

'There are more things to find out about in this house,' he said to himself, 'than all my family could find out in all their lives. I shall certainly stay and find out.'

He spent all that day roaming over the house. He nearly drowned himself in the bath-tubs, put his nose into the ink on a writing-table, and burnt it on the end of the big man's cigar, for he climbed up in the big man's lap to see how writing was done. At nightfall he ran into Teddy's nursery to watch how kerosene-lamps were lighted, and when Teddy went to bed Rikki-tikki climbed up too; but he was a restless companion, because he had to get up and attend to every noise all through the night, and find out what made it. Teddy's mother and father came in, the last thing, to look at their boy, and Rikki-tikki was awake on the pillow. 'I don't like that,' said Teddy's mother; 'he may bite the child.' 'He'll do no such thing,' said the father. 'Teddy's safer with that little beast than if he had a bloodhound to watch him. If a snake came into the nursery now –'

But Teddy's mother wouldn't think of anything so awful.

Early in the morning Rikki-tikki came to early breakfast in the verandah riding on Teddy's shoulder, and they gave him banana and some boiled egg; and he sat on all their laps one after the other, because every well-brought-up mongoose always hopes to be a house-mongoose some day and have rooms to run about in, and Rikki-tikki's mother (she used to live in the General's house at Segowlee) had carefully told Rikki what to do if ever he came across white men.

Then Rikki-tikki went out into the garden to see what was to be seen. It was a large garden, only half cultivated, with bushes as big as summerhouses of Marshal Niel roses, lime and orange trees, clumps of bamboos, and thickets of high grass. Rikki-tikki licked his lips. 'This is a splendid hunting-ground,' he said, and his tail grew bottle-brushy at the thought of it, and he scuttled up and down the garden, snuffing here and there till he heard very sorrowful voices in a thorn-bush.

It was Darzee, the tailor-bird, and his wife. They had made a beautiful nest by pulling two big leaves together and stitching them up the edges with fibres, and had filled the hollow with cotton and downy fluff. The nest swayed to and fro, as they sat on the rim and cried.

'What is the matter?' asked Rikki-tikki.

'We are very miserable,' said Darzee. 'One of our babies fell out of the nest yesterday, and Nag ate him.'

'H'm!' said Rikki-tikki, 'that is very sad – but I am a stranger here. Who is Nag?'

Darzee and his wife only cowered down in the nest without answering, for from the thick grass at the foot of the bush there came a low hiss – a horrid cold sound that made Rikki-tikki jump back two clear feet. Then inch by inch out of the grass rose up the head and spread hood of Nag, the big black cobra, and he was five feet long from tongue to tail. When he had lifted one-third of himself clear of the ground, he stayed balancing to and fro exactly as a dandelion-tuft balances in the wind, and he looked at Rikki-tikki with the wicked snake's eyes that never change their expression, whatever the snake may be thinking of.

'Who is Nag?' said he. '*I* am Nag. The great god Brahm [3] put his mark upon all our people when the first cobra spread his hood to keep the sun off Brahm as he slept. Look, and be afraid!'

He spread out his hood more than ever, and Rikki-tikki saw the spectacle-mark on the back of it that looks exactly like the eye part of a hook-and-eye fastening. He was afraid for the minute; but it is impossible for a mongoose to stay frightened for any length of time, and though Rikki-tikki had never met a live cobra before, his mother had fed him on dead ones, and he knew that all a grown mongoose's business in life was to fight and eat snakes. Nag knew that too, and at the bottom of his cold heart he was afraid.

'Well,' said Rikki-tikki, and his tail began to fluff up again, 'marks or no marks, do you think it is right for you to eat fledglings out of a nest?'

Nag was thinking to himself, and watching the least little movement in the grass behind Rikki-tikki. He knew that mongooses in the garden meant death sooner or later for him and his family, but he wanted to get Rikki-tikki off his guard. So he dropped his head a little, and put it on one side.

'Let us talk,' he said. 'You eat eggs. Why should not I eat birds?'

'Behind you! Look behind you!' sang Darzee.

Rikki-tikki knew better than to waste time in staring. He jumped up in the air as high as he could go, and just under him whizzed by the head of Nagaina, Nag's wicked wife. She had crept up behind him as he was talking, to make an end of him; and he heard her savage hiss as the stroke missed. He came down almost across her back, and if he had been an old mongoose he would have known that then was the time to break her back with one bite; but he was afraid of the terrible lashing return-stroke of the cobra. He bit, indeed, but did not bite long enough, and he jumped clear of the whisking tail, leaving Nagaina torn and angry.

'Wicked, wicked Darzee!' said Nag, lashing up as high as he could reach toward the nest in the thorn-bush; but Darzee had built it out of reach of snakes, and it only swayed to and fro.

Rikki-tikki felt his eyes growing red and hot (when a mongoose's eyes grow red, he is angry), and he sat back on his tail and hind legs like a little kangaroo, and looked all round him, and chattered with rage. But Nag and Nagaina had disappeared into the grass. When a snake misses its stroke, it never says anything or gives any sign of what it means to do next. Rikki-tikki did not care to follow them, for he did not feel sure that he could manage two snakes at once. So he trotted off to the gravel path near the house, and sat down to think. It was a serious matter for him.

If you read the old books of natural history, you will find they say that when the mongoose fights the snake and happens to get bitten, he runs off and eats some herb that cures him. That is not true. The victory is only a matter of quickness of eye and quickness of foot – snake's blow against mongoose's jump – and as no eye can follow the motion of a snake's head when it strikes, that makes things much more wonderful than any magic herb. Rikki-tikki knew he was a young mongoose, and it made him all the more pleased to think that he had managed to escape a blow from behind. It gave him confidence in himself, and when Teddy came running down the path, Rikki-tikki was ready to be petted.

But just as Teddy was stooping, something flinched a little in the dust, and a tiny voice said: 'Be careful. I am death!' It was Karait, the dusty brown snakeling that lies for choice on the dusty earth; and his bite is as dangerous as the cobra's. But he is so small that nobody thinks of him, and so he does the more harm to people.

Rikki-tikki's eyes grew red again, and he danced up to Karait with the peculiar rocking, swaying motion that he had inherited from his family. It looks very funny, but it is so perfectly balanced a gait that you can fly off from it at any angle you please; and in dealing with snakes this is an advantage. If Rikki-tikki had only known, he was doing a much more dangerous thing than fighting Nag, for Karait is so small, and can turn so quickly, that unless Rikki bit him close to the back of the head, he would get the return-stroke in his eye or lip. But Rikki did not know: his eyes were all red, and he rocked back and forth, looking for a good place to hold. Karait struck out. Rikki jumped sideways and tried to run in, but the wicked little dusty grey head lashed within a fraction of his shoulder, and he had to jump over the body, and the head followed his heels close.

Teddy shouted to the house: 'Oh, look here! Our mongoose is killing a snake'; and Rikki-tikki heard a scream from Teddy's mother. His father ran out with a stick, but by the time he came up, Karait had lunged out once too far, and Rikki-tikki had sprung, jumped on the snake's back, dropped his head far between his fore-legs, bitten as high up the back as he could get hold, and rolled away. That bite paralysed Karait, and Rikki-tikki was just going to eat him up from the tail, after the custom of his family at dinner, when he remembered that a full meal makes a slow mongoose, and if he wanted all his strength and quickness ready, he must keep himself thin.

He went away for a dust-bath under the castor-oil bushes, while Teddy's father beat the dead Karait. 'What is the use of that?' thought Rikki-tikki. 'I have settled it all'; and then Teddy's mother picked him up from the dust and hugged him, crying that he had saved Teddy from death, and Teddy's father said that he was a providence, and Teddy looked on with big scared eyes. Rikki-tikki was rather amused at all the fuss, which, of course, he did not understand. Teddy's mother might just as well have petted Teddy for playing in the dust. Rikki was thoroughly enjoying himself.

That night, at dinner, walking to and fro among the wine-glasses on the table, he could have stuffed himself three times over with nice things; but he remembered Nag and Nagaina, and though it was very pleasant to be patted and petted by Teddy's mother, and to sit on Teddy's shoulder, his eyes would get red from time to time, and he would go off into his long war-cry of '*Rikk-tikk-tikki-tikki-tchk!*'

Teddy carried him off to bed, and insisted on Rikki-tikki sleeping under his chin. Rikki-tikki was too well bred to bite or scratch, but as soon as Teddy was asleep he went off for his nightly walk round the house, and in the dark he ran up against Chuchundra, the musk-rat, creeping round by the wall. Chuchundra is a broken-hearted little beast. He whimpers and cheeps all the night, trying to make up his mind to run into the middle of the room, but he never gets there.

'Don't kill me,' said Chuchundra, almost weeping. 'Rikki-tikki, don't kill me.'

'Do you think a snake-killer kills musk-rats?' said Rikki-tikki scornfully.

'Those who kill snakes get killed by snakes,' said Chuchundra, more sorrowfully than ever. 'And how am I to be sure that Nag won't mistake me for you some dark night?'

'There's not the least danger,' said Rikki-tikki; 'but Nag is in the garden, and I know you don't go there.'

'My cousin Chua, the rat, told me –' said Chuchundra, and then he stopped.

'Told you what?'

'H'sh! Nag is everywhere, Rikki-tikki. You should have talked to Chua in the garden.'

'I didn't – so you must tell me. Quick, Chuchundra, or I'll bite you!'

Chuchundra sat down and cried till the tears rolled off his whiskers. 'I am a very poor man,' he sobbed. 'I never had spirit enough to run out into the middle of the room. H'sh! I mustn't tell you anything. Can't you *hear*, Rikki-tikki?'

Rikki-tikki listened. The house was as still as still, but he thought he could just catch the faintest *scratch-scratch* in the world – a noise as faint as that of a wasp walking on a window-pane – the dry scratch of a snake's scales on brickwork.

'That's Nag or Nagaina,' he said to himself; 'and he is crawling into the bath-room sluice. You're right, Chuchundra; I should have talked to Chua.'

He stole off to Teddy's bath-room, but there was nothing there, and then to Teddy's mother's bath-room. At the bottom of the smooth plaster wall there was a brick pulled out to make a sluice for the bath-water, and as Rikki-tikki stole in by the masonry curb where the bath is put, he heard Nag and Nagaina whispering together outside in the moonlight.

'When the house is emptied of people,' said Nagaina to her husband, '*he* will have to go away, and then the garden will be our own again. Go in quietly, and remember that the big man who killed Karait is the first one to bite. Then come out and tell me, and we will hunt for Rikki-tikki together.'

'But are you sure that there is anything to be gained by killing the people?' said Nag.

'Everything. When there were no people in the bungalow, did we have any mongoose in the garden? So long as the bungalow is empty, we are king and queen of the garden; and remember that as soon as our eggs in the melon-bed hatch (as they may tomorrow), our children will need room and quiet.'

'I had not thought of that,' said Nag. 'I will go, but there is no need that we should hunt for Rikki-tikki afterward. I will kill the big man and his wife, and the child if I can, and come away quietly. Then the bungalow will be empty, and Rikki-tikki will go.'

Rikki-tikki tingled all over with rage and hatred at this, and then Nag's head came through the sluice, and his five feet of cold body followed it. Angry as he was, Rikki-tikki was very frightened as he saw the size of the big cobra. Nag coiled himself up, raised his head, and looked into the bath-room in the dark, and Rikki could see his eyes glitter.

'Now, if I kill him here, Nagaina will know; and if I fight him on the open floor, the odds are in his favour. What am I to do?' said Rikki-tikki-tavi.

Nag waved to and fro, and then Rikki-tikki heard him drinking from the biggest water-jar that was used to fill the bath. 'That is good,' said the snake. 'Now, when Karait was killed, the big man had a stick. He may have that stick still, but when he comes in to bathe in the morning he will not have a stick. I shall wait here till he comes. Nagaina – do you hear me? – I shall wait here in the cool till daytime.'

There was no answer from outside, so Rikki-tikki knew Nagaina had gone away. Nag coiled himself down, coil by coil, round the bulge at the bottom of the water-jar, and Rikki-tikki stayed still as death. After an hour he began to move, muscle by muscle, toward the jar. Nag was asleep, and Rikki-tikki looked at his big back, wondering which would be the best place for a good hold. 'If I don't break his back at the first jump,' said Rikki, 'he can still fight; and if he fights – O Rikki!' He looked at the thickness of the neck below the hood, but that was too much for him; and a bite near the tail would only make Nag savage.

'It must be the head,' he said at last; 'the head above the hood; and when I am once there, I must not let go.'

Then he jumped. The head was lying a little clear of the water-jar, under the curve of it; and, as his teeth met, Rikki braced his back against the bulge of the red earthenware to hold down the head. This gave him just one second's purchase, and he made the most of it. Then he was battered to and fro as a rat is shaken by a dog – to and fro on the floor, up and down, and round in great circles; but his eyes were red, and he held on as the body cart-whipped over the floor, upsetting the tin dipper and the soap-dish and the flesh-brush, and banged against the tin side of the bath. As he held he closed his jaws tighter and tighter, for he made sure he would be banged to death, and, for the honour of his family, he preferred to be found with his teeth locked. He was dizzy, aching, and felt shaken to pieces when something went off like a thunderclap just behind him; a hot wind knocked him senseless, and red fire singed his fur. The big man had been wakened by the noise, and had fired both barrels of a shot-gun into Nag just behind the hood.

Rikki-tikki held on with his eyes shut, for now he was quite sure he was dead; but the head did not move, and the big man picked him up and said: 'It's the mongoose again, Alice; the little chap has saved *our* lives now.' Then Teddy's mother came in with a very white face, and saw what was left of Nag, and Rikki-tikki dragged himself to Teddy's bedroom and spent half the rest of the night shaking himself tenderly to find out whether he really was broken into forty pieces, as he fancied.

When morning came he was very stiff, but well pleased with his doings. 'Now I have Nagaina to settle with, and she will be worse than five Nags, and there's no knowing when the eggs she spoke of will hatch. Goodness! I must go and see Darzee,' he said.

Without waiting for breakfast, Rikki-tikki ran to the thorn-bush where Darzee was singing a song of triumph at the top of his voice. The news of Nag's death was all over the garden, for the sweeper had thrown the body on the rubbish-heap.

'Oh, you stupid tuft of feathers!' said Rikki-tikki angrily. 'Is this the time to sing?'

'Nag is dead – is dead – is dead!' sang Darzee. 'The valiant Rikki-tikki caught him by the head and held fast. The big man brought the bang-stick, and Nag fell in two pieces! He will never eat my babies again.'

'All that's true enough; but where's Nagaina?' said Rikki-tikki, looking carefully round him.

'Nagaina came to the bath-room sluice and called for Nag,' Darzee went on; 'and Nag came out on the end of a stick – the sweeper picked him up on the end of a stick and threw him upon the rubbish-heap. Let us sing about the great, the red-eyed Rikki-tikki!' and Darzee filled his throat and sang.

'If I could get up to your nest, I'd roll all your babies out!' said Rikki-tikki. 'You don't know when to do the right thing at the right time. You're safe enough in your nest there, but it's war for me down here. Stop singing a minute, Darzee.'

'For the great, the beautiful Rikki-tikki's sake I will stop,' said Darzee. 'What is it, O Killer of the terrible Nag?'

'Where is Nagaina, for the third time?'

'On the rubbish-heap by the stables, mourning for Nag. Great is Rikki-tikki with the white teeth.'

'Bother my white teeth! Have you ever heard where she keeps her eggs?'

'In the melon-bed, on the end nearest the wall, where the sun strikes nearly all day. She hid them there weeks ago.'

'And you never thought it worth while to tell me? The end nearest the wall, you said?'

'Rikki-tikki, you are not going to eat her eggs?'

'Not eat exactly; no. Darzee, if you have a grain of sense you will fly off to the stables and pretend that your wing is broken, and let Nagaina chase you away to this bush. I must get to the melon-bed, and if I went there now she'd see me.'

Darzee was a feather-brained little fellow who could never hold more than one idea at a time in his head; and just because he knew that Nagaina's children were born in eggs like his own, he didn't think at first that it was fair to kill them. But his wife was a sensible bird, and she knew that cobra's eggs meant young cobras later on; so she flew off from the nest, and left Darzee to keep the babies warm, and continue his song about the death of Nag. Darzee was very like a man in some ways.

She fluttered in front of Nagaina by the rubbish-heap, and cried out, 'Oh, my wing is broken! The boy in the house threw a stone at me and broke it.' Then she fluttered more desperately than ever.

Nagaina lifted up her head and hissed, 'You warned Rikki-tikki when I would have killed him. Indeed and truly, you've chosen a bad place to be lame in.' And she moved toward Darzee's wife, slipping along over the dust.

'The boy broke it with a stone!' shrieked Darzee's wife.

'Well! It may be some consolation to you when you're dead to know that I shall settle accounts with the boy. My husband lies on the rubbish-heap this morning, but before night the boy in the house will lie very still. What is the use of running away? I am sure to catch you. Little fool, look at me!'

Darzee's wife knew better than to do *that*, for a bird who looks at a snake's eyes gets so frightened that she cannot move. Darzee's wife fluttered on, piping sorrowfully, and never leaving the ground, and Nagaina quickened her pace.

Rikki-tikki heard them going up the path from the stables, and he raced for the end of the melon-patch near the wall. There, in the warm litter about the melons, very cunningly hidden, he found twenty-five eggs, about the size of a bantam's eggs, but with whitish skin instead of shell.

'I was not a day too soon,' he said; for he could see the baby cobras curled up inside the skin, and he knew that the minute they were hatched they could each kill a man or a mongoose. He bit off the tops of the eggs as fast as he could, taking care to crush the young cobras, and turned over the litter from time to time to see whether he had missed any. At last there were only three eggs left, and Rikki-tikki began to chuckle to himself, when he heard Darzee's wife screaming:

'Rikki-tikki, I led Nagaina toward the house, and she has gone into the verandah, and – oh, come quickly – she means killing!'

Rikki-tikki smashed two eggs, and tumbled backward down the melon-bed with the third egg in his mouth, and scuttled to the verandah as hard as he could put foot to the ground. Teddy and his mother and father were there at early breakfast; but Rikki-tikki saw that they were not eating anything. They sat stone-still, and their faces were white. Nagaina was coiled up on the matting by Teddy's chair, within easy striking-distance of Teddy's bare leg, and she was swaying to and fro singing a song of triumph.

'Son of the big man that killed Nag,' she hissed, 'stay still. I am not ready yet. Wait a little. Keep very still, all you three. If you move I strike, and if you do not move I strike. Oh, foolish people, who killed my Nag!'

Teddy's eyes were fixed on his father, and all his father could do was to whisper, 'Sit still, Teddy. You mustn't move. Teddy, keep still.'

Then Rikki-tikki came up and cried: 'Turn round, Nagaina; turn and fight!'

'All in good time,' said she, without moving her eyes. 'I will settle my account with *you* presently. Look at your friends, Rikki-tikki. They are still and white; they are afraid. They dare not move, and if you come a step nearer I strike.'

'Look at your eggs,' said Rikki-tikki, 'in the melon-bed near the wall. Go and look, Nagaina.'

The big snake turned half round, and saw the egg on the verandah. 'Ah-h! Give it to me,' she said.

Rikki-tikki put his paws one on each side of the egg, and his eyes were blood-red. 'What price for a snake's egg? For a young cobra? For a young king-cobra? For the last – the very last of the brood? The ants are eating all the others down by the melon-bed.'

Nagaina spun clear round, forgetting everything for the sake of the one egg; and Rikki-tikki saw Teddy's father shoot out a big hand, catch Teddy by the shoulder, and drag him across the little table with the tea-cups, safe and out of reach of Nagaina.

'Tricked! Tricked! Tricked! *Rikk-tck-tck!*' chuckled Rikki-tikki. 'The boy is safe, and it was I – I – I that caught Nag by the hood last night in the bath-room.' Then he began to jump up and down, all four feet together, his head close to the floor. 'He threw me to and fro, but he could not shake me off. He was dead before the big man blew him in two. I did it. *Rikki-tikki-tck-tck!* Come then, Nagaina. Come and fight with me. You shall not be a widow long.'

Nagaina saw that she had lost her chance of killing Teddy, and the egg lay between Rikki-tikki's paws. 'Give me the egg, Rikki-tikki. Give me the last of my eggs, and I will go away and never come back,' she said, lowering her hood.

'Yes, you will go away, and you will never come back; for you will go to the rubbish-heap with Nag. Fight, widow! The big man has gone for his gun! Fight!'

Rikki-tikki was bounding all round Nagaina, keeping just out of reach of her stroke, his little eyes like hot coals. Nagaina gathered herself together, and flung out at him. Rikki-tikki jumped up and backward. Again and again and again she struck, and each time her head came with a whack on the matting of the verandah, and she gathered herself together like a watch-spring. Then Rikki-tikki danced in a circle to get behind her, and Nagaina spun round to keep her head to his head, so that the rustle of her tail on the matting sounded like dry leaves blown along by the wind.

He had forgotten the egg. It still lay on the verandah, and Nagaina came nearer and nearer to it, till at last, while Rikki-tikki was drawing breath, she caught it in her mouth, turned to the verandah steps, and flew like an arrow down the path, with Rikki-tikki behind her. When the cobra runs for her life, she goes like a whip-lash flicked across a horse's neck.

Rikki-tikki knew that he must catch her, or all the trouble would begin again. She headed straight for the long grass by the thorn-bush, and as he was running Rikki-tikki heard Darzee still singing his foolish little song of triumph. But Darzee's wife was wiser. She flew off her nest as Nagaina came along, and flapped her wings about Nagaina's head. If Darzee had helped they might have turned her; but Nagaina only lowered her hood and went on. Still, the instant's delay brought Rikki-tikki up to her, and as she plunged into the rat-hole where she and Nag used to live, his little white teeth were clenched on her tail, and he went down with her – and very few mongooses, however wise and old they may be, care to follow a cobra into its hole. It was dark in the hole; and Rikki-tikki never knew when it might open out and give Nagaina room to turn and strike at him. He held on savagely, and struck out his feet to act as brakes on the dark slope of the hot, moist earth.

Then the grass by the mouth of the hole stopped waving, and Darzee said: 'It is all over with Rikki-tikki! We must sing his death-song. Valiant Rikki-tikki is dead! For Nagaina will surely kill him underground.'

So he sang a very mournful song that he made up on the spur of the minute, and just as he got to the most touching part the grass quivered again, and Rikki-tikki, covered with dirt, dragged himself out of the hole leg by leg, licking his whiskers. Darzee stopped with a little shout. Rikki-tikki shook some of the dust out of his fur and sneezed. 'It is all over,' he said. 'The widow will never come out again.' And the red ants that live between the grass stems heard him, and began to troop down one after another to see if he had spoken the truth.

Rikki-tikki curled himself up in the grass and slept where he was – slept and slept till it was late in the afternoon, for he had done a hard day's work.

'Now,' he said, when he awoke, 'I will go back to the house. Tell the Coppersmith, Darzee, and he will tell the garden that Nagaina is dead.'

The Coppersmith is a bird who makes a noise exactly like the beating of a little hammer on a copper pot; and the reason he is always making it is because he is the town-crier to every Indian garden, and tells all the news to everybody who cares to listen. As Rikki-tikki went up the path, he heard his 'attention' notes like a tiny dinner-gong; and then the steady '*Ding-dong-tock!* Nag is dead – *dong!* Nagaina is dead! *Ding-dong-tock!*' That set all the birds in the garden singing, and the frogs croaking; for Nag and Nagaina used to eat frogs as well as little birds.

When Rikki got to the house, Teddy and Teddy's mother (she looked very white still, for she had been fainting) and Teddy's father came out and almost cried over him; and that night he ate all that was given him till he could eat no more, and went to bed on Teddy's shoulder, where Teddy's mother saw him when she came to look late at night.

'He saved our lives and Teddy's life,' she said to her husband. 'Just think, he saved all our lives.'

Rikki-tikki woke up with a jump, for all the mongooses are light sleepers.

'Oh, it's you,' said he. 'What are you bothering for? All the cobras are dead; and if they weren't, I'm here.'

Rikki-tikki had a right to be proud of himself; but he did not grow too proud, and he kept that garden as a mongoose should keep it, with tooth and jump and spring and bite, till never a cobra dared show its head inside the walls.

The Miracle of Purun Bhagat [1]

The night we felt the Earth would move
    We stole and plucked him by the hand,
Because we loved him with the love
    That knows but cannot understand.

And when the roaring hillside broke,
    And all our world fell down in rain,
We saved him, we the Little Folk;
    But lo! he will not come again!

Mourn now, we saved him for the sake
    Of such poor love as wild ones may.
Mourn ye! Our brother does not wake
    And his own kind drive us away!
                        Dirge of the Langurs. [2]

There was once a man in India who was Prime Minister of one of the semi-independent native States in the north-western part of the country. He was a Brahmin,[3] so high-caste that caste ceased to have any particular meaning for him; and his father had been an important official in the gay-coloured tag-rag and bob-tail of an old-fashioned Hindoo Court. But as Purun Dass grew up he realized that the ancient order of things was changing, and that if anyone wished to get on he must stand well with the English, and imitate all the English believed to be good. At the same time a native official must keep his own master's favour. This was a difficult game, but the quiet, close-mouthed, young Brahmin, helped by a good English education at a Bombay University, played it coolly, and rose, step by step, to be Prime Minister of the kingdom. That is to say, he held more real power than his master, the Maharajah.

When the old king – who was suspicious of the English, their railways and telegraphs – died, Purun Dass stood high with his young successor, who had been tutored by an Englishman; and between them, though he always took care that his master should have the credit, they established schools for little girls, made roads, and started State dispensaries and shows of agricultural implements, and published a yearly blue-book on the 'Moral and Material Progress of the State', and the Foreign Office and the Government of India were delighted. Very few native States take up English progress without reservations, for they will not believe, as Purun Dass showed he did, that what is good for the Englishman must be twice as good for the Asiatic. The Prime Minister became the honoured friend of Viceroys and Governors, and Lieutenant-Governors, and medical missionaries, and common missionaries, and hard-riding English officers who came to shoot in the State preserves, as well as of whole hosts of tourists who travelled up and down India in the cold weather, showing how things ought to be managed. In his spare time he would endow scholarships for the study of medicine and manufactures on strictly English lines, and write letters to the *Pioneer*,[4] the greatest Indian daily paper, explaining his master's aims and objects.

At last he went to England on a visit, and had to pay enormous sums to the priests when he came back; for even so high-caste a Brahmin as Purun Dass lost caste by crossing the black sea. In London he met and talked with everyone worth knowing – men whose names go all over the world – and saw a great deal more than he said. He was given honorary degrees by learned universities, and he made speeches and talked of Hindu social reform to English ladies in evening dress, till all London cried, 'This is the most fascinating man we have ever met at dinner since cloths were first laid!'

When he returned to India there was a blaze of glory, for the Viceroy himself made a special visit to confer upon the Maharajah the Grand Cross of the Star of India – all diamonds and ribbons and enamel; and at the same ceremony, while the cannon boomed, Purun Dass was made a Knight Commander of the Order of the Indian Empire; so that his name stood Sir Purun Dass, K.C.I.E.

That evening at dinner in the big Viceregal tent he stood up with the badge and the collar of the Order on his breast, and replying to the toast of his master's health, made a speech that few Englishmen could have surpassed.

Next month, when the city had returned to its sun-baked quiet, he did a thing no Englishman would have dreamed of doing, for, so far as the world's affairs went, he died. The jewelled order of his knighthood returned to the Indian Government, and a new Prime Minister was appointed to the charge of affairs, and a great game of General Post began in all the subordinate appointments. The priests knew what had happened and the people guessed; but India is the one place in the world where a man can do as he pleases and nobody asks why; and the fact that Dewan[5] Sir Purun Dass, K.C.I.E., had resigned position, palace, and power, and taken up the begging-bowl and ochre-coloured dress of a Sunnyasi or holy man, was considered nothing extraordinary. He had been, as the Old Law recommends, twenty years a youth, twenty years a fighter – though he had never carried a weapon in his life – and twenty years head of a household. He had used his wealth and his power for what he knew both to be worth; he had taken honour when it came his way; he had seen men and cities far and near, and men and cities had stood up and honoured him. Now he would let these things go, as a man drops the cloak he needs no longer.

Behind him, as he walked through the city gates, an antelope skin and brass-handled crutch under his arm, and a begging-bowl of polished brown *coco-de-mer* [6] in his hand, barefoot, alone, with eyes cast on the ground – behind him they were firing salutes from the bastions in honour of his happy successor. Purun Dass nodded. All that life was ended; and he bore it no more ill-will or good-will than a man bears to a colourless dream of the night. He was a Sunnyasi – a houseless, wandering mendicant, depending on his neighbours for his daily bread; and so long as there is a morsel to divide in India neither priest nor beggar starves. He had never in his life tasted meat, and very seldom eaten even fish. A five-pound-note would have covered his personal expenses for food through any one of the many years in which he had been absolute master of millions of money. Even when he was being lionized in London he had held before him his dream of peace and quiet – the long, white, dusty Indian road, printed all over with bare feet, the incessant, slow-moving traffic, and the sharp-smelling wood-smoke curling up under the fig-trees in the twilight, where the wayfarers sat at their evening meal.

When the time came to make that dream true the Prime Minister took the proper steps, and in three days you might more easily have found a bubble in the trough of the long Atlantic seas than Purun Dass among the roving, gathering, separating millions of India.

At night his antelope skin was spread where the darkness overtook him – sometimes in a Sunnyasi monastery by the roadside; sometimes by a mud pillar shrine of Kala Pir, [7] where the Jogis, [8] who are another misty division of holy men, would receive him as they do those who know what castes and divisions are worth; sometimes on the outskirts of a little Hindu village, where the children would steal up with the food their parents had prepared; and sometimes on the pitch of the bare grazing-grounds where the flame of his stick fire waked the drowsy camels. It was all one to Purun Dass – or Purun Bhagat, as he called himself now. Earth, people, and food were all one. But, unconsciously, his feet drew him away northward and eastward; from the south to Rohtak; from Rohtak to Kurnool; from Kurnool to ruined Samanah, and then up-stream along the dried bed of the Gugger river that fills only when the rain falls in the hills, till, one day, he saw the far line of the great Himalayas.

Then Purun Bhagat smiled, for he remembered that his mother was of Rajput Brahmin birth, from Kulu way – a Hill-woman, always homesick for the snows – and that the least touch of Hill blood draws a man in the end back to where he belongs.

'Yonder,' said Purun Bhagat, breasting the lower slopes of the Sewaliks, where the cacti stand up like seven-branched candlesticks, 'yonder I shall sit down and get knowledge'; and the cool wind of the Himalayas whistled about his ears as he trod the road that led to Simla.[9]

The last time he had come that way it had been in state, with a clattering cavalry escort, to visit the gentlest and most affable of Viceroys; and the two had talked for an hour together about mutual friends in London, and what the Indian common folk really thought of things. This time Purun Bhagat paid no calls, but leaned on the rail of the Mall, watching the glorious view of the Plains spread out forty miles below, till a native Mohammedan policeman told him he was obstructing traffic; and Purun Bhagat salaamed reverently to the Law, because he knew the value of it, and was seeking for a Law of his own. Then he moved on, and slept that night in an empty hut at Chota Simla, which looks like the very last end of the earth, but it was only the beginning of his journey. He followed the Himalaya-Thibet road, the little ten-foot track that is blasted out of solid rock, or strutted out on timbers over gulfs a thousand feet deep; that dips into warm, wet, shut-in valleys, and climbs across bare, grassy hill-shoulders where the sun strikes like a burning-glass; or turns through dripping, dark forests where the tree-ferns dress the trunks from head to heel, and the pheasant calls to his mate. And he met Thibetan herdsmen with their dogs and flocks of sheep, each sheep with a little bag of borax on his back, and wandering woodcutters, and cloaked and blanketed Lamas from Thibet, coming into India on pilgrimage, and envoys of little solitary Hill-states, posting furiously on ring-streaked and piebald ponies, or the cavalcade of a Rajah paying a visit; or else for a long, clear day he would see nothing more than a black bear grunting and rooting down below in the valley. When he first started, the roar of the world he had left still rang in his ears, as the roar of a tunnel rings a little after the train has passed through; but when he had put the Mutteeanee Pass behind him that was all done, and Purun Bhagat was alone with himself, walking, wondering, and thinking, his eyes on the ground, and his thoughts with the clouds.

One evening he crossed the highest pass he had met till then – it had been a two days' climb – and came out on a line of snow-peaks that belted all the horizon – mountains from fifteen to twenty thousand feet high, looking almost near enough to hit with a stone, though they were fifty or sixty miles away. The pass was crowned with dense, dark forest – deodar, walnut, wild cherry, wild olive, and wild pear but mostly deodar, which is the Himalayan cedar; and under the shadow of the deodars stood a deserted shrine to Kali[10] –who is Durga, who is Sitala, who is sometimes worshipped against the smallpox.

Purun Dass swept the stone floor clean, smiled at the grinning statue, made himself a little mud fireplace at the back of the shrine, spread his antelope skin on a bed of fresh pine needles, tucked his *bairagi* – his brass-handled crutch – under his armpit, and sat down to rest.

Immediately below him the hillside fell away, clean and cleared for fifteen hundred feet, to where a little village of stone-walled houses, with roofs of beaten earth, clung to the steep tilt. All round it tiny terraced fields lay out like aprons of patchwork on the knees of the mountain, and cows no bigger than beetles grazed between the smooth stone circles of the threshing-floors. Looking across the valley the eye was deceived by the size of things, and could not at first realize that what seemed to be low scrub, on the opposite mountain-flank, was in truth a forest of hundred-foot pines. Purun Bhagat saw an eagle swoop across the enormous hollow, but the great bird dwindled to a dot ere it was half-way over. A few bands of scattered clouds strung up and down the valley, catching on a shoulder of the hills, or rising up and dying out when they were level with the head of the pass. And 'Here shall I find peace,' said Purun Bhagat.

Now, a Hill-man makes nothing of a few hundred feet up or down, and as soon as the villagers saw the smoke in the deserted shrine, the village priest climbed up the terraced hillside to welcome the stranger.

When he met Purun Bhagat's eyes – the eyes of a man used to control thousands – he bowed to the earth, took the begging-bowl without a word, and returned to the village, saying, 'We have at last a holy man. Never have I seen such a man. He is of the plains – but pale coloured – a Brahmin of the Brahmins.' Then all the housewives of the village said, 'Think you he will stay with us?' and each did her best to cook the most savoury meal for the Bhagat. Hill-food is very simple, but with buck-wheat and Indian corn, and rice and red pepper, and little fish out of the stream in the little valley, and honey from the flue-like hives built in the stone walls, and dried apricots, and turmeric, and wild ginger, and bannocks of flour, a devout woman can make good things; and it was a full bowl that the priest carried to the Bhagat. Was he going to stay? asked the priest. Would he need a *chela* – a disciple – to beg for him? Had he a blanket against the cold weather? Was the food good?

Purun Bhagat ate, and thanked the giver. It was in his mind to stay. That was sufficient, said the priest. Let the begging-bowl be placed outside the shrine, in the hollow made by those two twisted roots, and daily should the Bhagat be fed; for the village felt honoured that such a man – he looked timidly into the Bhagat's face – should tarry among them.

That day saw the end of Purun Bhagat's wanderings. He had come to the place appointed for him – the silence and the space. After this, time stopped, and he, sitting at the mouth of the shrine, could not tell whether he were alive or dead; a man with control of his limbs, or a part of the hills, and the clouds, and the shifting rain, and sunlight. He would repeat a Name softly to himself a hundred hundred times, till, at each repetition, he seemed to move more and more out of his body, sweeping up to the doors of some tremendous discovery; but, just as the door was opening, his body would drag him back, and, with grief, he felt he was locked up again in the flesh and bones of Purun Bhagat.

Every morning the filled begging-bowl was laid silently in the crotch of the roots outside the shrine. Sometimes the priest brought it; sometimes a Ladakhi trader, lodging in the village, and anxious to get merit, trudged up the path; but, more often, it was the woman who had cooked the meal overnight; and she would murmur, hardly above her breath: 'Speak for me before the gods, Bhagat. Speak for such an one, the wife of so-and-so!' Now and then some bold child would be allowed the honour, and Purun Bhagat would hear him drop the bowl and run as fast as his little legs could carry him, but the Bhagat never came down to the village. It was laid out like a map at his feet. He could see the evening gatherings held on the circle of the threshing-floors, because that was the only level ground; could see the wonderful unnamed green of the young rice, the indigo blues of the Indian corn; the dock-like patches of buckwheat, and, in its season, the red bloom of the amaranth, whose tiny seeds, being neither grain nor pulse, make a food that can be lawfully eaten by Hindus in time of fasts.

When the year turned, the roofs of the huts were all little squares of purest gold, for it was on the roofs that they laid out their cobs of the corn to dry. Hiving and harvest, rice-sowing and husking, passed before his eyes, all embroidered down there on the many-sided fields, and he thought of them all, and wondered what they all led to at the long last.

Even in populated India a man cannot a day sit still before the wild things run over him as though he were a rock; and in that wilderness very soon the wild things, who knew Kali's Shrine well, came back to look at the intruder. The *langurs*, the big grey-whiskered monkeys of the

Himalayas, were, naturally, the first, for they are alive with curiosity; and when they had upset the begging-bowl, and rolled it round the floor, and tried their teeth on the brass-handled crutch, and made faces at the antelope skin, they decided that the human being who sat so still was harmless. At evening, they would leap down from the pines, and beg with their hands for things to eat, and then swing off in graceful curves. They liked the warmth of the fire, too, and huddled round it till Purun Bhagat had to push them aside to throw on more fuel; and in the morning, as often as not, he would find a furry ape sharing his blanket. All day long, one or other of the tribe would sit by his side, staring out at the snows, crooning and looking unspeakably wise and sorrowful.

After the monkeys came the *barasingh*, that big deer which is like our red deer, but stronger. He wished to rub off the velvet of his horns against the cold stones of Kali's statue, and stamped his feet when he saw the man at the shrine. But Purun Bhagat never moved, and, little by little, the royal stag edged up and nuzzled his shoulder. Purun Bhagat slid one cool hand along the hot antlers, and the touch soothed the fretted beast, who bowed his head, and Purun Bhagat very softly rubbed and ravelled off the velvet. Afterwards, the *barasingh* brought his doe and fawn – gentle things that mumbled on the holy man's blanket – or would come alone at night, his eyes green in the fire-flicker, to take his share of fresh walnuts. At last, the musk-deer, the shyest and almost the smallest of the deerlets, came, too, her big, rabbity ears erect; even brindled, silent *mushick-nabha* [11] must needs find out what the light in the shrine meant, and drop her moose-like nose into Purun Bhagat's lap, coming and going with the shadows of the fire. Purun Bhagat called them all 'my brothers', and his low call of '*Bhai! Bhai!*' [12] would draw them from the forest at noon if they were within earshot. The Himalayan black bear, moody and suspicious – Sona, who has the V-shaped white mark under his chin – passed that way more than once; and since the Bhagat showed no fear, Sona showed no anger, but watched him, and came closer, and begged a share of the caresses, and a dole of bread or wild berries. Often, in the still dawns, when the Bhagat would climb to the very crest of the notched pass to watch the red day walking along the peaks of the snows, he would find Sona shuffling and grunting at his heels, thrusting a curious forepaw under fallen trunks, and bringing it away with a *whoof* of impatience; or his early steps would wake Sona where he lay curled up, and the great brute, rising erect, would think to fight, till he heard the Bhagat's voice and knew his best friend.

Nearly all hermits and holy men who live apart from the big cities have the reputation of being able to work miracles with the wild things, but all the miracle lies in keeping still, in never making a hasty movement, and, for a long time, at least, in never looking directly at a visitor. The villagers saw the outlines of the *barasingh* stalking like a shadow through the dark forest behind the shrine; saw the *minaul*, the Himalayan pheasant, blazing in her best colours before Kali's statue; and the *langurs* on their haunches, inside, playing with the walnut shells. Some of the children, too, had heard Sona singing to himself, bear-fashion, behind the fallen rocks, and the Bhagat's reputation as miracle-worker stood firm.

Yet nothing was further from his mind than miracles. He believed that all things were one big Miracle, and when a man knows that much he knows something to go upon. He knew for a certainty that there was nothing great and nothing little in this world; and day and night he strove to think out his way into the heart of things, back to the place whence his soul had come.

So thinking, his untrimmed hair fell down about his shoulders, the stone slab at the side of the antelope-skin was dented into a little hole by the foot of his brass-handled crutch, and the place between the tree-trunks, where the begging-bowl rested day after day, sunk and wore into a hollow almost as smooth as the brown shell itself; and each beast knew his exact place at the fire. The fields changed their colours with the seasons; the threshing-floors filled and emptied, and filled again and again; and again and again, when winter came, the *langurs* frisked among the branches feathered with light snow, till the mother-monkeys brought their sad-eyed little babies up from the warmer valleys with the spring. There were few changes in the village. The priest was older, and many of the little children who used to come with the begging-dish sent their own children now; and when you asked of the villagers how long their holy man had lived in Kali's Shrine at the head of the pass, they answered, 'Always.'

Then came such summer rains as had not been known in the Hills for many seasons. Through three good months the valley was wrapped in cloud and soaking mist – steady, unrelenting downfall, breaking off into thunder-shower after thunder-shower. Kali's Shrine stood above the clouds, for the most part, and there was a whole month in which the Bhagat never caught a glimpse of his village. It was packed away under a white floor of cloud that swayed and shifted and rolled on itself and bulged upward, but never broke from its piers – the streaming flanks of the valley.

All that time he heard nothing but the sound of a million little waters, overhead from the trees, and underfoot along the ground, soaking through the pine-needles, dripping from the tongues of draggled fern, and spouting in newly-torn muddy channels down the slopes. Then the sun came out, and drew forth the good incense of the deodars and the rhododendrons, and that far-off, clean smell the Hill People call 'the smell of the snows'. The hot sunshine lasted for a week, and then the rains gathered together for their last downpour, and the water fell in sheets that flayed off the skin of the ground and leaped back in mud. Purun Bhagat heaped his fire high that night, for he was sure his brothers would need warmth; but never a beast came to the shrine, though he called and called till he dropped asleep, wondering what had happened in the woods.

It was in the black heart of the night, the rain drumming like a thousand drums, that he was roused by a plucking at his blanket, and, stretching out, felt the little hand of a *langur*. 'It is better here than in the trees,' he said sleepily, loosening a fold of blanket; 'take it and be warm.' The monkey caught his hand and pulled hard. 'Is it food, then?' said Purun Bhagat. 'Wait awhile, and I will prepare some.' As he kneeled to throw fuel on the fire the *langur* ran to the door of the shrine, crooned, and ran back again, plucking at the man's knee.

'What is it? What is thy trouble, Brother?' said Purun Bhagat, for the *langur's* eyes were full of things that he could not tell. 'Unless one of thy caste be in a trap – and none set traps here – I will not go into that weather. Look, Brother, even the *barasingh* comes for shelter.'

The deer's antlers clashed as he strode into the shrine, clashed against the grinning statue of Kali. He lowered them in Purun Bhagat's direction and stamped uneasily, hissing through his half-shut nostrils.

'Hai! Hai! Hai!' said the Bhagat, snapping his fingers. 'Is *this* payment for a night's lodging?' But the deer pushed him towards the door, and as he did so Purun Bhagat heard the sound of something opening with a sigh, and saw two slabs of the floor draw away from each other, while the sticky earth below smacked its lips.

'Now I see,' said Purun Bhagat. 'No blame to my brothers that they did not sit by the fire tonight. The mountain is falling. And yet – why should I go?' His eye fell on the empty begging-bowl, and his face changed. 'They have given me good food daily since – since I came, and, if I am not swift, tomorrow there will not be one mouth in the valley. Indeed, I must go and warn them below. Back there, Brother! Let me get to the fire.'

The *barasingh* backed unwillingly as Purun Bhagat drove a torch deep into the flame, twirling it till it was well lit. 'Ah! ye came to warn me,' he said, rising. 'Better than that we shall do, better than that. Out, now, and lend my thy neck, Brother, for I have but two feet.'

The Miracle of Purun Bhagat

He clutched the bristling withers of the *barasingh* with his right hand, held the torch away with his left, and stepped out of the shrine into the desperate night. There was no breath of wind, but the rain nearly drowned the torch as the great deer hurried down the slope, sliding on his haunches. As soon as they were clear of the forest more of the Bhagat's brothers joined them. He heard, though he could not see, the *langurs* pressing about him, and behind them the *uhh! uhh!* of Sona. The rain matted his long white hair into ropes; the water splashed beneath his bare feet, and his yellow robe clung to his frail old body, but he stepped down steadily, leaning against the *barasingh*. He was no longer a holy man, but Sir Purun Dass, K.C.I.E., Prime Minister of no small State, a man accustomed to command, going out to save life. Down the steep plashy path they poured all together, the Bhagat and his brothers, down and down till the deer clicked and stumbled on the wall of a threshing-floor, and snorted because he smelt Man. Now they were at the head of the one crooked village street, and the Bhagat beat with his crutch at the barred windows of the blacksmith's house as his torch blazed up in the shelter of the eaves. 'Up and out!' cried Purun Bhagat; and he did not know his own voice, for it was years since he had spoken aloud to a man. 'The hill falls! The hill is falling! Up and out, oh, you within!'

'It is our Bhagat,' said the blacksmith's wife. 'He stands among his beasts. Gather the little ones and give the call.'

It ran from house to house, while the beasts, cramped in the narrow way, surged and huddled round the Bhagat, and Sona puffed impatiently.

The people hurried into the street – they were no more than seventy souls all told – and in the glare of their torches they saw their Bhagat holding back the terrified *barasingh*, while the monkeys plucked piteously at his skirts, and Sona sat on his haunches and roared.

'Across the valley and up the next hill!' shouted Purun Bhagat. 'Leave none behind! We follow!'

Then the people ran as only Hill-folk can run, for they knew that in a landslip you must climb for the highest ground across the valley. They fled, splashing through the little river at the bottom, and panted up the terraced fields on the far side, while the Bhagat and his brethren followed. Up and up the opposite mountain they climbed, calling to each other by name – the roll-call of the village – and at their heels toiled the big *barasingh*, weighted by the failing strength of Purun Bhagat. At last the deer stopped in the shadow of a deep pine-wood, five hundred feet up the hillside. His instinct, that had warned him of the coming slide, told him he would be safe here.

Purun Bhagat dropped fainting by his side, for the chill of the rain and that fierce climb was killing him; but first he called to the scattered torches ahead, 'Stay and count your numbers'; then, whispering to the deer as he saw the lights gather in a cluster: 'Stay with me, Brother. Stay – till – I – go!'

There was a sigh in the air that grew to a mutter, and a mutter that grew to a roar, and a roar that passed all sense of hearing, and the hillside on which the villagers stood was hit in the darkness, and rocked to the blow. Then a note as steady, deep, and true as the deep C of the organ drowned everything for perhaps five minutes, while the very roots of the pines quivered to it. It died away, and the sound of the rain falling on miles of hard ground and grass changed to the muffled drums of water on soft earth. That told its own tale.

Never a villager – not even the priest – was bold enough to speak to the Bhagat who had saved their lives. They crouched under the pines and waited till the day. When it came they looked across the valley, and saw that what had been forest, and terraced field, and track-threaded grazing-ground was one raw, red, fan-shaped smear, with a few trees flung head-down on the scarp. That red ran high up the hill of their refuge, damming back the little river, which had begun to spread into a brick-coloured lake. Of the village, of the road to the shrine, of the shrine itself, and the forest behind, there was no trace. For one mile in width and two thousand feet in sheer depth the mountain-side had come away bodily, planed clean from head to heel.

And the villagers, one by one, crept through the wood to pray before their Bhagat. They saw the *barasingh* standing over him, who fled when they came near, and they heard the *langurs* wailing in the branches, and Sona moaning up the hill; but their Bhagat was dead, sitting cross-legged, his back against a tree, his crutch under his armpit, and his face turned to the north-east.

The priest said: 'Behold a miracle after a miracle, for in this very attitude must all Sunnyasis be buried! Therefore, where he now is we will build the temple to our holy man.'

They built the temple before a year was ended, a little stone and earth shrine, and they called the hill the Bhagat's Hill, and they worship there with lights and flowers and offerings to this day. But they do not know that the saint of their worship is the late Sir Purun Dass, K.C.I.E., D.C.L., Ph.D.,[13] etc., once Prime Minister of the progressive and enlightened State of Mohiniwala, and honorary or corresponding member of more learned and scientific societies than will ever do any good in this world or the next.

The Maltese Cat [1]

They had good reason to be proud, and better reason to be afraid, all twelve of them; for, though they had fought their way, game by game, up the teams entered for the polo tournament, they were meeting the Archangels that afternoon in the final match; and the Archangels' men were playing with half-a-dozen ponies apiece. As the game was divided into six quarters of eight minutes each, that meant a fresh pony after every halt. The Skidars' [2] team, even supposing there were no accidents, could only supply one pony for every other change; and two to one is heavy odds. Again, as Shiraz, the grey Syrian, pointed out, they were meeting the pink and pick of the polo ponies of Upper India; ponies that had cost from a thousand rupees each, while they themselves were a cheap lot gathered, often from country carts, by their masters who belonged to a poor but honest native infantry regiment.

'Money means pace and weight,' said Shiraz, rubbing his black silk nose dolefully along his neat-fitting boot, 'and by the maxims of the game as I know it –'

'Ah, but we aren't playing the maxims,' said the Maltese Cat. 'We're playing the game, and we've the great advantage of knowing the game. Just think a stride, Shiraz. We've pulled up from bottom to second place in two weeks against all those fellows on the ground here; and that's because we play with our heads as well as with our feet.'

'It makes me feel undersized and unhappy all the same,' said Kittiwynk, a mouse-coloured mare with a red browband and the cleanest pair of legs that ever an aged pony owned. 'They've twice our size, these others.'

Kittiwynk looked at the gathering and sighed. The hard, dusty Umballa polo-ground was lined with thousands of soldiers, black and white, not counting hundreds and hundreds of carriages, and drags, and dog-carts, and ladies with brilliant-coloured parasols, and officers in uniform and out of it, and crowds of natives behind them; and orderlies on camels who had halted to watch the game, instead of carrying letters up and down the station, and native horse-dealers running about on thin-eared Biluchi mares, looking for a chance to sell a few first-class polo ponies. Then there were the ponies of thirty teams that had entered for the Upper India Free For All Cup – nearly every pony of worth and dignity from Mhow to Peshawar, from Allahabad to Multan; prize ponies, Arabs, Syrian, Barb, country bred, Deccanee, Waziri, and Kabul ponies of every colour and shape and temper that you could imagine. Some of them were in mat-roofed stables close to the polo-ground, but most were under saddle while their masters, who had been defeated in the earlier games, trotted in and out and told each other exactly how the game should be played.

It was a glorious sight, and the come-and-go of the little quick hoofs, and the incessant salutations of ponies that had met before on other polo-grounds or racecourses were enough to drive a four-footed thing wild.

But the Skidars' team were careful not to know their neighbours, though half the ponies on the ground were anxious to scrape acquaintance with the little fellows that had come from the North, and, so far, had swept the board.

'Let's see,' said a soft, golden-coloured Arab, who had been playing very badly the day before, to the Maltese Cat, 'didn't we meet in Abdul Rahman's stable in Bombay four seasons ago? I won the Paikpattan Cup next season, you may remember.'

'Not me,' said the Maltese Cat politely. 'I was at Malta then, pulling a vegetable cart. I don't race. I play the game.'

'O-oh!' said the Arab, cocking his tail and swaggering off.

'Keep yourselves to yourselves,' said the Maltese Cat to his companions. 'We don't want to rub noses with all those goose-rumped half-breeds of Upper India. When we've won this cup they'll give their shoes to know us.'

'*We* shan't win the cup,' said Shiraz. 'How do you feel?'

'Stale as last night's feed when a musk-rat has run over it,' said Polaris, a rather heavy-shouldered grey, and the rest of the team agreed with him.

'The sooner you forget that the better,' said the Maltese Cat cheerfully. 'They've finished tiffin [3] in the big tent. We shall be wanted now. If your saddles are not comfy, kick. If your bits aren't easy, rear, and let the *saises* know whether your boots are tight.'

Each pony had his *sais*, his groom, who lived and ate and slept with the pony, and had betted a great deal more than he could afford on the result of the game. There was no chance of anything going wrong, and, to make sure, each *sais* was shampooing the legs of his pony to the last minute. Behind the *saises* sat as many of the Skidars' regiment as had leave to attend the match – about half the native officers, and a hundred or two dark, black-bearded men with the regimental pipers nervously fingering the big beribboned bagpipes. The Skidars were what they call a Pioneer regiment; and the bagpipes made the national music of half the men. The native officers held bundles of polo-sticks, long cane-handled mallets, and as the grand-stand filled after lunch they arranged themselves by ones and twos at different points round the ground, so that if a stick were broken the player would not have far to ride for a new one. An impatient British cavalry band struck up 'If you want to know the time, ask a p'leeceman!' and the two umpires in light dust-coats danced out on two little excited ponies. The four players of the Archangels' team followed, and the sight of their beautiful mounts made Shiraz groan again.

'Wait till we know,' said the Maltese Cat. 'Two of 'em are playing in blinkers, and that means they can't see to get out of the way of their own side, or they *may* shy at the umpires' ponies. They've *all* got white web reins that are sure to stretch or slip!'

'And,' said Kittiwynk, dancing to take the stiffness out of her, 'they carry their whips in their hands instead of on their wrists. Hah!'

'True enough. No man can manage his stick and his reins, and his whip that way,' said the Maltese Cat. 'I've fallen over every square yard of the Malta ground, and *I* ought to know.' He quivered his little flea-bitten [4] withers just to show how satisfied he felt; but his heart was not so light. Ever since he had drifted into India on a troopship, taken, with an old rifle, as part payment for a racing debt, the Maltese Cat had played and preached polo to the Skidars' team on the Skidars' stony polo-ground. Now a polo-pony is like a poet. If he is born with a love for the game he can be made. The Maltese Cat knew that bamboos grew solely in order that polo-balls might be turned from their roots, that grain was given to ponies to keep them in hard condition, and that ponies were shod to prevent them slipping on a turn. But, besides all these things, he knew every trick and device of the finest game of the world, and for two seasons he had been teaching the others all he knew or guessed.

'Remember,' he said for the hundredth time as the riders came up, 'we *must* play together, and you *must* play with your heads. Whatever happens, follow the ball. Who goes out first?'

Kittiwynk, Shiraz, Polaris, and a short high little bay fellow with tremendous hocks and no withers worth speaking of (he was called Corks) were being girthed up, and the soldiers in the background stared with all their eyes.

'I want you men to keep quiet,' said Lutyens, the captain of the team, 'and especially *not* to blow your pipes.'

'Not if we win, Captain Sahib?' asked a piper.

'If we win, you can do what you please,' said Lutyens, with a smile, as he slipped the loop of his stick over his wrist, and wheeled to canter to his place. The Archangels' ponies were a little bit above themselves on account of the many-coloured crowd so close to the ground. Their riders were excellent players, but they were a team of crack players instead of a crack team; and that made all the difference in the world. They honestly meant to play together, but it is very hard for four men, each the best of the team he is picked from, to remember that in polo no brilliancy of hitting or riding makes up for playing alone. Their captain shouted his orders to them by name, and it is a curious thing that if you call his name aloud in public after an Englishman you make him hot and fretty. Lutyens said nothing to his men because it had all been said before. He pulled up Shiraz, for he was playing 'back', to guard the goal. Powell on Polaris was half-back, and Macnamara and Hughes on Corks and Kittiwynk were forwards. The tough bamboo-root ball was put into the middle of the ground one hundred and fifty yards from the ends, and Hughes crossed sticks, heads-up, with the captain of the Archangels, who saw fit to play forward, and that is a place from which you cannot easily control the team. The little click as the cane-shafts met was heard all over the ground, and then Hughes made some sort of quick wrist-stroke that just dribbled the ball a few yards. Kittiwynk knew that stroke of old, and followed as a cat follows a mouse. While the captain of the Archangels was wrenching his pony round Hughes struck with all his strength, and next instant Kittiwynk was away, Corks followed close behind her, their little feet pattering like rain-drops on glass.

'Pull out to the left,' said Kittiwynk between her teeth, 'it's coming our way, Corks!'

The back and half-back of the Archangels were tearing down on her just as she was within reach of the ball. Hughes leaned forward with a loose rein, and cut it away to the left almost under Kittiwynk's feet, and it hopped and skipped off to Corks, who saw that, if he were not quick, it would run beyond the boundaries. That long bouncing drive gave the Archangels time to wheel and send three men across the ground to head off Corks. Kittiwynk stayed where she was, for she knew the game. Corks was on the ball half a fraction of a second before the others came up, and Macnamara, with a back-handed stroke, sent it back across the ground to Hughes, who saw the way clear to the Archangels' goal, and smacked the ball in before anyone quite knew what had happened.

'That's luck,' said Corks, as they changed ends. 'A goal in three minutes for three hits and no riding to speak of.'

'Don't know,' said Polaris. 'We've made 'em angry too soon. Shouldn't wonder if they try to rush us off our feet next time.'

'Keep the ball hanging then,' said Shiraz. 'That wears out every pony that isn't used to it.'

Next time there was no easy galloping across the ground. All the Archangels closed up as one man, but there they stayed, for Corks, Kittiwynk, and Polaris were somewhere on the top of the ball, marking time among the rattling sticks, while Shiraz circled about outside, waiting for a chance.

'*We* can do this all day,' said Polaris, ramming his quarters into the side of another pony. 'Where do you think you're shoving to?'

'I'll – I'll be driven in an *ekka* [5] if I know,' was the gasping reply, 'and I'd give a week's feed to get my blinkers off. I can't see anything.'

'The dust is rather bad. Whew! That was one for my off hock. Where's the ball, Corks?'

'Under my tail. At least a man's looking for it there. This is beautiful. They can't use their sticks, and it's driving 'em wild. Give old blinkers a push and he'll go over!'

'Here, don't touch me! I can't see. I'll – I'll back out, I think,' said the pony in blinkers, who knew that if you can't see all round your head you cannot prop yourself against a shock.

Corks was watching the ball where it lay in the dust close to his near fore with Macnamara's shortened stick tap-tapping it from time to time. Kittiwynk was edging her way out of the scrimmage, whisking her stump of a tail with nervous excitement.

'Ho! They've got it,' she snorted. 'Let me out!' and she galloped like a rifle-bullet just behind a tall lanky pony of the Archangels, whose rider was swinging up his stick for a stroke.

'Not today, thank you,' said Hughes, as the blow slid off his raised stick, and Kittiwynk laid her shoulder to the tall pony's quarters, and shoved him aside just as Lutyens on Shiraz sent the ball where it had come from, and the tall pony went skating and slipping away to the left. Kittiwynk, seeing that Polaris had joined Corks in the chase for the ball up the ground, dropped into Polaris's place, and then time was called.

The Skidars' ponies wasted no time in kicking or fuming. They knew each minute's rest meant so much gain, and trotted off to the rails and their *saises*, who began to scrape and blanket and rub them at once.

'Whew!' said Corks, stiffening up to get all the tickle out of the big vulcanite scraper. 'If we were playing pony for pony we'd bend those Archangels double in half an hour. But they'll bring out fresh ones, and fresh ones, and fresh ones after that – you see.'

'Who cares?' said Polaris. 'We've drawn first blood. Is my hock swelling?'

'Looks puffy,' said Corks. 'You must have had rather a wipe. Don't let it stiffen. You'll be wanted again in half an hour.'

'What's the game like?' said the Maltese Cat.

'Ground's like your shoe, except where they've put too much water on it,' said Kittiwynk. 'Then it's slippery. Don't play in the centre. There's a bog there. I don't know how their next four are going to behave, but we kept the ball hanging and made 'em lather for nothing. Who goes out? Two Arabs and a couple of countrybreds! That's bad. What a comfort it is to wash your mouth out!'

Kitty was talking with a neck of a leather-covered soda-water bottle between her teeth and trying to look over her withers at the same time. This gave her a very coquettish air.

'What's bad?' said Grey Dawn, giving to the girth and admiring his well-set shoulders.

'You Arabs can't gallop fast enough to keep yourselves warm – that's what Kitty means,' said Polaris, limping to show that his hock needed attention. 'Are you playing "back", Grey Dawn?'

'Looks like it,' said Grey Dawn, as Lutyens swung himself up. Powell mounted the Rabbit, a plain bay countrybred much like Corks, but with mulish ears. Macnamara took Faiz Ullah, a handy short-backed little red Arab with a long tail, and Hughes mounted Benami, an old and sullen brown beast, who stood over in front more than a polo pony should.

'Benami looks like business,' said Shiraz. 'How's your temper, Ben?' The old campaigner hobbled off without answering, and the Maltese Cat looked at the new Archangel ponies prancing about on the ground. They were four beautiful blacks, and they saddled big enough and strong enough to eat the Skidars' team and gallop away with the meal inside them.

'Blinkers again,' said the Maltese Cat. 'Good enough!'

'They're chargers – cavalry chargers!' said Kittiwynk indignantly. '*They'll* never see thirteen three [6] again.'

'They've all been fairly measured and they've all got their certificates,' said the Maltese Cat, 'or they wouldn't be here. We must take things as they come along, and keep our eyes on the ball.'

The game began, but this time the Skidars were penned to their own end of the ground, and the watching ponies did not approve of that.

'Faiz Ullah is shirking, as usual,' said Polaris, with a scornful grunt.

'Faiz Ullah is eating whip,' said Corks. They could hear the leather-thonged polo quirt lacing the little fellow's well-rounded barrel. Then the Rabbit's shrill neigh came across the ground. 'I can't do all the work,' he cried.

'Play the game, don't talk,' the Maltese Cat whickered; and all the ponies wriggled with excitement, and the soldiers and the grooms gripped the railings and shouted. A black pony with blinkers had singled out old Benami, and was interfering with him in every possible way. They could see Benami shaking his head up and down and flapping his underlip.

'There'll be a fall in a minute,' said Polaris. 'Benami is getting stuffy.'

The game flickered up and down between goal-post and goal-post, and the black ponies were getting more confident as they felt they had the legs of the others. The ball was hit out of a little scrimmage, and Benami and the Rabbit followed it; Faiz Ullah only too glad to be quiet for an instant.

The blinkered black pony came up like a hawk, with two of his own side behind him, and Benami's eye glittered as he raced. The question was which pony should make way for the other; each rider was perfectly willing to risk a fall in a good cause. The black who had been driven nearly crazy by his blinkers trusted to his weight and his temper; but Benami knew how to apply his weight and how to keep his temper. They met, and there was a cloud of dust. The black was lying on his side with all the breath knocked out of his body. The Rabbit was a hundred yards up the ground with the ball, and Benami was sitting down. He had slid nearly ten yards, but he had had his revenge, and sat cracking his nostrils till the black pony rose.

'That's what you get for interfering. Do you want any more?' said Benami, and he plunged into the game. Nothing was done because Faiz Ullah would not gallop, though Macnamara beat him whenever he could spare a second. The fall of the black pony had impressed his companions tremendously, and so the Archangels could not profit by Faiz Ullah's bad behaviour.

But as the Maltese Cat said, when time was called and the four came back blowing and dripping, Faiz Ullah ought to have been kicked all round Umballa. If he did not behave better next time, the Maltese Cat promised to pull out his Arab tail by the root and eat it.

There was no time to talk, for the third four were ordered out.

The third quarter of a game is generally the hottest, for each side thinks that the others must be pumped; and most of the winning play in a game is made about that time.

Lutyens took over the Maltese Cat with a pat and a hug, for Lutyens valued him more than anything else in the world. Powell had Shikast, a little grey rat with no pedigree and no manners outside polo; Macnamara mounted Bamboo, the largest of the team, and Hughes took Who's Who, *alias* The Animal. He was supposed to have Australian blood in his veins, but he looked like a clothes horse, and you could whack him on the legs with an iron crow-bar without hurting him.

They went out to meet the very flower of the Archangels' team, and when Who's Who saw their elegantly booted legs and their beautiful satiny skins he grinned a grin through his light, well-worn bridle.

'My word!' said Who's Who. 'We must give 'em a little football. Those gentlemen need a rubbing down.'

'No biting,' said the Maltese Cat warningly, for once or twice in his career Who's Who had been known to forget himself in that way.

'Who said anything about biting? I'm not playing tiddlywinks. I'm playing the game.'

The Archangels came down like a wolf on the fold, for they were tired of football and they wanted polo. They got it more and more. Just after the game began, Lutyens hit a ball that was coming towards him rapidly, and it rose in the air, as a ball sometimes will, with the whirr of a frightened partridge. Shikast heard, but could not see it for the minute, though he looked everywhere and up into the air as the Maltese Cat had taught him. When he saw it ahead and overhead, he went forward with Powell as fast as he could put foot to ground. It was then that Powell, a quiet and level-headed man as a rule, became inspired and played a stroke that sometimes comes off successfully on a quiet afternoon of long practice. He took his stick in both hands, and standing up in his stirrups, swiped at the ball in the air, Munipore fashion. There was one second of paralysed astonishment, and then all four sides of the ground went up in a yell of applause and delight as the ball flew true (you could see the amazed Archangels ducking in their saddles to get out of the line of flight, and looking at it with open mouths), and the regimental pipes of the Skidars squealed from the railings as long as the piper had breath.

Shikast heard the stroke; but he heard the head of the stick fly off at the same time. Nine hundred and ninety-nine ponies out of a thousand would have gone tearing on after the ball with a useless player pulling at their heads, but Powell knew him, and he knew Powell; and the instant he felt Powell's right leg shift a trifle on the saddle-flap he headed to the boundary, where a native officer was frantically waving a new stick. Before the shouts had ended Powell was armed again.

Once before in his life the Maltese Cat had heard that very same stroke played off his own back, and had profited by the confusion it made. This time he acted on experience, and leaving Bamboo to guard the goal in case of accidents, came through the others like a flash, head and tail low, Lutyens standing up to ease him – swept on and on before the other side knew what was the matter, and nearly pitched on his head between the Archangels' goal-post as Lutyens tipped the ball in after a straight scurry of a hundred and fifty yards. If there was one thing more than another upon which the Maltese Cat prided himself it was on this quick, streaking kind of run half across the ground. He did not believe in taking balls round the field unless you were clearly over-matched. After this they gave the Archangels five minutes football, and an expensive fast pony hates football because it rumples his temper.

Who's Who showed himself even better than Polaris in this game. He did not permit any wriggling away, but bored joyfully into the scrimmage as if he had his nose in a feed-box, and were looking for something nice. Little Shikast jumped on the ball the minute it got clear, and every time an Archangel pony followed it he found Shikast standing over it asking what was the matter.

'If we can live through this quarter,' said the Maltese Cat, 'I sha'n't care. Don't take it out of yourselves. Let them do the lathering.'

So the ponies, as their riders explained afterwards, 'shut up'. The Archangels kept them tied fast in front of their goal, but it cost the Archangels' ponies all that was left of their tempers; and ponies began to kick, and men began to repeat compliments, and they chopped at the legs of Who's Who, and he set his teeth and stayed where he was, and the dust stood up like a tree over the scrimmage till that hot quarter ended.

They found the ponies very excited and confident when they went to their *saises*; and the Maltese Cat had to warn them that the worst of the game was coming.

'Now *we* are all going in for the second time,' said he, 'and *they* are trotting out fresh ponies. You'll think you can gallop, but you'll find you can't; and then you'll be sorry.'

'But two goals to nothing is a halter-long lead,' said Kittiwynk prancing.

'How long does it take to get a goal?' the Maltese Cat answered. 'For pity sake, don't run away with the notion that the game is half-won just because we happen to be in luck now. They'll ride you into the grandstand if they can; you must *not* give 'em a chance. Follow the ball.'

'Football, as usual?' said Polaris. 'My hock's half as big as a nose-bag.'

'Don't let them have a look at the ball if you can help it. Now leave me alone. I must get all the rest I can before the last quarter.'

He hung down his head and let all his muscles go slack; Shikast, Bamboo, and Who's Who copying his example.

'Better not watch the game,' he said. 'We aren't playing, and we shall only take it out of ourselves if we grow anxious. Look at the ground and pretend it's fly-time.'

They did their best, but it was hard advice to follow. The hoofs were drumming and the sticks were rattling all up and down the ground, and yells of applause from the English troops told that the Archangels were pressing the Skidars hard. The native soldiers behind the ponies groaned and grunted, and said things in undertones, and presently they heard a long-drawn shout and a clatter of hurrahs!

'One to the Archangels,' said Shikast, without raising his head. 'Time's nearly up. Oh, my sire and dam!'

'Faiz Ullah,' said the Maltese Cat, 'if you don't play to the last nail in your shoes this time, I'll kick you on the ground before all the other ponies.'

'I'll do my best when my time comes,' said the little Arab sturdily.

The *saises* looked at each other gravely as they rubbed their ponies' legs. This was the first time when long purses began to tell, and everybody knew it. Kittiwynk and the others came back with the sweat dripping over their hoofs and their tails telling sad stories.

'They're better than we are,' said Shiraz. 'I knew how it would be.'

'Shut your big head,' said the Maltese Cat; 'we've one goal to the good yet.'

'Yes, but it's two Arabs and two countrybreds to play now,' said Corks. 'Faiz Ullah, remember!' He spoke in a biting voice.

As Lutyens mounted Grey Dawn he looked at his men, and they did not look pretty. They were covered with dust and sweat in streaks. Their yellow boots were almost black, their wrists were red and lumpy, and their eyes seemed two inches deep in their heads, but the expression in the eyes was satisfactory.

'Did you take anything [7] at tiffin?' said Lutyens, and the team shook their heads. They were too dry to talk.

'All right. The Archangels did. They are worse pumped than we are.'

'They've got the better ponies,' said Powell. 'I sha'n't be sorry when this business is over.'

That fifth quarter was a sad one in every way. Faiz Ullah played like a little red demon; and the Rabbit seemed to be everywhere at once, and Benami rode straight at anything and everything that came in his way, while the umpires on their ponies wheeled like gulls outside the shifting game. But the Archangels had the better mounts – they had kept their racers till late in the game – and never allowed the Skidars to play football. They hit the ball up and down the width of the ground till Benami and the rest were outpaced. Then they went forward, and time and again Lutyens and Grey Dawn were just, and only just, able to send the ball away with a long splitting back-hander. Grey Dawn forgot that he was an Arab; and turned from grey to blue as he galloped. Indeed, he forgot too well, for he did not keep his eyes on the ground as an Arab should, but stuck out his nose and scuttled for the dear honour of the game. They had watered the ground once or twice between the quarters, and a careless waterman had emptied the last of his skinful all in one place near the Skidars' goal. It was close to the end of play, and for the tenth time Grey Dawn was bolting after a ball when his near hind foot slipped on the greasy mud and he rolled over and over, pitching Lutyens just clear of the goal-post; and the triumphant Archangels made their goal. Then time was called – two goals all; but Lutyens had to be helped up, and Grey Dawn rose with his near hind leg strained somewhere.

'What's the damage?' said Powell, his arm round Lutyens.

'Collar-bone, of course,' said Lutyens between his teeth. It was the third time he had broken it in two years, and it hurt him.

Powell and the others whistled. 'Game's up,' said Hughes.

'Hold on. We've five good minutes yet, and it isn't my right hand,' said Lutyens. 'We'll stick it out.'

'I say,' said the captain of the Archangels, trotting up. 'Are you hurt, Lutyens? We'll wait if you care to put in a substitute. I wish – I mean – the fact is, you fellows deserve this game if any team does. Wish we could give you a man or some of our ponies – or something.'

'You're awfully good, but we'll play it to a finish, I think.'

The captain of the Archangels stared for a little. 'That's not half bad,' he said, and went back to his own side, while Lutyens borrowed a scarf from one of his native officers and made a sling of it. Then an Archangel galloped up with a big bath-sponge and advised Lutyens to put it under his arm-pit to ease his shoulder, and between them they tied up his left arm scientifically, and one of the native officers leaped forward with four long glasses that fizzed and bubbled.

The team looked at Lutyens piteously, and he nodded. It was the last quarter, and nothing would matter after that. They drank out the dark golden drink, and wiped their moustaches, and things looked more hopeful.

The Maltese Cat had put his nose into the front of Lutyens' shirt, and was trying to say how sorry he was.

'He knows,' said Lutyens, proudly. 'The beggar knows. I've played him without a bridle before now – for fun.'

'It's no fun now,' said Powell. 'But we haven't a decent substitute.'

'No,' said Lutyens. 'It's the last quarter, and we've got to make our goal and win. I'll trust the Cat.'

'If you fall this time you'll suffer a little,' said Macnamara.

'I'll trust the Cat,' said Lutyens.

'You hear that?' said the Maltese Cat proudly to the others. 'It's worth while playing polo for ten years to have that said of you. Now then, my sons, come along. We'll kick up a little bit, just to show the Archangels *this* team haven't suffered.'

And, sure enough, as they went on to the ground the Maltese Cat, after satisfying himself that Lutyens was home in the saddle, kicked out three or four times, and Lutyens laughed. The reins were caught up anyhow in the tips of his strapped hand, and he never pretended to rely on them. He knew the Cat would answer to the least pressure of the leg, and by way of showing off – for his shoulder hurt him very much – he bent the little fellow in a close figure-of-eight in and out between the goal-posts. There was a roar from the native officers and men, who dearly loved a piece of *dugabashi* (horse-trick work), as they called it, and the pipes very quietly and scornfully droned out the first bars of a common bazar-tune called 'Freshly Fresh and Newly New', just as a warning to the other regiments that the Skidars were fit. All the natives laughed.

'And now,' said the Cat, as they took their place, 'remember that this is the last quarter, and follow the ball!'

'Don't need to be told,' said Who's Who.

'Let me go on. All those people on all four sides will begin to crowd in – just as they did at Malta. You'll hear people calling out, and moving forward and being pushed back, and that is going to make the Archangel ponies very unhappy. But if a ball is struck to the boundary, you go after it, and let the people get out of your way. I went over the pole of a four-in-hand once, and picked a game out of the dust by it. Back me up when I run, and follow the ball.'

There was a sort of an all-round sound of sympathy and wonder as the last quarter opened, and then there began exactly what the Maltese Cat had foreseen. People crowded in close to the boundaries, and the Archangels' ponies kept looking sideways at the narrowing space. If you know how a man feels to be cramped at tennis – not because he wants to run out of the court, but because he likes to know that he can at a pinch – you will guess how ponies must feel when they are playing in a box of human beings.

'I'll bend some of those men if I can get away,' said Who's Who, as he rocketed behind the ball; and Bamboo nodded without speaking. They were playing the last ounce in them, and the Maltese Cat had left the goal undefended to join them. Lutyens gave him every order that he could to bring him back, but this was the first time in his career that the little wise grey had ever played polo on his own responsibility, and he was going to make the most of it.

'What are you doing here?' said Hughes, as the Cat crossed in front of him and rode off an Archangel.

'The Cat's in charge – mind the goal!' shouted Lutyens, and bowing forward hit the ball full, and followed on, forcing the Archangels towards their own goal.

'No football,' said the Cat. 'Keep the ball by the boundaries and cramp 'em. Play open order, and drive 'em to the boundaries.'

Across and across the ground in big diagonals flew the ball, and whenever it came to a flying rush and a stroke close to the boundaries the Archangel ponies moved stiffly. They did not care to go headlong at a wall of men and carriages, though if the ground had been open they could have turned on a sixpence.

'Wriggle her up the sides,' said the Cat. 'Keep her close to the crowd. They hate the carriages. Shikast, keep her up this side.'

Shikast with Powell lay left and right behind the uneasy scuffle of an open scrimmage, and every time the ball was hit away Shikast galloped on it at such an angle that Powell was forced to hit it towards the boundary; and when the crowd had been driven away from that side, Lutyens would send the ball over to the other, and Shikast would slide desperately after it till his friends came down to help. It was billiards, and no football, this time – billiards in a corner pocket; and the cues were not well chalked.

'If they get us out in the middle of the ground they'll walk away from us. Dribble her along the sides,' cried the Cat.

So they dribbled all along the boundary, where a pony could not come on their right-hand side; and the Archangels were furious, and the umpires had to neglect the game to shout at the people to get back, and several blundering mounted policemen tried to restore order, all close to the scrimmage, and the nerves of the Archangels' ponies stretched and broke like cob-webs.

Five or six times an Archangel hit the ball up into the middle of the ground, and each time the watchful Shikast gave Powell his chance to send it back, and after each return, when the dust had settled, men could see that the Skidars had gained a few yards.

Every now and again there were shouts of ''Side! Off side!' from the spectators; but the teams were too busy to care, and the umpires had all they could do to keep their maddened ponies clear of the scuffle.

At last Lutyens missed a short easy stroke, and the Skidars had to fly back helter-skelter to protect their own goal, Shikast leading. Powell stopped the ball with a backhander when it was not fifty yards from the goal-posts, and Shikast spun round with a wrench that nearly hoisted Powell out of his saddle.

'Now's our last chance,' said the Cat, wheeling like a cockchafer on a pin. 'We've got to ride it out. Come along.'

Lutyens felt the little chap take a deep breath, and, as it were, crouch under his rider. The ball was hopping towards the right-hand boundary, an Archangel riding for it with both spurs and a whip; but neither spur nor whip would make his pony stretch himself as he neared the crowd. The Maltese Cat glided under his very nose, picking up his hind legs sharp, for there was not a foot to spare between his quarters and the other pony's bit. It was as neat an exhibition as fancy figure-skating. Lutyens hit with all the strength he had left, but the stick slipped a little in his hand, and the ball flew off to the left instead of keeping close to the boundary. Who's Who was far across the ground, thinking hard as he galloped. He repeated, stride for stride, the Cat's manoeuvres with another Archangel pony, nipping the ball away from under his bridle, and clearing his opponent by half a fraction of an inch, for Who's Who was clumsy behind. Then he drove away towards the right as the Maltese Cat came up from the left; and Bamboo held a middle course exactly between them. The three were making a sort of Government-broad-arrow-shaped attack; and there was only the Archangels' back to guard the goal; but immediately behind them were three Archangels racing all they knew, and mixed up with them was Powell, sending Shikast along on what he felt was their last hope. It takes a very good man to stand up to the rush of seven crazy ponies in the last quarters of a cup game, when men are riding with their necks for sale, and the ponies are delirious. The Archangels' back missed his stroke, and pulled aside just in time to let the rush go by. Bamboo and Who's Who shortened stride to give the Maltese Cat room, and Lutyens got the goal with a clean, smooth, smacking stroke that was heard all over the field. But there was no stopping the ponies. They poured through the goal-posts in one mixed mob, winners and losers together, for the pace had been terrific. The Maltese Cat knew by experience what would happen, and, to save Lutyens, turned to the right with one last effort that strained a back-sinew beyond hope of repair. As he did so he heard the right-hand goal-post crack as a pony cannoned into it – crack, splinter, and fall like a mast. It had been sawed three parts through in case of accidents, but it upset the pony nevertheless, and he blundered into another, who blundered into the left-hand post, and then there was confusion and dust and wood. Bamboo was lying on the ground, seeing stars; an Archangel pony rolled beside him, breathless and angry; Shikast had sat down dog-fashion to avoid falling over the others, and was sliding along on his little bobtail in a cloud of dust; and Powell was sitting on the ground, hammering with his stick and trying to cheer. All the others were shouting at the top of what was left of their voices, and the men who had been spilt were shouting too. As soon as the people saw no one was hurt, ten thousand native and English shouted and clapped and yelled, and before anyone could stop them the pipers of the Skidars broke on to the ground, with all the native officers and men behind them, and marched up and down, playing a wild Northern tune called 'Zakhme Bagān', and through the insolent blaring of the pipes and the high-pitched native yells you could hear the Archangels' band hammering, 'For they are all jolly good fellows', and then reproachfully to the losing team, 'Ooh, Kafoozalum! Kafoozalum! Kafoozalum!'

Besides all these things and many more, there was a Commander-in-Chief, and an Inspector-General of Cavalry, and the principal veterinary officer in all India, standing on the top of a regimental coach, yelling like school-boys; and brigadiers and colonels and commissioners, and hundreds of pretty ladies joined the chorus. But the Maltese Cat stood with his head down, wondering how many legs were left to him; and Lutyens watched the men and ponies pick themselves out of the wreck of the two goal-posts, and he patted the Cat very tenderly.

'I say,' said the captain of the Archangels, spitting a pebble out of his mouth, 'will you take three thousand [8] for that pony – as he stands?'

'No, thank you. I've an idea he's saved my life,' said Lutyens, getting off and lying down at full length. Both teams were on the ground too, waving their boots in the air, and coughing and drawing deep breaths, as the *saises* ran up to take away the ponies, and an officious water-carrier sprinkled the players with dirty water till they sat up.

'My Aunt!' said Powell, rubbing his back and looking at the stumps of the goal-posts, 'That was a game!'

They played it over again, every stroke of it, that night at the big dinner, when the Free-for-All Cup was filled and passed down the table, and emptied and filled again, and everybody made most eloquent speeches. About two in the morning, when there might have been some singing, a wise little, plain little, grey little head looked in through the open door.

'Hurrah! Bring him in,' said the Archangels; and his *sais*, who was very happy indeed, patted the Maltese Cat on the flank, and he limped in to the blaze of light and the glittering uniforms, looking for Lutyens. He was used to messes, and men's bedrooms, and places where ponies are not usually encouraged, and in his youth had jumped on and off a mess-table for a bet. So he behaved himself very politely, and ate bread dipped in salt, and was petted all round the table, moving gingerly; and they drank his health, because he had done more to win the Cup than any man or horse on the ground.

That was glory and honour enough for the rest of his days, and the Maltese Cat did not complain much when the veterinary surgeon said that he would be no good for polo any more. When Lutyens married, his wife did not allow him to play, so he was forced to be an umpire; and his pony on these occasions was a flea-bitten grey with a neat polo-tail, lame all round, but desperately quick on his feet, and, as everybody knew, Past Pluperfect Prestissimo Player of the Game.

⨭ Red Dog [1] ⨮

For our white and our excellent nights − for the nights of swift running,
   Fair ranging, far-seeing, good hunting, sure cunning!
For the smells of the dawning, untainted, ere dew has departed!
For the rush through the mist, and the quarry blind-started!
For the cry of our mates when the *sambhur* [2] has wheeled and is standing at bay,
   For the risk and the riot of night!
For the sleep at the lair-mouth by day −
    It is met, and we go to the fight.
      Bay! O Bay!

It was after the letting in of the Jungle [3] that the pleasantest part of Mowgli's [4] life began. He had the good conscience that comes from paying a just debt; and all the Jungle was his friend, for all the Jungle was afraid of him. The things that he did and saw and heard when he was wandering from one people to another, with or without his four companions, would make many, many stories, each as long as this one. So you will never be told how he met and escaped from the Mad Elephant of Mandla, who killed two-and-twenty bullocks drawing eleven carts of coined silver to the Government Treasury, and scattered the shiny rupees in the dust; how he fought Jacala, the Crocodile, all one long night in the Marshes of the North, and broke his skinning knife on the brute's back-plates; how he found a new and longer knife round the neck of a man who had been killed by a wild boar, and how he tracked that boar and killed him as a fair price for the knife; how he was caught up in the Great Famine by the moving of the deer, and nearly crushed to death in the swaying hot herds; how he saved Hathi [5] the Silent from being caught in a pit with a stake at the bottom, and how next day he himself fell into a very cunning leopard-trap, and how Hathi broke the thick wooden bars to pieces about him; how he milked the wild buffaloes in the swamp, and how −

But we must tell one tale at a time. Father and Mother Wolf died, and Mowgli rolled a big boulder against the mouth of the cave and cried the Death Song over them, and Baloo grew very old and stiff, and even Bagheera, whose nerves were steel and whose muscles were iron, seemed slower at the kill. Akela [6] turned from grey to milky white with pure age;

287

his ribs stuck out, and he walked as though he had been made of wood, and Mowgli killed for him. But the young wolves, the children of the disbanded Seeonee Pack, throve and increased, and when there were some forty of them, masterless, clean-footed five-year-olds, Akela told them that they ought to gather themselves together and follow the Law, and run under one head, as befitted the Free People.

This was not a matter in which Mowgli gave advice, for, as he said, he had eaten sour fruit, and he knew the tree it hung from; but when Phao, son of Phaona (his father was the Grey Tracker in the days of Akela's headship), fought his way to the leadership of the Pack according to the Jungle Law, and when the old calls and the old songs began to ring under the stars once more, Mowgli came to the Council Rock for memory's sake. If he chose to speak the Pack waited till he had finished, and he sat at Akela's side on the rock above Phao. Those were the days of good hunting and good sleeping. No stranger cared to break into the jungles that belonged to Mowgli's people, as they called the Pack, and the young wolves grew fat and strong, and there were many cubs to bring to the Looking-over. Mowgli always attended a Looking-over, for he remembered the night when a black panther brought a naked brown baby into the pack, and the long call, 'Look, look well, O Wolves,' made his heart flutter with strange feelings. Otherwise, he would be far away in the jungle; tasting, touching, seeing, and feeling new things.

One twilight when he was trotting leisurely across the ranges to give Akela the half of a buck that he had killed, while his four wolves were jogging behind him, sparring a little and tumbling one over another for joy of being alive, he heard a cry that he had not heard since the bad days of Shere Khan.[7] It was what they call in the Jungle the *Pheeal*, a kind of shriek that the jackal gives when he is hunting behind a tiger, or when there is some big killing afoot. If you can imagine a mixture of hate, triumph, fear, and despair, with a kind of leer running through it, you will get some notion of the *Pheeal* that rose and sank and wavered and quivered far away across the Waingunga. The Four began to bristle and growl. Mowgli's hand went to his knife and he too checked as though he had been turned into stone.

'There is no Striped One would dare kill here,' he said, at last.

'That is not the cry of the Forerunner,' said Grey Brother. 'It is some great killing. Listen!'

It broke out again, half sobbing and half chuckling, just as though the jackal had soft human lips. Then Mowgli drew deep breath, and ran to the Council Rock, overtaking in his way hurrying wolves of the Pack.

Phao and Akela were on the Rock together, and below them, every nerve strained, sat the others. The mothers and the cubs were cantering to their lairs; for when the *Pheeal* cries is no time for weak things to be abroad.

They could hear nothing except the Waingunga gurgling in the dark and the evening winds among the tree-tops, till suddenly across the river a wolf called. It was no wolf of the Pack, for those were all at the rock. The note changed to a long despairing bay; and 'Dhole!' it said, 'Dhole! Dhole! Dhole!' In a few minutes they heard tired feet on the rocks, and a gaunt, dripping wolf, streaked with red on his flanks, his right fore-paw useless, and his jaws white with foam, flung himself into the circle and lay gasping at Mowgli's feet.

'Good hunting? Under whose headship?' said Phao gravely.

'Good hunting! Won-tolla am I,' was the answer. He meant that he was a solitary wolf, fending for himself, his mate, and his cubs in some lonely lair. Won-tolla means an outlier – one who lies out from any pack. When he panted they could see his heart shake him backwards and forwards.

'What moves?' said Phao, for that is the question all the Jungle asks after the *Pheeal*.

'The dhole, the dhole of the Dekkan [8] – Red Dog, the Killer! They came north from the south saying the Dekkan was empty and killing out by the way. When this moon was new there were four to me – my mate and three cubs. She would teach them to kill on the grass plains, hiding to drive the buck, as we do who are of the open. At midnight I heard them together full tongue on the trail. At the dawn-wind I found them stiff in the grass – four, Free people, four when this moon was new! Then sought I my Blood-Right and found the dhole.'

'How many?' said Mowgli: the Pack growled deep in their throats.

'I do not know. Three of them will kill no more, but at the last they drove me like the buck; on three legs they drove me. Look, Free People!'

He thrust out his mangled fore-foot, all dark with dried blood. There were cruel bites low down on his side, and his throat was torn and worried.

'Eat,' said Akela, rising up from the meat Mowgli had brought him; the outlier flung himself on it famishing.

'This shall be no loss,' he said humbly when he had taken off the edge of his hunger. 'Give me a little strength, Free People, and I also will kill! My lair is empty that was full when this moon was new, and the Blood Debt is not all paid.'

Phao heard his teeth crack on a haunch-bone and grunted approvingly. 'We shall need those jaws,' said he. 'Were their cubs with the dhole?' 'Nay, nay. Red hunters all: grown dogs of their pack, heavy and strong.'

That meant that the dhole, the red hunting-dog of the Dekkan, was moving to fight, and the wolves knew well that even the tiger will surrender a new kill to the dhole. They drive straight through the Jungle, and what they meet they pull down and tear to pieces. Though they are not as big nor half as cunning as the wolf, they are very strong and very numerous. The dhole, for instance, do not begin to call themselves a pack till they are a hundred strong, whereas forty wolves make a very fair pack. Mowgli's wanderings had taken him to the edge of the high grassy downs of the Dekkan, and he had often seen the fearless dholes sleeping and playing and scratching themselves among the little hollows and tussocks that they use for lairs. He despised and hated them because they did not smell like the Free People, because they did not live in caves, and above all, because they had hair between their toes while he and his friends were clean-footed. But he knew, for Hathi had told him, what a terrible thing a dhole hunting pack was. Hathi himself moves aside from their line, and until they are all killed, or till game is scarce, they go forward killing as they go.

Akela knew something of the dholes, too; he said to Mowgli quietly: 'It is better to die in the Full Pack than leaderless and alone. It is good hunting, and – my last. But, as men live, thou hast very many more nights and days, Little Brother. Go north and lie down, and if any wolf live after the dhole has gone by he shall bring thee word of the fight.'

'Ah,' said Mowgli, quite gravely, 'must I go to the marshes and catch little fish and sleep in a tree, or must I ask help of the *bandar-log*⁹ and eat nuts while the pack fights below?'

'It is to the death,' said Akela. 'Thou hast never met the dhole – the Red Killer. Even the Striped One –'

'Aowa! Aowa!' said Mowgli pettingly. 'I have killed one striped ape. Listen now: There was a wolf, my father, and there was a wolf, my mother, and there was an old grey wolf (not too wise: he is white now) was my father and my mother. Therefore I –' he raised his voice, 'I say that when the dhole come, and if the dhole come, Mowgli and the Free People are of one skin for that hunting; and I say, by the Bull that bought me, by the bull Bagheera paid for me in the old days which ye of the Pack do not remember, *I* say, that the Trees and the River may hear and hold fast if I forget; *I* say that this my knife shall be as a tooth to the Pack – and I do not think it is so blunt. This is my Word which has gone from me.'

'Thou dost not know the dhole, man with a wolf's tongue,' Won-tolla cried. 'I look only to clear my blood debt against them ere they have me in many pieces. They move slowly, killing out as they go, but in two days a little strength will come back to me and I turn again for my blood debt. But for *ye*, Free People, my counsel is that ye go north and eat but little for a while till the dhole are gone. There is no sleep in this hunting.'

'Hear the Outlier!' said Mowgli with a laugh. 'Free People, we must go north and eat lizards and rats from the bank, lest by any chance we meet the dhole. He must kill out our hunting grounds while we lie hid in the north till it please him to give us our own again. He is a dog – and the pup of a dog – red, yellow-bellied, lairless, and haired between every toe! He counts his cubs six and eight at the litter, as though he were Chikai, the little leaping rat. Surely we must run away, Free People, and beg leave of the peoples of the north for the offal of dead cattle! Ye know the saying: "North are the vermin; South are the lice. *We* are the Jungle." Choose ye, O choose. It is good hunting! For the Pack – for the Full Pack – for the lair and the litter; for the in-kill and the out-kill; for the mate that drives the doe and the little, little cub within the cave, it is met – it is met – it is met!'

The Pack answered with one deep crashing bark that sounded in the night like a tree falling. 'It is met,' they cried.

'Stay with these,' said Mowgli to his Four. 'We shall need every tooth. Phao and Akela must make ready the battle. I go to count the dogs.'

'It is death!' Won-tolla cried, half rising. 'What can such an hairless one do against the Red Dog. Even the Striped One, remember –'

'Thou art indeed an outlier,' Mowgli called back, 'but we will speak when the dholes are dead. Good hunting all!'

He hurried off into the darkness wild with excitement, hardly looking where he set foot, and the natural consequence was that he tripped full length over Kaa's great coils where the python lay watching a deer-path near the river.

'Kssha!' said Kaa angrily. 'Is this jungle work to stamp and ramp and undo a night's hunting – when the game are moving so well, too?'

'The fault was mine,' said Mowgli, picking himself up. 'Indeed I was seeking thee, Flathead, but each time we meet thou art longer and broader by the length of my arm. There is none like thee in the Jungle, wise, old, strong, and most beautiful Kaa.'

'Now whither does *this* trail lead?' Kaa's voice was gentler. 'Not a moon since there was a Manling with a knife threw stones at my head and called me bad little tree-cat names because I lay asleep in the open.'

Selected Stories

'Ay, and turned every driven deer to all the winds, and Mowgli was hunting, and this same Flathead was too deaf to hear his whistle and leave the deer-roads free,' Mowgli answered composedly, sitting down among the painted coils.

'Now this same Manling comes with soft, tickling words to this same Flathead, telling him that he is wise, and strong, and beautiful, and this same old Flathead believes and coils a place, thus, for this same stone-throwing Manling and ... Art thou at ease now? Could Bagheera give thee so good a resting-place?'

Kaa had, as usual, made a sort of soft half-hammock of himself under Mowgli's weight. The boy reached out in the darkness and gathered in the supple cable-like neck till Kaa's head rested on his shoulder, and then he told him all that had happened in the jungle that night.

'Wise I may be,' said Kaa at the end, 'but deaf I surely am. Else I should have heard the *Pheeal*. Small wonder the eaters-of-grass are uneasy. How many be the dhole?'

'I have not seen yet. I came hot foot to thee. Thou art older than Hathi. But, oh, Kaa,' – here Mowgli wriggled with joy, 'it will be good hunting! Few of us will see another moon.'

'Dost *thou* strike in this? Remember thou art a man; and remember what pack cast thee out. Let the wolf look to the dog. *Thou* art a man.'

'Last year's nuts are this year's black earth,' said Mowgli. 'It is true that I am a man, but it is in my stomach that this night I have said that I am a wolf. I called the River and the Trees to remember. I am of the Free People, Kaa, till the dhole has gone by.'

'Free People,' Kaa grunted. 'Free thieves! And thou has tied thyself into the Death-knot for the sake of the memory of dead wolves! This is no good hunting.'

'It is my Word which I have spoken. The Trees know, the River knows. Till the dhole have gone by my Word comes not back to me.'

'Ngssh! That changes all trails. I had thought to take thee away with me to the northern marshes, but the Word – even the Word of a little, naked, hairless Manling – is the Word. Now I, Kaa, say –'

'Think well, Flathead, lest thou tie thyself into the Death-knot also. I need no word from thee, for well I know –'

'Be it so, then,' said Kaa. 'I will give no Word; but what is in thy stomach to do when the dhole come?'

'They must swim the Waingunga. I thought to meet them with my knife in the shallows, the Pack behind me; and so stabbing and thrusting we might turn them down stream, or cool their throats a little.'

292

Red Dog

'The dhole do not turn and their throats are hot,' said Kaa. 'There will be neither Manling nor wolf-cub when that hunting is done, but only dry bones.'

'Alala! If we die we die. It will be most good hunting. But my stomach is young, and I have not seen many Rains. I am not wise nor strong. Hast thou a better plan, Kaa?'

'I have seen a hundred and a hundred Rains. Ere Hathi cast his milk-tushes my trail was big in the dust. By the First Egg I am older than many trees, and I have seen all that the Jungle has done.'

'But *this* is new hunting,' said Mowgli. 'Never before has the dhole crossed our trail.'

'What is has been. What will be is no more than a forgotten year striking backwards. Be still while I count those my years.'

For a long hour Mowgli lay back among the coils, playing with his knife, while Kaa, his head motionless on the ground, thought of all that he had seen and known since the day he came from the egg. The light seemed to go out of his eyes and leave them like stale opals, and now and again he made little stiff passes with his head to right and left, as though he were hunting in his sleep. Mowgli dozed quietly, for he knew that there is nothing like sleep before hunting, and he was trained to take it at any hour of the day or night.

Then he felt Kaa grow bigger and broader below him as the huge python puffed himself out, hissing with the noise of a sword drawn from a steel scabbard.

'I have seen all the dead seasons,' Kaa said at last, 'and the great trees and the old elephants and the rocks that were bare and sharp-pointed ere the moss grew. Art *thou* still alive, Manling?'

'It is only a little after moonrise,' said Mowgli. 'I do not understand –'

'Hssh! I am again Kaa. I knew it was but a little time. Now we will go to the river, and I will show thee what is to be done against the dhole.'

He turned, straight as an arrow, for the main stream of the Waingunga, plunging in a little above the pool that hid the Peace Rock, Mowgli at his side.

'Nay, do not swim. I go swiftly. My back, Little Brother.'

Mowgli tucked his left arm round Kaa's neck, dropped his right close to his body and straightened his feet. Then Kaa breasted the current as he alone could, and the ripple of the checked water stood up in a frill round Mowgli's neck and his feet were waved to and fro in the eddy under the python's lashing sides. A mile or so above the Peace Rock the Waingunga narrows between a gorge of marble rocks from eighty to a hundred feet high, and the current runs like a mill-race between and over all manner of ugly stones. But Mowgli did not trouble his head about the water: no water in the world could have given him a moment's fear. He was looking at the gorge on either side and sniffing uneasily, for there was a sweetish-sourish smell in the air, very like the smell of a big ant-hill on a hot day. Instinctively he lowered himself in the water, only raising his head to breathe, and Kaa came to anchor with a double twist of his tail round a sunken rock, holding Mowgli in the hollow of a coil, while the water raced by.

'This is the Place of Death,' said the boy. 'Why do we come here?'

'They sleep,' said Kaa. 'Hathi will not turn aside for the Striped One. Yet Hathi and the Striped One together turn aside for the dhole, and the dhole they say turns aside for nothing. And yet for whom do the Little People of the Rocks turn aside? Tell me, Master of the Jungle, who is the Master of the Jungle?'

'These,' Mowgli whispered. 'It is the Place of Death. Let us go.'

'Nay, look well, for they are asleep. It is as it was when I was not the length of thy arm.'

The split and weatherworn rocks of the gorge of the Waingunga had been used since the beginning of the Jungle by the Little People of the Rocks – the busy, furious, black, wild bees of India; and, as Mowgli knew well, all trails turned off half a mile away from their country. For centuries the Little People had hived and swarmed from cleft to cleft and swarmed again, staining the white marble with stale honey, and made their combs tall and deep and black in the dark of the inner caves, and neither man nor beast nor fire nor water had ever touched them. The length of the gorge on both sides was hung as it were with black shimmery velvet curtains, and Mowgli sank as he looked, for those were the clotted millions of the sleeping bees. There were other lumps and festoons and things like decayed tree-trunks studded on the face of the rock – the old comb of past years, or new cities built in the shadow of the windless gorge – and huge masses of spongy, rotten trash had rolled down and stuck among the trees and creepers that clung to the rock-face. As he listened he heard more than once the rustle and slide of a honey-loaded comb turning over or falling away somewhere in the dark galleries; then a booming of angry wings and the sullen drip, drip, drip, of the wasted honey, guttering along till it lipped over some ledge in the open and sluggishly trickled down on the twigs. There was a tiny little beach, not five feet broad, on one side of the river, and that was piled high with the rubbish of uncounted years. There lay dead bees, drones, sweepings, stale combs, and wings of marauding moths and beetles that had strayed in after honey, all tumbled in smooth piles of the finest black dust. The mere sharp smell of it was enough to frighten anything that had no wings, and knew what the Little People were.

Kaa moved up stream again till he came to a sandy bar at the head of the gorge.

'Here is this season's kill,' said he. 'Look!'

On the bank lay the skeletons of a couple of young deer and a buffalo. Mowgli could see that no wolf nor jackal had touched the bones, which were laid out naturally.

'They came beyond the line, they did not know,' murmured Mowgli, 'and the Little People killed them. Let us go ere they awake.'

'They do not wake till the dawn,' said Kaa. 'Now I will tell thee. A hunted buck from the south, many, many Rains ago, came hither from the south, not knowing the jungle, a pack on his trail. Being made blind by fear he leaped from above, the pack running by sight, for they were hot and blind on the trail. The sun was high, and the Little People were many and very angry. Many, too, were those of the pack who leaped into the Waingunga, but they were dead ere they took water. Those who did not leap died also in the rocks above. But the buck lived.'

'How?'

'Because he came first, running for his life, leaping ere the Little People were aware, and was in the river when they gathered to kill. The pack, following, was altogether lost under the weight of the Little People, who had been roused by the feet of that buck.'

'The buck lived?' Mowgli repeated slowly.

'At least he did not die *then*, though none waited his coming down with a strong body to hold him safe against the water, as a certain old fat, deaf, yellow Flathead would wait for a Manling – yea, though there were all the dholes of the Dekkan on his trail. What is in thy stomach?'

Kaa's head lay on Mowgli's wet shoulder, and his tongue quivered by the boy's ear. There was a long silence before Mowgli whispered:

'It is to pull the very whiskers of Death, but – Kaa, thou art, indeed, the wisest of all the Jungle.'

'So many have said. Look now, if the dholes follow thee –'

'As surely they will follow. Ho! ho! I have many little thorns under my tongue to prick into their hides.'

'If they follow thee hot and blind, looking only at thy shoulders, those who do not die up above will take water either here or lower down, for the Little People will rise up and cover them. Now the Waingunga is hungry water, and they will have no Kaa to hold them, but will go down, such as live, to the shallows by the Seeonee lairs, and there thy Pack may meet them by the throat.'

'Ahai! Eowawa! Better could not be till the Rains fall in the dry season. There is now only the little matter of the run and the leap. I will make me known to the dholes, so that they shall follow me very closely.'

'Hast thou seen the rocks above thee? From the landward side?'

'Indeed no. That I had forgotten.'

'Go look. It is all rotten ground, cut and full of holes. One of thy clumsy feet set down without seeing would end the hunt. See, I leave thee here, and for thy sake only I will carry word to the Pack that they may know where to look for the dhole. For myself, I am not of one skin with *any* wolf.'

When Kaa disliked an acquaintance he could be more unpleasant than any of the Jungle people, except perhaps Bagheera. He swam down stream, and opposite the Rock he came on Phao and Akela listening to the night noises.

'Hssh! dogs,' he said cheerfully. 'The dhole will come down stream. If ye be not afraid ye can kill them in the shallows.'

'When come they?' said Phao. 'And where is my man-cub?' said Akela.

'They come when they come,' said Kaa. 'Wait and see. As for *thy* man-cub, from whom thou hast taken his Word and so laid him open to Death, *thy* man-cub is with *me*, and if he be not already dead the fault is none of thine, bleached dog! Wait here for the dhole, and be glad that the man-cub and I strike on thy side.'

Kaa flashed up stream again and moored himself in the middle of the gorge, looking upwards at the line of the cliff. Presently he saw Mowgli's head move against the stars: then there was a whizz in the air, the keen clean *schloop* of a body falling feet first; next minute the body was at rest again in the loop of Kaa's body.

'It is no leap by night,' said Mowgli quietly. 'I have jumped twice as far for sport; but that is an evil place above – low bushes and gullies that go down deep – all full of the Little People. I have put big stones one above the other by the side of three gullies. These I shall throw down with my feet in running, and the Little People will rise up behind me angry.'

'That is man's cunning,' said Kaa. 'Thou art wise, but the Little People are always angry.'

'Nay, at twilight all wings near and far rest for awhile. I will play with the dhole at twilight, for the dhole hunts best by day. He follows now Won-tolla's blood-trail.'

'Chil [10] does not leave a dead ox, or the dhole a blood-trail,' said Kaa.

'Then I will make him a new blood-trail – of his own blood if I can, and give him dirt to eat. Thou wilt stay here, Kaa, till I come with my dholes?'

'Ay, but what if they kill thee in the Jungle, or the Little People kill thee before thou canst leap down to the river?'

'When tomorrow comes we will kill tomorrow,' said Mowgli, quoting a Jungle saying; and again, 'When I am dead it is time to sing the Death Song. Good hunting, Kaa.'

He loosed his arm from the python's neck and went down the gorge like a log in a freshet, paddling towards the far bank, where he found slack water, and laughing aloud from sheer happiness. There was nothing Mowgli liked better than, as he himself said, 'to pull the whiskers of Death' and make the Jungle feel that he was their overlord. He had often, with Baloo's help, robbed bees' nests in single trees, and he knew that the Little People disliked the smell of wild garlic. So he gathered a small bundle of it, tied it up with a bark string, and then followed Won-tolla's blood-trail as it ran southerly from the lairs, for some five miles, looking at the trees with his head on one side and chuckling as he looked.

'Mowgli the Frog have I been,' said he to himself, 'Mowgli the Wolf have I said that I am. Now Mowgli the Ape must I be before I am Mowgli the Buck. At the end I shall be Mowgli the Man. Ho!' and he slid his thumb along the eighteen-inch blade of his knife.

Won-tolla's trail, all rank with dark blood-spots, ran under a forest of thick trees that grew close together and stretched away north-eastward, gradually growing thinner and thinner to within two miles of the Bee Rocks. From the last tree to the low scrub of the Bee Rocks was open country, where there was hardly cover enough to hide a wolf. Mowgli trotted along under the trees, judging distances between branch and branch, occasionally climbing up a trunk and taking a trial leap from one tree to another, till he came to the open ground, which he studied very carefully for an hour. Then he turned, picked up Won-tolla's trail where he had left it, settled himself in a tree with an outrunning branch some eight feet from the ground, hung his bunch of garlic in a safe crotch, and sat still sharpening his knife on the sole of his foot.

A little before midday when the sun was very warm, he heard the patter of feet and smelt the abominable smell of the dhole pack as they trotted steadily and pitilessly along Won-tolla's trail. Seen from above the red dhole does not look half the size of a wolf, but Mowgli knew how strong his feet and jaws were. He watched the sharp bay head of the leader snuffing along the trail and gave him 'Good hunting!'

The brute looked up and his companions halted behind him, scores and scores of red dogs with low-hung tails, heavy shoulders, weak quarters, and bloody mouths. The dholes are a very silent people as a rule, and they have no manners even in their own Dekkan. Fully two hundred must have gathered below him, but he could see that the leaders sniffed hungrily on Won-tolla's trail, and tried to drag the pack forward. That would never do, or they would be at the lairs in broad daylight, and Mowgli meant to hold them under his tree till twilight.

'By whose leave do ye come here?' said Mowgli.

'All jungles are our jungle,' was the reply, and the dhole that gave it bared his white teeth. Mowgli looked down with a smile and imitated perfectly the sharp chitter-chatter of Chikai, the leaping rat of the Dekkan, meaning the dholes to understand that he considered them no better than Chikai. The pack closed up round the tree trunk and the leader bayed savagely, calling Mowgli a tree-ape. For an answer Mowgli stretched down one naked leg and wriggled his bare toes just above the leader's head. That was enough, and more than enough to wake the pack to stupid rage. Those who have hair between their toes do not care to be reminded of it. Mowgli caught his foot away as the leader leaped and said sweetly: 'Dog, red dog! Go back to the Dekkan and eat lizards. Go to Chikai thy brother, dog, dog, red, red dog! There is hair between every toe!' He twiddled his toes a second time.

'Come down ere we starve thee out, hairless ape,' yelled the pack, and this was exactly what Mowgli wanted. He laid himself down along the branch, his cheek to the bark, his right arm free, and for some five minutes he told the pack what he thought and knew about them, their manners, their customs, their mates, and their puppies. There is no speech in the world so rancorous and so stinging as the language the Jungle People use to show scorn and contempt. When you come to think of it you will see how this must be so. As Mowgli told Kaa, he had many little thorns under his tongue, and slowly and deliberately he drove the dholes from silence to growls, from growls to yells, and from yells to hoarse slavery ravings. They tried to answer his taunts, but a cub might as well have tried to answer Kaa in a rage, and all the while Mowgli's right hand lay crooked at his side, ready for action, his feet locked round the branch. The big bay leader had leaped many times into the air, but Mowgli dared not risk a false blow. At last, made furious beyond his natural strength, he bounded up seven or eight feet clear of the ground. Then Mowgli's hand shot out like the head of a tree-snake, and gripped him by the scruff of his neck, and the branch shook with the jar as his weight fell back, and Mowgli was almost wrenched on to the ground. But he never loosed his grip, and inch by inch he hauled the beast, hanging like a drowned jackal, up on the branch. With his left hand he reached for his knife and cut off the red, bushy tail, flinging the dhole back to earth again. That was all he needed. The dhole would not go forward on Won-tolla's trail now till they had killed Mowgli, or Mowgli had killed them. He saw them settle down in circles with a quiver of the haunches that meant revenge to the death, and so he climbed to a higher crotch, settled his back comfortably and went to sleep.

After three or four hours he waked and counted the pack. They were all there, silent, husky, and dry, with eyes of steel. The sun was beginning to sink. In half an hour the Little People of the Rocks would be ending their labours, and, as you know, the dhole does not fight well in the twilight.

'I did not need such faithful watchers,' he said, standing up on a branch, 'but I will remember this. Ye be true dholes, but to my thinking too much of one kind. For that reason I do not give the big lizard-eater his tail again. Art thou not pleased, Red Dog?'

'I myself will tear out thy stomach,' yelled the leader, biting the foot of the tree.

'Nay, but consider, wise rat of Dekkan. There will now be many litters of little tailless red dogs, yea, with raw red stumps that sting when the sand is hot. Go home, Red Dog, and cry that an ape has done this. Ye will not go? Come then with me, and I will make ye very wise.'

He moved monkey-fashion into the next tree, and so on and the next and the next, the pack following with lifted hungry heads. Now and then he would pretend to fall, and the pack would tumble one over the other in their haste to be in at the death. It was a curious sight – the boy with the knife that shone in the low sunlight as it sifted through the upper branches, and the silent pack with their red coats all aflame huddling and following below. When he came to the last tree he took the garlic and rubbed himself all over carefully, and the dholes yelled with scorn. 'Ape with a wolf's tongue, dost thou think to cover thy scent?' they said. 'We will follow to the death.'

'Take thy tail,' said Mowgli, flinging it back along the course he had taken. The pack naturally rushed back a little when they smelt the blood. 'And follow now – to the death!'

He had slipped down the tree trunk, and headed like the wind in bare feet for the Bee Rocks, before the dholes saw what he would do.

They gave one deep howl and settled down to the long lobbing canter that can, at the last, run down anything that lives. Mowgli knew their pack pace to be much slower than that of the wolves, or he would never have risked a two-mile run in full sight. They were sure that the boy was theirs at last, and he was sure that he had them to play with as he pleased. All his trouble was to keep them sufficiently hot behind him to prevent them turning off too soon. He ran cleanly, evenly, and springily; the tailless leader not five yards behind him; and the pack stringing out over perhaps a quarter of a mile of ground, crazy and blind with the rage of slaughter. So he kept his distance by ear, reserving his last effort for the rush across the Bee Rocks.

The Little People had gone to sleep in the early twilight, for it was not the season of late blossoming flowers; but as Mowgli's first footfalls rang hollow on the hollow ground he heard a sound as though all the earth were humming. Then he ran as he had never run in his life before, spurned aside one – two – three of the piles of stones into the dark sweet-smelling gullies; heard a roar like the roar of the sea in a cave, saw with the tail of his eye the air grow dark behind him, saw the current of the Waingunga far below, and a flat, diamond-shaped head in the water; leaped outward with all his strength, the tailless dhole snapping at his shoulder in mid-air, and dropped feet first to the safety of the river, breathless and triumphant. There was not a sting on his body, for the smell of garlic had checked the Little People for just the few seconds that carried him across the rocks. When he rose Kaa's coils were steadying him and things were bounding over the edge of the cliff – great lumps, it seemed, of clustered bees falling like plummets; and as each lump touched water the bees flew upward and the body of a dhole whirled down stream. Overhead they could hear furious short yells that were drowned in a roar like thunder – the roar of the wings of the Little People of the Rocks. Some of the dholes, too, had fallen into the gullies that communicated with the underground caves, and there choked, and fought, and snapped among the tumbled honeycombs, and at last, borne up dead on the heaving waves of bees beneath them, shot out of some hole in the river face, to roll over on the black rubbish heaps. There were dholes who had leaped short into the trees on the cliffs, and the bees blotted out their shapes; but the greater number of them, maddened by the stings, had flung themselves into the river; and, as Kaa said, the Waingunga was hungry water.

Kaa held Mowgli fast till the boy had recovered his breath.

'We may not stay here,' he said. 'The Little People are roused indeed. Come!'

Swimming low and diving as often as he could, Mowgli went down the river with the knife in his hand.

'Slowly, slowly!' said Kaa. 'One tooth does not kill a hundred unless it be a cobra's, and many of the dholes took water swiftly when they saw the Little People rise. *They* are unhurt.'

'The more work for my knife, then. Phai! How the Little People follow.' Mowgli sank again. The face of the water was blanketed with wild bees buzzing sullenly and stinging all they found.

'Nothing was ever yet lost by silence,' said Kaa – no sting could penetrate his scales – 'and thou hast all the long night for the hunting. Hear them howl!'

Nearly half the pack had seen the trap their fellows rushed into, and, turning sharp aside, had flung themselves into the water where the gorge broke down in steep banks. Their cries of rage and their threats against the 'tree-ape' who had brought them to their shame mixed with the yells and growls of those who had been punished by the Little People. To remain ashore was death, and every dhole knew it. The pack was swept along the current, down and down to the rocks of the Peace Pool, but even there the angry Little People followed and forced them to the water again. Mowgli could hear the voice of the tailless leader bidding his people hold on and kill out every wolf in Seeonee. But he did not waste his time in listening.

'One kills in the dark behind us!' snapped a dhole. 'Here is tainted water!'

Mowgli had dived forward like an otter, twitched a struggling dhole under water before he could open his mouth, and dark, oily rings rose in the Peace Pool as the body plopped up, turning on its side. The dholes tried to turn, but the current forced them by, and the Little People darted at their heads and ears, and they could hear the challenge of the Seeonee Pack growing louder and deeper in the gathering darkness ahead. Again Mowgli dived, and again a dhole went under and rose dead, and again the clamour broke out at the rear of the pack, some howling that it was best to go ashore, others calling on their leader to lead them back to the Dekkan, and others bidding Mowgli show himself and be killed.

'They come to the fight with two stomachs and many voices,' said Kaa. 'The rest is with thy brethren below yonder. The Little People go back to sleep, and I will turn also. I do not help wolves.'

A wolf came running along the bank on three legs, leaping up and down, laying his sideways close to the ground, hunching his back, and breaking a couple of feet into the air, as though he were playing with his cubs. It was Won-tolla, the Outlier, and he said never a word, but continued his horrible sport beside the dholes. They had been long in the water now, and were swimming laboriously, their coats drenched and heavy, and their bushy tails dragging like sponges, so tired and shaken that they, too, were silent, watching the pair of blazing eyes that moved abreast of them.

'This is no good hunting,' said one at last.

'Good hunting!' said Mowgli as he rose boldly at the brute's side and sent the long knife home behind the shoulder, pushing hard to avoid the dying snap.

'Art thou there, man-cub?' said Won-tolla, from the bank.

'Ask of the dead, Outlier,' Mowgli replied. 'Have none come down stream? I have filled these dogs' mouths with dirt; I have tricked them in the broad daylight, and their leader lacks his tail, but here be some few for thee still. Whither shall I drive them?'

'I will wait,' said Won-tolla. 'The long night is before me, and I shall see well.'

Nearer and nearer came the bay of the Seeonee wolves. 'For the Pack, for the full Pack it is met!' and a bend in the river drove the dholes forward among the sands and shoals opposite the Seeonee lairs.

Then they saw their mistake. They should have landed half a mile higher up and rushed the wolves on dry ground. Now it was too late. The bank was lined with burning eyes, and except for the horrible *Pheeal* cry that had never stopped since sundown there was no sound in the jungle. It seemed as though Won-tolla was fawning on them to come ashore; and 'Turn and take hold!' said the leader of the dholes. The entire pack flung themselves at the shore, threshing and squattering through the shoal water till the face of the Waingunga was all white and torn, and the great ripples went from side to side like bow-waves from a boat. Mowgli followed the rush, stabbing and slicing as the dholes, huddled together, rushed up the river-beach in a wave.

Then the long fight began, heaving and straining and splitting and scattering and narrowing and broadening along the red wet sands, and over and between the tangled tree-roots, and through and among the bushes, and in and out of the grass clumps, for even now the dholes were two to one. But they met wolves fighting for all that made the pack, and not only the short, deep-chested white-tusked hunters of the pack, but the wild-eyed lahinis – the she-wolves of the lair, as the saying is – fighting for their litters, with here and there a yearling wolf, his first coat still half woolly, tugging and grappling by their sides. A wolf, you must know, flies at the throat or snaps at the flank, while a dhole by preference bites low, so when the dholes were struggling out of the water and had to raise their heads the odds were with the wolves; on dry land the wolves suffered, but in the water or on land Mowgli's knife came and went the same. The Four had worked their way to his aid. Grey Brother, crouched between the boy's knees, protected his stomach, while the others guarded his back and either side, or stood over him when the shock of a leaping, yelling dhole who had thrown himself on the steady blade bore him down. For the rest, it was one tangled confusion – a locked and swaying mob that moved from right to left and from left to right along the bank, and also ground round and round slowly on its centre. Here would be a heaving mound, like a water-blister in a whirlpool, which would break like a water-blister, and throw up four or five mangled dogs, each striving to get back to the centre; here would be a single wolf borne down by two or three dholes dragging them forward, and sinking the while; here a yearling cub would be held up by the pressure round him, though he had been killed early in the fight, while his mother, crazed with dumb rage, rolled over snapping and passing on; and in the middle of the thickest fight, perhaps, one wolf and one dhole, forgetting everything else, would be manoeuvring for first hold till they were swept away by a rush of yelling fighters. Once Mowgli passed Akela, a dhole on either flank, and his all but toothless jaws closed over the loins of a third; and once he saw Phaon, his teeth set in the throat of a dhole, tugging the unwilling beast forward till the yearlings could finish him. But the bulk of the fight was blind flurry and smother in the dark; hit, trip, and tumble, yelp, groan and worry-worry-worry round him and behind him and above him.

As the night wore on the quick giddy-go-round motion increased. The dholes were wearied and afraid to attack the stronger wolves, though they did not yet dare to run away; but Mowgli felt that the end was coming soon, and contented himself with striking to cripple. The yearlings were growing bolder; there was time to breathe; and now the mere flicker of the knife would sometimes turn a dhole aside.

'The meat is very near the bone,' Grey Brother gasped. He was bleeding from a score of flesh-wounds.

'But the bone is yet to be cracked,' said Mowgli. 'Aowawa! *Thus* do we do in the Jungle!' The red blade ran like a flame along the side of a dhole whose hind-quarters were hidden by the weight of a clinging wolf.

'My kill!' snorted the wolf through his wrinkled nostrils. 'Leave him to me!'

'Is thy stomach *still* empty, Outlier?' said Mowgli. Won-tolla was fearfully punished, but his grip had paralysed the dhole, who could not turn round and reach him.

'By the Bull that bought me,' Mowgli cried, with a bitter laugh, 'it is the tailless one!' And indeed it was the big bay-coloured leader.

'It is not wise to kill cubs and lahinis,' Mowgli went on philosophically, wiping the blood out of his eyes, 'unless one also kills the lair-father, and it is in my stomach that this lair-father kills thee.'

A dhole leaped to his leader's aid, but before his teeth had found Won-tolla's flank, Mowgli's knife was in his chest, and Grey Brother took what was left.

'And thus do we do in the Jungle,' said Mowgli.

Won-tolla said not a word, only his jaws were closing and closing on the backbone as life ebbed. The dhole shuddered, his head dropped and he lay still, and Won-tolla dropped above him.

'Huh! The Blood debt is paid,' said Mowgli. 'Sing the song, Won-tolla.'

'He hunts no more,' said Grey Brother, 'and Akela too is silent, this long time.'

'The bone is cracked!' thundered Phao, son of Phaon. 'They go! Kill, kill out, O hunters of the Free People!'

Dhole after dhole was slinking away from those dark and bloody sands to the river, to the thick jungle, up stream or down stream as he saw the road clear.

'The debt! The debt!' shouted Mowgli. 'Pay the debt! They have slain the Lone Wolf! Let not a dog go!'

He was flying to the river, knife in hand, to check any dhole who dared to take water, when, from under a mound of nine dead, rose Akela's head and forequarters, and Mowgli dropped on his knees beside the Lone Wolf.

'Said I not it would be my last fight?' Akela gasped. 'It is good hunting. And thou, Little Brother?'

'I live, having killed many.'

'Even so. I die, and I would – I would die by thee, Little Brother.'

Mowgli took the terrible scarred head on his knees, and put his arms round the torn neck.

'It is long since the old days of Shere Khan and a man-cub that rolled naked in the dust,' coughed Akela.

'Nay, nay, I am a wolf. I am of one skin with the Free People,' Mowgli cried. 'It is no will of mine that I am a man.'

'Thou art a man, Little Brother, wolfling of my watching. Thou art all a man, or else the Pack had fled before the dhole. My life I owe to thee, and today thou hast saved the Pack even as once I saved thee. Hast thou forgotten? All debts are paid now. Go to thine own people. I tell thee again, eye of my eye, this hunting is ended. Go to thine own people.'

'I will never go. I will hunt alone in the Jungle. I have said it.'

'After the summer come the rains, and after the rains comes the spring. Go back before thou art driven.'

'Who will drive me?'

'Mowgli will drive Mowgli. Go back to thy people. Go to man.'

'When Mowgli drives Mowgli I will go,' Mowgli answered.

'There is no more for thee,' said Akela. 'Now I would speak to my kind. Little Brother, canst thou raise me to my feet? I also am a leader of the Free People.'

Very carefully and gently Mowgli raised Akela to his feet, both arms round him, and the Lone Wolf drew a deep breath and began the Death Song that a leader of the Pack should sing when he dies. It gathered strength as he went on, lifting and lifting and ringing far across the river, till it came to the last 'Good hunting!' and Akela shook himself clear of Mowgli for an instant, and leaping into the air, fell backwards dead upon his last and most terrible kill.

Mowgli sat with his head on his knees, careless of anything else, while the last of the dying dholes were being overtaken and run down by the merciless lahinis. Little by little the cries died away, and the wolves came back limping as their wounds stiffened to take stock of the dead. Fifteen of the pack, as well as half a dozen lahinis, were dead by the river, and of the others not one was unmarked. Mowgli sat through it all till the cold daybreak, when Phao's wet red muzzle was dropped in his hand, and Mowgli drew back to show the gaunt body of Akela.

'Good hunting!' said Phao, as though Akela were still alive, and then over his bitten shoulder to the others: 'Howl, dogs! A wolf has died tonight!'

But of all the pack of two hundred fighting dholes, Red Dogs of the Dekkan, whose boast is that no living thing in the Jungle dare stand before them, not one returned to the Dekkan to carry that news.

﹛ The Ship that Found Herself [1] ﹜

It was her first voyage, and though she was but a cargo-steamer of twenty-five hundred tons, she was the very best of her kind, the outcome of forty years of experiments and improvements in framework and machinery; and her designers and owner thought as much of her as though she had been the *Lucania*. Anyone can make a floating hotel that will pay expenses, if he puts enough money into the saloon, and charges for private baths, suites of rooms, and such like; but in these days of competition and low freights every square inch of a cargo-boat must be built for cheapness, great hold-capacity, and a certain steady speed. This boat was, perhaps, two hundred and forty feet long and thirty-two feet wide, with arrangements that enabled her to carry cattle on her main and sheep on her upper deck if she wanted to; but her great glory was the amount of cargo that she could store away in her holds. Her owners – they were a very well known Scotch firm – came round with her from the north, where she had been launched and christened and fitted, to Liverpool, where she was to take cargo for New York; and the owner's daughter, Miss Frazier, went to and fro on the clean decks, admiring the new paint and the brass work, and the patent winches, and particularly the strong, straight bow, over which she had cracked a bottle of champagne when she named the steamer the *Dimbula*. It was a beautiful September afternoon, and the boat in all her newness – she was painted lead-colour with a red funnel – looked very fine indeed. Her house-flag was flying, and her whistle from time to time acknowledged the salutes of friendly boats, who saw that she was new to the High and Narrow Seas and wished to make her welcome.

'And now,' said Miss Frazier, delightedly, to the captain, 'she's a real ship, isn't she? It seems only the other day father gave the order for her, and now – and now – isn't she a beauty!' The girl was proud of the firm, and talked as though she were the controlling partner.

'Oh, she's no so bad,' the skipper replied cautiously. 'But I'm sayin' that it takes more than christenin' to mak' a ship. In the nature o' things, Miss Frazier, if ye follow me, she's just irons and rivets and plates put into the form of a ship. She has to find herself yet.'

'I thought father said she was exceptionally well found.'

'So she is,' said the skipper, with a laugh. 'But it's this way wi' ships,

Miss Frazier. She's all here, but the parrts of her have not learned to work together yet. They've had no chance.'

'The engines are working beautifully. I can hear them.'

'Yes, indeed. But there's more than engines to a ship. Every inch of her, ye'll understand, has to be livened up and made to work wi' its neighbour – sweetenin' her, we call it, technically.'

'And how will you do it?' the girl asked.

'We can no more than drive and steer her, and so forth; but if we have rough weather this trip – it's likely – she'll learn the rest by heart! For a ship, ye'll obsairve, Miss Frazier, is in no sense a reegid body closed at both ends. She's a highly complex structure o' various an' conflictin' strains, wi' tissues that must give an' tak' accordin' to her personal modulus of elasteecity.'[2] Mr Buchanan, the chief engineer, was coming towards them. 'I'm sayin' to Miss Frazier, here, that our little *Dimbula* has to be sweetened yet, and nothin' but a gale will do it. How's all wi' your engines, Buck?'

'Well enough – true by plumb an' rule, o' course; but there's no spontaneeity yet.' He turned to the girl. 'Take my word, Miss Frazier, and maybe ye'll comprehend later; even after a pretty girl's christened a ship it does not follow that there's such a thing as a ship under the men that work her.'

'I was sayin' the very same, Mr Buchanan,' the skipper interrupted.

'That's more metaphysical than I can follow,' said Miss Frazier, laughing.

'Why so? Ye're good Scotch, an' – I knew your mother's father, he was fra' Dumfries – ye've a vested right in metapheesics, Miss Frazier, just as ye have in the *Dimbula*,' the engineer said.

'Eh, well, we must go down to the deep watters, an' earn Miss Frazier her deevidends. Will you not come to my cabin for tea?' said the skipper. 'We'll be in dock the night, and when you're goin' back to Glasgie ye can think of us loadin' her down an' drivin' her forth – all for your sake.'

In the next few days they stowed some four thousand tons' dead weight into the *Dimbula*, and took her out from Liverpool. As soon as she met the lift of the open water, she naturally began to talk. If you lay your ear to the side of the cabin the next time you are in a steamer, you will hear hundreds of little voices in every direction, thrilling and buzzing, and whispering and popping, and gurgling and sobbing and squeaking exactly like a telephone in a thunder-storm. Wooden ships shriek and growl and grunt, but iron vessels throb and quiver through all their hundreds of ribs and thousands of rivets. The *Dimbula* was very strongly built, and every piece of her had a letter or number, or both, to describe it; and every piece had been hammered, or forged, or rolled, or punched by man, and had lived in the roar and rattle of the shipyard for months. Therefore, every piece had its own separate voice in exact proportion to the amount of trouble spent upon it. Cast-iron, as a rule, says very little; but mild steel plates and wrought-iron, and ribs and beams that have been much bent and welded and riveted, talk continuously. Their conversation, of course, is not half as wise as our human talk, because they are all, though they do not know it, bound down one to the other in a black darkness, where they cannot tell what is happening near them, nor what will overtake them next.

As soon as she had cleared the Irish coast a sullen, grey-headed old wave of the Atlantic climbed leisurely over her straight bows, and sat down on her steam-capstan used for hauling up the anchor. Now the capstan and the engine that drive it had been newly painted red and green; besides which, nobody likes being ducked.

'Don't you do that again,' the capstan sputtered through the teeth of his cogs. 'Hi! Where's the fellow gone?'

The wave had slouched overside with a plop and a chuckle; but 'Plenty more where he came from,' said a brother-wave, and went through and over the capstan, who was bolted firmly to an iron plate on the iron deck-beams below.

'Can't you keep still up there?' said the deck-beams. 'What's the matter with you? One minute you weigh twice as much as you ought to, and the next you don't!'

'It isn't my fault,' said the capstan. 'There's a green brute outside that comes and hits me on the head.'

'Tell that to the shipwrights. You've been in position for months and you've never wriggled like this before. If you aren't careful you'll strain *us*.'

'Talking of strain,' said a low, rasping, unpleasant voice, 'are any of you fellows – you deck-beams, we mean – aware that those exceedingly ugly knees of yours happen to be riveted into our structure – *ours?*'

'Who might you be?' the deck-beams inquired.

'Oh, nobody in particular,' was the answer. 'We're only the port and starboard upper-deck stringers; and if you persist in heaving and hiking like this, we shall be reluctantly compelled to take steps.'

Now the stringers of the ship are long iron girders, so to speak, that run lengthways from stern to bow. They keep the iron frames (what are called ribs in a wooden ship) in place, and also help to hold the ends of the deck-beams, which go from side to side of the ship. Stringers always consider themselves most important, because they are so long.

'You will take steps – will you?' This was a long echoing rumble. It came from the frames – scores and scores of them, each one about eighteen inches distant from the next, and each riveted to the stringers in four places. 'We think you will have a certain amount of trouble in *that*'; and thousands and thousands of the little rivets that held everything together whispered: 'You will. You will! Stop quivering and be quiet. Hold on, brethren! Hold on! Hot Punches! What's that?'

Rivets have no teeth, so they cannot chatter with fright; but they did their best as a fluttering jar swept along the ship from stern to bow, and she shook like a rat in a terrier's mouth.

An unusually severe pitch, for the sea was rising, had lifted the big throbbing screw nearly to the surface, and it was spinning round in a kind of soda-water – half sea and half air – going much faster than was proper, because there was no deep water for it to work in. As it sank again, the engines – and they were triple expansion, three cylinders in a row – snorted through all their three pistons. 'Was that a joke, you fellow outside? It's an uncommonly poor one. How are we to do our work if you fly off the handle that way?'

'I didn't fly off the handle,' said the screw, twirling huskily at the end of the screw-shaft. 'If I had, you'd have been scrap-iron by this time. The sea dropped away from under me, and I had nothing to catch on to. That's all.'

'That's all, d'you call it?' said the thrust-block, whose business it is to take the push of the screw; for if a screw had nothing to hold it back it would crawl right into the engine-room. (It is the holding back of the screwing action that gives the drive to a ship.) 'I know I do my work deep down and out of sight, but I warn you I expect justice. All I ask for is bare justice. Why can't you push steadily and evenly, instead of whizzing like a whirligig, and making me hot under all my collars.' The thrust-block had six collars, each faced with brass, and he did not wish to get them heated.

All the bearings that supported the fifty feet of screw-shaft as it ran to the stern whispered: 'Justice – give us justice.'

'I can only give you what I can get,' the screw answered. 'Look out! It's coming again!'

He rose with a roar as the *Dimbula* plunged, and 'whack – flack – whack – whack' went the engines, furiously, for they had little to check them.

'I'm the noblest outcome of human ingenuity – Mr Buchanan says so,' squealed the high-pressure cylinder. 'This is simply ridiculous!' The piston went up savagely, and choked, for half the steam behind it was mixed with dirty water. 'Help! Oiler! Fitter! Stoker! Help! I'm choking,' it gasped. 'Never in the history of maritime invention has such a calamity overtaken one so young and strong. And if I go, who's to drive the ship?'

'Hush! oh, hush!' whispered the Steam, who, of course, had been to sea many times before. He used to spend his leisure ashore in a cloud, or a gutter, or a flower-pot, or a thunder-storm, or anywhere else where water was needed. 'That's only a little priming, a little carrying-over, as they call it. It'll happen all night, on and off. I don't say it's nice, but it's the best we can do under the circumstances.'

'What difference can circumstances make? I'm here to do my work – on clean, dry steam. Blow circumstances!' the cylinder roared.

'The circumstances will attend to the blowing. I've worked on the North Atlantic run a good many times – it's going to be rough before morning.'

'It isn't distressingly calm now,' said the extra-strong frames – they were called web-frames – in the engine-room. 'There's an upward thrust that we don't understand, and there's a twist that is very bad for our brackets and diamond-plates, and there's a sort of west-north-westerly pull that follows the twist, which seriously annoys us. We mention this because we happened to cost a good deal of money, and we feel sure that the owner would not approve of our being treated in this frivolous way.'

'I'm afraid the matter is out of the owner's hands for the present,' said the Steam, slipping into the condenser. 'You're left to your own devices till the weather betters.'

'I wouldn't mind the weather,' said a flat bass voice below; 'it's this confounded cargo that's breaking my heart. I'm the garboard-strake, and I'm twice as thick as most of the others, and I ought to know something.'

The garboard-strake is the lowest plate in the bottom of a ship, and the *Dimbula's* garboard-strake was nearly three-quarters of an inch mild steel.

'The sea pushes me up in a way I should never have expected,' the strake grunted, 'and the cargo pushes me down, and, between the two, I don't know what I'm supposed to do.'

'When in doubt, hold on,' rumbled the Steam, making head in the boilers.

'Yes; but there's only dark, and cold, and hurry, down here; and how do I know whether the other plates are doing their duty? Those bulwark-plates up above, I've heard, ain't more than five-sixteenths of an inch thick – scandalous, I call it.'

'I agree with you,' said a huge web-frame by the main cargo-hatch.

He was deeper and thicker than all the others, and curved half-way across the ship in the shape of half an arch, to support the deck where deck-beams would have been in the way of cargo coming up and down. 'I work entirely unsupported, and I observe that I am the sole strength of this vessel, so far as my vision extends. The responsibility, I assure you, is enormous. I believe the money-value of the cargo is over one hundred and fifty thousand pounds. Think of that!'

'And every pound of it is dependent on my personal exertions.' Here spoke a sea-valve that communicated directly with the water outside, and was seated not very far from the garboard-strake. 'I rejoice to think that I am a Prince-Hyde Valve, with best Pará rubber facings. Five patents cover me – I mention this without pride – five separate and several patents, each one finer than the other. At present I am screwed fast. Should I open, you would immediately be swamped. This is incontrovertible!'

Patent things always use the longest words they can. It is a trick that they pick up from their inventors.

'That's news,' said a big centrifugal bilge-pump. 'I had an idea that you were employed to clean decks and things with. At least, I've used you for that more than once. I forget the precise number, in thousands, of gallons which I am guaranteed to throw per hour; but I assure you, my complaining friends, that there is not the least danger. I alone am capable of clearing any water that may find its way here. By my Biggest Deliveries, we pitched then!'

The sea was getting up in workmanlike style. It was a dead westerly gale, blown from under a ragged opening of green sky, narrowed on all sides by fat, grey clouds; and the wind bit like pincers as it fretted the spray into lacework on the flanks of the waves.

'I tell you what it is,' the foremast telephoned down its wire-stays. 'I'm up here, and I can take a dispassionate view of things. There's an organized conspiracy against us. I'm sure of it, because every single one of these waves is heading directly for our bows. The whole sea is concerned in it – and so's the wind. It's awful!'

'What's awful?' said a wave, drowning the capstan for the hundredth time.

'This organized conspiracy on your part,' the capstan gurgled, taking his cue from the mast.

'Organized bubbles and spindrift! There has been a depression in the Gulf of Mexico. Excuse me!' He leaped overside; but his friends took up the tale one after another.

'Which has advanced –' That wave hove green water over the funnel.

'As far as Cape Hatteras –' He drenched the bridge.

'And is now going out to sea – to sea – to sea!' The third went free in three surges, making a clean sweep of a boat, which turned bottom up and sank in the darkening troughs alongside, while the broken falls whipped the davits.

'That's all there is to it,' seethed the white water roaring through the scuppers. 'There's no animus in our proceedings. We're only meteorological corollaries.'

'Is it going to get any worse?' said the bow-anchor chained down to the deck, where he could only breathe once in five minutes.

'Not knowing, can't say. Wind may blow a bit by midnight. Thanks awfully. Good-bye.'

The wave that spoke so politely had travelled some distance aft, and found itself all mixed up on the deck amidships, which was a well-deck sunk between high bulwarks. One of the bulwark plates, which was hung on hinges to open outward, had swung out, and passed the bulk of the water back to the sea again with a clean smack.

'Evidently that's what I'm made for,' said the plate, closing again with a sputter of pride. 'Oh, no, you don't, my friend!'

The top of a wave was trying to get in from the outside, but as the plate did not open in that direction, the defeated water spurted back.

'Not bad for five-sixteenths of an inch,' said the bulwark-plate. 'My work, I see, is laid down for the night'; and it began opening and shutting, as it was designed to do, with the motion of the ship.

'We are not what you might call idle,' groaned all the frames together, as the *Dimbula* climbed a big wave, lay on her side at the top, and shot into the next hollow, twisting in the descent. A huge swell pushed up exactly under her middle, and her bow and stern hung free with nothing to support them. Then one joking wave caught her up at the bow, and another at the stern, while the rest of the water slunk away from under her just to see how she would like it; so she was held up at her two ends only, and the weight of the cargo and the machinery fell in the groaning iron keels and bilge-stringers.

'Ease off! Ease off, there!' roared the garboard-strake. 'I want one-eighth of an inch fair play. D'you hear me, you rivets!'

'Ease off! Ease off!' cried the bilge-stringers. 'Don't hold us so tight to the frames!'

'Ease off!' grunted the deck-beams, as the *Dimbula* rolled fearfully. 'You've cramped our knees into the stringers, and we can't move. Ease off, you flat-headed little nuisances.'

Then two converging seas hit the bows, one on each side, and fell away in torrents of streaming thunder.

'Ease off!' shouted the forward collision-bulkhead. 'I want to crumple up, but I'm stiffened in every direction. Ease off, you dirty little forge-filings. Let me breathe!'

All the hundreds of plates that are riveted to the frames, and make the outside skin of every steamer, echoed the call, for each plate wanted to shift and creep a little, and each plate, according to its position, complained against the rivets.

'We can't help it! *We* can't help it!' they murmured in reply. 'We're put here to hold you, and we're going to do it; you never pull us twice in the same direction. If you'd say what you were going to do next, we'd try to meet your views.'

'As far as I could feel,' said the upper-deck planking, and that was four inches thick, 'every single iron near me was pushing or pulling in opposite directions. Now, what's the sense of that? My friends, let us all pull together.'

'Pull any way you please,' roared the funnel, 'so long as you don't try your experiments on *me*. I need fourteen wire ropes, all pulling in different directions, to hold me steady. Isn't that so?'

'We believe you, my boy!' whistled the funnel-stays through their clinched teeth, as they twanged in the wind from the top of the funnel to the deck.

'Nonsense! We must all pull together,' the decks repeated. 'Pull lengthways.'

'Very good,' said the stringers; 'then stop pushing sideways when you get wet. Be content to run gracefully fore and aft, and curve in at the ends as we do.'

'No – no curves at the end! A very slight workmanlike curve from side to side, with a good grip at each knee, and little pieces welded on,' said the deck-beams.

'Fiddle!' cried the iron pillars of the deep, dark hold. 'Who ever heard of curves? Stand up straight; be a perfectly round column, and carry tons of good solid weight – like that! There!' A big sea smashed on the deck above, and the pillars stiffened themselves to the load.

'Straight up and down is not bad,' said the frames, who ran that way in the sides of the ship, 'but you must also expand yourselves sideways. Expansion is the law of life, children. Open out! open out!'

'Come back!' said the deck-beams, savagely, as the upward heave of the sea made the frames try to open. 'Come back to your bearings, you slack-jawed irons!'

'Rigidity! Rigidity! Rigidity!' thumped the engines. 'Absolute, un-varying rigidity – rigidity!'

'You see!' whined the rivets in chorus. 'No two of you will ever pull alike, and – and you blame it all on us. We only know how to go through a plate and bite down on both sides so that it can't, and mustn't, and shan't move.'

'I've got one-fraction of an inch play, at any rate,' said the garboard-strake, triumphantly. So he had, and all the bottom of the ship felt the easier for it.

'Then we're no good,' sobbed the bottom rivets. 'We were ordered – we were ordered – never to give; and we've given, and the sea will come in, and we'll all go to the bottom together! First we're blamed for everything unpleasant, and now we haven't the consolation of having done our work.'

'Don't say I told you,' whispered the Steam, consolingly; 'but, between you and me and the last cloud I came from, it was bound to happen sooner or later. You *had* to give a fraction, and you've given without knowing it. Now, hold on, as before.'

'What's the use?' a few hundred rivets chattered. 'We've given – we've given; and the sooner we confess that we can't keep the ship together, and go off our little heads, the easier it will be. No rivet forged can stand this strain.'

'No one rivet was ever meant to. Share it among you,' the Steam answered.

'The others can have my share. I'm going to pull out,' said a rivet in one of the forward plates.

'If you go, others will follow,' hissed the Steam. 'There's nothing so contagious in a boat as rivets going. Why, I knew a little chap like you – he was an eighth of an inch fatter, though – on a steamer – to be sure, she was only twelve hundred tons, now I come to think of it – in exactly the same place as you are. He pulled out in a bit of a bobble of a sea, not half as bad as this, and he started all his friends on the same butt-strap, and the plates opened like a furnace door, and I had to climb into the nearest fog-bank, while the boat went down.'

'Now that's peculiarly disgraceful,' said the rivet. 'Fatter than me, was he, and in a steamer not half our tonnage? Reedy little peg! I blush for the family, sir.' He settled himself more firmly than ever in his place, and the Steam chuckled.

'You see,' he went on, quite gravely, 'a rivet, and especially a rivet in your position, is really the one indispensable part of the ship.'

The Steam did not say that he had whispered the very same thing to every single piece of iron aboard. There is no sense in telling too much truth.

The Ship that Found Herself

And all that while the little *Dimbula* pitched and chopped, and swung and slewed, and lay down as though she were going to die, and got up as though she had been stung, and threw her nose round and round in circles half a dozen times as she dipped; for the gale was at its worst. It was inky black, in spite of the tearing white froth on the waves, and, to top everything, the rain began to fall in sheets, so that you could not see your hand before your face. This did not make much difference to the ironwork below, but it troubled the foremast a good deal.

'Now it's all finished,' he said dismally. 'The conspiracy is too strong for us. There is nothing left but to –'

'*Hurraar! Brrrraaah! Brrrrrrp!*' roared the Steam through the fog-horn, till the decks quivered. 'Don't be frightened, below. It's only me, just throwing out a few words, in case anyone happens to be rolling round tonight.'

'You don't mean to say there's anyone except *us* on the sea in such weather?' said the funnel in a husky snuffle.

'Scores of 'em,' said the steam, clearing its throat; '*Rrrrraaa! Brraaaaa! Prrrrp!* It's a trifle windy up here; and, Great Boilers! how it rains!'

'We're drowning,' said the scuppers. They had been doing nothing else all night, but this steady thrash of rain above them seemed to be the end of the world.

'That's all right. We'll be easier in an hour or two. First the wind and then the rain: Soon you may make sail again! *Grrraaaaaah! Drrrraaaa! Drrrp!* I have a notion that the sea is going down already. If it does you'll learn something about rolling. We've only pitched till now. By the way, aren't you chaps in the hold a little easier than you were?'

There was just as much groaning and straining as ever, but it was not so loud or squeaky in tone; and when the ship quivered she did not jar stiffly, like a poker hit on the floor, but gave with a supple little waggle, like a perfectly balanced golf-club.

'We have made a most amazing discovery,' said the stringers, one after another. 'A discovery that entirely changes the situation. We have found, for the first time in the history of ship-building, that the inward pull of the deck-beams and the outward thrust of the frames locks us, as it were, more closely in our places, and enables us to endure a strain which is entirely without parallel in the records of marine architecture.'

The Steam turned a laugh quickly into a roar up the fog-horn. 'What massive intellects you great stringers have,' he said softly, when he had finished.

'We also,' began the deck-beams, 'are discoverers and geniuses. We are of opinion that the support of the hold-pillars materially helps us. We find that we lock up on them when we are subjected to a heavy and singular weight of sea above.'

Here the *Dimbula* shot down a hollow, lying almost on her side – righting at the bottom with a wrench and a spasm.

'In these cases – are you aware of this, Steam? – the plating at the bows, and particularly at the stern – we would also mention the floors beneath us – help *us* to resist any tendency to spring.' The frames spoke, in the solemn, awed voice which people use when they have just come across something entirely new for the very first time.

'I'm only a poor puffy little flutterer,' said the Steam, 'but I have to stand a good deal of pressure in my business. It's all tremendously interesting. Tell us some more. You fellows are so strong.'

'Watch us and you'll see,' said the bow-plates, proudly. 'Ready, behind there! Here's the Father and Mother of Waves coming! Sit tight, rivets all!' A great sluicing comber thundered by, but through the scuffle and confusion the Steam could hear the low, quick cries of the ironwork as the various strains took them – cries like these: 'Easy, now – easy! *Now* push for all your strength! Hold out! Give a fraction! Hold up! Pull in! Shove crossways! Mind the strain at the ends! Grip, now! Bite tight! Let the water get away from under – and there she goes!'

The wave raced off into the darkness, shouting, 'Not bad, that, if it's your first run!' and the drenched and ducked ship throbbed to the beat of the engines inside her. All three cylinders were white with the salt spray that had come down through the engine-room hatch; there was white fur on the canvas-bound steam-pipes, and even the bright-work deep below was speckled and soiled; but the cylinders had learned to make the most of steam that was half water, and were pounding along cheerfully.

'How's the noblest outcome of human ingenuity hitting it?' said the Steam, as he whirled through the engine-room.

'Nothing for nothing in this world of woe,' the cylinders answered, as though they had been working for centuries, 'and precious little for seventy-five pounds' head. We've made two knots this last hour and a quarter! Rather humiliating for eight hundred horse-power, isn't it?'

'Well, it's better than drifting astern, at any rate. You seem rather less – how shall I put it? – stiff in the back than you were.'

'If you'd been hammered as we've been this night, you wouldn't be stiff – iff – iff, either. Theoreti – retti – retti – cally, of course, rigidity is the thing. Purr – purr – practically, there has to be a little give and take. *We* found that out by working on our sides for five minutes at a stretch – chch – chh. How's the weather?'

'Sea's going down fast,' said the Steam.

'Good business,' said the high-pressure cylinder. 'Whack her up, boys. They've given us five pounds more steam'; and he began humming the first bars of 'Said the young Obadiah to the old Obadiah', which, as you may have noticed, is a pet tune among engines not built for high speed. Racing-liners with twin-screws sing 'The Turkish Patrol' and the overture to the 'Bronze Horse', and 'Madame Angot', till something goes wrong, and then they render Gounod's 'Funeral March of a Marionette', with variations.

'You'll learn a song of your own some fine day,' said the Steam, as he flew up the fog-horn for one last bellow.

Next day the sky cleared and the sea dropped a little, and the *Dimbula* began to roll from side to side till every inch of iron in her was sick and giddy. But luckily they did not all feel ill at the same time: otherwise she would have opened out like a wet paper box.

The Steam whistled warnings as he went about his business: it is in this short, quick roll and tumble that follows a heavy sea that most of the accidents happen, for then everything thinks that the worst is over and goes off guard. So he orated and chattered till the beams and frames and floors and stringers and things had learned how to lock down and lock up on one another, and endure this new kind of strain.

They found ample time to practise, for they were sixteen days at sea, and it was foul weather till within a hundred miles of New York. The *Dimbula* picked up her pilot, and came in covered with salt and red rust. Her funnel was dirty grey from top to bottom; two boats had been carried away; three copper ventilators looked like hats after a fight with the police; the bridge had a dimple in the middle of it; the house that covered the steam steering-gear was split as with hatchets; there was a bill for small repairs in the engine-room almost as long as the screw-shaft; the forward cargo-hatch fell into bucket-staves when they raised the iron cross-bars; and the steam-capstan had been badly wrenched on its bed. Altogether, as the skipper said, it was 'a pretty general average'.

'But she's soupled,' he said to Mr Buchanan. 'For all her dead weight she rode like a yacht. Ye mind that last blow off the Banks? I am proud of her, Buck.'

'It's vera good,' said the chief engineer, looking along the dishevelled decks. 'Now, a man judgin' superfeecially would say we were a wreck, but we know otherwise – by experience.'

Naturally everything in the *Dimbula* fairly stiffened with pride, and the foremast and the forward collision-bulkhead, who are pushing creatures, begged the Steam to warn the Port of New York of their arrival. 'Tell those big boats all about us,' they said. 'They seem to take us quite as a matter of course.'

It was a glorious, clear, dead calm morning, and in single file, with less than half a mile between each, their bands playing and their tugboats shouting and waving handkerchiefs, were the *Majestic*, the *Paris*, the *Touraine*, the *Servia*, the *Kaiser Wilhelm II*, and the *Werkendam*, all statelily going out to sea. As the *Dimbula* shifted her helm to give the great boats clear way, the Steam (who knows far too much to mind making an exhibition of himself now and then) shouted:

'Oyez! Oyez! Oyez! Princes, Dukes, and Barons of the High Seas! Know ye by these presents, we are the *Dimbula*, fifteen days nine hours from Liverpool, having crossed the Atlantic with four thousand ton of cargo for the first time in our career! We have not foundered. We are here. 'Eer! 'Eer! We are not disabled. But we have had a time wholly unparalleled in the annals of ship-building! Our decks were swept! We pitched; we rolled! We thought we were going to die! *Hi! Hi!* But we didn't. We wish to give notice that we have come to New York all the way across the Atlantic, through the worst weather in the world; and we are the *Dimbula!* We are – arr – ha – ha – ha-r-r-r!'

The beautiful line of boats swept by as steadily as the procession of the Seasons. The *Dimbula* heard the *Majestic* say, 'Hmph!' and the *Paris* grunted, 'How!' and the *Touraine* said, 'Oui!' with a little co-quettish flicker of steam; and the *Servia* said, 'Haw!' and the *Kaiser* and the *Werkendam* said, 'Hoch!' Dutch fashion – and that was absolutely all.

'I did my best,' said the Steam, gravely, 'but I don't think they were much impressed with us, somehow. Do you?'

'It's simply disgusting,' said the bow-plates. 'They might have seen what we've been through. There isn't a ship on the sea that has suffered as we have – is there, now?'

'Well, I wouldn't go so far as that,' said the Steam, 'because I've worked on some of those boats and sent them through weather quite as bad as the fortnight that we've had, in six days; and some of them are a little over ten thousand tons, I believe. Now I've seen the *Majestic*, for instance, ducked from her bows to her funnel; and I've helped the *Arizona*, I think she was, to back off an iceberg she met with one dark night; and I had to run out of the *Paris*'s engine-room, one day, because there was thirty foot of water in it. Of course, I don't deny –' The Steam shut off suddenly, as a tug-boat, loaded with a political club and a brass band, that had been to see a New York Senator off to Europe, crossed their bows, going to Hoboken. There was a long silence that reached, without a break, from the cut-water to the propeller-blades of the *Dimbula*.

Then a new, big voice said slowly and thickly, as though the owner had just waked up: 'It's my conviction that I have made a fool of myself.'

The Steam knew what had happened at once; for when a ship finds herself all the talking of the separate pieces ceases and melts into one voice, which is the soul of the ship.

'Who are you?' he said, with a laugh.

'I am the *Dimbula*, of course. I've never been anything else except that – and a fool!'

The tugboat, which was doing its very best to be run down, got away just in time, its band playing clashily and brassily a popular but impolite air:

> In the days of old Rameses – are you on?
> In the days of old Rameses – are you on?
> In the days of old Rameses,
> That story had paresis,[3]
> Are you on – are you on – are you on?

'Well, I'm glad you've found yourself,' said the Steam. 'To tell the truth I was a little tired of talking to all those ribs and stringers. Here's Quarantine. After that we'll go to our wharf and clean up a little, and – next month we'll do it all over again.'

William the Conqueror [1]

I have done one braver thing
Than all the worthies did;
And yet a braver thence doth spring,
Which is to keep that hid.
The Undertaking.[2]

'Is it officially declared yet?'

'They've gone as far as to admit extreme local scarcity, and they've started relief-works in one or two districts, the paper says.'

'That means it will be declared as soon as they can make sure of the men and the rolling-stock. Shouldn't wonder if it were as bad as the Big Famine.'

'Can't be,' said Scott, turning a little in the long cane chair. 'We've had fifteen-anna [3] crops in the north, and Bombay and Bengal report more than they know what to do with. They'll be able to check it before it gets out of hand. It will only be local.'

Martyn picked up the *Pioneer* [4] from the table, read through the telegrams once more, and put up his feet on the chair-rests. It was a hot, dark, breathless evening, heavy with the smell of the newly-watered Mall. The flowers in the Club gardens were dead and black on their stalks, the little lotus-pond was a circle of caked mud, and the tamarisk-trees were white with the dust of days. Most of the men were at the band-stand in the public gardens – from the Club verandah you could hear the native Police band hammering stale waltzes – or on the polo-ground or in the high-walled fives-court, hotter than a Dutch oven. Half a dozen grooms, squatted at the heads of their ponies, waited their masters' return. From time to time a man would ride at a foot-pace into the Club compound, and listlessly loaf over to the whitewashed barracks beside the main building. These were supposed to be chambers. Men lived in them, meeting the same faces night after night at dinner, and drawing out their office-work till the latest possible hour, that they might escape that doleful company.

'What are you going to do?' said Martyn, with a yawn. 'Let's have a swim before dinner.'

'Water's hot,' said Scott. 'I was at the bath today.'

'Play you game o' billiards – fifty up.'

'It's a hundred and five in the hall now. Sit still and don't be so abominably energetic.'

A grunting camel swung up to the porch, his badged and belted rider fumbling a leather pouch.

'*Kubber-kargaz – ki – yektraaa*,'[5] the man whined, handing down the newspaper extra – a slip printed on one side only, and damp from the press. It was pinned on the green baize-board, between notices of ponies for sale and fox-terriers missing.

Martyn rose lazily, read it, and whistled. 'It's declared!' he cried. 'One, two, three – eight districts go under the operations of the Famine Code[6] *ek dum*.[7] They've put Jimmy Hawkins in charge.'

'Good business!' said Scott, with the first sign of interest he had shown. 'When in doubt hire a Punjabi.[8] I worked under Jimmy when I first came out and he belonged to the Punjab. He has more *bundobust*[9] than most men.'

'Jimmy's a Jubilee Knight[10] now,' said Martyn. 'He was a good chap, even though he is a thrice-born civilian[11] and went to the Benighted Presidency.[12] What unholy names these Madras districts rejoice in – all *ungas* or *rungas* or *pillays* or *polliums*.'

A dog-cart drove up, and a man entered, mopping his head. He was editor of the one daily paper[13] at the capital of a province of twenty-five million natives and a few hundred white men, and as his staff was limited to himself and one assistant, his office hours ran variously from ten to twenty a day.

'Hi, Raines; you're supposed to know everything,' said Martyn, stopping him. 'How's this Madras "scarcity" going to turn out?'

'No one knows as yet. There's a message as long as your arm coming in on the telephone. I've left my cub to fill it out. Madras has owned she can't manage it alone, and Jimmy seems to have a free hand in getting all the men he needs. Arbuthnot's warned to hold himself in readiness.'

' "Badger" Arbuthnot?'

'The Peshawur chap. Yes, and the *Pi* wires that Ellis and Clay have been moved from the North-West already, and they've taken half a dozen Bombay men, too. It's *pukka*[14] famine, by the looks of it.'

'They're nearer the scene of action than we are; but if it comes to indenting on the Punjab this early, there's more in this than meets the eye,' said Martyn.

'Here today and gone tomorrow. Didn't come to stay for ever,' said Scott, dropping one of Marryat's novels, and rising to his feet. 'Martyn, your sister's waiting for you.'

A rough grey horse was backing and shifting at the edge of the verandah, where the light of a kerosene-lamp fell on a brown calico habit and a white face under a grey felt hat.

'Right, O,' said Martyn. 'I'm ready. Better come and dine with us if you've nothing to do, Scott. William, is there any dinner in the house?'

'I'll go home first and see,' was the rider's answer. 'You can drive him over – at eight, remember.'

Scott moved leisurely to his room, and changed into the evening-dress of the season and the country: spotless white linen from head to foot, with a broad silk *cummerbund*. Dinner at the Martyns was a decided improvement on the goat-mutton, twiney-tough fowl, and tinned entrées of the Club. But it was a great pity Martyn could not afford to send his sister to the Hills for the hot weather. As an Acting District Superintendent of Police, Martyn drew the magnificent pay of six hundred depreciated silver rupees a month, and his little four-roomed bungalow said just as much. There were the usual blue-and-white striped jail-made rugs on the uneven floor; the usual glass-studded Amritsar *phulkaris*[15] draped to nails driven into the flaking whitewash of the walls; the usual half-dozen chairs that did not match, picked up at sales of dead men's effects; and the usual streaks of black grease where the leather punka-thong ran through the wall. It was as though everything had been unpacked the night before to be repacked next morning. Not a door in the house was true on its hinges. The little windows, fifteen feet up, were darkened with wasp-nests, and lizards hunted flies between the beams of the wood-ceiled roof. But all this was part of Scott's life. Thus did people live who had such an income; and in a land where each man's pay, age, and position are printed in a book, that all may read, it is hardly worth while to play at pretences in word or deed. Scott counted eight years' service in the Irrigation Department, and drew eight hundred rupees a month, on the understanding that if he served the State faithfully for another twenty-two years he could retire on a pension of some four hundred rupees a month. His working life, which had been spent chiefly under canvas or in temporary shelters where a man could sleep, eat, and write letters, was bound up with the opening and guarding of irrigation canals, the handling of two or three thousand workmen of all castes and creeds, and the payment of vast sums of coined silver. He had finished that spring, not without credit, the last section of the great Mosuhl Canal, and – much against his will, for he hated office work – had been sent in to serve during the hot weather on the accounts and supply side of the Department, with sole charge of the sweltering sub-office at the capital of the Province. Martyn knew this; William, his sister, knew it; and everybody knew it.

Scott knew, too, as well as the rest of the world, that Miss Martyn had come out to India four years before, to keep house for her brother, who, as everyone, again, knew, had borrowed the money to pay for her passage, and that she ought, as all the world said, to have married long ago. Instead of this, she had refused some half a dozen subalterns, a civilian twenty years her senior, one major, and a man in the Indian Medical Department. This, too, was common property. She had 'stayed down three hot weathers', as the saying is, because her brother was in debt and could not afford the expense of her keep at even a cheap hill-station. Therefore her face was white as bone, and in the centre of her forehead was a big silvery scar about the size of a shilling – the mark of a Delhi sore, which is the same as a 'Bagdad date'. This comes from drinking bad water, and slowly eats into the flesh till it is ripe enough to be burned out with acids.

None the less William had enjoyed herself hugely in her four years. Twice she had been nearly drowned while fording a river on horseback; once she had been run away with on a camel; had witnessed a midnight attack of thieves on her brother's camp; had seen justice administered, with long sticks, in the open under trees; could speak Urdu and even rough Punjabi with a fluency that was envied by her seniors; had altogether fallen out of the habit of writing to her aunts in England, or cutting the pages of the English magazines; had been through a very bad cholera year, seeing sights unfit to be told; and had wound up her experiences by six weeks of typhoid fever, during which her head had been shaved; and hoped to keep her twenty-third birthday that September. It is conceivable that her aunts would not have approved of a girl who never set foot on the ground if a horse were within hail; who rode to dances with a shawl thrown over her skirt; who wore her hair cropped and curling all over her head; who answered indifferently to the name of William or Bill; whose speech was heavy with the flowers of the vernacular; who could act in amateur theatricals, play on the banjo, rule eight servants and two horses, their accounts and their diseases, and look men slowly and deliberately between the eyes – yea, after they had proposed to her and been rejected.

'I like men who do things,' she had confided to a man in the Educational Department, who was teaching the sons of cloth merchants and dyers the beauty of Wordsworth's 'Excursion' in annotated cram-books; and when he grew poetical, William explained that she 'didn't understand poetry very much; it made her head ache', and another broken heart took refuge at the Club. But it was all William's fault. She delighted in hearing men talk of their own work, and that is the most fatal way of bringing a man to your feet.

Scott had known her more or less for some three years, meeting her, as a rule, under canvas when his camp and her brother's joined for a day on the edge of the Indian Desert. He had danced with her several times at the big Christmas gatherings, when as many as five hundred white people came into the station; and he had always a great respect for her housekeeping and her dinners.

She looked more like a boy than ever when, after their meal, she sat, one foot tucked under her, on the leather camp-sofa, rolling cigarettes for her brother, her low forehead puckered beneath the dark curls as she twiddled the papers. She stuck out her rounded chin when the tobacco stayed in place, and, with a gesture as true as a school-boy's throwing a stone, tossed the finished article across the room to Martyn, who caught it with one hand, and continued his talk with Scott. It was all 'shop' – canals and the policing of canals; the sins of villagers who stole more water than they had paid for, and the grosser sin of native constables who connived at the thefts; of the transplanting bodily of villages to newly-irrigated ground, and of the coming fight with the desert in the south when the Provincial funds should warrant the opening of the long-surveyed Luni Protective Canal System. And Scott spoke openly of his great desire to be put on one particular section of the work where he knew the land and the people, and Martyn sighed for a billet in the Himalayan foot-hills, and spoke his mind of his superiors, and William rolled cigarettes and said nothing, but smiled gravely on her brother because he was happy.

At ten Scott's horse came to the door, and the evening was ended.

The lights of the two low bungalows in which the daily paper was printed showed bright across the road. It was too early to try to find sleep, and Scott drifted over to the editor. Raines, stripped to the waist like a sailor at a gun, lay in a long chair, waiting for night telegrams. He had a theory that if a man did not stay by his work all day and most of the night he laid himself open to fever; so he ate and slept among his files.

'Can you do it?' he said drowsily. 'I didn't mean to bring you over.'

'About what? I've been dining at the Martyns'.'

'The famine, of course, Martyn's warned for it, too. They're taking men where they can find 'em. I sent a note to you at the Club just now, asking if you could do us a letter once a week from the south – between two and three columns, say. Nothing sensational, of course, but just plain facts about who is doing what, and so forth. Our regular rates – ten rupees a column.'

'Sorry, but it's out of my line,' Scott answered, staring absently at the map of India on the wall. 'It's rough on Martyn – very. Wonder what he'll do with his sister. Wonder what the deuce they'll do with me? I've no famine experience. This is the first I've heard of it. *Am* I ordered?'

'Oh, yes. Here's the wire. They'll put you on relief-works,' Raines went on, 'with a horde of Madrassis dying like flies; one native apothecary and half a pint of cholera-mixture among the ten thousand of you. It comes of your being idle for the moment. Every man who isn't doing two men's work seems to have been called upon. Hawkins evidently believes in Punjabis. It's going to be quite as bad as anything they have had in the last ten years.'

'It's all in the day's work, worse luck. I suppose I shall get my orders officially sometime tomorrow. I'm glad I happened to drop in. Better go and pack my kit now. Who relieves me here – do you know?'

Raines turned over a sheaf of telegrams. 'McEuan,' said he, 'from Murree.'[16]

Scott chuckled. 'He thought he was going to be cool all summer. He'll be very sick about this. Well, no good talking. Night.'

Two hours later, Scott, with a clear conscience, laid himself down to rest on a string cot in a bare room. Two worn bullock-trunks, a leather water-bottle, a tin ice-box, and his pet saddle sewed up in sacking were piled at the door, and the Club secretary's receipt for last month's bill was under his pillow. His orders came next morning, and with them an unofficial telegram from Sir James Hawkins, who did not forget good men, bidding him report himself with all speed at some unpronounceable place fifteen hundred miles to the south, for the famine was sore in the land, and white men were needed.

A pink and fattish youth arrived in the red-hot noonday, whimpering a little at fate and famines, which never allowed anyone three months' peace. He was Scott's successor – another cog in the machinery, moved forward behind his fellow, whose services, as the official announcement ran, 'were placed at the disposal of the Madras Government for famine duty until further orders'. Scott handed over the funds in his charge, showed him the coolest corner in the office, warned him against excess of zeal, and, as twilight fell, departed from the Club in a hired carriage, with his faithful body servant, Faiz Ullah, and a mound of disordered baggage atop, to catch the Southern Mail at the loopholed and bastioned railway-station. The heat from the thick brick walls struck him across the face as if it had been a hot towel, and he reflected that there were at least five nights and four days of travel before him. Faiz Ullah, used to the chances of service, plunged into the crowd on the stone platform, while Scott, a black cheroot between his teeth, waited till his compartment should be set away. A dozen native policemen, with their rifles and bundles, shouldered into the press of Punjabi farmers, Sikh craftsmen, and greasy-locked Afreedee pedlars, escorting with all pomp Martyn's uniform-case, water-bottles, ice-box, and bedding-roll. They saw Faiz Ullah's lifted hand, and steered for it.

'My Sahib and your Sahib,' said Faiz Ullah to Martyn's man, 'will travel together. Thou and I, O brother, willl thus secure the servants' places close by, and because of our masters' authority none will dare to disturb us.'

When Faiz Ullah reported all things ready, Scott settled down coatless and bootless on the broad leather-covered bunk. The heat under the iron-arched roof of the station might have been anything over a hundred degrees. At the last moment Martyn entered, hot and dripping.

'Don't swear,' said Scott, lazily; 'it's too late to change your carriage; and we'll divide the ice.'

'What are you doing here?' said the policeman.

'Lent to the Madras Government, same as you. By Jove, it's a bender of a night! Are you taking any of your men down?'

'A dozen. Suppose I'll have to superintend relief distributions. Didn't know you were under orders too.'

'I didn't till after I left you last night. Raines had the news first. My orders came this morning. McEuan relieved me at four, and I got off at once. Shouldn't wonder if it wouldn't be a good thing – this famine – if we come through it alive.'

'Jimmy ought to put you and me to work together,' said Martyn; and then, after a pause: 'My sister's here.'

'Good business,' said Scott, heartily. 'Going to get off at Umballa, I suppose, and go up to Simla. Who'll she stay with there?'

'No-o; that's just the trouble of it. She's going down with me.'

Scott sat bolt upright under the oil lamp as the train jolted past Tarn-Taran station. 'What! You don't mean you couldn't afford –'

'Oh, I'd have scraped up the money somehow.'

'You might have come to me, to begin with,' said Scott, stiffly; 'we aren't altogether strangers.'

'Well, you needn't be stuffy about it. I might, but – you don't know my sister. I've been explaining and exhorting and entreating and commanding and all the rest of it all day – lost my temper since seven this morning, and haven't got it back yet – but she wouldn't hear of any compromise. A woman's entitled to travel with her husband if she wants to, and William says she's on the same footing. You see, we've been together all our lives, more or less, since my people died. It isn't as if she were an ordinary sister.'

'All the sisters I've ever heard of would have stayed where they were well off.'

'She's as clever as a man, confound her,' Martyn went on. 'She broke up the bungalow over my head while I was talking at her. Settled the whole *subchiz* [outfit] in three hours – servants, horses, and all. I didn't get my orders till nine.'

'Jimmy Hawkins won't be pleased,' said Scott. 'A famine's no place for a woman.'

'Mrs Jim – I mean Lady Jim's in camp with him. At any rate, she says she will look after my sister. William wired down to her on her own responsibility, asking if she could come, and knocked the ground from under me by showing me her answer.'

Scott laughed aloud. 'If she can do that she can take care of herself, and Mrs Jim won't let her run into any mischief. There aren't many women, sisters or wives, who would walk into a famine with their eyes open. It isn't as if she didn't know what these things mean. She was through the Jaloo cholera last year.'

The train stopped at Amritsar, and Scott went back to the ladies' compartment, immediately behind their carriage. William, a cloth riding-cap on her curls, nodded affably.

'Come in and have some tea,' she said. 'Best thing in the world for heat-apoplexy.'

'Do I look as if I were going to have heat-apoplexy?'

'Never can tell,' said William, wisely. 'It's always best to be ready.'

She had arranged her belongings with the knowledge of an old campaigner. A felt-covered water-bottle hung in the draught of one of the shuttered windows; a tea-set of Russian china, packed in a wadded basket, stood ready on the seat; and a travelling spirit-lamp was clamped against the woodwork above it.

William served them generously, in large cups, hot tea, which saves the veins of the neck from swelling inopportunely on a hot night. It was characteristic of the girl that, her plan of action once settled, she asked for no comments on it. Life with men who had a great deal of work to do, and very little time to do it in, had taught her the wisdom of effacing as well as of fending for herself. She did not by word or deed suggest that she would be useful, comforting, or beautiful in their travels, but continued about her business serenely: put the cups back without clatter when tea was ended, and made cigarettes for her guests.

'This time last night,' said Scott, 'we didn't expect – er – this kind of thing, did we?'

'I've learned to expect anything,' said William. 'You know, in our service, we live at the end of the telegraph; but, of course, this ought to be a good thing for us all, departmentally – if we live.'

'It knocks us out of the running in our own Province,' Scott replied, with equal gravity. 'I hoped to be put on the Luni Protective Works this cold weather; but there's no saying how long the famine may keep us.'

'Hardly beyond October, I should think,' said Martyn. 'It will be ended, one way or the other, then.'

'And we've nearly a week of this,' said William. 'Sha'n't we be dusty when it's over?'

For a night and a day they knew their surroundings; and for a night and a day, skirting the edge of the great Indian Desert on a narrow-gauge line, they remembered how in the days of their apprenticeship they had come by that road from Bombay. Then the languages in which the names of the stations were written changed, and they launched south into a foreign land, where the very smells were new. Many long and heavily-laden grain trains were in front of them, and they could feel the hand of Jimmy Hawkins from far off. They waited in extemporized sidings blocked by processions of empty trucks returning to the north, and were coupled on to slow, crawling trains, and dropped at midnight, Heaven knew where; but it was furiously hot; and they walked to and fro among sacks, and dogs howled.

Then they came to an India more strange to them than to the un-travelled Englishman – the flat, red India of palm-tree, palmyra-palm, and rice, the India of the picture-books, of *Little Henry and His Bearer* [17] – all dead and dry in the baking heat. They had left the incessant passenger-traffic of the north and west far and far behind them. Here the people crawled to the side of the train, holding their little ones in their arms; and a loaded truck would be left behind, men and women clustering round and above it like ants by spilled honey. Once in the twilight they saw on a dusty plain a regiment of little brown men, each bearing a body over his shoulder; and when the train stopped to leave yet another truck, they perceived that the burdens were not corpses, but only foodless folk picked up beside their dead oxen by a corps of Irregular troops. Now they met more white men, here one and there two, whose tents stood close to the line, and who came armed with written authorities and angry words to cut off a truck. They were too busy to do more than nod at Scott and Martyn, and stare curiously at William, who could do nothing except make tea, and watch how her men staved off the rush of wailing, walking skeletons, putting them down three at a time in heaps, with their own hands uncoupling the marked trucks, or taking receipts from the hollow-eyed, weary white men, who spoke another argot than theirs.

They ran out of ice, out of soda-water, and out of tea; for they were six days and seven nights on the road, and it seemed to them like seven times seven years.

At last, in a dry, hot dawn, in a land of death, lit by long red fires of railway sleepers, where they were burning the dead, they came to their destination, and were met by Jim Hawkins, the Head of the Famine, unshaven, unwashed, but cheery, and entirely in command of affairs.

Martyn, he decreed, then and there, was to live on trains till further orders; was to go back with empty trucks, filling them with starving people as he found them, and dropping them at a famine-camp on the edge of the Eight Districts. He would pick up supplies and return, and his constables would guard the loaded grain-cars, also picking up people, and would drop them at a camp a hundred miles south. Scott – Hawkins was very glad to see Scott again – would, that same hour, take charge of a convoy of bullock-carts, and would go south, feeding as he went, to yet another famine-camp, far from the rail, where he would leave his starving – there would be no lack of starving on the route – and wait for orders by telegraph. Generally, Scott was in all small things to do what he thought best.

William bit her underlip. There was no one in the wide world like her one brother, but Martyn's orders gave him no discretion. She came out, masked with dust from head to foot, a horse-shoe wrinkle on her forehead, put there by much thinking during the past week, but as self-possessed as ever. Mrs Jim – who should have been Lady Jim, but that no one remembered to call her aright – took possession of her with a little gasp.

'Oh, I'm so glad you're here,' she almost sobbed. 'You oughtn't to, of course, but there – there isn't another woman in the place, and we must help each other, you know; and we've all the wretched people and the little babies they are selling.'

'I've seen some,' said William.

'Isn't it ghastly? I've bought twenty; they're in our camp; but won't you have something to eat first? We've more than ten people can do here; and I've got a horse for you. Oh, I'm so glad you've come! You're a Punjabi too, you know.'

'Steady, Lizzie,' said Hawkins, over his shoulder. 'We'll look after you, Miss Martyn. Sorry I can't ask you to breakfast, Martyn. You'll have to eat as you go. Leave two of your men to help Scott. These poor devils can't stand up to load carts. Saunders' (this to the engine-driver, half asleep in the cab), 'back down and get those empties away. You've 'line clear' to Anundrapillay; they'll give you orders north of that. Scott, load up your carts from that B. P. P. truck, and be off as soon as you can. The Eurasian in the pink shirt is your interpreter and guide. You'll find an apothecary of sorts tied to the yoke of the second wagon. He's been trying to bolt; you'll have to look after him. Lizzie, drive Miss Martyn to camp, and tell them to send the red horse down here for me.'

Scott, with Faiz Ullah and two policemen, was already busy on the carts, backing them up to the truck and unbolting the sideboards quietly, while the others pitched in the bags of millet and wheat. Hawkins watched him for as long as it took to fill one cart.

'That's a good man,' he said. 'If all goes well I shall work him – hard.' This was Jim Hawkins's notion of the highest compliment one human being could pay another.

An hour later Scott was under way; the apothecary threatening him with the penalties of the law for that he, a member of the Subordinate Medical Department, had been coerced and bound against his will and all laws governing the liberty of the subject; the pink-shirted Eurasian begging leave to see his mother, who happened to be dying some three miles away: 'Only verree, verree short leave of absence, and will presently return, sar –'; the two constables, armed with staves, bringing up the rear; and Faiz Ullah, a Mohammedan's contempt for all Hindoos and foreigners in every line of his face, explaining to the drivers that though Scott Sahib was a man to be feared on all fours, he, Faiz Ullah, was Authority itself.

The procession creaked past Hawkins's camp – three stained tents under a clump of dead trees; behind them the famine-shed where a crowd of hopeless ones tossed their arms around the cooking-kettles.

'Wish to Heaven William had kept out of it,' said Scott to himself, after a glance. 'We'll have cholera, sure as a gun, when the Rains come.'

But William seemed to have taken kindly to the operations of the Famine Code, which, when famine is declared, supersede the workings of the ordinary law. Scott saw her, the centre of a mob of weeping women, in a calico riding-habit and blue-grey felt hat with a gold puggaree.[18]

'I want fifty rupees, please. I forgot to ask Jack before he went away. Can you lend it me? It's for condensed milk for the babies,' said she.

Scott took the money from his belt, and handed it over without a word. 'For goodness sake take care of yourself,' he said.

'Oh, I shall be all right. We ought to get the milk in two days. By the way, the orders are, I was to tell you, that you're to take one of Sir Jim's horses. There's a grey Cabuli here that I thought would be just your style, so I've said you'd take him. Was that right?'

'That's awfully good of you. We can't either of us talk much about style, I'm afraid.'

Scott was in a weather-stained drill shooting-kit, very white at the seams and a little frayed at the wrists. William regarded him thoughtfully, from his pith helmet to his greased ankle-boots. 'You look very nice, I think. Are you sure you've everything you'll need – quinine, chlorodyne, and so on?'

'Think so,' said Scott, patting three or four of his shooting-pockets as the horse was led up, and he mounted and rode alongside his convoy.

'Good-bye,' he cried.

'Good-bye, and good luck,' said William. 'I'm awfully obliged for the money.' She turned on a spurred heel and disappeared into the tent, while the carts pushed on past the famine-sheds, past the roaring lines of the thick, fat fires, down to the baked Gehenna [19] of the South.

II

> So let us melt and make no noise,
>   No tear-floods nor sigh-tempests move;
>   'Twere profanation of our joys
>   To tell the laity our love.
>   *A Valediction.* [20]

It was punishing work, even though he travelled by night and camped by day; but within the limits of his vision there was no man whom Scott could call master. He was as free as Jimmy Hawkins – freer, in fact, for the Government held the Head of the Famine tied neatly to a telegraph-wire, and if Jimmy had ever regarded telegrams seriously, the death-rate of that famine would have been much higher than it was.

At the end of a few days' crawling Scott learned something of the size of the India which he served; and it astonished him. His carts, as you know, were loaded with wheat, millet, and barley, good food-grains needing only a little grinding. But the people to whom he brought the life-giving stuffs were rice-eaters. They knew how to hull rice in their mortars, but they knew nothing of the heavy stone querns of the North, and less of the material that the white man convoyed so laboriously. They

clamoured for rice – unhusked paddy, such as they were accustomed to
– and, when they found that there was none, broke away weeping from
the sides of the cart. What was the use of these strange hard grains that
choked their throats? They would die. And then and there there were
many of them kept their word. Others took their allowance, and bartered
enough millet to feed a man through a week for a few handfuls of rotten
rice saved by some less unfortunate. A few put their shares into the rice-
mortars, pounded it, and made a paste with foul water; but they were
very few. Scott understood dimly that many people in the India of the
South ate rice, as a rule, but he had spent his service in a grain Province,
had seldom seen rice in the blade or the ear, and least of all would have
believed that, in time of deadly need, men would die at arm's length of
plenty, sooner than touch food they did not know. In vain the interpreters
interpreted; in vain his two policemen showed by vigorous pantomime
what should be done. The starving crept away to their bark and weeds,
grubs, leaves, and clay, and left the open sacks untouched. But sometimes
the women laid their phantoms of children at Scott's feet, looking back
as they staggered away.

Faiz Ullah opined it was the will of God that these foreigners should
die, and therefore it remained only to give orders to burn the dead. None
the less there was no reason why the Sahib should lack his comforts, and
Faiz Ullah, a campaigner of experience, had picked up a few lean goats
and had added them to the procession. That they might give milk for the
morning meal, he was feeding them on the good grain that these im-
beciles rejected. 'Yes,' said Faiz Ullah; 'if the Sahib thought fit, a little
milk might be given to some of the babies'; but, as the Sahib well knew,
babies were cheap, and, for his own part, Faiz Ullah held that there was
no Government order as to babies. Scott spoke forcefully to Faiz Ullah
and the two policemen, and bade them capture goats where they could
find them. This they most joyfully did, for it was a recreation, and many
ownerless goats were driven in. Once fed, the poor brutes were willing
enough to follow the carts, and a few days' good food – food such as
human beings died for lack of – set them in milk again.

'But I am no goatherd,' said Faiz Ullah. 'It is against my *izzat* [my
honour].'

'When we cross the Bias River²¹ again we will talk of *izzat*,' Scott
replied. 'Till that day thou and the policemen shall be sweepers to the
camp, if I give the order.'

'Thus, then, it is done,' grunted Faiz Ullah, 'if the Sahib will have it
so'; and he showed how a goat should be milked, while Scott stood over
him.

'Now we will feed them,' said Scott; 'thrice a day we will feed them'; and he bowed his back to the milking, and took a horrible cramp.

When you have to keep connection unbroken between a restless mother of kids and a baby who is at the point of death, you suffer in all your system. But the babies were fed. Morning, noon and evening Scott would solemnly lift them out one by one from their nest of gunny-bags[22] under the cart-tilts. There were always many who could do no more than breathe, and the milk was dropped into their toothless mouths drop by drop, with due pauses when they choked. Each morning, too, the goats were fed; and since they would straggle without a leader, and since the natives were hirelings, Scott was forced to give up riding, and pace slowly at the head of his flocks, accommodating his step to their weaknesses. All this was sufficiently absurd, and he felt the absurdity keenly; but at least he was saving life, and when the women saw that their children did not die, they made shift to eat a little of the strange foods, and crawled after the carts, blessing the master of the goats.

'Give the women something to live for,' said Scott to himself, as he sneezed in the dust of a hundred little feet, 'and they'll hang on somehow. But this beats William's condensed-milk trick all to pieces. I shall never live it down, though.'

He reached his destination very slowly, found that a rice-ship had come in from Burmah, and that stores of paddy were available; found also an overworked Englishman in charge of the shed, and, loading the carts, set back to cover the ground he had already passed. He left some of the children and half his goats at the famine-shed. For this he was not thanked by the Englishman, who had already more stray babies than he knew what to do with. Scott's back was suppled to stooping now, and he went on with his wayside ministrations in addition to distributing the paddy. More babies and more goats were added unto him; but now some of the babies wore rags, and beads round their wrists or necks. '*That*,' said the interpreter, as though Scott did not know, 'signifies that their mothers hope in eventual contingency to resume them offeecially.'

'The sooner the better,' said Scott; but at the same time he marked, with the pride of ownership, how this or that little Ramasawmy was putting on flesh like a bantam. As the paddy-carts were emptied he headed for Hawkins's camp by the railway, timing his arrival to fit in with the dinner-hour, for it was long since he had eaten at a cloth. He had no desire to make any dramatic entry, but an accident of the sunset ordered it that, when he had taken off his helmet to get the evening breeze, the low light should fall across his forehead, and he could not see what was before him; while one waiting at the tent door beheld, with new eyes, a young man, beautiful as Paris,[23] a god in a halo of golden dust, walking slowly at the head of his flocks, while at his knee ran small naked Cupids. But she laughed – William, in a slate-coloured blouse, laughed consumedly till Scott, putting the best face he could upon the matter, halted his armies and bade her admire the kindergarten. It was an unseemly sight, but the proprieties had been left ages ago, with the tea-party at Amritsar Station, fifteen hundred miles to the northward.

'They are coming on nicely,' said William. 'We've only five-and-twenty here now. The women are beginning to take them away again.'

'Are you in charge of the babies, then?'

'Yes – Mrs Jim and I. We didn't think of goats, though. We've been trying condensed milk and water.'

'Any losses?'

'More than I care to think of,' said William, with a shudder. 'And you?'

Scott said nothing. There had been many little burials along his route – many mothers who had wept when they did not find again the children they had trusted to the care of the Government.

Then Hawkins came out carrying a razor, at which Scott looked hungrily, for he had a beard that he did not love. And when they sat down to dinner in the tent he told his tale in few words, as it might have been an official report. Mrs Jim snuffled from time to time, and Jim bowed his head judicially; but William's grey eyes were on the clean-shaven face, and it was to her that Scott seemed to speak.

'Good for the Pauper Province!'[24] said William, her chin in her hand, as she leaned forward among the wine-glasses. Her cheeks had fallen in, and the scar on her forehead was more prominent than ever, but the well-turned neck rose roundly as a column from the ruffle of the blouse which was the accepted evening-dress in camp.

'It was awfully absurd at times,' said Scott. 'You see I didn't know much about milking or babies. They'll chaff my head off, if the tale goes north.'

'Let 'em,' said William, haughtily. 'We've all done coolie-work since we came. I know Jack has.' This was to Hawkins's address, and the big man smiled blandly.

'Your brother's a highly efficient officer, William,' said he, 'and I've done him the honour of treating him as he deserves. Remember, I write the confidential reports.'

'Then you must say that William's worth her weight in gold,' said Mrs Jim. 'I don't know what we should have done without her. She has been everything to us.' She dropped her hand upon William's, which

was rough with much handling of reins, and William patted it softly.
Jim beamed on the company. Things were going well with his world.
Three of his more grossly incompetent men had died, and their places
had been filled by their betters. Every day brought the rains nearer.
They had put out the famine in five of the Eight Districts, and, after all,
the death-rate had not been too heavy – things considered. He looked
Scott over carefully, as an ogre looks over a man, and rejoiced in his
thews and iron-hard condition.

'He's just the least bit in the world tucked up,'[25] said Jim to himself,
'but he can do two men's work yet.' Then he was aware that Mrs Jim
was telegraphing to him, and according to the domestic code the message
ran: 'A clear case. Look at them!'

He looked and listened. All that William was saying was: 'What can
you expect of a country where they call a *bhistee* [a water-carrier] a *tunni-cutch?*' and all that Scott answered was: 'I shall be precious glad to get
back to the Club. Save me a dance at the Christmas ball, won't you?'

'It's a far cry from here to the Lawrence Hall,'[26] said Jim. 'Better
turn in early, Scott. It's paddy-carts tomorrow; you'll begin loading at
five.'

'Aren't you going to give Mr Scott one day's rest?'

'Wish I could, Lizzie. 'Fraid I can't. As long as he can stand up we
must use him.'

'Well, I've had one Europe evening, at least ... By Jove, I'd nearly
forgotten! What do I do about those babies of mine?'

'Leave them here,' said William – 'we are in charge of that – and as
many goats as you can spare. I must learn how to milk now.'

'If you care to get up early enough tomorrow I'll show you. I have to
milk, you see; and, by the way, half of 'em have beads and things round
their necks. You must be careful not to take 'em off, in case the mothers
turn up.'

'You forget I've had some experience here.'

'I hope to goodness you won't overdo.' Scott's voice was unguarded.

'I'll take care of her,' said Mrs Jim, telegraphing hundred-word
messages as she carried William off, while Jim gave Scott his orders for
the coming campaign. It was very late – nearly nine o'clock.

'Jim, you're a brute,' said his wife, that night; and the Head of the
Famine chuckled.

'Not a bit of it, dear. I remember doing the first Jandiala Settlement[27]
for the sake of a girl in a crinoline; and she was slender, Lizzie. I've
never done as good a piece of work since. *He*'ll work like a demon.'

'But you might have given him one day.'

'And let things come to a head now? No, dear; it's their happiest time.'

'I don't believe either of the dears know what's the matter with them. Isn't it beautiful? Isn't it lovely?'

'Getting up at three to learn to milk, bless her heart! Ye gods, why must we grow old and fat?'

'She's a darling. She has done more work under me –'

'Under *you!* The day after she came she was in charge and you were her subordinate, and you've stayed there ever since. She manages you almost as well as you manage me.'

'She doesn't, and that's why I love her. She's as direct as a man – as her brother.'

'Her brother's weaker than she is. He's always coming to me for orders; but he's honest, and a glutton for work. I confess I'm rather fond of William, and if I had a daughter –'

The talk ended there. Far away in the Derajat[28] was a child's grave more than twenty years old, and neither Jim nor his wife spoke of it any more.

'All the same, you're responsible,' Jim added, after a moment's silence.

'Bless 'em!' said Mrs Jim, sleepily.

Before the stars paled, Scott, who slept in an empty cart, waked and went about his work in silence; it seemed at that hour unkind to rouse Faiz Ullah and the interpreter. His head being close to the ground, he did not hear William till she stood over him in the dingy old riding-habit, her eyes still heavy with sleep, a cup of tea and a piece of toast in her hands. There was a baby on the ground, squirming in a piece of blanket, and a six-year-old child peered over Scott's shoulder.

'Hai, you little rip,' said Scott, 'how the deuce do you expect to get your rations if you aren't quiet?'

A cool white hand steadied the brat, who forthwith choked as the milk gurgled into his mouth.

'Mornin',' said the milker. 'You've no notion how these little fellows can wriggle.'

'Oh, yes, I have.' She whispered, because the world was asleep. 'Only I feed them with a spoon or a rag. Yours are fatter than mine . . . And you've been doing this day after day, twice a day?' The voice was almost lost.

'Yes; it was absurd. Now you try,' he said, giving place to the girl. 'Look out! A goat's not a cow.'

The goat protested against the amateur, and there was a scuffle, in which Scott snatched up the baby. Then it was all to do over again, and

William laughed softly and merrily. She managed, however, to feed two babies, and a third.

'Don't the little beggars take it well!' said Scott. 'I trained 'em.'

They were very busy and interested, when, lo! it was broad daylight, and before they knew, the camp was awake, and they kneeled among the goats, surprised by the day, both flushed to the temples. Yet all the round world rolling up out of the darkness might have heard and seen all that had passed between them.

'Oh,' said William, unsteadily, snatching up the tea and toast. 'I had this made for you. It's stone-cold now. I thought you mightn't have anything ready so early. Better not drink it. It's – it's stone-cold.'

'That's awfully kind of you. It's just right. It's awfully good of you, really. I'll leave my kids and goats with you and Mrs Jim; and, of course, anyone in camp can show you about the milking.'

'Of course,' said William; and she grew pinker and pinker and statelier and more stately, as she strode back to her tent, fanning herself vigorously with the saucer.

There were shrill lamentations through the camp when the elder children saw their nurse move off without them. Faiz Ullah unbent so far as to jest with the policemen, and Scott turned purple with shame because Hawkins, already in the saddle, roared.

A child escaped from the care of Mrs Jim, and, running like a rabbit, clung to Scott's boot, William pursuing with long, easy strides.

'I will not go – I will not go!' shrieked the child, twining his feet round Scott's ankle. 'They will kill me here. I do not know these people.'

'I say,' said Scott, in broken Tamil, 'I say, she will do you no harm. Go with her and be well fed.'

'Come!' said William, panting, with a wrathful glance at Scott, who stood helpless and, as it were, hamstrung.

'Go back,' said Scott quickly to William. 'I'll send the little chap over in a minute.'

The tone of authority had its effect, but in a way Scott did not exactly intend. The boy loosened his grasp, and said with gravity, 'I did not know the woman was thine. I will go.' Then he cried to his companions, a mob of three-, four-, and five-year-olds waiting on the success of his venture ere they stampeded: 'Go back and eat. It is our man's woman. She will obey his orders.'

Jim collapsed where he sat; Faiz Ullah and the two policemen grinned; and Scott's orders to the cartmen flew like hail.

'That is the custom of the Sahibs when truth is told in their presence,' said Faiz Ullah. 'The time comes that I must seek new service. Young wives, especially such as speak our language and have knowledge of the ways of the Police, make great trouble for honest butlers in the matter of weekly accounts.'

What William thought of it all she did not say, but when her brother, ten days later, came to camp for orders, and heard of Scott's performances, he said, laughing: 'Well, that settles it. He'll be *Bakri* Scott to the end of his days.' (*Bakri*, in the northern vernacular, means a goat.) 'What a lark! I'd have given a month's pay to have seen him nursing famine babies. I fed some with *conjee* [rice-water], but that was all right.'

'It's perfectly disgusting,' said his sister, with blazing eyes. 'A man does something like – like that – and all you other men think of is to give him an absurd nickname, and then you laugh and think it's funny.'

'Ah,' said Mrs Jim, sympathetically.

'Well, *you* can't talk, William. You christened little Miss Demby the Button-quail last cold weather; you know you did. India's the land of nicknames.'

'That's different,' William replied. 'She was only a girl, and she hadn't done anything except walk like a quail, and she *does*. But it isn't fair to make fun of a man.'

'Scott won't care,' said Martyn. 'You can't get a rise out of old Scotty. I've been trying for eight years, and you've only known him for three. How does he look?'

'He looks very well,' said William, and went away with a flushed cheek. '*Bakri* Scott, indeed!' Then she laughed to herself, for she knew the country of her service. 'But it will be *Bakri* all the same'; and she repeated it under her breath several times slowly, whispering it into favour.

When he returned to his duties on the railway, Martyn spread the name far and wide among his associates, so that Scott met it as he led his paddy-carts to war. The natives believed it to be some English title of honour, and the cart-drivers used it in all simplicity till Faiz Ullah, who did not approve of foreign japes, broke their heads. There was very little time for milking now, except at the big camps, where Jim had extended Scott's idea, and was feeding large flocks on the useless northern grains. Enough paddy had come into the Eight Districts to hold the people safe, if it were only distributed quickly; and for that purpose no one was better than the big Canal officer, who never lost his temper, never gave an unnecessary order, and never questioned an order given. Scott pressed on, saving his cattle, washing their galled necks daily, so that no time should be lost on the road; reported himself with his rice at the minor famine-sheds, unloaded, and went back light by forced night-march to the next distributing centre, to find Hawkins's unvarying telegram: 'Do it again.' And he did it again and again, and yet again, while Jim Hawkins, fifty miles away, marked off on a big map the tracks of his wheels gridironing the stricken lands. Others did well – Hawkins reported at the end that they all did well – but Scott was the most excellent, for he kept good coined rupees by him, and paid for his own cart-repairs on the spot, and ran to meet all sorts of unconsidered extras, trusting to be recouped later. Theoretically, the Government should have paid for every shoe and linchpin, for every hand employed in the loading; but Government vouchers cash themselves slowly, and intelligent and efficient clerks write at great length, contesting unauthorized expenditures of eight annas. The man who wishes to make his work a success must draw on his own bank-account of money or other things as he goes.

'I told you he'd work,' said Jimmy to his wife at the end of six weeks. 'He's been in sole charge of a couple of thousand men up north on the Mosuhl Canal for a year, and he gives one less trouble than young Martyn with his ten constables; and I'm morally certain – only Government doesn't recognize moral obligations – that he's spent about half his pay to grease his wheels. Look at this, Lizzie, for one week's work! Forty miles in two days with twelve carts; two days' halt building a famine-shed for young Rogers (Rogers ought to have built it himself, the idiot!). Then forty miles back again, loading six carts on the way, and distributing all Sunday. Then in the evening he pitches in a twenty-page demi-official to me, saying that the people where he is might be "advantageously employed on relief-work", and suggesting that he put 'em to work on some broken-down old reservoir he's discovered, so as to have a good water-supply when the Rains come. He thinks he can caulk the dam in a fortnight. Look at his marginal sketches – aren't they clear and good? I knew he was *pukka*, but I didn't know he was as *pukka* as this!'

'I must show these to William,' said Mrs Jim. 'The child's wearing herself out among the babies.'

'Not more than you are, dear. Well, another two months ought to see us out of the wood. I'm sorry it's not in my power to recommend you for a V.C.'

William sat late in her tent that night, reading through page after page of the square handwriting, patting the sketches of proposed repairs to the reservoir, and wrinkling her eyebrows over the columns of figures of estimated water-supply.

'And he finds time to do all this,' she cried to herself, 'and . . . well, I also was present. I've saved one or two babies.'

She dreamed for the twentieth time of the god in the golden dust, and woke refreshed to feed loathsome black children, scores of them, wastrels picked up by the wayside, their bones almost breaking their skin, terrible and covered with sores.

Scott was not allowed to leave his cart-work, but his letter was duly forwarded to the Government, and he had the consolation, not rare in India, of knowing that another man was reaping where he had sown. That also was discipline profitable to the soul.

'He's much too good to waste on canals,' said Jimmy. 'Anyone can oversee coolies. You needn't be angry, William: he can – but I need my pearl among bullock-drivers, and I've transferred him to the Khanda district, where he'll have it all to do over again. He should be marching now.'

'He's *not* a coolie,' said William, furiously. 'He ought to be doing his regulation work.'

'He's the best man in his service, and that's saying a good deal; but if you *must* use razors to cut grindstones, why, I prefer the best cutlery.'

'Isn't it almost time we saw him again?' said Mrs Jim. 'I'm sure the poor boy hasn't had a respectable meal for a month. He probably sits on a cart and eats sardines with his fingers.'

'All in good time, dear. Duty before decency – wasn't it Mr Chucks[29] said that?'

'No; it was Midshipman Easy,' William laughed. 'I sometimes wonder how it will feel to dance or listen to a band again, or sit under a roof. I can't believe that I ever wore a ball-frock in my life.'

'One minute,' said Mrs Jim, who was thinking. 'If he goes to Khanda, he passes within five miles of us. Of course he'll ride in.'

'Oh, no he won't,' said William.

'How do you know, dear?'

'It'll take him off his work. He won't have time.'

'He'll make it,' said Mrs Jim, with a twinkle.

'It depends on his own judgment. There's absolutely no reason why he shouldn't, if he thinks fit,' said Jim.

'He won't see fit,' William replied, without sorrow or emotion. 'It wouldn't be him if he did.'

'One certainly gets to know people rather well in times like these,' said Jim, drily; but William's face was serene as ever, and, even as she prophesied, Scott did not appear.

The Rains fell at last, late, but heavily; and the dry, gashed earth was red mud, and servants killed snakes in the camp, where everyone was weather-bound for a fortnight – all except Hawkins, who took horse and splashed about in the wet, rejoicing. Now the Government decreed that

William the Conqueror

seed-grain should be distributed to the people, as well as advances of money for the purchase of new oxen; and the white men were doubly worked for this new duty, while William skipped from brick to brick laid down on the trampled mud, and dosed her charges with warming medicines that made them rub their little round stomachs; and the milch-goats throve on the rank grass. There was never a word from Scott in the Khanda district, away to the south-east, except the regular telegraphic report to Hawkins. The rude country roads had disappeared; his drivers were half mutinous; one of Martyn's loaned policemen had died of cholera; and Scott was taking thirty grains of quinine a day to fight the fever that comes if one works hard in heavy rain; but those were things he did not consider necessary to report. He was, as usual, working from a base of supplies on a railway line, to cover a circle of fifteen miles radius, and since full loads were impossible, he took quarter-loads, and toiled four times as hard by consequence; for he did not choose to risk an epidemic which might have grown uncontrollable by assembling villagers in thousands at the relief-sheds. It was cheaper to take Government bullocks, work them to death, and leave them to the crows in the wayside sloughs.

That was the time when eight years of clean living and hard condition told, though a man's head were ringing like a bell from the cinchona,[30] and the earth swayed under his feet when he stood and under his bed when he slept. If Hawkins had seen fit to make him a bullock-driver, that, he thought, was entirely Hawkins's own affair. There were men in the North who would know what he had done; men of thirty years' service in his own department who would say that it was 'not half bad'; and above, immeasurably above all men of all grades, there was William in the thick of the fight, who would approve because she understood. He had so trained his mind that it would hold fast to the mechanical routine of the day, though his own voice sounded strange in his own ears, and his hands, when he wrote, grew large as pillows or small as peas at the end of his wrists. That steadfastness bore his body to the telegraph-office at the railway-station, and dictated a telegram to Hawkins, saying that the Khanda district was, in his judgment, now safe, and he 'waited further orders'.

The Madrassee telegraph-clerk did not approve of a large, gaunt man falling over him in a dead faint, not so much because of the weight, as because of the names and blows that Faiz Ullah dealt him when he found the body rolled under a bench. Then Faiz Ullah took blankets and quilts and coverlets where he found them, and lay down under them at his master's side, and bound his arms with a tent-rope, and filled him

341

with a horrible stew of herbs, and set the policeman to fight him when he wished to escape from the intolerable heat of his coverings, and shut the door of the telegraph-office to keep out the curious for two nights and one day; and when a light engine came down the line, and Hawkins kicked in the door, Scott hailed him weakly, but in a natural voice, and Faiz Ullah stood back and took all the credit.

'For two nights, Heaven-born, he was *pagal*,'[31] said Faiz Ullah. 'Look at my nose, and consider the eye of the policeman. He beat us with his bound hands; but we sat upon him, Heaven-born, and though his words were *tez*,[32] we sweated him. Heaven-born, never has been such a sweat! He is weaker now than a child; but the fever has gone out of him, by the grace of God. There remains only my nose and the eye of the constabeel. Sahib, shall I ask for my dismissal because my Sahib has beaten me?' And Faiz Ullah laid his long thin hand carefully on Scott's chest to be sure that the fever was all gone, ere he went out to open tinned soups and discourage such as laughed at his swelled nose.

'The district's all right,' Scott whispered. 'It doesn't make any difference. You got my wire? I shall be fit in a week. Can't understand how it happened. I shall be fit in a few days.'

'You're coming into camp with us,' said Hawkins.

'But look here – but –'

'It's all over except the shouting. We sha'n't need you Punjabis any more. On my honour, we sha'n't. Martyn goes back in a few weeks; Arbuthnot's returned already; Ellis and Clay are putting the last touches to a new feeder-line the Government's built as relief-work. Morten's dead – he was a Bengal man, though; you wouldn't know him. 'Pon my word, you and Will – Miss Martyn – seem to have come through it as well as anybody.'

'Oh, how is she?' The voice went up and down as he spoke.

'She was in great form when I left her. The Roman Catholic Missions are adopting the unclaimed babies to turn them into little priests; the Basil Mission is taking some, and the mothers are taking the rest. You should hear the little beggars howl when they're sent away from William. She's pulled down a bit, but so are we all. Now, when do you suppose you'll be able to move?'

'I can't come into camp in this state. I won't,' he replied pettishly.

'Well, you *are* rather a sight, but from what I gathered there it seemed to me they'd be glad to see you under any conditions. I'll look over your work here, if you like, for a couple of days, and you can pull yourself together while Faiz Ullah feeds you up.'

Scott could walk dizzily by the time Hawkins's inspection was ended, and he flushed all over when Jim said of his work in the district that it was 'not half bad', and volunteered, further, that he had considered Scott his right-hand man through the famine, and would feel it his duty to say as much officially.

So they came back by rail to the old camp; but there were no crowds near it, the long fires in the trenches were dead and black, and the famine-sheds stood almost empty.

'You see!' said Jim. 'There isn't much more for us to do. Better ride up and see the wife. They've pitched a tent for you. Dinner's at seven. I'll see you then.'

Riding at a foot-pace, Faiz Ullah by his stirrup, Scott came to William in the brown-calico riding-habit, sitting at the dining-tent door, her hands in her lap, white as ashes, thin and worn, with no lustre in her hair. There did not seem to be any Mrs Jim on the horizon, and all that William could say was: 'My word, how pulled down you look!'

'I've had a touch of fever. You don't look very well yourself.'

'Oh, I'm fit enough. We've stamped it out. I suppose you know?'

Scott nodded. 'We shall all be returned in a few weeks. Hawkins told me.'

'Before Christmas, Mrs Jim says. Sha'n't you be glad to go back? I can smell the wood-smoke already'; William sniffed. 'We shall be in time for all the Christmas doings. I don't suppose even the Punjab Government would be base enough to transfer Jack till the new year?'

'It seems hundreds of years ago – the Punjab and all that – doesn't it? Are you glad you came?'

'Now it's all over, yes. It has been ghastly here. You know we had to sit still and do nothing, and Sir Jim was away so much.'

'Do nothing! How did you get on with the milking?'

'I managed it somehow – after you taught me.'

Then the talk stopped with an almost audible jar. Still no Mrs Jim.

'That reminds me I owe you fifty rupees for the condensed milk. I thought perhaps you'd be coming here when you were transferred to the Khanda district, and I could pay you then; but you didn't.'

'I passed within five miles of the camp. It was in the middle of a march, you see, and the carts were breaking down every few minutes, and I couldn't get 'em over the ground till ten o'clock that night. But I wanted to come awfully. You knew I did, didn't you?'

'I – believe – I – did,' said William, facing him with level eyes. She was no longer white.

'Did you understand?'

'Why you didn't ride in? Of course I did.'

'Why?'

'Because you couldn't, of course. I knew that.'

'Did you care?'

'If you had come in – but I knew you wouldn't – but if you *had*, I should have cared a great deal. You know I should.'

'Thank God I didn't! Oh, but I wanted to! I couldn't trust myself to ride in front of the carts, because I kept edging 'em over here, don't you know?'

'I knew, you wouldn't,' said William, contentedly. 'Here's your fifty.'

Scott bent forward and kissed the hand that held the greasy notes. Its fellow patted him awkwardly but very tenderly on the head.

'And *you* knew, too, didn't you?' said William, in a new voice.

'No, on my honour, I didn't. I hadn't the – the cheek to expect anything of the kind, except . . . I say, were you out riding anywhere the day I passed by to Khanda?'

William nodded, and smiled after the manner of an angel surprised in a good deed.

'Then it was just a speck I saw of your habit in the –'

'Palm-grove on the Southern cart-road. I saw your helmet when you came up from the nullah [33] by the temple – just enough to be sure that you were all right. D'you care?'

This time Scott did not kiss her hand, for they were in the dusk of the dining-tent, and, because William's knees were trembling under her, she had to sit down in the nearest chair, where she wept long and happily, her head on her arms; and when Scott imagined that it would be well to comfort her, she needed nothing of the kind; she ran to her own tent; and Scott went out into the world, and smiled upon it largely and idiotically. But when Faiz Ullah brought him a drink, he found it necessary to support one hand with the other, or the good whisky and soda would have been spilled abroad. There are fevers and fevers.

But it was worse – much worse – the strained, eye-shirking talk at dinner till the servants had withdrawn, and worst of all when Mrs Jim, who had been on the edge of weeping from the soup down, kissed Scott and William, and they drank one whole bottle of champagne, hot, because there was no ice, and Scott and William sat outside the tent in the starlight till Mrs Jim drove them in for fear of more fever.

Apropos of these things and some others William said: 'Being engaged is abominable, because, you see, one has no official position. We must be thankful that we've lots of things to do.'

'Things to do!' said Jim, when that was reported to him. 'They're neither of them any good any more. I can't get five hours' work a day out of Scott. He's in the clouds half the time.'

'Oh, but they're so beautiful to watch, Jimmy. It will break my heart when they go. Can't you do anything for him?'

'I've given the Government the impression – at least, I hope I have – that he personally conducted the entire famine. But all he wants is to get on to the Luni Canal Works, and William's just as bad. Have you ever heard 'em talking of barrage and aprons and wastewater? It's their style of spooning, I suppose.'

Mrs Jim smiled tenderly. 'Ah, that's in the intervals – bless 'em.'

And so Love ran about the camp unrebuked in broad daylight, while men picked up the pieces and put them neatly away of the Famine in the Eight Districts.

Morning brought the penetrating chill of the Northern December, the layers of wood-smoke, the dusty grey blue of the tamarisks, the domes of ruined tombs, and all the smell of the white Northern plains, as the mail-train ran on to the mile-long Sutlej Bridge. William, wrapped in a *poshteen* – silk-embroidered sheepskin jacket trimmed with rough astrakhan – looked out with moist eyes and nostrils that dilated joyously. The South of pagodas and palm-trees, the over-populated Hindu South, was done with. Here was the land she knew and loved, and before her lay the good life she understood, among folk of her own caste and mind.

They were picking them up at almost every station now – men and women coming in for the Christmas Week, with racquets, with bundles of polo-sticks, with dear and bruised cricket-bats, with fox-terriers and saddles. The greater part of them wore jackets like William's, for the Northern cold is as little to be trifled with as the Northern heat. And William was among them and of them, her hands deep in her pockets, her collar turned up over her ears, stamping her feet on the platforms as she walked up and down to get warm, visiting from carriage to carriage, and everywhere being congratulated. Scott was with the bachelors at the far end of the train, where they chaffed him mercilessly about feeding babies and milking goats; but from time to time he would stroll up to William's window, and murmur: 'Good enough, isn't it?' and William would answer with sighs of pure delight: 'Good enough, indeed.' The large open names of the home towns were good to listen to. Umballa, Ludianah, Phillour, Jullundur, they rang like the coming marriage-bells in her ears, and William felt deeply and truly sorry for all strangers and outsiders – visitors, tourists, and those fresh-caught for the service of the country.

It was a glorious return, and when the bachelors gave the Christmas ball, William was, unofficially, you might say, the chief and honoured guest among the stewards, who could make things very pleasant for their friends. She and Scott danced nearly all the dances together, and sat out the rest in the big dark gallery overlooking the superb teak floor, where the uniforms blazed, and the spurs clinked, and the new frocks and four hundred dancers went round and round till the draped flags on the pillars flapped and bellied to the whirl of it.

About midnight half a dozen men who did not care for dancing came over from the Club to play 'Waits', and – that was a surprise the stewards had arranged – before anyone knew what had happened, the band stopped, and hidden voices broke into 'Good King Wenceslaus', and William in the gallery hummed and beat time with her foot:

> Mark my footsteps well, my page,
> Tread thou in them boldly.
> Thou shalt feel the winter's rage
> Freeze thy blood less coldly!

'Oh, I hope they are going to give us another! Isn't it pretty, coming out of the dark in that way? Look – look down. There's Mrs Gregory wiping her eyes!'

'It's like home, rather,' said Scott. 'I remember –'

'H'sh! Listen! – dear.' And it began again:

> When shepherds watched their flocks by night –

'A-h-h!' said William, drawing closer to Scott.

> All seated on the ground,
> The Angel of the Lord came down,
> And glory shone around.
> 'Fear not,' said he (for mighty dread
> Had seized their troubled mind);
> 'Glad tidings of great joy I bring
> To you and all mankind.'

This time it was William that wiped her eyes.

🍸 The Devil and the Deep Sea [1] 🍸

'All supplies very bad and dear, and there are no facilities for even the smallest repairs.'   *Sailing Directions.*

Her nationality was British, but you will not find her house-flag in the list of our mercantile marine. She was a nine-hundred ton, iron, schooner-rigged, screw cargo-boat, differing externally in no way from any other tramp of the sea. But it is with steamers as it is with men. There are those who will for a consideration sail extremely close to the wind; and, in the present state of a fallen world, such people and such steamers have their use. From the hour that the *Aglaia* first entered the Clyde – new, shiny, and innocent, with a quart of cheap champagne trickling down her cutwater – Fate and her owner, who was also her captain, decreed that she should deal with embarrassed crowned heads, fleeing Presidents, financiers of over-extended ability, women to whom change of air was imperative, and the lesser law-breaking Powers. Her career led her sometimes into the Admiralty Courts, where the sworn statements of her skipper filled his brethren with envy. The mariner cannot tell or act a lie in the face of the sea, or mislead a tempest; but, as lawyers have discovered, he makes up for chances withheld when he returns to shore, an affidavit in either hand.

The *Aglaia* figured with distinction in the great *Mackinaw* salvage case. It was her first slip from virtue, and she learned how to change her name, but not her heart, and to run across the sea. As the *Guiding Light* she was very badly wanted in a South American port for the little matter of entering harbour at full speed, colliding with a coal-hulk and the State's only man-of-war, just as that man-of-war was going to coal. She put to sea without explanations, though three forts fired at her for half an hour. As the *Julia M'Gregor* she had been concerned in picking up from a raft certain gentlemen who should have stayed in Noumea,[2] but who preferred making themselves vastly unpleasant to authority in quite another quarter of the world; and as the *Shah-in-Shah* she had been overtaken on the high seas, indecently full of munitions of war, by the cruiser of an agitated Power at issue with its neighbour. That time she was very nearly sunk, and her riddled hull gave eminent lawyers of two countries great profit. After a season she reappeared as the *Martin Hunt*, painted a dull slate colour, with pure saffron funnel, and boats of robin's-egg blue, engaging in the Odessa trade till she was invited (and the invitation could not well be disregarded) to keep away from Black Sea ports altogether.

She had ridden through many waves of depression. Freights might drop out of sight, Seamen's Unions throw spanners and nuts at certificated masters, or stevedores combine till cargo perished on the dockhead; but the boat of many names came and went, busy, alert, and inconspicuous always. Her skipper made no complaint of hard times, and port officers observed that her crew signed and signed again with the regularity of Atlantic liner boatswains. Her name she changed as occasion called; her well-paid crew never; and a large percentage of the profits of her voyages was spent with an open hand on her engine-room. She never troubled the underwriters, and very seldom stopped to talk with a signal-station; for her business was urgent and private.

But an end came to her tradings, and she perished in this manner. Deep peace brooded over Europe, Asia, Africa, America, Australasia, and Polynesia. The Powers dealt together more or less honestly; banks paid their depositors to the hour; diamonds of price came safely to the hands of their owners; republics rested content with their dictators; diplomats found no one whose presence in the least incommoded them; monarchs lived openly with their lawfully wedded wives. It was as though the whole earth had put on its best Sunday bib and tucker; and business was very bad for the *Martin Hunt*. The great, virtuous calm engulfed her, slate sides, yellow funnel, and all, but cast up in another hemisphere the steam-whaler *Haliotis*, black and rusty, with a manure-coloured funnel, a litter of dingy white boats, and an enormous stove, or furnace, for boiling blubber on her forward well-deck. There could be no doubt that her trip was successful, for she lay at several ports not too well known, and the smoke of her trying-out [3] insulted the beaches.

Anon she departed, at the speed of the average London four-wheeler, and entered a semi-inland sea, warm, still, and blue, which is, perhaps, the most strictly preserved water in the world. There she stayed for a certain time, and the great stars of those mild skies beheld her playing puss-in-the-corner among islands where whales are never found. All that time she smelt abominably, and the smell, though fishy, was not wholesome. One evening calamity descended upon her from the island of Pygang-Watai, and she fled, while her crew jeered at a fat black-and-brown gunboat puffing far behind. They knew to the last revolution the capacity of every boat, on those seas, that they were anxious to avoid. A British ship with a good conscience does not, as a rule, flee from the man-of-war of a foreign Power, and it is also considered a breach of etiquette to stop and search British ships at sea. These things the skipper of the *Haliotis* did not pause to prove, but held on at an inspiriting eleven knots an hour till nightfall. One thing only he overlooked.

The Power that kept an expensive steam-patrol moving up and down those waters (they had dodged the two regular ships of the station with an ease that bred contempt) had newly brought up a third and a fourteen-knot boat with a clean bottom to help the work; and that was why the *Haliotis*, driving hard from the east to the west, found herself at daylight in such a position that she could not help seeing an arrangement of four flags, a mile and a half behind, which read: 'Heave to, or take the consequences!'

She had her choice, and she took it, and the end came when, presuming on her lighter draught, she tried to draw away northward over a friendly shoal. The shell that arrived by way of the Chief Engineer's cabin was some five inches in diameter, with a practice, not a bursting, charge. It had been intended to cross her bows, and that was why it knocked the framed portrait of the Chief Engineer's wife – and she was a very pretty girl – on to the floor, splintered his wash-hand stand, crossed the alleyway into the engine-room, and striking on a grating, dropped directly in front of the forward engine, where it burst, neatly fracturing both the bolts that held the connecting-rod to the forward crank.

What follows is worth consideration. The forward engine had no more work to do. Its released piston-rod, therefore, drove up fiercely, with nothing to check it, and started most of the nuts of the cylinder-cover. It came down again, the full weight of the steam behind it, and the foot of the disconnected connecting-rod, useless as the leg of a man with a sprained ankle, flung out to the right and struck the starboard, or right-hand, cast-iron supporting-column of the forward engine, cracking it clean through about six inches above the base, and wedging the upper portion outwards three inches towards the ship's side. There the connecting-rod jammed. Meantime, the after engine, being as yet un-embarrassed, went on with its work, and in so doing brought round at its next revolution the crank of the forward engine, which smote the already jammed connecting-rod, bending it and therewith the piston-rod cross-head – the big cross-piece that slides up and down so smoothly.

The cross-head jammed sideways in the guides, and, in addition to putting further pressure on the already broken starboard supporting column, cracked the port, or left-hand supporting column in two or three places. There being nothing more that could be made to move, the engines brought up, all standing, with a hiccup that seemed to lift the *Haliotis* a foot out of the water; and the engine-room staff, opening every steam outlet that they could find in the confusion, arrived on deck somewhat scalded, but calm. There was a sound below of things happening – a rushing, clicking, purring, grunting, rattling noise that did not last for more than a minute. It was the machinery adjusting itself on the spur of the moment, to a hundred altered conditions. Mr Wardrop, one foot on the upper grating, inclined his ear sideways, and groaned. You cannot stop engines working at twelve knots an hour in three seconds without disorganizing them. The *Haliotis* slid forward in a cloud of steam, shrieking like a wounded horse. There was nothing more to do. The five-inch shell with a reduced charge had settled the situation. And when you are full, all three holds, of strictly preserved pearls; when you have cleaned out the Tanna Bank, the Sea-Horse Bank, and four other banks from one end to the other of the Amanala Sea – when you have ripped out the very heart of a rich Government monopoly so that five years will not repair your wrong-doings – you must smile and take what is in store. But the skipper reflected, as a launch put out from the man-of-war, that he had been bombarded on the high seas, with the British flag – several of them – picturesquely disposed above him, and tried to find comfort in the thought.

'Where,' said the stolid naval lieutenant hoisting himself aboard, 'where are those dam' pearls?'

They were there beyond evasion. No affidavit could do away with the fearful smell of decayed oysters, the diving-dresses, and the shell-littered hatches. They were there to the value of seventy thousand pounds, more or less; and every pound poached.

The man-of-war was annoyed; for she had used up many tons of coal, she had strained her tubes, and, worse than all, her officers and crew had been hurried. Everyone on the *Haliotis* was arrested and rearrested several times, as each officer came aboard; then they were told by what they esteemed to be the equivalent of a midshipman that they were to consider themselves prisoners, and finally were put under arrest.

'It's not the least good,' said the skipper, suavely. 'You'd much better send us a tow –'

'Be still – you are arrest!' was the reply.

'Where the devil do you expect we are going to escape to? We're helpless. You've got to tow us into somewhere, and explain why you fired on us. Mr Wardrop, we're helpless, aren't we?'

'Ruined from end to end,' said the man of machinery. 'If she rolls, the forward cylinder will come down and go through her bottom. Both columns are clean cut through. There's nothing to hold anything up.'

The council of war clanked off to see if Mr Wardrop's words were true. He warned them that it was as much as a man's life was worth to enter the engine-room, and they contented themselves with a distant inspection through the thinning steam. The *Haliotis* lifted to the long, easy swell, and the starboard supporting-column ground a trifle, as a man grits his teeth under the knife. The forward cylinder was depending on that unknown force men call the pertinacity of materials, which now and then balances that other heartbreaking power, the perversity of inanimate things.

'You see!' said Mr Wardrop, hurrying them away. 'The engines aren't worth their price as old iron.'

'We tow,' was the answer. 'Afterwards we shall confiscate.'

The man-of-war was short-handed, and did not see the necessity for putting a prize-crew aboard the *Haliotis*. So she sent one sub-lieutenant, whom the skipper kept very drunk, for he did not wish to make the tow too easy, and, moreover, he had an inconspicuous little rope hanging from the stern of his ship.

Then they began to tow at an average speed of four knots an hour. The *Haliotis* was very hard to move, and the gunnery-lieutenant, who had fired the five-inch shell, had leisure to think upon consequences. Mr Wardrop was the busy man. He borrowed all the crew to shore up the cylinders, with spars and blocks, from the bottom and sides of the ship. It was a day's risky work; but anything was better than drowning at the end of a tow-rope; and if the forward cylinder had fallen, it would have made its way to the sea-bed, and taken the *Haliotis* after.

'Where are we going to, and how long will they tow us?' he asked of the skipper.

'God knows! and this prize-lieutenant's drunk. What do you think you can do?'

'There's just the bare chance,' Mr Wardrop whispered, though no one was within hearing – 'there's just the bare chance o' repairin' her, if a man knew how. They've twisted the very guts out of her, bringing her up with that jerk; but I'm saying that, with time and patience, there's just the chance of making steam yet. *We* could do it.'

The skipper's eye brightened. 'Do you mean,' he began, 'that she is any good?'

'Oh no,' said Mr Wardrop. 'She'll need three thousand pounds in repairs, at the lowest, if she's to take the sea again, an' that apart from any injury to her structure. She's like a man fallen down five pair o' stairs. We can't tell for months what has happened; but we know she'll never be good again without a new inside. Ye should see the condenser-tubes an' the steam connections to the donkey,[4] for two things only. I'm not afraid of them repairin' her. I'm afraid of them stealin' things.'

'They've fired on us. They'll have to explain that.'

'Our reputation's not good enough to ask for explanations. Let's take what we have and be thankful. Ye would not have consuls rememberin' the *Guidin' Light*, an' the *Shah-in-Shah*, an' the *Aglaia* at this most alarmin' crisis. We've been no better than pirates these ten years. Under Providence we're no worse than thieves now. We've much to be thankful for – if we e'er get back to her.'

'Make it your own way, then,' said the skipper, 'if there's the least chance –'

'I'll leave none,' said Mr Wardrop – 'none that they'll dare to take. Keep her heavy on the tow, for we need time.'

The skipper never interfered with the affairs of the engine-room, and Mr Wardrop – an artist in his profession – turned to and composed a work terrible and forbidding. His background was the dark-grained sides of the engine-room; his material the metals of power and strength, helped out with spars, baulks, and ropes. The man-of-war towed sullenly and viciously. The *Haliotis* behind her hummed like a hive before swarming. With extra and totally unneeded spars her crew blocked up the space round the forward engine till it resembled a statue in its scaffolding, and the butts of the shores interfered with every view that a dispassionate eye might wish to take. And that the dispassionate mind might be swiftly shaken out of its calm, the well-sunk bolts of the shores were wrapped round untidily with loose ends of ropes, giving a studied effect of most dangerous insecurity. Next, Mr Wardrop took up a collection from the after engine, which, as you will remember, had not been affected in the general wreck. The cylinder escape-valve he abolished with a flogging-hammer. It is difficult in far-off ports to come by such valves, unless, like Mr Wardrop, you keep duplicates in store. At the same time men took off the nuts of two of the great holding-down bolts that serve to keep the engines in place on their solid bed. An engine violently arrested in mid-career may easily jerk off the nut of a holding-down bolt, and this accident looked very natural.

Passing along the tunnel, he removed several shaft coupling-bolts and nuts, scattering other and ancient pieces of iron under foot. Cylinder-bolts he cut off to the number of six from the after engine cylinder, so that it might match its neighbour, and stuffed the bilge- and feed-pumps with cotton-waste. Then he made a neat bundle of the various odds and ends that he had gathered from the engines – little things like nuts and valve-spindles, all carefully tallowed – and retired with them under the floor of the engine-room, where he sighed, being fat, as he passed from manhole to manhole of the double bottom, and in a fairly dry submarine compartment hid them. Any engineer, particularly in an unfriendly port, has a right to keep his spare stores where he chooses; and the foot of one of the cylinder shores blocked all entrance into the regular storeroom, even if that had not been already closed with steel wedges. In conclusion, he disconnected the after engine, laid piston and connecting-rod, carefully tallowed, where it would be most inconvenient to the casual visitor, took out three of the eight collars of the thrust-block, hid them where only he could find them again, filled the boilers by hand, wedged the sliding doors of the coal-bunkers, and rested from his labours. The engine-room was a cemetery, and it did not need the contents of an ash-lift through the skylight to make it any worse.

He invited the skipper to look at the completed work.

'Saw ye ever such a forsaken wreck as that?' said he proudly. 'It almost frights *me* to go under those shores. Now, what d'you think they'll do to us?'

'Wait till we see,' said the skipper. 'It'll be bad enough when it comes.'

He was not wrong. The pleasant days of towing ended all too soon, though the *Haliotis* trailed behind her a heavily weighted jib stayed out into the shape of a pocket; and Mr Wardrop was no longer an artist of imagination, but one of seven-and-twenty prisoners in a prison full of insects. The man-of-war had towed them to the nearest port, not to the headquarters of the colony, and when Mr Wardrop saw the dismal little harbour, with its ragged line of Chinese junks, its one crazy tug, and the boat-building shed that, under the charge of a philosophical Malay, represented a dockyard, he sighed and shook his head.

'I did well,' he said. 'This is the habitation o' wreckers an' thieves. We're at the uttermost ends of the earth. Think you they'll ever know in England?'

'Doesn't look like it,' said the skipper.

They were marched ashore with what they stood up in, under a generous escort, and were judged according to the customs of the country, which, though excellent, are a little out of date. There were the pearls; there were the poachers; and there sat a small but hot Governor. He consulted for a while, and then things began to move with speed, for he did not wish to keep a hungry crew at large on the beach, and the man-of-war had gone up the coast. With a wave of his hand – a stroke of the pen was not necessary – he consigned them to the *blakgang-tana*, the black-country, and the hand of the Law removed them from his sight and the knowledge of men. They were marched into the palms, and the black-country swallowed them up – all the crew of the *Haliotis*.

Deep peace continued to brood over Europe, Asia, Africa, America, Australasia, and Polynesia.

It was the firing that did it. They should have kept their counsel, but when a few thousand foreigners are bursting with joy over the fact that a ship under the British flag had been fired at on the high seas, news travels quickly; and when it came out that the pearl stealing crew had not been allowed access to their consul (there was no consul within a few hundred miles of that lonely port) even the friendliest of Powers has a right to ask questions. The great heart of the British public was beating furiously on account of the performance of a notorious race-horse, and had not a throb to waste on distant accidents; but somewhere deep in the hull of the ship of State there is machinery which more or less accurately takes charge of foreign affairs. That machinery began to revolve, and who so shocked and surprised as the Power that had captured the *Haliotis*? It explained that colonial governors and far-away men-of-war were difficult to control, and promised that it would most certainly make an example both of the Governor and the vessel. As for the crew, reported to be pressed into military service in tropical climes, it would produce them as soon as possible, and it would apologize, if necessary. Now, no apologies were needed. When one nation apologizes to another, millions of amateurs who have no earthly concern with the difficulty hurl themselves into the strife and embarrass the trained specialist. It was requested that the crew be found, if they were still alive – they had been eight months beyond knowledge – and it was promised that all would be forgotten.

The little Governor of the little port was pleased with himself. Seven-and-twenty white men made a very compact force to throw away on a war that had neither beginning nor end – a jungle-and-stockade fight that flickered and smouldered through the wet, hot years in the hills a hundred miles away, and was the heritage of every wearied official. He had, he thought, deserved well of his country; and if only someone would buy the unhappy *Haliotis*, moored in the harbour below his verandah, his cup would be full. He looked at the neatly silvered lamps that he had taken from her cabins, and thought of much that might be turned to account. But his countrymen in that moist climate had no spirit. They would peep into the silent engine room, and shake their heads. Even the men-of-war would not tow her farther up the coast, where the Governor believed that she could be repaired. She was a bad bargain; but her cabin carpets were undeniably beautiful, and his wife approved of her mirrors.

Three hours later cables were bursting round him like shells, for, though he knew it not, he was being offered as a sacrifice by the nether to the upper millstone, and his superiors had no regard for his feelings. He had, said the cables, grossly exceeded his power, and failed to report on events. He would, therefore – at this he cast himself back in his hammock – produce the crew of the *Haliotis*. He would send for them, and, if that failed, he would put his dignity on a pony and fetch them himself. He had no conceivable right to make pearl-poachers serve in any war. He would be held responsible.

Next morning the cables wished to know whether he had found the crew of the *Haliotis*. They were to be found, freed and fed – he was to feed them – till such time as they could be sent to the nearest English port in a man-of-war. If you abuse a man long enough in great words flashed over the sea-beds, things happen. The Governor sent inland swiftly for his prisoners, who were also soldiers; and never was a militia regiment more anxious to reduce its strength. No power short of death could make these mad men wear the uniform of their service. They would not fight, except with their fellows, and it was for that reason the regiment had not gone to war, but stayed in a stockade, reasoning with the new troops. The autumn campaign had been a fiasco, but here were the Englishmen. All the regiment marched back to guard them, and the hairy enemy, armed with blow-pipes, rejoiced in the forest. Five of the crew had died, but there lined up on the Governor's verandah two-and-twenty men marked about the legs with the scars of leech-bites. A few of them wore fringes that had once been trousers; the others used loin-cloths of gay patterns; and they existed beautifully but simply in the Governor's verandah; and when he came out they sang at him. When you have lost seventy thousand pounds' worth of pearls, your pay, your ship, and all your clothes, and have lived in bondage for eight months beyond the faintest pretences of civilization, you know what true independence means, for you become the happiest of created things – natural man.

The Governor told the crew that they were evil, and they asked for food. When he saw how they ate, and when he remembered that none of the pearl patrol-boats were expected for two months, he sighed. But the crew of the *Haliotis* lay down in the verandah, and said that they were pensioners of the Governor's bounty. A grey-bearded man, fat and bald-headed, his one garment a green and yellow loin-cloth, saw the *Haliotis* in the harbour, and bellowed with joy. The men crowded to the verandah-rail, kicking aside the long cane chairs. They pointed, gesticulated, and argued freely, without shame. The militia regiment sat down in the Governor's garden. The Governor retired to his hammock – it was as easy to be killed lying as standing – and his women squeaked from the shuttered rooms.

'She sold?' said the grey-bearded man, pointing to the *Haliotis*. He was Mr Wardrop.

'No good,' said the Governor, shaking his head. 'No one come buy.'

'He's taken my lamps, though,' said the skipper. He wore one leg of a pair of trousers, and his eyes wandered along the verandah. The Governor quailed. There were cuddy⁵ camp-stools and the skipper's writing-table in plain sight.

'They've cleaned her out, o' course,' said Mr Wardrop. 'They would. We'll go aboard and take an inventory. See!' He waved his hands over the harbour. 'We – live – there – now. Sorry?'

The Governor smiled a smile of relief.

'He's glad of that,' said one of the crew, reflectively. 'I don't wonder.'

They flocked down to the harbour-front, the militia regiment clattering behind, and embarked themselves in what they found – it happened to be the Governor's boat. Then they disappeared over the bulwarks of the *Haliotis*, and the Governor prayed that they might find occupation inside.

Mr Wardrop's first bound took him to the engine-room; and when the others were patting the well-remembered decks, they heard him giving God thanks that things were as he had left them. The wrecked engines stood over his head untouched; no inexpert hand had meddled with his shores; the steel wedges of the store-room were rusted home; and, best of all, the hundred and sixty tons of good Australian coal in the bunkers had not diminished.

'I don't understand it,' said Mr Wardrop. 'Any Malay knows the use o' copper. They ought to have cut away the pipes. And with Chinese junks coming here, too. It's a special interposition o' Providence.'

'You think so,' said the skipper, from above. 'There's only been one thief here, and he's cleaned her out of all *my* things, anyhow.'

Here the skipper spoke less than the truth, for under the planking of his cabin, only to be reached by a chisel, lay a little money which never drew any interest – his sheet-anchor to windward. It was all in clean sovereigns that pass current the world over, and might have amounted to more than a hundred pounds.

'He's left me alone. Let's thank God,' repeated Mr Wardrop.

'He's taken everything else; look!'

The *Haliotis*, except as to her engine-room, had been systematically and scientifically gutted from one end to the other, and there was strong evidence that an unclean guard had camped in the skipper's cabin to regulate that plunder. She lacked glass, plate, crockery, cutlery, mattresses, cuddy carpets and chairs, all boats, and her copper ventilators. These things had been removed, with her sails and as much of the wire rigging as would not imperil the safety of the masts.

'He must have sold those,' said the skipper. 'The other things are in his house, I suppose.'

Every fitting that could be prized or screwed out was gone. Port, starboard, and masthead lights; teak gratings; sliding sashes of the deckhouse; the captain's chest of drawers, with charts and chart-table; photographs, brackets, and looking-glasses; cabin doors; rubber cuddy-mats; hatch-irons; half the funnel-stays; cork fenders; carpenter's grindstone and tool-chest; holy-stones, swabs, squeegees; all cabin and pantry lamps; galley fittings *en bloc*; flags and flag-locker; clocks, chronometers; the forward compass and the ship's bell and belfry, were among the missing.

There were great scarred marks on the deck-planking, over which the cargo-derricks had been hauled. One must have fallen by the way, for the bulwark-rails were smashed and bent and the side-plates bruised.

'It's the Governor,' said the skipper. 'He's been selling her on the instalment plan.'

'Let's go up with spanners and shovels, and kill 'em all,' shouted the crew. 'Let's drown him, and keep the woman!'

'Then we'll be shot by that black-and-tan regiment – *our* regiment. What's the trouble ashore? They've camped our regiment on the beach.'

'We're cut off, that's all. Go and see what they want,' said Mr Wardrop. 'You've the trousers.'

In his simple way the Governor was a strategist. He did not desire that the crew of the *Haliotis* should come ashore again, either singly or in detachments, and he proposed to turn their steamer into a convict-hulk. They would wait – he explained this from the quay to the skipper in the barge – and they would continue to wait till the man-of-war came along, exactly where they were. If one of them set foot ashore, the entire regiment would open fire, and he would not scruple to use the two cannon of the town. Meantime food would be sent daily in a boat under an armed escort. The skipper, bare to the waist, and rowing, could only grind his teeth; and the Governor improved the occasion, and revenged himself for the bitter words in the cables, by telling what he thought of the morals and manners of the crew. The barge returned to the *Haliotis* in silence, and the skipper climbed aboard, white on the cheek-bones and blue about the nostrils.

'I knew it,' said Mr Wardrop; 'and they won't give us good food, either. We shall have bananas morning, noon, and night, an' a man can't work on fruit. *We* know that.'

Then the skipper cursed Mr Wardrop for importing frivolous side-issues into the conversation; and the crew cursed one another, and the *Haliotis*, the voyage, and all that they knew or could bring to mind. They sat down in silence on the empty decks, and their eyes burned in their heads. The green harbour water chuckled at them overside. They looked at the palm-fringed hills inland, at the white houses above the harbour road, at the single tier of native craft by the quay, at the stolid soldiery sitting round the two cannon, and, last of all, at the blue bar of the horizon. Mr Wardrop was buried in thought, and scratched imaginary lines with his untrimmed finger-nails on the planking.

'I make no promise,' he said at last, 'for I can't say what may or may not have happened to them. But here's the ship, and here's us.'

There was a little scornful laughter at this, and Mr Wardrop knitted his brows. He recalled that in the days when he wore trousers he had been chief engineer of the *Haliotis*.

'Harland, Mackesy, Noble, Hay, Naughton, Fink, O'Hara, Trumbull.'

'Here, sir!' The instinct of obedience waked to answer the roll-call of the engine-room.

'Below!'

They rose and went.

'Captain, I'll trouble you for the rest of the men as I want them. We'll get my stores out, and clear away the shores we don't need, and then we'll patch her up. *My* men will remember that they're in the *Haliotis* — under me.'

He went into the engine-room, and the others stared. They were used to the accidents of the sea, but this was beyond their experience. None who had seen the engine-room believed that anything short of new engines from end to end could stir the *Haliotis* from her moorings.

The engine-room stores were unearthed, and Mr Wardrop's face, red with the filth of the bilges and the exertion of travelling on his stomach, lit with joy. The spare gear of the *Haliotis* had been unusually complete, and two-and-twenty men, armed with screw-jacks, differential blocks, tackle, vices, and a forge or so, can look Kismet [6] between the eyes without winking. The crew were ordered to replace the holding-down and shaft-bearing bolts, and return the collars of the thrust-block. When they had finished, Mr Wardrop delivered a lecture on repairing compound engines without the aid of the shops, and the men sat about on the cold machinery. The cross-head jammed in the guides leered at them drunkenly, but offered no help. They ran their fingers hopelessly into the cracks of the starboard supporting-column, and picked at the ends of the ropes round the shores, while Mr Wardrop's voice rose and fell echoing, till the quick tropic night closed down over the engine-room skylight.

Next morning the work of reconstruction began.

It has been explained that the foot of the connecting-rod was forced against the foot of the starboard supporting-column, which it had cracked through and driven outward towards the ship's skin. To all appearance the job was more than hopeless, for rod and column seemed to have been welded into one. But herein Providence smiled on them for one moment to hearten them through the weary weeks ahead. The second engineer – more reckless than resourceful – struck at random with a cold chisel into the cast-iron of the column, and a greasy, grey flake of metal flew from under the imprisoned foot of the connecting-rod, while the rod itself fell away slowly, and brought up with a thunderous clang somewhere in the dark of the crank-pit. The guide-plates above were still jammed fast in the guides, but the first blow had been struck. They spent the rest of the day grooming the donkey-engine, which stood immediately forward of the engine-room hatch. Its tarpaulin, of course, had been stolen, and eight warm months had not improved the working parts. Further, the last dying hiccup of the *Haliotis* seemed – or it might have been the Malay from the boat-house – to have lifted the thing bodily on its bolts, and set it down inaccurately as regarded its steam connections.

'If we only had one single cargo-derrick!' Mr Wardrop sighed. 'We can take the cylinder-cover off by hand, if we sweat; but to get the rod out o' the piston's not possible unless we use steam. Well, there'll be steam the morn, if there's nothing else. She'll fizzle!'

Next morning men from the shore saw the *Haliotis* through a cloud, for it was as though the decks smoked. Her crew were chasing steam through the shaken and leaky pipes to its work in the forward donkey-engine; and where oakum failed to plug a crack, they stripped off their loin-cloths for lapping, and swore, half-boiled and mother-naked. The donkey-engine worked – at a price – the price of constant attention and furious stoking – worked long enough to allow a wire rope (it was made up of a funnel and a foremast-stay) to be led into the engine-room and made fast on the cylinder-cover of the forward engine. That rose easily enough, and was hauled through the skylight and on to the deck; many hands assisting the doubtful steam. Then came the tug of war, for it was necessary to get to the piston and the jammed piston-rod. They removed two of the piston junk-ring studs, screwed in two strong iron eye-bolts by way of handles, doubled the wire rope, and set half-a-dozen men to smite with an extemporized battering-ram at the end of the piston-rod, where it peered through the piston, while the donkey-engine hauled upwards on the piston itself. After four hours of this killing work the piston-rod suddenly slipped, and the piston rose with a jerk, knocking one or two men over into the engine-room. But when Mr Wardrop declared that the piston had not split, they cheered, and thought nothing of their wounds; and the donkey-engine was hastily stopped: its boiler was no thing to tamper with.

And day by day their supplies reached them by boat. The skipper humbled himself once more before the Governor, and as a concession had leave to get drinking-water from the Malay boat-builder on the quay. It was not good drinking-water, but the Malay was anxious to supply anything in his power, if he were paid for it.

Now, when the jaws of the forward engine stood, as it were, stripped and empty, they began to wedge up the shores of the cylinder itself. That work alone filled the better part of three days – warm and sticky days, when the hands slipped and sweat ran into the eyes. When the last wedge was hammered home there was no longer an ounce of weight on the supporting-columns; and Mr Wardrop rummaged the ship for boiler-plate three-quarters of an inch thick, where he could find it. There was not much available, but what there was was more than beaten gold to him. In one desperate forenoon the entire crew, naked and lean, haled back, more or less into place, the starboard supporting-column, which, as you remember, was cracked clean through. Mr Wardrop found them asleep where they had finished the work, and gave them a day's rest, smiling upon them as a father while he drew chalk-marks about the cracks. They woke to new and more trying labour; for over each one of those cracks a plate of three-quarter-inch boiler-iron was to be worked hot, the rivet-holes being drilled by hand. All that time they were fed on fruits, chiefly bananas, with some sago.

Those were the days when men swooned over the ratchet-drill and the hand-forge, and where they fell they had leave to lie unless their bodies were in the way of their fellows' feet. And so, patch upon patch, and a patch over all, the starboard supporting-column was clouted; but when they thought all was secure, Mr Wardrop decreed that the noble patchwork would never support working engines: at the best, it could only hold the guide-bars approximately true. The dead weight of the cylinders must be borne by vertical struts; and, therefore, a gang would repair to the bows, and take out, with files, the big bow-anchor davits, each of which was some three inches in diameter. They threw hot coals at Wardrop, and threatened to kill him, those who did not weep (they were ready to weep on the least provocation); but he hit them with iron bars heated at the end, and they limped forward, and the davits came with them when they returned. They slept sixteen hours on the strength of it, and in three days two struts were in place, bolted from the foot of the starboard supporting-column to the under side of the cylinder. There remained now the port, or condenser-column, which, though not so badly cracked as its fellow, had also been strengthened in four places with boiler-plate patches, but needed struts. They took away the main stanchions of the bridge for that work, and, crazy with toil, did not see till all was in place that the rounded bars of iron must be flattened from top to bottom to allow the air-pump levers to clear them. It was Wardrop's oversight, and he wept bitterly before the men as he gave the order to unbolt the struts and flatten them with hammer and the flame. Now the broken engine was underpinned firmly, and they took away the wooden shores from under the cylinders, and gave them to the robbed bridge, thanking God for even half a day's work on gentle, kindly wood instead of the iron that had entered into their souls. Eight months in the back-country among the leeches, at a temperature of 85° moist, is very bad for the nerves.

They had kept the hardest work to the last, as boys save Latin prose, and, worn though they were, Mr Wardrop did not dare to give them rest. The piston-rod and connecting-rod were to be straightened, and this was a job for a regular dockyard with every appliance. They fell to it, cheered by a little chalk-showing of work done and time consumed which Mr Wardrop wrote up on the engine-room bulkhead. Fifteen days had gone – fifteen days of killing labour – and there was hope before them.

It is curious that no man knows how the rods were straightened. The crew of the *Haliotis* remember that week very dimly, as a fever patient remembers the delirium of a long night. There were fires everywhere, they say; the whole ship was one consuming furnace, and the hammers were never still. Now, there could not have been more than one fire at the most, for Mr Wardrop distinctly recalls that no straightening was done except under his own eye. They remember, too, that for many years voices gave orders which they obeyed with their bodies, but their minds were abroad on all the seas. It seems to them that they stood through days and nights slowly sliding a bar backwards and forwards through a white glow that was part of the ship. They remember an intolerable noise in their burning heads from the walls of the stoke-hole, and they remember being savagely beaten by men whose eyes seemed asleep. When their shift was over they would draw straight lines in the air, anxiously and repeatedly, and would question one another in their sleep, crying, 'Is she straight?'

At last – they do not remember whether this was by day or by night – Mr Wardrop began to dance clumsily, and wept the while; and they too danced and wept, and went to sleep twitching all over; and when they woke, men said that the rods were straightened, and no one did any work for two days, but lay on the decks and ate fruit. Mr Wardrop would go below from time to time, and pat the two rods where they lay, and they heard him singing hymns.

Then his trouble of mind went from him, and at the end of the third day's idleness he made a drawing in chalk upon the deck, with letters of the alphabet at the angles. He pointed out that, though the piston-rod was more or less straight, the piston-rod cross-head – the thing that had been jammed sideways in the guides – had been badly strained, and had cracked the lower end of the piston-rod. He was going to forge and shrink a wrought-iron collar on the neck of the piston-rod where it joined the cross-head, and from the collar he would bolt a Y-shaped piece of iron whose lower arms should be bolted into the cross-head. If anything more were needed, they could use up the last of the boiler-plate.

So the forges were lit again, and men burned their bodies, but hardly felt the pain. The finished connection was not beautiful, but it seemed strong enough – at least, as strong as the rest of the machinery; and with that job their labours came to an end. All that remained was to connect up the engines, and to get food and water. The skipper and four men dealt with the Malay boat-builder – by night chiefly; it was no time to haggle over the price of sago and dried fish. The others stayed aboard and replaced piston, piston-rod, cylinder-cover, cross-head, and bolts, with the aid of the faithful donkey-engine. The cylinder-cover was hardly steam-proof, and the eye of science might have seen in the connecting-rod a flexure something like that of a Christmas-tree candle which has melted and been straightened by hand over a stove, but, as Mr Wardrop said, 'She didn't hit anything.'

As soon as the last bolt was in place, men tumbled over one another in their anxiety to get to the hand starting-gear, the wheel and the worm,[7] by which some engines can be moved when there is no steam aboard.

They nearly wrenched off the wheel, but it was evident to the blindest eye that the engines stirred. They did not revolve in their orbits with any enthusiasm, as good machines should; indeed, they groaned not a little; but they moved over and came to rest in a way which proved that they still recognized man's hand. Then Mr Wardrop sent his slaves into the darker bowels of the engine-room and the stoke-hole, and followed them with a flare-lamp. The boilers were sound, but would take no harm from a little scaling and cleaning. Mr Wardrop would not have anyone over-zealous, for he feared what the next stroke of the tool might show. 'The less we know about her now,' said he, 'the better for us all, I'm thinkin'. Ye'll understand me when I say that this is in no sense regular en-gineerin'.'

As his raiment, when he spoke, was his grey beard and uncut hair, they believed him. They did not ask too much of what they met, but polished and tallowed and scraped it to a false brilliancy.

'A lick of paint would make me easier in my mind,' said Mr Wardrop, plaintively. 'I know half the condenser-tubes are started; and the pro-peller-shaftin' 's God knows how far out of the true, and we'll need a new air-pump, an' the main-steam leaks like a sieve, and there's worse each way I look; but – paint's like clothes to a man, an' ours is near all gone.'

The skipper unearthed some stale ropy paint of the loathsome green that they used for the galleys of sailing-ships, and Mr Wardrop spread it abroad lavishly to give the engines self-respect.

His own was returning day by day, for he wore his loin-cloth continu-ously; but the crew, having worked under orders, did not feel as he did. The completed work satisfied Mr Wardrop. He would at the last have made shift to run to Singapore, and gone home, without vengeance taken, to show his engines to his brethren in the craft; but the others and the captain forbade him. They had not yet recovered their self-respect.

'It would be safer to make what ye might call a trial trip, but beggars mustn't be choosers; an' if the engines will go over to the hand gear, the probability – I'm only saying it's a probability – the chance is that they'll hold up when we put steam on her.'

'How long will you take to get steam?' said the skipper.

'God knows! Four hours – a day – half a week. If I can raise sixty pound I'll not complain.'

'Be sure of her first; we can't afford to go out half a mile, and break down.'

'My soul and body, man, we're one continous breakdown, fore an' aft! We might fetch Singapore, though.'

'We'll break down at Pygang-Watai, where we can do good,' was the answer, in a voice that did not allow argument. 'She's *my* boat, and – I've had eight months to think in.'

No man saw the *Haliotis* depart, though many heard her. She left at two in the morning, having cut her moorings, and it was none of her crew's pleasure that the engines should strike up a thundering half-seas-over chanty that echoed among the hills. Mr Wardrop wiped away a tear as he listened to the new song.

'She's gibberin' – she's just gibberin',' he whimpered. 'Yon's the voice of a maniac.'

And if engines have any soul, as their masters believe, he was quite right. There were outcries and clamours, sobs and bursts of chattering laughter, silences where the trained ear yearned for the clear note, and torturing reduplications where there should have been one deep voice. Down the screw-shaft ran murmurs and warnings, while a heart-diseased flutter without told that the propeller needed re-keying.

'How does she make it?' said the skipper.

'She moves, but – but she's breakin' my heart. The sooner we're at Pygang-Watai, the better. She's mad, and we're waking the town.'

'Is she at all near safe?'

'What do *I* care how safe she is! She's mad. Hear that, now! To be sure, nothing's hittin' anything, and the bearin's are fairly cool, but – can ye not hear?'

'If she goes,' said the skipper, 'I don't care a curse. And she's *my* boat, too.'

She went, trailing a fathom of weed behind her. From a slow two knots an hour she crawled up to a triumphant four. Anything beyond that made the struts quiver dangerously, and filled the engine-room with steam. Morning showed her out of sight of land, and there was a visible ripple under her bows; but she complained bitterly in her bowels, and, as though the noise had called it, there shot along across the purple sea a swift, dark proa,[8] hawk-like and curious, which presently ranged alongside and wished to know if the *Haliotis* were helpless. Ships, even the steamers of the white men, had been known to break down in those waters, and the honest Malay and Javanese traders[9] would sometimes aid them in their own peculiar way. But this ship was not full of lady passengers and well-dressed officers. Men, white, naked and savage, swarmed down her sides – some with red-hot iron bars and others with large hammers – threw themselves upon those innocent inquiring strangers, and, before any man could say what had happened, were in full possession of the proa, while the lawful owners bobbed in the water overside. Half an hour later the proa's cargo of sago and tripang,[10] as well as a doubtful-minded compass, was in the *Haliotis*. The two huge triangular mat sails, with their seventy-foot yards, had followed the cargo, and were being fitted to the stripped masts of the steamer.

They rose, they swelled, they filled, and the empty steamer visibly laid over as the wind took them. They gave her nearly three knots an hour, and what better could men ask? But if she had been forlorn before, this new purchase made her horrible to see. Imagine a respectable charwoman in the tights of a ballet-dancer rolling drunk along the streets, and you will come to some faint notion of the appearance of that nine-hundred-ton well-decked once schooner-rigged cargo-boat as she staggered under her new help, shouting and raving across the deep. With steam and sail that marvellous voyage continued; and the bright-eyed crew looked over the rail, desolate, unkempt, unshorn, shamelessly clothed – beyond the decencies.

At the end of the third week she sighted the island of Pygang-Watai, whose harbour is the turning-point of a pearling sea-patrol. Here the gunboats stay for a week ere they retrace their line. There is no village at Pygang-Watai, only a stream of water, some palms, and a harbour safe to rest in till the first violence of the south-east monsoon has blown itself out. They opened up the low coral beach, with its mound of white-washed coal ready for supply, the deserted huts for the sailors, and the flagless flagstaff.

Next day there was no *Haliotis* – only a little proa rocking in the warm rain at the mouth of the harbour, whose crew watched with hungry eyes the smoke of a gunboat on the horizon.

Months afterwards there were a few lines in an English newspaper to the effect that some gunboat of some foreign Power had broken her back at the mouth of some far-away harbour by running at full speed into a sunken wreck.

'Bread upon the Waters' [1]

If you remember my improper friend Brugglesmith, you will also bear in mind his friend McPhee, Chief Engineer of the *Breslau*, whose dingey Brugglesmith tried to steal. His apologies for the performances of Brugglesmith may one day be told in their proper place: the tale before us concerns McPhee. He was never a racing engineer, and took special pride in saying as much before the Liverpool men; but he had a thirty-two years' knowledge of machinery and the humours of ships. One side of his face had been wrecked through the bursting of a pressure-gauge in the days when men knew less than they do now; and his nose rose grandly out of the wreck, like a club in a public riot. There were cuts and lumps on his head, and he would guide your forefinger through his short, iron-grey hair and tell you how he had come by his trademarks. He owned all sorts of certificates of extra-competency, and at the bottom of his cabin chest of drawers, where he kept the photograph of his wife, were two or three Royal Humane Society medals for saving lives at sea. Professionally – it was different when crazy steerage-passengers jumped overboard – professionally, McPhee does not approve of saving life at sea, and he has often told me that a new hell is awaiting stokers and trimmers who sign for a strong man's pay and fall sick the second day out. He believes in throwing boots at fourth and fifth engineers when they wake him up at night with word that a bearing is red-hot, all because a lamp's glare is reflected red from the twirling metal. He believes that there are only two poets in the world: one being Robert Burns, of course, and the other Gerald Massey.[2] When he has time for novels, he reads Wilkie Collins and Charles Reade – chiefly the latter – and knows whole pages of *Very Hard Cash* by heart. In the saloon his table is next to the captain's, and he drinks only water while his engines work.

He was good to me when we first met, because I did not ask questions, and believed in Charles Reade as a most shamefully neglected author. Later he approved of my writings to the extent of one pamphlet of twenty-four pages that I wrote for Holdock, Steiner, and Chase, owners of the line, when they bought some ventilating patent and fitted it to the cabins of the *Breslau*, *Spandau*, and *Koltzau*. The purser of the *Breslau* recommended me to Holdock's secretary for the job; and Holdock, who is a Wesleyan Methodist, invited me to his house, and gave me dinner with the governess when the others had finished, and placed the plans and specifications in my hand, and I wrote the pamphlet that same afternoon. It was called 'Comfort in the Cabin', and brought me seven pound ten, cash down – an important sum of money in those days; and the governess, who was teaching Master John Holdock his scales, told me that Mrs Holdock had told her to keep an eye on me, in case I went away with coats from the hat-rack. McPhee liked that pamphlet enormously, for it was composed in the Bouverie-Byzantine style,[3] with baroque and rococo embellishments; and afterward he introduced me to Mrs McPhee, who succeeded Dinah[4] in my heart; for Dinah was half a world away, and it is wholesome and antiseptic to love such a woman as Janet McPhee. They lived in a little twelve-pound house, close to the shipping. When McPhee was away Mrs McPhee read the Lloyd's column in the papers, and called on the wives of senior engineers of equal social standing. Once or twice, too, Mrs Holdock visited Mrs McPhee in a brougham with celluloid fittings, and I have reason to believe that, after she had played owner's wife long enough, they talked scandal. The Holdocks lived in an old-fashioned house with a big brick garden not a mile from the McPhees, for they stayed by their money as their money stayed by them; and in summer you met their brougham solemnly junketing by Theydon Bois or Loughton. But I was Mrs McPhee's friend, for she allowed me to convoy her westward, sometimes, to theatres, where she sobbed or laughed or shivered with a simple heart; and she introduced me to a new world of doctors' wives, captains' wives, and engineers' wives, whose whole talk and thought centred in and about ships and lines of ships you have never heard of. There were sailing-ships, with stewards and mahogany and maple saloons, trading to Australia, taking cargoes of consumptives and hopeless drunkards for whom a sea-voyage was recommended; there were frouzy little West African boats, full of rats and cockroaches, where men died anywhere but in their bunks; there were Brazilian boats whose cabins could be hired for merchandise that went out loaded nearly awash; there were Zanzibar and Mauritius steamers, and wonderful reconstructed boats that plied to the other side of Borneo. These were loved and known, for they earned our bread and a little butter, and we despised the big Atlantic boats, and made fun of the P. & O. and Orient liners, and swore by our respective owners – Wesleyan, Baptist, or Presbyterian, as the case might be.

I had only just come back to England when Mrs McPhee invited me to dinner at three o'clock in the afternoon, and the notepaper was almost bridal in its scented creaminess. When I reached the house I saw that there were new curtains in the window that must have cost forty-five shillings a pair; and as Mrs McPhee drew me into the little marble-paper hall, she looked at me keenly, and cried:

'Have ye not heard? What d'ye think o' the hat-rack?'

Now, that hat-rack was oak – thirty shillings at least. McPhee came downstairs with a sober foot – he steps as lightly as a cat, for all his weight, when he is at sea – and shook hands in a new and awful manner – a parody of old Holdock's style when he says good-bye to his skippers. I perceived at once that a legacy had come to him, but I held my peace, though Mrs McPhee begged me every thirty seconds to eat a great deal and say nothing. It was rather a mad sort of meal, because McPhee and his wife took hold of hands like little children (they always do after voyages), and nodded and winked and choked and gurgled, and hardly ate a mouthful.

A female servant came in and waited; though Mrs McPhee had told me time and again that she would thank no one to do her housework while she had her health. But this was a servant with a cap, and I saw Mrs McPhee swell and swell under her *garance*-coloured [5] gown. There is no small free-board to Janet McPhee, nor is *garance* any subdued tint; and with all this unexplained pride and glory in the air I felt like watching fireworks without knowing the festival. When the maid had removed the cloth she brought a pineapple that would have cost half a guinea at that season (only McPhee has his own way of getting such things), and a Canton china bowl of dried lichis, and a glass plate of preserved ginger, and a small jar of sacred and imperial chow-chow [6] that perfumed the room. McPhee gets it from a Dutchman in Java, and I think he doctors it with liqueurs. But the crown of the feast was some Madeira of the kind you can only come by if you know the wine and the man. A little maize-wrapped fig of clotted Madeira cigars went with the wine, and the rest was a pale blue smoky silence; Janet, in her splendour, smiling on us two, and patting McPhee's hand.

'We'll drink,' said McPhee slowly, rubbing his chin, 'to the eternal damnation o' Holdock, Steiner, and Chase.'

Of course I answered 'Amen', though I had made seven pound ten shillings out of the firm. McPhee's enemies were mine, and I was drinking his Madeira.

'Ye've heard nothing?' said Janet. 'Not a word, not a whisper?'

'Not a word, nor a whisper. On my word, I have not.'

'Tell him, Mac,' said she; and that is another proof of Janet's goodness and wifely love. A smaller woman would have babbled first, but Janet is five feet nine in her stockings.

'We're rich,' said McPhee. I shook hands all round.

'We're damned rich,' he added. I shook hands all round a second time.

'I'll go to sea no more – unless – there's no sayin' – a private yacht, maybe – wi' a small an' handy auxiliary.'

'It's not enough for *that*,' said Janet. 'We're fair rich – well-to-do, but no more. A new gown for church, and one for the theatre. We'll have it made west.'

'How much is it?' I asked.

'Twenty-five thousand pounds.' I drew a long breath. 'An' I've been earnin' twenty-five an' twenty pound a month!' The last words came away with a roar, as though the wide world was conspiring to beat him down.

'All this time I'm waiting,' I said. 'I know nothing since last September. Was it left you?'

They laughed aloud together. 'It was left,' said McPhee, choking. 'Ou, ay, it was left. That's vara good. Of course it was left. Janet, d'ye note that? It was left. Now if you'd put *that* in your pamphlet it would have been vara jocose. It *was* left.' He slapped his thigh and roared till the wine quivered in the decanter.

The Scotch are a great people, but they are apt to hang over a joke too long, particularly when no one can see the point but themselves.

'When I rewrite my pamphlet I'll put it in, McPhee. Only I must know something more first.'

McPhee thought for the length of half a cigar, while Janet caught my eye and led it round the room to one new thing after another – the new vine-pattern carpet, the new chiming rustic clock between the models of the Colombo outrigger-boats, the new inlaid sideboard with a purple cut-glass flower-stand, the fender of gilt and brass, and last, the new black-and-gold piano.

'In October o' last year the Board sacked me,' began McPhee. 'In October o' last year the *Breslau* came in for winter overhaul. She'd been runnin' eight months – two hunder an' forty days – an' I was three days makin' up my indents, when she went to dry-dock. All told, mark you, it was this side o' three hunder pound – to be preceese, two hunder an' eighty-six pound four shillings. There's not another man could ha' nursed the *Breslau* for eight months to that tune. Never again – never again! They may send their boats to the bottom, for aught I care.'

'There's no need,' said Janet softly. 'We're done wi' Holdock, Steiner, and Chase.'

'It's irritatin', Janet, it's just irritatin'. I ha' been justified from first to last, as the world knows, but – but I canna forgie 'em. Ay, wisdom is justified o' her children; an' any other man than me wad ha' made the indent eight hunder. Hay was our skipper – ye'll have met him. They shifted him to the *Torgau*, an' bade me wait for the *Breslau* under young Bannister. Ye'll obsairve there'd been a new election on the Board. I heard the shares were sellin' hither an' yon, an' the major part of the Board was new to me. The old Board would ne'er ha' done it. They trusted me. But the new Board was all for reorganization. Young Steiner – Steiner's son – the Jew, was at the bottom of it, an' they did not think it worth their while to send me word. The first *I* knew – an' I was Chief Engineer – was the notice of the line's winter sailin's, and the *Breslau* timed for sixteen days between port an' port! Sixteen days, man! She's a good boat, but eighteen is her summer time, mark you. Sixteen was sheer, flytin', kitin' nonsense, an' so I told young Bannister.

'"We've got to make it," he said. "Ye should not ha' sent in a three hunder pound indent."

'"Do they look for their boats to be run on air?" I said. "The Board is daft."

'"E'en tell 'em so," he says. "I'm a married man, an' my fourth's on the ways now, she says."'

'A boy – wi' red hair,' Janet put in. Her own hair is the splendid red-gold that goes with a creamy complexion.

'My word, I was an angry man that day! Forbye I was fond o' the old *Breslau*, I look for a little consideration from the Board after twenty years' service. There was Board meetin' on Wednesday; an I sat overnight in the engine-room, takin' figures to support my case. Well, I put it fair and square before them all. "Gentlemen," I said, "I've run the *Breslau* eight seasons, an' I believe there's no fault to find wi' my wark. But if ye haud to this" – I waggled the advertisement at 'em – "this that *I*'ve never heard of it till I read it at breakfast, I do assure you on my professional reputation, she can never do it. That is to say, she can for a while, but at a risk no thinkin' man would run."

'"What the deil d'ye suppose we pass your indent for?" says old Holdock. "Man, we're spendin' money like watter."

'"I'll leave it in the Board's hands," I said, "if two hunder an' eighty-seven pound is anything beyond right and reason for eight months." I might ha' saved my breath, for the Board was new since the last election, an' there they sat, the damned deevidend-huntin' ship-chandlers, deaf as the adders o' Scripture.[7]

'"We must keep faith wi' the public," said young Steiner.

'"Keep faith wi' the *Breslau* then," I said. "She's served you well, an' your father before you. She'll need her bottom restiffenin', an' new bed-plates, an' turnin' out the forward boilers, an' re-turnin' all three cylinders, an' refacin' all guides, to begin with. It's a three months' job."

'"Because one employé is afraid?" says young Steiner. "Maybe a piano in the Chief Engineer's cabin would be more to the point."

'I crushed my cap in my hands, an' thanked God we'd no bairns an' a bit put by.

'"Understand, gentlemen," I said. "If the *Breslau* is made a sixteen-day boat, ye'll find another engineer."

'"Bannister makes no objection," said Holdock.

'"I'm speakin' for myself," I said. "Bannister has bairns." An' then I lost my temper. "Ye can run her into Hell an' out again if ye pay pilotage," I said, "but ye run without me."

'"That's insolence," said young Steiner.

'"At your pleasure," I said, turnin' to go.

'"Ye can consider yourself dismissed. We must preserve discipline among our employés," said old Holdock, an' he looked round to see that the Board was with him. They knew nothin' – God forgie 'em – an' they nodded me out o' the Line after twenty years – after twenty years.

'I went out an' sat down by the hall porter to get my wits again. I'm thinkin' I swore at the Board. Then auld McRimmon – o' McNaughton and McRimmon – came oot o' his office, that's on the same floor, an' looked at me, proppin' up one eyelid wi' his forefinger. Ye know they call him the Blind Deevil, forbye he's onythin' but blind, an' no deevil in his dealin's wi' me – McRimmon o' the Black Bird Line.

'"What's here, Mister McPhee?" said he.

'I was past prayin' for by then. "A Chief Engineer sacked after twenty years' service because he'll not risk the *Breslau* on the new timin', an' be damned to ye, McRimmon," I said.

'The auld man sucked in his lips an' whistled. "Ah," said he, "the new timin'. I see!" He doddered into the Board-room I'd just left, an' the Dandie-dog that is just his blind man's leader stayed wi' me. *That* was providential. In a minute he was back again. "Ye've cast your bread on the watter, McPhee, an' be damned to you," he says. "Whaur's my dog? My word, is he on your knee? There's more discernment in a dog than a Jew. What garred ye curse your Board, McPhee? It's expensive."

'"They'll pay more for the *Breslau*," I said. "Get off my knee, ye smotherin' beastie."

'"Bearin's hot, eh?" said McRimmon. "It's thirty year since a man daur curse me to my face. Time was I'd ha' cast ye doon the stairway for that."

'"Forgie's all!" I said. He was wearin' to eighty, as I knew. "I was wrong, McRimmon; but when a man's shown the door for doin' his plain duty he's not always ceevil."

'"So I hear," says McRimmon. "Ha' ye ony objection to a tramp freighter? It's only fifteen a month, but they say the Blind Deevil feeds a man better than others. She's my *Kite*. Come ben. Ye can thank Dandie, here. I'm no used to thanks. An' noo," says he, "what possessed ye to throw up your berth wi' Holdock?"

'"The new timin'," said I. "The *Breslau* will not stand it."

'"Hoot, oot," said he. "Ye might ha' crammed her a little – enough to show ye were drivin' her – an' brought her in twa days behind. What's easier than to say ye slowed for bearin's, eh? All my men do it, and – I believe 'em."

'"McRimmon," says I, "what's her virginity to a lassie?"

'He puckered his dry face an' twisted in his chair. "The warld an' a'," says he. "My God, the vara warld an' a'! But what ha' you or me to do wi' virginity, this late along?"

'"This," I said. "There's just one thing that each one of us in his trade or profession will *not* do for ony consideration whatever. If I run to time I run to time, barrin' always the risks o' the high seas. Less than that, under God, I have not done. More than that, by God, I will not do! There's no trick o' the trade I'm not acquaint wi' –"

'"So I've heard," says McRimmon, dry as a biscuit.

'"But yon matter o' fair runnin' 's just my Shekinah,[8] ye'll understand. I daurna tamper wi' *that*. Nursing weak engines is fair craftsmanship; but what the Board ask is cheatin', wi' the risk o' manslaughter addeetional. Ye'll note I know my business."

'There was some more talk, an' next week I went aboard the *Kite*, twenty-five hunder ton, simple compound,[9] a Black Bird tramp. The deeper she rode, the better she'd steam. I've snapped as much as eleven out of her, but eight point three was her fair normal. Good food forward an' better aft, all indents passed wi'out marginal remarks, the best coal, new donkeys,[10] and good crews. There was nothin' the old man would not do, except paint. That was his deeficulty. Ye could no more draw paint than his last teeth from him. He'd come down to dock, an' his boats a scandal all along the watter, an' he'd whine an' cry an' say they looked all he could desire. Every owner has his *non plus ultra*,[11] I've obsairved. Paint was McRimmon's. But you could get round his engines without riskin' your life, an', for all his blindness, I've seen him reject five flawed intermediates, one after the other, on a nod from me; an' his cattle-fittin's were guaranteed for North Atlantic winter weather. Ye ken what *that* means? McRimmon an' the Black Bird Line, God bless him!

'Oh, I forgot to say she would lie down an' fill her forward deck green, an' snore away into a twenty-knot gale forty-five to the minute, three an' a half knots an hour, the engines runnin' sweet an' true as a bairn breathin' in its sleep. Bell was skipper; an' forbye there's no love lost between crews an' owners, we were fond o' the auld Blind Deevil an' his dog, an' I'm thinkin' he liked us. He was worth the windy side o' twa million sterlin', an' no friend to his own blood-kin. Money's an awfu' thing – overmuch – for a lonely man.

'I'd taken her out twice, there an' back again, when word came o' the *Breslau*'s breakdown, just as I prophesied. Calder was her engineer – he's not fit to run a tug down the Solent – and he fairly lifted the engines off the bed-plates, an' they fell down in heaps, by what I heard. So she filled from the after-stuffin'-box to the after-bulkhead, an' lay star-gazing, with seventy-nine squealin' passengers in the saloon, till the *Camaralzaman* o' Ramsey and Gold's Carthagena Line gave her a tow to the tune o' five thousand seven hunder an' forty pound, wi' costs in the Admiralty Court. She was helpless, ye'll understand, an' in no case to meet ony weather. Five thousand seven hunder an' forty pounds, *with* costs, an' exclusive o' new engines! They'd ha' done better to ha' kept me – on the old timin'.

'But, even so, the new Board were all for retrenchment. Young Steiner, the Jew, was at the bottom of it. They sacked men right an' left that would not eat the dirt the Board gave 'em. They cut down repairs; they fed crews wi' leavin's an' scrapin's; and, reversin' McRimmon's practice, they hid their defeeciencies wi' paint an' cheap gildin'. *Quem Deus vult perrdere prrius dementat*,[12] ye remember.

'In January we went to dry-dock, an' in the next dock lay the *Grotkau*, their big freighter that was the *Dolabella* o' Piegan, Piegan, and Walsh's Line in '84 – a Clyde-built iron boat, a flat-bottomed, pigeon-breasted, under-engined, bull-nosed bitch of a five thousand ton freighter, that would neither steer, nor steam, nor stop when ye asked her. Whiles she'd attend to her helm, whiles she'd take charge, whiles she'd wait to scratch herself, an' whiles she'd buttock into a dockhead. But Holdock and Steiner had bought her cheap, and painted her all over like the Hoor[13] o'

Babylon, an' we called her the *Hoor* for short.' (By the way, McPhee kept to that name throughout the rest of his tale; so you must read accordingly.) 'I went to see young Bannister – he had to take what the Board gave him, an' he an' Calder were shifted together from the *Breslau* to this abortion – an' talkin' to him I went into the dock under her. Her plates were pitted till the men that were paint, paint, paintin' her laughed at it. But the warst was at the last. She'd a great clumsy iron twelve-foot Thresher propeller – Aitcheson designed the *Kite*'s – and just on the tail o' the shaft, behind the boss, was a red weepin' crack ye could ha' put a penknife to. Man, it was an awfu' crack!

'"When d'ye ship a new tail-shaft?" I said to Bannister.

'He knew what I meant. "Oh, yon's a superfeecial flaw," says he, not lookin' at me.

'"Superfeecial Gehenna!"[14] I said. "Ye'll not take her oot wi' a solution o' continuity that like."

'"They'll putty it up this evening," he said. "I'm a married man, an' – ye used to know the Board."

'I e'en said what was gie'd me in that hour. Ye know how a dry-dock echoes. I saw young Steiner standin' listenin' above me, an', man, he used language provocative of a breach o' the peace. I was a spy and a disgraced employé, an' a corrupter o' young Bannister's morals, an' he'd prosecute me for libel. He went away when I ran up the steps – I'd ha' thrown him into the dock if I'd caught him – an' there I met McRimmon, wi' Dandie pullin' on the chain, guidin' the auld man among the railway lines.

'"McPhee," said he, "ye're no paid to fight Holdock, Steiner, Chase, and Company, Limited, when ye meet. What's wrong between you?"

'"No more than a tail-shaft rotten as a kail-stump. For ony sakes go and look, McRimmon. It's a comedietta."

'"I'm feared o' yon conversational Hebrew," said he. "Whaur's the flaw, an' what like?"

'"A seven-inch crack just behind the boss. There's no power on earth will fend it just jarrin' off."

'"When?"

'"That's beyon' my knowledge," I said.

'"So it is; so it is," said McRimmon. "We've all oor leemitations. Ye're certain it was a crack?"

'"Man, it's a crevasse," I said, for there were no words to describe the magnitude of it. "An' young Bannister's sayin' it's no more than a superfeecial flaw!"

'"Weel, I tak' it oor business is to mind oor business. If ye've ony

friends aboard her, McPhee, why not bid them to a bit dinner at Radley's?"

'"I was thinkin' o' tea in the cuddy,"[15] I said. "Engineers o' tramp
freighters cannot afford hotel prices."

'"Na! na!" says the auld man, whimperin'. "Not the cuddy. They'll
laugh at my *Kite*, for she's no plastered with paint like the *Hoor*. Bid
them to Radley's, McPhee, an' send me the bill. Thank Dandie, here,
man. I'm no used to thanks." Then he turned him round. (I was just
thinkin' the vara same thing.)

'"Mister McPhee," said he, "this is *not* senile dementia."

'"Preserve's!" I said, clean jumped oot o' mysel'. "I was but thinkin'
you're fey, McRimmon."

'Dod, the auld deevil laughed till he nigh sat down on Dandie. "Send
me the bill," says he. "I'm lang past champagne, but tell me how it tastes
the morn."

'Bell and I bid young Bannister and Calder to dinner at Radley's.
They'll have no laughin' an' singin' there, but we took a private room —
like yacht-owners fra' Cowes.'

McPhee grinned all over, and lay back to think.

'And then?' said I.

'We were no drunk in ony preceese sense o' the word, but Radley's
showed me the dead men. There were six magnums o' dry champagne
an' maybe a bottle o' whisky.'

'Do you mean to tell me that you four got away with a magnum and a
half apiece, besides whisky?' I demanded.

McPhee looked down upon me from between his shoulders with
toleration.

'Man, we were not settin' down to drink,' he said. 'They no more than
made us wutty. To be sure, young Bannister laid his head on the table
an' greeted like a bairn, an' Calder was all for callin' on Steiner at two in
the morn' an' painting him galley-green; but they'd been drinkin' the
afternoon. Lord, how they twa cursed the Board, an' the *Grotkau*, an'
the tail-shaft, an' the engines, an' a'? They didna talk o' superfeecial
flaws that night. I mind young Bannister an' Calder shakin' hands on a
bond to be revenged on the Board at ony reasonable cost this side o'
losing their certificates. Now mark ye how false economy ruins business.
The Board fed them like swine (I have good reason to know it), an' I've
obsairved wi' my ain people that if ye touch his stomach ye wauken the
deil in a Scot. Men will tak' a dredger across the Atlantic if they're well
fed, and fetch her somewhere on the broadside o' the Americas; but bad
food's bad service the warld over.

'The bill went to McRimmon, an' he said no more to me till the week-end, when I was at him for more paint, for we'd heard the *Kite* was chartered Liverpool-side.

'"Bide whaur ye're put," said the Blind Deevil. "Man, do ye wash in champagne? The *Kite*'s no leavin' here till I gie the order, an' – how am I to waste paint on her, wi' the *Lammergeyer* docked for who knows how long, an' a'?"

'She was our big freighter – M'Intyre was engineer – an' I knew she'd come from overhaul not three months. That morn I met McRimmon's head-clerk – ye'll not know him – fair bitin' his nails off wi' mortification.

'"The auld man's gone gyte,"[16] says he. "He's withdrawn the *Lammergeyer*."

'"Maybe he has reasons," says I.

'"Reasons! He's daft!"

'"He'll no be daft till he begins to paint," I said.

'"That's just what he's done – and South American freights higher than we'll live to see them again. He's laid her up to paint her – to paint her – to paint her!" says the little clerk, dancin' like a hen on a hot plate. "Five thousand ton o' potential freight rottin' in dry-dock, man; an' he dolin' the paint out in quarter-pound-tins, for it cuts him to the heart, mad though he is. An' the *Grotkau* – the *Grotkau* of all conceivable bottoms – soaking up every pound that should be ours at Liverpool!"

'I was staggered wi' this folly – considerin' the dinner at Radley's in connection wi' the same.

'"Ye may well stare, McPhee," says the head-clerk. "There's engines, an' rollin' stock, an' iron bridges – d'ye know what freights are noo? – an' pianos, an' millinery, an' fancy Brazil cargo o' every species pourin' into the *Grotkau* – the *Grotkau* o' the Jerusalem firm – and the *Lammergeyer*'s bein' painted!"

'Losh, I thought he'd drop dead wi' the fits.

'I could say no more than "Obey orders, if ye break owners," but on the *Kite* we believed McRimmon was mad; an' McIntyre of the *Lammergeyer* was for lockin' him up by some patent legal process he'd found in a book o' maritime law. An' a' that week South American freights rose an' rose. It was sinfu'!

'Syne Bell got orders to tak' the *Kite* round to Liverpool in water-ballast, and McRimmon came to bid's good-bye, yammerin' an' whinin' o'er the acres o' paint he'd lavished on the *Lammergeyer*.

'"I look to you to retrieve it," says he. "I look to you to reimburse me! 'Fore God, why are ye not cast off? Are ye dawdlin' in dock for a purpose?"

'"What odds, McRimmon?" says Bell. "We'll be a day behind the fair at Liverpool. The *Grotkau*'s got all the freight that might ha' been ours an' the *Lammergeyer*'s." McRimmon laughed an' chuckled — the pairfect eemage o' senile dementia. Ye ken his eyebrows wark up an' down like a gorilla's.

'"Ye're under sealed orders," said he, tee-heein' an' scratchin' himself. "Yon's they" — to be opened *seriatim*.[17]

'Says Bell, shufflin' the envelopes when the auld man had gone ashore: "We're to creep round a' the south coast, standin' in for orders — this weather, too. There's no question o' his lunacy now."

'Well, we buttocked the auld *Kite* along — vara bad weather we made — standin' in alongside for telegraphic orders, which are the curse o' skippers. Syne we made over to Holyhead, an' Bell opened the last envelope for the last instructions. I was wi' him in the cuddy, an' he threw it over to me, cryin': "Did ye ever know the like, Mac?"

'I'll no say what McRimmon had written, but he was far from mad. There was a sou'-wester brewin' when we made the mouth o' the Mersey, a bitter cold morn wi' a grey-green sea and a grey-green sky — Liverpool weather, as they say; an' there we lay choppin', an' the men swore. Ye canna keep secrets aboard ship. They thought McRimmon was mad, too.

'Syne we saw the *Grotkau* rollin' oot on the top o' flood, deep an' double deep, wi' her new-painted funnel an' her new-painted boats an' a'. She looked her name, an', moreover, she coughed like it. Calder tauld me at Radley's what ailed his engines, but my own ear would ha' told me twa mile awa', by the beat o' them. Round we came, plungin' an' squatterin' in her wake, an' the wind cut wi' good promise o' more to come. By six it blew hard but clear, an' before the middle watch it was a sou'wester in airnest.

'"She'll edge into Ireland, this gait," says Bell. I was with him on the bridge, watchin' the *Grotkau*'s port light. Ye canna see green so far as red, or we'd ha' kept to leeward. We'd no passengers to consider, an' (all eyes being on the *Grotkau*) we fair walked into a liner rampin' home to Liverpool. Or, to be preceese, Bell no more than twisted the *Kite* oot from under her bows, and there was a little damnin' betwix' the twa bridges. Noo a passenger' — McPhee regarded me benignantly — 'wad ha' told the papers that as soon as he got to the Customs. We stuck to the *Grotkau*'s tail that night an' the next twa days — she slowed down to five knots by my reckonin' — and we lapped along the weary way to the Fastnet.'

'But you don't go by the Fastnet to get to any South American port, do you?' I said.

'*We* do not. We prefer to go as direct as may be. But we were followin' the *Grotkau*, an' she'd no walk into that gale for ony consideration. Knowin' what I did to her discredit, I couldna blame young Bannister. It was warkin' up to a North Atlantic winter gale, snow an' sleet an' a perishin' wind. Eh, it was like the Deil walkin' abroad o' the surface o' the deep, whuppin' off the top o' the waves before he made up his mind. They'd bore up against it so far, but the minute she was clear o' the Skelligs she fair tucked up her skirts an' ran for it by Dunmore Head. Wow, she rolled!

'"She'll be makin' Smerwick," says Bell.

'"She'd ha' tried for Ventry by noo if she meant that," I said.

'"They'll roll the funnel oot o' her, this gait," says Bell. "Why canna Bannister keep her head to sea?"

'"It's the tail-shaft. Ony rollin's better than pitchin' wi' superfeecial cracks in the tail-shaft. Calder knows that much," I said.

'"It's ill wark retreevin' steamers this weather," said Bell. His beard and whiskers were frozen to his oilskin, an' the spray was white on the weather side of him. Pairfect North Atlantic winter weather!

'One by one the sea raxed away our three boats, an' the davits were crumpled like rams' horns.

'"Yon's bad," said Bell, at the last. "Ye canna pass a hawser wi'oot a boat." Bell was a vara judeecious man – for an Aberdonian.

'I'm not one that fashes himself for eventualities outside the engine-room, so I e'en slipped down betwixt waves to see how the *Kite* fared. Man, she's the best geared boat of her class that ever left the Clyde! Kinloch, my second, knew her as well as I did. I found him dryin' his socks on the mainsteam, an' combin' his whiskers wi' the comb Janet gied me last year, for the warld an' a' as though we were in port. I tried the feed, speered[18] into the stoke-hole, thumbed all bearin's, spat on the thrust for luck, gied 'em my blessin', an' took Kinloch's socks before I went up to the bridge again.

'Then Bell handed me the wheel, an' went below to warm himself. When he came up my gloves were frozen to the spokes an' the ice clicked over my eye-lids. Pairfect North Atlantic winter weather, as I was sayin'.

'The gale blew out by night, but we lay in smotherin' cross-seas that made the auld *Kite* chatter from stem to stern. I slowed to thirty-four, I mind – no, thirty-seven. There was a long swell the morn, an' the *Grotkau* was headin' into it west awa'.

'"She'll win to Rio yet, tail-shaft or no tail-shaft," says Bell.

'"Last night shook her," I said. "She'll jar it off yet, mark my word."

'We were then, maybe, a hunder and fifty mile west-sou'west o' Slyne Head, by dead reckonin'. Next day we made a hunder an' thirty – ye'll note we were not racin' boats – an' the day after a hunder and sixty-one, an' that made us, we'll say, Eighteen an' a bittock west, an' maybe Fifty-one an' a bittock north, crossin' all the North Atlantic liner lanes on the long slant, always in sight o' the *Grotkau*, creepin' up by night and fallin' awa' by day. After the gale, it was cold weather wi' dark nights.

'I was in the engine-room on Friday night, just before the middle watch, when Bell whustled down the tube: "She's done it"; an' up I came.

'The *Grotkau* was just a fair distance south, an' one by one she ran up the three red lights in a vertical line – the sign of a steamer not under control.

'"Yon's a tow for us," said Bell, lickin' his chops. "She'll be worth more than the *Breslau*. We'll go down to her, McPhee!"

'"Bide a while," I said. "The seas fair throng wi' ships here."

'"Reason why," said Bell. "It's a fortune gaun beggin'. What d'ye think, man?"

'"Gie her till daylight. She knows we're here. If Bannister needs help he'll loose a rocket."

'"Wha told ye Bannister's need? We'll ha' some rag-an'-bone tramp snappin' her up under oor nose," said he; an' he put the wheel over. We were gaun slow.

'"Bannister wad like better to go home on a liner an' eat in the saloon. Mind ye what they said o' Holdock and Steiner's food that night at Radley's? Keep her awa', man – keep her awa'. A tow's a tow, but a derelict's big salvage."

'"E-eh!" said Bell. "Yon's an inshot o' yours, Mac. I love ye like a brother. We'll bide whaur we are till daylight"; an' he kept her awa'.

'Syne up went a rocket forward, an' twa on the bridge, an' a blue light aft. Syne a tar-barrel forward again.

'"She's sinkin'," said Bell. "It's all gaun, an' I'll get no more than a pair o' night-glasses for pickin' up young Bannister – the fool!"

'"Fair an' soft again," I said. "She's signallin' to the south of us. Bannister knows as well as I that one rocket would bring the *Kite*. He'll no be wastin' fireworks for nothin'. Hear her ca'!"

'The *Grotkau* whustled an' whustled for five minutes, an' then there were more fireworks – a regular exhibeetion.

'"That's no for men in the regular trade," says Bell. "Ye're right, Mac. That's for a cuddy full o' passengers." He blinked through the night-glasses when it lay a bit thick to southward.

'"What d'ye make of it?" I said.

'"Liner," he says. "Yon's her rocket. Ou, ay; they've waukened the gold-strapped skipper, an' – noo they've waukened the passengers. They're turnin' on the electrics, cabin by cabin. Yon's another rocket! They're comin' up to help the perishin' in deep watters."

'"Gie me the glass," I said. But Bell danced on the bridge, clean dementit. "Mails – mails – mails!" said he. "Under contract wi' the Government for the due conveyance o' the mails; an' as such, Mac, ye'll note, she may rescue life at sea, but she canna tow! – she canna tow! Yon's her night-signal. She'll be up in half an hour!"

'"Gowk!"[19] I said, "an' we blazin' here wi' all oor lights. Oh, Bell, but ye're a fool."

'He tumbled off the bridge forward, an' I tumbled aft, an' before ye could wink our lights were oot, the engine-room hatch was covered, an' we lay pitch-dark, watchin' the lights o' the liner come up that the *Grotkau*'d been signallin' for. Twenty knot an hour she came, every cabin lighted, an' her boats swung awa'. It was grandly done, an' in the inside of an hour. She stopped like Mrs Holdock's machine; down went the gangway, down went the boats, an' in ten minutes we heard the passengers cheerin', an' awa' she fled.

'"They'll tell o' this all the days they live," said Bell. "A rescue at sea by night, as pretty as a play. Young Bannister an' Calder will be drinkin' in the saloon, an' six months hence the Board o' Trade 'll gie the skipper a pair o' binoculars. It's vara philanthropic all round.'

'We lay by till day – ye may think we waited for it wi' sore eyes – an' there sat the *Grotkau*, her nose a bit cocked, just leerin' at us. She looked pairfectly rideeculous.

'"She'll be fillin' aft," says Bell; "for why is she down by the stern? The tail-shaft's punched a hole in her, an' – we've no boats. There's three hunder thousand pound sterlin', at a conservative estimate, droonin' before our eyes. What's to do?" An' his bearin's got hot again in a minute; for he was an incontinent man.

'"Run her as near as ye daur," I said. "Gie me a jacket an' a life-line, an' I'll swum for it." There was a bit lump of a sea, an' it was cold in the wind – vara cold; but they'd gone overside like passengers, young Bannister an' Calder an' a', leaving the gangway down on the lee-side. It would ha' been a flyin' in the face o' manifest Providence to overlook the invitation. We were within fifty yards o' her while Kinloch was garmin' me all over wi' oil behind the galley; an' as we ran past I went outboard for the salvage o' three hunder thousand pound. Man, it was perishin' cold, but I'd done my job judgmatically, an' came scrapin' all along her side slap on the lower gratin' o' the gangway. No one more astonished than me, I assure ye. Before I'd caught my breath I'd skinned both my knees on the gratin', an' was climbing up before she rolled again. I made my line fast to the rail, an' squattered aft to young Bannister's cabin, whaur I dried me wi' everything in his bunk, an' put on every conceivable sort o' rig I found till the blood was circulatin'. Three pair drawers, I mind I found – to begin upon – an' I needed them all. It was the coldest cold I remember in all my experience.

'Syne I went aft to the engine-room. The *Grotkau* sat on her own tail, as they say. She was vara short-shafted, an' her gear was all aft. There was four or five foot o' water in the engine-room slummockin' to and fro, black an' greasy; maybe there was six foot. The stoke-hold doors were screwed home, an' the stoke-hold was tight enough, but for a minute the mess in the engine-room deceived me. Only for a minute, though, an' that was because I was not, in a manner o' speakin', as calm as ordinar'. I looked again to mak' sure. 'Twas just black wi' bilge: dead watter that must ha' come in fortuitously, ye ken.'

'McPhee, I'm only a passenger,' I said, 'but you don't persuade me that six foot o' water can come into an engine-room fortuitously.'

'Who's tryin' to persuade one way or the other?' McPhee retorted. 'I'm statin' the facts o' the case – the simple, natural facts. Six or seven foot o' dead watter in the engine-room is a vara depressin' sight if ye think there's like to be more comin'; but I did not consider that such was likely, and so, ye'll note, I was not depressed.'

'That's all very well, but I want to know about the water,' I said.

'I've told ye. There was six feet or more there, wi' Calder's cap floatin' on top.'

'Where did it come from?'

'Weel, in the confusion o' things after the propeller had dropped off an' the engines were racin' an' a', it's vara possible that Calder might ha' lost it off his head an' no troubled himself to pick it up again. I remember seein' that cap on him at Southampton.'

'I don't want to know about the cap. I'm asking where the water came from, and what it was doing there, and why you were so certain that it wasn't a leak, McPhee?'

'For good reason – for good an' sufficient reason.'

'Give it to me, then.'

'Weel, it's a reason that does not properly concern myself only. To be preceese, I'm of opinion that it was due, the watter, in part to an error o' judgment in another man. We can a' mak' mistakes.'

'Oh, I beg your pardon! Go on.'

'I got me to the rail again, an', "What's wrang?" said Bell, hailin'.

'"She'll do," I said. "Send's o'er a hawser, an' a man to help steer. I'll pull him in by the life-line."

'I could see heads bobbin' back an' forth, an' a whuff or two o' strong words. Then Bell said: "They'll not trust themselves – one of 'em – in this watter – except Kinloch, an' I'll no spare him."

'"The more salvage to me, then," I said. "I'll make shift *solo*."

'Says one dock-rat at this: "D'ye think she's safe?"

'"I'll guarantee ye nothing," I said, "except, maybe, a hammerin' for keepin' me this long."

'Then he sings out: "There's no more than one life-belt, an' they canna find it, or I'd come."

'"Throw him over, the Jezebel," I said, for I was oot o' patience; an' they took haud o' that volunteer before he knew what was in store, and hove him over in the bight of the life-line. So I e'en hauled him upon the sag of it, hand-over-fist – a vara welcome recruit when I'd tilted the salt watter out of him; for, by the way, he could not swum.

'Syne they bent a twa-inch rope to the life-line, an' a hawser to that, an' I led the rope o'er the drum of a hand-winch forward, an' we sweated the hawser inboard an' made it fast to the *Grotkau's* bitts.[20]

'Bell brought the *Kite* so close I feared she'd roll in an' do the *Grotkau's* plates a mischief. He hove anither life-line to me, an' went astern, an' we had all the weary winch-work to do again wi' a second hawser. For all that, Bell was right: we'd a long tow before us, an' though Providence had helped us that far, there was no sense in leavin' too much to its keepin'. When the second hawser was fast, I was wet wi' sweat, an' I cried Bell to tak' up his slack an' go home. The other man was by way o' helpin' the work wi' askin' for drinks, but I e'en told him he must hand reef an' steer, beginnin' with steerin', for I was goin' to turn in. He steered – ou, ay, he steered, in a manner o' speakin'. At the least, he grippit the spokes an' twiddled 'em an' looked wise, but I doubt if the *Hoor* ever felt it. I turned in there an' then to young Bannister's bunk, an' slept past expression. I waukened ragin' wi' hunger, a fair lump o' sea runnin', the *Kite* snorin' awa' four knots an hour; an' the *Grotkau* slappin' her nose under, an' yawin' an' standin' over at discretion. She was a most disgracefu' tow. But the shameful thing of all was the food. I raxed me a meal fra galley-shelves an' pantries an' lazareetes[21] an' cubby-holes that I would not ha' gied to the mate of a Cardiff collier; an' ye ken we say a Cardiff mate will eat clinkers to save waste. I'm sayin' it was simply vile! The crew had written what *they* thought of it on the new paint o' the fo'c'sle, but I had not a decent soul wi' me to complain on. There was nothin' for me to do save watch the hawsers an' the *Kite's* tail squatterin' down in white watter when she lifted to a sea; so I got steam on the after donkey-pump, an' pumped oot the engine-room. There's no sense in leavin' watter loose in a ship. When she was dry, I went doun the shaft-tunnel, an' found she was leakin' a little through the stuffin'-box, but nothin' to make wark. The propeller had e'en jarred off, as I knew it must, an' Calder had been waitin' for it to go wi' his hand on the gear. He told me as much when I met him ashore. There was nothin' started or strained. It had just slipped awa' to the bed o' the Atlantic as easy as a man dyin' wi' due warnin' – a most providential business for all concerned. Syne I took stock o' the *Grotkau's* upper works. Her boats had been smashed on the davits, an' here an' there was the rail missin', an' a ventilator or two had fetched awa', an' the bridge-rails were bent by the seas; but her hatches were tight, and she'd taken no sort of harm. Dod, I came to hate her like a human bein', for I was eight weary days aboard, starvin' – ay, starvin' – within a cable's length o' plenty. All day I lay in the bunk reading the *Woman-Hater*, the grandest book Charlie Reade ever wrote, an' pickin' a toothful here an' there. It was weary weary work. Eight days, man, I was aboard the *Grotkau*, an' not one full meal did I make. Sma' blame her crew would not stay by her. The other man? Oh, I warked him to keep him crack.[22] I warked him wi' a vengeance.

'It came on to blow when we fetched soundin's, an' that kept me standin' by the hawsers, lashed to the capstan, breathin' betwixt green seas. I near died o' cauld an' hunger, for the *Grotkau* towed like a barge, an' Bell howkit her along through or over. It was vara thick up-Channel, too. We were standin' in to make some sort o' light, and we near walked over twa three fishin'-boats, an' they cried us we were o'erclose to Falmouth. Then we were near cut down by a drunken foreign fruiter that was blunderin' between us an' the shore, and it got thicker and thicker that night, an' I could feel by the tow Bell did not know whaur he was. Losh, we knew in the morn, for the wind blew the fog oot like a candle, an' the sun came clear; and as surely as McRimmon gied me my cheque, the shadow o' the Eddystone[23] lay across our tow-rope! We were that near – ay, we were that near! Bell fetched the *Kite* round with the jerk that came close to tearin' the bitts out o' the *Grotkau*; an' I mind I thanked my Maker in young Bannister's cabin when we were inside Plymouth breakwater.

'The first to come aboard was McRimmon, wi' Dandie. Did I tell you our orders were to take anything found into Plymouth? The auld deil had just come down overnight, puttin' two an' two together from what

Calder had told him when the liner landed the *Grotkau's* men. He had preceesely hit oor time. I'd hailed Bell for something to eat, an' he sent it o'er in the same boat wi' McRimmon, when the auld man came to me. He grinned an' slapped his legs and worked his eyebrows the while I ate.

"'How do Holdock, Steiner, and Chase feed their men?" said he.

"'Ye can see," I said, knockin' the top off another beer-bottle. "I did not take to be starved, McRimmon."

"'Nor to swim, either," said he, for Bell had tauld him how I carried the line aboard. "Well, I'm thinkin' you'll be no loser. What freight could we ha' put into the *Lammergeyer* would equal salvage on four hunder thousand pounds – hull and cargo? Eh, McPhee? This cuts the liver out o' Holdock, Steiner, Chase, and Company, Limited. Eh, McPhee? An' I'm sufferin' from senile dementia now? Eh, McPhee? An' I'm not daft, am I, till I begin to paint the *Lammergeyer*? Eh, McPhee? Ye may weel lift your leg, Dandie! I ha' the laugh o' them all. Ye found watter in the engine-room?"

"'To speak wi'oot prejudice," I said, "there was some watter."

"'They thought she was sinkin' after the propeller went. She filled with extraordinary rapeedity. Calder said it grieved him an' Bannister to abandon her."

'I thought o' the dinner at Radley's, an' what like o' food I'd eaten for eight days.

"'It would grieve them sore," I said.

"'But the crew would not hear o' stayin' an' takin' their chances. They're gaun up an' down saying' they'd ha' starved first."

"'They'd ha' starved if they'd stayed," said I.

"'I tak' it, fra Calder's account, there was a mutiny a'most."

"'Ye know more than I, McRimmon," I said. "Speakin' wi'oot prejudice, for we're all in the same boat, *who* opened the bilge-cock?"

"'Oh, that's it – is it?" said the auld man, an' I could see he was surprised. "A bilge-cock, ye say?"

"'I believe it was a bilge-cock. They were all shut when I came aboard, but someone had flooded the engine-room eight feet over all, and shut it off with the worm-an'-wheel gear from the second gratin' afterwards."

"'Losh!" said McRimmon. "The ineequity o' man's beyond belief. But it's awfu' discreditable to Holdock, Steiner, and Chase, if that came oot in court."

"'It's just my own curiosity," I said.

"'Aweel, Dandie's afflicted wi' the same disease. Dandie, strive against curiosity, for it brings a little dog into traps an' suchlike. Whaur was the *Kite* when yon painted liner took off the *Grotkau's* people?"

'"Just there or thereabouts," I said.

'"An' which o' you twa thought to cover your lights?" said he, winkin'.

'"Dandie," I said to the dog, "we must both strive against curiosity. It's an unremunerative business. What's our chance o' salvage, Dandie?"

'He laughed till he choked. "Tak' what I gie you, McPhee, an' be content," he said. "Lord, how a man wastes time when he gets old. Get aboard the *Kite*, mon, as soon as ye can. I've clear forgot there's a Baltic charter yammerin' for you at London. That'll be your last voyage, I'm thinkin', excep' by way o' pleasure."

'Steiner's men were comin' aboard to take charge an' tow her round, an' I passed young Steiner in a boat as I went to the *Kite*. He looked down his nose; but McRimmon pipes up: "Here's the man ye owe the *Grotkau* to – at a price, Steiner – at a price! Let me introduce Mister McPhee to you. Maybe ye've met before; but ye've vara little luck in keeping your men – ashore or afloat!"

'Young Steiner looked angry enough to eat him as he chuckled an' whustled in his dry old throat.

'"Ye've not got your award yet," Steiner says.

'"Na, na," says the auld man, in a screech ye could hear to the Hoe, "but I've twa million sterlin', an' no bairns, ye Judeeas Apella,[24] if ye mean to fight; an' I'll match ye p'und for p'und till the last p'und's oot. Ye ken *me*, Steiner? I'm McRimmon o' McNaughten and McRimmon!"

'"Dod," he said betwix' his teeth, sittin' back in the boat, "I've waited fourteen year to break that Jew-firm, an' God be thankit I'll do it now."

'The *Kite* was in the Baltic while the auld man was warking his warks, but I know the assessors valued the *Grotkau*, all told, at over three hunder and sixty thousand – her manifest was a treat o' richness – and McRimmon got a third for salvin' an abandoned ship. Ye see, there's vast deeference between towin' a ship wi' men on her and pickin' up a derelict – a vast deeference – in pounds sterlin'. Moreover, twa three o' the *Grotkau's* crew were burnin' to testify about food, an' there was a note o' Calder to the Board in regard to the tail-shaft that would ha' been vara damagin' if it had come into court. They knew better than to fight.

'Syne the *Kite* came back, and McRimmon paid off me an' Bell personally, and the rest of the crew *pro rata*, I believe it's ca'ed. My share – oor share, I should say – was just twenty-five thousand pounds sterlin'.

385

At this point Janet jumped up and kissed him.

'Five-and-twenty thousand pound sterlin'. Noo, I'm fra the North, and I'm not the like to fling money awa' rashly, but I'd gie six months' pay – one hunder an' twenty pound – to know *who* flooded the engine-room of the *Grotkau*. I'm fairly well acquaint wi' McRimmon's eedio-syncrasies, and *he*'d no hand in it. It was not Calder, for I've asked him, an' he wanted to fight me. It would be in the highest degree unprofessional o' Calder – not fightin', but openin' bilge-cocks – but for a while I thought it was him. Ay, I judged it might be him – under temptation.'

'What's your theory?' I demanded.

'Weel, I'm inclined to think it was one o' those singular providences that remind us we're in the hands o' Higher Powers.'

'It couldn't open and shut itself?'

'I did not mean that; but some half-starvin' oiler or, maybe, trimmer must ha' opened it a while to mak' sure o' leavin' the *Grotkau*. It's a demoralizin' thing to see an engine-room flood up after any accident to the gear – demoralizin' and deceptive both. Aweel, the man got what he wanted, for they went aboard the liner cryin' that the *Grotkau* was sinkin'. But it's curious to think o' the consequences. In a' human probability, he's bein' damned in heaps at the present moment aboard another tramp-freighter; an' here am I, wi' five-an-twenty thousand pounds invested, resolute to go to sea no more – providential's the preceese word – except as a passenger, ye'll understand, Janet.'

McPhee kept his word. He and Janet went for a voyage as passengers in the first-class saloon. They paid seventy pounds for their berths; and Janet found a very sick woman in the second-class saloon, so that for sixteen days she lived below, and chatted with the stewardesses at the foot of the second-saloon stairs while her patient slept. McPhee was a passenger for exactly twenty-four hours. Then the engineers' mess – where the oilcloth tables are – joyfully took him to its bosom, and for the rest of the voyage that company was richer by the unpaid services of a highly certificated engineer.

❴ 'They' [1] ❵

One view called me to another; one hill top to its fellow, half across the county, and since I could answer at no more trouble than the snapping forward of a lever, I let the county flow under my wheels. The orchid-studded flats of the East gave way to the thyme, ilex, and grey grass of the Downs; these again to the rich cornland and fig-trees of the lower coast, where you carry the beat of the tide on your left hand for fifteen level miles; and when at last I turned inland through a huddle of rounded hills and woods I had run myself clean out of my known marks. Beyond that precise hamlet [2] which stands godmother to the capital of the United States, I found hidden villages where bees, the only things awake, boomed in eighty-foot lindens that overhung grey Norman churches; miraculous brooks diving under stone bridges built for heavier traffic than would ever vex them again; tithe-barns larger than their churches, and an old smithy that cried out aloud how it had once been a hall of the Knights of the Temple. Gipsies I found on a common where the gorse, bracken, and heath fought it out together up a mile of Roman road; and a little farther on I disturbed a red fox rolling dog-fashion in the naked sunlight.

As the wooded hills closed about me I stood up in the car to take the bearings of that great Down whose ringed head is a landmark for fifty miles across the low countries. I judged that the lie of the country would bring me across some westward-running road that went to his feet, but I did not allow for the confusing veils of the woods. A quick turn plunged me first into a green cutting brim-full of liquid sunshine, next into a gloomy tunnel where last year's dead leaves whispered and scuffled about my tyres. The strong hazel stuff meeting overhead had not been cut for a couple of generations at least, nor had any axe helped the moss-cankered oak and beech to spring above them. Here the road changed frankly into a carpeted ride on whose brown velvet spent primrose-clumps showed like jade, and a few sickly, white-stalked blue-bells nodded together. As the slope favoured I shut off the power and slid over the whirled leaves, expecting every moment to meet a keeper; but I only heard a jay, far off, arguing against the silence under the twilight of the trees.

Still the track descended. I was on the point of reversing and working

387

my way back on the second speed ere I ended in some swamp, when I saw sunshine through the tangle ahead and lifted the brake.

It was down again at once. As the light beat across my face my fore-wheels took the turf of a great still lawn from which sprang horsemen ten feet high with levelled lances, monstrous peacocks, and sleek round-headed maids of honour – blue, black, and glistening – all of clipped yew. Across the lawn – the marshalled woods besieged it on three sides – stood an ancient house of lichened and weather-worn stone, with mullioned windows and roofs of rose-red tile. It was flanked by semicircular walls, also rose-red, that closed the lawn on the fourth side, and at their feet a box hedge grew man-high. There were doves on the roof about the slim brick chimneys, and I caught a glimpse of an octagonal dove-house behind the screening wall.

Here, then, I stayed; a horseman's green spear laid at my breast; held by the exceeding beauty of that jewel in that setting.

'If I am not packed off for a trespasser, or if this knight does not ride a wallop at me,' thought I, 'Shakespeare and Queen Elizabeth at least must come out of that half-open garden door and ask me to tea.'

A child appeared at an upper window, and I thought the little thing waved a friendly hand. But it was to call a companion, for presently another bright head showed. Then I heard a laugh among the yew-peacocks, and turning to make sure (till then I had been watching the house only) I saw the silver of a fountain behind a hedge thrown up against the sun. The doves on the roof cooed to the cooing water; but between the two notes I caught the utterly happy chuckle of a child absorbed in some light mischief.

The garden door – heavy oak sunk deep in the thickness of the wall – opened further: a woman in a big garden hat set her foot slowly on the time-hollowed stone step and as slowly walked across the turf. I was forming some apology when she lifted up her head and I saw that she was blind.

'I heard you,' she said. 'Isn't that a motor car?'

'I'm afraid I've made a mistake in my road. I should have turned off up above – I never dreamed –' I began.

'But I'm very glad. Fancy a motor car coming into the garden! It will be such a treat –' She turned and made as though looking about her. 'You – you haven't seen anyone, have you – perhaps?'

'No one to speak to, but the children seemed interested at a distance.'

'Which?'

'I saw a couple up at the window just now, and I think I heard a little chap in the grounds.'

'They'

'Oh, lucky you!' she cried, and her face brightened. 'I hear them, of course, but that's all. You've seen them and heard them?'

'Yes,' I answered. 'And if I know anything of children, one of them's having a beautiful time by the fountain yonder. Escaped, I should imagine.'

'You're fond of children?'

I gave her one or two reasons why I did not altogether hate them.

'Of course, of course,' she said. 'Then you understand. Then you won't think it foolish if I ask you to take your car through the gardens, once or twice – quite slowly. I'm sure they'd like to see it. They see so little, poor things. One tries to make their life pleasant, but –' she threw out her hands towards the woods. 'We're so out of the world here.'

'That will be splendid,' I said. 'But I can't cut up your grass.'

She faced to the right. 'Wait a minute,' she said. 'We're at the South gate, aren't we? Behind those peacocks there's a flagged path. We call it the Peacocks' Walk. You can't see it from here, they tell me, but if you squeeze along by the edge of the wood you can turn at the first peacock and get on to the flags.'

It was sacrilege to wake that dreaming house-front with the clatter of machinery, but I swung the car to clear the turf, brushed along the edge of the wood and turned in on the broad stone path where the fountain-basin lay like one star-sapphire.

'May I come too?' she cried. 'No, please don't help me. They'll like it better if they see me.'

She felt her way lightly to the front of the car, and with one foot on the step she called: 'Children, oh, children! Look and see what's going to happen!'

The voice would have drawn lost souls from the Pit, for the yearning that underlay its sweetness, and I was not surprised to hear an answering shout behind the yews. It must have been the child by the fountain, but he fled at our approach, leaving a little toy boat in the water. I saw the glint of his blue blouse among the still horsemen.

Very disposedly we paraded the length of the walk and at her request backed again. This time the child had got the better of his panic, but stood far off and doubting.

'The little fellow's watching us,' I said. 'I wonder if he'd like a ride.'

'They're very shy still. Very shy. But, oh, lucky you to be able to see them! Let's listen.'

I stopped the machine at once, and the humid stillness, heavy with the scent of box, cloaked us deep. Shears I could hear where some gardener was clipping; a mumble of bees and broken voices that might have been the doves.

'Oh, unkind!' she said weariedly.

'Perhaps they're only shy of the motor. The little maid at the window looks tremendously interested.'

'Yes?' She raised her head. 'It was wrong of me to say that. They are really fond of me. It's the only thing that makes life worth living – when they're fond of you, isn't it? I daren't think what the place would be without them. By the way, is it beautiful?'

'I think it is the most beautiful place I have ever seen.'

'So they all tell me. I can feel it, of course, but that isn't quite the same thing.'

'Then have you never –?' I began, but stopped abashed.

'Not since I can remember. It happened when I was only a few months old, they tell me. And yet I must remember something, else how could I dream about colours. I see light in my dreams, and colours, but I never see *them*. I only hear them just as I do when I'm awake.'

'It's difficult to see faces in dreams. Some people can, but most of us haven't the gift,' I went on, looking up at the window where the child stood all but hidden.

'I've heard that too,' she said. 'And they tell me that one never sees a dead person's face in a dream. Is that true?'

'I believe it is – now I come to think of it.'

'But how is it with yourself – yourself?' The blind eyes turned towards me.

'I have never seen the faces of my dead in any dream,' I answered.

'Then it must be as bad as being blind.'

The sun had dipped behind the woods and the long shades were possessing the insolent horsemen one by one. I saw the light die from off the top of a glossy-leaved lance and all the brave hard green turn to soft black. The house, accepting another day at end, as it had accepted an hundred thousand gone, seemed to settle deeper into its rest among the shadows.

'Have you ever wanted to?' she said after the silence.

'Very much sometimes,' I replied. The child had left the window as the shadows closed upon it.

'Ah! So've I, but I don't suppose it's allowed . . . Where d'you live?'

'Quite the other side of the county – sixty miles and more, and I must be going back. I've come without my big lamp.'

'But it's not dark yet. I can feel it.'

'I'm afraid it will be by the time I get home. Could you lend me someone to set me on my road at first? I've utterly lost myself.'

'I'll send Madden with you to the cross-roads. We are so out of the world, I don't wonder you were lost! I'll guide you round to the front of the house; but you will go slowly, won't you, till you're out of the grounds? It isn't foolish, do you think?'

'I promise you I'll go like this,' I said, and let the car start herself down the flagged path.

We skirted the left wing of the house, whose elaborately cast lead guttering alone was worth a day's journey; passed under a great rose-grown gate in the red wall, and so round to the high front of the house which in beauty and stateliness as much excelled the back as that all others I had seen.

. 'Is it so very beautiful?' she said wistfully when she heard my raptures. 'And you like the lead-figures too? There's the old azalea garden behind. They say that this place must have been made for children. Will you help me out, please? I should like to come with you as far as the cross-roads, but I mustn't leave them. Is that you, Madden? I want you to show this gentleman the way to the cross-roads. He has lost his way but – he has seen them.'

A butler appeared noiselessly at the miracle of old oak that must be called the front door, and slipped aside to put on his hat. She stood looking at me with open blue eyes in which no sight lay, and I saw for the first time that she was beautiful.

'Remember,' she said quietly, 'if you are fond of them you will come again,' and disappeared within the house.

The butler in the car said nothing till we were nearly at the lodge gates, where catching a glimpse of a blue blouse in the shrubbery I swerved amply lest the devil that leads little boys to play should drag me into child-murder.

'Excuse me,' he asked of a sudden, 'but why did you do that, Sir?'

'The child yonder.'

'Our young gentleman in blue?'

'Of course.'

'He runs about a good deal. Did you see him by the fountain, Sir?'

'Oh, yes, several times. Do we turn here?'

'Yes, Sir. And did you 'appen to see them upstairs too?'

'At the upper window? Yes.'

'Was that before the mistress come out to speak to you, Sir?'

'A little before that. Why d'you want to know?'

He paused a little. 'Only to make sure that – that they had seen the car, Sir, because with children running about, though I'm sure you're driving particularly careful, there might be an accident. That was all, Sir. Here are the cross-roads. You can't miss your way from now on. Thank you, Sir, but that isn't *our* custom, not with –'

'I beg your pardon,' I said, and thrust away the British silver.

'Oh, it's quite right with the rest of 'em as a rule. Good-bye, Sir.'

He retired into the armour-plated conning tower of his caste and walked away. Evidently a butler solicitous for the honour of his house, and interested, probably through a maid, in the nursery.

Once beyond the signposts at the cross-roads I looked back, but the crumpled hills interlaced so jealously that I could not see where the house had lain. When I asked its name at a cottage along the road, the fat woman who sold sweetmeats there gave me to understand that people with motor cars had small right to live – much less to 'go about talking like carriage folk'. They were not a pleasant-mannered community.

When I retraced my route on the map that evening I was little wiser. Hawkin's Old Farm appeared to be the Survey title of the place, and the old County Gazetteer, generally so ample, did not allude to it. The big house of those parts was Hodnington Hall, Georgian with early Victorian embellishments, as an atrocious steel engraving attested. I carried my difficulty to a neighbour – a deep-rooted tree of that soil – and he gave me a name of a family which conveyed no meaning.

A month or so later – I went again, or it may have been that my car took the road of her own volition. She over-ran the fruitless Downs, threaded every turn of the maze of lanes below the hills, drew through the high-walled woods, impenetrable in their full leaf, came out at the cross-roads where the butler had left me, and a little farther on developed an internal trouble which forced me to turn her in on a grass way-waste that cut into a summer-silent hazel wood. So far as I could make sure by the sun and a six-inch Ordnance map, this should be the road flank of that wood which I had first explored from the heights above. I made a mighty serious business of my repairs and a glittering shop of my repair kit, spanners, pump, and the like, which I spread out orderly upon a rug. It was a trap to catch all childhood, for on such a day, I argued, the children would not be far off. When I paused in my work I listened, but the wood was so full of the noises of summer (though the birds had mated) that I could not at first distinguish these from the tread of small cautious feet stealing across the dead leaves. I rang my bell in an alluring manner, but the feet fled, and I repented, for to a child a sudden noise is very real terror. I must have been at work half an hour when I heard in the wood the voice of the blind woman crying: 'Children, oh, children! Where are you?' and the stillness made slow to close on the perfection of that cry. She came towards me, half feeling her way between the tree boles, and though a child it seemed clung to her skirt, it swerved into the leafage like a rabbit as she drew nearer.

'Is that you?' she said, 'from the other side of the county?'

'Yes, it's me from the other side of the county.'

'Then why didn't you come through the upper woods? They were there just now.'

'They were here a few minutes ago. I expect they knew my car had broken down, and came to see the fun.'

'Nothing serious, I hope? How do cars break down?'

'In fifty different ways. Only mine has chosen the fifty first.'

She laughed merrily at the tiny joke, cooed with delicious laughter, and pushed her hat back.

'Let me hear,' she said.

'Wait a moment,' I cried, 'and I'll get you a cushion.'

She set her foot on the rug all covered with spare parts, and stooped above it eagerly. 'What delightful things!' The hands through which she saw glanced in the chequered sunlight. 'A box here – another box! Why you've arranged them like playing shop!'

'I confess now that I put it out to attract them. I don't need half those things really.'

'How nice of you! I heard your bell in the upper wood. You say they were here before that?'

'I'm sure of it. Why are they so shy? That little fellow in blue who was with you just now ought to have got over his fright. He's been watching me like a Red Indian.'

'It must have been your bell,' she said. 'I heard one of them go past me in trouble when I was coming down. They're shy – so shy even with me.' She turned her face over her shoulder and cried again: 'Children, oh, children! Look and see!'

'They must have gone off together on their own affairs,' I suggested, for there was a murmur behind us of lowered voices broken by the sudden squeaking giggles of childhood. I returned to my tinkerings and she leaned forward, her chin on her hand, listening interestedly.

'How many are they?' I said at last. The work was finished, but I saw no reason to go.

Her forehead puckered a little in thought. 'I don't quite know,' she said simply. 'Sometimes more – sometimes less. They come and stay with me because I love them, you see.'

'That must be very jolly,' I said, replacing a drawer, and as I spoke I heard the inanity of my answer.

'You – you aren't laughing at me,' she cried. 'I – I haven't any of my own. I never married. People laugh at me sometimes about them because – because –'

'Because they're savages,' I returned. 'It's nothing to fret for. That sort laugh at everything that isn't in their own fat lives.'

'I don't know. How should I? I only don't like being laughed at about *them*. It hurts; and when one can't see . . . I don't want to seem silly,' her chin quivered like a child's as she spoke, 'but we blindies have only one skin, I think. Everything outside hits straight at our souls. It's different with you. You've such good defences in your eyes – looking out – before anyone can really pain you in your soul. People forget that with us.'

I was silent reviewing that inexhaustible matter – the more than inherited (since it is also carefully taught) brutality of the Christian peoples, beside which the mere heathendom of the West Coast nigger is clean and restrained. It led me a long distance into myself.

'Don't do that!' she said of a sudden, putting her hands before her eyes.
'What?'
She made a gesture with her hand.
'That! It's – it's all purple and black. Don't! That colour hurts.'

'But, how in the world do you know about colours?' I exclaimed, for here was a revelation indeed.

'Colours as colours?' she asked.

'No. *Those* Colours which you saw just now.'

'You know as well as I do,' she laughed, 'else you wouldn't have asked that question. They aren't in the world at all. They're in *you* – when you went so angry.'

'D'you mean a dull purplish patch, like port wine mixed with ink?' I said.

'I've never seen ink or port wine, but the colours aren't mixed. They are separate – all separate.'

'Do you mean black streaks and jags across the purple?'

She nodded. 'Yes – if they are like this,' and zig-zagged her finger again, 'but it's more red than purple – that bad colour.'

'And what are the colours at the top of the – whatever you see?'

Slowly she leaned forward and traced on the rug the figure of the Egg[3] itself.

'I see them so,' she said, pointing with a grass stem, 'white, green, yellow, red, purple, and when people are angry or bad, black across the red – as you were just now.'

'Who told you anything about it – in the beginning?' I demanded.

'About the colours? No one. I used to ask what colours were when I was little – in table-covers and curtains and carpets, you see – because some colours hurt me and some made me happy. People told me; and when I got older that was how I saw people.' Again she traced the outline of the Egg which it is given to very few of us to see.

'All by yourself?' I repeated.

'All by myself. There wasn't anyone else. I only found out afterwards that other people did not see the Colours.'

She leaned against the tree-bole plaiting and unplaiting chance-plucked grass stems. The children in the wood had drawn nearer. I could see them with the tail of my eye frolicking like squirrels.

'Now I am sure you will never laugh at me,' she went on after a long silence. 'Nor at *them*.'

'Goodness! No!' I cried, jolted out of my train of thought. 'A man who laughs at a child – unless the child is laughing too – is a heathen!'

'I didn't mean that, of course. You'd never laugh *at* children, but I thought – I used to think – that perhaps you might laugh about *them*. So now I beg your pardon . . . What are you going to laugh at?'

I had made no sound, but she knew.

'At the notion of your begging my pardon. If you had done your duty as a pillar of the State and a landed proprietress you ought to have summoned me for trespass when I barged through your woods the other day. It was disgraceful of me – inexcusable.'

She looked at me, her head against the tree trunk – long and steadfastly – this woman who could see the naked soul.

'How curious,' she half whispered. 'How very curious.'

'Why, what have I done?'

'You don't understand . . . and yet you understood about the Colours. Don't you understand?'

She spoke with a passion that nothing had justified, and I faced her bewilderedly as she rose. The children had gathered themselves in a roundel behind a bramble bush. One sleek head bent over something smaller, and the set of the little shoulders told me that fingers were on lips. They, too, had some child's tremendous secret. I alone was hopelessly astray there in the broad sunlight.

'No,' I said, and shook my head as though the dead eyes could note. 'Whatever it is, I don't understand yet. Perhaps I shall later – if you'll let me come again.'

'You will come again,' she answered. 'You will surely come again and walk in the wood.'

'Perhaps the children will know me well enough by that time to let me play with them – as a favour. You know what children are like.'

'It isn't a matter of favour but of right,' she replied, and while I wondered what she meant, a dishevelled woman plunged round the bend of the road, loose-haired, purple, almost lowing with agony as she ran. It was my rude, fat friend of the sweetmeat shop. The blind woman heard and stepped forward. 'What is it, Mrs Madehurst?' she asked.

The woman flung her apron over her head and literally grovelled in the dust, crying that her grandchild was sick to death, that the local doctor was away fishing, that Jenny the mother was at her wits' end, and so forth, with repetitions and bellowings.

'Where's the next nearest doctor?' I asked between paroxysms.

'Madden will tell you. Go round to the house and take him with you. I'll attend to this. Be quick!' She half supported the fat woman into the shade. In two minutes I was blowing all the horns of Jericho under the front of the House Beautiful, and Madden, in the pantry, rose to the crisis like a butler and a man.

A quarter of an hour at illegal speeds caught us a doctor five miles away. Within the half-hour we had decanted him, much interested in motors, at the door of the sweetmeat shop, and drew up the road to await the verdict.

'Useful things cars,' said Madden, all man and no butler. 'If I'd had one when mine took sick she wouldn't have died.'

'How was it?' I asked.

'Croup. Mrs Madden was away. No one knew what to do. I drove eight miles in a tax cart[4] for the doctor. She was choked when we came back. This car 'd ha' saved her. She'd have been close on ten now.'

'I'm sorry,' I said. 'I thought you were rather fond of children from what you told me going to the cross-roads the other day.'

'Have you seen 'em again, Sir – this mornin'?'

'Yes, but they're well broke to cars. I couldn't get any of them within twenty yards of it.'

He looked at me carefully as a scout considers a stranger – not as a menial should lift his eyes to his divinely appointed superior.

'I wonder why,' he said just above the breath that he drew.

We waited on. A light wind from the sea wandered up and down the long lines of the woods, and the wayside grasses, whitened already with summer dust, rose and bowed in sallow waves.

A woman, wiping the suds off her arms, came out of the cottage next the sweetmeat shop.

'I've be'n listenin' in de back-yard,' she said cheerily. 'He says Arthur's

396

unaccountable bad. Did ye hear him shruck just now? Unaccountable bad. I reckon t'will come Jenny's turn to walk in de wood nex' week along, Mr Madden.'

'Excuse me, Sir, but your lap-robe is slipping,' said Madden deferentially. The woman started, dropped a curtsey, and hurried away.

'What does she mean by "walking in the wood"?' I asked.

'It must be some saying they use hereabouts. I'm from Norfolk myself,' said Madden. 'They're an independent lot in this county. She took you for a chauffeur, Sir.'

I saw the Doctor come out of the cottage followed by a draggle-tailed wench who clung to his arm as though he could make treaty for her with Death. 'Dat sort,' she wailed – 'dey're just as much to us dat has 'em as if dey was lawful born. Just as much – just as much! An' God he'd be just as pleased if you saved 'un, Doctor. Don't take it from me. Miss Florence will tell ye de very same. Don't leave 'im, Doctor!'

'I know, I know,' said the man; 'but he'll be quiet for a while now. We'll get the nurse and the medicine as fast as we can.' He signalled me to come forward with the car, and I strove not to be privy to what followed; but I saw the girl's face, blotched and frozen with grief, and I felt the hand without a ring clutching at my knees when we moved away.

The Doctor was a man of some humour, for I remember he claimed my car under the Oath of Æsculapius,[5] and used it and me without mercy. First we convoyed Mrs Madehurst and the blind woman to wait by the sick bed till the nurse should come. Next we invaded a neat county town for prescriptions (the Doctor said the trouble was cerebro-spinal meningitis), and when the County Institute, banked and flanked with scared market cattle, reported itself out of nurses for the moment we literally flung ourselves loose upon the county. We conferred with the owners of great houses – magnates at the ends of overarching avenues whose big-boned womenfolk strode away from their tea-tables to listen to the imperious Doctor. At last a white-haired lady sitting under a cedar of Lebanon and surrounded by a court of magnificent Borzois – all hostile to motors – gave the Doctor, who received them as from a princess, written orders which we bore many miles at top speed, through a park, to a French nunnery, where we took over in exchange a pallid-faced and trembling Sister. She knelt at the bottom of the tonneau telling her beads without pause till, by short cuts of the Doctor's invention, we had her to the sweetmeat shop once more. It was a long afternoon crowded with mad episodes that rose and dissolved like the dust of our wheels; cross-sections of remote and incomprehensible lives through which we raced at right angles; and I went home in the dusk, wearied out, to dream of the clashing horns of cattle; round-eyed nuns walking in a garden of graves; pleasant tea-parties beneath shaded trees; the carbolic-scented, grey-painted corridors of the County Institute; the steps of shy children in the wood, and the hands that clung to my knees as the motor began to move.

I had intended to return in a day or two, but it pleased Fate to hold me from that side of the county, on many pretexts, till the elder and the wild rose had fruited. There came at last a brilliant day, swept clear from the south-west, that brought the hills within hand's reach – a day of unstable airs and high filmy clouds. Through no merit of my own I was free, and set the car for the third time on that known road. As I reached the crest of the Downs I felt the soft air change, saw it glaze under the sun; and, looking down at the sea, in that instant beheld the blue of the Channel turn through polished silver and dulled steel to dingy pewter. A laden collier hugging the coast steered outward for deeper water, and, across copper-coloured haze, I saw sails rise one by one on the anchored fishing-fleet. In a deep dene behind me an eddy of sudden wind drummed through sheltered oaks, and spun aloft the first dry sample of autumn leaves. When I reached the beach road the sea-fog fumed over the brickfields, and the tide was telling all the groins of the gale beyond Ushant. In less than an hour summer England vanished in chill grey. We were again the shut island of the North, all the ships of the world bellowing at our perilous gates; and between their outcries ran the piping of bewildered gulls. My cap dripped moisture, the folds of the rug held it in pools or sluiced it away in runnels, and the salt-rime stuck to my lips.

Inland the smell of autumn loaded the thickened fog among the trees, and the drip became a continuous shower. Yet the late flowers – mallow of the wayside, scabious of the field, and dahlia of the garden – showed gay in the mist, and beyond the sea's breath there was little sign of decay in the leaf. Yet in the villages the house doors were all open, and bare-legged, bare-headed children sat at ease on the damp doorsteps to shout 'pip-pip' at the stranger.

I made bold to call at the sweetmeat shop, where Mrs Madehurst met me with a fat woman's hospitable tears. Jenny's child, she said, had died two days after the nun had come. It was, she felt, best out of the way, even though insurance offices, for reasons which she did not pretend to follow, would not willingly insure such stray lives. 'Not but what Jenny didn't tend to Arthur as though he'd come all proper at de end of de first year – like Jenny herself.' Thanks to Miss Florence, the child had been buried with a pomp which, in Mrs Madehurst's opinion, more than covered the small irregularity of its birth. She described the coffin, within and without, the glass hearse, and the evergreen lining of the grave.

'But how's the mother?' I asked.

'Jenny? Oh, she'll get over it. I've felt dat way with one or two o' my own. She'll get over. She's walkin' in de wood now.'

'In this weather?'

Mrs Madehurst looked at me with narrowed eyes across the counter.

'I dunno but it opens de 'eart like. Yes, it opens de 'eart. Dat's where losin' and bearin' comes so alike in de long run, we do say.'

Now the wisdom of the old wives is greater than that of all the Fathers,[6] and this last oracle sent me thinking so extendedly as I went up the road, that I nearly ran over a woman and a child at the wooded corner by the lodge gates of the House Beautiful.

'Awful weather!' I cried, as I slowed dead for the turn.

'Not so bad,' she answered placidly out of the fog. 'Mine's used to 'un. You'll find yours indoors, I reckon.'

Indoors, Madden received me with professional courtesy, and kind inquiries for the health of the motor, which he would put under cover.

I waited in a still, nut-brown hall, pleasant with late flowers and warmed with a delicious wood fire – a place of good influence and great peace. (Men and women may sometimes, after great effort, achieve a creditable lie; but the house, which is their temple, cannot say anything save the truth of those who have lived in it.) A child's cart and a doll lay on the black-and-white floor, where a rug had been kicked back. I felt that the children had only just hurried away – to hide themselves, most like – in the many turns of the great adzed staircase that climbed statelily out of the hall, or to crouch at gaze behind the lions and roses of the carven gallery above. Then I heard her voice above me, singing as the blind sing – from the soul:

> In the pleasant orchard-closes.

And all my early summer came back at the call.

> In the pleasant orchard-closes,
> God bless all our gains say we –
> But may God bless all our losses,
> Better suits with our degree.[7]

She dropped the marring fifth line, and repeated –

> Better suits with our degree!

I saw her lean over the gallery, her linked hands white as pearl against the oak.

'Is that you – from the other side of the county?' she called.

'Yes, me – from the other side of the county,' I answered, laughing.

'What a long time before you had to come here again.' She ran down the stairs, one hand lightly touching the broad rail. 'It's two months and four days. Summer's gone!'

'I meant to come before, but Fate prevented.'

'I knew it. Please do something to that fire. They won't let me play with it, but I can feel it's behaving badly. Hit it!'

I looked on either side of the deep fireplace, and found but a half-charred hedge-stake with which I punched a black log into flame.

'It never goes out, day or night,' she said, as though explaining. 'In case anyone comes in with cold toes, you see.'

'It's even lovelier inside than it was out,' I murmured. The red light poured itself along the age-polished dusky panels till the Tudor roses and lions of the gallery took colour and motion. An old eagle-topped convex mirror gathered the picture into its mysterious heart, distorting afresh the distorted shadows, and curving the gallery lines into the curves of a ship. The day was shutting down in half a gale as the fog turned to stringy scud. Through the uncurtained mullions of the broad window I could see valiant horsemen of the lawn rear and recover against the wind that taunted them with legions of dead leaves.

'Yes, it must be beautiful,' she said. 'Would you like to go over it? There's still light enough upstairs.'

I followed her up the unflinching, wagon-wide staircase to the gallery whence opened the thin fluted Elizabethan doors.

'Feel how they put the latch low down for the sake of the children.' She swung a light door inward.

'By the way, where are they?' I asked. 'I haven't even heard them today.'

She did not answer at once. Then, 'I can only hear them,' she replied softly. 'This is one of their rooms – everything ready, you see.'

She pointed into a heavily-timbered room. There were little low gate tables and children's chairs. A doll's house, its hooked front half open, faced a great dappled rocking-horse, from whose padded saddle it was but a child's scramble to the broad window-seat overlooking the lawn. A toy gun lay in a corner beside a gilt wooden cannon.

'Surely they've only just gone,' I whispered. In the failing light a door creaked cautiously. I heard the rustle of a frock and the patter of feet – quick feet through a room beyond.

'I heard that,' she cried triumphantly. 'Did you? Children, oh, children! Where are you?'

The voice filled the walls that held it lovingly to the last perfect note, but there came no answering shout such as I had heard in the garden. We hurried on from room to oak-floored room; up a step here, down three steps there; among a maze of passages; always mocked by our quarry. One might as well have tried to work an unstopped warren with a single ferret. There were bolt-holes innumerable – recesses in walls, embrasures of deep slitten windows now darkened, whence they could start up behind us; and abandoned fireplaces, six feet deep in the masonry, as well as the tangle of communicating doors. Above all, they had the twilight for their helper in our game. I had caught one or two joyous chuckles of evasion, and once or twice had seen the silhouette of a child's frock against some darkening window at the end of a passage; but we returned empty-handed to the gallery, just as a middle-aged woman was setting a lamp in its niche.

'No, I haven't seen her either this evening, Miss Florence,' I heard her say, 'but that Turpin he says he wants to see you about his shed.'

'Oh, Mr Turpin must want to see me very badly. Tell him to come to the hall, Mrs Madden.'

I looked down into the hall whose only light was the dulled fire, and deep in the shadow I saw them at last. They must have slipped down while we were in the passages, and now thought themselves perfectly hidden behind an old gilt leather screen. By child's law, my fruitless chase was as good as an introduction, but since I had taken so much trouble I resolved to force them to come forward later by the simple trick, which children detest, of pretending not to notice them. They lay close, in a little huddle, no more than shadows except when a quick flame betrayed an outline.

'And now we'll have some tea,' she said. 'I believe I ought to have offered it you at first, but one doesn't arrive at manners somehow when one lives alone and is considered – h'm – peculiar.' Then with very pretty scorn, 'Would you like a lamp to see to eat by?'

'The firelight's much pleasanter, I think.' We descended into that delicious gloom and Madden brought tea.

I took my chair in the direction of the screen ready to surprise or be surprised as the game should go, and at her permission, since a hearth is always sacred, bent forward to play with the fire.

'Where do you get these beautiful short faggots from?' I asked idly. 'Why, they are tallies!'

'Of course,' she said. 'As I can't read or write I'm driven back on the early English tally for my accounts. Give me one and I'll tell you what it meant.'

I passed her an unburned hazel-tally, about a foot long, and she ran her thumb down the nicks.

'This is the milk-record for the home farm for the month of April last year, in gallons,' said she. 'I don't know what I should have done without tallies. An old forester of mine taught me the system. It's out of date now for everyone else; but my tenants respect it. One of them's coming now to see me. Oh, it doesn't matter. He has no business here out of office hours. He's a greedy, ignorant man – very greedy or – he wouldn't come here after dark.'

'Have you much land then?'

'Only a couple of hundred acres in hand, thank goodness. The other six hundred are nearly all let to folk who knew my folk before me, but this Turpin is quite a new man – and a highway robber.'

'But are you sure I shan't be –?'

'Certainly not. You have the right. He hasn't any children.'

'Ah, the children!' I said, and slid my low chair back till it nearly touched the screen that hid them. 'I wonder whether they'll come out for me.'

There was a murmur of voices – Madden's and a deeper note – at the low, dark side door, and a ginger-headed, canvas-gaitered giant of the unmistakable tenant-farmer type stumbled or was pushed in.

'Come to the fire, Mr Turpin,' she said.

'If – if you please, Miss, I'll – I'll be quite as well by the door.' He clung to the latch as he spoke like a frightened child. Of a sudden I realized that he was in the grip of some almost overpowering fear.

'Well?'

'About that new shed for the young stock – that was all. These first autumn storms settin' in . . . but I'll come again, Miss.' His teeth did not chatter much more than the door latch.

'I think not,' she answered levelly. 'The new shed – m'm. What did my agent write you on the 15th?'

'I – fancied p'raps that if I came to see you – ma – man to man like, Miss. But –'

His eyes rolled into every corner of the room wide with horror. He half opened the door through which he had entered, but I noticed it shut again – from without and firmly.

'He wrote what I told him,' she went on. 'You are overstocked already. Dunnett's Farm never carried more than fifty bullocks – even in Mr Wright's time. And *he* used cake. You've sixty-seven and you don't cake. You've broken the lease in that respect. You're dragging the heart out of the farm.'

'I'm – I'm getting some minerals – superphosphates – next week. I've as good as ordered a truck-load already. I'll go down to the station tomorrow about 'em. Then I can come and see you man to man like, Miss, in the daylight . . . That gentleman's not going away, is he?' He almost shrieked.

I had only slid the chair a little farther back, reaching behind me to tap on the leather of the screen, but he jumped like a rat.

'No. Please attend to me, Mr Turpin.' She turned in her chair and faced him with his back to the door. It was an old and sordid little piece of scheming that she forced from him – his plea for the new cow-shed at his landlady's expense, that he might with the covered manure pay his next year's rent out of the valuation after, as she made clear, he had bled the enriched pastures to the bone. I could not but admire the intensity of his greed, when I saw him out-facing for its sake whatever terror it was that ran wet on his forehead.

I ceased to tap the leather – was, indeed, calculating the cost of the shed – when I felt my relaxed hands taken and turned softly between the soft hands of a child. So at last I had triumphed. In a moment I would turn and acquaint myself with those quick-footed wanderers . . .

The little brushing kiss fell in the centre of my palm – as a gift on which the fingers were, once, expected to close: as the all-faithful half-reproachful signal of a waiting child not used to neglect even when grown-ups were busiest – a fragment of the mute code devised very long ago.

Then I knew. And it was as though I had known from the first day when I looked across the lawn at the high window.

I heard the door shut. The woman turned to me in silence, and I felt that she knew.

What time passed after this I cannot say. I was roused by the fall of a log, and mechanically rose to put it back. Then I returned to my place in the chair very close to the screen.

'Now you understand,' she whispered, across the packed shadows.

'Yes, I understand – now. Thank you.'

'I – I only hear them.' She bowed her head in her hands. 'I have no right, you know – no other right. I have neither borne nor lost – neither borne nor lost!'

'Be very glad then,' said I, for my soul was torn open within me.

'Forgive me!'

She was still, and I went back to my sorrow and my joy.

'It was because I loved them so,' she said at last, brokenly. '*That* was why it was, even from the first – even before I knew that they – they were all I should ever have. And I loved them so!'

She stretched out her arms to the shadows and the shadows within the shadow.

'They came because I loved them – because I needed them. I – I must have made them come. Was that wrong, think you?'

'No – no.'

'I – I grant you that the toys and – and all that sort of thing were nonsense, but – but I used to so hate empty rooms myself when I was little.' She pointed to the gallery. 'And the passages all empty . . . And how could I ever bear the garden door shut? Suppose –'

'Don't! For pity's sake, don't!' I cried. The twilight had brought a cold rain with gusty squalls that plucked at the leaded windows.

'And the same thing with keeping the fire in all night. *I* don't think it so foolish – do you?'

I looked at the broad brick hearth, saw, through tears I believe, that there was no unpassable iron [8] on or near it, and bowed my head.

'I did all that and lots of other things – just to make believe. Then they came. I heard them, but I didn't know that they were not mine by right till Mrs Madden told me –'

'The butler's wife? What?'

'One of them – I heard – she saw. And knew. Hers! *Not* for me. I didn't know at first. Perhaps I was jealous. Afterwards, I began to understand that it was only because I loved them, not because – . . . Oh, you *must* bear or lose,' she said piteously. 'There is no other way – and yet they love me. They must! Don't they?'

There was no sound in the room except the lapping voices of the fire, but we two listened intently, and she at least took comfort from what she heard. She recovered herself and half rose. I sat still in my chair by the screen.

'Don't think me a wretch to whine about myself like this, but – but I'm all in the dark, you know, and *you* can see.'

In truth I could see, and my vision confirmed me in my resolve, though that was like the very parting of spirit and flesh. Yet a little longer I would stay since it was the last time.

'You think it is wrong, then?' she cried sharply, though I had said nothing.

'Not for you. A thousand times no. For you it is right . . . I am grateful to you beyond words. For me it would be wrong. For me only . . .'

'Why?' she said, but passed her hand before her face as she had done at our second meeting in the wood. 'Oh, I see,' she went on simply as a child. 'For you it would be wrong.' Then with a little indrawn laugh, 'and, d'you remember, I called you lucky – once – at first. You who must never come here again!'

She left me to sit a little longer by the screen, and I heard the sound of her feet die out along the gallery above.

⨍ The Mother Hive [1] ⨍

If the stock had not been old and overcrowded, the Wax-moth would never have entered; but where bees are too thick on the comb there must be sickness or parasites. The heat of the hive had risen with the June honey-flow, and though the fanners worked, until their wings ached, to keep people cool, everybody suffered.

A young bee crawled up the greasy, trampled alighting-board. 'Excuse me,' she began, 'but it's my first honey-flight. Could you kindly tell me if this is my –'

'– own hive?' the Guard snapped. 'Yes! Buzz in, and be foul-brooded to you! Next!'

'Shame!' cried half-a-dozen old workers with worn wings and nerves, and there was a scuffle and a hum.

The little grey Wax-moth, pressed close in a crack in the alighting-board, had waited this chance all day. She scuttled in like a ghost, and, knowing the senior bees would turn her out at once, dodged into a brood-frame, where youngsters who had not yet seen the winds blow or the flowers nod discussed life. Here she was safe, for young bees will tolerate any sort of stranger. Behind her came the bee who had been slanged by the Guard.

'What is the world like, Melissa?' [2] said a companion.

'Cruel! I brought in a full load of first-class stuff, and the Guard told me to go and be foul-brooded!' She sat down in the cool draught across the combs.

'If you'd only heard,' said the Wax-moth silkily, 'the insolence of the Guard's tone when she cursed our sister! It aroused the Entire Community.' She laid an egg. She had stolen in for that purpose.

'There *was* a bit of a fuss on the Gate,' Melissa chuckled. 'You were there, Miss –?' She did not know how to address the slim stranger.

'Don't call me "Miss". I'm a sister to all in affliction – just a working-sister. My heart bled for you beneath your burden.' The Wax-moth caressed Melissa with her soft feelers and laid another egg.

'You mustn't lay here,' cried Melissa. 'You aren't a Queen.'

'My dear child, I give you my most solemn word of honour those aren't eggs. Those are my principles, and I am ready to die for them.' She raised her voice a little above the rustle and tramp round her. 'If you'd like to kill me, pray do.'

'Don't be unkind, Melissa,' said a young bee, impressed by the chaste folds of the Wax-moth's wing, which hid her ceaseless egg-dropping.

'*I* haven't done anything,' Melissa answered. 'She's doing it all.'

'Ah, don't let your conscience reproach you later, but when you've killed me, write me, at least, as one that loved her fellow-workers.'

Laying at every sob, the Wax-moth backed into a crowd of young bees, and left Melissa bewildered and annoyed. So she lifted up her little voice in the darkness and cried, 'Stores!' till a gang of cell-fillers hailed her, and she left her load with them.

'I'm afraid I foul-brooded you just now,' said a voice over her shoulder. 'I'd been on the Gate for three hours, and one would foul-brood the Queen herself after that. No offence meant.'

'None taken,' Melissa answered cheerily. 'I shall be on guard myself, some day. What's next to do?'

'There's a rumour of Death's Head Moths about. Send a gang of youngsters to the Gate, and tell them to narrow it in with a couple of stout scrap-wax pillars. It'll make the Hive hot, but we can't have Death's Headers in the middle of our honey-flow.'

'My Only Wings! I should think not!' Melissa had all a sound bee's hereditary hatred against the big, squeaking, feathery Thief of the Hives. 'Tumble out!' she called across the youngsters' quarters. 'All you who aren't feeding babies, show a leg. Scrap-wax pillars for the Ga-ate!' She chanted the order at length.

'That's nonsense,' a downy, day-old bee answered. 'In the first place, I never heard of a Death's Header coming into a hive. People don't *do* such things. In the second, building pillars to keep 'em out is purely a Cypriote trick, unworthy of British bees. In the third, if you trust a Death's Head, he will trust you. Pillar-building shows lack of confidence. Our dear sister in grey says so.'

'Yes. Pillars are un-English and provocative, and a waste of wax that is needed for higher and more practical ends,' said the Wax-moth from an empty store-cell.

'The safety of the Hive is the highest thing I've ever heard of. You mustn't teach us to refuse work,' Melissa began.

'You misunderstand me as usual, love. Work's the essence of life; but to expend precious unreturning vitality and real labour against imaginary danger, *that* is heartbreakingly absurd! If I can only teach a – a little toleration – a little ordinary kindness here towards that absurd old bogey you call the Death's Header, I shan't have lived in vain.'

'She *hasn't* lived in vain, the darling!' cried twenty bees together. 'You should see her saintly life, Melissa! She just devotes herself to spreading her principles, and – and – she looks lovely!'

An old, baldish bee came up the comb.

'Pillar-workers for the Gate! Get out and chew scraps. Buzz off!' she said. The Wax-moth slipped aside.

The young bees trooped down the frame, whispering.

'What's the matter with 'em?' said the oldster. 'Why do they call each other "ducky" and "darling". Must be the weather.' She sniffed suspiciously. 'Horrid stuffy smell here. Like stale quilts. Not Wax-moth, I hope, Melissa?'

'Not to my knowledge,' said Melissa, who, of course, only knew the Wax-moth as a lady with principles, and had never thought to report her presence. She had always imagined Wax-moths to be like blood-red dragon-flies.

'You had better fan out this corner for a little,' said the old bee and passed on. Melissa dropped her head at once, took firm hold with her fore-feet, and fanned obediently at the regulation stroke – three hundred beats to the second. Fanning tries a bee's temper, because she must always keep in the same place where she never seems to be doing any good, and, all the while, she is wearing out her only wings. When a bee cannot fly, a bee must not live; and a bee knows it. The Wax-moth crept forth, and caressed Melissa again.

'I see,' she murmured, 'that at heart you are one of Us.'

'I work with the Hive,' Melissa answered briefly.

'It's the same thing. We and the Hive are one.'

'Then why are your feelers different from ours? Don't cuddle so.'

'Don't be provincial, *carissima*.[3] You can't have all the world alike – yet.'

'But why do you lay eggs?' Melissa insisted. 'You lay 'em like a Queen – only you drop them in patches all over the place. I've watched you.'

'Ah, Brighteyes, so you've pierced my little subterfuge? Yes, they are eggs. By and by they'll spread our principles. Aren't you glad?'

'You gave me your most solemn word of honour that they were not eggs.'

'That was my little subterfuge, dearest – for the sake of the Cause. Now I must reach the young.' The Wax-moth tripped towards the fourth brood-frame where the young bees were busy feeding the babies.

It takes some time for a sound bee to realize a malignant and continuous lie. 'She's very sweet and feathery,' was all that Melissa thought, 'but her talk sounds like ivy honey tastes. I'd better get to my field-work again.'

She found the Gate in a sulky uproar. The youngsters told off to the pillars had refused to chew scrap-wax because it made their jaws ache, and were clamouring for virgin stuff.

'Anything to finish the job!' said the badgered Guards. 'Hang up, some of you, and make wax for these slack-jawed sisters.'

Before a bee can make wax she must fill herself with honey. Then she climbs to safe foothold and hangs, while other gorged bees hang on to her in a cluster. There they wait in silence till the wax comes. The scales are either taken out of the maker's pockets by the workers, or tinkle down on the workers while they wait. The workers chew them (they are useless unchewed) into the all-supporting, all-embracing Wax of the Hive.

But now, no sooner was the wax cluster in position than the workers below broke out again.

'Come down!' they cried. 'Come down and work! Come on, you Levantine parasites! Don't think to enjoy yourselves up there while we're sweating down here!'

The cluster shivered, as from hooked fore-foot to hooked hind-foot it telegraphed uneasiness. At last a worker sprang up, grabbed the lowest wax-maker, and swung, kicking, above her companions.

'I can make wax too!' she bawled. 'Give me a full gorge and I'll make tons of it.'

'Make it, then,' said the bee she had grappled. The spoken word snapped the current through the cluster. It shook and glistened like a cat's fur in the dark. 'Unhook!' it murmured. 'No wax for anyone today.'

'You lazy thieves! Hang up at once and produce our wax,' said the bees below.

'Impossible! The sweat's gone. To make your wax we must have stillness, warmth, and food. Unhook! Unhook!'

They broke up as they murmured, and disappeared among the other bees, from whom, of course, they were undistinguishable.

''Seems as if we'd have to chew scrap-wax for these pillars, after all,' said a worker.

'Not by a whole comb,' cried the young bee who had broken the cluster. 'Listen here! I've studied the question more than twenty minutes. It's as simple as falling off a daisy. You've heard of Cheshire, Root and Langstroth?'

They had not, but they shouted 'Good old Langstroth!' just the same.

'Those three know all that there is to be known about making hives. One or t'other of 'em must have made ours, and if they've made it, they're bound to look after it. Ours is a "Guaranteed Patent Hive". You can see it on the label behind.'

'Good old guarantee! Hurrah for the label behind!' roared the bees.

'Well, such being the case, *I* say that when we find they've betrayed us, we can exact from them a terrible vengeance.'

'Good old vengeance! Good old Root! 'Nuff said! Chuck it!' The crowd cheered and broke away as Melissa dived through.

'D'you know where Langstroth, Root and Cheshire live if you happen to want 'em?' she asked of the proud and panting orator.

'Gum me if I know they ever lived at all! But aren't they beautiful names to buzz about? Did you see how it worked up the sisterhood?'

'Yes, but it didn't defend the Gate,' she replied.

'Ah, perhaps that's true, but think how delicate *my* position is, sister. I've a magnificent appetite, and I don't like working. It's bad for the mind. My instinct tells me that I can act as a restraining influence on others. They would have been worse, but for me.'

But Melissa had already risen clear, and was heading for a breadth of virgin white clover, which to an overtired bee is as soothing as plain knitting to a woman.

'I think I'll take this load to the nurseries,' she said, when she had finished. 'It was always quiet there in my day,' and she topped off with two little pats of pollen for the babies.

She was met on the fourth brood-comb by a rush of excited sisters all buzzing together.

'One at a time! Let me put down my load. Now, what is it, Sacharissa?' she said.

'Grey Sister – that fluffy one, I mean – she came and said we ought to be out in the sunshine gathering honey, because life was short. She said any old bee could attend to our babies, and some day old bees would. That isn't true, Melissa, is it? No old bees can take us away from our babies, can they?'

'Of course not. You feed the babies while your heads are soft. When your heads harden, you go on to field-work. Anyone knows that.'

'We told her so! We *told* her so; but she only waved her feelers, and said we could all lay eggs like Queens if we chose. And I'm afraid lots of the weaker sisters believe her, and are trying to do it. *So* unsettling!'

Sacharissa sped to a sealed worker-cell whose lid pulsated, as the bee within began to cut its way out.

'Come along, precious!' she murmured, and thinned the frail top from the other side. A pale, damp, creased thing hoisted itself feebly on to the comb. Sacharissa's note changed at once. 'No time to waste! Go up the frame and preen yourself!' she said. 'Report for nursing-duty in my ward tomorrow evening at six. Stop a minute. What's the matter with your third right leg?'

The young bee held it out in silence – unmistakably a drone leg incapable of packing pollen.

'Thank you. You needn't report till the day after tomorrow.' Sacharissa turned to her companion. 'That's the fifth oddity hatched in my ward since noon. I don't like it.'

'There's always a certain number of 'em,' said Melissa. 'You can't stop a few working sisters from laying, now and then, when they overfeed themselves. They only raise dwarf drones.'

'But we're hatching out drones with workers' stomachs; workers with drones' stomachs; and albinos and mixed-leggers who can't pack pollen – like that poor little beast yonder. I don't mind dwarf drones any more than you do (they all die in July), but this steady hatch of oddities frightens me, Melissa!'

'How narrow of you! They are all so delightfully clever and unusual and interesting,' piped the Wax-moth from a crack above them. 'Come here, you dear, downy duck, and tell us all about your feelings.'

'I wish she'd go!' Sacharissa lowered her voice. 'She meets these – er – oddities as they dry out, and cuddles 'em in corners.'

'I suppose the truth is that we're over-stocked and too well fed to swarm,' said Melissa.

'That *is* the truth,' said the Queen's voice behind them. They had not heard the heavy royal footfall which sets empty cells vibrating. Sacharissa offered her food at once. She ate and dragged her weary body forward. 'Can you suggest a remedy?' she said.

'New principles!' cried the Wax-moth from her crevice. 'We'll apply them quietly – later.'

'Suppose we sent out a swarm?' Melissa suggested. 'It's a little late, but it might ease us off.'

'It would save us, but – I know the Hive! You shall see for yourself.' The old Queen cried the Swarming Cry, which to a bee of good blood should be what the trumpet was to Job's war-horse.[4] In spite of her immense age (three years), it rang between the cañon-like frames as a pibroch rings in a mountain pass; the fanners changed their note, and repeated it up in every gallery; and the broad-winged drones, burly and eager, ended it on one nerve-thrilling outbreak of bugles: '*La Reine le veult!*[5] Swarm! Swar-rm! Swar-r-rm!*'

But the roar which should follow the Call was wanting. They heard a broken grumble like the murmur of a falling tide.

'Swarm? What for? Catch me leaving a good bar-frame Hive, with fixed foundations, for a rotten old oak out in the open where it may rain any minute! *We're* all right! It's a "Patent Guaranteed Hive". Why do they want to turn us out? Swarming be gummed! Swarming was invented to cheat a worker out of her proper comforts. Come on off to bed!'

The noise died out as the bees settled in empty cells for the night.

'You hear?' said the Queen. 'I know the Hive!'

'Quite between ourselves, *I* taught them that,' cried the Wax-moth. 'Wait till my principles develop, and you'll see the light from a new quarter.'

'You speak truth for once,' the Queen said suddenly, for she recognized the Wax-moth. 'That Light will break into the top of the Hive. A Hot Smoke will follow it, and your children will not be able to hide in any crevice.'

'Is it possible?' Melissa whispered. 'I – we have sometimes heard a legend like it.'

'It is no legend,' the old Queen answered. 'I had it from my mother, and she had it from hers. After the Wax-moth has grown strong, a Shadow will fall across the gate; a Voice will speak from behind a Veil; there will be Light, and Hot Smoke, and earthquakes, and those who live will see everything that they have done, all together in one place, burned up in one great Fire.' The old Queen was trying to tell what she had been told of the Bee Master's dealings with an infected hive in the apiary, two or three seasons ago; and, of course, from her point of view the affair was as important as the Day of Judgment.

'And then?' asked horrified Sacharissa.

'Then, I have heard that a little light will burn in a great darkness, and perhaps the world will begin again. Myself, I think not.'

'Tut! Tut!' the Wax-moth cried. 'You good, fat people always prophesy ruin if things don't go exactly your way. But I grant you there will be changes.'

There were. When her eggs hatched, the wax was riddled with little tunnels, coated with the dirty clothes of the caterpillars. Flannelly lines ran through the honey-stores, the pollen-larders, the foundations, and, worst of all, through the babies in their cradles, till the Sweeper Guards spent half their time tossing out useless little corpses. The lines ended in a maze of sticky webbing on the face of the comb. The caterpillars could not stop spinning as they walked, and as they walked everywhere, they smarmed and garmed [6] everything. Even where it did not hamper the bees' feet, the stale, sour smell of the stuff put them off their work; though some of the bees who had taken to egg-laying said it encouraged them to be mothers and maintain a vital interest in life.

When the caterpillars became moths, they made friends with the ever-increasing Oddities – albinos, mixed-leggers, single-eyed composites, faceless drones, half-queens and laying sisters; and the ever-dwindling band of the old stock worked themselves bald and fray-winged to feed their queer charges. Most of the Oddities would not, and many, on account of their malformations, could not, go through a day's field-work; but the Wax-moths, who were always busy on the brood-comb, found pleasant home occupations for them. One albino, for instance, divided the number of pounds of honey in stock by the number of bees in the Hive, and proved that if every bee only gathered honey for seven and three-quarter minutes a day, she would have the rest of the time to herself, and could accompany the drones on their mating flights. The drones were not at all pleased.

Another, an eyeless drone with no feelers, said that all brood-cells should be perfect circles, so as not to interfere with the grub or the workers. He proved that the old six-sided cell was solely due to the workers building against each other on opposite sides of the wall, and that if there were no interference, there would be no angles. Some bees tried the new plan for a while, and found it cost eight times more wax than the old six-sided specification; and, as they never allowed a cluster to hang up and make wax in peace, real wax was scarce. However, they eked out their task with varnish stolen from new coffins at funerals, and it made them rather sick. Then they took to cadging round sugar-factories and breweries, because it was easiest to get their material from those places, and the mixture of glucose and beer naturally fermented in store and blew the store-cells out of shape, besides smelling abominably. Some of the sound bees warned them that ill-gotten gains never prosper, but the Oddities at once surrounded them and balled them to death. That was a punishment they were almost as fond of as they were of eating, and they expected the sound bees to feed them. Curiously enough the age-old instinct of loyalty and devotion towards the Hive made the sound bees do this, though their reason told them they ought to slip away and unite with some other healthy stock in the apiary.

'What about seven and three-quarter minutes' work now?' said Melissa one day as she came in. 'I've been at it for five hours, and I've only half a load.'

'Oh, the Hive subsists on the Hival Honey which the Hive produces,' said a blind Oddity squatting in a store-cell.

'But honey is gathered from flowers outside – two miles away sometimes,' cried Melissa.

'Pardon me,' said the blind thing, sucking hard. 'But this is the Hive, is it not?'

'It was. Worse luck, it is.'

'And the Hival Honey is here, is it not?' It opened a fresh store-cell to prove it.

'Ye-es, but it won't be long at this rate,' said Melissa.

'The rates have nothing to do with it. This Hive produces the Hival Honey. You people never seem to grasp the economic simplicity that underlies all life.'

'Oh, me!' said poor Melissa, 'haven't you ever been beyond the Gate?'

'Certainly not. A fool's eyes are in the ends of the earth. Mine are in my head.' It gorged till it bloated.

Melissa took refuge in her poorly-paid field-work and told Sacharissa the story.

'Hut!' said that wise bee, fretting with an old maid of a thistle. 'Tell us something new. The Hive's full of such as him – it, I mean.'

'What's the end to be? All the honey going out and none coming in. Things *can't* last this way!' said Melissa.

'Who cares?' said Sacharissa. 'I know now how drones feel the day before they're killed. A short life and a merry one for me!'

'If it only were merry! But think of those awful, solemn, lop-sided Oddities waiting for us at home – crawling and clambering and preaching – and dirtying things in the dark.'

'I don't mind that so much as their silly songs, after we've fed 'em, all about "work among the merry, merry blossoms",' said Sacharissa from the deeps of a stale Canterbury bell.

'I do. How's our Queen?' said Melissa.

'Cheerfully hopeless, as usual. But she lays an egg now and then.'

'Does she so?' Melissa backed out of the next bell with a jerk. 'Suppose, now, we sound workers tried to raise a Princess in some clean corner?'

'You'd be put to it to find one. The Hive's all wax-moth and muckings. But – Well?'

'A Princess might help us in the time of the Voice behind the Veil that the Queen talks of. And anything is better than working for Oddities that chirrup about work that they can't do, and waste what we bring home.'

'Who cares?' said Sacharissa. 'I'm with you, for the fun of it. The Oddities would ball us to death, if they knew. Come home, and we'll begin.'

There is no room to tell how the experienced Melissa found a far-off frame so messed and mishandled by abandoned cell-building experiments that, for very shame, the bees never went there. How in that ruin she blocked out a Royal Cell of sound wax, but disguised by rubbish till it looked like a kopje [7] among deserted kopjes. How she prevailed upon the hopeless Queen to make one last effort and lay a worthy egg. How the Queen obeyed and died. How her spent carcass was flung out on the rubbish heap, and how a multitude of laying sisters went about dropping drone-eggs where they listed, and said there was no more need of Queens. How, covered by this confusion, Sacharissa educated certain young bees to educate certain new-born bees in the almost lost art of making Royal Jelly. How the nectar for it was won out of hours in the teeth of chill winds. How the hidden egg hatched true – no drone, but Blood Royal. How it was capped, and how desperately they worked to feed and double-feed the now swarming Oddities, lest any break in the food-supplies should set them to instituting inquiries, which, with songs about work, was their favourite amusement. How in an auspicious hour, on a moonless night, the Princess came forth – a Princess indeed – and how Melissa smuggled her into a dark empty honey-magazine, to bide her time; and how the drones, knowing she was there, went about singing the deep disreputable love-songs of the old days – to the scandal of the laying-sisters, who do not think well of drones. These things are written in the Book of Queens, which is laid up in the hollow of the Great Ash Ygdrasil. [8]

After a few days the weather changed again and became glorious. Even the Oddities would now join the crowd that hung out on the alighting-board, and would sing of work among the merry, merry blossoms till an untrained ear might have received it for the hum of a working hive. Yet, in truth, their store-honey had been eaten long ago. They lived from day to day on the efforts of the few sound bees, while the Wax-moth fretted and consumed again their already ruined wax. But the sound bees never mentioned these matters. They knew, if they did, the Oddities would hold a meeting and ball them to death.

'Now you see what we have done,' said the Wax-moths. 'We have created New Material, a New Convention, a New Type, as we said we would.'

'And new possibilities for us,' said the laying-sisters gratefully. 'You have given us a new life's work, vital and paramount.'

'More than that,' chanted the Oddities in the sunshine; 'you have created a new heaven and a new earth. Heaven, cloudless and accessible' (it was a perfect August evening) 'and Earth teeming with the merry, merry blossoms, waiting only our honest toil to turn them all to good.

The – er – Aster, and the Crocus, and the – er – Ladies' Smock in her season, the Chrysanthemum after her kind, and the Guelder Rose bringing forth abundantly withal.'

'Oh, Holy Hymettus!'⁹ said Melissa, awestruck. 'I knew they didn't know how honey was made, but they've forgotten the Order of the Flowers! What will become of them?'

A Shadow fell across the alighting-board as the Bee Master and his son came by. The Oddities crawled in and a Voice behind a Veil said: 'I've neglected the old Hive too long. Give me the smoker.'

Melissa heard and darted through the gate. 'Come, oh come!' she cried. 'It is the destruction the Old Queen foretold. Princess, come!'

'Really, you are too archaic for words,' said an Oddity in an alley-way. 'A cloud, I admit, may have crossed the sun; but why hysterics? Above all, why Princesses so late in the day? Are you aware it's the Hival Tea-time? Let's sing grace.'

Melissa clawed past him with all six legs. Sacharissa had run to what was left of the fertile brood-comb. 'Down and out!' she called across the brown breadth of it. 'Nurses, guards, fanners, sweepers – out! Never mind the babies. They're better dead. Out, before the Light and the Hot Smoke!'

The Princess's first clear fearless call (Melissa had found her) rose and drummed through all the frames. *'La Reine le veult! Swarm! Swar-rm! Swar-r-rm!'*

The Hive shook beneath the shattering thunder of a stuck-down quilt being torn back.

'Don't be alarmed, dears,' said the Wax-moths. 'That's our work. Look up, and you'll see the dawn of the New Day.'

Light broke in the top of the hive as the Queen had prophesied – naked light on the boiling, bewildered bees.

Sacharissa rounded up her rearguard, which dropped headlong off the frame, and joined the Princess's detachment thrusting toward the Gate. Now panic was in full blast, and each sound bee found herself embraced by at least three Oddities. The first instinct of a frightened bee is to break into the stores and gorge herself with honey; but there were no stores left, so the Oddities fought the sound bees.

'You must feed us, or we shall die!' they cried, holding and clutching and slipping, while the silent scared earwigs and little spiders twisted between their legs. 'Think of the Hive, traitors! The Holy Hive!'

'You should have thought before!' cried the sound bees. 'Stay and see the dawn of your New Day.'

They reached the Gate at last over the soft bodies of many to whom they had ministered.

'On! Out! Up!' roared Melissa in the Princess's ear. 'For the Hive's sake! To the Old Oak!'

The Princess left the alighting-board, circled once, flung herself at the lowest branch of the Old Oak, and her little loyal swarm – you could have covered it with a pint mug – followed, hooked, and hung.

'Hold close!' Melissa gasped. 'The old legends have come true! Look!'

The Hive was half hidden by smoke, and Figures moved through the smoke. They heard a frame crack stickily, saw it heaved high and twirled round between enormous hands – a blotched, bulged, and perished horror of grey wax, corrupt brood, and small drone-cells, all covered with crawling Oddities, strange to the sun.

'Why, this isn't a hive! This is a museum of curiosities,' said the Voice behind the Veil. It was only the Bee Master talking to his son.

'Can you blame 'em, father?' said a second voice. 'It's rotten with Wax-moth. See here!'

Another frame came up. A finger poked through it, and it broke away in rustling flakes of ashy rottenness.

'Number Four Frame! That was your mother's pet comb once,' whispered Melissa to the Princess. 'Many's the good egg I've watched her lay there.'

'Aren't you confusing *post hoc* with *propter hoc*?'[10] said the Bee Master. 'Wax-moth only succeed when weak bees let them in.' A third frame crackled and rose into the light. 'All this is full of laying workers' brood. That never happens till the stock's weakened. Phew!'

He beat it on his knee like a tambourine, and it also crumbled to pieces.

The little swarm shivered as they watched the dwarf drone-grubs squirm feebly on the grass. Many sound bees had nursed on that frame, well knowing their work was useless; but the actual sight of even useless work destroyed disheartens a good worker.

'No, they have some recuperative power left,' said the second voice. 'Here's a Queen cell!'

'But it's tucked away among – What on earth *has* come to the little wretches? They seem to have lost the instinct of cell-building.' The father held up the frame where the bees had experimented in circular cell-work. It looked like the pitted head of a decaying toadstool.

'Not altogether,' the son corrected. 'There's one line, at least, of perfectly good cells.'

'My work,' said Sacharissa to herself. 'I'm glad Man does me justice before –'

That frame, too, was smashed out and thrown atop of the others and the foul earwiggy quilts.

As frame after frame followed it, the swarm beheld the upheaval, exposure, and destruction of all that had been well or ill done in every cranny of their Hive for generations past. There was black comb so old that they had forgotten where it hung; orange, buff, and ochre-varnished store-comb, built as bees were used to build before the days of artificial foundations; and there was a little, white, frail new work. There were sheets on sheets of level, even brood-comb that had held in its time unnumbered thousands of unnamed workers; patches of obsolete drone-comb, broad and high-shouldered, showing to what marks the male grub was expected to grow; and two inch deep honey-magazines, empty, but still magnificent: the whole gummed and glued into twisted scrap-work, awry on the wires, half-cells, beginnings abandoned, or grandiose, weak-walled, composite cells pieced out with rubbish and capped with dirt.

Good or bad, every inch of it was so riddled by the tunnels of the Wax-moth that it broke in clouds of dust as it was flung on the heap.

'Oh, see!' cried Sacharissa. 'The Great Burning that Our Queen foretold. Who can bear to look?'

A flame crawled up the pile of rubbish, and they smelt singeing wax.

The Figures stooped, lifted the Hive and shook it upside down over the pyre. A cascade of Oddities, chips of broken comb, scale, fluff, and grubs slid out, crackled, sizzled, popped a little, and then the flames roared up and consumed all that fuel.

'We must disinfect,' said a Voice. 'Get me a sulphur-candle, please.'

The shell of the Hive was returned to its place, a light was set in its sticky emptiness, tier by tier the Figures built it up, closed the entrance, and went away. The swarm watched the light leaking through the cracks all the long night. At dawn one Wax-moth came by, fluttering impudently.

'There has been a miscalculation about the New Day, my dears,' she began; 'one can't expect people to be perfect all at once. That was our mistake.'

'No, the mistake was entirely ours,' said the Princess.

'Pardon me,' said the Wax-moth. 'When you think of the enormous upheaval – call it good or bad – which our influence brought about, you will admit that we, and we alone –'

'You?' said the Princess. 'Our stock was not strong. So *you* came – as any other disease might have come. Hang close, all my people.'

When the sun rose, Veiled Figures came down, and saw their swarm at the bough's end waiting patiently within sight of the old Hive – a handful, but prepared to go on.

⚡ Marklake Witches ¹ ⚡

When Dan took up boat-building, Una ² coaxed Mrs Vincey, the farmer's wife at Little Lindens, to teach her to milk. Mrs Vincey milks in the pasture in summer, which is different from milking in the shed, because the cows are not tied up, and until they know you they will not stand still. After three weeks Una could milk *Red Cow* or *Kitty Shorthorn* quite dry, without her wrists aching, and then she allowed Dan to look. But milking did not amuse him, and it was pleasanter for Una to be alone in the quiet pastures with quiet-spoken Mrs Vincey. So, evening after evening, she slipped across to Little Lindens, took her stool from the fern-clump beside the fallen oak, and went to work, her pail between her knees, and her head pressed hard into the cow's flank. As often as not, Mrs Vincey would be milking cross *Pansy* at the other end of the pasture, and would not come near till it was time to strain and pour off.

Once, in the middle of a milking, *Kitty Shorthorn* boxed Una's ear with her tail.

'You old pig!' said Una, nearly crying, for a cow's tail can hurt.

'Why didn't you tie it down, child?' said a voice behind her.

'I meant to, but the flies are so bad I let her off – and this is what she's done!' Una looked round, expecting Puck, and saw a curly-haired girl, not much taller than herself, but older, dressed in a curious high-waisted, lavender-coloured riding-habit, with a high hunched collar and a deep cape and a belt fastened with a steel clasp. She wore a yellow velvet cap and tan gauntlets, and carried a real hunting-crop. Her cheeks were pale except for two pretty pink patches in the middle, and she talked with little gasps at the end of her sentences, as though she had been running.

'You don't milk so badly, child,' she said, and when she smiled her teeth showed small and even and pearly.

'Can you milk?' Una asked, and then flushed, for she heard Puck's chuckle.

He stepped out of the fern and sat down, holding *Kitty Shorthorn's* tail. 'There isn't much,' he said, 'that Miss Philadelphia doesn't know about milk – or, for that matter, butter and eggs. She's a great housewife.'

'Oh,' said Una. 'I'm sorry I can't shake hands. Mine are all milky; but Mrs Vincey is going to teach me butter-making this summer.'

'Ah! *I*'m going to London this summer,' the girl said, 'to my aunt in Bloomsbury.' She coughed as she began to hum, '"Oh, what a town! What a wonderful metropolis!"'

'You've got a cold,' said Una.

'No. Only my stupid cough. But it's vastly better than it was last winter. It will disappear in London air. Everyone says so. D'you like doctors, child?'

'I don't know any,' Una replied. 'But I'm sure I shouldn't.'

'Think yourself lucky, child. I beg your pardon,' the girl laughed, for Una frowned.

'I'm not a child, and my name's Una,' she said.

'Mine's Philadelphia. But everybody except René calls me Phil. I'm Squire Buicksteed's daughter – over at Marklake yonder.' She jerked her little round chin towards the south behind Dallington. 'Sure-ly you know Marklake?'

'We went a picnic to Marklake Green once,' said Una. 'It's awfully pretty. I like all those funny little roads that don't lead anywhere.'

'They lead over our land,' said Philadelphia stiffly, 'and the coach road is only four miles away. One can go anywhere from the Green. I went to the Assize Ball at Lewes last year.' She spun round and took a few dancing steps, but stopped with her hand to her side.

'It gives me a stitch,' she explained. 'No odds. 'Twill go away in London air. That's the latest French step, child. René taught it me. D'you hate the French, chi – Una?'

'Well, I hate French, of course, but I don't mind Mam'selle. She's rather decent. Is René your French governess?'

Philadelphia laughed till she caught her breath again.

'Oh no!' René's a French prisoner – on parole. That means he's promised not to escape till he has been properly exchanged for an Englishman. He's only a doctor, so I hope they won't think him worth exchanging. My Uncle captured him last year in the *Ferdinand* privateer, off Belle Isle, and he cured my Uncle of a r-r-raging toothache. Of course, after *that* we couldn't let him lie among the common French prisoners at Rye, and so he stays with us. He's of very old family – a Breton, which is nearly next door to being a true Briton, my father says – and he wears his hair clubbed – not powdered. *Much* more becoming, don't you think?'

'I don't know what you're –' Una began, but Puck, the other side of the pail, winked, and she went on with her milking.

'He's going to be a great French physician [3] when the war is over. He makes me bobbins for my lace-pillow now – he's very clever with his hands; but he'd doctor our people on the Green if they would let him. Only our Doctor – Dr Break – says he's an emp – or imp something – worse than impostor. But my Nurse says –'

'Nurse! You're ever so old. What have you got a nurse for?' Una finished milking, and turned round on her stool as *Kitty Shorthorn* grazed off.

'Because I can't get rid of her. Old Cissie nursed my mother, and she says she'll nurse me till she dies. The idea! She never lets me alone. She thinks I'm delicate. She has grown infirm in her understanding, you know. Mad – quite mad, poor Cissie!'

'Really mad?' said Una. 'Or just silly?'

'Crazy I should say – from the things she does. Her devotion to me is terribly embarrassing. You know I have all the keys of the Hall except the brewery and the tenants' kitchen. I give out all stores and the linen and plate.'

'How jolly! I love store-rooms and giving out things.'

'Ah, it's a great responsibility you'll find when you come to my age. Last year Dad said I was fatiguing myself with my duties, and he actually wanted me to give up the keys to old Amoore, our housekeeper. I wouldn't. I hate her. I said, "No, sir. I am Mistress of Marklake Hall just as long as I live, because I'm never going to be married, and I shall give out stores and linen till I die!" '

'And what did your father say?'

'Oh, I threatened to pin a dishclout to his coat-tail. He ran away. Everyone's afraid of Dad, except me.' Philadelphia stamped her foot. 'The idea! If I can't make my own father happy in his own house, I'd like to meet the woman that can, and – and – I'd have the living hide off her!'

She cut with her long-thonged whip. It cracked like a pistol-shot across the still pasture. *Kitty Shorthorn* threw up her head and trotted away.

'I beg your pardon,' Philadelphia said; 'but it makes me furious. Don't you hate those ridiculous old quizzes with their feathers and fronts, who come to dinner and call you "child" in your own chair at your own table?'

'I don't always come to dinner,' said Una, 'but I hate being called "child". Please tell me about store-rooms and giving out things.'

'Ah, it's a great responsibility – particularly with that old cat Amoore looking at the lists over your shoulder. And such a shocking thing happened last summer! Poor crazy Cissie, my Nurse that I was telling you of, she took three solid silver tablespoons.'

'Took! But isn't that stealing?' Una cried.

'Hsh!' said Philadelphia, looking round at Puck. 'All I say is she took them without my leave. I made it right afterwards. So, as Dad says – and he's a magistrate – it wasn't a legal offence; it was only compounding a felony.'

'It sounds awful,' said Una.

'It was. My dear, I was furious! I had had the keys for ten months, and I'd never lost anything before. I said nothing at first, because a big house offers so many chances of things being mislaid, and coming to hand later. "Fetching up in the lee-scuppers", my Uncle calls it. But next week I spoke to old Cissie about it when she was doing my hair at night, and she said I wasn't to worry my heart for trifles!'

'Isn't it like 'em?' Una burst out. 'They see you're worried over something that really matters, and they say, "Don't worry"; as if *that* did any good!'

'I quite agree with you, my dear; quite agree with you! I told Ciss the spoons were solid silver, and worth forty shillings, so if the thief were found, he'd be tried for his life.'

'Hanged, do you mean?' Una said.

'They ought to be; but Dad says no jury will hang a man nowadays for a forty-shilling theft. They transport 'em into penal servitude at the uttermost ends of the earth beyond the seas, for the term of their natural life. I told Cissie that, and I saw her tremble in my mirror. Then she cried, and caught hold of my knees, and I couldn't for my life understand what it was all about – she cried so. *Can* you guess, my dear, what that poor crazy thing had done? It was midnight before I pieced it together. She had given the spoons to Jerry Gamm, the Witchmaster on the Green, so that he might put a charm on me! Me!'

'Put a charm on you? Why?'

'That's what *I* asked; and then I saw how mad poor Cissie was! You know this stupid little cough of mine? It will disappear as soon as I go to London. She was troubled about *that*, and about my being so thin, and she told me Jerry had promised her, if she would bring him three silver spoons, that he'd charm my cough away and make me plump – "flesh-up", she said. I couldn't help laughing; but it was a terrible night! I had to put Cissie into my own bed, and stroke her hand till she cried herself to sleep. What else could I have done? When she woke, and I coughed – I suppose I *can* cough in my own room if I please – she said that she'd killed me, and asked me to have her hanged at Lewes sooner than send her to the uttermost ends of the earth away from me.'

'How awful! What did you do, Phil?'

'Do? I rode off at five in the morning to talk to Master Jerry, with a new lash on my whip. Oh, I was *furious*! Witchmaster or no witchmaster, I meant to –'

'Ah! what's a Witchmaster?'

'A master of witches, of course. *I* don't believe there are witches; but people say every village has a few, and Jerry was the master of all ours at Marklake. He has been a smuggler, and a man-of-war's man, and now he pretends to be a carpenter and joiner – he can make almost anything – but he really is a white wizard. He cures people by herbs and charms. He can cure them after Dr Break has given them up, and that's why Dr Break hates him so. He used to make me toy carts, and charm off my warts when I was a child.' Philadelphia spread out her hands with the delicate shiny little nails. 'It isn't counted lucky to cross him. He has his ways of getting even with you, they say. But *I* wasn't afraid of Jerry! I saw him working in his garden, and I leaned out of my saddle and double-thonged him between the shoulders, over the hedge. Well, my dear, for the first time since Dad gave him to me, my *Troubadour* (I wish you could see the sweet creature!) shied across the road, and I spilled out into the hedge-top. *Most* undignified! Jerry pulled me through to his side and brushed the leaves off me. I was horribly pricked, but I didn't care. "Now, Jerry," I said, "I'm going to take the hide off you first, and send you to Lewes afterwards. You well know why." "Oh!" he said, and he sat down among his bee-hives. "Then I reckon you've come about old Cissie's business, my dear." "I reckon I just about have," I said. "Stand away from these hives. I can't get at you there." "That's why I be where I be," he said. "If you'll excuse me, Miss Phil, I don't hold with bein' flogged before breakfast, at my time o' life." He's a huge big man, but he looked so comical squatting among the hives that – I know I oughtn't to – I laughed, and he laughed. I always laugh at the wrong time. But I soon recovered my dignity, and I said, "Then give me back what you made poor Cissie steal!"

'"Your pore Cissie," he said. "She's a hatful o' trouble. But you shall have 'em, Miss Phil. They're all ready put by for you." And, would you believe it, the old sinner pulled my three silver spoons out of his dirty pocket, and polished them on his cuff! "Here they be," he says, and he gave them to me, just as cool as though I'd come to have my warts charmed. That's the worst of people having known you when you were young. But I preserved my composure. "Jerry," I said, "what in the world are we to do? If you'd been caught with these things on you, you'd have been hanged."

'"I know it," he said. "But they're yours now."

'"But you made my Cissie steal them," I said.

'"That I didn't," he said. "Your Cissie, she was pickin' at me and tarrifyin' me all the long day an' every day for weeks, to put a charm on you, Miss Phil, and take away your little spitty cough."

'"Yes, I knew that, Jerry, and to make me flesh up!" I said. "I'm much obliged to you, but I'm not one of your pigs!"

'"Ah! I reckon she've been talking to you, then," he said. "Yes, she give me no peace, and bein' tarrified – for I don't hold with old women – I laid a task on her which I thought 'ud silence her. *I* never reckoned the old scrattle 'ud risk her neckbone at Lewes Assizes for your sake, Miss Phil. But she did. She up an' stole, I tell ye, as cheerful as a tinker. You might ha' knocked me down with any one of them liddle spoons when she brung 'em in her apron."

'"Do you mean to say, then, that you did it to try my poor Cissie?" I screamed at him.

'"What else for, dearie?" he said. "*I* don't stand in need of hedge-stealings. I'm a freeholder, with money in the bank; and now I won't trust women no more! Silly old besom! I do beleft she'd ha' stole the Squire's big fob-watch, if I'd required her."

'"Then you're a wicked, wicked old man," I said, and I was so angry that I couldn't help crying, and of course that made me cough.

'Jerry was in a fearful taking. He picked me up and carried me into his cottage – it's full of foreign curiosities – and he got me something to eat and drink, and he said he'd be hanged by the neck any day if it pleased me. He said he'd even tell old Cissie he was sorry. That's a great come-down for a Witchmaster, you know.

'I was ashamed of myself for being so silly, and I dabbed my eyes and said, "The least you can do now is to give poor Ciss some sort of a charm for me."

'"Yes, that's only fair dealings," he said. "You know the names of the Twelve Apostles, dearie? You say them names, one by one, before your open window, rain or storm, wet or shine, five times a day fasting. But mind you, 'twixt every name you draw in your breath through your nose, right down to your pretty liddle toes, as long and as deep as you can, and let it out slow through your pretty liddle mouth. There's virtue for your cough in those names spoke that way. And I'll give you something you can see, moreover. Here's a stick of maple which is the warmest tree in the wood."'

'That's true,' Una interrupted. 'You can feel it almost as warm as yourself when you touch it.'

'"It's cut one inch long for your every year," Jerry said. "That's sixteen inches. You set it in your window so that it holds up the sash, and thus you keep it, rain or shine, or wet or fine, day and night. I've said words over it which will have virtue on your complaints."

'"I haven't any complaints, Jerry," I said. "It's only to please Cissie."

'"I know that as well as you do, dearie," he said. And – and that was all that came of my going to give him a flogging. I wonder whether he made poor *Troubadour* shy when I lashed at him? Jerry has his ways of getting even of people.'

'I wonder,' said Una. 'Well, did you try the charm? Did it work?'

'What nonsense! I told René about it, of course, because he's a doctor. He's going to be a most famous doctor. That's why our doctor hates him. René said, "Oho! Your Master Gamm, he is worth knowing," and he put up his eyebrows – like this. He made joke of it all. He can see my window from the carpenter's shed, where he works, and if ever the maple stick fell down, he pretended to be in a fearful taking till I propped the window up again. He used to ask me whether I had said my Apostles properly, and how I took my deep breaths. Oh yes, and the next day, though he had been there ever so many times before, he put on his new hat and paid Jerry Gamm a visit of state – as a fellow-physician. Jerry never guessed René was making fun of him, and so he told René about the sick people in the village, and how he cured them with herbs after Dr Break had given them up. Jerry could talk smugglers' French, of course, and I had taught René plenty of English, if only he wasn't so shy. They called each other Monsieur Gamm and Mosheur Lanark, just like gentlemen. I suppose it amused poor René. He hasn't much to do, except to fiddle about in the carpenter's shop. He's like all the French prisoners – always making knick-knacks; and Jerry had a little lathe at his cottage, and so – and so – René took to being with Jerry much more than I approved of. The Hall is so big and empty when Dad's away, and I will *not* sit with old Amoore – she talks so horridly about everyone – specially about René.

'I was rude to René, I'm afraid; but I was properly served out for it. One always is. You see Dad went down to Hastings to pay his respects to the General who commanded the brigade there, and to bring him to the Hall afterwards. Dad told me he was a very brave soldier from India – he was Colonel of Dad's regiment, the Thirty-third Foot, after Dad left the Army, and then he changed his name from Wesley to Wellesley,[4] or else the other way about; and Dad said I was to get out all the silver for him, and I knew that meant a big dinner. So I sent down to the sea for early mackerel, and had *such* a morning in the kitchen and the store-rooms. Old Amoore nearly cried.

'However, my dear, I made all my preparations in ample time, but the fish didn't arrive – it never does – and I wanted René to ride to Pevensey and bring it himself. He had gone over to Jerry, of course, as he always used, unless I requested his presence beforehand. *I* can't send for René every time I want him. He should be there. Now, don't you ever do what I did, child, because it's in the highest degree unladylike; but – but one of our woods runs up to Jerry's garden, and if you climb – it's ungenteel, but I can climb like a kitten – there's an old hollow oak just above the pigsty where you can hear and see everything below. Truthfully, I only went to tell René about the mackerel, but I saw him and Jerry sitting on the seat playing with wooden toy trumpets. So I slipped into the hollow, and choked down my cough, and listened. René had never shown *me* any of these trumpets.'

'Trumpets? Aren't you too old for trumpets?' said Una.

'They weren't real trumpets, because Jerry opened his shirt collar, and René put one end of his trumpet against Jerry's chest, and put his ear to the other. Then Jerry put his trumpet against René's chest, and listened while René breathed and coughed. I was afraid *I* would cough too.

'"This hollywood one is the best," said Jerry. "'Tis won'erful like hearin' a man's soul whisperin' in his innards; but unless I've a buzzin' in my ears, Mosheur Lanark, you make much about the same kind o' noises as old Gaffer Macklin – but not quite so loud as young Copper. It sounds like breakers on a reef – a long way off. Comprenny?"

'"Perfectly," said René. "I drive on the breakers. But before I strike, I shall save hundreds, thousands, millions perhaps, by my little trumpets. Now tell me what sounds the old Gaffer Macklin have made in his chest, and what the young Copper also."

'Jerry talked for nearly a quarter of an hour about sick people in the village, while René asked questions. Then he sighed, and said, "You explain very well, Monsieur Gamm, but if only I had your opportunities to listen for myself! Do you think these poor people would let me listen to them through my trumpet – for a little money? No?" – René's as poor as a church mouse.

'"They'd kill you, Mosheur. It's all I can do to coax 'em to abide it, and I'm Jerry Gamm," said Jerry. He's very proud of his attainments.

'"Then these poor people are alarmed – No?" said René.

'"They've had it in for me for some time back because o' my tryin' your trumpets on their sick; and I reckon by the talk at the alehouse they won't stand much more. Tom Dunch an' some of his kidney was drinkin' themselves riot-ripe when I passed along after noon. Charms an' mutterin's and bits o' red wool and black hens is in the way o' nature to these fools, Mosheur; but anything likely to do 'em real service is devil's work by their estimation. If I was you, I'd go home before they come." Jerry spoke quite quietly, and René shrugged his shoulders.

'"I am prisoner on parole, Monsieur Gamm," he said. "I have no home."

'Now that was unkind of René. He's often told me that he looked on England as his home. I suppose it's French politeness.

'"Then we'll talk o' something that matters," said Jerry. "Not to name no names, Mosheur Lanark, what might be your own opinion o' someone who ain't old Gaffer Macklin nor young Copper? Is that person better or worse?"

'"Better – for time that is," said René. He meant for the time being, but I never could teach him some phrases.

'"I thought so too," said Jerry. "But how about time to come?"

'René shook his head, and then he blew his nose. You don't know how odd a man looks blowing his nose when you are sitting directly above him.

'"I've thought that too," said Jerry. He rumbled so deep i could scarcely catch. "It don't make much odds to me, because I'm old. But you're young, Mosheur – you're young," and he put his hand on René's knee, and René covered it with his hand. I didn't know they were such friends.

'"Thank you, *mon ami*," said René. "I am much oblige. Let us return to our trumpet-making. But I forget" – he stood up – "it appears that you receive this afternoon!"

'You can't see into Gamm's Lane from the oak, but the gate opened, and fat little Doctor Break stumped in, mopping his head, and half-a-dozen of our people followed him, very drunk.

'You ought to have seen René bow; he does it beautifully.

'"A word with you, Laennec," said Dr Break. "Jerry has been practising some devilry or other on these poor wretches, and they've asked me to be arbiter."

'"Whatever that means, I reckon it's safer than asking you to be doctor," said Jerry, and Tom Dunch, one of our carters, laughed.

'"That ain't right feeling of you, Tom," Jerry said, "seeing how clever Dr Break put away your thorn in the flesh last winter." Tom's wife had died at Christmas, though Dr Break bled her twice a week. He danced with rage.

'"This is all beside the mark," he said. "These good people are willing to testify that you've been impudently prying into God's secrets by means of some papistical contrivance which this person" – he pointed to poor René – "has furnished you with. Why, here are the things themselves!" René was holding a trumpet in his hand.

'Then all the men talked at once. They said old Gaffer Macklin was dying from stitches in his side where Jerry had put the trumpet – they called it the devil's ear-piece; and they said it left round red witchmarks on people's skins, and dried up their lights, and made 'em spit blood, and threw 'em into sweats. Terrible things they said. You never heard such a noise. I took advantage of it to cough.

'René and Jerry were standing with their backs to the pigsty. Jerry fumbled in his big flap pockets and fished up a pair of pistols. You ought to have seen the men give back when he cocked his. He passed one to René.

'"Wait! Wait!" said René. "I will explain to the doctor if he permits." He waved a trumpet at him, and the men at the gate shouted, "Don't touch it, Doctor! Don't lay a hand to the thing."

'"Come, come!" said René. "You are not so big fool as you pretend, Dr Break. No?"

'Dr Break backed toward the gate, watching Jerry's pistol, and René followed him with his trumpet, like a nurse trying to amuse a child, and put the ridiculous thing to his ear to show how it was used, and talked of *la Gloire*, and *la Humanité*, and *la Science*, while Dr Break watched Jerry's pistol and swore. I nearly laughed aloud.

'"Now listen! Nów listen!" said René. "This will be moneys in your pockets, my dear *confrère*.[5] You will become rich."

'Then Dr Break said something about adventurers who could not earn an honest living in their own country creeping into decent houses and taking advantage of gentlemen's confidence to enrich themselves by base intrigues.

'René dropped his absurd trumpet and made one of his best bows. I knew he was angry from the way he rolled his "r's".

'"Ver-r-ry good," said he. "For that I shall have much pleasure to kill you now and here. Monsieur Gamm" – another bow to Jerry – "you will please lend him your pistol, or he shall have mine. I give you my word I know not which is best; and if he will choose a second from his friends over there" – another bow to our drunken yokels at the gate – "we will commence."

'"That's fair enough," said Jerry. "Tom Dunch, you owe it to the doctor to be his second. Place your man."

'"No," said Tom. "No mixin' in gentry's quarrels for me." And he shook his head and went out, and the others followed him.

'"Hold on," said Jerry. "You've forgot what you set out to do up at the alehouse just now. You was goin' to search me for witchmarks; you was goin' to duck me in the pond; you was goin' to drag all my bits o' sticks out o' my little cottage here. What's the matter with you? Wouldn't you like to be with your old woman tonight, Tom?"

'But they didn't even look back, much less come. They ran to the village alehouse like hares.

'"No matter for these canaille," [6] said René, buttoning up his coat so as not to show any linen. All gentlemen do that before a duel, Dad says – and he's been out five times. "You shall be his second, Monsieur Gamm. Give him the pistol."

'Dr Break took it as if it was red-hot, but he said that if René resigned his pretensions in certain quarters he would pass over the matter. René bowed deeper than ever.

'"As for that," he said, "if you were not the ignorant which you are, you would have known long ago that the subject of your remarks is not for any living man."

'I don't know what the subject of his remarks might have been, but he spoke in a simply dreadful voice, my dear, and Dr Break turned quite white, and said René was a liar; and then René caught him by the throat, and choked him black.

'Well, my dear, as if this wasn't deliciously exciting enough, just exactly at that minute I heard a strange voice on the other side of the hedge say, "What's this? What's this, Bucksteed?" and there was my father and Sir Arthur Wesley on horseback in the lane; and there was René kneeling on Dr Break, and there was I up in the oak, listening with all my ears.

'I must have leaned forward too much, and the voice gave me such a start that I slipped. I had only time to make one jump on to the pigsty roof – another, before the tiles broke, on to the pigsty wall – and then I bounced down into the garden, just behind Jerry, with my hair full of bark. Imagine the situation!'

'Oh, I cant!' Una laughed till she nearly fell off the stool.

'Dad said, "Phil – a – del – phia!" and Sir Arthur Wesley said, "Good Ged!" and Jerry put his foot on the pistol René had dropped. But René was splendid. He never even looked at me. He began to untwist Dr Break's neckcloth as fast as he'd twisted it, and asked him if he felt better.

'"What's happened? What's happened?" said Dad.

'"A fit!" said René. "I fear my *confrère* has had a fit. Do not be alarmed. He recovers himself. Shall I bleed you a little, my dear Doctor?"

Dr Break was very good too. He said, "I am vastly obliged, Monsieur Laennec, but I am restored now." And as he went out of the gate he told Dad it was a syncope [7] – I think. Then Sir Arthur said, "Quite right, Bucksteed. Not another word! They are both gentlemen." And he took off his cocked hat to Dr Break and René.

'But poor Dad wouldn't let well alone. He kept saying, "Philadelphia, what does all this mean?"

'"Well, sir," I said, "I've only just come down. As far as I could see, it looked as though Dr Break has had a sudden seizure." That was quite true – if you'd seen René seize him. Sir Arthur laughed. "Not much change there, Bucksteed," he said. "She's a lady – a thorough lady."

'"Heaven knows she doesn't look like one," said poor Dad. "Go home, Philadelphia."

'So I went home, my dear – don't laugh so! – right under Sir Arthur's nose – a most enormous nose – feeling as though I were twelve years old, going to be whipped. Oh, I *beg* your pardon, child!'

'It's all right,' said Una. 'I'm getting on for thirteen. I've never been whipped, but I know how you felt. All the same, it must have been funny!'

'Funny! If you'd heard Sir Arthur jerking out, "Good Ged, Bucksteed!" every minute as they rode behind me; and poor Dad saying, "'Pon my honour, Arthur, I can't account for it!" Oh, how my cheeks tingled when I reached my room! But Cissie had laid out my very best evening dress, the white satin one, vandyked [8] at the bottom with spots of morone [9] foil, and the pearl knots, you know, catching up the drapery from the left shoulder. I had poor mother's lace tucker and her coronet comb.'

'Oh, you lucky!' Una murmured. '*And* gloves?'

'French kid, my dear' – Philadelphia patted her shoulder – 'and morone satin shoes and a morone and gold crape fan. That restored my calm. Nice things always do. I wore my hair banded on my forehead with a little curl over the left ear. And when I descended the stairs, *en grande tenue*,[10] old Amoore curtsied to me without my having to stop and look at her, which alas! is too often the case. Sir Arthur highly approved of the dinner, my dear: the mackerel *did* come in time. We had all the Marklake silver out, and he toasted my health, and he asked me where my little bird's-nesting sister was. I *know* he did it to quiz me, so I looked him straight in the face, my dear, and I said, "I always send her to the nursery, Sir Arthur, when I receive guests at Marklake Hall."'

'Oh, how chee– clever of you. What did he say?' Una cried.

'He said, "Not much change there, Bucksteed. Ged, I deserved it," and he toasted me again. They talked about the French and what a shame it was that Sir Arthur only commanded a brigade at Hastings, and he told Dad of a battle in India at a place called Assaye.[11] Dad said it was a terrible fight, but Sir Arthur described it as though it had been a whist-party – I suppose because a lady was present.'

'Of course you were the lady; I wish I'd seen you,' said Una.

'I wish you had, child. I had *such* a triumph after dinner. René and Dr Break came in. They had quite made up their quarrel, and they told me they had the highest esteem for each other, and I laughed and said, "I heard every word of it up in the tree." You never saw two men so frightened in your life, and when I said, "What *was* 'the subject of your remarks', René?" neither of them knew where to look. Oh, I quizzed them unmercifully. They'd seen me jump off the pigsty roof, remember.'

'But what *was* the subject of their remarks?' said Una.

'Oh, Dr Break said it was a professional matter, so the laugh was turned on me. I was horribly afraid it might have been something unladylike and indelicate. But *that* wasn't my triumph. Dad asked me to play on the harp. Between just you and me, child, I had been practising a new song from London – I don't always live in trees – for weeks; and I gave it them for a surprise.'

'What was it?' said Una. 'Sing it.'

'"I have given my heart to a flower." Not very difficult fingering, but r-r-ravishing sentiment.'

Philadelphia coughed and cleared her throat.

'I've a deep voice for my age and size,' she explained. 'Contralto, you know, but it ought to be stronger,' and she began, her face all dark against the last of the soft pink sunset:

> 'I have given my heart to a flower,
> Though I know it is fading away,
> Though I know it will live but an hour
> And leave me to mourn its decay!

'Isn't that touchingly sweet? Then the last verse – I wish I had my harp, dear – goes as low as my register will reach.' She drew in her chin, and took a deep breath:

> 'Ye desolate whirlwinds that rave,
> I charge you be good to my dear!
> She is all – she is all that I have,
> And the time of our parting is near!'

'Beautiful!' said Una. 'And did they like it?'

'Like it? They were overwhelmed – *accablés*,[12] as René says. My dear, if I hadn't seen it, I shouldn't have believed that I could have drawn tears, genuine tears, to the eyes of four grown men. But I did! René simply couldn't endure it! He's all French sensibility. He hid his face and said, "*Assez Mademoiselle! C'est plus fort que moi! Assez!*"[13] And Sir Arthur blew his nose and said, "Good Ged! This is worse than Assaye!" While Dad sat with the tears simply running down his cheeks.'

'And what did Dr Break do?'

'He got up and pretended to look out of the window, but I saw his little fat shoulders jerk as if he had the hiccoughs. That *was* a triumph. I never suspected him of sensibility.'

'Oh, I wish I'd seen! I wish I'd been you,' said Una, clasping her hands. Puck rustled and rose from the fern, just as a big blundering cockchafer flew smack against Una's cheek.

When she had finished rubbing the place, Mrs Vincey called to her that *Pansy* had been fractious, or she would have come long before to help her strain and pour off.

'It didn't matter,' said Una; 'I just waited. Is that old *Pansy* barging about the lower pasture now?'

'No,' said Mrs Vincey, listening. 'It sounds more like a horse being galloped middlin' quick through the woods; but there's no road there. I reckon it's one of Gleason's colts loose. Shall I see you up to the house, Miss Una?'

'Gracious no! thank you. What's going to hurt me?' said Una, and she put her stool away behind the oak, and strolled home through the gaps that old Hobden kept open for her.

⁅ The Knife and the Naked Chalk ¹ ⁆

The children went to the seaside for a month, and lived in a flint village
on the bare windy chalk Downs, quite thirty miles away from home.
They made friends with an old shepherd, called Mr Dudeney, who had
known their father when their father was little. He did not talk like their
own people in the Weald of Sussex, and he used different names for
farm things, but he understood how they felt, and let them go with him.
He had a tiny cottage about half a mile from the village, where his wife
made mead from thyme honey, and nursed sick lambs in front of a coal
fire, while Old Jim, who was Mr Dudeney's sheep-dog's father, lay at
the door. They brought up beef bones for Old Jim (you must never give a
sheep-dog mutton bones), and if Mr Dudeney happened to be far in the
Downs, Mrs Dudeney would tell the dog to take them to him, and he did.

One August afternoon when the village water-cart had made the street
smell specially townified, they went to look for their shepherd as usual,
and, as usual, Old Jim crawled over the door-step and took them in
charge. The sun was hot, the dry grass was very slippery, and the
distances were very distant.

'It's just like the sea,' said Una, when Old Jim halted in the shade of a
lonely flint barn on a bare rise. 'You see where you're going, and – you
go there, and there's nothing between.'

Dan slipped off his shoes. 'When we get home I shall sit in the woods
all day,' he said.

'Whuff!' said Old Jim, to show he was ready, and struck across a long
rolling stretch of turf. Presently he asked for his beef bone.

'Not yet,' said Dan. 'Where's Mr Dudeney? Where's master?'

Old Jim looked as if he thought they were mad, and asked again.

'Don't you give it him,' Una cried. 'I'm not going to be left howling in
a desert.'

'Show, boy! Show!' said Dan, for the Downs seemed as bare as the
palm of your hand.

Old Jim sighed, and trotted forward. Soon they spied the blob of Mr
Dudeney's hat against the sky a long way off.

'Right! All right!' said Dan. Old Jim wheeled round, took his bone
carefully between his blunted teeth, and returned to the shadow of the
old barn, looking just like a wolf. The children went on. Two kestrels

hung bivvering [2] and squealing above them. A gull flapped lazily along the white edge of the cliffs. The curves of the Downs shook a little in the heat, and so did Mr Dudeney's distant head.

They walked toward it very slowly and found themselves staring into a horse-shoe-shaped hollow a hundred feet deep, whose steep sides were laced with tangled sheep-tracks. The flock grazed on the flat at the bottom, under charge of Young Jim. Mr Dudeney sat comfortably knitting on the edge of the slope, his crook between his knees. They told him what Old Jim had done.

'Ah, he thought you could see my head as soon as he did. The closeter you be to the turf the more you see things. You look warm-like,' said Mr Dudeney.

'We be,' said Una, flopping down. '*And* tired.'

'Set beside o' me here. The shadow'll begin to stretch out in a little while, and a heat-shake o' wind will come up with it that'll overlay your eyes like so much wool.'

'We don't want to sleep,' said Una indignantly; but she settled herself as she spoke, in the first strip of early afternoon shade.

'O' course not. You come to talk with me same as your father used. *He* didn't need no dog to guide him to Norton Pit.'

'Well, he belonged here,' said Dan, and laid himself down at length on the turf.

'He did. And what beats me is why he went off to live among them messy trees in the Weald, when he might ha' stayed here and looked all about him. There's no profit to trees. They draw the lightning, and sheep shelter under 'em, and *so*, like as not, you'll lose a half score ewes struck dead in one storm. Tck! Your father knew that.'

'Trees aren't messy.' Una rose on her elbow. 'And what about firewood? I don't like coal.'

'Eh? You lie a piece more up-hill and you'll lie more natural,' said Mr Dudeney, with his provoking deaf smile. 'Now press your face down and smell to the turf. That's Southdown thyme which makes our Southdown mutton beyond compare, and, my mother told me, 'twill cure anything except broken necks, or hearts. I forget which.'

They sniffed, and somehow forgot to lift their cheeks from the soft thymy cushions.

'You don't get nothing like that in the Weald. Watercress, maybe?' said Mr Dudeney.

'But we've water – brooks full of it – where you paddle in hot weather,' Una replied, watching a yellow-and-violet-banded snail-shell close to her eye.

'Brooks flood. Then you must shift your sheep – let alone foot-rot afterward. I put more dependence on a dew-pond any day.'

'How's a dew-pond made?' said Dan, and tilted his hat over his eyes. Mr Dudeney explained.

The air trembled a little as though it could not make up its mind whether to slide into the Pit or move across the open. But it seemed easiest to go down-hill, and the children felt one soft puff after another slip and sidle down the slope in fragrant breaths that baffed [3] on their eyelids. The little whisper of the sea by the cliffs joined with the whisper of the wind over the grass, the hum of insects in the thyme, the ruffle and rustle of the flock below, and a thickish mutter deep in the very chalk beneath them. Mr Dudeney stopped explaining, and went on with his knitting.

They were roused by voices. The shadow had crept half-way down the steep side of Norton's Pit, and on the edge of it, his back to them, Puck sat beside a half-naked man who seemed busy at some work. The wind had dropped, and in that funnel of ground every least noise and movement reached them like whispers up a water-pipe.

'That is clever,' said Puck, leaning over. 'How truly you shape it!'

'Yes, but what does The Beast care for a brittle flint tip? Bah!' The man flicked something contemptuously over his shoulder. It fell between Dan and Una – a beautiful dark-blue flint arrow-head still hot from the maker's hand.

The man reached for another stone, and worked away like a thrush with a snail-shell.

'Flint work is fool's work,' he said at last. 'One does it because one always did it, but when it comes to dealing with The Beast – no good!' He shook his shaggy head.

'The Beast was dealt with long ago. He has gone,' said Puck.

'He'll be back at lambing-time. *I* know him.' He chipped very carefully, and the flints squeaked.

'Not he. Children can lie out on the Chalk now all day through and go home safe.'

'Can they? Well, call The Beast by his True Name, and I'll believe it,' the man replied.

'Surely!' Puck leaped to his feet, curved his hands round his mouth and shouted: 'Wolf! Wolf!'

Norton's Pit threw back the echo from its dry sides – 'Wuff! Wuff!' like Young Jim's bark.

'You see? You hear?' said Puck. 'Nobody answers. Grey Shepherd is gone. Feet-in-the-Night has run off. There are no more wolves.'

'Wonderful!' The man wiped his forehead as though he were hot. 'Who drove him away? You?'

'Many men through many years, each working in his own country. Were you one of them?' Puck answered.

The man slid his sheepskin cloak to his waist, and without a word pointed to his side, which was all seamed and blotched with scars. His arms too were dimpled from shoulder to elbow with horrible white dimples.

'I see,' said Puck. 'It is The Beast's mark. What did you use against him?'

'Hand, hammer, and spear, as our fathers did before us.'

'So? Then how' – Puck twitched aside the man's dark-brown cloak – 'how did a Flint-worker come by *that*? Show, man, show!' He held out his little hand.

The man slipped a long dark iron knife, almost a short sword, from his belt, and after breathing on it, handed it hilt-first to Puck, who took it with his head on one side, as you should when you look at the works of a watch, squinted down the dark blade, and very delicately rubbed his forefinger from the point to the hilt.

'Good!' said he, in a surprised tone.

'It should be. The Children of the Night made it,' the man answered.

'So I see by the iron. What might it have cost you?'

'This!' The man raised his hand to his cheek. Puck whistled like a Weald starling.

'By the Great Rings of the Chalk!' he cried. 'Was *that* your price? Turn sunward that I may see better, and shut your eye.'

He slipped his hand beneath the man's chin and swung him till he faced the children up the slope. They saw that his right eye was gone, and the eyelid lay shrunk. Quickly Puck turned him round again, and the two sat down.

'It was for the sheep. The sheep are the people,' said the man, in an ashamed voice. 'What else could I have done?[4] *You* know, Old One.'

Puck sighed a little fluttering sigh. 'Take the knife. I listen.'

The man bowed his head, drove the knife into the turf, and while it still quivered said: 'This is witness between us that I speak the thing that has been. Before my Knife and the Naked Chalk I speak. Touch!'

Puck laid a hand on the hilt. It stopped shaking. The children wriggled a little nearer.

'I am of the People of the Worked Flint. I am the one son of the Priestess who sells the Winds to the Men of the Sea. I am the Buyer of the Knife – the Keeper of the People,' the man began, in a sort of singing shout. 'These are my names in this country of the Naked Chalk, between the Trees and the Sea.'

'Yours was a great country. Your names are great too,' said Puck.

'One cannot feed some things on names and songs'; the man hit himself on the chest. 'It is better – always better – to count one's children safe round the fire, their Mother among them.'

'Ahai!' said Puck. 'I think this will be a very old tale.'

'I warm myself and eat at any fire that I choose, but there is no *one* to light me a fire or cook my meat. I sold all that when I bought the Magic Knife for my people. It was not right that The Beast should master man. What else could I have done?'

'I hear. I know. I listen,' said Puck.

'When I was old enough to take my place in the Sheepguard, The Beast gnawed all our country like a bone between his teeth. He came in behind the flocks at watering-time, and watched them round the Dewponds; he leaped into the folds between our knees at the shearing; he walked out alongside the grazing flocks, and chose his meat on the hoof while our boys threw flints at him; he crept by night into the huts, and licked the babe from between the mother's hands; he called his companions and pulled down men in broad daylight on the Naked Chalk. No – not always did he do so! *This* was his cunning! He would go away for a while to let us forget him. A year – two years perhaps – we neither smelt, nor heard, nor saw him. When our flocks had increased; when our men did not always look behind them; when children strayed from the fenced places; when our women walked alone to draw water – back, back, back came the Curse of the Chalk, Grey Shepherd, Feet-in-the Night – The Beast, The Beast, The Beast!

'He laughed at our little brittle arrows and our poor blunt spears. He learned to run in under the stroke of the hammer. I think he knew when there was a flaw in the flint. Often it does not show till you bring it down on his snout. Then – *Pouf!* – the false flint falls all to flinders, and you are left with the hammer-handle in your fist, and his teeth in your flank! I have felt them. At evening, too, in the dew, or when it has misted and rained, your spear-head lashings slack off, though you have kept them beneath your cloak all day. You are alone – but so close to the home ponds that you stop to tighten the sinews with hands, teeth, and a piece of driftwood. You bend over and pull – so! That is the minute for which he has followed you since the stars went out. "Aarh!" he says. "Wurr-aarh!" he says.' (Norton's Pit gave back the growl like a pack of real wolves.) 'Then he is on your right shoulder feeling for the vein in your neck, and – perhaps your sheep run on without you. To fight The

Selected Stories

Beast is nothing, but to be despised by The Beast when he fights you –
that is like his teeth in the heart! Old One, why is it that men desire so
greatly, and can do so little?'

'I do not know. Did you desire so much?' said Puck.

'I desired to master The Beast. It is not right that The Beast should
master man. But my people were afraid. Even my Mother, the Priestess,
was afraid when I told her what I desired. We were accustomed to be
afraid of The Beast. When I was made a man, and a maiden – she was a
Priestess – waited for me at the Dew-ponds, The Beast flitted from off
the Chalk. Perhaps it was a sickness; perhaps he had gone to his Gods to
learn how to do us new harm. But he went, and we breathed more freely.
The women sang again; the children were not so much guarded; our
flocks grazed far out. I took mine yonder' – he pointed inland to the
hazy line of the Weald – 'where the new grass was best. They grazed
north. I followed till we were close to the Trees' – he lowered his voice –
'close *there* where the Children of the Night live.' He pointed north
again.

'Ah, now I remember a thing,' said Puck. 'Tell me, why did your
people fear the Trees so extremely?'

'Because the Gods hate the Trees and strike them with lightning. We
can see them burning for days all along the Chalk's edge. Besides, all the
Chalk knows that the Children of the Night, though they worship our
Gods, are magicians. When a man goes into their country, they change
his spirit; they put words into his mouth; they make him like talking
water. But a voice in my heart told me to go toward the north. While I
watched my sheep there I saw three Beasts chasing a man, who ran
toward the Trees. By this I knew he was a Child of the Night. We Flint-
workers fear the Trees more than we fear The Beast. He had no hammer;
he carried a knife like this one. A Beast leaped at him. He stretched out
his knife. The Beast fell dead. The other Beasts ran away howling,
which they would never have done from a Flint-worker. The man went
in among the Trees. I looked for the dead Beast. He had been killed in a
new way – by a single deep, clean cut, without bruise or tear, which had
split his bad heart. Wonderful! So I saw that the man's knife was magic,
and I thought how to get it – thought strongly how to get it.

'When I brought the flocks to the shearing, my Mother the Priestess
asked me, "What is the new thing which you have seen and I see in your
face?" I said, "It is a sorrow to me"; and she answered, "All new things
are sorrow. Sit in my place, and eat sorrow." I sat down in her place by
the fire, where she talks to the ghosts in winter, and two voices spoke in
my heart. One voice said, "Ask the Children of the Night for the Magic

438

Knife. It is not fit that The Beast should master man." I listened to that voice.

'One voice said, "If you go among the Trees, the Children of the Night will change your spirit. Eat and sleep here." The other voice said, "Ask for the Knife." I listened to that voice.

'I said to my Mother in the morning, "I go away to find a thing for the people, but I do not know whether I shall return in my own shape." She answered, "Whether you live or die, or are made different, I am your Mother."'

'True,' said Puck. 'The Old Ones themselves cannot change men's mothers even if they would.'

'Let us thank the Old Ones! I spoke to my Maiden, the Priestess who waited for me at the Dew-ponds. She promised fine things too.' The man laughed. 'I went away to that place where I had seen the magician with the knife. I lay out two days on the short grass before I ventured among the Trees. I felt my way before me with a stick. I was afraid of the terrible talking Trees. I was afraid of the ghosts in the branches; of the soft ground underfoot; of the red and black waters. I was afraid, above all, of the Change. It came!'

They saw him wipe his forehead once again, and his strong back-muscles quivered till he laid his hand on the knife-hilt.

'A fire without a flame burned in my head; an evil taste grew in my mouth; my eyelids shut hot over my eyes; my breath was hot between my teeth, and my hands were like the hands of a stranger. I was made to sing songs and to mock the Trees, though I was afraid of them. At the same time I saw myself laughing, and I was very sad for this fine young man, who was myself. Ah! The Children of the Night know magic.'

'I think that is done by the Spirits of the Mist. They change a man if he sleeps among them,' said Puck. 'Had you slept in any mists?'

'Yes – but *I* know it was the Children of the Night. After three days I saw a red light behind the Trees, and I heard a heavy noise. I saw the Children of the Night dig red stones from a hole, and lay them in fires. The stones melted like tallow, and the men beat the soft stuff with hammers. I wished to speak to these men, but the words were changed in my mouth, and all I could say was, "Do not make that noise. It hurts my head." By this I knew that I was bewitched, and I clung to the Trees, and prayed the Children of the Night to take off their spells. They were cruel. They asked me many questions which they would never allow me to answer. They changed my words between my teeth till I wept. Then they led me into a hut and covered the floor with hot stones and dashed water on the stones, and sang charms till the sweat poured off me like water. I slept. When I waked, my own spirit – not the strange, shouting thing – was back in my body, and I was like a cool bright stone on the shingle between the sea and the sunshine. The magicians came to hear me – women and men – each wearing a Magic Knife. Their Priestess was their Ears and their Mouth.

'I spoke. I spoke many words that went smoothly along like sheep in order when their shepherd, standing on a mound, can count those coming, and those far off getting ready to come. I asked for Magic Knives for my people. I said that my people would bring meat, and milk, and wool, and lay them in the short grass outside the Trees, if the Children of the Night would leave Magic Knives for our people to take away. They were pleased. Their Priestess said, "For whose sake have you come?" I answered, "The sheep are the people. If The Beast kills our sheep, our people die. So I come for a Magic Knife to kill The Beast."

'She said, "We do not know if our God will let us trade with the people of the Naked Chalk. Wait till we have asked."

'When they came back from the Question place (their Gods are our Gods), their Priestess said, "The God needs a proof that your words are true." I said, "What is the proof?" She said, "The God says that if you have come for the sake of your people you will give him your right eye to be put out; but if you have come for any other reason you will not give it. This proof is between you and the God. We ourselves are sorry."

'I said, "This is a hard proof. Is there no other road?"

'She said, "Yes. You can go back to your people with your two eyes in your head if you choose. But then you will not get any Magic Knives for your people."

'I said, "It would be easier if I knew that I were to be killed."

'She said, "Perhaps the God knew this too. See! I have made my knife hot."

'I said, "Be quick, then!" With her knife heated in the flame she put out my right eye. She herself did it. I am the son of a Priestess. She was a Priestess. It was not work for any common man.'

'True! Most true,' said Puck. 'No common man's work, that. And, afterwards?'

'Afterwards I did not see out of that eye any more. I found also that a one eye does not tell you truly where things are. Try it!'

At this Dan put his hand over one eye, and reached for the flint arrow-head on the grass. He missed it by inches. 'It's true,' he whispered to Una. 'You can't judge distances a bit with only one eye.'

Puck was evidently making the same experiment, for the man laughed at him.

'I know it is so,' said he. 'Even now I am not always sure of my blow. I stayed with the Children of the Night till my eye healed. They said I was the son of Tyr,[5] the God who put his right hand in a Beast's mouth. They showed me how they melted their red stone and made the Magic Knives of it. They told me the charms they sang over the fires and at the beatings. I can sing many charms.' Then he began to laugh like a boy.

'I was thinking of my journey home,' he said, 'and of the surprised Beast. He had come back to the Chalk. I saw him – I smelt his lairs as soon as ever I left the Trees. He did not know I had the Magic Knife – I hid it under my cloak – the Knife that the Priestess gave me. Ho! Ho! That happy day was too short! See! A Beast would wind me. "Wow!" he would say, "here is my Flint-worker!" He would come leaping, tail in air; he would roll; he would lay his head between his paws out of merriness of heart at his warm, waiting meal. He would leap – and, oh, his eye in mid-leap when he saw – when he saw the knife held ready for him! It pierced his hide as a rush pierces curdled milk. Often he had no time to howl. I did not trouble to flay any beasts I killed. Sometimes I missed my blow. Then I took my little flint hammer and beat out his brains as he cowered. He made no fight. He knew the knife! But The Beast is very cunning. Before evening all The Beasts had smelt the blood on my knife, and were running from me like hares. *They* knew! Then I walked as a man should – the Master of The Beast!

'So came I back to my Mother's house. There was a lamb to be killed. I cut it in two halves with my knife, and I told her all my tale. She said, "This is the work of a God." I kissed her and laughed. I went to my Maiden who waited for me at the Dew-ponds. There was a lamb to be killed. I cut it in two halves with my knife, and told her all my tale. She said, "It is the work of a God." I laughed, but she pushed me away, and being on my blind side, ran off before I could kiss her. I went to the Men of the Sheepguard at watering-time. There was a sheep to be killed for their meat. I cut it in two halves with my knife, and told them all my tale. They said, "It is the work of a God." I said, "We talk too much about Gods. Let us eat and be happy, and tomorrow I will take you to the Children of the Night, and each man will find a Magic Knife."

'I was glad to smell our sheep again; to see the broad sky from edge to edge, and to hear the sea. I slept beneath the stars in my cloak. The men talked among themselves.

'I led them, the next day, to the Trees, taking with me meat, wool, and curdled milk, as I had promised. We found the Magic Knives laid out on the grass, as the Children of the Night had promised. They watched us from among the Trees. Their Priestess called to me and said, "How is it with your people?" I said, "Their hearts are changed. I cannot see their hearts as I used to." She said, "That is because you have only one eye. Come to me and I will be both your eyes." But I said, "I must show my people how to use their knives against The Beast, as you showed me how to use my knife." I said this because the Magic Knife does not balance like the flint. She said, "What you have done, you have done for the sake of a woman, and not for the sake of your people." I asked of her, "Then why did the God accept my right eye, and why are you so angry?" She answered, "Because any man can lie to a God, but no man can lie to a woman. And I am not angry with you. I am only very sorrowful for you. Wait a little, and you will see out of your one eye why I am sorry." So she hid herself.

'I went back with my people, each one carrying his knife, and making it sing in the air – *tssee-sssse*. The Flint never sings. It mutters – *ump-ump*. The Beast heard. The Beast saw. *He* knew! Everywhere he ran away from us. We all laughed. As we walked over the grass my Mother's brother – the Chief on the Man's Side – he took off his Chief's necklace of yellow sea-stones.'

'How? Eh? Oh, I remember! Amber,' said Puck.

'And would have put them on my neck. I said, "No, I am content. What does my one eye matter if my other eye sees fat sheep and fat children running about safely?" My Mother's brother said to them, "I told you he would never take such things." Then they began to sing a song in the Old Tongue – *The Song of Tyr*. I sang with them, but my mother's brother said, "This is *your* song, oh, Buyer of the Knife. Let *us* sing it, Tyr."

'Even then I did not understand, till I saw that – that no man stepped on my shadow; and I knew that they thought me to be a God, like the God Tyr, who gave his right hand to conquer a Great Beast.'

'By the Fire in the Belly of the Flint, was that so?' Puck rapped out.

'By my Knife and the Naked Chalk, so it was! They made way for my shadow as though it had been a Priestess walking to the Barrows of the Dead. I was afraid. I said to myself, "My Mother and my Maiden will know I am not Tyr." But *still* I was afraid with the fear of a man who falls into a steep flint-pit while he runs, and feels that it will be hard to climb out.

'When we came to the Dew-ponds all our people were there. The men showed their knives and told their tale. The sheepguards also had seen The Beast flying from us. The Beast went west across the river in packs

– howling! He knew the Knife had come to the Naked Chalk at last – at last! *He* knew! So my work was done. I looked for my Maiden among the Priestesses. She looked at me, but she did not smile. She made the sign to me that our Priestesses must make when they sacrifice to the Old Dead in the Barrows. I would have spoken, but my Mother's brother made himself my Mouth, as though I had been one of the Old Dead in the Barrows for whom our Priests speak to the people on Midsummer mornings.'

'I remember. Well I remember those Midsummer mornings!' said Puck.

'Then I went away angrily to my Mother's house. She would have knelt before me. Then I was more angry, but she said, "Only a God would have spoken to me thus, a Priestess. A man would have feared the punishment of the Gods." I looked at her and laughed. I could not stop my unhappy laughing. They called me from the door by the name of Tyr himself. A young man with whom I had watched my first flocks, and chipped my first arrow, and fought my first Beast, called me by that name in the Old Tongue. He asked my leave to take my Maiden. His eyes were lowered, his hands were on his forehead. He was full of the fear of a God, but of *me*, a man, he had no fear when he asked. I did not kill him. I said, "Call the maiden." She came also without fear – this very one that had waited for me, that had talked with me by our Dew-ponds. Being a Priestess, she lifted her eyes to me. As I look on a hill or a cloud, so she looked at me. She spoke in the Old Tongue which Priestesses use when they make prayers to the Old Dead in the Barrows. She asked leave that she might light the fire in my companion's house – and that I should bless their children. I did not kill her. I heard my own voice, little and cold, say, "Let it be as you desire," and they went away hand in hand. My heart grew little and cold, a wind shouted in my ears; my eye darkened. I said to my Mother, "Can a God die?" I heard her say, "What is it? What is it, my son?" and I fell into darkness full of hammer-noises. I was not.'

'Oh, poor – poor God!' said Puck. 'And your wise Mother?'

'*She* knew. As soon as I dropped she knew. When my spirit came back I heard her whisper on my ear, "Whether you live or die, or are made different, I am your Mother." That was good – better even than the water she gave me and the going away of the sickness. Though I was ashamed to have fallen down, yet I was very glad. She was glad too. Neither of us wished to lose the other. There is only the one Mother for the one son. I heaped the fire for her, and barred the doors, and sat at her feet as before I went away, and she combed my hair, and sang.

I said at last, "What is to be done to the people who say that I am Tyr?"

'She said, "He who has done a God-like thing must bear himself like a God. I see no way out of it. The people are now your sheep till you die. You cannot drive them off."

'I said, "This is a heavier sheep than I can lift." She said, "In time it will grow easy. In time perhaps you will not lay it down for any maiden anywhere. Be wise – be very wise, my son, for nothing is left you except the words, and the songs, and the worship of a God."'

'Oh, poor God!' said Puck. 'But those are not altogether bad things.'

'I know they are not; but I would sell them all – all – all for one small child of my own, smearing himself with the ashes of our own house-fire.'

He wrenched his knife from the turf, thrust it into his belt and stood up.

'And yet, what else could I have done?' he said. 'The sheep are the people.'

'It is a very old tale,' Puck answered. 'I have heard the like of it not only on the Naked Chalk, but also among the Trees – under Oak, and Ash, and Thorn.'[6]

The afternoon shadows filled all the quiet emptiness of Norton's Pit. The children heard the sheep bells and Young Jim's busy bark above them, and they scrambled up the slope to the level.

'We let you have your sleep out,' said Mr Dudeney, as the flock scattered before them. 'It's making for tea-time now.'

'Look what I've found,' said Dan, and held up a little blue flint arrow-head as fresh as though it had been chipped that very day.

'Oh,' said Mr Dudeney, 'the closeter you be to the turf the more you're apt to see things. I've found 'em often. Some says the fairies made 'em, but I says they was made by folks like ourselves – only a goodish time back. They're lucky to keep. Now, you couldn't ever have slept – not to any profit – among your father's trees same as you've laid out on Naked Chalk – could you?'

'One doesn't want to sleep in the woods,' said Una.

'Then what's the good of 'em?' said Mr Dudeney. 'Might as well set in the barn all day. Fetch 'em 'long, Jim boy!'

The Downs, that looked so bare and hot when they came, were full of delicious little shadow-dimples; the smell of the thyme and the salt mixed together on the south-west drift from the still sea; their eyes dazzled with the low sun, and the long grass under it looked golden. The sheep knew where their fold was, so Young Jim came back to his master, and they all four strolled home, the scabious-heads swishing about their ankles, and their shadows streaking behind them like the shadows of giants.

He had suffered from the disease of the century [2] since his early youth, and before he was thirty he was heavily marked with it. He and a few friends had rearranged Heaven very comfortably, but the reorganization of Earth, which they called Society, was even greater fun. It demanded Work in the shape of many taxi-rides daily; hours of brilliant talk with brilliant talkers; some sparkling correspondence; a few silences (but on the understanding that their own turn should come soon) while other people expounded philosophies; and a fair number of picture-galleries, tea-fights, concerts, theatres, music-halls, and cinema shows; the whole trimmed with love-making to women whose hair smelt of cigarette-smoke. Such strong days sent Frankwell Midmore back to his flat assured that he and his friends had helped the World a step nearer the Truth, the Dawn, and the New Order.

His temperament, he said, led him more towards concrete data than abstract ideas. People who investigate detail are apt to be tired at the day’s end. The same temperament, or it may have been a woman, made him early attach himself to the Immoderate Left of his Cause in the capacity of an experimenter in Social Relations. And since the Immoderate Left contains plenty of women anxious to help earnest inquirers with large independent incomes to arrive at evaluations of essentials, Frankwell Midmore’s lot was far from contemptible.

At that hour Fate chose to play with him. A widowed aunt, widely separated by nature, and more widely by marriage, from all that Midmore’s mother had ever been or desired to be, died and left him possessions. Mrs Midmore, having that summer embraced a creed which denied the existence of death, naturally could not stoop to burial; but Midmore had to leave London for the dank country at a season when Social Regeneration works best through long, cushioned conferences, two by two, after tea. There he faced the bracing ritual of the British funeral, and was wept at across the raw grave by an elderly coffin-shaped female with a long nose, who called him ‘Master Frankie’; and there he was congratulated behind an echoing top-hat by a man he mistook for a mute, who turned out to be his aunt’s lawyer. He wrote his mother next day, after a bright account of the funeral:

‘So far as I can understand, she has left me between four and five

446

hundred a year. It all comes from Ther Land, as they call it down here. The unspeakable attorney, Sperrit, and a green-eyed daughter, who hums to herself as she tramps but is silent on all subjects except "huntin'", insisted on taking me to see it. Ther Land is brown and green in alternate slabs like chocolate and pistachio cakes, speckled with occasional peasants who do not utter. In case it should not be wet enough there is a wet brook in the middle of it. Ther House is by the brook. I shall look into it later. If there should be any little memento of Jenny that you care for, let me know. Didn't you tell me that mid-Victorian furniture is coming into the market again? Jenny's old maid – it is called Rhoda Dolbie – tells me that Jenny promised it thirty pounds a year. The will does not. Hence, I suppose, the tears at the funeral. But that is close on ten per cent of the income. I fancy Jenny has destroyed all her private papers and records of her *vie intime*,[3] if, indeed, life be possible in such a place. The Sperrit man told me that if I had means of my own I might come and live on Ther Land. I didn't tell him how much I would pay not to! I cannot think it right that any human being should exercise mastery over others in the merciless fashion our tom-fool social system permits; so, as it is all mine, I intend to sell it whenever the unholy Sperrit can find a purchaser.'

And he went to Mr Sperrit with the idea next day, just before returning to town.

'Quite so,' said the lawyer. 'I see your point, of course. But the house itself is rather old-fashioned – hardly the type purchasers demand nowadays. There's no park, of course, and the bulk of the land is let to a life-tenant, a Mr Sidney. As long as he pays his rent, he can't be turned out, and even if he didn't' – Mr Sperrit's face relaxed a shade – 'you might have a difficulty.'

'The property brings four hundred a year, I understand,' said Midmore.

'Well, hardly – ha-ardly. Deducting land and income tax, tithes, fire insurance, cost of collection and repairs of course, it returned two hundred and eighty-four pounds last year. The repairs are rather a large item – owing to the brook. I call it Liris – out of Horace,[4] you know.'

Midmore looked at his watch impatiently.

'I suppose you can find somebody to buy it?' he repeated.

'We will do our best, of course, if those are your instructions. Then, that is all except' – here Midmore half rose, but Mr Sperrit's little grey eyes held his large brown ones firmly – 'except about Rhoda Dolbie, Mrs Werf's maid. I may tell you that we did not draw up your aunt's last will. She grew secretive towards the last – elderly people often do –

and had it done in London. I expect her memory failed her, or she mislaid her notes. She used to put them in her spectacle-case ... My motor only takes eight minutes to get to the station, Mr Midmore ... but, as I was saying, whenever she made her will with *us*, Mrs Werf always left Rhoda thirty pounds per annum. Charlie, the wills!' A clerk with a baldish head and a long nose dealt documents on to the table like cards, and breathed heavily behind Midmore. 'It's in no sense a legal obligation, of course,' said Mr Sperrit. 'Ah, that one is dated January the 11th, eighteen eighty-nine.'

Midmore looked at his watch again and found himself saying with no good grace: 'Well, I suppose she'd better have it – for the present at any rate.'

He escaped with an uneasy feeling that two hundred and fifty-four pounds a year was not exactly four hundred, and that Charlie's long nose annoyed him. Then he returned, first-class, to his own affairs.

Of the two, perhaps three, experiments in Social Relations which he had then in hand, one interested him acutely. It had run for some months and promised most variegated and interesting developments, on which he dwelt luxuriously all the way to town. When he reached his flat he was not well prepared for a twelve-page letter explaining, in the diction of the Immoderate Left which rubricates its I's and illuminates its T's, that the lady had realized greater attractions in another Soul. She re-stated, rather than pleaded, the gospel of the Immoderate Left as her justification, and ended in an impassioned demand for her right to express herself in and on her own life, through which, she pointed out, she could pass but once. She added that if, later, she should discover Midmore was 'essentially complementary to her needs', she would tell him so. That Midmore had himself written much the same sort of epistle – barring the hint of return – to a woman of whom his needs for self-expression had caused him to weary three years before, did not assist him in the least. He expressed himself to the gas-fire in terms essential but not complimentary. Then he reflected on the detached criticism of his best friends and her best friends, male and female, with whom he and she and others had talked so openly while their gay adventure was in flower. He recalled, too – this must have been about midnight – her analysis from every angle, remote and most intimate, of the mate to whom she had been adjudged under the base convention which is styled marriage. Later, at that bad hour when the cattle wake for a little, he remembered her in other aspects and went down into the hell appointed; desolate, desiring, with no God to call upon. About eleven o'clock next morning Eliphaz [5] the Temanite, Bildad the Shuhite, and

Zophar the Naamathite called upon him 'for they had made appointment together' to see how he took it; but the janitor told them that Job had gone – into the country, he believed.

Midmore's relief when he found his story was not written across his aching temples for Mr Sperrit to read – the defeated lover, like the successful one, believes all earth privy to his soul – was put down by Mr Sperrit to quite different causes. He led him into a morning-room. The rest of the house seemed to be full of people, singing to a loud piano idiotic songs about cows, and the hall smelt of damp cloaks.

'It's our evening to take the winter cantata,' Mr Sperrit explained. 'It's "High Tide on the Coast of Lincolnshire". I hoped you'd come back. There are scores of little things to settle. As for the house, of course, it stands ready for you at any time. I couldn't get Rhoda out of it – nor could Charlie for that matter. She's the sister, isn't she, of the nurse who brought you down here when you were four, she says, to recover from measles?'

'Is she? Was I?' said Midmore through the bad tastes in his mouth. 'D'you suppose I could stay there the night?'

Thirty joyous young voices shouted appeal to someone to leave their 'pipes of parsley 'ollow – 'ollow – 'ollow!' Mr Sperrit had to raise his voice above the din.

'Well, if I asked you to stay *here*, I should never hear the last of it from Rhoda. She's a little cracked, of course, but the soul of devotion and capable of anything. *Ne sit ancillae*,[6] you know.'

'Thank you. Then I'll go. I'll walk.' He stumbled out dazed and sick into the winter twilight, and sought the square house by the brook.

It was not a dignified entry, because when the door was unchained and Rhoda exclaimed, he took two valiant steps into the hall and then fainted – as men sometimes will after twenty-two hours of strong emotion and little food.

'I'm sorry,' he said when he could speak. He was lying at the foot of the stairs, his head on Rhoda's lap.

'Your 'ome is your castle, sir,' was the reply in his hair. 'I smelt it wasn't drink. You lay on the sofa till I get your supper.'

She settled him in a drawing-room hung with yellow silk, heavy with the smell of dead leaves and oil lamp. Something murmured soothingly in the background and overcame the noises in his head. He thought he heard horses' feet on wet gravel and a voice singing about ships and flocks and grass. It passed close to the shuttered bay-window.

'But each will mourn his own, she saith,
And sweeter woman ne'er drew breath
Than my son's wife, Elizabeth ...
Cusha – cusha – cusha – calling.'

The hoofs broke into a canter as Rhoda entered with the tray. 'And then I'll put you to bed,' she said. 'Sidney's coming in the morning.' Midmore asked no questions. He dragged his poor bruised soul to bed and would have pitied it all over again, but the food and warm sherry and water drugged him to instant sleep.

Rhoda's voice wakened him, asking whether he would have ''ip, foot, or sitz', which he understood were the baths of the establishment. 'Suppose you try all three,' she suggested. 'They're all yours, you know, sir.'

He would have renewed his sorrows with the daylight, but her words struck him pleasantly. Everything his eyes opened upon was his very own to keep for ever. The carved four-post Chippendale bed, obviously worth hundreds; the wavy walnut William and Mary chairs – he had seen worse ones labelled twenty guineas apiece; the oval medallion mirror; the delicate eighteenth-century wire fireguard; the heavy brocaded curtains were his – all his. So, too, a great garden full of birds that faced him when he shaved; a mulberry tree, a sun-dial, and a dull, steel-coloured brook that murmured level with the edge of a lawn a hundred yards away. Peculiarly and privately his own was the smell of sausages and coffee that he sniffed at the head of the wide square landing, all set round with mysterious doors and Bartolozzi[7] prints. He spent two hours after breakfast in exploring his new possessions. His heart leaped up at such things as sewing-machines, a rubber-tyred bath-chair in a tiled passage, a malachite-headed Malacca cane, boxes and boxes of unopened stationery, seal-rings, bunches of keys, and at the bottom of a steel-net reticule a little leather purse with seven pounds ten shillings in gold and eleven shillings in silver.

'You used to play with that when my sister brought you down here after your measles,' said Rhoda as he slipped the money into his pocket. 'Now, this was your pore dear auntie's business-room.' She opened a low door. 'Oh, I forgot about Mr Sidney! There he is.' An enormous old man with rheumy red eyes that blinked under downy white eyebrows sat in an Empire chair, his cap in his hands. Rhoda withdrew sniffing. The man looked Midmore over in silence, then jerked a thumb towards the door. 'I reckon she told you who I be,' he began. 'I'm the only farmer you've got. Nothin' goes off my place 'thout it walks on its own feet. What about my pig-pound?'

'Well, what about it?' said Midmore.

'That's just what I be come about. The County Councils are getting more particular. Did ye know there was swine fever at Pashell's? There *be*. It'll 'ave to be in brick.'

'Yes,' said Midmore politely.

'I've bin at your aunt that was, plenty times about it. I don't say she wasn't a just woman, but she didn't read the lease same way I did. I be used to bein' put upon, but there's no doing any longer 'thout that pig-pound.'

'When would you like it?' Midmore asked. It seemed the easiest road to take.

'Any time or other suits me, I reckon. He ain't thrivin' where he is, an' I paid eighteen shillin' for him.' He crossed his hands on his stick and gave no further sign of life.

'Is that all?' Midmore stammered.

'All now – excep'' – he glanced fretfully at the table beside him – 'excep' my usuals. Where's that Rhoda?'

Midmore rang the bell. Rhoda came in with a bottle and a glass. The old man helped himself to four stiff fingers, rose in one piece, and stumped out. At the door he cried ferociously: 'Don't suppose it's any odds to you whether I'm drowned or not, but them floodgates want a wheel and winch, they do. I be too old for liftin' 'em with the bar – my time o' life.'

'Good riddance if 'e was drowned,' said Rhoda. 'But don't you mind him. He's only amusin' himself. Your pore dear auntie used to give 'im 'is usual – 'tisn't the whisky *you* drink – an' send 'im about 'is business.'

'I see. Now, is a pig-pound the same thing as a pig-sty?'

Rhoda nodded. ''E needs one, too, but 'e ain't entitled to it. You look at 'is lease – third drawer on the left in that Bombay cab'net – an' next time 'e comes you ask 'im to read it. That'll choke 'im off, because 'e can't!'

There was nothing in Midmore's past to teach him the message and significance of a hand-written lease of the late 'eighties, but Rhoda interpreted.

'It don't mean anything reelly,' was her cheerful conclusion, 'excep' you mustn't get rid of him anyhow, an' 'e can do what 'e likes always. Lucky for us 'e *do* farm; and if it wasn't for 'is woman –'

'Oh, there's a Mrs Sidney, is there?'

'Lor, *no*! The Sidneys don't marry. They keep. That's his fourth since – to my knowledge. He was a takin' man from the first.'

'Any families?'

'They'd be grown up by now if there was, wouldn't they? But you can't spend all your days considerin' 'is interests. That's what gave your pore aunt 'er indigestion. 'Ave you seen the gun-room?'

Midmore held strong views on the immorality of taking life for pleasure. But there was no denying that the late Colonel Werf's seventy-guinea breechloaders were good at their filthy job. He loaded one, took it out and pointed – merely pointed – it at a cock-pheasant which rose out of a shrubbery behind the kitchen, and the flaming bird came down in a long slant on the lawn, stone dead. Rhoda from the scullery said it was a lovely shot, and told him lunch was ready.

He spent the afternoon gun in one hand, a map in the other, beating the bounds of his lands. They lay altogether in a shallow, uninteresting valley, flanked with woods and bisected by a brook. Up stream was his own house; down stream, less than half a mile, a low red farm-house squatted in an old orchard, beside what looked like small lock-gates on the Thames. There was no doubt as to ownership. Mr Sidney saw him while yet far off, and bellowed at him about pig-pounds and flood-gates. These last were two great sliding shutters of weedy oak across the brook, which were prised up inch by inch with a crowbar along a notched strip of iron, and when Sidney opened them they at once let out half the water. Midmore watched it shrink between its aldered banks like some conjuring trick. This, too, was his very own.

'I see,' he said. 'How interesting! Now, what's that bell for?' he went on, pointing to an old ship's bell in a rude belfry at the end of an outhouse. 'Was that a chapel once?' The red-eyed giant seemed to have difficulty in expressing himself for the moment and blinked savagely.

'Yes,' he said at last. 'My chapel. When you 'ear that bell ring you'll 'ear something. Nobody but me ud put up with it – but I reckon it don't make any odds to you.' He slammed the gates down again, and the brook rose behind them with a suck and a grunt.

Midmore moved off, conscious that he might be safer with Rhoda to hold his conversational hand. As he passed the front of the farm-house a smooth fat woman, with neatly parted grey hair under a widow's cap, curtsied to him deferentially through the window. By every teaching of the Immoderate Left she had a perfect right to express herself in any way she pleased, but the curtsey revolted him. And on his way home he was hailed from behind a hedge by a manifest idiot with no roof to his mouth, who hallooed and danced round him.

'What did that beast want?' he demanded of Rhoda at tea.

'Jimmy? He only wanted to know if you 'ad any telegrams to send. 'E'll go anywhere so long as 'tisn't across running water. That gives 'im 'is seizures. Even talkin' about it for fun like makes 'im shake.'

'But why isn't he where he can be properly looked after?'

'What 'arm's 'e doing? 'E's a love-child, but 'is family can pay for 'im. If 'e was locked up 'e'd die all off at once, like a wild rabbit. Won't you, please, look at the drive, sir?'

Midmore looked in the fading light. The neat gravel was pitted with large roundish holes, and there was a punch or two of the same sort on the lawn.

'That's the 'unt comin' 'ome,' Rhoda explained. 'Your pore dear auntie always let 'em use our drive for a short cut after the Colonel died. The Colonel wouldn't so much because he preserved;[8] but your auntie was always an 'orsewoman till 'er sciatica.'

'Isn't there someone who can rake it over or – or something?' said Midmore vaguely.

'Oh yes. You'll never see it in the morning, but – you was out when they came 'ome an' Mister Fisher – he's the Master – told me to tell you with 'is compliments that if you wasn't preservin' and cared to 'old to the old understandin', 'is gravel-pit is at your service same as before. 'E thought, perhaps, you mightn't know, and it 'ad slipped my mind to tell you. It's good gravel, Mister Fisher's, and it binds beautiful on the drive. We 'ave to draw it, o' course, from the pit, but –'

Midmore looked at her helplessly.

'Rhoda,' said he, 'what am I supposed to do?'

'Oh, let 'em come through,' she replied. 'You never know. You may want to 'unt yourself some day.'

That evening it rained and his misery returned on him, the worse for having been diverted. At last he was driven to paw over a few score books in a panelled room called the library, and realized with horror what the late Colonel Werf's mind must have been in its prime. The volumes smelt of a dead world as strongly as they did of mildew. He opened and thrust them back, one after another, till crude coloured illustrations of men on horses held his eye. He began at random and read a little, moved into the drawing-room with the volume, and settled down by the fire still reading. It was a foul world into which he peeped for the first time – a heavy-eating, hard-drinking hell of horse-copers, swindlers, matchmaking mothers, economically dependent virgins selling themselves blushingly for cash and lands: Jews, tradesmen, and an ill-considered spawn of Dickens-and-horsedung characters (I give Midmore's own criticism), but he read on, fascinated, and behold, from the pages leaped, as it were, the brother to the red-eyed man of the brook, bellowing at a landlord (here Midmore realized that *he* was that very animal) for new barns; and another man who, like himself again, objected to hoof-marks on gravel. Outrageous as thought and conception were, the stuff seemed to have the rudiments of observation. He dug out other volumes by the same author, till Rhoda came in with a silver candlestick.

'Rhoda,' said he, 'did you ever hear about a character called James Pigg – and Batsey?'[9]

'Why, o' course,' said she. 'The Colonel used to come into the kitchen in 'is dressin'-gown an' read us all those Jorrockses.'

'Oh, Lord!' said Midmore, and went to bed with a book called *Handley Cross* under his arm, and a lonelier Columbus into a stranger world the wet-ringed moon never looked upon.

Here we omit much. But Midmore never denied that for the epicure in sensation the urgent needs of an ancient house, as interpreted by Rhoda pointing to daylight through attic-tiles held in place by moss, gives an edge to the pleasure of Social Research elsewhere. Equally he found that the reaction following prolonged research loses much of its grey terror if one knows one can at will bathe the soul in the society of plumbers (all the water-pipes had chronic appendicitis), village idiots (Jimmy had taken Midmore under his weak wing and camped daily at the drive-gates), and a giant with red eyelids whose every action is an unpredictable outrage.

Towards spring Midmore filled his house with a few friends of the Immoderate Left. It happened to be the day when, all things and Rhoda working together, a cartload of bricks, another of sand, and some bags of lime had been despatched to build Sidney his almost daily-demanded pig-pound. Midmore took his friends across the flat fields with some idea of showing them Sidney as a type of 'the peasantry'. They hit the minute when Sidney, hoarse with rage, was ordering bricklayer, mate, carts and all off his premises. The visitors disposed themselves to listen.

'You never give me no notice about changin' the pig,' Sidney shouted. The pig – at least eighteen inches long – reared on end in the old sty and smiled at the company.

'But, my good man –' Midmore opened.

'I ain't! For aught you know I be a dam' sight worse than you be. You can't come and be'ave arbit'ry with me. You *are* be'avin' arbit'ry! All you men go clean away an' don't set foot on my land till I bid ye.'

'But you asked' – Midmore felt his voice jump up – 'to have the pig-pound built.'

''Spose I did. That's no reason you shouldn't send me notice to change the pig. 'Comin' down on me like this 'thout warnin'! That pig's got to be got into the cowshed an' all.'

'Then open the door and let him run in,' said Midmore.

'Don't you be'ave arbit'ry with *me*! Take all your dam' men 'ome off my land. I won't be treated arbit'ry.'

The carts moved off without a word, and Sidney went into the house and slammed the door.

'Now, I hold that is enormously significant,' said a visitor. 'Here you have the logical outcome of centuries of feudal oppression – the frenzy of fear.' The company looked at Midmore with grave pain.

'But he *did* worry my life out about his pig-sty,' was all Midmore found to say.

Others took up the parable and proved to him if he only held true to the gospels of the Immoderate Left the earth would soon be covered with 'jolly little' pig-sties, built in the intervals of morris-dancing by 'the peasant' himself.

Midmore felt grateful when the door opened again and Mr Sidney invited them all to retire to the road which, he pointed out, was public. As they turned the corner of the house, a smooth-faced woman in a widow's cap curtsied to each of them through the window.

Instantly they drew pictures of that woman's lot, deprived of all vehicle for self-expression – 'the set grey life and apathetic end',[10] one quoted – and they discussed the tremendous significance of village theatricals. Even a month ago Midmore would have told them all that he knew and Rhoda had dropped about Sidney's forms of self-expression. Now, for some strange reason, he was content to let the talk run on from village to metropolitan and world drama.

Rhoda advised him after the visitors left that 'if he wanted to do that again' he had better go up to town.

'But we only sat on cushions on the floor,' said her master.

'They're too old for romps,' she retorted, 'an' it's only the beginning of things. I've seen what *I've* seen. Besides, they talked and laughed in the passage going to their baths – such as took 'em.'

'Don't be a fool, Rhoda,' said Midmore. No man – unless he has loved her – will casually dismiss a woman on whose lap he has laid his head.

'Very good,' she snorted, 'but that cuts both ways. An' now, you go down to Sidney's this evenin' and put him where he ought to be. He was in his right about you givin' 'im notice about changin' the pig, but he 'adn't any right to turn it up before your company. No manners, no pig-pound. He'll understand.'

Midmore did his best to make him. He found himself reviling the old man in speech and with a joy quite new in all his experience. He wound up – it was a plagiarism from a plumber – by telling Mr Sidney that he looked like a turkey-cock, had the morals of a parish bull, and need never hope for a new pig-pound as long as he or Midmore lived.

'Very good,' said the giant. 'I reckon you thought you 'ad something against me, and now you've come down an ' told it me like man to man. Quite right. I don't bear malice. Now, you send along those bricks an' sand, an' I'll make do to build the pig-pound myself. If you look at my lease you'll find out you're bound to provide me materials for the repairs. Only – only I thought there'd be no 'arm in my askin' you to do it throughout like.'

Midmore fairly gasped. 'Then, why the devil did you turn my carts back when – when I sent them up here to do it throughout for you?'

Mr Sidney sat down on the floodgates, his eyebrows knitted in thought.

'I'll tell you,' he said slowly. ''Twas too dam' like cheatin' a suckin' baby. My woman, she said so too.'

For a few seconds the teachings of the Immoderate Left, whose humour is all their own, wrestled with those of Mother Earth, who has her own humours. Then Midmore laughed till he could scarcely stand. In due time Mr Sidney laughed too – crowing and wheezing crescendo till it broke from him in roars. They shook hands, and Midmore went home grateful that he had held his tongue among his companions.

When he reached his house he met three or four men and women on horseback, very muddy indeed, coming down the drive. Feeling hungry himself, he asked them if they were hungry. They said they were, and he bade them enter. Jimmy took their horses, who seemed to know him. Rhoda took their battered hats, led the women upstairs for hairpins, and presently fed them all with tea-cakes, poached eggs, anchovy toast, and drinks from a coromandel-wood liqueur case which Midmore had never known that he possessed.

'And I *will* say,' said Miss Connie Sperrit, her spurred foot on the fender and a smoking muffin in her whip hand, 'Rhoda does one top-hole. She always did since I was eight.'

'Seven, Miss, was when you began to 'unt,' said Rhoda, setting down more buttered toast.

'And so,' the M.F.H. was saying to Midmore, 'when he got to your brute Sidney's land, we had to whip 'em off. It's a regular Alsatia [11] for 'em. They know it. Why' – he dropped his voice – 'I don't want to say anything against Sidney as your tenant, of course, but I do believe the old scoundrel's perfectly capable of putting down poison.'

'Sidney's capable of anything,' said Midmore with immense feeling;

but once again he held his tongue. They were a queer community; yet when they had stamped and jingled out to their horses again, the house felt hugely big and disconcerting.

This may be reckoned the conscious beginning of his double life. It ran in odd channels that summer – a riding school, for instance, near Hayes Common and a shooting ground near Wormwood Scrubs. A man who has been saddle-galled or shoulder-bruised for half the day is not at his London best of evenings; and when the bills for his amusements come in he curtails his expenses in other directions. So a cloud settled on Midmore's name. His London world talked of a hardening of heart and a tightening of purse-strings which signified disloyalty to the Cause. One man, a confidant of the old expressive days, attacked him robustiously and demanded account of his soul's progress. It was not furnished, for Midmore was calculating how much it would cost to repave stables so dilapidated that even the village idiot apologized for putting visitors' horses into them. The man went away, and served up what he had heard of the pig-pound episode as a little newspaper sketch, calculated to annoy. Midmore read it with an eye as practical as a woman's, and since most of his experiences had been among women, at once sought out a woman to whom he might tell his sorrow at the disloyalty of his own familiar friend. She was so sympathetic that he went on to confide how his bruised heart – she knew all about it – had found solace, with a long O, in another quarter which he indicated rather carefully in case it might be betrayed to other loyal friends. As his hints pointed directly towards facile Hampstead, and as his urgent business was the purchase of a horse from a dealer, Beckenham way, he felt he had done good work. Later, when his friend, the scribe, talked to him alluringly of 'secret gardens' and those so-laces to which every man who follows the Wider Morality is entitled, Midmore lent him a five-pound note which he had got back on the price of a ninety-guinea bay gelding. So true it is, as he read in one of the late Colonel Werf's books, that 'the young man of the present day would sooner lie under an imputation against his morals than against his knowledge of horse-flesh.'[12]

Midmore desired more than he desired anything else at that moment to ride and, above all, to jump on a ninety-guinea bay gelding with black points and a slovenly habit of hitting his fences. He did not wish many people except Mr Sidney, who very kindly lent his soft meadow behind the flood-gates, to be privy to the matter, which he rightly foresaw would take him to the autumn. So he told such friends as hinted at country week-end visits that he had practically let his newly inherited house. The rent, he said, was an object to him, for he had lately lost large sums through ill-considered benevolences. He would name no names, but they could guess. And they guessed loyally all round the circle of his acquaintance as they spread the news that explained so much.

There remained only one couple of his once intimate associates to pacify. They were deeply sympathetic and utterly loyal, of course, but as curious as any of the apes whose diet they had adopted. Midmore met them in a suburban train, coming up to town, not twenty minutes after he had come off two hours' advanced tuition (one guinea an hour) over hurdles in a hall. He had, of course, changed his kit, but his too heavy bridle-hand shook a little among the newspapers. On the inspiration of the moment, which is your natural liar's best hold, he told them that he was condemned to a rest-cure. He would lie in semi-darkness drinking milk, for weeks and weeks, cut off even from letters. He was astonished and delighted at the ease with which the usual lie confounds the unusual intellect. They swallowed it as swiftly as they recommended him to live on nuts and fruit; but he saw in the woman's eyes the exact reason she would set forth for his retirement. After all, she had as much right to express herself as he purposed to take for himself; and Midmore believed strongly in the fullest equality of the sexes.

That retirement made one small ripple in the strenuous world. The lady who had written the twelve-page letter ten months before sent him another of eight pages, analysing all the motives that were leading her back to him – should she come? – now that he was ill and alone. Much might yet be retrieved, she said, out of the waste of jarring lives and piteous misunderstandings. It needed only a hand.

But Midmore needed two, next morning very early, for a devil's diversion, among wet coppices, called 'cubbing'.[13]

'You haven't a bad seat,' said Miss Sperrit through the morning-mists. 'But you're worrying him.'

'He pulls so,' Midmore grunted.

'Let him alone, then. Look out for the branches,' she shouted, as they whirled up a splashy ride. Cubs were plentiful. Most of the hounds attached themselves to a straight-necked youngster of education who scuttled out of the woods into the open fields below.

'Hold on!' someone shouted. 'Turn 'em, Midmore. That's your brute Sidney's land. It's all wire.'

'Oh, Connie, stop!' Mrs Sperrit shrieked as her daughter charged at a boundary-hedge.

'Wire be damned! I had it all out a fortnight ago. Come on!' This was Midmore, buffeting into it a little lower down.

'*I* knew that!' Connie cried over her shoulder, and she flitted across the open pasture, humming to herself.

'Oh, of course! If some people have private information, they can afford to thrust.' This was a snuff-coloured habit into which Miss Sperrit had cannoned down the ride.

'What! Midmore got Sidney to heel? *You* never did that, Sperrit.' This was Mr Fisher, M.F.H., enlarging the breach Midmore had made.

'No, confound him!' said the father testily. 'Go on, sir! *Injecto ter pulvere* [14] – you've kicked half the ditch into my eye already.'

They killed that cub a little short of the haven his mother had told him to make for – a two-acre Alsatia of a gorse-patch to which the M.F.H. had been denied access for the last fifteen seasons. He expressed his gratitude before all the field and Mr Sidney, at Mr Sidney's farm-house door.

'And if there should be any poultry claims –' he went on.

'There won't be,' said Midmore. 'It's too like cheating a sucking child, isn't it, Mr Sidney?'

'You've got me!' was all the reply. 'I be used to bein' put upon, but you've got me, Mus' Midmore.'

Midmore pointed to a new brick pig-pound built in strict disregard of the terms of the life-tenant's lease. The gesture told the tale to the few who did not know, and they shouted.

Such pagan delights as these were followed by pagan sloth of evenings when men and women elsewhere are at their brightest. But Midmore preferred to lie out on a yellow silk couch, reading works of a debasing vulgarity; or, by invitation, to dine with the Sperrits and savages of their kidney. These did not expect flights of fancy or phrasing. They lied, except about horses, grudgingly and of necessity, not for art's sake; and, men and women alike, they expressed themselves along their chosen lines with the serene indifference of the larger animals. Then Midmore would go home and identify them, one by one, out of the natural-history books by Mr Surtees, on the table beside the sofa. At first they looked upon him coolly, but when the tale of the removed wire and the recaptured gorse had gone the rounds, they accepted him for a person willing to play their games. True, a faction suspended judgment for a while, because they shot, and hoped that Midmore would serve the glorious mammon of pheasant-raising rather than the unkempt god of fox-hunting. But after he had shown his choice, they did not ask by what intellectual process he had arrived at it. He hunted three, sometimes four, times a week, which necessitated not only one bay gelding (£94 : 10s.), but a mannerly white-stockinged chestnut (£114), and a black mare, rather long in the back but with a mouth of silk (£150), who so evidently preferred to carry a lady that it would have been cruel to have baulked her. Besides, with that handling she could be sold at a profit. And besides, the hunt was a quiet, intimate, kindly little hunt, not anxious for strangers, of good report in the *Field*, the servant of one M.F.H., given to hospitality, riding well its own horses, and, with the exception of Midmore, not novices. But as Miss Sperrit observed, after the M.F.H. had said some things to him at a gate: 'It *is* a pity you don't know as much as your horse, but you will in time. It takes years and yee-ars. I've been at it for fifteen and I'm only just learning. But you've made a decent kick-off.'

So he kicked off in wind and wet and mud, wondering quite sincerely why the bubbling ditches and sucking pastures held him from day to day, or what so-lace he could find on off days in chasing grooms and bricklayers round outhouses.

To make sure he up-rooted himself one week-end of heavy mid-winter rain, and re-entered his lost world in the character of Galahad fresh from a rest-cure. They all agreed, with an eye over his shoulder for the next comer, that he was a different man; but when they asked him for the symptoms of nervous strain, and led him all through their own, he realized he had lost much of his old skill in lying. His three months' absence, too, had put him hopelessly behind the London field. The movements, the allusions, the slang of the game had changed. The couples had rearranged themselves or were re-crystallizing in fresh triangles, whereby he put his foot in it badly. Only one great soul (he who had written the account of the pig-pound episode) stood untouched by the vast flux of time, and Midmore lent him another fiver for his integrity. A woman took him, in the wet forenoon, to a pronouncement on the Oneness of Impulse in Humanity, which struck him as a poly-syllabic *résumé* of Mr Sidney's domestic arrangements, plus a clarion call to 'shock civilization into common-sense'.

'And you'll come to tea with me tomorrow?' she asked, after lunch, nibbling cashew nuts from a saucer. Midmore replied that there were great arrears of work to overtake when a man had been put away for so long.

'But you've come back like a giant refreshed . . . I hope that Daphne' – this was the lady of the twelve and the eight-page letter – 'will be with us too. She has misunderstood herself, like so many of us,' the woman murmured, 'but I think eventually . . .' she flung out her thin little hands. 'However, these are things that each lonely soul must adjust for itself.'

'Indeed, yes,' said Midmore with a deep sigh. The old tricks were sprouting in the old atmosphere like mushrooms in a dung-pit. He passed into an abrupt reverie, shook his head, as though stung by tumultuous memories, and departed without any ceremony of farewell to catch a mid-afternoon express where a man meets associates who talk horse, and weather as it affects the horse, all the way down. What worried him most was that he had missed a day with the hounds.

He met Rhoda's keen old eyes without flinching; and the drawing-room looked very comfortable that wet evening at tea. After all, his visit to town had not been wholly a failure. He had burned quite a bushel of letters at his flat. A flat – here he reached mechanically toward the worn volumes near the sofa – a flat was a consuming animal. As for Daphne ... he opened at random on the words: 'His lordship then did as desired and disclosed a *tableau* of considerable strength and variety.' Midmore reflected: 'And I used to think ... But she wasn't ... We were all babblers and skirters together ... I didn't babble much – thank goodness – but I skirted.' He turned the pages backward for more *Sortes Surteesianae*,[15] and read: 'When at length they rose to go to bed it struck each man as he followed his neighbour upstairs, that the man before him walked very crookedly.' He laughed aloud at the fire.

'What about tomorrow?' Rhoda asked, entering with garments over her shoulder. 'It's never stopped raining since you left. You'll be plastered out of sight an' all in five minutes. You'd better wear your next best, 'adn't you? I'm afraid they've shrank. 'Adn't you best try 'em on?'

'Here?' said Midmore.

''Suit yourself. I bathed you when you wasn't larger than a leg o' lamb,' said the ex-ladies'-maid.

'Rhoda, one of these days I shall get a valet, and a married butler.'

'There's many a true word spoke in jest. But nobody's huntin' tomorrow.'

'Why? Have they cancelled the meet?'

'They say it only means slipping and over-reaching in the mud, and they all 'ad enough of that today. Charlie told me so just now.'

'Oh!' It seemed that the word of Mr Sperrit's confidential clerk had weight.

'Charlie came down to help Mr Sidney lift the gates,' Rhoda continued.

'The flood-gates? They are perfectly easy to handle now. I've put in a wheel and a winch.'

'When the brook's really up they must be took clean out on account of the rubbish blockin' 'em. That's why Charlie came down.'

461

Midmore grunted impatiently. 'Everybody has talked to me about that brook ever since I came here. It's never done anything yet.'

'This 'as been a dry summer. If you care to look now, sir, I'll get you a lantern.'

She paddled out with him into a large wet night. Half-way down the lawn her light was reflected on shallow brown water, pricked through with grass blades at the edges. Beyond that light, the brook was strangling and kicking among hedges and tree-trunks.

'What on earth will happen to the big rose-bed?' was Midmore's first word.

'It generally 'as to be restocked after a flood. Ah!' she raised her lantern. 'There's two garden-seats knockin' against the sun-dial. Now, that won't do the roses any good.'

'This is too absurd. There ought to be some decently thought-out system – for – for dealing with this sort of thing.' He peered into the rushing gloom. There seemed to be no end to the moisture and the racket. In town he had noticed nothing.

'It can't be 'elped,' said Rhoda. 'It's just what it does do once in just so often. We'd better go back.'

All earth under foot was sliding in a thousand liquid noises towards the hoarse brook. Somebody wailed from the house: ''Fraid o' the water! Come 'ere! 'Fraid o' the water!'

'That's Jimmy. Wet always takes 'im that way,' she explained. The idiot charged into them, shaking with terror.

'Brave Jimmy! How brave of Jimmy! Come into the hall. What Jimmy got now?' she crooned. It was a sodden note which ran: 'Dear Rhoda – Mr Lotten, with whom I rode home this afternoon, told me that if this wet keeps up, he's afraid the fish-pond he built last year, where Coxen's old mill-dam was, will go, as the dam did once before, he says. If it does it's bound to come down the brook. It may be all right, but perhaps you had better look out. C. S.'

'If Coxen's dam goes, that means . . . I'll 'ave the drawing-room carpet up at once to be on the safe side. The claw-'ammer is in the libery.'

'Wait a minute. Sidney's gates are out, you said?'

'Both. He'll need it if Coxen's pond goes . . . I've seen it once.'

'I'll just slip down and have a look at Sidney. Light the lantern again, please, Rhoda.'

'You won't get *him* to stir. He's been there since he was born. But *she* don't know anything. I'll fetch your waterproof and some top-boots.'

"'Fraid o' the water! 'Fraid o' the water!' Jimmy sobbed, pressed against a corner of the hall, his hands to his eyes.

'All right, Jimmy. Jimmy can help play with the carpet,' Rhoda answered, as Midmore went forth into the darkness and the roarings all round. He had never seen such an utterly unregulated state of affairs. There was another lantern reflected on the streaming drive.

'Hi! Rhoda! Did you get my note? I came down to make sure. I thought, afterwards, Jimmy might funk the water!'

'It's me – Miss Sperrit,' Midmore cried. 'Yes, we got it, thanks.'

'You're back, then. Oh, good! . . . Is it bad down with you?'

'I'm going to Sidney's to have a look.'

'You won't get *him* out. Lucky I met Bob Lotten. I told him he hadn't any business impounding water for his idiotic trout without rebuilding the dam.'

'How far up is it? I've only been there once.'

'Not more than four miles as the water will come. He says he's opened all the sluices.'

She had turned and fallen into step beside him, her hooded head bowed against the thinning rain. As usual she was humming to herself.

'Why on earth did you come out in this weather?' Midmore asked.

'It was worse when you were in town. The rain's taking off now. If it wasn't for that pond, I wouldn't worry so much. There's Sidney's bell. Come on!' She broke into a run. A cracked bell was jangling feebly down the valley.

'Keep on the road!' Midmore shouted. The ditches were snorting bank-full on either side, and towards the brook-side the fields were afloat and beginning to move in the darkness.

'Catch me going off it! There's his light burning all right.' She halted undistressed at a little rise. 'But the flood's in the orchard. Look!' She swung her lantern to show a front rank of old apple-trees reflected in still, out-lying waters beyond the half-drowned hedge. They could hear above the thud-thud of the gorged flood-gates, shrieks in two keys as monotonous as a steam-organ.

'The high one's the pig.' Miss Sperrit laughed.

'All right! I'll get *her* out. You stay where you are, and I'll see you home afterwards.'

'But the water's only just over the road,' she objected.

'Never mind. Don't you move. Promise?'

'All right. You take my stick, then, and feel for holes in case anything's washed out anywhere. This *is* a lark!'

Midmore took it, and stepped into the water that moved sluggishly as yet across the farm road which ran to Sidney's front door from the raised and metalled public road. It was half way up to his knees when he knocked. As he looked back Miss Sperrit's lantern seemed to float in mid-ocean.

'You can't come in or the water'll come with you. I've bunged up all the cracks,' Mr Sidney shouted from within. 'Who be ye?'

'Take me out! Take me out!' the woman shrieked, and the pig from his sty behind the house urgently seconded the motion.

'I'm Midmore! Coxen's old mill-dam is likely to go, they say. Come out!'

'I told 'em it would when they made a fish-pond of it. 'Twasn't ever puddled proper. But it's a middlin' wide valley. She's got room to spread ... Keep still, or I'll take and duck you in the cellar! ... You go 'ome, Mus' Midmore, an' take the law o' Mus' Lotten soon's you've changed your socks.'

'Confound you, aren't you coming out?'

'To catch my death o' cold? I'm all right where I be. I've seen it before. But you can take *her*. She's no sort o' use or sense ... Climb out through the window. Didn't I tell you I'd plugged the door-cracks, you fool's daughter?' The parlour window opened, and the woman flung herself into Midmore's arms, nearly knocking him down. Mr Sidney leaned out of the window, pipe in mouth.

'Take her 'ome,' he said, and added oracularly:

> 'Two women in one house,
> Two cats an' one mouse,
> Two dogs an' one bone –
> Which I will leave alone.

I've seen it before.' Then he shut and fastened the window.

'A trap! A trap! You had ought to have brought a trap for me. I'll be drowned in this wet,' the woman cried.

'Hold up! You can't be any wetter than you are. Come along!' Midmore did not at all like the feel of the water over his boot-tops.

'Hooray! Come along!' Miss Sperrit's lantern, not fifty yards away, waved cheerily.

The woman threshed towards it like a panic-stricken goose, fell on her knees, was jerked up again by Midmore, and pushed on till she collapsed at Miss Sperrit's feet.

'But you won't get bronchitis if you go straight to Mr Midmore's house,' said the unsympathetic maiden.

'O Gawd! O Gawd! I wish our 'eavenly Father 'ud forgive me my sins an' call me 'ome,' the woman sobbed. 'But I won't go to '*is* 'ouse! I won't.'

'All right, then. Stay here. Now, if we run,' Miss Sperrit whispered to Midmore, 'she'll follow us. Not too fast!'

They set off at a considerate trot, and the woman lumbered behind them, bellowing, till they met a third lantern – Rhoda holding Jimmy's hand. She had got the carpet up, she said, and was escorting Jimmy past the water that he dreaded.

'That's all right,' Miss Sperrit pronounced. 'Take Mrs Sidney back with you, Rhoda, and put her to bed. I'll take Jimmy with me. You aren't afraid of the water now, are you, Jimmy?'

'Not afraid of anything now.' Jimmy reached for her hand. 'But get away from the water quick.'

'I'm coming with you,' Midmore interrupted.

'You most certainly are not. You're drenched. She threw you twice. Go home and change. You may have to be out again all night. It's only half-past seven now. I'm perfectly safe.' She flung herself lightly over a stile, and hurried uphill by the footpath, out of reach of all but the boasts of the flood below.

Rhoda, dead silent, herded Mrs Sidney to the house.

'You'll find your things laid out on the bed,' she said to Midmore as he came up. 'I'll attend to – to this. *She*'s got nothing to cry for.'

Midmore raced into dry kit, and raced uphill to be rewarded by the sight of the lantern just turning into the Sperrits' gate. He came back by way of Sidney's farm, where he saw the light twinkling across three acres of shining water, for the rain had ceased and the clouds were stripping overhead, though the brook was noisier than ever. Now there was only that doubtful mill-pond to look after – that and his swirling world abandoned to himself alone.

'We shall have to sit up for it,' said Rhoda after dinner. And as the drawing-room commanded the best view of the rising flood, they watched it from there for a long time, while all the clocks of the house bore them company.

''Tisn't the water, it's the mud on the skirting-board after it goes down that I mind,' Rhoda whispered. 'The last time Coxen's mill broke, I remember it came up to the second – no, third – step o' Mr Sidney's stairs.'

'What did Sidney do about it?'

'He made a notch on the step. 'E said it was a record. Just like 'im.'

'It's up to the drive now,' said Midmore after another long wait. 'And the rain stopped before eight, you know.'

'Then Coxen's dam '*as* broke, and that's the first of the flood-water.' She stared out beside him. The water was rising in sudden pulses – an inch or two at a time, with great sweeps and lagoons and a sudden increase of the brook's proper thunder.

'You can't stand all the time. Take a chair,' Midmore said presently.

Rhoda looked back into the bare room. 'The carpet bein' up *does* make a difference. Thank you, sir, I *will* 'ave a set-down.'

'Right over the drive now,' said Midmore. He opened the window and leaned out. 'Is that wind up the valley, Rhoda?'

'No, that's *it*! But I've seen it before.'

There was not so much a roar as the purposeful drive of a tide across a jagged reef, which put down every other sound for twenty minutes. A wide sheet of water hurried up to the little terrace on which the house stood, pushed round either corner, rose again and stretched, as it were, yawning beneath the moonlight, joined other sheets waiting for them in unsuspected hollows, and lay out all in one. A puff of wind followed.

'It's right up to the wall now. I can touch it with my finger.' Midmore bent over the window-sill.

'I can 'ear it in the cellars,' said Rhoda dolefully. 'Well, we've done what we can! I think I'll 'ave a look.' She left the room and was absent half an hour or more, during which time he saw a full-grown tree hauling itself across the lawn by its naked roots. Then a hurdle knocked against the wall, caught on an iron foot-scraper just outside, and made a square-headed ripple. The cascade through the cellar-windows diminished.

'It's dropping,' Rhoda cried, as she returned. 'It's only tricklin' into my cellars now.'

'Wait a minute. I believe – I believe I can see the scraper on the edge of the drive just showing!'

In another ten minutes the drive itself roughened and became gravel again, tilting all its water towards the shrubbery.

'The pond's gone past,' Rhoda announced. 'We shall only 'ave the common flood to contend with now. You'd better go to bed.'

'I ought to go down and have another look at Sidney before daylight.'

'No need. You can see 'is light burnin' from all the upstairs windows.'

'By the way. I forgot about *her*. Where've you put her?'

'In my bed.' Rhoda's tone was ice. 'I wasn't going to undo a room for *that* stuff.'

'But it – it couldn't be helped,' said Midmore. 'She was half drowned. One mustn't be narrow-minded, Rhoda, even if her position isn't quite – er – regular.'

'Pfff! I wasn't worryin' about that.' She leaned forward to the window. 'There's the edge of the lawn showin' now. It falls as fast as it rises. Dearie' – the change of tone made Midmore jump – 'didn't you know that I was 'is first? *That*'s what makes it so hard to bear.' Midmore looked at the long lizard-like back and had no words.

She went on, still talking through the black window-pane:

'Your pore dear auntie was very kind about it. She said she'd make all allowances for one, but no more. Never any more . . . Then, you didn't know 'oo Charlie was all this time?'

'Your nephew, I always thought.'

'Well, well,' she spoke pityingly. 'Everybody's business being nobody's business, I suppose no one thought to tell you. But Charlie made 'is own way for 'imself from the beginnin'! . . . But *her* upstairs, she never produced anything. Just an 'ousekeeper, as you might say. Turned over an' went to sleep straight off. She 'ad the impudence to ask me for 'ot sherry-gruel.'

'Did you give it to her,' said Midmore.

'Me? Your sherry? No!'

The memory of Sidney's outrageous rhyme at the window, and Charlie's long nose (he thought it looked interested at the time) as he passed the copies of Mrs Werf's last four wills, overcame Midmore without warning.

'This damp is givin' you a cold,' said Rhoda, rising. 'There you go again! Sneezin's a sure sign of it. Better go to bed. You can't do anythin' excep'' – she stood rigid, with crossed arms – 'about me.'

'Well. What about you?' Midmore stuffed the handkerchief into his pocket.

'Now you know about it, what are you goin' to do – sir?'

She had the answer on her lean cheek before the sentence was finished.

'Go and see if you can get us something to eat, Rhoda. And beer.'

'I expec' the larder'll be in a swim,' she replied, 'but old bottled stuff don't take any harm from wet.' She returned with a tray, all in order, and they ate and drank together, and took observations of the falling flood till dawn opened its bleared eyes on the wreck of what had been a fair garden. Midmore, cold and annoyed, found himself humming:

> 'That flood strewed wrecks upon the grass,
>   That ebb swept out the flocks to sea.

There isn't a rose left, Rhoda!

'An awesome ebb and flow it was
To many more than mine and me.
But each will mourn his . . .

It'll cost me a hundred.'

'Now we know the worst,' said Rhoda, 'we can go to bed. I'll lay on the kitchen sofa. His light's burnin' still.'

'And *she*?'

'Dirty old cat! You ought to 'ear 'er snore!'

At ten o'clock in the morning, after a maddening hour in his own garden on the edge of the retreating brook, Midmore went off to confront more damage at Sidney's. The first thing that met him was the pig, snowy white, for the water had washed him out of his new sty, calling on high heaven for breakfast. The front door had been forced open, and the flood had registered its own height in a brown dado on the walls. Midmore chased the pig out and called up the stairs.

'I be abed o' course. Which step 'as she rose to?' Sidney cried from above. 'The fourth? Then it's beat all records. Come up.'

'Are you ill?' Midmore asked as he entered the room. The red eyelids blinked cheerfully. Mr Sidney, beneath a sumptuous patch-work quilt, was smoking.

'Nah! I'm only thankin' God I ain't my own landlord. Take that cheer. What's she done?'

'It hasn't gone down enough for me to make sure.'

'Them floodgates o' yourn 'll be middlin' far down the brook by now; an' your rose-garden have gone after 'em. I saved my chickens, though. You'd better get Mus' Sperrit to take the law o' Lotten an' 'is fish-pond.'

'No, thanks. I've trouble enough without that.'

'Hev ye?' Mr Sidney grinned. 'How did ye make out with those two women o' mine last night? I lay they fought.'

'You infernal old scoundrel!' Midmore laughed.

'I be – an' then again I bain't,' was the placid answer. 'But, Rhoda, *she* wouldn't ha' left me last night. Fire or flood, she wouldn't.'

'Why didn't you ever marry her?' Midmore asked.

'Waste of good money. She was willin' without.'

There was a step on the gritty mud below, and a voice humming. Midmore rose quickly saying: 'Well, I suppose you're all right now.'

'I be. I ain't a landlord, nor I ain't young – nor anxious. Oh, Mus' Midmore! Would it make any odds about her thirty pounds comin' regular if I married her? Charlie said maybe 'twould.'

468

'Did he?' Midmore turned at the door. 'And what did Jimmy say about it?'

'Jimmy?' Mr Sidney chuckled as the joke took him. 'Oh, *he's* none o' mine. He's Charlie's look-out.'

Midmore slammed the door and ran downstairs.

'Well, this is a – sweet – mess,' said Miss Sperrit in shortest skirts and heaviest riding-boots. 'I had to come down and have a look at it. "The old mayor climbed the belfry tower." Been up all night nursing your family?'

'Nearly that! Isn't it cheerful?' He pointed through the door to the stairs with small twig-drift on the last three treads.

'It's a record, though,' said she, and hummed to herself:

> 'That flood strewed wrecks upon the grass,
> That ebb swept out the flocks to sea.'

'You're always singing that, aren't you?' Midmore said suddenly as she passed into the parlour where slimy chairs had been stranded at all angles.

'Am I? Now I come to think of it I believe I do. They say I always hum when I ride. Have you noticed it?'

'Of course I have. I notice every –'

'Oh,' she went on hurriedly. 'We had it for the village cantata last winter – "The Brides of Enderby".'

'No! "High Tide on the Coast of Lincolnshire".' For some reason Midmore spoke sharply.

'Just like that.' She pointed to the befouled walls. 'I say . . . Let's get this furniture a little straight . . . You know it too?'

'Every word, since you sang it, of course.'

'When?'

'The first night I ever came down. You rode past the drawing-room window in the dark singing it – "And sweeter woman –"'

'I thought the house was empty then. Your aunt always let us use that short cut. Ha–hadn't we better get this out into the passage? It'll all have to come out anyhow. You take the other side.' They began to lift a heavyish table. Their words came jerkily between gasps and their faces were as white as – a newly washed and very hungry pig.

'Look out!' Midmore shouted. His legs were whirled from under him, as the table, grunting madly, careened and knocked the girl out of sight.

The wild boar of Asia could not have cut down a couple more scientifically, but this little pig lacked his ancestor's nerve and fled shrieking over their bodies.

'Are you hurt, darling?' was Midmore's first word, and 'No – I'm only winded – dear,' was Miss Sperrit's, as he lifted her out of her corner, her hat over one eye and her right cheek a smear of mud.

They fed him a little later on some chicken-feed that they found in Sidney's quiet barn, a pail of buttermilk out of the dairy, and a quantity of onions from a shelf in the back-kitchen.

'Seed-onions, most likely,' said Connie. 'You'll hear about this.'

'What does it matter? They ought to have been gilded. We must buy him.'

'And keep him as long as he lives,' she agreed. 'But I think I ought to go home now. You see, when I came out I didn't expect . . . Did you?'

'No! Yes . . . It had to come . . . But if anyone had told me an hour ago! . . . Sidney's unspeakable parlour – and the mud on the carpet.'

'Oh, I say! Is my cheek clean now?'

'Not quite. Lend me your hanky again a minute, darling . . . What a purler you came!'

'You can't talk. Remember when your chin hit that table and you said "blast"! I was just going to laugh.'

'You didn't laugh when I picked you up. You were going "oo-oo-oo" like a little owl.'

'My dear child –'

'Say that again!'

'My dear child. (Do you really like it? I keep it for my best friends.) My *dee-ar* child, I thought I was going to be sick there and then. He knocked every ounce of wind out of me – the angel! But I must really go.'

They set off together, very careful not to join hands or take arms.

'Not across the fields,' said Midmore at the stile. 'Come round by – by your own place.'

She flushed indignantly.

'It will be yours in a little time,' he went on, shaken with his own audacity.

'Not so much of your little times, if you please!' She shied like a colt across the road; then instantly, like a colt, her eyes lit with new curiosity as she came in sight of the drive-gates.

'And not quite so much of your airs and graces, Madam,' Midmore returned, 'or I won't let you use our drive as a short cut any more.'

'Oh, I'll be good. I'll be good.' Her voice changed suddenly. 'I swear I'll try to be good, dear. I'm not much of a thing at the best. What made *you* . . .'

'I'm worse – worse! Miles and oceans worse. But what does it matter now?'

They halted beside the gate-pillars.

'I see!' she said, looking up the sodden carriage sweep to the front door porch where Rhoda was slapping a wet mat to and fro. '*I* see . . . Now, I really must go home. No! Don't you come. I must speak to Mother first all by myself.'

He watched her up the hill till she was out of sight.

⟨ Mary Postgate [1] ⟩

Of Miss Mary Postgate, Lady McCausland wrote that she was 'thoroughly conscientious, tidy, companionable, and ladylike. I am very sorry to part with her, and shall always be interested in her welfare.'

Miss Fowler engaged her on this recommendation, and to her surprise, for she had had experience of companions, found that it was true. Miss Fowler was nearer sixty than fifty at the time, but though she needed care she did not exhaust her attendant's vitality. On the contrary, she gave out, stimulatingly and with reminiscences. Her father had been a minor Court official in the days when the Great Exhibition of 1851 had just set its seal on Civilization made perfect. Some of Miss Fowler's tales, none the less, were not always for the young. Mary was not young, and though her speech was as colourless as her eyes or her hair, she was never shocked. She listened unflinchingly to every one; said at the end, 'How interesting!' or 'How shocking!' as the case might be, and never again referred to it, for she prided herself on a trained mind, which 'did not dwell on these things'. She was, too, a treasure at domestic accounts, for which the village tradesmen, with their weekly books, loved her not. Otherwise she had no enemies; provoked no jealousy even among the plainest; neither gossip nor slander had ever been traced to her; she supplied the odd place at the Rector's or the Doctor's table at half an hour's notice; she was a sort of public aunt to very many small children of the village street, whose parents, while accepting everything, would have been swift to resent what they called 'patronage'; she served on the Village Nursing Committee as Miss Fowler's nominee when Miss Fowler was crippled by rheumatoid arthritis, and came out of six months' fortnightly meetings equally respected by all the cliques.

And when Fate threw Miss Fowler's nephew, an unlovely orphan of eleven, on Miss Fowler's hands, Mary Postgate stood to her share of the business of education as practised in private and public schools. She checked printed clothes-lists, and unitemized bills of extras; wrote to Head and House masters, matrons, nurses and doctors, and grieved or rejoiced over half-term reports. Young Wyndham Fowler repaid her in his holidays by calling her 'Gatepost', 'Postey', or 'Packthread', by thumping her between her narrow shoulders, or by chasing her bleating, round the garden, her large mouth open, her large nose high in air, at a stiff-necked shamble very like a camel's. Later on he filled the house with clamour, argument, and harangues as to his personal needs, likes and dislikes, and the limitations of 'you women', reducing Mary to tears of physical fatigue, or, when he chose to be humorous, of helpless laughter. At crises, which multiplied as he grew older, she was his ambassadress and his interpretress to Miss Fowler, who had no large sympathy with the young; a vote in his interest at the councils on his future; his sewing-woman, strictly accountable for mislaid boots and garments; always his butt and his slave.

And when he decided to become a solicitor, and had entered an office in London; when his greeting had changed from 'Hullo, Postey, you old beast,' to 'Mornin', Packthread,' there came a war which, unlike all wars that Mary could remember, did not stay decently outside England and in the newspapers, but intruded on the lives of people whom she knew. As she said to Miss Fowler, it was 'most vexatious'. It took the Rector's son who was going into business with his elder brother; it took the Colonel's nephew on the eve of fruit-farming in Canada; it took Mrs Grant's son who, his mother said, was devoted to the ministry; and, very early indeed, it took Wynn Fowler, who announced on a postcard that he had joined the Flying Corps and wanted a cardigan waistcoat.

'He must go, and he must have the waistcoat,' said Miss Fowler. So Mary got the proper-sized needles and wool, while Miss Fowler told the men of her establishment – two gardeners and an odd man, aged sixty – that those who could join the Army had better do so. The gardeners left. Cheape, the odd man, stayed on, and was promoted to the gardener's cottage. The cook, scorning to be limited in luxuries, also left, after a spirited scene with Miss Fowler, and took the housemaid with her. Miss Fowler gazetted Nellie, Cheape's seventeen-year-old daughter, to the vacant post; Mrs Cheape to the rank of cook, with occasional cleaning bouts; and the reduced establishment moved forward smoothly.

Wynn demanded an increase in his allowance. Miss Fowler, who always looked facts in the face, said, 'He must have it. The chances are he won't live long to draw it, and if three hundred makes him happy –'

Wynn was grateful, and came over, in his tight-buttoned uniform, to say so. His training centre was not thirty miles away, and his talk was so technical that it had to be explained by charts of the various types of machines. He gave Mary such a chart.

'And you'd better study it, Postey,' he said. 'You'll be seeing a lot of 'em soon.' So Mary studied the chart, but when Wynn next arrived to swell and exalt himself before his womenfolk, she failed badly in cross-examination, and he rated her as in the old days.

'You *look* more or less like a human being,' he said in his new Service voice. 'You *must* have had a brain at some time in your past. What have you done with it? Where d'you keep it? A sheep would know more than you do, Postey. You're lamentable. You are less use than an empty tin can, you dowey old cassowary.'

'I suppose that's how your superior officer talks to *you*?' said Miss Fowler from her chair.

'But Postey doesn't mind,' Wynn replied. 'Do you, Packthread?'

'Why? Was Wynn saying anything? I shall get this right next time you come,' she muttered, and knitted her pale brows again over the diagrams of Taubes, Farmans, and Zeppelins.

In a few weeks the mere land and sea battles which she read to Miss Fowler after breakfast passed her like idle breath. Her heart and her interest were high in the air with Wynn, who had finished 'rolling' (whatever that might be) and had gone on from a 'taxi' to a machine more or less his own. One morning it circled over their very chimneys, alighted on Vegg's Heath, almost outside the garden gate, and Wynn came in, blue with cold, shouting for food. He and she drew Miss Fowler's bath-chair, as they had often done, along the Heath foot-path to look at the biplane. Mary observed that 'it smelt very badly'.

'Postey, I believe you think with your nose,' said Wynn. 'I know you don't with your mind. Now, what type's that?'

'I'll go and get the chart,' said Mary.

'You're hopeless! You haven't the mental capacity of a white mouse,' he cried, and explained the dials and the sockets for bomb-dropping till it was time to mount and ride the wet clouds once more.

'Ah!' said Mary, as the stinking thing flared upward. 'Wait till our Flying Corps gets to work! Wynn says it's much safer than in the trenches.'

'I wonder,' said Miss Fowler. 'Tell Cheape to come and tow me home again.'

'It's all downhill. I can do it,' said Mary, 'if you put the brake on.' She laid her lean self against the pushing-bar and home they trundled.

'Now, be careful you aren't heated and catch a chill,' said overdressed Miss Fowler.

'Nothing makes me perspire,' said Mary. As she bumped the chair under the porch she straightened her long back. The exertion had given her a colour, and the wind had loosened a wisp of hair across her forehead. Miss Fowler glanced at her.

'What do you ever think of, Mary?' she demanded suddenly.

'Oh, Wynn says he wants another three pairs of stockings – as thick as we can make them.'

'Yes. But I mean the things that women think about. Here you are, more than forty –'

'Forty-four,' said truthful Mary.

'Well?'

'Well?' Mary offered Miss Fowler her shoulder as usual.

'And you've been with me ten years now.'

'Let's see,' said Mary. 'Wynn was eleven when he came. He's twenty now, and I came two years before that. It must be eleven.'

'Eleven! And you've never told me anything that matters in all that while. Looking back, it seems to me that *I*'ve done all the talking.'

'I'm afraid I'm not much of a conversationalist. As Wynn says, I haven't the mind. Let me take your hat.'

Miss Fowler, moving stiffly from the hip, stamped her rubber-tipped stick on the tiled hall floor. 'Mary, aren't you *anything* except a companion? Would you *ever* have been anything except a companion?'

Mary hung up the garden hat on its proper peg. 'No,' she said after consideration. 'I don't imagine I ever should. But I've no imagination, I'm afraid.'

She fetched Miss Fowler her eleven-o'clock glass of Contrexeville.[2]

That was the wet December when it rained six inches to the month, and the women went abroad as little as might be. Wynn's flying chariot visited them several times, and for two mornings (he had warned her by postcard) Mary heard the thresh of his propellers at dawn. The second time she ran to the window, and stared at the whitening sky. A little blur passed overhead. She lifted her lean arms towards it.

That evening at six o'clock there came an announcement in an official envelope that Second Lieutenant W. Fowler had been killed during a trial flight. Death was instantaneous. She read it and carried it to Miss Fowler.

'I never expected anything else,' said Miss Fowler; 'but I'm sorry it happened before he had done anything.'

The room was whirling round Mary Postgate, but she found herself quite steady in the midst of it.

'Yes,' she said. 'It's a great pity he didn't die in action after he had killed somebody.'

'He was killed instantly. That's one comfort,' Miss Fowler went on.

'But Wynn says the shock of a fall kills a man at once – whatever happens to the tanks,' quoted Mary.

The room was coming to rest now. She heard Miss Fowler say impatiently, 'But why can't we cry, Mary?' and herself replying, 'There's nothing to cry for. He has done his duty as much as Mrs Grant's son did.'

'And when he died, *she* came and cried all the morning,' said Miss Fowler. 'This only makes me feel tired – terribly tired. Will you help me to bed, please, Mary? – And I think I'd like the hot-water bottle.'

So Mary helped her and sat beside, talking of Wynn in his riotous youth.

'I believe,' said Miss Fowler suddenly, 'that old people and young people slip from under a stroke like this. The middle-aged feel it most.'

'I expect that's true,' said Mary, rising. 'I'm going to put away the things in his room now. Shall we wear mourning?'

'Certainly not,' said Miss Fowler. 'Except, of course, at the funeral. I can't go. You will. I want you to arrange about his being buried here. What a blessing it didn't happen at Salisbury!'

Everyone, from the Authorities of the Flying Corps to the Rector, was most kind and sympathetic. Mary found herself for the moment in a world where bodies were in the habit of being despatched by all sorts of conveyances to all sorts of places. And at the funeral two young men in buttoned-up uniforms stood beside the grave and spoke to her afterwards.

'You're Miss Postgate, aren't you?' said one. 'Fowler told me about you. He was a good chap – a first-class fellow – a great loss.'

'Great loss!' growled his companion. 'We're all awfully sorry.'

'How high did he fall from?' Mary whispered.

'Pretty nearly four thousand feet, I should think, didn't he? You were up that day, Monkey?'

'All of that,' the other child replied. 'My bar made three thousand, and I wasn't as high as him by a lot.'

'Then *that's* all right,' said Mary. 'Thank you very much.'

They moved away as Mrs Grant flung herself weeping on Mary's flat chest, under the lych-gate, and cried, '*I* know how it feels! *I* know how it feels!'

'But both his parents are dead,' Mary returned, as she fended her off. 'Perhaps they've all met by now,' she added vaguely as she escaped towards the coach.

'I've thought of that too,' wailed Mrs Grant; 'but then he'll be practically a stranger to them. Quite embarrassing!'

Mary faithfully reported every detail of the ceremony to Miss Fowler, who, when she described Mrs Grant's outburst, laughed aloud.

'Oh, how Wynn would have enjoyed it! He was always utterly unreliable at funerals. D'you remember –' And they talked of him again, each piecing out the other's gaps. 'And now,' said Miss Fowler, 'we'll pull up the blinds and we'll have a general tidy. That always does us good. Have you seen to Wynn's things?'

'Everything – since he first came,' said Mary. 'He was never de-structive – even with his toys.'

They faced that neat room.

'It can't be natural not to cry,' Mary said at last. 'I'm *so* afraid you'll have a reaction.'

'As I told you, we old people slip from under the stroke. It's you I'm afraid for. Have you cried yet?'

'I can't. It only makes me angry with the Germans.'

'That's sheer waste of vitality,' said Miss Fowler. 'We must live till the war's finished.' She opened a full wardrobe. 'Now, I've been thinking things over. This is my plan. All his civilian clothes can be given away – Belgian refugees, and so on.'

Mary nodded. 'Boots, collars, and gloves?'

'Yes. We don't need to keep anything except his cap and belt.'

'They came back yesterday with his Flying Corps clothes' – Mary pointed to a roll on the little iron bed.

'Ah, but keep his Service things. Someone may be glad of them later. Do you remember his sizes?'

'Five feet eight and a half; thirty-six inches round the chest. But he told me he's just put on an inch and a half. I'll mark it on a label and tie it on his sleeping-bag.'

'So that disposes of *that*,' said Miss Fowler, tapping the palm of one hand with the ringed third finger of the other. 'What waste it all is! We'll get his old school trunk tomorrow and pack his civilian clothes.'

'And the rest?' said Mary. 'His books and pictures and the games and the toys – and – and the rest?'

'My plan is to burn every single thing,' said Miss Fowler. 'Then we shall know where they are and no one can handle them afterwards. What do you think?'

'I think that would be much the best,' said Mary. 'But there's such a lot of them.'

'We'll burn them in the destructor,' said Miss Fowler.

This was an open-air furnace for the consumption of refuse; a little circular four-foot tower of pierced brick over an iron grating. Miss Fowler had noticed the design in a gardening journal years ago, and had had it built at the bottom of the garden. It suited her tidy soul, for it saved unsightly rubbish-heaps, and the ashes lightened the stiff clay soil.

Mary considered for a moment, saw her way clear, and nodded again. They spent the evening putting away well-remembered civilian suits, underclothes that Mary had marked, and the regiments of very gaudy socks and ties. A second trunk was needed, and, after that, a little packing case, and it was late next day when Cheape and the local carrier lifted them to the cart. The Rector luckily knew of a friend's son, about five feet eight and a half inches high, to whom a complete Flying Corps outfit would be most acceptable, and sent his gardener's son down with a barrow to take delivery of it. The cap was hung up in Miss Fowler's bedroom, the belt in Miss Postgate's; for, as Miss Fowler said, they had no desire to make tea-party talk of them.

'That disposes of *that*,' said Miss Fowler. 'I'll leave the rest to you, Mary. I can't run up and down the garden. You'd better take the big clothes-basket and get Nellie to help you.'

'I shall take the wheel-barrow and do it myself,' said Mary, and for once in her life closed her mouth.

Miss Fowler, in moments of irritation, had called Mary deadly methodical. She put on her oldest waterproof and gardening-hat and her ever-slipping goloshes, for the weather was on the edge of more rain. She gathered fire-lighters from the kitchen, a half-scuttle of coals, and a faggot of brushwood. These she wheeled in the barrow down the mossed paths to the dank little laurel shrubbery where the destructor stood under the drip of three oaks. She climbed the wire fence into the Rector's glebe just behind, and from his tenant's rick pulled two large armfuls of good hay, which she spread neatly on the fire-bars. Next, journey by journey, passing Miss Fowler's white face at the morning-room window each time, she brought down in the towel-covered clothes-basket, on the wheelbarrow, thumbed and used Hentys, Marryats, Levers, Stevensons, Baroness Orczys, Garvices, schoolbooks, and atlases, unrelated piles of the *Motor Cyclist*, the *Light Car*, and catalogues of Olympia Exhibitions; the remnants of a fleet of sailing-ships from nine-penny cutters to a three-guinea yacht; a prep.-school dressing-gown; bats from three-and-sixpence to twenty-four shillings; cricket and tennis balls; disintegrated steam and clockwork locomotives with their twisted rails; a grey and red tin model of a submarine; a dumb gramophone and cracked records; golf-clubs that had to be broken across the knee, like his walking-sticks, and an assegai; photographs of private and public school cricket and football elevens, and his O.T.C. on the line of march; kodaks, and film-rolls; some pewters, and one real silver cup, for boxing competitions and Junior Hurdles; sheaves of school photographs; Miss Fowler's photograph; her own which he had borne off in fun and (good care she took not to ask!) had never returned; a playbox with a secret drawer; a load of flannels, belts, and jerseys, and a pair of spiked shoes unearthed in the attic; a packet of all the letters that Miss Fowler and she had ever written to him, kept for some absurd reason through all these years; a five-day attempt at a diary; framed pictures of racing motors in full Brooklands career, and load upon load of undistinguishable wreckage of tool-boxes, rabbit-hutches, electric batteries, tin soldiers, fret-saw outfits, and jig-saw puzzles.

Miss Fowler at the window watched her come and go, and said to herself, 'Mary's an old woman. I never realized it before.'

After lunch she recommended her to rest.

'I'm not in the least tired,' said Mary. 'I've got it all arranged. I'm going to the village at two o'clock for some paraffin. Nellie hasn't enough, and the walk will do me good.'

She made one last quest round the house before she started, and found that she had overlooked nothing. It began to mist as soon as she had skirted Vegg's Heath, where Wynn used to descend – it seemed to her that she could almost hear the beat of his propellers overhead, but there was nothing to see. She hoisted her umbrella and lunged into the blind wet till she had reached the shelter of the empty village. As she came out of Mr Kidd's shop with a bottle full of paraffin in her string shopping-bag, she met Nurse Eden, the village nurse, and fell into talk with her, as usual, about the village children. They were just parting opposite the 'Royal Oak', when a gun, they fancied, was fired immediately behind the house. It was followed by a child's shriek dying into a wail.

'Accident!' said Nurse Eden promptly, and dashed through the empty bar, followed by Mary. They found Mrs Gerritt, the publican's wife, who could only gasp and point to the yard, where a little cart-lodge was sliding sideways amid a clatter of tiles. Nurse Eden snatched up a sheet drying before the fire, ran out, lifted something from the ground, and flung the sheet round it. The sheet turned scarlet and half her uniform too, as she bore the load into the kitchen. It was little Edna Gerritt, aged nine, whom Mary had known since her perambulator days.

'Am I hurted bad?' Edna asked, and died between Nurse Eden's dripping hands. The sheet fell aside and for an instant, before she could shut her eyes, Mary saw the ripped and shredded body.

'It's a wonder she spoke at all,' said Nurse Eden. 'What in God's name was it?'

'A bomb,' said Mary.

'One o' the Zeppelins?'

'No. An aeroplane. I thought I heard it on the Heath, but I fancied it was one of ours. It must have shut off its engines as it came down. That's why we didn't notice it.'

'The filthy pigs!' said Nurse Eden, all white and shaken. 'See the pickle I'm in! Go and tell Dr Hennis, Miss Postgate.' Nurse looked at the mother, who had dropped face down on the floor. 'She's only in a fit. Turn her over.'

Mary heaved Mrs Gerritt right side up, and hurried off for the doctor. When she told her tale, he asked her to sit down in the surgery till he got her something.

'But I don't need it, I assure you,' said she. 'I don't think it would be wise to tell Miss Fowler about it, do you? Her heart is so irritable in this weather.'

Dr Hennis looked at her admiringly as he packed up his bag.

'No. Don't tell anybody till we're sure,' he said, and hastened to the 'Royal Oak', while Mary went on with the paraffin. The village behind her was as quiet as usual, for the news had not yet spread. She frowned a little to herself, her large nostrils expanded uglily, and from time to time she muttered a phrase which Wynn, who never restrained himself before his women-folk, had applied to the enemy. 'Bloody pagans! They *are* bloody pagans. But,' she continued, falling back on the teaching that had made her what she was, 'one mustn't let one's mind dwell on these things.'

Before she reached the house Dr Hennis, who was also a special constable, overtook her in his car.

'Oh, Miss Postgate,' he said, 'I wanted to tell you that that accident at the "Royal Oak" was due to Gerritt's stable tumbling down. It's been dangerous for a long time. It ought to have been condemned.'

'I thought I heard an explosion too,' said Mary.

'You might have been misled by the beams snapping. I've been looking at 'em. They were dry-rotted through and through. Of course, as they broke, they would make a noise just like a gun.'

'Yes?' said Mary politely.

'Poor little Edna was playing underneath it,' he went on, still holding her with his eyes, 'and that and the tiles cut her to pieces, you see?'

'I saw it,' said Mary, shaking her head. 'I heard it too.'

'Well, we cannot be sure.' Dr Hennis changed his tone completely. 'I know both you and Nurse Eden (I've been speaking to her) are perfectly trustworthy, and I can rely on you not to say anything – yet at least. It is no good to stir up people unless –'

'Oh, I never do – anyhow,' said Mary, and Dr Hennis went on to the county town.

After all, she told herself, it might, just possibly, have been the collapse of the old stable that had done all those things to poor little

Edna. She was sorry she had even hinted at other things, but Nurse Eden was discretion itself. By the time she reached home the affair seemed increasingly remote by its very monstrosity. As she came in, Miss Fowler told her that a couple of aeroplanes had passed half an hour ago.

'I thought I heard them,' she replied, 'I'm going down to the garden now. I've got the paraffin.'

'Yes, but – what *have* you got on your boots? They're soaking wet. Change them at once.'

Not only did Mary obey but she wrapped the boots in a newspaper, and put them into the string bag with the bottle. So, armed with the longest kitchen poker, she left.

'It's raining again,' was Miss Fowler's last word, 'but – I know you won't be happy till that's disposed of.'

'It won't take long. I've got everything down there, and I've put the lid on the destructor to keep the wet out.'

The shrubbery was filling with twilight by the time she had completed her arrangements and sprinkled the sacrificial oil. As she lit the match that would burn her heart to ashes, she heard a groan or a grunt behind the dense Portugal laurels.

'Cheape?' she called impatiently, but Cheape, with his ancient lumbago, in his comfortable cottage would be the last man to profane the sanctuary. 'Sheep,' she concluded, and threw in the fusee. The pyre went up in a roar, and the immediate flame hastened night around her.

'How Wynn would have loved this!' she thought, stepping back from the blaze.

By its light she saw, half hidden behind a laurel not five paces away, a bareheaded man sitting very stiffly at the foot of one of the oaks. A broken branch lay across his lap – one booted leg protruding from beneath it. His head moved ceaselessly from side to side, but his body was as still as the tree's trunk. He was dressed – she moved sideways to look more closely – in a uniform something like Wynn's, with a flap buttoned across the chest. For an instant, she had some idea that it might be one of the young flying men she had met at the funeral. But their heads were dark and glossy. This man's was as pale as a baby's, and so closely cropped that she could see the disgusting pinky skin beneath. His lips moved.

'What do you say?' Mary moved towards him and stooped.

'Laty! Laty! Laty!' [3] he muttered, while his hands picked at the dead wet leaves. There was no doubt as to his nationality. It made her so angry that she strode back to the destructor, though it was still too hot to use the poker there. Wynn's books seemed to be catching well. She looked up at the oak behind the man; several of the light upper and two or three rotten lower branches had broken and scattered their rubbish on the shrubbery path. On the lowest fork a helmet with dependent strings showed like a bird's-nest in the light of a long-tongued flame. Evidently this person had fallen through the tree. Wynn had told her that it was quite possible for people to fall out of aeroplanes. Wynn told her too, that trees were useful things to break an aviator's fall, but in this case the aviator must have been broken or he would have moved from his queer position. He seemed helpless except for his horrible rolling head. On the other hand, she could see a pistol case at his belt – and Mary loathed pistols. Months ago, after reading certain Belgian reports together, she and Miss Fowler had had dealings with one – a huge revolver with flat-nosed bullets, which latter, Wynn said, were forbidden by the rules of war to be used against civilized enemies. 'They're good enough for us,' Miss Fowler had replied. 'Show Mary how it works.' And Wynn, laughing at the mere possibility of any such need, had led the craven winking Mary into the Rector's disused quarry, and had shown her how to fire the terrible machine. It lay now in the top-left-hand drawer of her toilet-table – a memento not included in the burning. Wynn would be pleased to see how she was not afraid.

She slipped up to the house to get it. When she came through the rain, the eyes in the head were alive with expectation. The mouth even tried to smile. But at sight of the revolver its corners went down just like Edna Gerritt's. A tear trickled from one eye, and the head rolled from shoulder to shoulder as though trying to point out something.

'Cassée. Tout cassée,'[4] it whimpered.

'What do you say?' said Mary disgustedly, keeping well to one side, though only the head moved.

'Cassée,' it repeated. 'Che me rends. Le médicin![5] Toctor!'

'Nein!' said she, bringing all her small German to bear with the big pistol. 'Ich haben der todt Kinder gesehn.'[6]

The head was still. Mary's hand dropped. She had been careful to keep her finger off the trigger for fear of accidents. After a few moments' waiting, she returned to the destructor, where the flames were falling, and churned up Wynn's charring books with the poker. Again the head groaned for the doctor.

'Stop that!' said Mary, and stamped her foot. 'Stop that, you bloody pagan!'

The words came quite smoothly and naturally. They were Wynn's own words, and Wynn was a gentleman who for no consideration on earth would have torn little Edna into those vividly coloured strips and strings. But this thing hunched under the oak-tree had done that thing. It was no question of reading horrors out of newspapers to Miss Fowler. Mary had seen it with her own eyes on the 'Royal Oak' kitchen table. She must not allow her mind to dwell upon it. Now Wynn was dead, and everything connected with him was lumping and rustling and tinkling under her busy poker into red black dust and grey leaves of ash. The thing beneath the oak would die too. Mary had seen death more than once. She came of a family that had a knack of dying under, as she told Miss Fowler, 'most distressing circumstances'. She would stay where she was till she was entirely satisfied that It was dead – dead as dear papa in the late 'eighties; aunt Mary in 'eighty-nine; mamma in 'ninety-one; cousin Dick in 'ninety-five; Lady McCausland's housemaid in 'ninety-nine; Lady McCausland's sister in nineteen hundred and one; Wynn buried five days ago; and Edna Gerritt still waiting for decent earth to hide her. As she thought – her underlip caught up by one faded canine, brows knit and nostrils wide – she wielded the poker with lunges that jarred the grating at the bottom, and careful scrapes round the brickwork above. She looked at her wrist-watch. It was getting on to half-past four, and the rain was coming down in earnest. Tea would be at five. If It did not die before that time, she would be soaked and would have to change. Meantime, and this occupied her, Wynn's things were burning well in spite of the hissing wet, though now and again a book-back with a quite distinguishable title would be heaved up out of the mass. The exercise of stoking had given her a glow which seemed to reach to the marrow of her bones. She hummed – Mary never had a voice – to herself. She had never believed in all those advanced views – though Miss Fowler herself leaned a little that way – of woman's work in the world; but now she saw there was much to be said for them. This, for instance, was *her* work – work which no man, least of all Dr Hennis, would ever have done. A man, at such a crisis, would be what Wynn called a 'sportsman'; would leave everything to fetch help, and would certainly bring It into the house. Now a woman's business was to make a happy home for – for a husband and children. Failing these – it was not a thing one should allow one's mind to dwell upon – but –

'Stop it!' Mary cried once more across the shadows. 'Nein, I tell you! Ich haben der todt Kinder gesehn.'

But it was a fact. A woman who had missed these things could still be useful – more useful than a man in certain respects. She thumped like a pavior through the settling ashes at the secret thrill of it. The rain was damping the fire, but she could feel – it was too dark to see – that her work was done. There was a dull red glow at the bottom of the destructor, not enough to char the wooden lid if she slipped it half over against the driving wet. This arranged, she leaned on the poker and waited, while an increasing rapture laid hold on her. She ceased to think. She gave herself up to feel. Her long pleasure was broken by a sound that she had waited for in agony several times in her life. She leaned forward and listened, smiling. There could be no mistake. She closed her eyes and drank it in. Once it ceased abruptly.

'Go on,' she murmured, half aloud. 'That isn't the end.'

Then the end came very distinctly in a lull between two rain-gusts. Mary Postgate drew her breath short between her teeth and shivered from head to foot. '*That's* all right,' said she contentedly, and went up to the house, where she scandalized the whole routine by taking a luxurious hot bath before tea, and came down looking, as Miss Fowler said when she saw her lying all relaxed on the other sofa, 'quite handsome!'

The Wish House [1]

The new Church Visitor had just left after a twenty minutes' call. During that time, Mrs Ashcroft had used such English as an elderly, experienced, and pensioned cook should, who had seen life in London. She was the readier, therefore, to slip back into easy, ancient Sussex ('t's softening to 'd's as one warmed) when the bus brought Mrs Fettley from thirty miles away for a visit, that pleasant March Saturday. The two had been friends since childhood; but, of late, destiny had separated their meetings by long intervals.

Much was to be said, and many ends, loose since last time, to be ravelled up on both sides, before Mrs Fettley, with her bag of quilt-patches, took the couch beneath the window commanding the garden, and the football-ground in the valley below.

'Most folk got out at Bush Tye for the match there,' she explained, 'so there weren't no one for me to cushion agin, the last five mile. An' she *do* just-about bounce ye.'

'You've took no hurt,' said her hostess. 'You don't brittle by agein', Liz.'

Mrs Fettley chuckled and made to match a couple of patches to her liking. 'No, or I'd ha' broke twenty year back. You can't ever mind when I was so's to be called round, can ye?'

Mrs Ashcroft shook her head slowly — she never hurried — and went on stitching a sack-cloth lining into a list-bound [2] rush tool-basket. Mrs Fettley laid out more patches in the Spring light through the geraniums on the window-sill, and they were silent awhile.

'What like's this new Visitor o' yourn?' Mrs Fettley inquired, with a nod towards the door. Being very short-sighted, she had, on her entrance, almost bumped into the lady.

Mrs Ashcroft suspended the big packing-needle judicially on high, ere she stabbed home. 'Settin' aside she don't bring much news with her yet, I dunno as I've anythin' special agin her.'

'Ourn, at Keyneslade,' said Mrs Fettley, 'she's full o' words an' pity, but she don't stay for answers. Ye can get on with your thoughts while she clacks.'

'This 'un don't clack. She's aimin' to be one o' those High Church nuns, like.'

'Ourn's married, but, by what they say, she've made no great gains of it . . .' Mrs Fettley threw up her sharp chin. 'Lord! How they dam' cherubim do shake the very bones o' the place!'

The tile-sided cottage trembled at the passage of two specially chartered forty-seat charabancs on their way to the Bush Tye match; a regular Saturday 'shopping' bus, for the county's capital, fumed behind them; while, from one of the crowded inns, a fourth car backed out to join the procession, and held up the stream of through pleasure-traffic.

'You're as free-tongued as ever, Liz,' Mrs Ashcroft observed.

'Only when I'm with you. Otherwhiles, I'm Granny – three times over. I lay that basket's for one o' your gran'chiller – ain't it?'

' 'Tis for Arthur – my Jane's eldest.'

'But he ain't workin' nowheres, is he?'

'No. 'Tis a picnic-basket.'

'You're let off light. My Willie, he's allus at me for money for them aireated wash-poles folk puts up in their gardens to draw the music from Lunnon, like. An' I give it 'im – pore fool me!'

'An' he forgets to give you the promise-kiss after, don't he?' Mrs Ashcroft's heavy smile seemed to strike inwards.

'He do. No odds 'twixt boys now an' forty year back. Take all an' give naught – an' we to put up with it! Pore fool we! Three shillin' at a time Willie'll ask me for!'

'They don't make nothin' o' money these days,' Mrs Ashcroft said.

'An' on'y last week,' the other went on, 'me daughter, she ordered a quarter pound suet at the butchers's; an' she sent it back to 'im to be chopped. She said she couldn't bother with choppin' it.'

'I lay he charged her, then.'

'I lay he did. She told me there was a whisk-drive that afternoon at the Institute, an' she couldn't bother to do the choppin'.'

'Tck!'

Mrs Ashcroft put the last firm touches to the basket-lining. She had scarcely finished when her sixteen-year-old grandson, a maiden of the moment in attendance, hurried up the garden-path shouting to know if the thing were ready, snatched it, and made off without acknowledgment. Mrs Fettley peered at him closely.

'They're goin' picnickin' somewheres,' Mrs Ashcroft explained.

'Ah,' said the other, with narrowed eyes. 'I lay *he* won't show much mercy to any he comes across, either. Now 'oo the dooce do he remind me of, all of a sudden?'

'They must look arter theirselves – same as we did.' Mrs Ashcroft began to set out the tea.

'No denyin' *you* could, Gracie,' said Mrs Fettley.

'What's in your head now?'

'Dunno ... But it come over me, sudden-like – about dat woman from Rye – I've slipped the name – Barnsley, wadn't it?'

'Batten – Polly Batten, you're thinkin' of.'

'That's it – Polly Batten. That day she had it in for you with a hay-fork – time we was all hayin' at Smalldene – for stealin' her man.'

'But you heered me tell her she had my leave to keep him?' Mrs Ashcroft's voice and smile were smoother than ever.

'I did – an' we was all looking that she'd prod the fork spang through your breastes when you said it.'

'No-oo. She'd never go beyond bounds – Polly. She shruck too much for reel doin's.'

'Allus seems to *me*,' Mrs Fettley said after a pause, 'that a man 'twixt two fightin' women is the foolishest thing on earth. Like a dog bein' called two ways.'

'Mebbe. But what set ye off on those times, Liz?'

'That boy's fashion o' carryin' his head an' arms. I haven't rightly looked at him since he's growed. Your Jane never showed it, but – *him*! Why, 'tis Jim Batten and his tricks come to life again! ... Eh?'

'Mebbe. There's some that would ha' made it out so – bein' barren-like, themselves.'

'Oho! Ah well! Dearie, dearie me, now! ... An' Jim Batten's been dead this –'

'Seven and twenty year,' Mrs Ashcroft answered briefly. 'Won't ye draw up, Liz?'

Mrs Fettley drew up to buttered toast, currant bread, stewed tea, bitter as leather, some home-preserved pears, and a cold boiled pig's tail to help down the muffins. She paid all the proper compliments.

'Yes. I dunno as I've ever owed me belly much,' said Mrs Ashcroft thoughtfully. 'We only go through this world once.'

'But don't it lay heavy on ye, sometimes?' her guest suggested.

'Nurse says I'm a sight liker to die o' me indigestion than me leg.' For Mrs Ashcroft had a long-standing ulcer on her shin, which needed regular care from the Village Nurse, who boasted (or others did, for her) that she had dressed it one hundred and three times already during her term of office.

'An' you that *was* so able, too! It's all come on ye before your full time, like. *I*'ve watched ye goin'.' Mrs Fettley spoke with real affection.

'Somethin's bound to find ye sometime. I've me 'eart left me still,' Mrs Ashcroft returned.

487

'You was always big-hearted enough for three. That's somethin' to look back on at the day's eend.'

'I reckon you've *your* back-lookin's, too,' was Mrs Ashcroft's answer.

'You know it. But I don't think much regardin' such matters excep' when I'm along with you, Gra'. Takes two sticks to make a fire.'

Mrs Fettley stared, with jaw half-dropped, at the grocer's bright calendar on the wall. The cottage shook again to the roar of the motor-traffic, and the crowded football-ground below the garden roared almost as loudly; for the village was well set to its Saturday leisure.

Mrs Fettley had spoken very precisely for some time without interruption, before she wiped her eyes. 'And,' she concluded, 'they read 'is death-notice to me, out o' the paper last month. O' course it wadn't any o' *my* becomin' concerns – let be I 'adn't set eyes on him for so long. O' course *I* couldn't say nor show nothin'. Nor I've no rightful call to go to Eastbourne to see 'is grave, either. I've been schemin' to slip over there by the 'bus some day; but they'd ask questions at 'ome past endurance. So I 'aven't even *that* to stay me.'

'But you've 'ad your satisfactions?'

'Godd! Yess! Those four years 'e was workin' on the rail near us. An' the other drivers they gave him a brave funeral, too.'

'Then you've naught to cast-up about. 'Nother cup o' tea?'

The light and air had changed a little with the sun's descent, and the two elderly ladies closed the kitchen-door against chill. A couple of jays squealed and skirmished through the undraped apple-trees in the garden. This time, the word was with Mrs Ashcroft, her elbows on the tea-table, and her sick leg propped on a stool . . .

'Well I never! But what did your 'usband say to that?' Mrs Fettley asked, when the deep-toned recital halted.

''E said I might go where I pleased for all of 'im. But seein' 'e was bedrid, I said I'd 'tend 'im out. 'E knowed I wouldn't take no advantage of 'im in that state. 'E lasted eight or nine week. Then he was took with a seizure-like; an' laid stone-still for days. Then 'e propped 'imself up abed an' says: "You pray no man'll ever deal with you like you've dealt with some." "An' you?" I says, for *you* know, Liz, what a rover 'e was. "It cuts both ways," says 'e, "but *I*'m death-wise, an' I can see what's comin' to you." He died a-Sunday an' was buried a-Thursday . . . An' yet I'd set a heap by him – one time or – did I ever?'

'You never told me that before,' Mrs Fettley ventured.

'I'm payin' ye for what ye told me just now. Him bein' dead, I wrote up, sayin' I was free for good, to that Mrs Marshall in Lunnon – which gave me my first place as kitchen-maid – Lord, how long ago! She was well pleased, for they two was both gettin' on, an' I knowed their ways. You remember, Liz, I used to go to 'em in service between whiles, for years – when we wanted money, or – or my 'usband was away – on occasion.'

''E *did* get that six months at Chichester, didn't 'e?' Mrs Fettley whispered. 'We never rightly won to the bottom of it.'

''E'd ha' got more, but the man didn't die.'

''None o' your doin's, was it, Gra'?'

'No! 'Twas the woman's husband this time. An' so, my man bein' dead, I went back to them Marshall's, as cook, to get me legs under a gentleman's table again, and be called with a handle to me name. That was the year you shifted to Portsmouth.'

'Cosham,' Mrs Fettley corrected. 'There was a middlin' lot o' new buildin' bein' done there. My man went first, an' got the room, an' I follered.'

'Well, then, I was a year-abouts in Lunnon, all at a breath, like, four meals a day an' livin' easy. Then, 'long towards autumn, they two went travellin', like, to France; keepin' me on, for they couldn't do without me. I put the house to rights for the caretaker, an' then I slipped down 'ere to me sister Bessie – me wages in me pockets, an' all 'ands glad to be'old of me.'

'That would be when I was at Cosham,' said Mrs Fettley.

'*You* know, Liz, there wasn't no cheap-dog pride to folk, those days, no more than there was cinemas nor whisk-drives. Man or woman 'ud lay hold o' any job that promised a shillin' to the backside of it, didn't they? I was all peaked up after Lunnon, an' I thought the fresh airs 'ud serve me. So I took on at Smalldene, obligin' with a hand at the early potato-liftin, stubbin' hens, an' such-like. They'd ha' mocked me sore in my kitchen in Lunnon, to see me in men's boots, an' me petticoats all shorted.'

'Did it bring ye any good?' Mrs Fettley asked.

''Twadn't for that I went. You know, 's'well's me, that na'un happens to ye till it *'as* 'appened. Your mind don't warn ye before'and of the road ye've took, till you're at the far eend of it. We've only a backwent view of our proceedin's.'

''Oo was it?'

''Arry Mockler.' Mrs Ashcroft's face puckered to the pain of her sick leg.

Mrs Fettley gasped. ''Arry? Bert Mockler's son! An' *I* never guessed!'

Mrs Ashcroft nodded. 'An' I told myself – *an*' I beleft it – that I wanted field-work.'

'What did ye get out of it?'

'The usuals. Everythin' at first – worse than naught after. I had signs an' warnings a-plenty, but I took no heed of 'em. For we was burnin' rubbish one day, just when we'd come to know how 'twas with – with both of us. 'Twas early in the year for burnin', an' I said so. "No!" says he. "The sooner dat old stuff's off an' done with," 'e says, "the better." 'Is face was harder'n rocks when he spoke. Then it come over me that I'd found me master, which I 'adn't ever before. I'd allus owned 'em, like.'

'Yes! Yes! They're yourn or you're theirn,' the other sighed. 'I like the right way best.'

'I didn't. But 'Arry did . . . 'Long then, it come time for me to go back to Lunnon. I couldn't. I clean couldn't! So, I took an' tipped a dollop o' scaldin' water out o' the copper one Monday mornin' over me left 'and and arm. Dat stayed me where I was for another fortnight.'

'Was it worth it?' said Mrs Fettley, looking at the silvery scar on the wrinkled fore-arm.

Mrs Ashcroft nodded. 'An' after that, we two made it up 'twixt us so's 'e could come to Lunnon for a job in a liv'ry-stable not far from me. 'E got it. *I* 'tended to that. There wadn't no talk nowhere. His own mother never suspicioned how 'twas. He just slipped up to Lunnon, an' there we abode that winter, not 'alf a mile 'tother from each.'

'Ye paid 'is fare an' all, though'; Mrs Fettley spoke convincedly.

Again Mrs Ashcroft nodded. 'Dere wadn't much I didn't do for him. 'E was me master, an' – O God, help us! – we'd laugh over it walkin' together after dark in them paved streets, an' me corns fair wrenchin' in me boots! I'd never been like that before. Ner he! Ner he!'

Mrs Fettley clucked sympathetically.

'An' when did ye come to the eend?' she asked.

'When 'e paid it all back again, every penny. Then I knowed, but I wouldn't *suffer* meself to know. "You've been mortal kind to me," he says. "Kind!" I said. "'Twixt *us*?" But 'e kep' all on tellin' me 'ow kind I'd been an' 'e'd never forget it all his days. I held it from off o' me for three evenin's, because I would *not* believe. Then 'e talked about not bein' satisfied with 'is job in the stables, an' the men there puttin' tricks on 'im, an' all they lies which a man tells when 'e's leavin' ye. I heard 'im out, neither 'elpin' nor 'inderin'. At the last, I took off a liddle brooch which he'd give me an' I says: "Dat'll do. *I* ain't askin' na'un'." An' I turned me round an' walked off to me own sufferin's. 'E didn't make 'em worse. 'E didn't come nor write after that. 'E slipped off 'ere back 'ome to 'is mother again.'

'An' 'ow often did ye look for 'en to come back?' Mrs Fettley demanded mercilessly.

'More'n once – more'n once! Goin' over the streets we'd used, I thought de very pave-stones 'ud shruck out under me feet.'

'Yes,' said Mrs Fettley. 'I dunno but dat don't 'urt as much as aught else. An' dat was all ye got?'

'No. 'Twadn't. That's the curious part, if you'll believe it, Liz.'

'I do. I lay you're further off lyin' now than in all your life, Gra'.'

'I am . . . An' I suffered, like I'd not wish my most arrantest enemies to. God's Own Name! I went through the hoop that spring! One part of it was headaches which I'd never known all me days before. Think o' *me* with an 'eddick! But I come to be grateful for 'em. They kep' me from thinkin' . . .'

''Tis like a tooth,' Mrs Fettley commented. 'It must rage an' rugg[3] till it tortures itself quiet on ye; an' then – then there's na'un left.'

'*I* got enough lef' to last me all *my* days on earth. It come about through our charwoman's liddle girl – Sophy Ellis was 'er name – all eyes an' elbers an' hunger. I used to give 'er vittles. Otherwhiles, I took no special notice of 'er, an' a sight less, o' course, when me trouble about 'Arry was on me. But – you know how liddle maids first feel it sometimes – she come to be crazy-fond o' me, pawin' an' cuddlin' all whiles; an' I 'adn't the 'eart to beat 'er off . . . One afternoon, early in spring 'twas, 'er mother 'ad sent 'er round to scutchel up what vittles she could off of us. I was settin' by the fire, me apern over me head, half-mad with the 'eddick, when she slips in. I reckon I was middlin' short with 'er. "Lor'!" she says. "Is *that* all? I'll take it off you in two-twos!" I told her not to lay a finger on me, for I thought she'd want to stroke my forehead; an' – I ain't that make. "*I* won't tech ye," she says, an' slips out again. She 'adn't been gone ten minutes 'fore me old 'eddick took off quick as bein' kicked. So I went about my work. Prasin'ly, Sophy comes back, an' creeps into my chair quiet as a mouse. 'Er eyes was deep in 'er 'ead an' 'er face all drawed. I asked 'er what 'ad 'appened. "Nothin'," she says. "On'y *I*'ve got it now." "Got what?" I says. "Your 'eddick," she says, all hoarse an' sticky-lipped. "I've took it on me." "Nonsense," I says, "it went of itself when you was out. Lay still an' I'll make ye a cup o' tea." "'Twon't do no good," she says, "till your time's up. 'Ow long do *your* 'eddicks last?" "Don't talk silly," I says, "or I'll send for the Doctor." It looked to me like she might be hatchin' de measles. "Oh, Mrs Ashcroft," she says, stretchin' out 'er liddle thin arms. "I *do* love ye." There wasn't any holdin' agin that. I took 'er into me lap an' made much of 'er. "Is it truly gone?" she says. "Yes," I says, "an' if 'twas you took it away, I'm truly grateful." "'*Twas* me,' she says, layin' 'er cheek to mine. "No one but me knows how." An' then she said she'd changed me 'eddick for me at a Wish 'Ouse.'

'Whatt?' Mrs Fettley spoke sharply.

'A Wish House. No! *I* 'adn't 'eard o' such things, either. I couldn't get it straight at first, but, puttin' all together, I made out that a Wish 'Ouse 'ad to be a house which 'ad stood unlet an' empty long enough for Some One, like, to come an' in'abit there. She said, a liddle girl that she'd played with in the livery-stables where 'Arry worked 'ad told 'er so. She said the girl 'ad belonged in a caravan that laid up, o' winters, in Lunnon. Gipsy, I judge.'

'Ooh! There's no sayin' what Gippos know, but *I*'ve never 'eard of a Wish 'Ouse, an' I know – some things,' said Mrs Fettley.

'Sophy said there was a Wish 'Ouse in Wadloes Road – just a few streets off, on the way to our green-grocer's. All you 'ad to do, she said, was to ring the bell an' wish your wish through the slit o' the letter-box. I asked 'er if the fairies give it 'er? "Don't ye know," she says, "there's no fairies in a Wish 'Ouse? There's on'y a Token."'

'Goo' Lord A'mighty! Where did she come by *that* word?' cried Mrs Fettley; for a Token is a wraith of the dead or, worse still, of the living.

'The caravan-girl 'ad told 'er, she said. Well, Liz, it troubled me to 'ear 'er, an' lyin' in me arms she must ha' felt it. "That's very kind o' you," I says, holdin' 'er tight, "to wish me 'eddick away. But why didn't ye ask somethin' nice for yourself?" "You can't do that," she says. "All you'll get at a Wish 'Ouse is leave to take someone else's trouble. I've took Ma's 'eadaches, when she's been kind to me; but this is the first time I've been able to do aught for you. Oh, Mrs Ashcroft, I *do* just-about love you." An' she goes on all like that. Liz, I tell you my 'air e'en a'most stood on end to 'ear 'er. I asked 'er what like a Token was. "I dunno," she says, "but after you've ringed the bell, you'll 'ear it run up from the basement, to the front door. Then say your wish," she says, "an' go away." "The Token don't open de door to ye, then?" I says. "Oh no," she says. "You on'y 'ear gigglin', like, be'ind the front door. Then you say you'll take the trouble off of 'oo ever 'tis you've chose for your love; an' ye'll get it," she says. I didn't ask no more – she was too 'ot an' fevered. I made much of 'er till it come time to light de gas, an' a liddle after that, 'er 'eddick – mine, I suppose – took off, an' she got down an' played with the cat.'

'Well, I never!' said Mrs Fettley. 'Did – did ye foller it up, anyways?'

'She askt me to, but I wouldn't 'ave no such dealin's with a child.'

'What *did* ye do, then?'

'Sat in me own room 'stid o' the kitchen when me 'eddicks come on. But it lay at de back o' me mind.'

''Twould. Did she tell ye more, ever?'

'No. Besides what the Gippo girl 'ad told 'er, she knew naught, 'cept that the charm worked. An', next after that – in May 'twas – I suffered the summer out in Lunnon. 'Twas hot an' windy for weeks, an' the streets stinkin' o' dried 'orse-dung blowin' from side to side an' lyin' level with the kerb. We don't get that nowadays. I 'ad my 'ol'day just before hoppin',[4] an' come down 'ere to stay with Bessie again. She noticed I'd lost flesh, an' was all poochy under the eyes.'

'Did ye see 'Arry?'

Mrs Ashcroft nodded. 'The fourth – no, the fifth day. Wednesday 'twas. I knowed 'e was workin' at Smalldene again. I asked 'is mother in the street, bold as brass. She 'adn't room to say much, for Bessie – you know 'er tongue – was talkin' full-clack. But that Wednesday, I was walkin' with one o' Bessie's chillern hangin' on me skirts, at de back o' Chanter's Tot. Prasin'ly, I felt 'e was be'ind me on the footpath, an' I knowed by 'is tread 'e'd changed 'is nature. I slowed, an' I heard 'im slow. Then I fussed a piece with the child, to force him past me, like. So 'e *ad* to come past. 'E just says "Good-evenin'", and goes on, tryin' to pull 'isself together.'

'Drunk, was he?' Mrs Fettley asked.

'Never! S'runk an' wizen; 'is clothes 'angin' on 'im like bags, an' the back of 'is neck whiter'n chalk. 'Twas all I could do not to oppen my arms an' cry after him. But I swallowed me spittle till I was back 'ome again an' the chillern abed. Then I says to Bessie after supper, "What in de world's come to 'Arry Mockler?" Bessie told me 'e'd been a-Hospital for two months, 'long o' cuttin' 'is foot wid a spade, muckin' out the old pond at Smalldene. There was poison in de dirt, an' it rooshed up 'is leg, like, an' come out all over him. 'E 'adn't been back to 'is job – carterin' at Smalldene – more'n a fortnight. She told me the Doctor said he'd go off, likely, with the November frostes; an' 'is mother 'ad told 'er that 'e didn't rightly eat nor sleep, an' sweated 'imself into pools, no odds 'ow chill 'e lay. An' spit terrible o' mornin's. "Dearie me," I says. "But, mebbe, hoppin' 'll set 'im right again," an' I licked me thread-point an' I fetched me needle's eye up to it an' I threads me needle under de lamp, steady as rocks. An' dat night (me bed was in de wash-house) I cried an' I cried. An' *you* know, Liz – for you've been with me in my throes – it takes summat to make me cry.'

'Yes; but chile-bearin' is on'y just pain,' said Mrs Fettley.

'I come round by cock-crow, an' dabbed cold tea on me eyes to take away the signs. Long towards nex' evenin' – I was settin' out to lay some flowers on me 'usband's grave, for the look o' the thing – I met 'Arry over against where the War Memorial is now. 'E was comin' back from 'is 'orses, so 'e couldn't *not* see me. I looked 'im all over, an' "'Arry," I says twix' me teeth, "come back an' rest-up in Lunnon." "I won't take it," he says, "for I can give ye naught." "I don't ask it," I says. "By God's Own Name, I don't ask na'un! On'y come up an' see a Lunnon doctor." 'E lifts 'is two 'eavy eyes at me: "'Tis past that, Gra'," 'e says. "I've but a few months left." "'Arry!" I says. "*My* man!" I says. I couldn't say no more. 'Twas all up in me throat. "Thank ye kindly, Gra'," 'e says (but 'e never says "my woman"), an' 'e went on up-street an' 'is mother – Oh, damn 'er! – she was watchin' for 'im, an' she shut de door be'ind 'im.'

Mrs Fettley stretched an arm across the table, and made to finger Mrs Ashcroft's sleeve at the wrist, but the other moved it out of reach.

'So I went on to the churchyard with my flowers, an' I remembered my 'usband's warnin' that night he spoke. 'E *was* death-wise, an' it *'ad* 'appened as 'e said. But as I was settin' down de jam-pot on the grave-mound, it come over me there was one thing I *could* do for 'Arry. Doctor or no Doctor, I thought I'd make a trial of it. So I did. Nex' mornin', a bill came down from our Lunnon green-grocer. Mrs Marshall, she'd lef' me petty cash for suchlike – o' course – but I tole Bess 'twas for me to come an' open the 'ouse. So I went up, afternoon train.'

'An' – but I know you 'adn't – 'adn't you no fear?'

'What for? There was nothin' front o' me but my own shame an' God's crooly. I couldn't ever get 'Arry – 'ow *could* I? I knowed it must go on burnin' till it burned me out.'

'Aie!' said Mrs Fettley, reaching for the wrist again, and this time Mrs Ashcroft permitted it.

'Yit 'twas a comfort to know I could try *this* for 'im. So I went an' I paid the green-grocer's bill, an' put 'is receipt in me hand-bag, an' then I stepped round to Mrs Ellis – our char – an' got the 'ouse-keys an' opened the 'ouse. First, I made me bed to come back to (God's Own Name! Me bed to lie upon!). Nex' I made me a cup o' tea an' sat down in the kitchen thinkin', till 'long towards dusk. Terrible close, 'twas. Then I dressed me an' went out with the receipt in me 'and-bag, feignin' to study it for an address, like. Fourteen, Wadloes Road, was the place – a liddle basement-kitchen 'ouse, in a row of twenty-thirty such, an' tiddy strips o' walled garden in front – the paint off the front doors, an' na'un done to na'un since ever so long. There wasn't 'ardly no one in the streets 'cept the cats. '*Twas* 'ot too! I turned into the gate bold as brass; up de steps I went an' I ringed the front-door bell. She pealed loud, like it do in an empty house. When she'd all ceased, I 'eard a cheer, like, pushed back on de floor o' the kitchen. Then I 'eard feet on de kitchen-stairs, like it might ha' been a heavy woman in slippers. They come up to de stairhead, acrost the hall – I 'eard the bare boards creak under 'em – an' at de front door dey stopped. I stooped me to the letter-box slit, an' I says: "Let me take everythin' bad that's in store for my man, 'Arry Mockler, for love's sake." Then, whatever it was 'tother side de door let its breath out, like, as if it 'ad been holdin' it for to 'ear better.'

'Nothin' was *said* to ye?' Mrs Fettley demanded.

'Na'un. She just breathed out – a sort of *A-ah*, like. Then the steps went back an' downstairs to the kitchen – all draggy – an' I heard the cheer drawed up again.'

'An' you abode on de doorstep, throughout all, Gra'?'

Mrs Ashcroft nodded.

'Then I went away, an' a man passin' says to me: "Didn't you know that house was empty?" "No," I says. "I must ha' been given the wrong number." An' I went back to our 'ouse, an' I went to bed; for I was fair flogged out. 'Twas too 'ot to sleep more'n snatches, so I walked me about, lyin' down betweens, till crack o' dawn. Then I went to the kitchen to make me a cup o' tea, an' I hitted meself just above the ankle on an old roastin'-jack o' mine that Mrs Ellis had moved out from the corner, her last cleanin'. An' so – nex' after that – I waited till the Marshalls come back o' their holiday.'

'Alone there? I'd ha' thought you'd 'ad enough of empty houses,' said Mrs Fettley, horrified.

'Oh, Mrs Ellis an' Sophy was runnin' in an' out soon's I was back, an' 'twixt us we cleaned de house again top-to-bottom. There's allus a hand's turn more to do in every house. An' that's 'ow 'twas with me that autumn an' winter, in Lunnon.'

'Then na'un hap – overtook ye for your doin's?'

Mrs Ashcroft smiled. 'No. Not then. 'Long in November I sent Bessie ten shillin's.'

'You was allus free-'anded,' Mrs Fettley interrupted.

'An' I got what I paid for, with the rest o' the news. She said the hoppin' 'ad set 'im up wonderful. 'E'd 'ad six weeks of it, and now 'e was back again carterin' at Smalldene. No odds to me '*ow* it 'ad 'appened – 'slong's it '*ad*. But I dunno as my ten shillin's eased me much. 'Arry bein' *dead*, like, 'e'd ha' been mine, till Judgment. 'Arry bein' alive, 'e'd like as not pick up with some woman middlin' quick. I raged over that. Come spring, I 'ad somethin' else to rage for. I'd growed a nasty little weepin' boil, like, on me shin, just above the boot-top, that wouldn't heal no shape. It made me sick to look at it, for I'm clean-fleshed by nature. Chop me all over with a spade, an' I'd heal like turf. Then Mrs Marshall she set 'er own doctor at me. 'E said I ought to ha' come to him at first go-off, 'stead o' drawin' all manner o' dyed stockin's over it for months. 'E said I'd stood up too much to me work, for it was settin' very close atop of a big swelled vein, like, behither the small o' me ankle. "Slow come, slow go," 'e says. "Lay your leg up on high an' rest it," he says, "an' 'twill ease off. Don't let it close up too soon. You've got a very fine leg, Mrs Ashcroft," 'e says. An' he put wet dressin's on it.'

''E done right.' Mrs Fettley spoke firmly. 'Wet dressin's to wet wounds. They draw de humours, same's a lamp-wick draws de oil.'

'That's true. An' Mrs Marshall was allus at me to make me set down more, an' dat nigh healed it up. An' then after a while they packed me off down to Bessie's to finish the cure; for I ain't the sort to sit down when I ought to stand up. You was back in the village then, Liz.'

'I was. I was, but – never did I guess!'

'I didn't desire ye to.' Mrs Ashcroft smiled. 'I saw 'Arry once or twice in de street, wonnerful fleshed up an' restored back. Then, one day I didn't see 'im, an' 'is mother told me one of 'is 'orses 'ad lashed out an' caught 'im on the 'ip. So 'e was abed an' middlin' painful. An' Bessie, she says to his mother, 'twas a pity 'Arry 'adn't a woman of 'is own to take the nursin' off 'er. And the old lady *was* mad! She told us that 'Arry 'ad never looked after any woman in 'is born days, an' as long as she was atop the mowlds, she'd contrive for 'im till 'er two 'ands dropped off. So I knowed she'd do watch-dog for me, 'thout askin' for bones.'

Mrs Fettley rocked with small laughter.

'That day,' Mrs Ashcroft went on, 'I'd stood on me feet nigh all the time, watchin' the doctor go in an' out; for they thought it might be 'is ribs, too. That made my boil break again, issuin' an' weepin'. But it turned out 'twadn't ribs at all, an' 'Arry 'ad a good night. When I heard that, nex' mornin', I says to meself, "I won't lay two an' two together *yit*. I'll keep me leg down a week, an' see what comes of it." It didn't hurt me that day, to speak of – 'seemed more to draw the strength out o' me like – an' 'Arry 'ad another good night. That made me persevere; but I didn't dare lay two an' two together till the week-end, an' then, 'Arry come forth e'en a'most 'imself again – na'un hurt outside ner in of him. I nigh fell on me knees in de wash-house when Bessie was up-street. "I've got ye now, my man," I says. "You'll take

your good from me 'thout knowin' it till my life's end. O God send
me long to live for 'Arry's sake!" I says. An' I dunno that didn't still
me ragin's.'

'For good?' Mrs Fettley asked.

'They come back, plenty times, but, let be how 'twould, I knowed I
was doin' for 'im. I *knowed* it. I took an' worked me pains on an' off, like
regulatin' my own range, till I learned to 'ave 'em at my commandments.
An' that was funny, too. There was times, Liz, when my trouble 'ud all
s'rink an' dry up, like. First, I used to try an' fetch it on again; bein'
fearful to leave 'Arry alone too long for anythin' to lay 'old of. Prasin'ly
I come to see that was a sign he'd do all right awhile, an' so I saved
myself.'

''Ow long for?' Mrs Fettley asked, with deepest interest.

'I've gone de better part of a year onct or twice with na'un more to
show than the liddle weepin' core of it, like. *All* s'rinked up an' dried off.
Then he'd inflame up – for a warnin' – an' I'd suffer it. When I
couldn't no more – an' I '*ad* to keep on goin' with my Lunnon work –
I'd lay me leg high on a cheer till it eased. Not too quick. I knowed by
the feel of it, those times, dat 'Arry was in need. Then I'd send another
five shillin's to Bess, or somethin' for the chillern, to find out if, mebbe,
'e'd took any hurt through my neglects. 'Twas *so*! Year in, year out, I
worked it dat way, Liz, an' 'e got 'is good from me 'thout knowin' – for
years and years.'

'But what did *you* get out of it, Gra'?' Mrs Fettley almost wailed. 'Did
ye see 'im reg'lar?'

'Times – when I was 'ere on me 'ol'days. An' more, now that I'm 'ere
for good. But 'e's never looked at me, ner any other woman 'cept 'is
mother. 'Ow I used to watch an' listen! So did she.'

'Years an' years!' Mrs Fettley repeated. 'An' where's 'e workin' at
now?'

'Oh, 'e's give up carterin' quite a while. He's workin' for one o' them
big tractorizin' firms – plowin' sometimes, an' sometimes off with lorries
– fur as Wales, I've 'eard. He comes 'ome to 'is mother 'tween whiles;
but I don't set eyes on him now, fer weeks on end. No odds! 'Is job
keeps 'im from continuin' in one stay anywheres.'

'But – just for de sake o' sayin' somethin' – s'pose 'Arry *did* get
married?' said Mrs Fettley.

Mrs Ashcroft drew her breath sharply between her still even and
natural teeth. '*Dat* ain't been required of me,' she answered. 'I reckon
my pains 'ull be counted agin that. Don't *you*, Liz?'

'It ought to be, dearie. It ought to be.'

'It *do* 'urt sometimes. You shall see it when Nurse comes. She thinks I don't know it's turned.'

Mrs Fettley understood. Human nature seldom walks up to the word 'cancer'.

'Be ye certain sure, Gra'?' she asked.

'I was sure of it when old Mr Marshall 'ad me up to 'is study an' spoke a long piece about my faithful service. I've obliged 'em on an' off for a goodish time, but not enough for a pension. But they give me a weekly 'lowance for life. I knew what *that* sinnified – as long as three years ago.'

'Dat don't *prove* it, Gra'.'

'To give fifteen bob a week to a woman 'oo'd live twenty year in the course o' nature? It *do*!'

'You're mistook! You're mistook!' Mrs Fettley insisted.

'Liz, there's *no* mistakin' when the edges are all heaped up, like – same as a collar. You'll see it. An' I laid out Dora Wickwood, too. *She* 'ad it under the arm-pit, like.'

Mrs Fettley considered awhile, and bowed her head in finality.

''Ow long d'you reckon 'twill allow ye, countin' from now, dearie?'

'Slow come, slow go. But if I don't set eyes on ye 'fore next hoppin', this'll be good-bye, Liz.'

'Dunno as I'll be able to manage by then – not 'thout I have a liddle dog to lead me. For de chillern, dey won't be troubled, an' – O Gra'! – I'm blindin' up – I'm blindin' up!'

'Oh, *dat* was why you didn't more'n finger with your quilt-patches all this while! I was wonderin' . . . But the pain *do* count, don't ye think, Liz? The pain *do* count to keep 'Arry – where I want 'im. Say it can't be wasted, like.'

'I'm sure of it – sure of it, dearie. You'll 'ave your reward.'

'I don't want no more'n this – *if* de pain is taken into de reckonin'.'

''Twill be – 'twill be, Gra'.'

There was a knock on the door.

'That's Nurse. She's before 'er time,' said Mrs Ashcroft. 'Open to 'er.'

The young lady entered briskly, all the bottles in her bag clicking. 'Evenin', Mrs Ashcroft,' she began. 'I've come raound a little earlier than usual because of the Institute dance to-na-ite. You won't ma-ind, will you?'

'Oh, no. Me dancin' days are over.' Mrs Ashcroft was the self-contained domestic at once. 'My old friend, Mrs Fettley 'ere, has been settin' talkin' with me a while.'

'I hope she 'asn't been fatiguing you?' said the Nurse a little frostily.

'Quite the contrary. It 'as been a pleasure. Only – only – just at the end I felt a bit – a bit flogged out like.'

'Yes, yes.' The Nurse was on her knees already, with the washes to hand. 'When old ladies get together they talk a deal too much, I've noticed.'

'Mebbe we do,' said Mrs Fettley, rising. 'So, now, I'll make myself scarce.'

'Look at it first, though,' said Mrs Ashcroft feebly. 'I'd like ye to look at it.'

Mrs Fettley looked, and shivered. Then she leaned over, and kissed Mrs Ashcroft once on the waxy yellow forehead, and again on the faded grey eyes.

'It *do* count, don't it – de pain?' The lips that still kept trace of their original moulding hardly more than breathed the words.

Mrs Fettley kissed them and moved towards the door.

❦ The Gardener [1] ❦

One grave to me was given,
    One watch till Judgment Day;
And God looked down from Heaven
    And rolled the stone away.

One day in all the years,
    One hour in that one day,
His Angel saw my tears,
    And rolled the stone away!

Everyone in the village knew that Helen Turrell did her duty by all her
world, and by none more honourably than by her only brother's unfortunate child. The village knew, too, that George Turrell had tried his
family severely since early youth, and were not surprised to be told that,
after many fresh starts given and thrown away, he, an Inspector of
Indian Police, had entangled himself with the daughter of a retired non-
commissioned officer, and had died of a fall from a horse a few weeks
before his child was born. Mercifully, George's father and mother were
both dead, and though Helen, thirty-five and independent, might well
have washed her hands of the whole disgraceful affair, she most nobly
took charge, though she was, at the time, under threat of lung trouble
which had driven her to the South of France. She arranged for the
passage of the child and a nurse from Bombay, met them at Marseilles,
nursed the baby through an attack of infantile dysentery due to the
carelessness of the nurse, whom she had had to dismiss, and at last, thin
and worn but triumphant, brought the boy late in the autumn, wholly
restored, to her Hampshire home.

All these details were public property, for Helen was as open as the
day, and held that scandals are only increased by hushing them up. She
admitted that George had always been rather a black sheep, but things
might have been much worse if the mother had insisted on her right to
keep the boy. Luckily, it seemed that people of that class would do
almost anything for money, and, as George had always turned to her in
his scrapes, she felt herself justified – her friends agreed with her – in
cutting the whole non-commissioned officer connection, and giving the
child every advantage. A christening, by the Rector, under the name of

Michael, was the first step. So far as she knew herself, she was not, she said, a child-lover, but, for all his faults, she had been very fond of George, and she pointed out that little Michael had his father's mouth to a line; which made something to build upon.

As a matter of fact, it was the Turrell forehead, broad, low, and well-shaped, with the widely spaced eyes beneath it, that Michael had most faithfully reproduced. His mouth was somewhat better cut than the family type. But Helen, who would concede nothing good to his mother's side, vowed he was a Turrell all over, and, there being no one to contradict, the likeness was established.

In a few years Michael took his place, as accepted as Helen had always been – fearless, philosophical, and fairly good-looking. At six, he wished to know why he could not call her 'Mummy', as other boys called their mothers. She explained that she was only his auntie, and that aunties were not quite the same as mummies, but that, if it gave him pleasure, he might call her 'Mummy' at bedtime, for a pet-name between themselves.

Michael kept his secret most loyally, but Helen, as usual, explained the fact to her friends; which when Michael heard, he raged.

'Why did you tell? *Why* did you tell?' came at the end of the storm.

'Because it's always best to tell the truth,' Helen answered, her arm round him as he shook in his cot.

'All right, but when the troof's ugly I don't think it's nice.'

'Don't you, dear?'

'No, I don't, and' – she felt the small body stiffen – 'now you've told, I won't call you "Mummy" any more – not even at bedtimes.'

'But isn't that rather unkind?' said Helen softly.

'I don't care! I don't care! You've hurted me in my insides and I'll hurt you back. I'll hurt you as long as I live!'

'Don't, oh, don't talk like that, dear! You don't know what –'

'I will! And when I'm dead I'll hurt you worse!'

'Thank goodness, I shall be dead long before you, darling.'

'Huh! Emma says, "Never know your luck."' (Michael had been talking to Helen's elderly, flat-faced maid.) 'Lots of little boys die quite soon. So'll I. *Then* you'll see!'

Helen caught her breath and moved towards the door, but the wail of 'Mummy! Mummy!' drew her back again, and the two wept together.

At ten years old, after two terms at a prep. school, something or somebody gave him the idea that his civil status was not quite regular.

He attacked Helen on the subject, breaking down her stammered defences with the family directness.

'Don't believe a word of it,' he said, cheerily, at the end. 'People wouldn't have talked like they did if my people had been married. But don't you bother, Auntie. I've found out all about my sort in English Hist'ry and the Shakespeare bits. There was William the Conqueror [2] to begin with, and – oh, heaps more, and they all got on first-rate. 'Twon't make any difference to you, my being *that* – will it?'

'As if anything could –' she began.

'All right. We won't talk about it any more if it makes you cry.' He never mentioned the thing again of his own will, but when, two years later, he skilfully managed to have measles in the holidays, as his temperature went up to the appointed one hundred and four he muttered of nothing else, till Helen's voice, piercing at last his delirium, reached him with assurance that nothing on earth or beyond could make any difference between them.

The terms at his public school and the wonderful Christmas, Easter, and Summer holidays followed each other, variegated and glorious as jewels on a string; and as jewels Helen treasured them. In due time Michael developed his own interests, which ran their courses and gave way to others; but his interest in Helen was constant and increasing throughout. She repaid it with all that she had of affection or could command of counsel and money; and since Michael was no fool, the War took him just before what was like to have been a most promising career.

He was to have gone up to Oxford, with a scholarship, in October. At the end of August he was on the edge of joining the first holocaust of public-school boys who threw themselves into the Line; [3] but the captain of his O.T.C., where he had been sergeant for nearly a year, headed him off and steered him directly to a commission in a battalion so new that half of it still wore the old Army red, and the other half was breeding meningitis through living overcrowdedly in damp tents. Helen had been shocked at the idea of direct enlistment.

'But it's in the family,' Michael laughed.

'You don't mean to tell me that you believed that old story all this time?' said Helen. (Emma, her maid, had been dead now several years.) 'I gave you my word of honour – and I give it again – that – that it's all right. It is indeed.'

'Oh, *that* doesn't worry me. It never did,' he replied valiantly. 'What I meant was, I should have got into the show earlier if I'd enlisted – like my grandfather.'

'Don't talk like that! Are you afraid of it's ending so soon, then?'

'No such luck. You know what K.[4] says.'

'Yes. But my banker told me last Monday it couldn't *possibly* last beyond Christmas – for financial reasons.'

''Hope he's right, but our Colonel – and he's a Regular – says it's going to be a long job.'

Michael's battalion was fortunate in that, by some chance which meant several 'leaves', it was used for coast-defence among shallow trenches on the Norfolk coast; thence sent north to watch the mouth of a Scotch estuary, and, lastly, held for weeks on a baseless rumour of distant service. But, the very day that Michael was to have met Helen for four whole hours at a railway-junction up the line, it was hurled out, to help make good the wastage of Loos, and he had only just time to send her a wire of farewell.

In France luck again helped the battalion. It was put down near the Salient,[5] where it led a meritorious and unexacting life, while the Somme was being manufactured; and enjoyed the peace of the Armentières and Laventie sectors when that battle began. Finding that it had sound views on protecting its own flanks and could dig, a prudent Commander stole it out of its own Division, under pretence of helping to lay telegraphs, and used it round Ypres at large.

A month later, and just after Michael had written Helen that there was nothing special doing and therefore no need to worry, a shell-splinter dropping out of a wet dawn killed him at once. The next shell uprooted and laid down over the body what had been the foundation of a barn wall, so neatly that none but an expert would have guessed that anything unpleasant had happened.

By this time the village was old in experience of war, and, English fashion, had evolved a ritual to meet it. When the postmistress handed her seven-year-old daughter the official telegram to take to Miss Turrell, she observed to the Rector's gardener: 'It's Miss Helen's turn now.' He replied, thinking of his own son: 'Well, he's lasted longer than some.' The child herself came to the front-door weeping aloud, because Master Michael had often given her sweets. Helen, presently, found herself pulling down the house-blinds one after one with great care, and saying earnestly to each: 'Missing *always* means dead.' Then she took her place in the dreary procession that was impelled to go through an inevitable series of unprofitable emotions. The Rector, of course, preached hope and prophesied word, very soon, from a prison camp. Several friends, too, told her perfectly truthful tales, but always about other women, to whom, after months and months of silence, their missing had been miraculously restored. Other people urged her to communicate with infallible Secretaries of organizations who could communicate with benevolent neutrals, who could extract accurate information from the most secretive of Hun prison commandants. Helen did and wrote and signed everything that was suggested or put before her.

Once, on one of Michael's leaves, he had taken her over a munition factory, where she saw the progress of a shell from blank-iron to the all but finished article. It struck her at the time that the wretched thing was never left alone for a single second; and 'I'm being manufactured into a bereaved next of kin,' she told herself, as she prepared her documents.

In due course, when all the organizations had deeply or sincerely regretted their inability to trace, etc., something gave way within her and all sensation – save of thankfulness for the release – came to an end in blessed passivity. Michael had died and her world had stood still and she had been one with the full shock of that arrest. Now she was standing still and the world was going forward, but it did not concern her – in no way or relation did it touch her. She knew this by the ease with which she could slip Michael's name into talk and incline her head to the proper angle, at the proper murmur of sympathy.

In the blessed realization of that relief, the Armistice with all its bells broke over her and passed unheeded. At the end of another year she had overcome her physical loathing of the living and returned young, so that she could take them by the hand and almost sincerely wish them well. She had no interest in any aftermath, national or personal, of the war, but, moving at an immense distance, she sat on various relief committees and held strong views – she heard herself delivering them – about the site of the proposed village War Memorial.

Then there came to her, as next of kin, an official intimation, backed by a page of a letter to her in indelible pencil, a silver identity-disc, and a watch, to the effect that the body of Lieutenant Michael Turrell had been found, identified, and re-interred [6] in Hagenzeele Third Military Cemetery – the letter of the row and the grave's number in that row duly given.

So Helen found herself moved on to another process of the manufacture – to a world full of exultant or broken relatives, now strong in the certainty that there was an altar upon earth where they might lay their love. These soon told her, and by means of time-tables made clear, how easy it was and how little it interfered with life's affairs to go and see one's grave.

'*So* different,' as the Rector's wife said, 'if he'd been killed in Mesopotamia, or even Gallipoli.'

The agony of being waked up to some sort of second life drove Helen across the Channel, where, in a new world of abbreviated titles, she learnt that Hagenzeele Third could be comfortably reached by an afternoon train which fitted in with the morning boat, and that there was a comfortable little hotel not three kilometres from Hagenzeele itself, where one could spend quite a comfortable night and see one's grave next morning. All this she had from a Central Authority who lived in a board and tar-paper shed on the skirts of a razed city full of whirling lime-dust and blown papers.

'By the way,' said he, 'you know your grave, of course?'

'Yes, thank you,' said Helen, and showed its row and number typed on Michael's own little typewriter. The officer would have checked it, out of one of his many books; but a large Lancashire woman thrust between them and bade him tell her where she might find her son, who had been corporal in the A.S.C.[7] His proper name, she sobbed, was Anderson, but, coming of respectable folk, he had of course enlisted under the name of Smith; and had been killed at Dickiebush, in early 'Fifteen. She had not his number nor did she know which of his two Christian names he might have used with his alias; but her Cook's tourist ticket expired at the end of Easter week, and if by then she could not find her child she should go mad. Whereupon she fell forward on Helen's breast; but the officer's wife came out quickly from a little bedroom behind the office, and the three of them lifted the woman on to the cot.

'They are often like this,' said the officer's wife, loosening the tight bonnet-strings. 'Yesterday she said he'd been killed at Hooge. Are you sure you know your grave? It makes such a difference.'

'Yes, thank you,' said Helen, and hurried out before the woman on the bed should begin to lament again.

Tea in a crowded mauve and blue striped wooden structure, with a false front, carried her still further into the nightmare. She paid her bill beside a stolid, plain-featured Englishwoman, who, hearing her inquire about the train to Hagenzeele, volunteered to come with her.

'I'm going to Hagenzeele myself,' she explained. 'Not to Hagenzeele Third; mine is Sugar Factory, but they call it La Rosière now. It's just south of Hagenzeele Three. Have you got your room at the hotel there?'

'Oh yes, thank you. I've wired.'

'That's better. Sometimes the place is quite full, and at others there's hardly a soul. But they've put bathrooms into the old Lion d'Or – that's the hotel on the west side of Sugar Factory – and it draws off a lot of people, luckily.'

'It's all new to me. This is the first time I've been over.'

'Indeed! This is my ninth time since the Armistice. Not on my own account. *I* haven't lost anyone, thank God – but, like everyone else, I've a lot of friends at home who have. Coming over as often as I do, I find it helps them to have someone just look at the – the place and tell them about it afterwards. And one can take photos for them, too. I get quite a list of commissions to execute.' She laughed nervously and tapped her slung Kodak. 'There are two or three to see at Sugar Factory this time, and plenty of others in the cemeteries all about. My system is to save them up, and arrange them, you know. And when I've got enough commissions for one area to make it worth while, I pop over and execute them. It *does* comfort people.'

'I suppose so,' Helen answered, shivering as they entered the little train.

'Of course it does. (Isn't it lucky we've got window-seats?) It must do or they wouldn't ask one to do it, would they? I've a list of quite twelve or fifteen commissions here' – she tapped the Kodak again – 'I must sort them out tonight. Oh, I forgot to ask you. What's yours?'

'My nephew,' said Helen. 'But I was very fond of him.'

'Ah, yes! I sometimes wonder whether *they* know after death? What do you think?'

'Oh, I don't – I haven't dared to think much about that sort of thing,' said Helen, almost lifting her hands to keep her off.

'Perhaps that's better,' the woman answered. 'The sense of loss must be enough, I expect. Well, I won't worry you any more.'

Helen was grateful, but when they reached the hotel Mrs Scarsworth (they had exchanged names) insisted on dining at the same table with her, and after the meal, in the little, hideous salon full of low-voiced relatives, took Helen through her 'commissions' with biographies of the dead, where she happened to know them, and sketches of their next of kin. Helen endured till nearly half-past nine, ere she fled to her room.

Almost at once there was a knock at her door and Mrs Scarsworth entered; her hands, holding the dreadful list, clasped before her.

'Yes – yes – *I* know,' she began. 'You're sick of me, but I want to tell you something. You – you aren't married, are you? Then perhaps you won't ... But it doesn't matter. I've *got* to tell someone. I can't go on any longer like this.'

'But please –' Mrs Scarsworth had backed against the shut door, and her mouth worked dryly.

'In a minute,' she said. 'You – you know about these graves of mine I was telling you about downstairs, just now? They really *are* commissions. At least several of them are.' Her eye wandered round the room. 'What extraordinary wall-papers they have in Belgium, don't you think? . . . Yes. I swear they are commissions. But there's *one*, d'you see, and – and he was more to me than anything else in the world. Do you understand?'

Helen nodded.

'More than anyone else. And, of course, he oughtn't to have been. He ought to have been nothing to me. But he *was*. He *is*. That's why I do the commissions, you see. That's all.'

'But why do you tell me?' Helen asked desperately.

'Because I'm *so* tired of lying. Tired of lying – always lying – year in and year out. When I don't tell lies I've got to act 'em and I've got to think 'em, always. *You* don't know what that means. He was everything to me that he oughtn't to have been – the one real thing – the only thing that ever happened to me in all my life; and I've had to pretend he wasn't. I've had to watch every word I said, and think out what lie I'd tell next, for years and years!'

'How many years?' Helen asked.

'Six years and four months before, and two and three-quarters after. I've gone to him eight times, since. Tomorrow'll make the ninth, and – and I can't – I *can't* go to him again with nobody in the world knowing. I want to be honest with someone before I go. Do you understand? It doesn't matter about *me*. I was never truthful, even as a girl. But it isn't worthy of *him*. So – so I – I had to tell you. I can't keep it up any longer. Oh, I can't!'

She lifted her joined hands almost to the level of her mouth, and brought them down sharply, still joined, to full arms' length below her waist. Helen reached forward, caught them, bowed her head over them, and murmured: 'Oh, my dear! My dear!' Mrs Scarsworth stepped back, her face all mottled.

'My God!' said she. 'Is *that* how you take it?'

Helen could not speak, and the woman went out; but it was a long while before Helen was able to sleep.

Next morning Mrs Scarsworth left early on her round of commissions, and Helen walked alone to Hagenzeele Third. The place was still in the making, and stood some five or six feet above the metalled road, which it flanked for hundreds of yards. Culverts across a deep ditch served for entrances through the unfinished boundary wall. She climbed a few wooden-faced earthen steps and then met the entire crowded level of the thing in one held breath. She did not know that Hagenzeele Third counted twenty-one thousand dead already. All she saw was a merciless sea of black crosses, bearing little strips of stamped tin at all angles across their faces. She could distinguish no order or arrangement in their mass; nothing but a waist-high wilderness as of weeds stricken dead, rushing at her. She went forward, moved to the left and the right hopelessly, wondering by what guidance she should ever come to her own. A great distance away there was a line of whiteness. It proved to be a block of some two or three hundred graves whose headstones had already been set, whose flowers were planted out, and whose new-sown grass showed green. Here she could see clear-cut letters at the ends of the rows, and, referring to her slip, realized that it was not here she must look.

A man knelt behind a line of headstones – evidently a gardener, for he was firming a young plant in the soft earth. She went towards him, her paper in her hand. He rose at her approach and without prelude or salutation asked: 'Who are you looking for?'

'Lieutenant Michael Turrell – my nephew,' said Helen slowly and word for word, as she had many thousands of times in her life.

The man lifted his eyes and looked at her with infinite compassion before he turned from the fresh-sown grass toward the naked black crosses.

'Come with me,' he said, 'and I will show you where your son lies.'

When Helen left the Cemetery she turned for a last look. In the distance she saw the man bending over his young plants; and she went away, supposing him to be the gardener.[8]

Notes

The Gate of the Hundred Sorrows

1. *The Gate of the Hundred Sorrows*: First published in the *Civil and Military Gazette*, 26 September 1884; collected in *Plain Tales from the Hills*, 1888.
2. *pice*: Coin of very small value.
3. *the City*: Lahore in the Punjab, where Kipling worked as a journalist on the *Civil and Military Gazette* from 1882 to 1887.
4. pukka: Proper.
5. chandoo-khanas: Opium dens.
6. *Baboos*: English-speaking, educated Bengalis; clerks.
7. *Anarkulli*: Area of Lahore.
8. *first chop*: Top quality.

The Story of Muhammad Din

1. *The Story of Muhammad Din*: First published in the *Civil and Military Gazette*, 8 September 1886; collected in *Plain Tales from the Hills*.
2. *Professor Peterson*: Then Professor of Sanscrit at Elphinstone College, Bombay.
3. khitmatgar: Table servant.
4. budmash: Evil-doer.
5. jail-khana: Prison.

The Other Man

1. *The Other Man*: First published in the *Civil and Military Gazette*, 15 November 1886; collected in *Plain Tales from the Hills*.
2. *Simla*: The summer capital of the Government of India, in the lower Himalayas.
3. *Jakko*: Mountain at Simla.
4. *P.W.D.*: Public Works Department.
5. *Terai hat*: A felt hat with a wide brim.
6. *tonga*: A light, two-wheeled carriage drawn by two horses, much used on the roads to and from Hill Stations.
7. bukshish: A tip.
8. *Peterhoff*: The Viceregal residence at Simla before Lord Dufferin had a grander Viceregal Lodge built. This was completed in 1887.

Selected Stories

Lispeth

1. *Lispeth*: First published in the *Civil and Military Gazette*, 29 November 1886; collected in *Plain Tales from the Hills*.
2. *Kotgarh*: A small settlement north-east of Simla.
3. *Moravian missionaries*: Representatives of a Protestant sect which originated in Czechoslovakia in the eighteenth century.
4. *Diana*: The virgin goddess of hunting.
5. *Narkunda*: About ten miles from Kotgarh.
6. *P. & O.*: The Peninsular and Oriental Steamship Company, whose ships plied between England and India.
7. *pahari*: Hill-man.
8. *Tarka Devi*: A Hindu goddess.

Venus Annodomini

1. *Venus Annodomini*: First published in the *Civil and Military Gazette*, 4 December 1886; collected in *Plain Tales from the Hills*.
2. *Number Eighteen in the Braccio Nuovo*: Presumably the copy in the Vatican gallery of the statue by Praxiteles of Venus Anadyomene (rising from the sea), with a pun on 'Annodomini' used as slang for old age.
3. *Bengal Civilian*: Member of the Bengal Civil Service.
4. *Mrs Hauksbee and Mrs Reiver*: Characters in other 'Plain Tales'.
5. *Ninon de L'Enclos*: A seventeenth-century Frenchwoman famous for her wit and beauty even in her old age.
6. *Darjiling*: The Hill Station for the Government of Bengal.

His Wedded Wife

1. *His Wedded Wife*: First published in the *Civil and Military Gazette*, 25 February 1887; collected in *Plain Tales from the Hills*.
2. *giants or beetles*: 'And the poor beetle that we tread upon / In corporal sufferance finds a pang as great / As when a giant dies' (*Measure for Measure*, Act III, Scene 1).
3. *Shikarris*: Literally, 'Hunters'; a fictional regiment.
4. *broke*: Cashiered.

In the Pride of his Youth

1. *In the Pride of his Youth*: First published in the *Civil and Military Gazette*, 5 May 1887; collected in *Plain Tales from the Hills*.
2. *weight-cloths*: Used in handicapping horses.

3. *Gravesend*: Where passengers embarked by tender on P. & O. liners for India.
4. *at 1–6⅞*: An exchange rate of one rupee for one shilling, six and seven-eighths pence (old currency, at twelve pennies to the shilling and twenty shillings to the pound).
5. *screw*: Slang for salary; in billiards an element of spin on the ball.

The Daughter of the Regiment

1. *The Daughter of the Regiment*: First published in the *Civil and Military Gazette*, 11 May 1887; collected in *Plain Tales from the Hills*.
2. *Jhansi*: A town south-west of Cawnpore.
3. *Pummeloe*: A large, orange-like fruit.
4. *Presidincy*: In the days of the East India Company Bengal, Bombay and Madras and the territories they controlled were known as Presidencies, each being governed by a Council headed by a President.
5. *Saint Lawrence*: Martyred by being broiled on a grid-iron.
6. *tope*: Grove.
7. lotah: A small brass pot.
8. *a three-year-ould*: A short-service soldier.
9. *Perhaps I will tell you . . .*: See 'In the Matter of a Private', *Soldiers Three and Other Stories*.

Thrown Away

1. *Thrown Away*: First published in *Plain Tales from the Hills*, 1888.
2. *lunge*: Make a horse canter in a circle while controlling it by a long rope.
3. *two-goldmohur*: The goldmohur was a coin worth fifteen rupees (about £1 sterling), so a two-goldmohur race would be an unimportant one.
4. *maiden*: A horse that has never won a race.
5. ekka: A one-horse carriage often used by Indians.
6. *Rest House*: For the use of officials travelling on business, but available to other travellers.
7. tetur: Partridge.
8. shikar-*kit*: Shooting-clothes.
9. *A country-bred*: As opposed to imported horses.
10. *Valley of the Shadow*: See Psalms 23:4.

Selected Stories
Beyond the Pale

1. *Beyond the Pale*: First published in *Plain Tales from the Hills*, 1888.
2. bustee: Quarter.
3. dhak: A tree sometimes known as 'Flame of the Forest'.
4. boorka: A long enveloping garment often worn by Moslem women.

A Wayside Comedy

1. *A Wayside Comedy*: First published in the *Week's News*, 21 January 1888; collected in *Under the Deodars*, 1888, and subsequently included in *Wee Willie Winkie and Other Stories*.
2. jhils: Marshy lakes.
3. *Samson . . . Gaza*: See Judges 16:29–30.
4. dâk: Stage of journey; used here in the sense of arrangements for travelling post (i.e., by relays of horses).
5. terai *hat*: A felt hat with a wide brim.
6. purdah: Curtain.
7. sais: Groom.

Dray Wara Yow Dee

1. *Dray Wara Yow Dee*: First published in the *Week's News*, 28 April 1888; collected in *In Black and White*, 1888; subsequently included in *Soldiers Three and Other Stories*.
2. *Thirteen-three*: Thirteen hands, three inches in height (4 feet 7 inches to the shoulder, the upper limit for a polo pony).
3. *Kursed . . .*: The reference is obscure.
4. *Imams*: Religious leaders and agents of divine illumination for Shi'ite Moslems.
5. *Tirah*: A valley in the North-West Frontier area.
6. *this accursed land*: Kipling was now working in Allahabad, far from the Punjab and the Frontier.
7. *Kamal*: A notorious freebooter whom Kipling later celebrated in 'The Ballad of East and West'.
8. *Jumrud*: A fort near Peshawar on the North-West Frontier.
9. *the Amir*: The ruler of Afghanistan.
10. *Thana*: Police station.
11. *Allah-al-Mumīt*: God the Giver of Death.
12. *Rahman*: An eighteenth-century Moslem sage.
13. *the Pindi camp*: At Rawalpindi where the Amir of Afghanistan visited the Viceroy in 1885; the Uzbegs were his cavalry escort. Kipling attended this Durbar as a special correspondent.
14. *the Fakr to the Isha*: The dawn prayer to the prayer after sunset.

Notes

15. *the Devil Atala . . .*: Reference unidentified.
16. *charpoy*: Bedstead.
17. *your Law*: The Arms Act which forbade the carrying of arms in British territory.
18. *Ali Musjid*: A fort in the Khyber Pass, beyond the bounds of British territory.
19. *Ghor Kuttri*: A Hindu temple in Peshawar, which was under British rule.
20. *not* Jamun *but* Ak: Not 'fruit tree' but 'twisted shrub'.
21. Alghias: Woe(?).
22. Djinns: Spirits or demons of Moslem mythology.
23. *Chenab*: One of the great rivers of the Punjab.

Little Tobrah

1. *Little Tobrah*: First published in the *Civil and Military Gazette*, 17 July 1888; collected in *Life's Handicap*, 1891.
2. *a forced voyage*: To penal servitude in the Andaman Islands in the Bay of Bengal.
3. *the other Black Water*: The ocean.
4. Bapri-bap: O Father – an exclamation of grief.
5. bunnia-*folk*: Corn-merchants.

Black Jack

1. *Black Jack*: First published in *Soldiers Three*, 1888; subsequently collected in *Soldiers Three and Other Stories*.
2. *Robert Buchanan*: Poet and novelist (1841–1901), author of *London Poems*, 1866.
3. *Corner Shop*: The Guard-Room cells.
4. *whip him on the peg*: Put him on a charge.
5. *kiddy*: Dish in which sailors measure their ration.
6. *peg*: Drink with soda.
7. *the Tyrone*: A fictional Irish regiment which figures, often as the Black Tyrone, in several of Kipling's works.
8. *wishful for to desert*: See 'The Madness of Private Ortheris' in *Plain Tales from the Hills*.
9. *the woman at Devizes*: Said to have been struck dead on committing perjury in 1753.
10. *crackin' on*: Swearing.
11. *palammers*: Slang for cards?
12. *stiffin'*: Swearing.
13. *Martini-Henry*: The new rifle which had superseded the Snider as standard issue in the British Army.

14. dooli: Covered litter.
15. *stoppages*: Stoppages of pay to cover the cost of damage to Government property.

On the City Wall

1. *On the City Wall*: First published in *In Black and White*, 1888; subsequently collected in *Soldiers Three and Other Stories*.
2. *Lilith*: Adam's first wife, according to Rabbinical tradition.
3. *jujube-tree*: A bush with plum-like fruit.
4. *chunam*: Plaster.
5. *Shiahs*: Adherents of one of the two main branches of Islam, as opposed to the more orthodox Sunnites.
6. *Sufis*: Adherents of a mystical and pantheistic Moslem sect.
7. *the Athenians*: See Acts 17:21: 'For all the Athenians . . . spent their time in nothing else, but either to tell, or to hear some new thing.'
8. *a Demnition Product*: 'Demnition' is a favourite epithet of Mr Mantalini in Dickens's *Nicholas Nickleby*.
9. sitar: Indian guitar.
10. *a great battle*: Pannipat in 1761, where the Afghans defeated the Mahrattas under the Peshwa or Chief Minister. See Kipling's poem 'With Scindia to Delhi'.
11. laonee: Ballad. The verses are from a novel *Lalun the Baragun or The Battle of Paniput*, by Mirza Murad Ali Beg (Bombay, 1884).
12. *Wahabi*: A member of a fanatical Moslem sect.
13. *Subadar*: Indian officer; 'Subadar Sahib' is a respectful form of address.
14. *Begums and Ranees*: Moslem and Hindu princesses.
15. *Sobraon*: Battle in which the British defeated the Sikhs in 1846.
16. *the Kuka rising*: The Kuka Movement was a Sikh sect which came into conflict with the British Government and fostered a rebellion in 1871–2. This was ruthlessly suppressed: its leader was imprisoned in Burma and many others were blown from cannons.
17. *'57*: The year of the Indian Mutiny.
18. *heterodox women*: The *hetairai* (companions) of ancient Athens were educated courtesans.
19. *Vizier*: Chief minister.
20. *Ladakh*: Area to the north of Kashmir.
21. Vox Populi *is* Vox Dei: The Voice of the People is the Voice of God.
22. *Sirkar*: Government.
23. *Din*: The Faith (cry of excited Moslems).
24. Hutt: Get out.
25. *lakh*: A hundred thousand.
26. bunnias: Merchants.
27. *It is expedient . . . people*: John 11:50: '. . . it is expedient for us, that one man should die for the people, and that the whole nation perish not'.

Notes

At the Pit's Mouth

1. *At the Pit's Mouth*: First published in *Under the Deodars*, 1888; subsequently collected in *Wee Willie Winkie and Other Stories*.
2. *Jean Ingelow*: Nineteenth-century poetess (1820–97), author of 'The High Tide on the Coast of Lincolnshire, 1571', from which these lines are taken.
3. *Tertium Quid*: Latin phrase meaning 'a third something'.
4. *Jakko*: Mountain at Simla.
5. *Observatory Hill*: Another feature of Simla topography, like Elysium, Summer Hill, etc., mentioned later in the story.
6. *banian*: Undershirt, singlet.
7. *ayahs*: Nursemaids.
8. *Medusa*: One of the Gorgons of Greek mythology – females with snakes for hair, whose gaze turned those who encountered them to stone.

The Man who would be King

1. *The Man who would be King*: First published in *The Phantom Rickshaw and Other Tales*, 1888; subsequently collected in *Wee Willie Winkie and Other Stories*.
2. *The Law, as quoted*: Presumably a principle of Freemasonry.
3. Backwoodsman: An allusion to the Allahabad *Pioneer*, for which Kipling was now working, having been transferred from the *Civil and Military Gazette* in autumn 1887.
4. *Residents*: British officials who acted as advisers to the rulers of independent 'Princely States' which did not come under direct British rule.
5. *for certain reasons*: The loafer is using Masonic phrases which the narrator, as a fellow-Mason, recognizes.
6. *Harun-al-Raschid*: Caliph of Baghdad in *The Arabian Nights*.
7. *Politicals*: Political agents or Residents (see note 4, above).
8. *Zenana*: Women's quarters where female members of the family were kept in seclusion.
9. *Mister Gladstone*: The great Liberal Prime Minister, whom Kipling saw as an enemy of Empire.
10. *Modred's shield*: Modred or Mordred, the nephew of King Arthur, carried a plain black shield.
11. *Sar-a*-whack: Win a kingdom of their own, as Sir James Brooke had done in Sarawak in 1841.
12. *Kafiristan*: A remote area of Afghanistan, hardly ever visited by Europeans in the nineteenth and even the twentieth century.
13. *Roberts' Army*: The British force under Sir Frederick (later Lord) Roberts, VC, in the Second Afghan War of 1878–80.
14. *Roum*: Constantinople.

15. *Pir Khan*: Pir is a title of Moslem saints or religious instructors, but the precise reference is unidentified.
16. *Roos*: Russians.
17. Huzrut: Respectful form of address.
18. *Hazar*: Caution (i.e., 'get ready').
19. *Martini*: A Martini-Henry rifle.
20. *Alexander . . . Semiramis*: Alexander the Great invaded India from the northeast; Semiramis was a mythical queen of Assyria.
21. *The Craft*: Freemasonry.
22. jezails: Long Afghan muskets.
23. *Rajah Brooke*: See note 11, above.
24. *our 'Fifty-Seven*: Our Indian Mutiny.
25. *in his habit as he lived*: A quotation from *Hamlet*, Act III, Scene 4: 'My father, in his habit as he lived!'
26. *The Son of God . . . his train*: From a hymn by Bishop Heber (1783–1826). The first line reads 'The Son of Man' in earlier editions of the story.

Baa Baa, Black Sheep

1. *Baa Baa, Black Sheep*: First published in the *Week's News*, 21 December 1888; collected in *Wee Willie Winkie and Other Stories*. This story is based on Kipling's own childhood experiences.
2. *When I was . . . place*: Cf. *As You Like It*, Act II, Scene 4: 'When I was at home I was in a better place'.
3. ayah: Nursemaid.
4. hamal: Porter.
5. Surti: From Surat, on the west coast of India.
6. *Ranee*: Hindu princess.
7. *Ghauts*: Hills parallel with the east and west coasts of south India.
8. *Nassick*: A Hill Station about a hundred miles from Bombay.
9. Belait: Originally meaning a kingdom or province, this word came to be used for Europe and then England. Hence 'Blighty' in soldiers' slang.
10. *Parel*: A suburb of Bombay.
11. *Apollo Bunder*: The main quay and landing-place at Bombay.
12. *broom*-gharri: Brougham (type of carriage).
13. *Sonny, my soul*: 'Sun of my soul' – the opening words of one verse of John Keble's 'Evening Hymn'.
14. *Navarino*: Naval battle of 1827 in which a British fleet under Admiral Codrington, together with French and Russian squadrons, destroyed the Turkish–Egyptian fleet, thus helping to ensure the national independence of Greece.
15. A. H. Clough: From his poem, 'Easter Day, Naples, 1849'.
16. Frank Fairlegh: A novel by Francis E. Smedley (1818–64).

Notes

17. *Tilbury*: A high two-wheeled carriage with a hood.
18. Cometh up as a Flower: A novel by Rhoda Broughton (1840–1920).
19. *Journeys end . . . know*: See *Twelfth Night*, Act II, Scene 3.
20. hubshi: Negro.
21. tout court: Just that.

The Head of the District

1. *The Head of the District*: First published in *Macmillan's Magazine* and New York *Tribune*, January 1890; collected in *Life's Handicap*, 1891.
2. *Man that is born . . . hill*: Cf. Job 14:1: 'Man that is born of a woman is of few days, and full of trouble.'
3. *the Very Greatest of All the Viceroys*: Probably Lord Ripon, Viceroy from 1880 to 1884, whose Liberal policies endeared him to Indians but antagonized the Anglo-Indian community.
4. *the Knight of the Drawn Sword*: The Commander-in-Chief (India) or the Military Member of Council.
5. peshbundi: Stratagem.
6. *civilians*: Members of the Indian Civil Service.
7. *his sisters and his cousins and his aunts*: Cf. Gilbert and Sullivan's *HMS Pinafore*.
8. *screw-gun*: Light artillery piece for mountain warfare, which could be dismantled, carried by mule and then re-assembled.
9. *Ghazis*: Fanatical Moslem warriors.
10. *Jehannum*: Hell.
11. *Akbar*: Mogul emperor of the sixteenth century.
12. *Belooch Beshaklis*: A fictional regiment.
13. *Tommy Dodd*: An innocent gambling game played at charity fêtes, with a pun here on roulette.

The Courting of Dinah Shadd

1. *The Courting of Dinah Shadd*: First published in *Macmillan's Magazine* and *Harper's Weekly*, March 1890; collected in *Life's Handicap*.
2. *Nordenfeldts*: Machine-guns.
3. *Eblis*: The devil, in Moslem mythology.
4. *lushin'*: Drinking.
5. *Wolseley was quite wrong*: Lord Wolseley, previously Sir Garnet Wolseley (1833–1913), was one of Britain's foremost generals. In the *Soldier's Pocket Book for Field Service* (1869) he had described war correspondents as 'those newly invented curses to armies, who eat the rations of fighting men and do no work at all'.

6. *the opinion of Polonius*: Cf. his advice to Laertes in *Hamlet* Act I, Scene 3: 'Beware/Of entrance to a quarrel, but being in,/Bear't that th' opposed may beware of thee.'
7. *Black Tyrone*: A fictional Irish regiment.
8. *in another place*: See 'The Solid Muldoon' in *Soldiers Three and Other Stories*.
9. *plastrons on his epigastrons*: Cloth facings on his midriff.
10. dah: Burmese sword.
11. *C.B.*: 'Confined to barracks' (Kipling).
12. *lost my tip*: Failed, 'came a cropper'.
13. *when he went mad with the home-sickness*: See 'The Madness of Private Ortheris' in *Plain Tales from the Hills*.
14. *Prometheus*: A Titan chained to a rock, in Greek mythology, with vultures tearing out his liver, as punishment for his stealing fire from heaven for the benefit of mankind.

The Man Who Was

1. *The Man Who Was*: First published in *Macmillan's Magazine* and *Harper's Weekly*, April 1890; collected in *Life's Handicap*.
2. *White Hussars*: A fictional regiment said to be based on the 9th Lancers.
3. *Black Tyrone*: A fictional Irish regiment.
4. *sotnia*: Squadron.
5. *Lushkar Light Horse*: Another fictional regiment.
6. *Punjab Frontier Force:* Irregular force under the control of the Punjab Government for policing the Frontier.
7. *sambhur, nilghai, markhor*: Large stag, great antelope, wild goat.
8. *dinner-slips*: Long white strips of cloth.
9. Shabash: Well done.
10. *Ressaidar*: Indian subaltern of irregular cavalry.
11. *Boot and saddle*: Trumpet signal to cavalry to mount.
12. *the pit whence he was digged*: Cf. Isaiah 51:1.
13. *before Sebastopol*: In the siege of Sebastopol in the Crimean War of 1854–6.

Without Benefit of Clergy

1. *Without Benefit of Clergy*: First published in *Macmillan's Magazine* and *Harper's Weekly*, June 1890; collected in *Life's Handicap*. The phrase 'benefit of clergy' refers to the right of clerics in the Middle Ages to be tried in special ecclesiastical courts, but Kipling uses it here to indicate that the lovers have gone through no church ceremony of marriage, nor have they any protection from fate or the consequences of their actions.
2. *Sheikh Badl*: Badl was a Rajput hero of the fourteenth century.

3. log: People.
4. Ya illah!: O God!
5. Tobah: penitence; an exclamation of strong negation (sc. 'No – shame!').
6. sitar: Indian guitar.
7. *Rajah Rasalu*: A king in Sialkot in the third and fourth centuries, about whom legends abound.
8. *scald-head*: One infected with ringworm; a term of general opprobrium.
9. janee: Beloved.
10. *burning-ghaut*: Place by a river for pyres for the dead.

On Greenhow Hill

1. *On Greenhow Hill*: First published in *Harper's Weekly*, 23 August 1890; collected in *Life's Handicap*.
2. Rivals: by Kipling's mother, Alice Kipling.
3. *Aurangabadis*: Fictional Indian regiment.
4. *tewed up*: Tied up, mixed up.
5. *Lotharius*: Lothario, the proverbial heartless libertine, from Nicholas Rowe's *The Fair Penitent* (1703).
6. *sumph*: Sump, the lowest part of a mine.
7. *jealoused*: Suspected.
8. *clemmed*: Pinched.
9. *brayed*: Pounded.
10. *the Widdy*: The Widow; i.e., Queen Victoria.
11. *Forders*: Drivers of hansom cabs, named after the manufacturers.
12. *boggart*: Ghost.
13. *tram*: A small vehicle on rails for carrying loads in a mine.
14. *fresh*: Tipsy.

'Rikki-Tikki-Tavi'

1. *'Rikki-Tikki-Tavi'*: First published in *St Nicholas Magazine* and *Pall Mall Magazine*, November 1893; collected in *The Jungle Book*, 1894.
2. *Nag*: 'Native name for the Cobra. Pronounced *Narg*' (Kipling).
3. *Brahm*: The supreme God of Hinduism.

The Miracle of Purun Bhagat

1. *The Miracle of Purun Baghat*: First published in New York *World*, *Pall Mall Gazette* and *Pall Mall Budget*, October 1894; collected in *The Second Jungle Book*, 1895. A *Baghat* is a Holy Man.
2. *Langurs*: Large monkeys.

3. *Brahmin*: A member of the highest priestly class.
4. *Pioneer*: Kipling himself had worked for this newspaper from late 1887 to early 1889.
5. *Dewan*: Chief Minister.
6. coco-de-mer: Coconut shell.
7. *Kala Pir*: The Black Saint (?).
8. *Jogis*: Yogis, followers of Yoga practices of meditation.
9. *Simla*: The summer capital of the Government of India, in the lower Himalayas.
10. *Kali*: Hindu goddess, wife of the great god Siva, associated with death and destruction.
11. mushick-nabha: A type of deer.
12. Bhai: Brother.
13. *D.C.L., Ph.D.*: Doctor of Civil Law, Doctor of Philosophy.

The Maltese Cat

1. *The Maltese Cat*: First published in *Pall Mall Gazette*, 26 and 27 June 1895; collected in *The Day's Work*, 1898.
2. *Archangels, Skidars*: Nicknames for fictional regiments.
3. *tiffin*: Lunch.
4. *flea-bitten*: Having a light coat spotted with patches of reddish hair.
5. *ekka*: A one-horse carriage often used by Indians.
6. *thirteen three*: Thirteen hands, three inches (four feet, seven inches to the shoulder), the maximum height for polo ponies under Calcutta Turf Club rules.
7. *anything*: i.e., to drink.
8. *three thousand*: Sc, rupees.

Red Dog

1. *Red Dog*: First published in the *Pall Mall Gazette*, 29 and 30 July 1895; collected in *The Second Jungle Book*.
2. sambhur: A large stag.
3. *the letting in of the Jungle*: See the story 'Letting in the Jungle' in *The Second Jungle Book*.
4. *Mowgli*: The central figure of the *Jungle Books*, a human child brought up by wolves and instructed by Baloo the bear and Bagheera the panther.
5. *Hathi*: The elephant.
6. *Akela*: The lone wolf, former leader of the pack.
7. *Shere Khan*: A tiger killed by Mowgli.
8. *Dekkan*: Central plateau of South India.
9. bandar-log: Monkey-people.
10. *Chil*: The kite.

Notes

The Ship that Found Herself

1. *The Ship that Found Herself*: First published in *The Idler*, December 1895; collected in *The Day's Work*. Kipling later modified, some of the ship's vital statistics.
2. *modulus of elasteecity*: A technical term for the ratio of stress imposed on a substance to the resulting strain within the elastic limit.
3. *paresis*: Partial paralysis, affecting power of movement.

William the Conqueror

1. *William the Conqueror*: First published in the *Gentlewoman* and *Ladies' Home Journal*, December 1895–January 1896; collected in *The Day's Work*.
2. The Undertaking: A poem by John Donne (1572–1631).
3. *fifteen-anna*: There were sixteen annas to a rupee, so fifteen-anna means almost the maximum.
4. Pioneer: See note 4 to 'The Miracle of Purun Baghat'.
5. Kubber-kargaz . . .: Newspaper-extra.
6. *the Famine Code*: Emergency regulations introduced in 1869.
7. ek dum: Immediately.
8. *a Punjabi*: i.e., an administrator who had served in the Punjab.
9. bundobust: Organization, or capacity to organize.
10. *a Jubilee Knight*: He had been knighted in Queen Victoria's Jubilee Honours in 1887.
11. *thrice-born civilian*: Very high caste (ironic). Brahmins, or members of the highest priestly class, were called twice-born once they had been initiated into their caste. A 'civilian' was a member of the Indian Civil Service.
12. *the Benighted Presidency*: Madras (cf. note 4 to 'The Daughter of the Regiment'); a contemptuous term used by North India men.
13. *the one daily paper . . .*: The *Civil and Military Gazette*, published in Lahore.
14. pukka: Genuine, proper.
15. phulkaris: Embroidered cotton sheets used as wall-hangings.
16. *Murree*: A Hill Station in North India.
17. Little Henry and His Bearer: By Mary Martha Sherwood (1775–1851), published in 1832.
18. *puggaree*: Turban, or, as here, scarf wound around a hat.
19. *Gehenna*: Hell.
20. A Valediction: A poem by John Donne.
21. *cross the Bias River*: i.e., return to the Punjab.
22. *gunny-bags*: Coarse sacking.
23. *Paris*: A son of King Priam and the lover of Helen of Troy.
24. *the Pauper Province*: i.e., the Punjab.
25. *tucked up*: Exhausted.
26. *the Lawrence Hall*: In Lahore.

27. *Settlement*: Review of tax assessments for Land Revenue over a given area, determining in the process the boundaries and ownership of all holdings.
28. *Derajat*: An area of the Punjab.
29. *Mr Chucks*: A character in one of Frederick Marryat's novels, *Peter Simple*, while Midshipman Easy is the hero of another.
30. *cinchona*: The shrub from which quinine derives.
31. pagal: Out of his mind.
32. *tez*: Fiery, hot.
33. *nullah*: Dry river bed.

The Devil and the Deep Sea

1. *The Devil and the Deep Sea*: First published in the *Graphic*, Christmas No., 1895; collected in *The Day's Work*.
2. *Noumea*: The capital of New Caledonia, the site of a French penal colony.
3. *trying-out*: Boiling whale blubber to extract oil.
4. *donkey*: Donkey engine, a small auxiliary used for loading cargo, etc.
5. *cuddy*: Cabin.
6. *Kismet*: Fate.
7. *worm*: A shaft with a spiral groove meshing with a toothed wheel.
8. *proa*: Swift Malay sailing vessel.
9. *the honest . . . traders*: i.e., pirates.
10. *tripang*: Edible sea-slug.

'Bread upon the Waters'

1. *'Bread upon the Waters'*: First published in the *Graphic* and *McClure's Magazine*, December 1896; collected in *The Day's Work*. For the title see Ecclesiastes 11:1: 'Cast thy bread upon the waters: for thou shalt find it after many days.' The opening sentence refers to the story 'Brugglesmith' in *Many Inventions*.
2. *Gerald Massey*: Poet, editor and author (1829–1907), associated with Christian Socialism.
3. *Bouverie-Byzantine style*: Elaborate journalese, Bouverie Street, off Fleet Street in London, being the place of publication of several newspapers.
4. *Dinah*: See 'The Courting of Dinah Shadd'.
5. garance: A red dye from the madder root.
6. *chow-chow*: Chinese preserve of ginger, orange peel etc., in syrup.
7. *deaf as the adders o' Scripture*: Psalms 58:4: 'even like the deaf adder which stoppeth her ears; which refuseth to hear the voice of the charmer: charm he never so wisely.'
8. *Shekinah*: Vision of the divine presence; with a sense here of what he reveres most.

Notes

9. *compound*: Engine with multiple stages in which steam used in one is used again in another.
10. *donkeys*: Donkey-engines; small auxiliary engines for loading cargo, etc.
11. non plus ultra: More correctly *ne plus ultra*: the ultimate limit (Latin).
12. Quem Deus vult . . . dementat: Whom God wishes to destroy he first drives mad (Latin).
13. *Hoor*: Whore. (Cf. Revelation 17:1–18.)
14. *Gehenna*: Hell.
15. *cuddy*: Cabin.
16. *gyte*: Mad.
17. seriatim: In sequence (Latin).
18. *speered*: Enquired.
19. *Gowk*: Idiot.
20. *bitts*: Strong posts on a ship's deck for securing mooring lines.
21. *lazareetes*: Sc. lazarettes, small lockers at the stern or between the decks of a ship.
22. *crack*: Up to the mark.
23. *Eddystone*: A lighthouse marking dangerous rocks.
24. *Judeeas Apella*: Sc. Judaeus Apella, Apella the Jew, in Horace, *Satires*, i:5.

'They'

1. *'They'*: First published in *Scribner's Magazine*, August 1904; collected in *Traffics and Discoveries*, 1904. Behind the delicate pathos of this story lies Kipling's grief at the death of his little daughter Josephine, aged six, in 1899.
2. *that precise hamlet*: Washington, in Sussex (though Washington, DC, is named after the first President of the United States, not after this village).
3. *the Egg*: A reference to the ancient belief that the world was egg-shaped and derived from an egg hatched by a Creator – sometimes this is termed the mundane egg. Here it seems to image spiritual reality.
4. *tax cart*: Light farm-cart exempt from taxation.
5. *Æsculapius*: God of medicine. The oath is the Hippocratic Oath (Hippocrates being 'the father of medicine' and a follower of Aesculapius) in which doctors undertake to practise their art for the benefit of their patients.
6. *the Fathers*: i.e., the Fathers of the Church.
7. *In the pleasant orchard-closes* . . .: From 'The Lost Bower' by Elizabeth Barrett Browning (1806–61).
8. *no unpassable iron*: Referring to the folklore belief that iron could drive away spirits or stop them from entering.

Selected Stories

The Mother Hive

1. *The Mother Hive*: First published in *Collier's Weekly*, 20 November 1908; collected in *Actions and Reactions*, 1909.
2. *Melissa*: Greek word for a bee.
3. carissima: dearest (Italian).
4. *what the trumpet was to Job's war-horse*: A summons to battle, joyfully accepted. ('He saith among the trumpets, Ha, ha; and he smelleth the battle afar off, the thunder of the captains, and the shouting' Job 39:2.)
5. La Reine le veult: The Queen wishes it. In parliamentary usage this phrase indicates the Royal Assent.
6. *garmed*: Smeared.
7. *kopje*: Boer word for small hill.
8. *Ygdrasil*: In Norse mythology the world-tree, connecting heaven, earth and hell.
9. *Hymettus*: Mountain near Athens, famous for its honey.
10. post hoc *with* propter hoc: *After this* with *because of this*.

Marklake Witches

1. *Marklake Witches*: First published in *Rewards and Fairies*, 1910.
2. *Dan and Una*: Dan and Una are based on Kipling's children John and Elsie, figure in *Puck of Pook's Hill* (1906) and *Rewards and Fairies* (1910), in both of which Puck, a benevolent hobgoblin, introduces them to characters who lived in Sussex in past ages.
3. *a great French physician*: Kipling is alluding to René Théophile Hyacinthe Laennec (1781–1826), a well-known French physician, later Professor of Medicine at the Collège de France, who began experiments which resulted in the development of the stethoscope.
4. *from Wesley to Wellesley*: Sir Arthur Wellesley, first Duke of Wellington (1769–1852), spelt his name 'Wesley' until 1798, when he adopted the form 'Wellesley'.
5. confrère: Colleague.
6. *canaille*: Roughs, rabble.
7. *syncope*: Fainting-fit.
8. *vandyked*: With a large series of points, forming a border.
9. *morone*: Maroon.
10. en grande tenue: In full dress.
11. *Assaye*: The battle in which Wellesley inflicted a major defeat on the Mahrattas in 1803.
12. accablés: Overwhelmed.
13. Assez ... Assez: Enough, Mademoiselle! It is too much for me! Enough!

Notes

The Knife and the Naked Chalk

1. *The Knife and the Naked Chalk*: First published in *Harper's Magazine*, December 1909; collected in *Rewards and Fairies*.
2. *bivvering*: Hovering.
3. *baffed*: Brushed.
4. *What else could I have done?*: The leitmotif, according to Kipling, of the stories in *Rewards and Fairies*. Cf. p. 422 above.
5. *Tyr*: The god of war and victory in Scandinavian mythology (the Teutonic Tiw), one of whose hands was bitten off by the demonic wolf Fenris, in whose mouth Tyr had placed it as a pledge.
6. *Oak, and Ash, and Thorn*: Used by Puck as a spell to make the children forget what they have heard, for the time being.

'My Son's Wife'

1. *'My Son's Wife'*: First published in *A Diversity of Creatures*, 1917, but attributed by Kipling to 1913. The title is provided by a phrase from Jean Ingelow's poem 'The High Tide on the Coast of Lincolnshire, 1571', which is quoted throughout the story (cf. 'At the Pit's Mouth', note 2).
2. *the disease of the century*: *Mal du siècle* – a pervasive sense of melancholy and disenchantment.
3. vie intime: Private and secret life.
4. *Liris – out of Horace*: Horace's *Odes*, iii:17, contains a reference to 'the Liris where it floods Marica's shores', and there is another reference to this stream in *Odes*, i:31.
5. *Eliphaz ... Naamathite*: Job's comforters (Job 2:11–13) who came to mourn with him in his misfortune.
6. Ne sit ancillae: From Horace, *Odes*, ii:4: 'Let not the love of thy handmaiden shame thee.'
7. *Bartolozzi*: Painter and engraver (1728–1815).
8. *preserved*: i.e., reared pheasants, which the hunt would have disturbed.
9. *James Pigg – and Batsey*: Characters in the works of R. S. Surtees (1805–64) which include *Handley Cross* (1843), and which portray the hunting world, especially the exploits of Mr Jorrocks, a London sportsman–grocer.
10. *'the set grey life and apathetic end'*: From Tennyson's poem, 'Love and Duty', 1842.
11. *Alsatia*: Whitefriars district of London which was once a sanctuary for criminals.
12. *the young man ... horse-flesh*: A not wholly accurate quotation from Surtees's *Handley Cross*.
13. *cubbing*: Hunting young foxes.
14. Injecto ter pulvere: Dust having been thrown on it three times (Latin).
15. Sortes Surteesianae: By analogy with *sortes Virgilianae* – a kind of divination

by opening Virgil's work at random and reading whatever lines presented themselves.

Mary Postgate

1. *Mary Postgate*: First published in *Nash's Magazine* and the *Century Magazine*, September 1915 (the month before Kipling's son John was killed in the Battle of Loos); collected in *A Diversity of Creatures*.
2. *Contrexeville*: French mineral water from the spa of that name.
3. *Laty*: Lady.
4. *Cassée. Tout cassée*: Broken. All broken (French).
5. *Che me rends. Le médicin*: I surrender. The doctor (French, with 'Che' for 'Je').
6. *Ich haben . . . gesehn*: I have seen the dead child (German).

The Wish House

1. *The Wish House*: First published in *Maclean's Magazine*, 15 October 1924; collected in *Debits and Credits*, 1926.
2. *list-bound*: Bound with cheap cloth-material.
3. *rugg*: Tear, pull violently.
4. *hoppin'*: 'Hop-picking' (Kipling).

The Gardener

1. *The Gardener*: First published in *McCall's Magazine*, April 1925; collected in *Debits and Credits*.
2. *William the Conqueror*: William was the illegitimate son of the Duke of Normandy.
3. *threw themselves into the Line*: Enlisted as privates so as to get to the Front quickly.
4. *K.*: Field Marshal Lord Kitchener (1850–1916), then Secretary of State for War.
5. *the Salient*: At Ypres.
6. *found, identified, and re-interred*: Kipling became a member of the Imperial War Graves Commission in 1917. His own son's body was never found after he was listed 'Missing' in October 1915.
7. *A.S.C.*: Army Service Corps.
8. *supposing him to be the gardener*: Cf. John 20:15: 'Jesus saith unto her, Woman, why weepest thou? whom seekest thou? She, supposing him to be the gardener, saith unto him, Sir, if thou have borne him hence, tell me where thou hast laid him . . .'

FOR THE BEST IN PAPERBACKS, LOOK FOR THE

In every corner of the world, on every subject under the sun, Penguin represents quality and variety – the very best in publishing today.

For complete information about books available from Penguin – including Pelicans, Puffins, Peregrines and Penguin Classics – and how to order them, write to us at the appropriate address below. Please note that for copyright reasons the selection of books varies from country to country.

In the United Kingdom: For a complete list of books available from Penguin in the U.K., please write to *Dept E.P., Penguin Books Ltd, Harmondsworth, Middlesex, UB7 0DA*

In the United States: For a complete list of books available from Penguin in the U.S., please write to *Dept BA, Penguin, 299 Murray Hill Parkway, East Rutherford, New Jersey 07073*

In Canada: For a complete list of books available from Penguin in Canada, please write to *Penguin Books Canada Ltd, 2801 John Street, Markham, Ontario L3R 1B4*

In Australia: For a complete list of books available from Penguin in Australia, please write to the *Marketing Department, Penguin Books Australia Ltd, P.O. Box 257, Ringwood, Victoria 3134*

In New Zealand: For a complete list of books available from Penguin in New Zealand, please write to the *Marketing Department, Penguin Books (NZ) Ltd, Private Bag, Takapuna, Auckland 9*

In India: For a complete list of books available from Penguin, please write to *Penguin Overseas Ltd, 706 Eros Apartments, 56 Nehru Place, New Delhi, 110019*

In Holland: For a complete list of books available from Penguin in Holland, please write to *Penguin Books Nederland B.V., Postbus 195, NL–1380AD Weesp, Netherlands*

In Germany: For a complete list of books available from Penguin, please write to *Penguin Books Ltd, Friedrichstrasse 10 – 12, D–6000 Frankfurt Main 1, Federal Republic of Germany*

In Spain: For a complete list of books available from Penguin in Spain, please write to *Longman Penguin España, Calle San Nicolas 15, E–28013 Madrid, Spain*

PENGUIN CLASSICS

PENGUIN CLASSICS

PENGUIN CLASSICS

Arnold Bennett	**The Old Wives' Tale**
Joseph Conrad	**Heart of Darkness**
	Nostromo
	The Secret Agent
	The Shadow-Line
	Under Western Eyes
E. M. Forster	**Howard's End**
	A Passage to India
	A Room With a View
	Where Angels Fear to Tread
Thomas Hardy	**The Distracted Preacher and Other Tales**
	Far From the Madding Crowd
	Jude the Obscure
	The Mayor of Casterbridge
	The Return of the Native
	Tess of the d'Urbervilles
	The Trumpet Major
	Under the Greenwood Tree
	The Woodlanders
Henry James	**The Aspern Papers** and **The Turn of the Screw**
	The Bostonians
	Daisy Miller
	The Europeans
	The Golden Bowl
	An International Episode and Other Stories
	Portrait of a Lady
	Roderick Hudson
	Washington Square
	What Maisie Knew
	The Wings of the Dove
D. H. Lawrence	**The Complete Short Novels**
	The Plumed Serpent
	The Rainbow
	Selected Short Stories
	Sons and Lovers
	The White Peacock
	Women in Love

Horatio Alger, Jr.	**Ragged Dick** and **Struggling Upward**
Phineas T. Barnum	**Struggles and Triumphs**
Ambrose Bierce	**The Enlarged Devil's Dictionary**
Kate Chopin	**The Awakening and Selected Stories**
Stephen Crane	**The Red Badge of Courage**
Richard Henry Dana, Jr.	**Two Years Before the Mast**
Frederick Douglass	**Narrative of the Life of Frederick Douglass, An American Slave**
Theodore Dreiser	**Sister Carrie**
Ralph Waldo Emerson	**Selected Essays**
Joel Chandler Harris	**Uncle Remus**
Nathaniel Hawthorne	**Blithedale Romance**
	The House of the Seven Gables
	The Scarlet Letter and Selected Tales
William Dean Howells	**The Rise of Silas Lapham**
Alice James	**The Diary of Alice James**
William James	**Varieties of Religious Experience**
Jack London	**The Call of the Wild and Other Stories**
	Martin Eden
Herman Melville	**Billy Budd, Sailor and Other Stories**
	Moby-Dick
	Redburn
	Typee
Frank Norris	**McTeague**
Thomas Paine	**Common Sense**
Edgar Allan Poe	**The Narrative of Arthur Gordon Pym of Nantucket**
	The Other Poe
	The Science Fiction of Edgar Allan Poe
	Selected Writings
Harriet Beecher Stowe	**Uncle Tom's Cabin**
Henry David Thoreau	**Walden and Civil Disobedience**
Mark Twain	**The Adventures of Huckleberry Finn**
	A Connecticut Yankee at King Arthur's Court
	Life on the Mississippi
	Pudd'nhead Wilson
	Roughing It
Edith Wharton	**The House of Mirth**

FOR THE BEST IN PAPERBACKS, LOOK FOR THE

A CHOICE OF PENGUIN FICTION

Monsignor Quixote   Graham Greene

Now filmed for television, Graham Greene's novel, like Cervantes' seventeenth-century classic, is a brilliant fable for its times. 'A deliciously funny novel' – *The Times*

The Dearest and the Best   Leslie Thomas

In the spring of 1940 the spectre of war turned into grim reality – and for all the inhabitants of the historic villages of the New Forest it was the beginning of the most bizarre, funny and tragic episode of their lives. 'Excellent' – *Sunday Times*

Earthly Powers   Anthony Burgess

Anthony Burgess's magnificent masterpiece, an enthralling, epic narrative spanning six decades and spotlighting some of the most vivid events and characters of our times. 'Enormous imagination and vitality . . . a huge book in every way' – Bernard Levin in the *Sunday Times*

The Penitent   Isaac Bashevis Singer

From the Nobel Prize-winning author comes a powerful story of a man who has material wealth but feels spiritually impoverished. 'Singer . . . restates with dignity the spiritual aspirations and the cultural complexities of a lifetime, and it must be said that in doing so he gives the Evil One no quarter and precious little advantage' – Anita Brookner in the *Sunday Times*

Paradise Postponed   John Mortimer

'Hats off to John Mortimer. He's done it again' – *Spectator*. A rumbustious, hilarious new novel from the creator of Rumpole, *Paradise Postponed* is now a major Thames Television series.

Animal Farm   George Orwell

The classic political fable of the twentieth century.

PENGUIN MODERN CLASSICS

The Collected Stories of Elizabeth Bowen

Seventy-nine stories – love stories, ghost stories, stories of childhood and of London during the Blitz – which all prove that 'the instinctive artist is there at the very heart of her work' – Angus Wilson

Tarr Wyndham Lewis

A strange picture of a grotesque world where human relationships are just fodder for a master race of artists, Lewis's extraordinary book remains 'a masterpiece of the period' – V. S. Pritchett

Chéri and The Last of Chéri Colette

Two novels that 'form the classic analysis of a love-affair between a very young man and a middle-aged woman' – Raymond Mortimer

Selected Poems 1923–1967 Jorge Luis Borges

A magnificent bilingual edition of the poetry of one of the greatest writers of today, conjuring up a unique world of invisible roses, uncaught tigers . . .

Beware of Pity Stefan Zweig

A cavalry officer becomes involved in the suffering of a young girl; when he attempts to avoid the consequences of his behaviour, the results prove fatal . . .

Valmouth and Other Novels Ronald Firbank

The world of Ronald Firbank – vibrant, colourful and fantastic – is to be found beneath soft deeps of velvet sky dotted with cognac clouds.

FOR THE BEST IN PAPERBACKS, LOOK FOR THE 🐧

PENGUIN MODERN CLASSICS

Death of a Salesman Arthur Miller

One of the great American plays of the century, this classic study of failure brings to life an unforgettable character: Willy Loman, the shifting and inarticulate hero who is nonetheless a unique individual.

The Echoing Grove Rosamund Lehmann

'No English writer has told of the pains of women in love more truly or more movingly than Rosamund Lehmann' – Marghenita Laski. 'This novel is one of the most absorbing I have read for years' – Simon Raven, *Listener*

Pale Fire Vladimir Nabokov

This book contains the last poem by John Slade, together with a Preface, notes and Index by his posthumous editor. But is the eccentric editor more than just haughty and intolerant – mad, bad, perhaps even dangerous . . .?

The Man Who Was Thursday G. K. Chesterton

This hilarious extravaganza concerns a secret society of revolutionaries sworn to destroy the world. But when Thursday turns out to be not a poet but a Scotland Yard detective, one starts to wonder about the identity of the others . . .

The Rebel Albert Camus

Camus's 'attempt to understand the time I live in' tries to justify innocence in an age of atrocity. 'One of the vital works of our time, compassionate and disillusioned, intelligent but instructed by deeply felt experience' – *Observer*

Letters to Milena Franz Kafka

Perhaps the greatest collection of love letters written in the twentieth century, they are an orgy of bliss and despair, of ecstasy and desperation poured out by Kafka in his brief two-year relationship with Milena Jesenska.

The Age of Reason Jean-Paul Sartre

The first part of Sartre's classic trilogy, set in the volatile Paris summer of 1938, is itself 'a dynamic, deeply disturbing novel' (Elizabeth Bowen) which tackles some of the major issues of our time.

Three Lives Gertrude Stein

A turning point in American literature, these portraits of three women – thin, worn Anna, patient, gentle Lena and the complicated, intelligent Melanctha – represented in 1909 one of the pioneering examples of modernist writing.

Doctor Faustus Thomas Mann

Perhaps the most convincing description of an artistic genius ever written, this portrait of the composer Leverkuhn is a classic statement of one of Mann's obsessive themes: the discord between genius and sanity.

The New Machiavelli H. G. Wells

This autobiography of a man who has thrown up a glittering political career and marriage to go into exile with the woman he loves also contains an illuminating Introduction by Melvyn Bragg.

The Collected Poems of Stevie Smith

Amused, amusing and deliciously barbed, this volume includes many poems which dwell on death; as a whole, though, as this first complete edition in paperback makes clear, Smith's poetry affirms an irrepressible love of life.

Rhinoceros / The Chairs / The Lesson Eugène Ionesco

Three great plays by the man who was one of the founders of what has come to be known as the Theatre of the Absurd.

RUDYARD KIPLING IN PENGUIN CLASSICS

Already published and forthcoming titles

'The most complete man of genius I have ever known' – Henry James

The Light That Failed
A Diversity of Creatures
The Day's Work
Debits and Credits
Wee Willie Winkie
Just So Stories
Traffics and Discoveries
Kim
The Jungle Books
Life's Handicap
Stalky and Co
Limits and Renewals
Something of Myself
Plain Tales From the Hills
Soldiers Three
Puck of Pook's Hill
Rewards and Fairies
Selected Poems
Selected Verse

'For my own part I worshipped Kipling at thirteen, loathed him at seventeen, enjoyed him at twenty, despised him at twenty-five, and now again rather admire him. The one thing that was never possible, if one had read him at all, was to forget him' – George Orwell

Also published in Penguin
Rudyard Kipling: His Life and Work
A literary biography by Charles Carrington